STATE OF FEAR

HarperCollins*Publishers*

MICHAEL CRICHTON

STATE OF FEAR

A NOVEL

HarperCollins books may be purchased for educational, business, or sales promotional use. For information, please write: Special Markets Department, HarperCollins Publishers Inc., 10 East 53rd Street, New York, NY 10022.

Grateful acknowledgment is made for permission to reprint from "You May Be Right" by Billy Joel, © 1980, Impulsive Music. All rights reserved; used by permission.

FIRST EDITION

DESIGNED BY LUCY ALBANESE

Printed on acid-free paper

Library of Congress Cataloging-in-Publication Data is available upon request.

ISBN 0-06-621413-0

04 05 06 07 08 ❖/RRD 10 9 8 7 6 5 4 3 2 1

There is something fascinating about science. One gets such wholesale returns of conjecture out of such a trifling investment of fact.

— MARK TWAIN

Within any important issue, there are always aspects no one wishes to discuss.

— GEORGE ORWELL

INTRODUCTION

In late 2003, at the Sustainable Earth Summit conference in Johannesburg, the Pacific island nation of Vanutu announced that it was preparing a lawsuit against the Environmental Protection Agency of the United States over global warming. Vanutu stood only a few feet above sea level, and the island's eight thousand inhabitants were in danger of having to evacuate their country because of rising sea levels caused by global warming. The United States, the largest economy in the world, was also the largest emitter of carbon dioxide and therefore the largest contributor to global warming.

The National Environmental Resource Fund, an American activist group, announced that it would join forces with Vanutu in the lawsuit, which was expected to be filed in the summer of 2004. It was rumored that wealthy philanthropist George Morton, who frequently backed environmental causes, would personally finance the suit, expected to cost more than $8 million. Since the suit would ultimately be heard by the sympathetic Ninth Circuit in San Francisco, the litigation was awaited with some anticipation.

But the lawsuit was never filed.

No official explanation for the failure to file has ever been given either by Vanutu or NERF. Even after the sudden disappearance of George Morton, an inexplicable lack of interest by the media has left the circumstances surrounding this lawsuit unexamined. Not until the end of 2004 did several former NERF board members begin to speak publicly about what had happened within that organization. Further revelations by Morton's staff, as well as by former members of the Los Angeles law firm of Hassle and Black, have added further detail to the story.

Thus it is now clear what happened to the progress of the Vanutu litigation between May and October of 2004, and why so many people died in remote parts of the world as a result.

MC
Los Angeles, 2004

STATE OF FEAR

From the Internal Report to the National Security Council (NSC) from the AASBC (Classified). Redacted portions from AASBC. Obtained FOIA 03/04/04.

    In retrospect the ▮▮▮▮▮▮▮ conspiracy was extremely well-planned. Preparations were under way for more than a year before the events themselves took place. There were preliminary ▮▮▮▮▮ as early as March ▮▮ 2003, and reports to the British ▮▮▮▮▮ ▮▮▮▮▮ and the German ▮▮ ▮▮▮▮.

    The first incident took place in Paris, in May of 2004. It is ▮▮ ▮▮▮▮▮ ▮▮▮▮▮ that the authorities ▮▮▮▮▮▮▮▮ But there now can be no doubt that what happened in Paris ▮▮▮▮▮▮, and the serious consequences that followed.

I

AKAMAI

In the darkness, he touched her arm and said, "Stay here." She did not move, just waited. The smell of salt water was strong. She heard the faint gurgle of water.

Then the lights came on, reflecting off the surface of a large open tank, perhaps fifty meters long and twenty meters wide. It might have been an indoor swimming pool, except for all the electronic equipment that surrounded it.

And the very strange device at the far end of the pool.

Jonathan Marshall came back to her, grinning like an idiot. *"Qu'est-ce que tu penses?"* he said, though he knew his pronunciation was terrible. "What do you think?"

"It is magnificent," the girl said. When she spoke English, her accent sounded exotic. In fact, everything about her was exotic, Jonathan thought. With her dark skin, high cheekbones, and black hair, she might have been a model. And she strutted like a model in her short skirt and spike heels. She was half Vietnamese, and her name was Marisa. "But no one else is here?" she said, looking around.

"No, no," he said. "It's Sunday. No one is coming."

Jonathan Marshall was twenty-four, a graduate student in physics from London, working for the summer at the ultra-modern Laboratoire Ondulatoire—the wave mechanics laboratory—of the French Marine

Institute in Vissy, just north of Paris. But the suburb was mostly the residence of young families, and it had been a lonely summer for Marshall. Which was why he could not believe his good fortune at meeting this girl. This extraordinarily beautiful and sexy girl.

"Show me what it does, this machine," Marisa said. Her eyes were shining. "Show me what it is you do."

"My pleasure," Marshall said. He moved to the large control panel and began to switch on the pumps and sensors. The thirty panels of the wave machine at the far end of the tank clicked, one after another.

He glanced back at her, and she smiled at him. "It is so complicated," she said. She came and stood beside him at the control panel. "Your research is recorded on cameras?"

"Yes, we have cameras in the ceiling, and on the sides of the tank. They make a visual record of the waves that are generated. We also have pressure sensors in the tanks that record pressure parameters of the passing wave."

"These cameras are on now?"

"No, no," he said. "We don't need them; we're not doing an experiment."

"Perhaps we are," she said, resting her hand on his shoulder. Her fingers were long and delicate. She had beautiful fingers.

She watched for a minute, then said, "This room, everything is so expensive. You must have great security, no?"

"Not really," he said. "Just cards to get in. And only one security camera." He gestured over his shoulder. "That one back in the corner."

She turned to look. "And that is turned on?" she said.

"Oh yes," he said. "That's always on."

She slid her hand to caress his neck lightly. "So is someone watching us now?"

"Afraid so."

"Then we should behave."

"Probably. Anyway, what about your boyfriend?"

"Him." She gave a derisive snort. "I have had enough of him."

• • •

Earlier that day, Marshall had gone from his small apartment to the café on rue Montaigne, the café he went to every morning, taking a journal article with him to read as usual. Then this girl had sat down at the next table, with her boyfriend. The couple had promptly fallen into an argument.

In truth, Marshall felt that Marisa and the boyfriend didn't seem to belong together. He was American, a beefy, red-faced fellow built like a footballer, with longish hair and wire-frame glasses that did not suit his thick features. He looked like a pig trying to appear scholarly.

His name was Jim, and he was angry with Marisa, apparently because she had spent the previous night away from him. "I don't know why you won't tell me where you were," he kept repeating.

"It is none of your business, that's why."

"But I thought we were going to have dinner together."

"Jimmy, I told you we were not."

"No, you told me you were. And I was waiting at the hotel for you. All night."

"So? No one made you. You could go out. Enjoy yourself."

"But I was waiting for you."

"Jimmy, you do not own me." She was exasperated by him, sighing, throwing up her hands, or slapping her bare knees. Her legs were crossed, and the short skirt rode up high. "I do as I please."

"That's clear."

"Yes," she said, and at that moment she turned to Marshall and said, "What is that you are reading? It looks very complicated."

At first Marshall was alarmed. She was clearly talking to him to taunt the boyfriend. He did not want to be drawn into the couple's dispute.

"It's physics," he said briefly, and turned slightly away. He tried to ignore her beauty.

"What kind of physics?" she persisted.

"Wave mechanics. Ocean waves."

"So, you are a student?"

"Graduate student."

"Ah. And clearly intelligent. You are English? Why are you in France?"

And before he knew it, he was talking to her, and she introduced the boyfriend, who gave Marshall a smirk and a limp handshake. It was still very uncomfortable, but the girl behaved as if it were not.

"So you work around here? What sort of work? A tank with a machine? Really, I can't imagine what you say. Will you show me?"

And now they were here, in the wave mechanics laboratory. And Jimmy, the boyfriend, was sulking in the parking lot outside, smoking a cigarette.

"What shall we do about Jimmy?" she said, standing beside Marshall while he worked at the control panel.

"He can't smoke in here."

"I will see that he does not. But I don't want to make him more angry. Can I let him in, do you think?"

Marshall felt disappointment flood through him. "Sure. I guess."

Then she squeezed his shoulder. "Don't worry, he is busy later with other business of his."

She went and opened the door at the back of the lab, and Jimmy came in. Marshall glanced back and saw him hanging back, hands in his pockets. Marisa came up to stand beside Marshall again, at the control panel.

"He's all right," she said. "Now show me."

The electric motors at the far end of the tank whirred, and the wave paddles generated the first wave. It was a small wave, and it rippled smoothly down the length of the tank, to splash on a slanted panel at the near end.

"So, this is a tidal wave?" she said.

"It is a simulation of a tsunami, yes," Marshall said, his fingers tapping the keyboard. On the control panel, displays showed temperature and pressure, generated false-color images of the wave.

"A simulation," she said. "Meaning what?"

"We can make waves up to one meter high in this tank," Marshall said. "But the real tsunamis are four, eight, ten meters high. Occasionally even more."

"A wave in the ocean that is ten meters?" Her eyes widened. "Really?" She was looking toward the ceiling, trying to imagine it.

Marshall nodded. That would be over thirty feet high, the height of a three-story building. And it would be moving at eight hundred kilometers an hour, roaring up to the shore.

"And when it comes to the shore?" she said. "Is that the slope at this end? It looks like a pebble texture on it. Is that the shore?"

"That's right," Marshall said. "How high the wave goes up the shore is a function of the angle of the slope. We can adjust the slope to any angle."

The boyfriend came forward, moving closer to the tank, but still he hung back. He never said a word.

Marisa was excited. "You can adjust it? How?"

"It is motorized."

"To any angle?" She giggled. "Show me *vingt-sept* degrees. Twenty-seven."

"Coming up." Marshall typed at the keyboard. With a slight grinding sound, the slope of the shore angled higher.

The American boyfriend went closer to the tank to look, drawn by the activity. It *was* fascinating, Marshall thought. Anybody would be interested. But the guy never spoke. He just stood and watched the pebbled surface tilt. Soon it stopped.

"So that is the slope?" she said.

"Yes," Marshall said. "Although in point of fact, twenty-seven degrees is fairly steep, more than the average shoreline in the real world. Maybe I should set it to—"

Her dark hand closed over his. "No, no," she said. Her skin was soft. "Leave it. Show me a wave. I want to see a wave."

Small waves were being generated every thirty seconds. They rippled along the length of the tank, with a slight whoosh. "Well, I first have to know the shape of the shoreline. Right now, it's flat beach, but if it was an inlet of some kind . . ."

"Will it change to make an inlet?"

"Of course."

"Really? Show me."

"What kind of inlet do you want? A harbor, a river, a bay . . ."

"Oh," she said, shrugging, "make a bay."

He smiled. "Fine. How big?"

With the whir of electric motors, the shoreline began to sink into a curve, the slope indenting into a bowl.

"Fantastic," she said. "Come on, Jonathan, show me the wave."

"Not yet. How big is the bay?"

"Oh . . ." She gestured in the air. "One mile. A bay of one mile. Now will you show me?" She leaned toward him. "I do not like to wait. You should know this."

He smelled her perfume. He typed quickly. "Here it comes," he said. "A big wave, coming into a one-mile bay, with a twenty-seven-degree slope."

There was a much louder whoosh as the next wave was generated at the far end of the tank, and then it rippled smoothly toward them, a raised line of water about six inches high.

"Oh!" Marisa pouted. "You promised me it would be *big*."

"Just wait," he said.

"It will grow?" she said, giggling. She put her hand on his shoulder again. Then the American glanced back, and gave her a dirty look. She jerked her chin in the air, defiant. But when he looked back at the tank, she took her hand away.

Marshall felt despondent again. She was just using him, he was a pawn in this game between them.

"You said it will grow?" she said.

"Yes," Marshall said, "the wave will grow as it comes to the shore. In deep water a tsunami is small, but in shallow water it builds. And the inlet will concentrate its power, so it goes higher."

The wave rose higher, and then smashed against the curved shore at the near end. It foamed white, and sloshed up the sides of the shore. It came up about five feet, he guessed.

"So it comes high," she said. "In the real world?"

"That's about forty, fifty feet," he said. "Fifteen meters."

"Ooh la la," she said, pursing her lips. "So a person cannot run away from this."

"Oh no," Marshall said. "You can't outrun a tidal wave. There was a wave in Hilo, Hawaii, in 1957, came right down the streets of the town, tall as the buildings, people ran from it but—"

"So that's it?" the American said. "That's all it does?" His voice was growly, like he needed to clear his throat.

"Don't mind him," she said quietly.

"Yes, that's what we do here," Marshall said. "We generate waves—"

"Jesus fucking A," the American said. "I could do that in my bathtub when I was six months old."

"Well," Marshall said, gesturing to the control panel, and the monitors displaying data, "we generate a lot of databases for researchers around the world who are—"

"Yeah, yeah. That's enough. Boring as whale shit. I'm leaving. You coming, Marisa, or not?" He stood and glared at her.

Marshall heard her suck in her breath.

"No," she said. "I am not."

The American turned and walked off, slamming the door loudly as he left.

Her apartment was just across the river from Notre Dame, and from the balcony in the bedroom he had a beautiful view of the cathedral, which was lighted at night. It was ten o'clock, but there was still a deep blue in the sky. He looked down at the street below, the lights of the cafés, the crowds walking on the streets. It was a busy and glamorous scene.

"Don't worry," she said, behind him. "If you're looking for Jimmy, he won't come here."

Actually, the thought hadn't occurred to him, until she mentioned it. "No?"

"No," she said. "He will go elsewhere. Jimmy has many women." She took a sip of red wine, then set the glass down on the bedside table. Unceremoniously, she pulled her top over her head and dropped her skirt. She was wearing nothing beneath.

Still in her high heels, she walked toward him. He must have seemed surprised, because she said, "I told you: I do not like to wait," and threw her arms around him and kissed him hard, fiercely, almost angrily. The next moments were awkward, trying to kiss while she tore off his clothes. She was breathing hard, almost panting. She never spoke. She was so passionate she seemed almost angry, and her beauty, the physical perfection of her dark body, intimidated him, but not for long.

Afterward she lay against him, her skin soft but her body taut beneath the surface. The bedroom ceiling had a soft glow from the church façade opposite. He was relaxed, but she seemed, if anything, to be energized, restless after making love. He wondered if she had really come, despite her moans and her final cries. And then abruptly, she got up.

"Anything wrong?"

She took a sip of wine. "To the toilet," she said, and turned away, passing through a door. She had left her wineglass. He sat up and took a sip, seeing the delicate pattern of her lipstick on the rim.

He looked at the bed and saw the dark streaks on the sheets from her heels. She had not taken them off until midway through their lovemaking. Now the heels were tossed away, coming to a stop beneath the window. Signs of their passion. He still felt, even now, as if he were in a dream. He had never been with a woman like this. Beautiful like this, living in a place like this. He wondered how much this apartment cost, the wood paneling, the perfect location . . .

He took another sip of wine. He could get used to this, he thought.

He heard water running in the bathroom. A humming sound, a tuneless song.

With a *bang!* the front door slammed open and three men burst into the bedroom. They were wearing dark raincoats and hats. Terrified, Marshall set the wineglass on the table—it fell—and dived for his clothes beside the bed to cover himself, but in an instant the men were on him, grabbing him with gloved hands. He yelled in alarm and panic as they threw him over, shoving him facedown on the bed. He was still yelling as they pushed his face into a pillow. He thought they were going to suffocate him, but they didn't. One man hissed, "Be quiet. Nothing will happen if you are quiet."

He didn't believe him, so he struggled, calling out again. Where was Marisa? What was she doing? It was happening so fast. One man was sitting on his back, knees digging into his spine, his cold shoes on Marshall's bare buttocks. He felt the man's hand on his neck, shoving him into the bed.

"Be quiet!" the man hissed again.

The other men had each taken one of his wrists, and they were pulling his arms wide, spread-eagling him on the bed. *They were getting ready to do something to him.* He felt terrified and vulnerable. He moaned, and somebody hit him on the back of the head. "Quiet!"

Everything was happening quickly, it was all impressionistic. Where was Marisa? Probably hiding in the bathroom, and he couldn't blame her. He heard a sloshing sound and saw a plastic baggie and something white in it, like a golf ball. They were placing the baggie under his armpit, on the fleshy part of his arm.

What the hell were they doing? He felt the water cold against his underarm, and he struggled but they held him tight, and then inside the water, something soft pressed against the arm, and he had a *sticky* sensation, like sticky chewing gum, something sticky and tugging against the flesh of his arm, and then he felt a little pinch. Nothing, hardly noticeable, a momentary sting.

The men were moving quickly, the baggie was removed, and at that

moment he heard two surprisingly loud gunshots and Marisa was screaming in rapid French—"*Salaud! Salopard! Bouge-toi le cul!*"—and the third
man had tumbled off Marshall's back and fallen to the ground, then scrambled up, and Marisa was still screaming, there were more shots, and he
could smell powder in the air, and the men fled. The door slammed, and
she came back, stark naked, babbling in French he could not understand,
something about *vacherie*, which he thought was a cow but he wasn't thinking straight. He was starting to tremble on the bed.

She came over and threw her arms around him. The barrel of the gun
was hot and he yelled, and she set it aside. "Oh Jonathan, I am so sorry,
so sorry." She cradled his head against her shoulder. "Please, you must
forgive me, it is all right now, I promise you."

Gradually his trembling stopped, and she looked at him. "Did they
hurt you?"

He shook his head, no.

"Good. I did not think so. Idiots! Friends of Jimmy, they think they
make a joke, to scare you. And me I am sure. But you are not hurt?"

He shook his head again. He coughed. "Perhaps," he said, finding his
voice at last. "Perhaps I should be going."

"Oh, no," she said. "No, no, you cannot do this to me."

"I don't feel—"

"Absolutely no," she said. She pushed closer to him, so her body was
touching his. "You must stay a while."

"Should we call the police?"

"*Mais non.* The police will do nothing. A quarrel of lovers. In France
we do not do this, call the police."

"But they broke in . . ."

"They are gone now," she said, whispering in his ear. He felt her
breath. "There is only us, now. Only us, Jonathan." Her dark body slid
down his chest.

It was after midnight when he was finally dressed and standing at the
window, looking out at Notre Dame. The streets were still crowded.

"Why will you not stay?" she said, pouting prettily. "I want you to stay. Don't you want to please me?"

"I'm sorry," he said. "I have to go. I don't feel very well."

"I will make you feel better."

He shook his head. In truth, he really did not feel well. He was experiencing waves of dizziness, and his legs felt oddly weak. His hands were trembling as he gripped the balcony.

"I'm sorry," he said again. "I have to leave."

"All right, then I will drive you."

Her car, he knew, was parked on the other side of the Seine. It seemed far to walk. But he just nodded numbly. "All right," he said.

She was in no rush. They strolled arm in arm, like lovers, along the embankment. They passed the houseboat restaurants tied up to the side, brightly lit, still busy with guests. Above them, on the other side of the river, rose Notre Dame, brilliantly lit. For a while, this slow walk, with her head on his shoulder, the soft words she spoke to him, made him feel better.

But soon he stumbled, feeling a kind of clumsy weakness coursing through his body. His mouth was very dry. His jaw felt stiff. It was difficult to speak.

She did not seem to notice. They had moved past the bright lights now, under one of the bridges, and he stumbled again. This time he fell on the stone embankment.

"My darling," she said, worried and solicitous, and helped him to his feet.

He said, "I think . . . I think . . ."

"Darling, are you all right?" She helped him to a bench, away from the river. "Here, just sit here for a moment. You will feel better in a moment."

But he did not feel better. He tried to protest, but he could not speak. In horror he realized he could not even shake his head. *Something was very wrong.* His whole body was growing weak, swiftly and astonishingly weak, and he tried to push up from the bench, but he could not move his limbs, he could not move his head. He looked at her, sitting beside him.

"Jonathan, what is wrong? Do you need a doctor?"

Yes, I need a doctor, he thought.

"Jonathan, this is not right . . ."

His chest was heavy. He was having trouble breathing. He looked away, staring straight ahead. He thought in horror: *I am paralyzed.*

"Jonathan?"

He tried to look at her. But now he could not even move his eyes. He could only look straight forward. His breathing was shallow.

"Jonathan?"

I need a doctor.

"Jonathan, can you look at me? Can you? No? You cannot turn your head?"

Somehow, her voice did not sound concerned. She sounded detached, clinical. Perhaps his hearing was affected. There was a rushing sound in his ears. It was harder and harder to breathe.

"All right, Jonathan, let's get you away from here."

She ducked her head under his arm and with surprising strength got him to his feet. His body was loose and floppy, sagging around her. He could not control where he looked. He heard the clicking of footsteps approaching and thought, *Thank God.* He heard a man's voice say in French, "Mademoiselle, do you need help?"

"Thank you, but no," she said. "Just too much to drink."

"Are you sure?"

"He does this all the time."

"Yes?"

"I can manage."

"Ah. Then I wish you *bonne nuit.*"

"*Bonne nuit,*" she said.

She continued on her way, carrying him. The footsteps became fainter. Then she paused, turned to look in all directions. And now . . . *she was moving him toward the river.*

"You are heavier than I thought," she said, in a conversational tone.

He felt a deep and profound terror. He was completely paralyzed. He could do nothing. His own feet were scraping over the stone.

Toward the river.

"I am sorry," she said, and she dropped him into the water.

It was a short fall, and a stunning sense of cold. He plunged beneath the surface, surrounded by bubbles and green, then black. He could not move, even in the water. He could not believe this was happening to him, he could not believe that he was dying this way.

Then slowly, he felt his body rise. Green water again, and then he broke the surface, on his back, turning slowly.

He could see the bridge, and the black sky, and Marisa, standing on the embankment. She lit a cigarette and stared at him. She had one hand on her hip, one leg thrust forward, a model's pose. She exhaled, smoke rising in the night.

Then he sank beneath the surface again, and he felt the cold and the blackness close in around him.

At three o'clock in the morning the lights snapped on in the Laboratoire Ondulatoire of the French Marine Institute, in Vissy. The control panel came to life. The wave machine began to generate waves that rolled down the tank, one after another, and crashed against the artificial shore. The control screens flashed three-dimensional images, scrolled columns of data. The data was transmitted to an unknown location somewhere in France.

At four o'clock, the control panel went dark, and the lights went out, and the hard drives erased any record of what had been done.

The twisting jungle road lay in shadow beneath the canopy of the Malay rain forest. The paved road was very narrow, and the Land Cruiser careened around the corners, tires squealing. In the passenger seat, a bearded man of forty glanced at his watch. "How much farther?"

"Just a few minutes," the driver said, not slowing. "We're almost there."

The driver was Chinese but he spoke with a British accent. His name was Charles Ling and he had flown over from Hong Kong to Kuala Lumpur the night before. He had met his passenger at the airport that morning, and they had been driving at breakneck speed ever since.

The passenger had given Ling a card that read "Allan Peterson, Seismic Services, Calgary." Ling didn't believe it. He knew perfectly well that there was a company in Alberta, ELS Engineering, that sold this equipment. It wasn't necessary to come all the way to Malaysia to see it.

Not only that, but Ling had checked the passenger manifest on the incoming flight, and there was no Allan Peterson listed. So this guy had come in on a different name.

Furthermore, he told Ling he was a field geologist doing independent consulting for energy companies in Canada, mostly evaluating potential oil sites. But Ling didn't believe that, either. You could spot those petroleum engineers a mile off. This guy wasn't one.

So Ling didn't know who the guy was. It didn't bother him. Mr. Peterson's credit was good; the rest was none of Ling's business. He had only one interest today, and that was to sell cavitation machines. And this looked like a big sale: Peterson was talking about three units, more than a million dollars in total.

He turned off the road abruptly, onto a muddy rut. They bounced through the jungle beneath huge trees, and suddenly came out into sunlight and a large opening. There was a huge semicircular gash in the ground, exposing a cliff of gray earth. A green lake lay below.

"What's this?" Peterson said, wincing.

"It was open-face mine, abandoned now. Kaolin."

"Which is . . . ?"

Ling thought, this is no geologist. He explained that kaolin was a mineral in clay. "It's used in paper and ceramics. Lot of industrial ceramics now. They make ceramic knives, incredibly sharp. They'll make ceramic auto engines soon. But the quality here was too low. It was abandoned four years ago."

Peterson nodded. "And where is the cavitator?"

Ling pointed toward a large truck parked at the edge of the cliff. "There." He drove toward it.

"Russians make it?"

"The vehicle and the carbon-matrix frame are Russian made. The electronics come from Taiwan. We assemble ourselves, in Kuala Lumpur."

"And is this your biggest model?"

"No, this is the intermediate. We don't have the largest one to show you."

They pulled alongside the truck. It was the size of a large earthmover; the cab of the Land Cruiser barely reached above the huge tires. In the center, hanging above the ground, was a large rectangular cavitation generator, looking like an oversize diesel generator, a boxy mass of pipes and wires. The curved cavitation plate was slung underneath, a few feet above the ground.

They climbed out of the car into sweltering heat. Ling's eyeglasses clouded over. He wiped them on his shirt. Peterson walked around the truck. "Can I get the unit without the truck?"

"Yes, we make transportable units. Seagoing containers. But usually clients want them mounted on vehicles eventually."

"I just want the units," Peterson said. "Are you going to demonstrate?"

"Right away," Ling said. He gestured to the operator, high up in the cab. "Perhaps we should step away."

"Wait a minute," Peterson said, suddenly alarmed. "I thought we were going to be alone. Who is that?"

"That's my brother," Ling said smoothly. "He's very trustworthy."

"Well . . ."

"Let's step away," Ling said. "We can see better from a distance."

The cavitation generator fired up, chugging loudly. Soon the noise blended with another sound, a deep humming that Ling always seemed to feel in his chest, in his bones.

Peterson must have felt it, too, because he moved back hastily.

"These cavitation generators are hypersonic," Ling explained, "producing a radially symmetric cavitation field that can be adjusted for focal point, rather like an optical lens, except we are using sound. In other words, we can focus the sound beam, and control how deep the cavitation will occur."

He waved to the operator, who nodded. The cavitation plate came down, until it was just above the ground. The sound changed, becoming deeper and much quieter. The earth vibrated slightly where they were standing.

"Jesus," Peterson said, stepping back.

"Not to worry," Ling said. "This is just low-grade reflection. The main energy vector is orthogonal, directed straight down."

About forty feet below the truck, the walls of the canyon suddenly seemed to blur, to become indistinct. Small clouds of gray smoke obscured the surface for a moment, and then a whole section of cliff gave way, and rumbled down into the lake below, like a gray avalanche. The whole area filled with smoke and dust.

As it began to clear, Ling said, "Now we will show how the beam is focused." The rumbling began again, and this time the cliff blurred much farther down, two hundred feet or more. Once again the gray sand gave way, this time sliding rather quietly into the lake.

"And it can focus laterally as well?" Peterson said.

Ling said it could. A hundred yards north of the truck, the cliff was shaken free, and again tumbled down.

"We can aim it in any direction, and any depth."

"Any depth?"

"Our big unit will focus at a thousand meters. Although no client has any use for such depths."

"No, no," Peterson said. "We don't need anything like that. But we want beam power." He wiped his hands on his trousers. "I've seen enough."

"Really? We have quite a few other techniques to demon—"

"I'm ready to go back." Behind his sunglasses, his eyes were unreadable.

"Very well," Ling said. "If you are sure—"

"I'm sure."

Driving back, Peterson said, "You ship from KL or Hong Kong?"

"From KL."

"With what restrictions?"

Ling said, "How do you mean?"

"Hypersonic cavitation technology in the US is restricted. It can't be exported without a license."

"As I said, we use Taiwanese electronics."

"Is it as reliable as the US technology?"

Ling said, "Virtually identical." If Peterson knew his business, he would know that the US had long ago lost the capacity to manufacture such advanced chipsets. The US cavitation chipsets were manufactured in Taiwan. "Why do you ask? Are you planning to export to the US?"

"No."

"Then there is no difficulty."

"What's your lead time?" Peterson said.

"We need seven months."

"I was thinking of five."

"It can be done. There will be a premium. For how many units?"

"Three," Peterson said.

Ling wondered why anyone would need three cavitation units. No geological survey company in the world owned more than one.

"I can fill that order," Ling said, "upon receipt of your deposit."

"You will have it wired to you tomorrow."

"And we are shipping where? Canada?"

"You will receive shipping instructions," Peterson said, "in five months."

Directly ahead, the curved spans of the ultra-modern airport designed by Kurokawa rose into the sky. Peterson had lapsed into silence. Driving up the ramp, Ling said, "I hope we are in time for your flight."

"What? Oh yes. We're fine."

"You're heading back to Canada?"

"Yes."

Ling pulled up at the international terminal, got out, and shook Peterson's hand. Peterson shouldered his day bag. It was his only luggage. "Well," Peterson said. "I'd better go."

"Safe flight."

"Thank you. You, too. Back to Hong Kong?"

"No," Ling said. "I have to go to the factory, and get them started."

"It's nearby?"

"Yes, in Pudu Raya. Just a few kilometers."

"All right, then." Peterson disappeared inside the terminal, giving a final wave. Ling got back in the car and drove away. But as he was heading down the ramp, he saw that Peterson had left behind his cell phone on the car seat. He pulled over to the curb, glancing back over his shoulder. But Peterson was gone. And the cell phone in his hand was lightweight, made of cheap plastic. It was one of those prepaid-card phones, the disposable ones. It couldn't be Peterson's main phone.

It occurred to Ling that he had a friend who might be able to trace the phone and the card inside it. Find out more about the purchaser. And Ling would like to know more. So he slipped the phone into his pocket and drove north, to the factory.

Richard Mallory looked up from his desk and said, "Yes?"

The man standing in the doorway was pale-complected, slender, and American-looking, with a blond crew cut. His manner was casual, his dress nondescript: dirty Adidas running shoes and a faded navy tracksuit. He looked as if he might be out for a jog and had stopped by the office for a moment.

And since this was Design/Quest, a hot graphics shop located on Butler's Wharf, a refurbished warehouse district below London's Tower Bridge, most of the employees in the office were casually dressed. Mallory was the exception. Since he was the boss, he wore slacks and a white shirt. And wingtip shoes that hurt his feet. But they were hip.

Mallory said, "Can I help you?"

"I've come for the package," the American said.

"I'm sorry. What package?" Mallory said. "If it's a DHL pickup, the secretary has it up front."

The American looked annoyed. "Don't you think you're overdoing it?" he said. "Just give me the fucking package."

"Okay, fine," Mallory said, getting up from behind the desk.

Apparently the American felt he had been too harsh, because in a quieter tone he said, "Nice posters," and pointed to the wall behind Mallory. "You do 'em?"

"We did," Mallory said. "Our firm."

There were two posters, side by side on the wall, both stark black with a hanging globe of the Earth in space, differing only in the tag line. One said "Save the Earth" and beneath it, "It's the Only Home We Have." The other said "Save the Earth" and beneath that, "There's Nowhere Else to Go."

Then off to one side was a framed photograph of a blond model in a T-shirt: "Save the Earth" and the copy line was "And Look Good Doing It."

"That was our 'Save the Earth' campaign," Mallory said. "But they didn't buy it."

"Who didn't?"

"International Conservation Fund."

He went past the American and headed down the back stairs to the garage. The American followed.

"Why not? They didn't like it?"

"No, they liked it," Mallory said. "But they got Leo as a spokesman, and used him instead. Campaign went to video spots."

At the bottom of the stairs, he swiped his card, and the door unlocked with a click. They stepped into the small garage beneath the building. It was dark except for the glare of daylight from the ramp leading to the street. Mallory noticed with annoyance that a van partly blocked the ramp. They always had trouble with delivery vans parking there.

He turned to the American. "You have a car?"

"Yes. A van." He pointed.

"Oh good, so that's yours. And somebody to help you?"

"No. Just me. Why?"

"It's bloody heavy," Mallory said. "It may just be wire, but it's half a million feet of it. Weighs seven hundred pounds, mate."

"I can handle it."

Mallory went to his Rover and unlocked the boot. The American whistled, and the van rumbled down the ramp. It was driven by a tough-looking woman with spiked hair, dark makeup.

Mallory said, "I thought you were alone."

"She doesn't know anything," the American said. "Forget her. She brought the van. She just drives."

Mallory turned to the open boot. There were stacked white boxes marked "Ethernet Cable (Unshielded)." And printed specifications.

"Let's see one," the American said.

Mallory opened a box. Inside was a jumble of fist-sized coils of very thin wire, each in shrink-wrap plastic. "As you see," he said, "it's guide wire. For anti-tank missiles."

"Is it?"

"That's what they told me. That's why it's wrapped that way. One coil of wire for each missile."

"I wouldn't know," the American said. "I'm just the delivery man." He went and opened the back of his van. Then he began to transfer the boxes, one at a time. Mallory helped.

The American said, "This guy tell you anything else?"

"Actually, he did," Mallory said. "He said somebody bought five hundred surplus Warsaw Pact rockets. Called Hotfire or Hotwire or something. No warheads or anything. Just the rocket bodies. The story is they were sold with defective guide wire."

"I haven't heard that."

"That's what he said. Missiles were bought in Sweden. Gothenburg, I think. Shipped out from there."

"Sounds like you're worried."

"I'm not worried," Mallory said.

"Like you're afraid you're mixed up in something."

"Not me."

"Sure about that?" the American said.

"Yes, of course I'm sure."

Most of the boxes were transferred to the van. Mallory started to sweat. The American seemed to be glancing at him out of the corner of his eye. Openly skeptical. He said, "So, tell me. What'd he look like, this guy?"

Mallory knew better than to answer that. He shrugged. "Just a guy."

"American?"

"I don't know."

"You don't know whether he was American or not?"

"I couldn't be sure of his accent."

"Why is that?" the American said.

"He might have been Canadian."

"Alone?"

"Yeah."

"Because I hear talk about some gorgeous woman. Sexy woman in high heels, tight skirt."

"I would have noticed a woman like that," Mallory said.

"You wouldn't be . . . leaving her out?" Another skeptical glance. "Keeping her to yourself?" Mallory noticed a bulge on the American's hip. Was it a gun? It might be.

"No. He was alone."

"Whoever the guy was."

"Yes."

"You ask me," the American said, "I'd be wondering why anybody needed half a million feet of wire for anti-tank missiles in the first place. I mean, for what?"

Mallory said, "He didn't say."

"And you just said, 'Right, mate, half a million feet of wire, leave it to me,' with never a question?"

"Seems like you're asking all the questions," Mallory said. Still sweating.

"And I have a reason," the American said. His tone turned ominous. "I got to tell you, pal. I don't like what I am hearing."

The last of the boxes were stacked in the van. Mallory stepped back. The American slammed the first door shut, then the second. As the second door closed, Mallory saw the driver standing there. The woman. She had been standing behind the door.

"I don't like it either," she said. She was wearing fatigues, army surplus stuff. Baggy trousers and high-laced boots. A bulky green jacket. Heavy gloves. Dark glasses.

"Now wait a minute," the American said.

"Give me your cell phone," she said. Holding out her hand for it. Her other hand was behind her back. As if she had a gun.

"Why?"

"Give it to me."

"Why?"

"I want to look at it, that's why."

"There's nothing unusual—"

"Give it to me."

The American pulled the cell phone out of his pocket and handed it to her. Instead of taking it, she grabbed his wrist and pulled him toward her. The cell phone clattered to the ground. She brought her other hand from around her back and quickly gripped the side of his neck with her gloved hand. She held him with both hands around his neck, as if she were strangling him.

For a moment he was stunned; then he began to struggle. "What the fuck are you doing?" he said. "What are you—hey!" He knocked her hands away and jumped back as if he had been burned. "What was that? What did you *do?*"

He touched his neck. A tiny trickle of blood ran down, just a few drops. There was red on his fingertips. Almost nothing.

"What did you do?" he said.

"Nothing." She was stripping off her gloves. Mallory could see she was doing it carefully. As if something were in the glove. Something she did not want to touch.

"Nothing?" the American said. "*Nothing?* Son of a bitch!" Abruptly, he turned and began to run up the ramp toward the street outside.

Calmly, she watched him go. She bent over, picked up the cell phone, and put it in her pocket. Then she turned to Mallory. "Go back to work."

He hesitated.

"You did a good job. I never saw you. You never saw me. Now go."

Mallory turned and walked to the back-stairs door. Behind him, he heard the woman slam the van door, and when he glanced back, he saw the van racing up the ramp into the glare of the street. The van turned right, and was gone.

• • •

Back in his office, his assistant, Elizabeth, came in with a mockup for the new ultralight computer ads for Toshiba. The shoot was tomorrow. These were the finals to go over. He shuffled through the boards quickly; Mallory had trouble concentrating.

Elizabeth said, "You don't like them?"

"No, no, they're fine."

"You look a little pale."

"I just, um . . . my stomach."

"Ginger tea," she said. "That's best. Shall I make some?"

He nodded, to get her out of the office. He looked out the window. Mallory's office had a spectacular view of the Thames, and the Tower Bridge off to the left. The bridge had been repainted baby blue and white (was that traditional or just a bad idea?), but to see it always made him feel good. Secure somehow.

He walked closer to the window, and stood looking at the bridge. He was thinking that when his best friend had asked if he would lend a hand in a radical environmental cause, it had sounded like something fun. A bit of secrecy, a bit of dash and derring-do. He had been promised that it would not involve anything violent. Mallory had never imagined he would be frightened.

But he was frightened now. His hands were shaking. He stuck them in his pockets as he stared out the window. Five hundred rockets? he thought. *Five hundred rockets.* What had he gotten himself into? Then, slowly, he realized that he was hearing sirens, and there were red lights flashing on the bridge railings.

There had been an accident on the bridge. And judging from the number of police and rescue vehicles, it was a serious accident.

One in which someone had died.

He couldn't help himself. Feeling a sense of panic, he left the office, went outside to the quay, and with his heart in his throat, hurried toward the bridge.

• • •

From the upper level of the red double-decker bus, the tourists were staring down, covering their mouths in horror. Mallory pushed through the crowd clustered near the front of the bus. He got close enough to see a half-dozen paramedics and police crouched around a body lying in the street. Above them stood the burly bus driver, in tears. He was saying that there was nothing he could have done, the man had stepped in front of the bus at the last moment. He must have been drunk, the driver said, because he was wobbling. It was almost as if he fell off the curb.

Mallory could not see the body; the policemen blocked his view. The crowd was nearly silent, just watching. Then one of the policemen stood, holding a red passport in his hands—a German passport. Thank God, Mallory thought, feeling a flood of relief that lasted until a moment later, when one of the paramedics stepped away and Mallory saw one leg of the victim—a faded black tracksuit and a dirty Adidas running shoe, now soaked with blood.

He felt a wave of nausea, and turned away, pushing back through the crowd. The faces stared past him, impassive or annoyed. But nobody even glanced at him. They were all looking at the body.

Except for one man, dressed like an executive in a dark suit and tie. He was looking directly at Mallory. Mallory met his eyes. The man nodded slightly. Mallory made no response. He just pushed through the last of the crowd and fled, hurrying back down the stairs to his office, and realizing that somehow, in some way that he did not understand, his life had changed forever.

TOKYO
TUESDAY, JUNE I
10:01 A.M.

IDEC, the International Data Environmental Consortium, was located in a small brick building adjacent to the campus of Keio Mita University. To the casual observer, IDEC was part of the university, and even showed the coat of arms (*"Calamus Gladio Fortior"*), but in fact it was independent. The center of the building consisted of a small conference room with a podium and two rows of five chairs facing a screen at the front.

At ten in the morning, IDEC director Akira Hitomi stood at the podium and watched as the American came in and took a seat. The American was a large man, not so tall but thick in the shoulders and chest, like an athlete. For such a large man he moved easily, quietly. The Nepali officer entered right behind him, dark-skinned and watchful. He took a seat behind the American and off to one side. At the podium, Hitomi nodded to them and said nothing.

The wood-paneled room darkened slowly, to allow eyes to adjust. On all sides, the wood panels slid silently away, exposing huge flat-panel screens. Some of the screens moved smoothly out from the walls.

At last, the main door closed and locked with a click. Only then did Hitomi speak.

"Good morning, Kenner-san." On the main screen it said "Hitomi Akira" in English and Japanese. "And good morning, Thapa-san."

Hitomi flipped open a very small, very thin silver laptop. "Today I will present data from the last twenty-one days, correct up to twenty minutes ago. These will be findings from our joint project, Akamai Tree."

The two visitors nodded. Kenner smiled in anticipation. As well he should, Hitomi thought. Nowhere else in the world could he see such a presentation, for Hitomi's agency was the world leader in the accumulation and manipulation of electronic data. Now images on the screens came up, glowing one after another. They showed what appeared to be a corporate logo: a green tree on a white background, and the lettering AKAMAI TREE DIGITAL NETWORK SOLUTIONS.

This name and image had been chosen for their similarity to actual Internet companies and their logos. For the last two years, Akamai Tree's network of servers actually consisted of carefully designed traps. They incorporated multilevel quad-check honeynets established in both business and academic domains. This enabled them to track backward from servers to user with an 87 percent success rate. They had baited the net starting last year, first with ordinary feed and then with increasingly juicy morsels.

"Our sites mirrored established geology, applied physics, ecology, civil engineering, and biogeography sites," Hitomi said. "To attract deep divers, typical data included information on the use of explosives in seismic recordings, the tests of the stability of structures to vibration and earthquake damage, and in our oceanographic sites, data on hurricanes, rogue waves, tsunamis, and so forth. All this is familiar to you."

Kenner nodded.

Hitomi continued: "We knew we had a disseminated enemy, and a clever one. Users often operate behind netnanny firewalls, or used AOL accounts with teen ratings, to imply they are juvenile pranksters or kiddie scripters. But they are nothing of the sort. They are well organized, patient, and unrelenting. In recent weeks, we have begun to understand more."

The screen changed, showing a list.

"Out of a mix of sites and discussion groups, our sys progs found the deep divers clustered on the following category topics:

Aarhus, Denmark
Argon/Oxygen Drives
Australian Military History
Caisson Seawalls
Cavitation (Solid)
Cellular Encryption
Controlled Demolition
Flood Mitigation
High-Voltage Insulators
Hilo, Hawaii
Mid-Ocean Relay Network (MORN)
Missionary Diaries of the Pacific
National Earthquake Information Center (NEIC)
National Environmental Resource Fund (NERF)
Network Data Encryption
Potassium Hydroxide
Prescott, Arizona
Rain Forest Disease Foundation (RFDF)
Seismic Signatures, Geological
Shaped Explosives (Timed)
Shinkai 2000
Solid Rocket Propellant Mixtures
Toxins and Neurotoxins
Wire-guided Projectiles

"An impressive, if mysterious list," Hitomi said. "However, we have filters to identify smees and high-performance clients. These are individuals attacking firewalls, setting trojans, wild spiders, and so forth. Many of them are looking for credit card lists. But not all." He tapped his little computer, and the images changed.

"We added each of these topics into the honeynet with increasing stickiness, finally including hints of forthcoming research data, which we exposed as e-mail exchanges among scientists in Australia, Germany, Canada, and Russia. We drew a crowd and watched the traffic. We eventually sorted a complex nodal North America—Toronto, Chicago, Ann Arbor, Montreal—with spines to both American coasts, as well as England, France, and Germany. This is a serious Alpha extremist group.

They may already have killed a researcher in Paris. We're awaiting data. But the French authorities can be . . . slow."

Kenner spoke for the first time. "And what's the current delta cellular?"

"Cellular traffic is accelerating. E-mail is heavily encrypted. STF rate is up. It is clear there is a project under way—global in scope, immensely complicated, extremely expensive."

"But we don't know what it is."

"Not yet."

"Then you'd better follow the money."

"We are doing it. Everywhere." Hitomi smiled grimly. "It is only a matter of time before one of these fishes takes the hook."

Nat Damon signed the paper with a flourish. "I've never been asked to sign a nondisclosure agreement before."

"I'm surprised," the man in the shiny suit said, taking the paper back. "I would have thought it was standard procedure. We don't want our proprietary information to be disclosed." He was a lawyer accompanying his client, a bearded man with glasses, wearing jeans and a work shirt. This bearded man said he was a petroleum geologist, and Damon believed him. He certainly looked like the other petroleum geologists he had dealt with.

Damon's company was called Canada Marine RS Technologies; from a tiny, cramped office outside Vancouver, Damon leased research submarines and remote submersibles to clients around the world. Damon didn't own these subs; he just leased them. The subs were located all over the world—in Yokohama, Dubai, Melbourne, San Diego. They ranged from fully operational fifty-foot submersibles with crews of six, capable of traveling around the globe, to tiny one-man diving machines and even smaller remote robotic vehicles that operated from a tender ship on the surface.

Damon's clients were energy and mining companies who used the subs for undersea prospecting or to check the condition of offshore rigs and platforms. His was a specialized business, and his little office at the back of a boat repair yard did not receive many visitors.

Yet these two men had come through his door just before closing time. The lawyer had done all of the talking; the client merely gave Damon a business card that said Seismic Services, with a Calgary address. That made sense; Calgary was a big city for hydrocarbon companies. Petro-Canada, Shell, and Suncor were all there, and many more. And dozens of small private consulting firms had sprung up there to do prospecting and research.

Damon took a small model down from the shelf behind him. It was a tiny white snub-nosed submarine with a bubble top. He set it on the table in front of the men.

"This is the vehicle I would recommend for your needs," he said. "The RS Scorpion, built in England just four years ago. Two-man crew. Diesel and electric power with closed cycle argon drive. Submerged, it runs on twenty percent oxygen, eighty percent argon. Solid, proven technology: potassium hydroxide scrubber, two-hundred-volt electrical, operational depth of two thousand feet, and 3.8 hours dive time. It's the equivalent of the Japanese Shinkai 2000, if you know that one, or the DownStar 80, of which there are four in the world, but they're all on long leases. The Scorpion is an excellent submarine."

The men nodded, and looked at each other. "And what kind of external manipulators are there?" the bearded man said.

"That's depth dependent," Damon said. "At lesser depths—"

"Let's say at two thousand feet. What external manipulators are there?"

"You want to collect samples at two thousand feet?"

"Actually, we're placing monitoring devices on the bottom."

"I see. Like radio devices? Sending data to the surface?"

"Something like that."

"How large are these devices?"

The bearded man held his hands two feet apart. "About so big."

"And they weigh what?"

"Oh, I don't know exactly. Maybe two hundred pounds."

Damon concealed his surprise. Usually petroleum geologists knew precisely what they were going to place. Exact dimensions, exact weight, exact specific gravity, all that. This guy was vague. But perhaps Damon was just being paranoid. He continued. "And these sensors are for geological work?"

"Ultimately. First we need information on ocean currents, flow rates, bottom temperatures. That kind of thing."

Damon thought: *For what?* Why did they need to know about currents? Of course, they might be sinking a tower, but nobody would do that in two thousand feet of water.

What were these guys intending to do?

"Well," he said, "if you want to place external devices, you have to secure them to the exterior of the hull prior to the dive. There are lateral shelves on each side—" he pointed to the model "—for that purpose. Once you're at depth, you have a choice of two remote arms to place the devices. How many devices are you talking about?"

"Quite a few."

"More than eight?"

"Oh yes. Probably."

"Well, then you're talking about multiple dives. You can only take eight, maybe ten external devices on any given dive." He talked on for a while, scanning their faces, trying to understand what lay behind the bland looks. They wanted to lease the sub for four months, starting in August of that year. They wanted the sub and the tender ship transported to Port Moresby, New Guinea. They would pick it up there.

"Depending on where you go, there are some required marine licenses—"

"We'll worry about that later," the lawyer said.

"Now, the crew—"

"We'll worry about that later, too."

"It's part of the contract."

"Then just write it in. However you do it."

"You'll return the tender to Moresby at the end of the lease period?"

"Yes."

Damon sat down in front of the desktop computer and began to fill in the estimate forms. There were, all in all, forty-three categories (not including insurance) that had to be filled out. At last he had the final number. "Five hundred and eighty three thousand dollars," he said.

The men didn't blink. They just nodded.

"Half in advance."

They nodded again.

"Second half in escrow account prior to your taking delivery in Port Moresby." He never required that with his regular customers. But for some reason, these two made him uneasy.

"That will be fine," the lawyer said.

"Plus twenty percent contingency, payable in advance."

That was simply unnecessary. But now he was trying to make these guys go away. It didn't work.

"That will be fine."

"Okay," Damon said. "Now, if you need to talk to your contracting company before you sign—"

"No. We're prepared to proceed now."

And then one of them pulled out an envelope and handed it to Damon.

"Tell me if this is satisfactory."

It was a check for $250,000. From Seismic Services, payable to Canada Marine. Damon nodded, and said it was. He put the check and the envelope on his desk, next to the submarine model.

Then one of the men said, "Do you mind if I make a couple of notes?" and picked up the envelope and scribbled on it. And it was only after they were gone that Damon realized they had given him the check and taken back the envelope. So there would be no fingerprints.

Or was he just being paranoid? The following morning, he was inclined to think so. When he went to Scotiabank to deposit the check, he stopped by to see John Kim, the bank manager, and asked him to find out if there were sufficient funds in the Seismic Services account to cover the check.

John Kim said he would check right away.

STANGFEDLIS
MONDAY, AUGUST 23
3:02 A.M.

Christ, it was cold, George Morton thought, climbing out of the Land Cruiser. The millionaire philanthropist stamped his feet and pulled on gloves, trying to warm himself. It was three o'clock in the morning, and the sky glowed red, with streaks of yellow from the still-visible sun. A bitter wind blew across the *Sprengisandur*, the rugged, dark plain in the interior of Iceland. Flat gray clouds hung low over the lava that stretched away for miles. The Icelanders loved this place. Morton couldn't see why.

In any case, they had reached their destination: directly ahead lay a huge, crumpled wall of dirt-covered snow and rock, stretching up to the mountains behind. This was Snorrajökul, one tongue of the huge Vatnajökull glacier, the largest ice cap in Europe.

The driver, a graduate student, climbed out and clapped his hands with delight. "Not bad at all! Quite warm! You are lucky, it's a pleasant August night." He was wearing a T-shirt, hiking shorts, and a light vest. Morton was wearing a down vest, a quilted windbreaker, and heavy pants. And he was still cold.

He looked back as the others got out of the backseat. Nicholas Drake, thin and frowning, wearing a shirt and tie and a tweed sport coat beneath his windbreaker, winced as the cold air hit him. With his thinning hair, wire-frame glasses, and pinched, disapproving manner, Drake conveyed a scholarly quality that in fact he cultivated. He did not want to be taken for what he was, a highly successful litigator who had retired to become the director of the National Environmental Resource Fund, a major American activist group. He had held the job at NERF for the last ten years.

Next, young Peter Evans bounced out of the car. Evans was the youngest of Morton's attorneys, and the one he liked best. Evans was twenty-eight and a junior associate of the Los Angeles firm of Hassle and Black. Now, even late at night, he remained cheerful and enthusiastic. He pulled on a Patagonia fleece and stuck his hands in his pockets, but otherwise gave no sign that the weather bothered him.

Morton had flown all of them in from Los Angeles on his Gulfstream G5 jet, arriving in Keflavík airport at nine yesterday morning. None of them had slept, but nobody was tired. Not even Morton, and he was sixty-five years old. He didn't feel the slightest sense of fatigue.

Just cold.

Morton zipped up his jacket and followed the graduate student down the rocky hill from the car. "The light at night gives you energy," the kid said. "Dr. Einarsson never sleeps more than four hours a night in the summer. None of us does."

"And where is Dr. Einarsson?" Morton asked.

"Down there." The kid pointed off to the left.

At first, Morton could see nothing at all. Finally he saw a red dot, and realized it was a vehicle. That was when he grasped the enormous size of the glacier.

Drake fell into step with Morton as they went down the hill. "George," he said, "you and Evans should feel free to go on a tour of the site, and let me talk to Per Einarsson alone."

"Why?"

"I expect Einarsson would be more comfortable if there weren't a lot of people standing around."

"But isn't the point that I'm the one who funds his research?"

"Of course," Drake said, "but I don't want to hammer that fact too hard. I don't want Per to feel compromised."

"I don't see how you can avoid it."

"I'll just point out the stakes," Drake said. "Help him to see the big picture."

"Frankly, I was looking forward to hearing this discussion," Morton said.

"I know," Drake said. "But it's delicate."

As they came closer to the glacier, Morton felt a distinct chill in the wind. The temperature dropped several degrees. They could see now the series of four large, tan tents arranged near the red Land Cruiser. From a distance, the tents had blended into the plain.

From one of the tents a very tall, blond man appeared. Per Einarsson threw up his hands and shouted, "Nicholas!"

"Per!" Drake raced forward.

Morton continued down the hill, feeling distinctly grouchy about being dismissed by Drake. Evans came up to walk alongside him. "I don't want to take any damn tour," Morton said.

"Oh, I don't know," Evans said, looking ahead. "It might be more interesting than we think." Coming out of one of the other tents were three young women in khakis, all blond and beautiful. They waved to the newcomers.

"Maybe you're right," Morton said.

Peter Evans knew that his client George Morton, despite his intense interest in all things environmental, had an even more intense interest in pretty women. And indeed, after a quick introduction to Einarsson, Morton happily allowed himself to be led away by Eva Jónsdóttir, who was tall and athletic, with short-cropped white blond hair and a radiant smile. She was Morton's type, Evans thought. She looked rather like Morton's beautiful assistant, Sarah Jones. He heard Morton say, "I had no idea so many women were interested in geology," and Morton and Eva drifted away, heading toward the glacier.

Evans knew he should accompany Morton. But perhaps Morton

wanted to take this tour alone. And more important, Evans's firm also represented Nicholas Drake, and Evans had a nagging concern about what Drake was up to. Not that it was illegal or unethical, exactly. But Drake could be imperious, and what he was going to do might cause embarrassment later on. So for a moment Evans stood there, wondering which way to go, which man to follow.

It was Drake who made the decision for him, giving Evans a slight, dismissive wave of his hand as he disappeared into the big tent with Einarsson. Evans took the hint, and ambled off toward Morton and the girl. Eva was chattering on about how 12 percent of Iceland was covered in glaciers, and how some of the glaciers had active volcanoes poking out from the ice.

This particular glacier, she said, pointing upward, was of the type called a surge glacier, because it had a history of rapid advances and retreats. At the moment, she said, the glacier was pushing forward at the rate of one hundred meters a day—the length of a football field, every twenty-four hours. Sometimes, when the wind died, you could actually hear it grinding forward. This glacier had surged more than ten kilometers in the last few years.

Soon they were joined by Ásdís Sveinsdóttir, who could have been Eva's younger sister. She paid flattering attention to Evans, asking him how his trip over had been, how he liked Iceland, how long he was staying in the country. Eventually, she mentioned that she usually worked in the office at Reykjavík, and had only come out for the day. Evans realized then that she was here doing her job. The sponsors were visiting Einarsson, and Einarsson had arranged for the visit to be memorable.

Eva was explaining that although surge-type glaciers were very common—there were several hundred of them in Alaska—the mechanism of the surges was not known. Nor was the mechanism behind the periodic advances and retreats, which differed for each glacier. "There is still so much to study, to learn," she said, smiling at Morton.

That was when they heard shouts coming from the big tent, and considerable swearing. Evans excused himself, and headed back to the tent. Somewhat reluctantly, Morton trailed after him.

Per Einarsson was shaking with anger. He raised his fists. "I tell you, no!" he yelled, and pounded the table.

Standing opposite him, Drake was very red in the face, clenching his teeth. "Per," he said, "I am asking you to consider the realities."

"You are not!" Einarsson said, pounding the table again. "The reality is what you do *not* want me to publish!"

"Now, Per—"

"The *reality*," he said, "is that in Iceland the first half of the twentieth century was warmer than the second half, as in Greenland.* The *reality* is that in Iceland, most glaciers lost mass after 1930 because summers warmed by .6 degrees Celsius, but since then the climate has become colder. The *reality* is that since 1970 these glaciers have been steadily advancing. They have regained half the ground that was lost earlier. Right now, eleven are surging. That is *the reality*, Nicholas! And I will not lie about it."

"No one has suggested you do," Drake said, lowering his voice and glancing at his newly arrived audience. "I am merely discussing how you word your paper, Per."

Einarsson raised a sheet of paper. "Yes, and you have *suggested* some wording—"

"Merely a suggestion—"

"That twists truth!"

"Per, with due respect, I feel you are exaggerating—"

"Am I?" Einarsson turned to the others and began to read. "This is what he wants me to say: 'The threat of global warming has melted glaciers throughout the world, and in Iceland as well. Many glaciers are shrinking dramatically, although paradoxically others are growing. How-

---

* P. Chylek, et al. 2004, "Global warming and the Greenland ice sheet," *Climatic Change* 63, 201–21. "Since 1940 . . . data have undergone predominantly a cooling trend. . . . The Greenland ice sheet and coastal regions are not following the current global warming trend."

ever, in all cases recent extremes in climate variability seem to be the cause . . . blah . . . blah . . . blah . . . *og svo framvegis.*' " He threw the paper down. "That is simply not true."

"It's just the opening paragraph. The rest of your paper will amplify."

"The opening paragraph is not true."

"Of course it is. It refers to 'extremes in climate variability.' No one can object to such vague wording."

"*Recent* extremes. But in Iceland these effects are not recent."

"Then take out 'recent.'"

"That is not adequate," Einarsson said, "because the implication of this paragraph is that we are observing the effects of global warming from greenhouse gases. Whereas in fact we are observing local climate patterns that are rather specific to Iceland and are unlikely to be related to any global pattern."

"And you can say so in your conclusion."

"But this opening paragraph will be a big joke among Arctic researchers. You think Motoyama or Sigurosson will not see through this paragraph? Or Hicks? Watanabe? Ísaksson? They will laugh and call me compromised. They will say I did it for grants."

"But there are other considerations," Drake said soothingly. "We must all be aware there are disinformation groups funded by industry— petroleum, automotive—who will seize on the report that some glaciers are growing, and use it to argue against global warming. That is what they always do. They snatch at anything to paint a false picture."

"How the information is used is not my concern. My concern is to report the truth as best I can."

"Very noble," Drake said. "Perhaps not so practical."

"I see. And you have brought the source of funding right here, in the form of Mr. Morton, so I do not miss the point?"

"No, no, Per," Drake said hastily. "Please, don't misunderstand—"

"I understand only too well. What is he doing here?" Einarsson was furious. "Mr. Morton? Do you approve of what I am being asked to do by Mr. Drake?"

It was at that point that Morton's cell phone rang, and with ill-concealed relief, he flipped it open. "Morton. Yes? Yes, John. Where are you? Vancouver? What time is it there?" He put his hand over the mouthpiece. "John Kim, in Vancouver. Scotiabank."

Evans nodded, though he had no idea who that was. Morton's financial operations were complex; he knew bankers all over the world. Morton turned and walked to the far side of the tent.

An awkward silence fell over the others as they waited. Einarsson stared at the floor, sucking in his breath, still furious. The blond women pretended to work, giving great attention to the papers they shuffled through. Drake stuck his hands in his pockets, looked at the roof of the tent.

Meanwhile, Morton was laughing. "Really? I hadn't heard that one," he said, chuckling. He glanced back at the others, and turned away again.

Drake said, "Look, Per, I feel we have gotten off on the wrong foot."

"Not at all," Einarsson said coldly. "We understand each other only too well. If you withdraw your support, you withdraw your support."

"Nobody is talking about withdrawing support . . ."

"Time will tell," he said.

And then Morton said, "*What?* They did *what?* Deposited to *what?* How much money are we—? Jesus Christ, John. This is *unbelievable!*" And still talking, he turned and walked out of the tent.

Evans hurried after him.

It was brighter, the sun now higher in the sky, trying to break through low clouds. Morton was scrambling up the slope, still talking on the phone. He was shouting, but his words were lost in the wind as Evans followed him.

They came to the Land Cruiser. Morton ducked down, using it as a shield against the wind. "Christ, John, do I have legal liability there? I mean—no, I didn't know a thing about it. What was the organization? Friends of the Planet Fund?"

Morton looked questioningly at Evans. Evans shook his head. He'd never heard of Friends of the Planet. And he knew most of the environmental organizations.

"Based where?" Morton was saying. "San Jose? California? Oh. Jesus.

What the hell is based in Costa Rica?" He cupped his hand over the phone. "Friends of the Planet Fund, San José, Costa Rica."

Evans shook his head.

"I never heard of them," Morton said, "and neither has my lawyer. And I don't remember—no, Ed, if it was a quarter of a million dollars, I'd remember. The check was issued where? I see. And my name was where? I see. Okay, thanks. Yeah. I will. Bye." He flipped the phone shut.

He turned to Evans.

"Peter," he said. "Get a pad and make notes."

Morton spoke quickly. Evans scribbled, trying to keep up. It was a complicated story that he took down as best he could.

John Kim, the manager of Scotiabank, Vancouver, had been called by a customer named Nat Damon, a local marine operator. Damon had deposited a check from a company called Seismic Services, in Calgary, and the check had bounced. It was for $300,000. Damon was nervous about whoever had written the check, and asked Kim to look into it.

John Kim could not legally make inquiries in the US, but the issuing bank was in Calgary, and he had a friend who worked there. He learned that Seismic Services was an account with a postal box for an address. The account was modestly active, receiving deposits every few weeks from only one source: The Friends of the Planet Foundation, based in San José, Costa Rica.

Kim placed a call down there. Then, about that time, it came up on his screen that the check had cleared. Kim called Damon and asked him if he wanted to drop the inquiry. Damon said no, check it out.

Kim had a brief conversation with Miguel Chavez at the Banco Credito Agricola in San José. Chavez said he had gotten an electronic deposit from the Moriah Wind Power Associates via Ansbach (Cayman) Ltd., a private bank on Grand Cayman island. That was all he knew.

Chavez called Kim back ten minutes later to say he had made inquiries at Ansbach and had obtained a record of a wire transfer that was paid into the Moriah account by the International Wilderness Preservation Society three days before that. And the IWPS transfer noted in the comment field, "G. Morton Research Fund."

John Kim called his Vancouver client, Nat Damon, to ask what the check was for. Damon said it was for the lease of a small two-man research submarine.

Kim thought that was pretty interesting, so he telephoned his friend George Morton to kid him a bit, and ask why he was leasing a submarine. And to his surprise, Morton knew absolutely nothing about it.

Evans finished taking down notes on the pad. He said, "This is what some bank manager in Vancouver told you?"

"Yes. A good friend of mine. Why are you looking at me that way?"

"Because it's a lot of information," Evans said. He didn't know the banking rules in Canada, to say nothing of Costa Rica, but he knew it was unlikely that any banks would freely exchange information in the way Morton had described. If the Vancouver manager's story was true, there was more to it that he wasn't telling. Evans made a note to check into it. "And do you know the International Wilderness Preservation Society, which has your check for a quarter of a million dollars?"

Morton shook his head. "Never heard of them."

"So you never gave them two hundred and fifty thousand dollars?"

Morton shook his head. "I'll tell you what I did do, in the last week," he said. "I gave two hundred and fifty grand to Nicholas Drake to cover a monthly operating shortfall. He told me he had some problem about a big contributor from Seattle not coming through for a week. Drake's asked me to help him out before like that, once or twice."

"You think that money ended up in Vancouver?"

Morton nodded.

"You better ask Drake about it," Evans said.

"I have no idea at all," Drake said, looking mystified. "Costa Rica? International Wilderness Preservation? My goodness, I can't imagine."

Evans said, "You know the International Wilderness Preservation Society?"

"Very well," Drake said. "They're excellent. We've worked closely with them on any number of projects around the world—the Everglades, Tiger Tops in Nepal, the Lake Toba preserve in Sumatra. The only thing I can think is that somehow George's check was mistakenly deposited in the wrong account. Or . . . I just don't know. I have to call the office. But it's late in California. It'll have to wait until morning."

Morton was staring at Drake, not speaking.

"George," Drake said, turning to him. "I'm sure this must make you feel very strange. Even if it's an honest mistake—as I am almost certain it is—it's still a lot of money to be mishandled. I feel terrible. But mistakes happen, especially if you use a lot of unpaid volunteers, as we do. But you and I have been friends for a long time. I want you to know that I will get to the bottom of this. And of course I will see that the money is recovered at once. You have my word, George."

"Thank you," Morton said.

They all climbed into the Land Cruiser.

The vehicle bounced over the barren plain. "Damn, those Icelanders are stubborn," Drake said, staring out the window. "They may be the most stubborn researchers in the world."

"He never saw your point?" Evans said.

"No," Drake said, "I couldn't make him understand. Scientists can't adopt that lofty attitude anymore. They can't say, 'I do the research, and I don't care how it is used.' That's out of date. It's irresponsible. Even in a seemingly obscure field like glacier geology. Because, like it or not, we're in the middle of a war—a global war of information versus disinformation. The war is fought on many battlegrounds. Newspaper op-eds. Television reports. Scientific journals. Websites, conferences, classrooms—and courtrooms, too, if it comes to that." Drake shook his head. "We have truth on our side, but we're outnumbered and outfunded. Today, the environmental movement is David battling Goliath. And Goliath is Aventis and Alcatel, Humana and GE, BP and Bayer, Shell and Glaxo-Wellcome—huge, global, corporate. These people are the implacable enemies of our planet, and Per Einarsson, out there on his glacier, is irresponsible to pretend it isn't happening."

Sitting beside Drake, Peter Evans nodded sympathetically, though in fact he took everything Drake was saying with a large grain of salt. The head of NERF was famously melodramatic. And Drake was pointedly ignoring the fact that several of the corporations he had named made substantial contributions to NERF every year, and three executives from those companies actually sat on Drake's board of advisors. That was true of many environmental organizations these days, although the reasons behind corporate involvement were much debated.

"Well," Morton said, "maybe Per will reconsider later on."

"I doubt it," Drake said gloomily. "He was angry. We've lost this battle, I'm sorry to say. But we do what we always do. Soldier on. Fight the good fight."

It was silent in the car for a while.

"The girls were damn good looking," Morton said. "Weren't they, Peter?"

"Yes," Evans said. "They were."

Evans knew that Morton was trying to lighten the mood in the car. But Drake would have none of it. The head of NERF stared morosely at the barren landscape, and shook his head mournfully at the snow-covered mountains in the distance.

Evans had traveled many times with Drake and Morton in the last couple of years. Usually, Morton could cheer everybody around him, even Drake, who was glum and fretful.

But lately Drake had become even more pessimistic than usual. Evans had first noticed it a few weeks ago, and had wondered at the time if there was illness in the family, or something else that was bothering him. But it seemed there was nothing amiss. At least, nothing that anyone would talk about. NERF was a beehive of activity; they had moved into a wonderful new building in Beverly Hills; fund-raising was at an all-time high; they were planning spectacular new events and conferences, including the Abrupt Climate Change Conference that would begin in two months. Yet despite these successes—or because of them?—Drake seemed more miserable than ever.

Morton noticed it, too, but he shrugged it off. "He's a lawyer," he said. "What do you expect? Forget about it."

By the time they reached Reykjavík, the sunny day had turned wet and chilly. It was sleeting at Keflavík airport, obliging them to wait while the wings of the white Gulfstream jet were de-iced. Evans slipped away to a corner of the hangar and, since it was still the middle of the night in the US, placed a call to a friend in banking in Hong Kong. He asked about the Vancouver story.

"Absolutely impossible," was the immediate answer. "No bank would divulge such information, even to another bank. There's an STR in the chain somewhere."

"An STR?"

"Suspicious transfer report. If it looks like money for drug trafficking or terrorism, the account gets tagged. And from then on, it's tracked. There are ways to track electronic transfers, even with strong encryption. But none of that tracking is ever going to wind up on the desk of a bank manager."

"No?"

"Not a chance. You'd need international law-enforcement credentials to see that tracking report."

"So this bank manager didn't do all this himself?"

"I doubt it. There is somebody else involved in this story. A policeman of some kind. Somebody you're not being told about."

"Like a customs guy, or Interpol?"

"Or something."

"Why would my client be contacted at all?"

"I don't know. But it's not an accident. Does your client have any radical tendencies?"

Thinking of Morton, Evans wanted to laugh. "Absolutely not."

"You quite sure, Peter?"

"Well, yes . . ."

"Because sometimes these wealthy donors amuse themselves, or justify themselves, by supporting terrorist groups. That's what happened with the IRA. Rich Americans in Boston supported them for decades. But times have changed. No one is amused any longer. Your client should be careful. And if you're his attorney, you should be careful, too. Hate to visit you in prison, Peter."

And he hung up.

The flight attendant poured Morton's vodka into a cut-glass tumbler. "No more ice, sweetie," Morton said, raising his hand. They were flying west, over Greenland, a vast expanse of ice and cloud in pale sun beneath them.

Morton sat with Drake, who talked about how the Greenland ice cap was melting. And the rate at which the Arctic ice was melting. And Canadian glaciers were receding. Morton sipped his vodka and nodded. "So Iceland is an anomaly?"

"Oh yes," Drake said. "An anomaly. Everywhere else, glaciers are melting at an unprecedented rate."

"It's good we have you, Nick," Morton said, putting his hand on Drake's shoulder.

Drake smiled. "And it's good we have *you*, George," he said. "We wouldn't be able to accomplish anything without your generous support. You've made the Vanutu lawsuit possible—and that's extremely important for the publicity it will generate. And as for your other grants, well . . . words fail me."

"Words never fail you," Morton said, slapping him on the back.

Sitting across from them, Evans thought they really were the odd couple. Morton, big and hearty, dressed casually in jeans and a workshirt, always seeming to burst from his clothes. And Nicholas Drake, tall and painfully thin, wearing a coat and tie, with his scrawny neck rising from the collar of a shirt that never seemed to fit.

In their manner, too, they were complete opposites. Morton loved to be around as many people as possible, loved to eat, and laugh. He had a penchant for pretty girls, vintage sports cars, Asian art, and practical jokes. His parties drew most of Hollywood to his Holmby Hills mansion; his charity functions were always special, always written up the next day.

Of course, Drake attended those functions, but invariably left early, sometimes before dinner. Often he pleaded illness—his own or a friend's. In fact, Drake was a solitary, ascetic man, who detested parties and noise. Even when he stood at a podium giving a speech, he conveyed an air of isolation, as if he were alone in the room. And, being Drake, he made it work for him. He managed to suggest that he was a lone messenger in the wilderness, delivering the truth the audience needed to hear.

Despite their differences in temperament, the two men had built a durable friendship that had lasted the better part of a decade. Morton, the heir to a forklift fortune, had the congenital uneasiness of inherited wealth. Drake had a good use for that money, and in return provided Morton with a passion, and a cause, that informed and guided Morton's life. Morton's name appeared on the board of advisors of the Audubon Society, the Wilderness Society, the World Wildlife Fund, and the Sierra Club. He was a major contributor to Greenpeace and the Environmental Action League.

All this culminated in two enormous gifts by Morton to NERF. The first was a grant of $1 million, to finance the Vanutu lawsuit. The second was a grant of $9 million to NERF itself, to finance future research and litigation on behalf of the environment. Not surprisingly, the NERF board had voted Morton their Concerned Citizen of the Year. A banquet in his honor was scheduled for later that fall, in San Francisco.

Evans sat across from the two men, idly thumbing through a magazine. But he had been shaken by the Hong Kong call, and found himself observing Morton with some care.

Morton still had his hand on Drake's shoulder, and was telling him a joke—as usual, trying to get Drake to laugh—but it seemed to Evans that he detected a certain distance on Morton's part. Morton had withdrawn, but didn't want Drake to notice.

This suspicion was confirmed when Morton stood up abruptly and headed for the cockpit. "I want to know about this damn electronic thing," he said. Since takeoff, they had been experiencing the effects of a major solar flare that rendered satellite telephones erratic or unusable. The pilots said the effect was heightened near the poles, and would soon diminish as they headed south.

And Morton seemed eager to make some calls. Evans wondered to whom. It was now four A.M. in New York, one A.M. in Los Angeles. Who was Morton calling? But of course it could concern any of his ongoing environmental projects—water purification in Cambodia, reforestation in Guinea, habitat preservation in Madagascar, medicinal plants in Peru. To say nothing of the German expedition to measure the thickness of the ice in Antarctica. Morton was personally involved in all these projects. He knew them in detail, knew the scientists involved, had visited the locations himself.

So it could be anything.

But somehow, Evans felt, it wasn't just anything.

Morton came back. "Pilots say it's okay now." He sat by himself in the front of the plane, reached for his headset, and pulled the sliding door shut for privacy.

Evans turned back to his magazine.

Drake said, "You think he's drinking more than usual?"

"Not really," Evans said.

"I worry."

"I wouldn't," Evans said.

"You realize," Drake said, "we are just five weeks from the banquet in his honor, in San Francisco. That's our biggest fund-raising event of the year. It will generate considerable publicity, and it'll help us launch the conference on Abrupt Climate Change."

"Uh-huh," Evans said.

"I'd like to ensure that the publicity focuses on environmental issues, and not anything else. Of a personal nature, if you know what I mean."

Evans said, "Isn't this a conversation you should be having with George?"

"Oh, I have. I only mention it to you because you spend so much time with him."

"I don't, really."

"You know he likes you, Peter," Drake said. "You're the son he never had or—hell, I don't know. But he *does* like you. And I'm just asking you to help us, if you can."

"I don't think he'll embarrass you, Nick."

"Just . . . keep an eye on him."

"Okay. Sure."

At the front of the plane, the sliding door opened. Morton said, "Mr. Evans? If you please."

Peter got up and went forward.

He slid the door shut behind him.

"I have been on the phone to Sarah," Morton said. Sarah Jones was his assistant in LA.

"Isn't it late?"

"It's her job. She's well paid. Sit down." Evans sat in the chair opposite. "Have you ever heard of the NSIA?"

"No."

"The National Security Intelligence Agency?"

Evans shook his head. "No. But there are twenty security agencies."

"Ever heard of John Kenner?"

"No . . ."

"Apparently he's a professor at MIT."

"No," Evans said. "Sorry. Does he have something to do with the environment?"

"He may. See what you can find out."

Evans turned to the laptop by his seat, and flipped open the screen. It was connected to the Internet by satellite. He started to type.

In a few moments he was looking at a picture of a fit-looking man with prematurely gray hair and heavy horn-rim glasses. The attached biography was brief. Evans read it aloud. "Richard John Kenner, William T. Harding Professor of Geoenvironmental Engineering."

"Whatever that means," Morton said.

"He is thirty-nine. Doctorate in civil engineering from Caltech at age twenty. Did his thesis on soil erosion in Nepal. Barely missed qualifying for the Olympic ski team. A JD from Harvard Law School. Spent the next four years in government. Department of the Interior, Office of Policy Analysis. Scientific advisor to the Intergovernmental Negotiating Committee. Hobby is mountain climbing; he was reported dead on Naya Khanga peak in Nepal, but he wasn't. Tried to climb K2, driven back by weather."

"K2," Morton said. "Isn't that the most dangerous peak?"

"I think so. Looks like he's a serious climber. Anyway, he then went to MIT, where I'd say his rise has been spectacular. Associate professor in '93. Director of the MIT Center for Risk Analysis in '95. William T. Harding Professor in '96. Consultant to the EPA, the Department of the Interior, the Department of Defense, the government of Nepal, God knows who else. Looks like a lot of corporations. And since 2002, on faculty leave."

"Meaning what?"

"It just says he's on leave."

"For the last two years?" Morton came and looked over Evans's shoulder. "I don't like it. The guy burns up the track at MIT, goes on leave, and never comes back. You think he got into trouble?"

"I don't know. But . . ." Evans was calculating the dates. "Professor Kenner got a doctorate from Caltech at twenty. Got his law degree from

Harvard in two years instead of three. Professor at MIT when he's twenty-eight . . ."

"Okay, okay, so he's smart," Morton said. "I still want to know why he's on leave. And why he's in Vancouver."

Evans said, "He's in Vancouver?"

"He's been calling Sarah from Vancouver."

"Why?"

"He wants to meet with me."

"Well," Evans said, "I guess you'd better meet with him."

"I will," Morton said. "But what do you think he wants?"

"I have no idea. Funding? A project?"

"Sarah says he wants the meeting to be confidential. He doesn't want anybody to be told."

"Well, that's not hard. You're on an airplane."

"No," Morton said, jerking his thumb. "He specifically doesn't want Drake to be told."

"Maybe I'd better attend this meeting," Evans said.

"Yes," Morton said. "Maybe you should."

The iron gates swung open, and the car drove up the shaded driveway to the house that slowly came into view. This was Holmby Hills, the wealthiest area of Beverly Hills. The billionaires lived here, in residences hidden from the street by high gates and dense foliage. In this part of town, security cameras were all painted green, and tucked back unobtrusively.

The house came into view. It was a Mediterranean-style villa, cream colored, and large enough for a family of ten. Evans, who had been speaking to his office, flipped his cell phone shut and got out as the car came to a stop.

Birds chirped in the ficus trees. The air smelled of the gardenia and jasmine that bordered the driveway. A hummingbird hung near the purple bougainvillea at the garage. It was, Evans thought, a typical California moment. Evans had been raised in Connecticut and schooled in Boston; even after five years in California, the place still seemed exotic to him.

He saw that another car was parked in front of the house: a dark gray sedan. It had government license plates.

From out of the front door came Morton's assistant, Sarah Jones, a tall blond woman of thirty, as glamorous as any movie star. Sarah was dressed in a white tennis skirt and pink top, her hair pulled back in a pony tail. Morton kissed her lightly on the cheek. "You playing today?"

"I was. My boss came back early." She shook Evans's hand and turned back to Morton. "Good trip?"

"Fine. Drake is morose. And he won't drink. It gets tiresome."

As Morton started toward the door, Sarah said, "I think I ought to tell you, they're here right now."

"Who is?"

"Professor Kenner. And another guy with him. Foreign guy."

"Really? But didn't you tell them they had to—"

"Make an appointment? Yes, I did. They seem to think that doesn't apply to them. They just sat down and said they'd wait."

"You should have called me—"

"They got here five minutes ago."

"Huh. Okay." He turned to Evans. "Let's go, Peter."

They went inside. Morton's living room looked out on the garden in back of the house. The room was decorated with Asian antiques, including a large stone head from Cambodia. Sitting erectly on the couch were two men. One was an American of middle height, with short gray hair and glasses. The other was very dark, compact, and very handsome despite the thin scar that ran down the left side of his face in front of his ear. They were dressed in cotton slacks and lightweight sport coats. Both men sat on the edge of the couch, very alert, as if they might spring up at any moment.

"Look military, don't they?" Morton muttered, as they went into the room.

The two men stood. "Mr. Morton, I'm John Kenner from MIT, and this is my colleague, Sanjong Thapa. A graduate student from Mustang. In Nepal."

Morton said, "And this is *my* colleague, Peter Evans."

They shook hands all around. Kenner's grip was firm. Sanjong Thapa gave a very slight bow as he shook hands. He spoke softly, with a British accent. "How do you do."

"I didn't expect you," Morton said, "so soon."

"We work quickly."

"So I see. What's this about?"

"I'm afraid we need your help, Mr. Morton." Kenner smiled pleasantly at Evans and Sarah. "And unfortunately, our discussion is confidential."

"Mr. Evans is my attorney," Morton said, "and I have no secrets from my assistant—"

"I'm sure," Kenner said. "You may take them into your confidence whenever you choose. But we must speak to you alone."

Evans said, "If you don't mind, I'd like to see some identification."

"Of course," Kenner said. Both men reached for wallets. Evans was shown Massachusetts driver's licenses, MIT faculty cards, and passports. Then they handed out business cards.

John Kenner, PhD
Center for Risk Analysis
Massachusetts Institute of Technology
454 Massachusetts Avenue
Cambridge, MA 02138

Sanjong Thapa, PhD
Research Associate
Department of Geoenvironmental Engineering
Building 4-C 323
Massachusetts Institute of Technology
Cambridge, MA 02138

There were telephone numbers, fax, e-mail. Evans turned the cards over. It all looked straightforward.

Kenner said, "Now, if you and Miss Jones will excuse us . . ."

They were outside, in the hallway, looking into the living room through the large glass doors. Morton was sitting on one couch. Kenner and Sanjong were on the other. The discussion was quiet. In fact, it looked to Evans just like one more of the endless investment meetings that Morton endured.

Evans picked up the hall phone and dialed a number. "Center for Risk Analysis," a woman said.

"Professor Kenner's office, please."

"One moment." Clicking. Another voice. "Center for Risk Analysis, Professor Kenner's office."

"Good afternoon," Evans said. "My name is Peter Evans, and I'm calling for Professor Kenner."

"I'm sorry, he is not in the office."

"Do you know where he is?"

"Professor Kenner is on extended leave."

"It is important that I reach him," Evans said. "Do you know how I could do that?"

"Well, it shouldn't be hard, since you are in Los Angeles and so is he."

So she had seen the caller ID, Evans thought. He would have imagined Morton had a blocked ID. But evidently not. Or perhaps the secretary in Massachusetts had a way to unblock it.

"Well," Evans said, "can you tell me—"

"I'm sorry, Mr. Evans," she said, "but I'm not able to help you further."

Click.

Sarah said, "What was that about?"

Before Evans could answer, a cell phone rang in the living room. He saw Kenner reach into his pocket, and answer briefly. Then he turned, looked at Evans, and waved.

Sarah said, "His office called him?"

"Looks like it."

"So I guess that's Professor Kenner."

"I guess it is," Evans said. "And we're dismissed."

"Come on," Sarah said. "I'll give you a ride home."

They walked past the open garage, the row of Ferraris glinting in the sun. Morton owned nine vintage Ferraris, which he kept in various garages. These included a 1947 Spyder Corsa, a 1956 Testa Rossa, and a 1959 California Spyder, each worth more than a million dollars. Evans knew this because he reviewed the insurance every time Morton bought another one. At the far end of the line was Sarah's black Porsche convertible. She backed it out, and he climbed in beside her.

Even by Los Angeles standards, Sarah Jones was an extremely beautiful woman. She was tall, with a honey-colored tan, shoulder-length blond hair, blue eyes, perfect features, very white teeth. She was athletic in the casual way that California people were athletic, generally showing up for work in a jogging suit or short tennis skirt. She played golf and tennis, scuba dived, mountain biked, skied, snowboarded, and God knew what else. Evans felt tired whenever he thought about it.

But he also knew that she had "issues," to use the California word. Sarah was the youngest child of a wealthy San Francisco family; her father was a powerful attorney who had held political office; her mother was a former high fashion model. Sarah's older brothers and sisters were all happily married, all successful, and all waiting for her to follow in their footsteps. She found her family's collective success a burden.

Evans had always wondered why she chose to work for Morton, another powerful and wealthy man. Or why she had come to Los Angeles at all, since her family regarded any address south of the Bay Bridge to be hopelessly tawdry. But she was good at her job, and devoted to Morton. And as George often said, her presence was aesthetically pleasing. And the actors and celebrities who attended Morton's parties agreed; she had dated several of them. Which further displeased her family.

Sometimes Evans wondered if everything she did was rebellion. Like her driving—she drove quickly, almost recklessly, shooting down Benedict Canyon, heading into Beverly Hills. "Do you want to go to the office, or your apartment?"

"My apartment," he said. "I have to pick up my car."

She nodded, swerved around a slow-moving Mercedes, then cut left down a side street. Evans took a deep breath.

"Listen," she said. "Do you know what netwar is?"

"What?" He wasn't sure he had heard her over the sound of the wind. "Netwar."

"No," he said. "Why?"

"I heard them talking about it, before you showed up. Kenner and that Sanjong guy."

Evans shook his head. "Doesn't ring a bell. You sure it wasn't net*ware?*"

"Might have been." She sped across Sunset, running a yellow light, and then downshifted as she came to Beverly. "You still on Roxbury?"

He said he was. He looked at her long legs, protruding from the short white skirt. "Who were you going to play tennis with?"

"I don't think you know him."

"It's not, uh . . ."

"No. That's over."

"I see."

"I'm serious, it's *over.*"

"Okay, Sarah. I hear you."

"You lawyers are all so suspicious."

"So, it's a lawyer you're playing with?"

"No, it is not a lawyer. I don't play with lawyers."

"What do you do with them?"

"As little as possible. Like everybody else."

"I'm sorry to hear that."

"Except you, of course," she said, giving him a dazzling smile.

She accelerated hard, making the engine scream.

Peter Evans lived in one of the older apartment buildings on Roxbury Drive in the flats of Beverly Hills. There were four units in his building, across the street from Roxbury Park. It was a nice park, a big green expanse, always busy. He saw Hispanic nannies chatting in groups while they minded the children of rich people, and several oldsters sitting in the sun. Off in a corner, a working mother in a business suit had taken off lunch to be with the kids.

The car screeched to a stop. "Here you are."

"Thanks," he said, getting out.

"Isn't it time to move? You've been here five years."

"I'm too busy to move," he said.

"Got your keys?"

"Yeah. But there's always one under the doormat." He reached in his pocket, jingled metal. "All set."

"See you." And she raced off, squealed around the corner, and was gone.

Evans walked through the little sunlit courtyard, and went up to his apartment, on the second floor. As always, he had found Sarah slightly distressing. She was so beautiful, and so flirtatious. He always had the feeling that she kept men at a distance by keeping them off balance. At least, she kept *him* off balance. He could never tell if she wanted him to ask her out or not. But considering his relationship with Morton, it was a bad idea. He would never do it.

As soon as he walked in the door, the phone began to ring. It was his assistant, Heather. She was going home early because she felt sick. Heather frequently felt sick toward the afternoon, in time to beat rush hour traffic. She tended to call in sick on Fridays or Mondays. Yet the firm showed a surprising reluctance to fire her; she had been there for years.

Some said she had had a relationship with Bruce Black, the founding partner, and that, ever since, Bruce lived in constant dread that his wife would find out, since she had all the money. Others claimed Heather was seeing another of the firm's partners, always unspecified. A third story was that she had been on the scene when the firm moved offices from one Century City skyscraper to another, in the course of which she stumbled on some incriminating documents, and copied them.

Evans suspected the truth was more mundane: that she was a clever woman who had worked in the firm long enough to know everything about wrongful termination suits, and now carefully gauged her repeated infractions against the cost and aggravation of their firing her. And in this way worked about thirty weeks a year.

Heather was invariably assigned to the best junior associate in the firm, on the assumption that a really good attorney wouldn't be hampered by her inconstancy. Evans had tried for years to get rid of her. He was promised a new assistant next year. He saw it as a promotion.

"I'm sorry you don't feel well," he told Heather dutifully. One had to go along with her pretense.

"It's just my stomach," she said. "I have to see the doctor."

"Are you going today?"

"Well, I'm trying to get an appointment . . ."

"All right, then."

"But I wanted to tell you they just set a big meeting for the day after tomorrow. Nine o'clock in the big conference room."

"Oh?"

"Mr. Morton just called it. Apparently ten or twelve people are called."

"You know who?"

"No. They didn't say."

Evans thought: Useless. "Okay," he said.

"And don't forget you have the arraignment for Morton's daughter next week. This time it's Pasadena, not downtown. And Margo Lane's calling about her Mercedes lawsuit. And that BMW dealer still wants to go forward."

"He still wants to sue the church?"

"He calls every other day."

"Okay. Is that it?"

"No, there's about ten others. I'll try to leave the list on your desk if I feel well enough . . ."

That meant she wouldn't. "Okay," he said.

"Are you coming in?"

"No, it's too late. I need to get some sleep."

"Then I'll see you tomorrow."

He realized he was very hungry. There was nothing to eat in the refrigerator except a container of yogurt of indeterminate age, some wilted celery, and a half-finished bottle of wine left over from his last date, about two weeks earlier. He had been seeing a girl named Carol who did product liability at another firm. They'd picked each other up in the gym and had begun a desultory, intermittent affair. They were both busy, and not especially interested in each other, to tell the truth. They met once or twice a week, had passionate sex, and then one of them would plead a breakfast appointment the next day and go home early. Sometimes they went to dinner as well, but not usually. Neither of them wanted to take the time.

He went into the living room to check his answering machine. There was no message from Carol, but there was a message from Janis, another girl he sometimes saw.

Janis was a trainer in the gym, the possessor of one of those LA bodies, perfectly proportioned and rock hard. Sex for Janis was an athletic event, involving multiple rooms, couches, and chairs, and it always left Evans feeling vaguely inadequate, as if his body fat weren't low enough for her. But he continued to see her, feeling vaguely proud that he could have a girl who looked so astonishing, even if the sex wasn't that good. And she was often available on short notice. Janis had a boyfriend who was older, a producer for a cable news station. He was out of town a lot, and she was restless.

Janis had left a message the night before. Evans didn't bother to call her back. With Janis it was always that night, or forget it.

Before Janis and Carol, there had been other women, more or less the same. Evans told himself he should find a more satisfying relationship. Something more serious, more adult. More suited to his age and station in life. But he was busy, and just took things as they came.

Meanwhile he was hungry.

He went back down to his car and drove to the nearest drive-in, a hamburger joint on Pico. They knew him there. He had a double cheeseburger and a strawberry shake.

He went home, intending to go to bed. Then he remembered that he owed Morton a call.

"I'm glad you called," Morton said, "I've just been going over some things with—going over some things. Where are we now on my donations to NERF? The Vanutu lawsuit, all that?"

"I don't know," Evans said. "The papers are drawn and signed, but I don't think anything's been paid yet."

"Good. I want you to hold off payments."

"Sure, no problem."

"Just for a while."

"Okay."

"There's no need to say anything to NERF."

"No, no. Of course not."

"Good."

Evans hung up. He went into the bedroom to get undressed. The phone rang again.

It was Janis. The exercise instructor.

"Hey," she said. "I was thinking about you, and I wondered what you were doing."

"As a matter of fact, I was going to go to bed."

"Oh. Pretty early for that."

"I just got in from Iceland."

"So you must be tired."

"Well," he said. "Not that tired."

"Want company?"

"Sure."

She giggled and hung up.

BEVERLY HILLS
TUESDAY, AUGUST 24
6:04 A.M.

Evans awoke to the sound of rhythmic gasping. He flung his hand across the bed, but Janis wasn't there. Her side of the bed was still warm. He raised his head slightly, yawning. In the warm morning light he saw one slender, perfectly formed leg rise above the foot of the bed, to be joined by the other leg. Then both legs slowly descended. Gasping. Then legs up again.

"Janis," he said, "what are you doing?"

"I have to warm up." She stood, smiling, naked and at ease, confident of her appearance, every muscle outlined. "I have a class at seven."

"What time is it?"

"Six."

He groaned, and buried his head in the pillow.

"You really should get up now," she said. "It shortens your lifespan to sleep in."

He groaned again. Janis was full of health information; it was her job. "How can it possibly shorten my life to sleep?"

"They did studies on rats. They didn't let them sleep, and you know what? They lived longer."

"Uh-huh. Would you mind turning on the coffee?"

"Okay," she said, "but you really should give up coffee . . ." She drifted out of the room.

He swung his feet onto the floor and said, "Haven't you heard? Coffee prevents strokes."

"It does not," she said, from the kitchen. "Coffee has nine hundred twenty-three different chemicals in it, and it is *not* good for you."

"New study," he said. It was true, too.

"Besides, it causes cancer."

"That's never been shown."

"And miscarriages."

"Not a concern for me."

"And nervous tension."

"Janis, please."

She came back, crossing her arms across her perfect breasts as she leaned against the doorjamb. He could see the veins in her lower abdomen, running down to her groin. "Well, you *are* nervous, Peter. You have to admit it."

"Only when I look at your body."

She pouted. "You don't take me seriously." She turned back into the kitchen, showing him her perfect, high glutes. He heard her open the refrigerator. "There's no milk."

"Black is fine."

He stood, and headed for the shower.

"Did you have any damage?" she said.

"From what?"

"From the earthquake. We had a little one, while you were gone. About 4.3."

"Not that I know."

"Well, it sure moved your TV."

He stopped in mid-stride. "What?"

"It moved your TV. Look for yourself."

The morning sunlight that slanted through the window clearly showed the faint outline where the base of the television had compressed the carpet. The TV had been moved about three inches from its former position. It was an old thirty-two-inch monitor, and damned heavy. It didn't move easily. Looking at it now gave Evans a chill.

"You're lucky," she said. "You have all those glass things on your mantel. They break all the time, even in a small quake. Do you have an insurance policy?"

He didn't answer. He was bent over, looking behind the television at the connections. Everything looked normal. But he hadn't looked behind his TV for about a year. He wouldn't really know.

"By the way," she said, "this is not organic coffee. You should at least drink organic. Are you listening to me?"

"Just a minute." He had crouched down in front of the television, looking for anything unusual beneath the set. He could see nothing out of the ordinary.

"And what is *this*?" she said.

He looked over. She was holding a donut in her hand. "Peter," Janis said severely, "do you know how much fat's in these things? You might as well just eat a stick of butter."

"I know . . . I should give them up."

"Well, you should. Unless you want to develop diabetes later in life. Why are you on the floor?"

"I was checking the TV."

"Why? Is it broken?"

"I don't think so." He got to his feet.

"The water is running in your shower," she said. "That's not environmentally conscious." She poured coffee, handed it to him. "Go and take your shower. I've got to get to my class."

When he came out of the shower, she was gone. He pulled the covers up over the bed (as close as he ever came to making it) and went into the closet to dress for the day.

The law firm of Hassle and Black occupied five floors of an office building in Century City. They were a forward-looking, socially aware firm. They represented many Hollywood celebrities and wealthy activists who were committed to environmental concerns. The fact that they also represented three of the biggest land developers in Orange County was less often publicized. But as the partners said, it kept the firm balanced.

Evans had joined the firm because of its many environmentally active clients, particularly George Morton. He was one of four attorneys who worked almost full-time for Morton, and for Morton's pet charity, the National Environmental Resource Fund, NERF.

Nevertheless, he was still a junior associate, and his office was small, with a window that looked directly at the flat glass wall of the skyscraper across the street.

Evans looked over the papers on his desk. It was the usual stuff that came to junior attorneys. There was a residential sublet, an employment agreement, written interrogatories for a bankruptcy, a form for the Franchise Tax Board, and two drafted letters threatening lawsuits on behalf of his clients—one for an artist against a gallery refusing to return his unsold paintings, and one for George Morton's mistress, who claimed that the parking attendant at Sushi Roku had scratched her Mercedes convertible while parking it.

The mistress, Margaret Lane, was an ex-actress with a bad temper and a propensity for litigation. Whenever George neglected her—which, in recent months, was increasingly often—she would find a reason to sue somebody. And the suit would inevitably land on Evans's desk. He made a note to call Margo; he didn't think she should proceed with this suit, but she would take convincing.

The next item was a spreadsheet from a Beverly Hills BMW dealer who claimed that the "What Would Jesus Drive?" campaign had hurt his business because it denigrated luxury cars. Apparently his dealership was a block from a church, and some parishioners had come around after services and harangued his sales staff. The dealer didn't like that, but it looked to Evans as if his sales figures were higher this year than last. Evans made a note to call him, too.

Then he checked his e-mails, sorting through twenty offers to enlarge his penis, ten offers for tranquilizers, and another ten to get a new mortgage now before rates started to rise. There were only a half-dozen e-mails of importance, the first from Herb Lowenstein, asking to see him. Lowenstein was the senior partner on Morton's account; he did mostly estate management, but handled other aspects of investments as well. For Morton, estate management was a full-time job.

Evans wandered down the hall to Herb's office.

Lisa, Herb Lowenstein's assistant, was listening on the phone. She hung up and looked guilty when Evans entered. "He's talking to Jack Nicholson."

"How is Jack?"

"He's good. Finishing a picture with Meryl. There were some problems."

Lisa Ray was a bright-eyed twenty-seven-year-old, and a dedicated gossip. Evans had long ago come to rely on her for office information of all sorts.

"What's Herb want me for?"

"Something about Nick Drake."

"What's this meeting about tomorrow at nine?"

"I don't *know*," she said, sounding amazed. "I can't find out a *thing.*

"Who called it?"

"Morton's accountants." She looked at the phone on her desk. "Oh, he's hung up. You can go right in."

Herb Lowenstein stood and shook Evans's hand perfunctorily. He was a pleasant-faced balding man, mild-mannered and slightly nerdy. His office was decorated with dozens of pictures of his family, stacked three and four deep on his desk. He got on well with Evans, if only because these days, whenever Morton's thirty-year-old daughter got arrested for cocaine possession, it was Evans who went downtown at midnight to post her bail. Lowenstein had done it for many years, and now was glad to sleep through the night.

"So," he said, "how was Iceland?"

"Good. Cold."

"Is everything okay?"

"Sure."

"I mean, between George and Nick. Everything okay there?"

"I think so. Why?"

"Nick is worried. He called me twice in the last hour."

"About what?"

"Where are we on George's NERF donation?"

"Nick's asking that?"

"Is there a problem about it?"

"George wants to hold off for a while."

"Why?"

"He didn't say."

"Is it this Kenner guy?"

"George didn't say. He just said, hold off." Evans wondered how Lowenstein knew about Kenner.

"What do I tell Nick?"

"Tell him it's in the works and we don't have a date for him yet."

"But there's not a problem with it, is there?"

"Not that I've been told," Evans said.

"Okay," Lowenstein said. "In this room. Tell me: Is there a problem?"

"There might be." Evans was thinking that George rarely held up charitable donations. And there had been a certain tension in the brief talk he had with him the night before.

"What's this meeting about tomorrow morning?" Lowenstein said. "The big conference room."

"Beats me."

"George didn't tell you?"

"No."

"Nick is very upset."

"Well, that's not unusual for Nick."

"Nick has heard of this Kenner guy. He thinks he's a troublemaker. Some kind of anti-environmental guy."

"I doubt that. He's a professor at MIT. In some environmental science."

"Nick thinks he's a troublemaker."

"I couldn't say."

"He overheard you and Morton talking about Kenner on the airplane."

"Nick should stop listening at keyholes."

"He's worried about his standing with George."

"Not surprising," Evans said. "Nick screwed up on a big check. Got deposited in the wrong account."

"I heard about that. It was an error by a volunteer. You can't blame Nick for that."

"It doesn't build confidence."

"It was deposited to the International Wilderness Preservation Society. A great organization. And the money is being transferred back, even as we speak."

"That's fine."

"Where are you in this?"

"Nowhere. I just do what the client says."

"But you advise him."

"If he asks me. He hasn't asked."

"It sounds like you've lost confidence yourself."

Evans shook his head. "Herb," he said. "I'm not aware of any problem. I'm aware of a delay. That's all."

"Okay," Lowenstein said, reaching for the phone. "I'll calm Nick down."

Evans went back to his office. His phone was ringing. He answered it. "What are you doing today?" Morton said.

"Not much. Paperwork."

"That can wait. I want you to go over and see how that Vanutu lawsuit is coming."

"Jeez, George, it's still pretty preliminary. I think the filing is several months away."

"Pay them a visit," Morton said.

"Okay, they're in Culver City, I'll call over there and—"

"No. Don't call. Just go."

"But if they're not expecting—"

"That's right. That's what I want. Let me know what you find out, Peter."

And he hung up.

The Vanutu litigation team had taken over an old warehouse south of Culver City. It was an industrial area, with potholes in the streets. There was nothing to see from the curb: just a plain brick wall, and a door with the street number in battered metal numerals. Evans pushed the buzzer and was admitted to a small walled-off reception area. He could hear the low murmur of voices from the other side of the wall, but he could see nothing at all.

Two armed guards stood on either side of the far door, leading into the warehouse itself. A receptionist sat at a small desk. She gave him an unfriendly look.

"And you are?"

"Peter Evans, Hassle and Black."

"To see?"

"Mr. Balder."

"You have an appointment?"

"No."

The receptionist looked disbelieving. "I will buzz his assistant."

"Thank you."

The receptionist talked on the phone in a low voice. He heard her mention the name of the law firm. Evans looked at the two guards. They were from a private security firm. They stared back at him, their faces blank, unsmiling.

The receptionist hung up and said, "Ms. Haynes will be out in a moment." She nodded to the guards.

One of them came over and said to Evans, "Just a formality, sir. May I see some identification?"

Evans gave him his driver's license.

"Do you have any cameras or recording equipment on your person?"

"No," Evans said.

"Any disks, drives, flash cards, or other computer equipment?"

"No."

"Are you armed, sir?"

"No."

"Would you mind raising your arms for a moment?" When Evans gave him a strange look, the guard said, "Just think of it like airport security," and he patted him down. But he was also clearly feeling for wires. He ran his fingers over the collar of Evans's shirt, felt the stitching in his jacket, ran his finger around his waistband, and then asked him to take off his shoes. Finally he passed an electronic wand over him.

"You guys are serious," Evans said.

"Yes we are. Thank you, sir."

The guard stepped away, resuming his place at the wall. There was no place to sit, so Evans just stood there and waited. It was probably two minutes before the door opened. An attractive but tough-looking woman in her late twenties, with short dark hair and blue eyes, wearing jeans and a white shirt, said, "Mr. Evans? I'm Jennifer Haynes." Her handshake was firm. "I work with John Balder. Come this way."

They went inside.

They were in a narrow corridor, with a locked door at the far end. Evans realized it was a security lock—two doors to get inside.

"What was that all about?" he said, indicating the guards.

"We've had a little trouble."

"What kind of trouble?"

"People want to know what's going on here."

"Uh-huh . . ."

"We've learned to be careful."

She held her card against the door, and it buzzed open.

They entered an old warehouse—a vast, high-ceilinged space, separated into large rooms by glass partitions. Immediately to his left, behind glass, Evans saw a room filled with computer terminals, each manned by a young person with a stack of documents beside their keyboard. In big lettering on the glass it said, "DATA-RAW."

To his right, there was a matching conference room labeled "SATELLITES/RADIOSONDE." Evans saw four people inside that room, busily discussing huge blowups of a graph on the wall, jagged lines on a grid.

Farther along there was another room marked "GENERAL CIRCULATION MODELS (GCMS)." Here the walls were plastered with large maps of the world, graphical representations in many colors.

"Wow," Evans said. "Big operation."

"Big lawsuit," Jennifer Haynes replied. "These are all our issue teams. They're mostly graduate students in climate science, not attorneys. Each team is researching a different issue for us." She pointed around the warehouse. "The first group does raw data, meaning processed data from the Goddard Institute for Space Studies at Columbia University, in New York, from the USHCN at Oak Ridge, Tennessee, and from Hadley Center in East Anglia, England. Those are the major sources of temperature data from around the world."

"I see," Evans said.

"Then the group over there works on satellite data. Orbiting satellites have recorded temperatures of the upper atmosphere since 1979, so there is more than a twenty-year record. We're trying to figure out what to do about it."

"What to do about it?"

"The satellite data's a problem," she said.

"Why?"

As though she hadn't heard him, she pointed to the next room. "The team there is doing comparative analyses of GCMs—meaning the computer-generated climate models—from the 1970s to the present. As you know, these models are immensely complex, manipulating a million variables or more at once. They are by far the most complex computer models ever created by man. We're dealing with American, British, and German models, primarily."

"I see . . ." Evans was starting to feel overwhelmed.

"And the team down there is doing sea-level issues. Around the corner is paleoclimate. Those're proxy studies, of course. And the final team is dealing with solar irradiance and aerosols. Then we have an off-site team at UCLA that is doing atmospheric feedback mechanisms, primarily focusing on cloud cover as it varies with temperature change. And that's about all of it." She paused, seeing the confusion on Evans's face. "I'm sorry. Since you work with George Morton, I assumed you were familiar with all this stuff."

"Who said I work with George Morton?"

She smiled. "We know our job, Mr. Evans."

They passed a final glass-walled room that had no label. It was filled with charts and huge photographs, and three-dimensional models of the earth set inside plastic cubes. "What's this?" he said.

"Our AV team. They prepare visuals for the jury. Some of the data is extremely complex, and we're trying to find the simplest and most forceful way to present it."

They walked on. Evans said, "Is it really that complicated?"

"That's correct," she said. "The island nation of Vanutu is actually four coral atolls in the southern Pacific, which have a maximum elevation of twenty feet above sea level. The eight thousand inhabitants of those islands are at risk of being flooded out by rising sea levels caused by global warming."

"Yes," Evans said. "I understand that. But why do you have so many people working on the science?"

She looked at him oddly. "Because we're trying to win the case."

"Yes . . ."

"And it's not an easy case to win."

"What do you mean?" Evans said. "This is global warming. Everybody knows that global warming is—"

A voice boomed from the other end of the warehouse. "Is *what?*"

A bald, bespectacled man came toward them. He had an ungainly gait, and looked like his nickname: the Bald Eagle. As always, John Balder was dressed all in blue: a blue suit, a blue shirt, and a blue tie. His manner was intense, his eyes narrowed as he looked at Evans. In spite of himself, Evans was intimidated to meet the famous litigator.

Evans extended his hand. "Peter Evans, Hassle and Black."

"And you work with George Morton?"

"Yes sir, I do."

"We are indebted to Mr. Morton's generosity. We strive to be worthy of his support."

"I'll tell him that, sir."

"I'm sure you will. You were speaking of global warming, Mr. Evans. Is it a subject that interests you?"

"Yes, sir, it does. And every concerned citizen of the planet."

"I certainly agree. But tell me. What *is* global warming, as you understand it?"

Evans tried to conceal his surprise. He hadn't expected to be quizzed. "Why do you ask?"

"We ask everybody who comes here. We're trying to get a feel for the general state of knowledge. What's global warming?"

"Global warming is the heating up of the earth from burning fossil fuels."

"Actually, that is not correct."

"It's not?"

"Not even close. Perhaps you'd try again."

Evans paused. It was obvious he was being interrogated by a fussy and precise legal mind. He knew the type only too well, from law school. He thought for a moment, choosing his words carefully. "Global warming is, uh, the heating up of the surface of the earth from the excess of carbon dioxide in the atmosphere that is produced by burning fossil fuels."

"Again, not correct."

"Why not?"

"Several reasons. At a minimum, I count four errors in the statement you just made."

"I don't understand," Evans said. "My statement—that's what global warming is."

"In fact, it is not." Balder's tone was crisp, authoritative. "Global warming is the *theory*—"

"—hardly a theory, anymore—"

"No, it is a *theory*," Balder said. "Believe me, I wish it were otherwise. But in fact, global warming is the *theory* that increased levels of carbon dioxide and certain other gases *are causing* an increase in the *average temperature* of the earth's *atmosphere* because of the so-called 'greenhouse effect.'"

"Well, okay," Evans said. "That's a more exact definition, but . . ."

"Mr. Evans, you yourself believe in global warming, I take it?"

"Of course."

"Believe in it strongly?"

"Sure. Everybody does."

"When you have a strongly held belief, don't you think it's important to express that belief accurately?"

Evans was starting to sweat. He really felt like he was back in law school. "Well, sir, I guess . . . not really, in this case. Because when you refer to global warming, everybody knows what you are talking about."

"Do they? I suspect that even you don't know what you are talking about."

Evans felt a burst of hot anger. Before he could check himself, he had blurted, "Look, just because I may not be expressing the fine details of the science—"

"I'm not concerned about *details*, Mr. Evans. I'm concerned about the *core* of your strongly held beliefs. I suspect you have no basis for those beliefs."

"With all due respect, that's ridiculous." He caught his breath. "Sir."

"You mean you do have such a basis?"

"Of course I do."

Balder looked at him thoughtfully. He seemed pleased with himself. "In that case, you can be a great help to this lawsuit. Would you mind giving us an hour of your time?"

"Uh . . . I guess so."

"Would you mind if we videotaped you?"

"No, but . . . why?"

Balder turned to Jennifer Haynes, who said, "We're trying to establish a baseline for what a well-informed person such as yourself knows about global warming. To help us refine our jury presentation."

"Sort of a mock jury of one?"

"Exactly. We've interviewed several people already."

"Okay," Evans said. "I guess I could schedule that at some point."

"*Now* is a good time," Balder said. He turned to Jennifer. "Get your team together in room four."

"Of course I'd like to help," Evans said, "but I came here to get an overview—"

"Because you've heard there are problems with the lawsuit? There aren't. But there are significant challenges," Balder said. He glanced at his watch. "I'm about to go into a meeting," he said. "You spend some time with Ms. Haynes, and when you're done, we'll talk about the litigation as I see it. Is that all right with you?"

There was nothing Evans could do but agree.

They put him in a conference room at the end of a long table, and aimed the video camera at him from the far end. Just like a deposition, he thought.

Five young people drifted into the room and took seats at the table. All were casually dressed, in jeans and T-shirts. Jennifer Haynes introduced them so quickly that Evans didn't catch their names. She explained that they were all graduate students in different scientific disciplines.

While they were setting up, Jennifer slipped into a chair beside his and said, "I'm sorry John was so rough on you. He's frustrated and under a lot of pressure."

"From the case?"

"Yes."

"What kind of pressure?"

"This session may give you some idea what we're dealing with." She turned to the others. "Are we ready?"

Heads nodded, notebooks flipped open. The camera light came on. Jennifer said, "Interview with Peter Evans, of Hassle and Black, on Tuesday, August twenty-fourth. Mr. Evans, we'd like to go over your views about the evidence that supports global warming. This isn't a test; we'd just like to clarify how you think about the issue."

"Okay," Evans said.

"Let's begin informally. Tell us what you know about the evidence for global warming."

"Well," Evans said, "I know that temperatures around the globe have risen dramatically in the last twenty or thirty years as a result of increases in carbon dioxide that is released by industry when fossil fuels are burned."

"Okay. And by a dramatic rise in temperature, you mean how much?"

"I think about a degree."

"Fahrenheit or Celsius?"

"Fahrenheit."

"And this rise has occurred over twenty years?"

"Twenty or thirty, yes."

"And earlier in the twentieth century?"

"Temperatures went up then, too, but not as fast."

"Okay," she said. "Now I am going to show you a graph . . ." She pulled out a graph* on foam core backing:

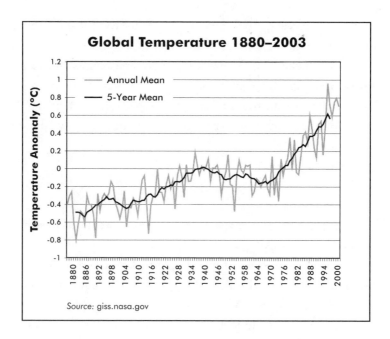

* All graphs are generated using tabular data from the following standard data sets: GISS (Columbia); CRU (East Anglia); GHCN and USHCN (Oak Ridge). See Appendix II for a full discussion.

"Does this look familiar to you?" she asked.

"I've seen it before," Evans said.

"It's taken from the NASA–Goddard data set used by the UN and other organizations. Do you consider the UN a trustworthy source?"

"Yes."

"So we can regard this graph as accurate? Unbiased? No monkey business?"

"Yes."

"Good. Do you know what this graph represents?"

Evans could read that much. He said, "It's the mean global temperature from all the weather stations around the world for the last hundred years or so."

"That's right," she said. "And how do you interpret this graph?"

"Well," he said, "it shows what I was describing." He pointed to the red line. "World temperatures have been rising since about 1890, but they start to go up steeply around 1970, when industrialization is most intense, which is the real proof of global warming."

"Okay," she said. "So the rapid increase in temperature since 1970 was caused by what?"

"Rising carbon dioxide levels from industrialization."

"Good. In other words, as the carbon dioxide goes up, the temperature goes up."

"Yes."

"All right. Now you mentioned the temperature started to rise from 1890, up to about 1940. And we see here that it did. What caused that rise? Carbon dioxide?"

"Um . . . I'm not sure."

"Because there was much less industrialization back in 1890, and yet look how temperatures go up. Was carbon dioxide rising in 1890?"

"I'm not sure."

"Actually, it was. Here is a graph showing carbon dioxide levels and temperature."

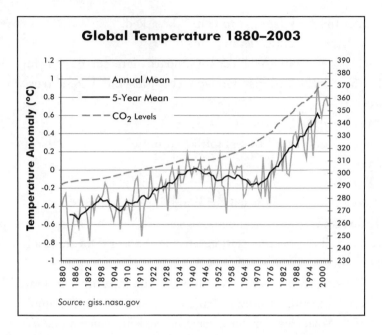

"Okay," Evans said. "Just what you would expect. Carbon dioxide goes up, and makes temperatures go up."

"Good," she said. "Now I want to direct your attention to the period from 1940 to 1970. As you see, during that period the global temperature actually went down. You see that?"

"Yes . . ."

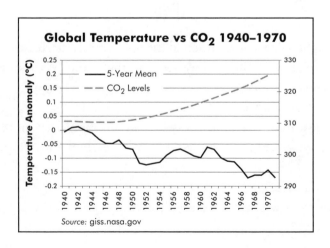

"Let me show you a closeup of that period." She took out another chart.

"This is a thirty-year period. One third of a century during which temperatures declined. Crops were damaged by frost in summer, glaciers in Europe advanced. What caused the decline?"

"I don't know."

"Was carbon dioxide rising during that period?"

"Yes."

"So, if rising carbon dioxide is the cause of rising temperatures, why didn't it cause temperatures to rise from 1940 to 1970?"

"I don't know," Evans said. "There must have been another factor. Or it could be an anomaly. There are anomalies within broad secular trends. Just look at the stock market."

"Does the stock market have anomalies that last thirty years?"

He shrugged. "Or it could have been soot. Or particulate matter in the air. There were a lot of particulates back then, before environmental laws took effect. Or maybe some other factor."

"These graphs show that carbon dioxide rose continuously, but temperature did not. It rose, then fell, then rose again. Even so, I take it you remain convinced that carbon dioxide has caused the most recent temperature rise?"

"Yes. Everybody knows that's the cause."

"Does this graph trouble you at all?"

"No," Evans said. "I admit it raises some questions, but then not everything is known about the climate. So, no. The graph doesn't trouble me."

"Okay, good. I'm glad to hear it. Let's move on. You said this graph was the average of weather stations around the world. How reliable is that weather data, do you think?"

"I have no idea."

"Well, for example, in the late nineteenth century, the data were generated by people going out to a little box and writing down the temperature twice a day. Maybe they forgot for a few days. Maybe somebody in their family was sick. They had to fill it in later."

"That was back then."

"Right. But how accurate do you think weather records are from Poland in the 1930s? Or Russian provinces since 1990?"

"Not very good, I would guess."

"And I would agree. So over the last hundred years, a fair number of reporting stations around the world may not have provided high-quality, reliable data."

"That could be," Evans said.

"Over the years, which country do you imagine has the best-maintained network of weather stations over a large area?"

"The US?"

"Right. I think there is no dispute about that. Here is another graph."

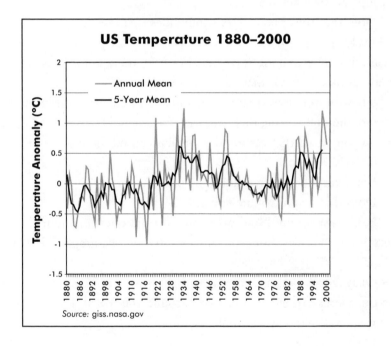

"Does this graph look like the first one we saw of world temperatures?"

"Not exactly."

"What is the change in temperature since 1880?"

"Looks like, uh, a third of a degree."

A third of a degree Celsius in a hundred and twenty years. Not very dramatic." She pointed to the graph. "And what was the warmest year of the last century?"

"Looks like 1934."

"Does this graph indicate to you that global warming is occurring?"

"Well. The temperature *is* going up."

"For the last thirty years, yes. But it went *down* for the previous thirty years. And current temperatures in the US are roughly the same as they were in the 1930s. So: Does this graph argue for global warming?"

"Yes," Evans said. "It's just not as dramatic in the US as it is in the rest of the world, but it's still happening."

"Does it trouble you that the most accurate temperature record shows the least warming?"

"No. Because global warming is a global phenomenon. It's not just the US."

"If you had to defend these graphs in a court of law, do you think you could persuade a jury of your position? Or would a jury look at the graph and say, this global warming stuff is nothing serious?"

"Leading the witness," he said, laughing.

In fact, Evans was feeling slightly uneasy. But only slightly. He'd heard such claims before, at environmental conferences. Industry hacks could slap together data that they had massaged and twisted, and give a convincing, well-prepared speech, and before Evans knew it, he'd start to doubt what he knew.

As if she were reading his mind, Jennifer said, "These graphs show solid data, Peter. Temperature records from Goddard Institute for Space Studies at Columbia University. Carbon dioxide levels from Mauna Loa and the Law Dome ice cores in Antarctica.* All generated by researchers who believe firmly in global warming."

"Yes," he said. "Because the overwhelming consensus of scientists

* D. M. Etheridge, et al., 1996, "Natural and anthropogenic changes in atmospheric CO_2 over the last 1,000 years from air in Antarctic ice and firn," *Journal of Geophysical Research* 101 (1996): 4115–28.

around the world is that global warming *is* happening and it *is* a major worldwide threat."

"Okay, good," she said smoothly. "I'm glad that none of this changes your views. Let's turn to some other questions of interest. David?"

One of the graduate students leaned forward. "Mr. Evans, I'd like to talk to you about land use, the urban heat island effect, and satellite data on the temperature of the troposphere."

Evans thought, *Oh Jesus*. But he just nodded. "Okay . . ."

"One of the issues we're trying to address concerns how surface temperatures change with land use. Are you familiar with that issue?"

"Not really, no." He looked at his watch. "Frankly, you people are working at a level of detail that is beyond me. I just listen to what the scientists say—"

"And we're preparing a lawsuit," Jennifer said, "based on what scientists say. This level of detail is where the suit will be fought."

"Fought?" Evans shrugged. "Who's going to fight it? Nobody with any stature. There isn't a reputable scientist in the world who doesn't believe in global warming."

"On that point, you are wrong," she said. "The defense will call full professors from MIT, Harvard, Columbia, Duke, Virginia, Colorado, UC Berkeley, and other prestigious schools. They will call the former president of the National Academy of Sciences. They may also call some Nobel Prize winners. They will bring in professors from England, from the Max Planck Institute in Germany, from Stockholm University in Sweden. These professors will argue that global warming is at best unproven, and at worst pure fantasy."

"Their research paid for by industry, no doubt."

"A few. Not all."

"Arch-conservatives. *Neocons*."

"The focus in litigation," she said, "will be on the data."

Evans looked at them and saw the concern on their faces. And he thought, *They really believe they might lose this thing.*

"But this is ridiculous," Evans said. "All you have to do is read the newspapers, or watch television—"

"Newspapers and television are susceptible to carefully orchestrated media campaigns. Lawsuits are not."

"Then forget mass media," Evans said, "and just read the scientific journals—"

"We do. They're not necessarily helpful to our side. Mr. Evans, we have a lot to go over. If you'd hold your protestations, we can get on with the issues."

It was at that moment that the phone buzzed, and Balder delivered him from his torment. "Send the guy from Hassle and Black into my office," he said. "I have ten minutes for him."

Balder was ensconced in a glass-walled office, with his feet up on a glass desk, working his way through a stack of briefs and research papers. He didn't take his feet down as Evans came in.

"You find it interesting?" he said. He meant the interrogation.

"In a way," Evans said. "But if you'll pardon my saying so, I get the sense they're worried they might lose."

"I have no doubt that we will win this case," Balder said. "No doubt whatsoever. But I don't want my people thinking that way! I want them worried as hell. I want my team running scared before any trial. And especially this one. We are bringing this suit against the EPA, and in anticipation of that, the agency has retained outside counsel in the person of Barry Beckman."

"Whew," Evans said. "Big guns."

Barry Beckman was the most famous litigator of his generation. A professor at Stanford Law School at twenty-eight, he left the university in his early thirties to go into private practice. He had already represented Microsoft, Toyota, Phillips, and a host of other multinationals. Beckman had an incredibly agile mind, a charming manner, a quick sense of humor, and a photographic memory. Everyone knew that when he argued before the Supreme Court (as he had done three times already) he cited document page numbers as he answered the Justices' questions. "Your honor, I believe you will find that in footnote 17 on the bottom of page 237." Like that.

"Barry has his faults," Balder said. "He has so much information at his fingertips that he can easily slip into irrelevance. He likes to hear himself talk. His arguments drift. I have beaten him once. And lost to him, once. But one thing is sure: We can expect an *extremely* well-prepared opposition."

"Isn't it a little unusual to hire an attorney before you've even filed?"

"It's a tactic," Balder said. "The current administration doesn't want to defend this lawsuit. They believe they will win, but they don't want the negative publicity that will accompany their brief against global warming. So they hope to intimidate us into dropping the case. And of course we never would. Especially now that we are fully funded, thanks to Mr. Morton."

"That's good," Evans said.

"At the same time, the challenges are significant. Barry will argue that there is insufficient evidence for global warming. He will argue that the supporting science is weak. He will argue that the predictions from ten and fifteen years ago have already been shown to be wrong. And he will argue that even leading proponents of global warming have publicly expressed doubts about whether it can be predicted, whether it is a serious problem—and indeed, whether it's occurring at all."

"Leading proponents have said that?"

Balder sighed. "They have. In journals."

"I've never read anything of that sort."

"The statements exist. Barry will dig them out." He shook his head. "Some experts have expressed different views at different times. Some have said rising carbon dioxide isn't a big problem; now they say it is. So far, we don't have a single expert witness that can't be turned. Or made to look very foolish on cross."

Evans nodded sympathetically. He was familiar with this circumstance. One of the first things you learned in law school was that the law was not about truth. It was about dispute resolution. In the course of resolving a dispute, the truth might or might not emerge. Often it did not. Prosecutors might know a criminal was guilty, and still be unable to convict him. It happened all the time.

"That's why," Balder said, "this case is going to hinge on the sea-level records in the Pacific. We are collecting all available data records now."

"Why does the case hinge on that?"

"Because I believe," Balder said, "that this is a case we should bait and switch. The case is about global warming, but that's not where the emotional impact is for a jury. Juries aren't comfortable reading graphs. And all this talk about tenths of a degree Celsius goes right over their heads. It's technical detail; it's the quibbles of experts; and it's incredibly boring for normal people.

"No, the jury will see this as a case about helpless, victimized, impoverished people being flooded out of their ancestral homelands. A case about the terror of sea levels rising precipitously—and inexplicably—with no conceivable cause *unless you accept that something extraordinary and unprecedented has affected the entire world* in recent years. Something that is causing the sea levels to rise and to threaten the lives of innocent men, women, and children."

"And that something is global warming."

Balder nodded. "The jury will have to draw their own conclusions. If we can show them a convincing record of rising sea levels, we will be on very strong ground. When juries see that damage has been done, they are inclined to blame *somebody.*"

"Okay." Evans saw where Balder was going. "So the sea-level data is important."

"Yes, but it needs to be solid, irrefutable."

"Is that so hard to obtain?"

Balder cocked an eyebrow. "Mr. Evans, do you know anything about the study of sea levels?"

"No. I just know that sea levels are rising around the world."

"Unfortunately, that claim is in considerable dispute."

"You're joking."

"It is well known," Balder said, "that I have no sense of humor."

"But sea level can't be disputed," Evans said. "It's too simple. You put a mark on a dock at high tide, measure it year after year, watch it go up . . . I mean, how difficult can it be?"

Balder sighed. "You think sea level is simple? Trust me, it's not. Have you ever heard of the geoid? No? The geoid is the equipotential surface of the earth's gravitational field that approximates the mean sea surface. That help you?"

Evans shook his head.

"Well, it is a core concept in the measurement of sea levels." Balder flipped through the stack of papers in front of him. "How about glacio-hydro-isostatic modeling? Eustatic and tectonic effects on shoreline dynamics? Holocene sedimentary sequences? Intertidal foraminifera distributions? Carbon analysis of coastal paleoenvironments? Aminostratigraphy? No? Not ringing a bell? Let me assure you, sea level is a fiercely debated specialty." He tossed the last of the papers aside. "That's what I'm working through now. But the disputes within the field give added importance to finding an unimpeachable set of data."

"And you are obtaining this data?"

"Waiting for them to arrive, yes. The Australians have several sets. The French have at least one in Moorea and perhaps another in Papeete. There is a set that was funded by the V. Allen Willy Foundation, but it may be of too short a duration. And other sets as well. We will have to see."

The intercom buzzed. The assistant said, "Mr. Balder, it's Mr. Drake on the line, from NERF."

"All right." Balder turned to Evans, extended a hand. "Nice talking with you, Mr. Evans. Again, our thanks to George. Tell him any time he wants to have a look around, he can drop by. We are always hard at work here. Good luck to you. Close the door on your way out."

Balder turned away, picking up the phone. Evans heard him say,

"Well, Nick, what the fuck is going on at NERF? Are you going to fix this for me, or not?"

Evans closed the door.

He walked out of Balder's office with a sense of nagging unease. Balder was one of the most persuasive men on the planet. He had known Evans was there on behalf of George Morton. He knew Morton was on the verge of making a huge contribution to the lawsuit. Balder should have been totally upbeat, radiating confidence. And he had, indeed, begun that way.

I have no doubt we will win this lawsuit.

But then, Evans had heard:

The challenges are significant.

I do not have a single expert witness who can't be turned.

This is a case we should bait and switch.

This case will hinge on sea-level records.

Sea level is a fiercely debated specialty.

We will have to see.

It certainly wasn't a conversation calculated to raise Evans's level of confidence. Neither, for that matter, was the video session he'd had with Jennifer Haynes, discussing the scientific problems the lawsuit would face.

But then, as he considered it, he decided that these expressions of doubt were actually a sign of confidence on the part of the legal team. Evans was an attorney himself; he had come to learn the issues surrounding the trial, and they had been forthright with him. It was a case they would win, even though it would not be easy, because of the complexity of the data and the short attention span of the jury.

So: would he recommend that Morton continue?

Of course he would.

Jennifer was waiting for him outside Balder's office. She said, "They're ready for you back in the conference room."

Evans said, "I'm really sorry, I can't. My schedule . . ."

"I understand," she said, "we'll do it another time. I was wondering if your schedule was really tight, or whether there was time for you and me to have lunch."

"Oh," Evans said, without missing a beat, "my schedule isn't that tight."

"Good," she said.

They had lunch in a Mexican restaurant in Culver City. It was quiet. There were a handful of film editors in the corner, from nearby Sony Studios. A couple of high school kids necking. A group of older women in sunhats.

They sat in a corner booth and both ordered the special. Evans said, "Balder seems to think the sea-level data is key."

"That's what Balder thinks. Frankly, I'm not so sure."

"Why is that?"

"Nobody's seen all the data. But even if it's high quality, it needs to show a substantial sea-level rise to impress a jury. It may not."

"How could it not?" Evans said. "With glaciers melting, and breaking off Antarctica—"

"Even so, it may not," she said. "You know the Maldive Islands in the Indian Ocean? They were concerned about flooding, so a team of Scandinavian researchers came in to study sea levels. The scientists found no rise in several centuries—and a fall in the last twenty years."

"A fall? Was that published?"

"Last year," she said. The food came; Jennifer gave a dismissive wave of her hand: enough shop talk for now. She ate her burrito with gusto, wiping her chin with the back of her hand. He saw a jagged white scar running from her palm down the underside of her forearm. She said, "God, I love this food. You can't get decent Mexican food in DC."

"Is that where you're from?"

She nodded. "I came out to help John."

"He asked you?"

"I couldn't turn him down." She shrugged. "So I see my boyfriend on alternate weekends. He comes out here, or I go back there. But if this trial goes forward, it will be a year, maybe two years. I don't think our relationship will make it."

"What does he do? Your boyfriend."

"Attorney."

Evans smiled. "Sometimes I think everyone's an attorney."

"Everyone is. He does securities law. Not my thing."

"What's your thing?"

"Witness prep and jury selection. Psychological analysis of the pool. That's why I'm in charge of the focus groups."

"I see."

"We know that most people we might put on the jury will have heard of global warming, and most will probably be inclined to think it is real."

"Jesus, I'd *hope* so," Evans said. "I mean, it's been an established fact for the last fifteen years."

"But we need to determine what people will believe in the face of contrary evidence."

"Such as?"

"Such as the graphs I showed you today. Or the satellite data. You know about the satellite data?"

Evans shook his head.

"The theory of global warming predicts that the upper atmosphere will warm from trapped heat, just like a greenhouse. The surface of the Earth warms later. But since 1979 we've had orbiting satellites that can continuously measure the atmosphere five miles up. They show that the upper atmosphere is warming much less than the ground is."

"Maybe there's a problem with the data—"

"Trust me, the satellite data have been re-analyzed dozens of times," she said. "They're probably the most intensely scrutinized data in the world. But the data from weather balloons agree with the satellites. They show much less warming than expected by the theory." She shrugged. "Another problem for us. We're working on it."

"How?"

"We think it'll prove too complex for a jury. The details of MSUs— microwave-sounding units, cross-track scanners with four-channel radiance analysis—and the questions about whether channel 2 has been corrected for diurnal drifts and inter-satellite offsets, time-varying non-linear instrumental responses . . . We hope it will make them throw up their hands. Anyway. Enough of all that." She wiped her face with her napkin and again he saw the white scar that ran down the underside of her arm.

"How'd you get that?" he said.

She shrugged. "In law school."

"And I thought my school was tough."

"I taught an inner-city karate class," she said. "Sometimes it went late. You want any more of these chips?"

"No," he said.

"Shall we get the check?"

"Tell me," he said.

"There's not a lot to tell. One night, I got in my car to drive home, and a kid jumped in the passenger seat and pulled a gun. Told me to start driving."

"Kid from your class?"

"No. An older kid. Late twenties."

"What'd you do?"

"I told him to get out. He told me to drive. So I started the car, and as I put it in gear I asked him where he wanted me to go. And he was stupid enough to point, so I hit him in the windpipe. I didn't hit him hard enough, and he got off a round, blew out the windshield. Then I hit him again with my elbow. Couple, three times."

"What happened to him?" he said.

"He died."

"Jesus," Evans said.

"Some people make bad decisions," she said. "What're you staring at me like that for? He was six-two and two-ten and had a record from here to Nebraska. Armed robbery, assault with a deadly weapon, attempted rape—you name it. You think I should feel sorry for him?"

"No," Evans said quickly.

"You do, I can see it in your eyes. A lot of people do. They go, He was just a kid, how could you do that? Let me tell you, people don't know what the hell they're talking about. One of us was going to get killed that night. I'm glad it wasn't me. But of course, it still bothers me."

"I'll bet."

"Sometimes I wake up in a cold sweat. Seeing the gunshot blow the windshield in front of my face. Realizing how close I came to dying. I was stupid. I should have killed him the first time."

Evans paused. He didn't know what to say.

"You ever had a gun at your head?" she said.

"No . . ."

"Then you have no idea how it feels, do you?"

"Was there trouble about it?" he said.

"You bet your ass there was trouble. For a while I thought I wasn't going to be able to practice law. They claimed I led him on. Do you believe that shit? I never saw the guy in my life. But then a very good attorney came to my rescue."

"Balder?"

She nodded. "That's why I'm here."

"And what about your arm?"

"Ah hell," she said, "the car crashed and I cut it on the broken glass." She signaled to the waitress. "What do you say we get the check?"

"I'll do that."

Minutes later they were back outside. Evans blinked in the milky midday light. They walked down the street. "So," Evans said. "I guess you're pretty good at karate."

"Good enough."

They came to the warehouse. He shook her hand.

"I'd really like to have lunch again some time," she said. She was so direct about it, he wondered whether it was personal, or whether she wanted him to know how the lawsuit was going. Because like Balder, much of what she had said was not encouraging.

"Lunch sounds great," he said.

"Not too long?"

"Deal."

"Will you call me?"

"Count on it," he said.

It was almost dark when he went home to his apartment and parked in the garage facing the alley. He was going up the back stairs when the landlady poked her head out the window. "You just missed them," she said.

"Who?"

"The cable repair people. They just left."

"I didn't call any cable repair people," he said. "Did you let them in?"

"Of course not. They said they would wait for you. They just left."

Evans had never heard of cable repair people waiting for anyone. "How long did they wait?"

"Not long. Maybe ten minutes."

"Okay."

He got up to the second-floor landing. A tag was hooked on his doorknob. "Sorry We Missed You." There was a check box to "Call again to reschedule service."

Then he saw the problem. The address was listed as 2119 Roxbury. His address was 2129 Roxbury. But the address was on the front door, not the back door. They'd just made a mistake. He lifted his doormat to check on the key he kept there. It was right where he'd left it. It hadn't been moved. There was even a ring of dust around it.

He unlocked the door and went inside. He went to the refrigerator, and saw the old container of yogurt. He needed to go to the supermarket but he was too tired. He checked the messages to see if Janis or Carol had called. They hadn't. Now of course there was the prospect of Jennifer Haynes, but she had a boyfriend, she lived in DC, and . . . he knew it would never work.

He thought of calling Janis, but decided not to. He took a shower, and was considering calling for pizza delivery. He lay down on the bed to relax for a minute before he called. And he fell immediately asleep.

The meeting was held in the big conference room on the fourteenth floor. Morton's four accountants were there; his assistant Sarah Jones; Herb Lowenstein, who did estate planning; a guy named Marty Bren, who did tax work for NERF, and Evans. Morton, who hated all financial meetings, paced restlessly.

"Let's get to it," he said. "I am supposedly giving ten million dollars to NERF, and we have signed papers, is that right?"

"Right," Lowenstein said.

"But now they want to attach a rider to the agreement?"

"Right," Marty Bren said. "It's pretty standard boilerplate for them." He shuffled through his papers. "Any charity wants to have full use of the money they receive, even when it is earmarked for a particular purpose. Maybe that purpose costs more or less than predicted, or it is delayed, or mired in litigation, or set aside for some other reason. In this case, the money has been earmarked for the Vanutu lawsuit, and the relevant phrase NERF wants to add is "said moneys to be used to defray the cost of the Vanutu litigation, including fees, filing, and copying costs . . . blah blah . . . or for other legal purposes, or for such other purposes as NERF shall see fit in its capacity as an environmental organization."

Morton said, "That's the phrase they want?"

"Boilerplate, as I said," Bren said.

"It's been in my previous donation agreements?"

"I don't recall offhand."

"Because," Morton said, "it sounds to me like they want to be able to pull the plug on this lawsuit, and spend the money elsewhere."

"Oh, I doubt that," Herb said.

"Why?" Morton said. "Why else would they want this boilerplate? Look, we had a signed deal. Now they want a change. Why?"

"It's not really a change," Bren said.

"It sure as hell is, Marty."

"If you look at the original agreement," Bren said calmly, "it says that any money not spent on the lawsuit goes to NERF for other purposes."

"But that's only if there's money left after the lawsuit ends," Morton said. "They can't spend it on anything else until the suit is decided."

"I think they imagine there may be long delays here."

"Why should there be delays?" Morton turned to Evans. "Peter? What is going on over there in Culver City?"

"It looks like the suit is going forward," Evans said. "They have a large operation. There must be forty people working on that one case. I don't think they plan to give it up."

"And are there problems with the suit?"

"There are certainly challenges," Evans said. "It's complicated litigation. They face strong opposing counsel. They're working hard."

"Why am I not convinced here?" Morton said. "Six months ago Nick Drake told me this damn lawsuit was a slam dunk and a great publicity opportunity, and now they want a bail-out clause."

"Maybe we should ask Nick."

"I got a better idea. Let's audit NERF."

Murmurs in the room. "I don't think you have that right, George."

"Make it part of the agreement."

"I'm not sure you can do that."

"They want a rider. I want a rider. What's the difference?"

"I'm not sure you can audit their entire operation—"

"George," Herb Lowenstein said. "You and Nick are friends of long standing. You're their Concerned Citizen of the Year. Auditing them seems a little out of character for your relationship."

"You mean it looks like I don't trust them?"

"Put bluntly, yes."

"I don't." Morton leaned on the table and looked at everyone sitting there. "You know what I think? They want to blow off the litigation and spend all the money on this conference on abrupt climate change that Nick is so excited about."

"They don't need ten million for a conference."

"I don't know what they need. He already misplaced two hundred and fifty thousand of my money. It ended up in fucking Vancouver. I don't know what he is doing anymore."

"Well, then you should withdraw your contribution."

"Ah ah," Marty Bren said. "Not so fast. I think they've already made financial commitments based on the reasonable expectation that the money was coming."

"Then give them some amount, and forget the rest."

"No," Morton said. "I'm not going to withdraw the grant. Peter Evans here says the litigation is going forward, and I believe him. Nick says that the two hundred and fifty grand was a mistake, and I believe him. I want you to ask for an audit and I want to know what happens. I will be out of town for the next three weeks."

"You will? Where?"

"I'm taking a trip."

"But we'll have to be able to reach you, George."

"I may be unreachable. Call Sarah. Or have Peter here get in touch with me."

"But George—"

"That's it, guys. Talk to Nick, see what he says. We'll be in contact soon."

And he walked out of the room, with Sarah hurrying after him.

Lowenstein turned to the others. "What the hell was that all about?"

Thunder rumbled ominously. Looking out the front windows of his office, Nat Damon sighed. He had always known that that submarine lease would mean trouble. After the check bounced, he had canceled the order, hoping that that would be the end of it. But it wasn't.

For weeks and weeks he had heard nothing, but then one of the men, the lawyer in the shiny suit, had come back unexpectedly to poke a finger in his face and tell him that he had signed a nondisclosure agreement and could not discuss any aspect of the submarine lease with anybody, or risk a lawsuit. "Maybe we'll win, and maybe we'll lose," the lawyer said. "But either way, you're out of business, friend. Your house is mortgaged. You're in debt for the rest of your life. So, think it over. And keep your mouth shut."

All during this, Damon's heart was pounding. Because the fact was, Damon had already been contacted by some sort of revenue service guy. A man named Kenner, who was coming to Damon's office that very afternoon. To ask a few questions, he had said.

Damon had been afraid that this Kenner would show up while the lawyer was still in his office, but now the lawyer was driving away. His car, a nondescript Buick sedan with Ontario plates, drove through the boatyard, and was gone.

Damon started to clean up the office, getting ready to go home. He was toying with the idea of leaving before Kenner arrived. Kenner was some revenue agent. Damon had done nothing wrong. He didn't have to meet any revenue agent. And if he did, what would he do, say he couldn't answer questions?

The next thing, he'd be subpoenaed or something. Dragged into court.

Damon decided to leave. There was more thunder, and the crack of distant lightning. A big storm was moving in.

As he was closing up, he saw that the lawyer had left his cell phone on the counter. He looked out to see if the lawyer was coming back for it. Not yet, but surely he would realize he had left it, and come back. Damon decided to leave before he showed up.

Hastily, he slipped the cell phone in his pocket, turned out the lights, and locked the office. The first drops of rain were spattering the pavement as he went to his car, parked right in front. He opened the door and was climbing into the car when the cell phone rang. He hesitated, not sure what to do. The phone rang insistently.

A jagged bolt of lightning crashed down, striking the mast of one of the ships in the boatyard. In the next instant there was a burst of light by the car, a blast of furious heat that knocked him to the ground. Dazed, he tried to get up.

He was thinking that his car had exploded, but it hadn't; the car was intact, the door blackened. Then he saw that his trousers were on fire. He stared stupidly at his own legs, not moving. He heard the rumble of thunder and realized that *he had been struck by lightning.*

My God, he thought. I was hit by lightning. He sat up and slapped at his trousers, trying to put out the fire. It wasn't working, and his legs were beginning to feel pain. He had a fire extinguisher inside the office.

Staggering to his feet, he moved unsteadily to his office. He was unlocking the door, his fingers fumbling, when there was another explosion. He felt a sharp pain in his ears, reached up, touched blood. He looked at his bloody fingertips, fell over, and died.

CENTURY CITY
THURSDAY, SEPTEMBER 2
12:34 P.M.

Under normal circumstances, Peter Evans spoke to George Morton every day. Sometimes twice a day. So after a week went by without hearing from him, Evans called his house. He spoke to Sarah.

"I have no idea what is going on," she said. "Two days ago he was in North Dakota. North Dakota! The day before that he was in Chicago. I think he might be in Wyoming today. He's made noises about going to Boulder, Colorado, but I don't know."

"What's in Boulder?" Evans said.

"I haven't a clue. Too early for snow."

"Has he got a new girlfriend?" Sometimes Morton disappeared when he was involved with a new woman.

"Not that I know," Sarah said.

"What's he doing?"

"I have no idea. It sounds like he has a shopping list."

"A shopping list?"

"Well," she said, "sort of. He wanted me to buy some kind of special GPS unit. You know, for locating position? Then he wanted some special video camera using CCD or CCF or something. Had to be rush-ordered from Hong Kong. And yesterday he told me to buy a new Ferrari from a guy in Monterey, and have it shipped to San Francisco."

"Another Ferrari?"

"I know," she said. "How many Ferraris can one man use? And this one doesn't seem up to his usual standards. From the e-mail pictures it looks kind of beat up."

"Maybe he's going to have it restored."

"If he was, he'd send it to Reno. That's where his car restorer is."

He detected a note of concern in her voice. "Is everything okay, Sarah?"

"Between you and me, I don't know," she said. "The Ferrari he bought is a 1972 365 GTS Daytona Spyder."

"So?"

"He already has one, Peter. It's like he doesn't know. And he sounds weird when you talk to him."

"Weird in what way?"

"Just . . . weird. Not his usual self at all."

"Who's traveling with him?"

"As far as I know, nobody."

Evans frowned. That was very odd. Morton hated being alone. Evans's immediate inclination was to disbelieve it.

"What about that guy Kenner and his Nepali friend?"

"Last I heard, they were going to Vancouver, and on to Japan. So they're not with him."

"Uh huh."

"When I hear from him, I'll let him know you called."

Evans hung up, feeling dissatisfied. On an impulse, he dialed Morton's cell phone. But he got the voice mail. "This is George. At the beep." And the quick beep.

"George, this is Peter Evans. Just checking in, to see if there's anything you need. Call me at the office if I can help."

He hung up, and stared out the window. Then he dialed again.

"Center for Risk Analysis."

"Professor Kenner's office, please."

In a moment he got the secretary. "This is Peter Evans, I'm looking for Professor Kenner."

"Oh yes, Mr. Evans. Dr. Kenner said you might call."

"He did?"

"Yes. Are you trying to reach Dr. Kenner?"

"Yes, I am."

"He's in Tokyo at the moment. Would you like his cell phone?"

"Please."

She gave him the number, and he wrote it down on his yellow pad. He was about to call when his assistant, Heather, came in to say that something at lunch had disagreed with her, and she was going home for the afternoon.

"Feel better," he said, sighing.

With her gone, he was obliged to answer his own phone, and the next call was from Margo Lane, George's mistress, asking where the hell George was. Evans was on the phone with her for the better part of half an hour.

And then Nicholas Drake walked into his office.

"I am very concerned," Drake said. He stood at the window, hands clasped behind his back, staring at the office building opposite.

"About what?"

"This Kenner person that George is spending so much time with."

"I don't know that they're spending time together."

"Of course they are. You don't seriously believe George is *alone*, do you?"

Evans said nothing.

"George is never alone. We both know that. Peter, I don't like this situation at all. Not at all. George is a good man—I don't have to tell you that—but he is susceptible to influence. Including the wrong influence."

"You think a professor at MIT is the wrong influence?"

"I've looked into Professor Kenner," Drake said, "and there are a few mysteries about him."

"Oh?"

"His résumé says he spent a number of years in government. Department of the Interior, Intergovernmental Negotiating Committee, and so on."

"Yes?"

"The Department of the Interior has no record of his working there."

Evans shrugged. "It was more than ten years ago. Government records being what they are . . ."

"Possibly," Drake said. "But there is more. Professor Kenner comes back to MIT, works there for eight years, very successfully. Consultant to the EPA, consultant to Department of Defense, God knows what else—and then he suddenly goes on extended leave, and no one seems to know what happened to him since. He just fell off the radar."

"I don't know," Evans said. "His card says he is Director of Risk Analysis."

"But he's on leave. I don't know what the hell he is doing these days. I don't know who supports him. I take it you've met him?"

"Briefly."

"And now he and George are great pals?"

"I don't know, Nick. I haven't seen or spoken to George in more than a week."

"He's off with Kenner."

"I don't know that."

"But you know that he and Kenner went to Vancouver."

"Actually, I didn't know."

"Let me lay it out for you plainly," Drake said. "I have it on good authority that John Kenner has unsavory connections. The Center for Risk Analysis is wholly funded by industry groups. I needn't say more. In addition, Mr. Kenner spent a number of years advising the Pentagon and in fact was so involved with them that he even underwent some sort of training for a period of time."

"You mean military training?"

"Yes. Fort Bragg and Harvey Point, in North Carolina," Drake said. "There is no question the man has military connections as well as industry connections. And I am told he is hostile toward mainstream environmental organizations. I hate to think of a man like that working on poor George."

"I wouldn't worry about George. He can see through propaganda."

"I hope so. But frankly I do not share your confidence. This military man shows up, and the next thing we know, George is trying to audit us. I mean, my God, why would he want to do that? Doesn't George realize what a waste of resources that involves? Time, money, everything? It would be a *tremendous* drag on my time."

"I wasn't aware an audit was going forward."

"It's being discussed. Of course, we have nothing to hide, and we can be audited at any time. I have always said so. But this is an especially busy time, with the Vanutu lawsuit starting up, and the conference on Abrupt Climate Change to be planned for. All that's in the next few weeks. I wish I could speak to George."

Evans shrugged. "Call his cell."

"I have. Have you?"

"Yes."

"He call you back?"

"No," Evans said.

Drake shook his head. "That man," he said, "is my Concerned Citizen of the Year, and I can't even get him on the phone."

Morton sat at a sidewalk table outside a café on Beverly Drive at eight in
the morning, waiting for Sarah to show up. His assistant was ordinarily
punctual, and her apartment was not far away. Unless she had taken up
with that actor again. Young people had so much time to waste on bad
relationships.

He sipped his coffee, glancing at the *Wall Street Journal* without much
interest. He had even less interest after an unusual couple sat down at the
next table.

The woman was petite and strikingly beautiful, with dark hair and
an exotic look. She might have been Moroccan; it was hard to judge
from her accent. Her clothing was chic and out of place in casual Los
Angeles—tight-fitting skirt, spike heels, Chanel jacket.

The man who accompanied her could not have been more different.
He was a red-faced, beefy American, with slightly piggish features, wearing a sweater, baggy khakis, and running shoes. He was as big as a football player. He slumped at the table and said, "I'll have a latte, sweetheart.
Nonfat. Grande."

She said, "I thought you would get one for me, like a gentleman."

"I'm not a gentleman," he said. "And you're no fucking lady. Not
after you didn't come home last night. So we can forget about ladies and
gentlemen, okay?"

She pouted. "*Chéri*, do not make a scene."

"Hey. I asked you to get a fucking latte. Who's making a scene?"

"But *chéri*—"

"You going to get it, or not?" He glared at her. "I've really had it with you, Marisa, you know that?"

"You don't own me," she said. "I do as I please."

"You've made that obvious."

During this conversation, Morton's paper had been slowly drifting downward. Now he folded it flat, set it on his knee, and pretended to read. But in fact he could not take his eyes off this woman. She was extremely beautiful, he decided, although not very young. She was probably thirty-five. Her maturity somehow made her more overtly sexual. He was captivated.

She said to the football player, "William, you are tiresome."

"You want me to leave?"

"Perhaps it is best."

"Oh, fuck you," he said, and slapped her.

Morton could not restrain himself. "Hey," he said, "take it easy there."

The woman gave him a smile. The beefy man stood up, fists bunched. "Mind your own fucking business!"

"You don't hit the lady, pal."

"How about just you and me?" he said, shaking his fist.

At that moment, a Beverly Hills cruiser drove by. Morton looked at it, and waved. The cruiser came over to the curb. "Everything all right?" one of the cops said.

"Just fine, officer," Morton said.

"Fuck this noise," the football player said, and turned away. He stalked off up the street.

The dark woman smiled at Morton. "Thank you for that."

"No problem. Did I hear you say you wanted a latte?"

She smiled again. She crossed her legs, exposing brown knees. "If you would be so kind."

Morton was standing to get it when Sarah called to him, "Hey,

George! Sorry to be late." She came jogging up in a tracksuit. As always, she looked very beautiful.

Anger flashed across the dark woman's features. It was fleeting, but Morton caught it and he thought, *Something is wrong here.* He didn't know this woman. She had no reason to be angry. Probably, he decided, she had wanted to teach the boyfriend a lesson. Even now the guy was hanging around at the end of the block, pretending to look in a shop window. But at this early hour, all the shops were closed.

"Ready to go?" Sarah said.

Morton made brief apologies to the woman, who made little gestures of indifference. He had the feeling now that she was French.

"Perhaps we will meet again," he said.

"Yes," she said, "but I doubt it. I am sorry. *Ça va.*"

"Have a nice day."

As they walked off, Sarah said, "Who was that?"

"I don't know. She sat down at the next table."

"Spicy little number."

He shrugged.

"Did I interrupt something? No? That's good." She handed Morton three manila folders. "This one's your contributions to NERF to date. This one is the agreement for the last contribution, so you have the language. And this one is the cashier's check you wanted. Be careful with that. It's a big number."

"Okay. It's not a problem. I'm leaving in an hour."

"You want to tell me where?"

Morton shook his head. "It's better you don't know."

Evans had heard nothing from Morton for almost two weeks. He could not remember ever having gone so long without contact with his client. He had lunch with Sarah, who was visibly anxious. "Do you hear from him at all?" he said.

"Not a word."

"What do the pilots say?"

"They're in Van Nuys. He's rented a different plane. I don't know where he is."

"And he's coming back . . ."

She shrugged. "Who knows?"

And so it was with considerable surprise that he received Sarah's call that day. "You better get going," she said. "George wants to see you right away."

"Where?"

"At NERF. In Beverly Hills."

"He's back?"

"I'll say."

It was a ten-minute drive from his offices in Century City to the NERF building. Of course the National Environmental Resource Fund was headquartered in Washington, DC, but they had recently opened a west coast office, in Beverly Hills. Cynics claimed that NERF had done it to be closer to the Hollywood celebrities who were so essential to their fund-raising. But that was just gossip.

Evans half expected to find Morton pacing outside, but he was nowhere in sight. Evans went into the reception area and was told that Morton was in the third-floor conference room. He walked up to the third floor.

The conference room was glass-walled on two sides. The interior was furnished with a large, boardroom-style table and eighteen chairs. There was an audiovisual unit in the corner for presentations.

Evans saw three people in the conference room, and an argument in progress. Morton stood at the front of the room, red-faced, gesticulating. Drake was also standing, pacing back and forth, pointing an angry finger at Morton, and shouting back at him. Evans also saw John Henley, the saturnine head of PR for NERF. He was bent over, making notes on a yellow legal pad. It was clearly an argument between Morton and Drake.

Evans was not sure what to do, so he stood there. After a moment, Morton saw him and made a quick jabbing motion, indicating that Evans should sit down outside. He did. And watched the argument through the glass.

It turned out there was a fourth person in the room as well. Evans hadn't seen him at first because he was hunched down behind the podium, but when that person stood, Evans saw a workman in clean, neatly pressed overalls carrying a briefcase-style toolbox and with a couple of electronic meters clipped to his belt. On his chest pocket a logo read AV NETWORK SYSTEMS.

The workman looked confused. Apparently Drake didn't want the workman in the room during the argument, whereas Morton seemed to like an audience. Drake wanted the guy to go; Morton insisted he stay. Caught in the middle, the workman looked uncomfortable, and ducked down out of sight again. But soon after, Drake prevailed, and the workman left.

As the workman walked past him, Evans said, "Rough day?"

The workman shrugged. "They got a lot of network problems in this building," he said. "Myself, I think it's bad Ethernet cable, or the routers are overheating . . ." And he walked on.

Back inside, the argument raged, fiercer than ever. It continued for another five minutes. The glass was almost entirely soundproof, but from time to time, when they shouted, Evans could hear a phrase. He heard Morton yell, "God damn it, I want to win!" and he heard Drake reply, "It's just too risky." Which made Morton even angrier.

And later Morton said, "Don't we have to fight for the most important issue facing our planet?" And Drake answered something about being practical, or facing reality. And Morton said, "Fuck reality!"

At which point the PR guy, Henley, glanced up and said, "My sentiments exactly." Or something like that.

Evans had the distinct impression that this argument concerned the Vanutu lawsuit, but it seemed to range over a number of other subjects as well.

And then, quite abruptly, Morton came out, slamming the door so hard that the glass walls shook. "Fuck those guys!"

Evans fell into step with his client. Through the glass, he saw the other two men huddle, whispering together.

"Fuck 'em!" George said loudly. He paused and looked back. "If we have right on our side, shouldn't we be telling the truth?"

Inside, Drake just shook his head sorrowfully.

"Fuck 'em," Morton said again, walking off.

Evans said, "You wanted me here?"

"Yes." Morton pointed. "You know who that other guy was?"

"Yes," he said. "John Henley."

"Correct. Those two guys *are* NERF," George said. "I don't care how many celebrity trustees they have on their letterhead. Or how many lawyers they keep on staff. Those two run the show, and everyone else rubberstamps. None of the trustees really knows anything about what is going on. Otherwise they wouldn't be a part of this. And let me tell you, I'm not going to be a part of this. Not anymore."

They started walking down the stairs.

"Meaning what?" Evans said to him.

"Meaning," Morton said, "I'm not giving them that ten-million-dollar grant for the lawsuit."

"You told them that?"

"No," he said, "I did not tell them that. And you will not tell them that either. I think I'll let it be a surprise, for later." He smiled grimly. "But draw up the papers now."

"Are you sure about this, George?"

"Don't piss me off, kid."

"I'm just asking—"

"And I said draw up the papers. So do it."

Evans said he would.

"*Today.*"

Evans said he would do it at once.

Evans waited until they got to the parking garage before he spoke again. He walked Morton to his waiting town car. His driver, Harry, opened the door for him. Evans said, "George, you have that NERF banquet honoring you next week. Is that still going ahead?"

"Absolutely," Morton said. "I wouldn't miss it for the world."

He got in the car, and Harry closed the door.

"Good day, sir," Harry said to Evans.

And the car drove off into the morning sunlight.

He called from his car: "Sarah."

"I know, I know."

"What is going on?"

"He won't tell me. But he's really angry, Peter. *Really* angry."

"I got that impression."

"And he just left again."

"What?"

"He left. Said he would be back in a week. In time to fly everybody up to San Francisco for the banquet."

Drake called Evans's cell phone. "What is going on, Peter?"

"I have no idea, Nick."

"The man's demented. The things he was saying . . . could you hear him?"

"No, actually."

"He's demented. I really am worried about him. I mean as a friend. To say nothing of our banquet next week. I mean, is he going to be all right?"

"I think so. He's taking a planeload of friends up there."

"Are you sure?"

"That's what Sarah says."

"Can I talk to George? Can you set something up?"

"My understanding," Evans said, "is that he just went out of town again."

"It's that damn Kenner. He's behind all this."

"I don't know what's going on with George, Nick. All I know is, he's coming to the banquet."

"I want you to promise me you'll deliver him."

"Nick," Evans said. "George does what he wants."

"That's what I'm afraid of."

Flying up on his Gulfstream, Morton brought several of the most prominent celebrity supporters of NERF. These included two rock stars, the wife of a comedian, an actor who played the president on a television series, a writer who had recently run for governor, and two environmental lawyers from other firms. Over white wine and smoked salmon canapés, the discussion became quite lively, focusing on what the United States, as the world's leading economy, should be doing to promote environmental sanity.

Uncharacteristically, Morton did not join in. Instead, he slumped in the back of the plane, looking irritable and gloomy. Evans sat beside him, keeping him company. Morton was drinking straight vodka. He was already on his second.

"I brought the papers cancelling your grant," Evans said, taking them out of his briefcase. "If you still want to do this."

"I do." Morton scribbled his signature, hardly looking at the documents. He said, "Keep those safe until tomorrow." He looked back at his guests, who were now trading statistics on species loss as the rain forests of the world were cut down. Off to one side, Ted Bradley, the actor who played the president, was talking about how he preferred his electric car—which, he pointed out, he had owned for many years now—to the new hybrids that were so popular. "There's no comparison," he was saying. "The hybrids are nice, but they're not the real thing."

At the center table, Ann Garner, who sat on the boards of environmental organizations, was arguing that Los Angeles needed to build more public transportation so that people could get out of their cars. Americans, she said, belched out more carbon dioxide than any other people on the planet, and it was disgraceful. Ann was the beautiful wife of a famous attorney, and always intense, especially on environmental issues.

Morton sighed. He turned to Evans. "Do you know how much pollution we're creating right this minute? We'll burn four hundred fifty gallons of aviation fuel to take twelve people to San Francisco. Just by making this trip, they're generating more pollution per capita than most people on the planet will generate in a year."

He finished his vodka, and rattled the ice in the glass irritably. He handed the glass to Evans, who dutifully signaled for more.

"If there's anything worse than a limousine liberal," Morton said, "it's a Gulfstream environmentalist."

"But George," Evans said. "You're a Gulfstream environmentalist."

"I know it," Morton said. "And I wish it bothered me more. But you know what? It doesn't. I *like* flying around in my own airplane."

Evans said, "I heard you were in North Dakota and Chicago."

"I was. Yes."

"What'd you do there?"

"I spent money. A lot of money. A *lot*."

Evans said, "You bought some art?"

"No. I bought something far more expensive than art. I bought integrity."

"You've always had integrity," Evans said.

"Oh, not my integrity," Morton said. "I bought somebody else's."

Evans didn't know what to say to that. For a minute he thought Morton was joking.

"I was going to tell you about it," Morton continued. "I got a list of numbers, kid, and I want you to get it to Kenner. It is very much—for later. Hello, Ann!"

Ann Garner was coming toward them. "So, George, are you back for a while? Because we need you here now. The Vanutu lawsuit, which thank God you are backing, and the climate change conference that Nick has scheduled, and it's so important—my God, George. This is crunch time."

Evans started to stand to let Ann take his seat, but Morton pushed him back down again.

"Ann," he said, "I must say you look more lovely than ever, but Peter and I are having a small business discussion."

She glanced at the papers, and Evans's open briefcase. "Oh. I didn't know I was interrupting."

"No, no, if you'd just give us a minute."

"Of course. I'm sorry." But she lingered. "This is so unlike you, George, doing business on the plane."

"I know," Morton said, "but, if you must know, I am feeling quite unlike myself these days."

That made her blink. She didn't know how to take it, so she smiled, nodded, and moved away. Morton said, "She looks wonderful. I wonder who did her work."

"Her work?"

"She's had more, in the last few months. I think eyes. Maybe chin. Anyway," he said, waving his hand, "about the list of numbers. You are to tell this to no one, Peter. *No one.* Not anyone in the law firm. And especially not anyone at—"

"George, damn it, why are you hiding back there?" Evans looked over his shoulder and saw Ted Bradley coming toward them. Ted was already drinking heavily, though it was only noon. "It hasn't been the same without you, George. My God, the world without Bradley is a boring world. Oops! I mean, without George Morton, is a boring world. Come on, George. Get up out of there. That man is a lawyer. Come and have a drink."

Morton allowed himself to be led away. He glanced over his shoulder at Evans. "Later," he said.

The Grand Ballroom of the Mark Hopkins Hotel was darkened for the after-dinner speeches. The audience was elegant, the men in tuxedos, the women in ball gowns. Beneath the ornate chandeliers, the voice of Nicholas Drake boomed from the podium.

"Ladies and gentlemen, it is no exaggeration to say that we face an environmental crisis of unprecedented proportions. Our forests are disappearing. Our lakes and rivers are polluted. The plants and animals that make up our biosphere are vanishing at unprecedented rates. Forty thousand species become extinct every year. That's fifty species every single day. At present rates, we will lose half of all species on our planet in the next few decades. It is the greatest extinction in the history of earth.

"And what is the texture of our own lives? Our food is contaminated with lethal pesticides. Our crops are failing from global warming. Our weather is growing worse, and more severe. Flooding, droughts, hurricanes, tornadoes. All around the globe. Our sea levels are rising—twenty-five feet in the next century, and possibly more. And most fearsome of all, new scientific evidence points to the specter of abrupt climate change, as a result of our destructive behavior. In short, ladies and gentlemen, we are confronted by a genuine global catastrophe for our planet."

Sitting at the center table, Peter Evans looked around at the audience. They were staring down at their plates, yawning, leaning over and talking to one another. Drake wasn't getting a lot of attention.

"They've heard it before," Morton growled. He shifted his heavy frame and gave a soft belch. He had been drinking steadily through the evening, and was now quite drunk.

". . . Loss of biodiversity, shrinking of habitat, destruction of the ozone layer . . ."

Nicholas Drake appeared tall and ungainly, his tuxedo ill-fitting. The collar of his shirt was bunched up around his scrawny neck. As always, he gave the impression of an impoverished but dedicated academic, a latter-day Ichabod Crane. Evans thought no one would ever guess that Drake was paid a third of a million dollars a year to head the Fund, plus another hundred thousand in expenses. Or that he had no science background at all. Nick Drake was a trial attorney, one of five who had started NERF many years before. And like all trial attorneys, he knew the importance of not dressing too well.

". . . the erosion of bio-reservoirs, the rise of ever more exotic and lethal diseases . . ."

"I wish he'd hurry up," Morton said. He drummed his fingers on the table. Evans said nothing. He had attended enough of these functions to know that Morton was always tense if he had to speak.

At the podium, Drake was saying ". . . glimmers of hope, faint rays of positive energy, and none more positive and hopeful than the man whose lifelong dedication we are here to honor tonight . . ."

"Can I get another drink?" Morton said, finishing the last of his martini. It was his sixth. He set the glass on the table with a thud. Evans turned to look for the waiter, raising his hand. He was hoping the waiter wouldn't come over in time. George had had enough.

". . . for three decades has dedicated his considerable resources and energy to making our world a better, healthier, saner place. Ladies and gentlemen, the National Environmental Resource Fund is proud . . ."

"Ah screw, never mind," Morton said. He tensed his body, ready to push back from the table. "I hate making a fool of myself, even for a good cause."

"Why should you make a fool of—" Evans began.

". . . my good friend and colleague and this year's concerned citizen . . . Mr. *George Morton!*"

The room filled with applause, and a spotlight hit Morton as he stood and headed toward the podium, a hunched bear of a man, physically powerful, solemn, head down. Evans was alarmed when Morton stumbled on the first step, and for a moment he feared his boss would fall backward, but Morton regained his balance, and as he stepped to the stage he seemed all right. He shook hands with Drake and moved to the podium, gripping it on both sides with his large hands. Morton looked out at the room, turning his head from side to side, surveying the audience. He did not speak.

He just stood there, and said nothing.

Ann Garner, sitting beside Evans, gave him a nudge. "Is he all right?"

"Oh yes. Absolutely," Evans said, nodding. But in truth, he wasn't sure.

Finally George Morton began to speak. "I'd like to thank Nicholas Drake and the National Environmental Resource Fund for this award, but I don't feel I deserve it. Not with all the work that remains to be done. Do you know, my friends, that we know more about the moon than we do about the Earth's oceans? That's a real environmental problem. We don't know enough about the planet we depend on for our very lives. But as Montaigne said three hundred years ago, 'Nothing is so firmly believed as that which is least known.'"

Evans thought: Montaigne? George Morton quoting Montaigne?

In the glare of the spotlight, Morton was distinctly weaving back and forth. He was gripping the podium for balance. The room was absolutely silent. People were not moving at all. Even the waiters had stopped moving between the tables. Evans held his breath.

"All of us in the environmental movement," Morton said, "have seen many wonderful victories over the years. We have witnessed the creation of the EPA. We have seen the air and water made cleaner, sewage treatment improved, toxic dumps cleaned up, and we have regulated common poisons like lead for the safety of all. These are real victories, my friends. We take justifiable pride in them. And we know more needs to be done."

The audience was relaxing. Morton was moving onto familiar ground.

"But will the work get done? I am not sure. I know my mood has been dark, since the death of my beloved wife, Dorothy."

Evans sat bolt upright in his chair. At the next table, Herb Lowenstein looked shocked, his mouth open. George Morton had no wife. Or rather, he had six ex-wives—none named Dorothy.

"Dorothy urged me to spend my money wisely. I always thought I did. Now I am less sure. I said before that we don't know enough. But I fear that today, the watchword of NERF has become, We don't sue enough."

You could hear breath sucked in sharply all around the room.

"NERF is a law firm. I don't know if you realize that. It was started by lawyers and it is run by lawyers. But I now believe money is better spent on research than litigation. And that is why I am withdrawing my funding for NERF, and why I am—"

For the next few moments Morton could not be heard above the excited jabber of the crowd. Everyone was talking loudly. There were scattered boos; some guests got up to leave. Morton continued to talk, seemingly oblivious to the effect he was having. Evans caught a few phrases: ". . . one environmental charity is under FBI investigation . . . complete lack of oversight . . ."

Ann Garner leaned over and hissed, *"Get him off there."*

"What do you want me to do?" Evans whispered.

"Go and get him. He's obviously drunk."

"That may be, but I can't—"

"You have to stop this."

But on the stage, Drake was already moving forward, saying "All right, thank you, George—"

"Because to tell the truth right now—"

"Thank you, George," Drake said again, moving closer. He was actually pushing against Morton's bulk, trying to shove him away from the podium.

"Okay, okay," Morton said, clinging to the podium. "I said what I did for Dorothy. My dear dead wife—"

"Thank you, George." Drake was applauding now, holding his hands up at head height, nodding to the audience to join with him. "Thank you."

". . . who I miss desperately . . ."

"Ladies and gentlemen, please join me in thanking—"

"Yeah, okay, I'm leaving."

To muted applause, Morton shambled off the stage. Drake immediately stepped up to the podium and signaled the band. They started into a rousing rendition of Billy Joel's "You May Be Right," which someone had told them was Morton's favorite song. It was, but it seemed a poor choice under the circumstances.

Herb Lowenstein leaned over from the next table and grabbed Evans by the shoulder, pulling him close. "Listen," he whispered fiercely. "*Get him out of here.*"

"I will," Evans said. "Don't worry."

"Did you know this was going to happen?"

"No, I swear to God."

Lowenstein released Evans just as George Morton returned to the table. The assembled group was stunned. But Morton was singing cheerfully with the music, "You may be right, I may be crazy . . ."

"Come on, George," Evans said, standing up. "Let's get out of here."

Morton ignored him. ". . . But it just may be a loo-natic you're looking for . . ."

"George? What do you say?" Evans took him by the arm. "Let's go."

". . . Turn out the light, don't try to save me . . ."

"I'm not trying to save you," Evans said.

"Then how about another damn martini?" Morton said, no longer singing. His eyes were cold, a little resentful. "I think I fucking earned it."

"Harry will have one for you in the car," Evans said, steering Morton away from the table. "If you stay here, you'll have to wait for it. And you don't want to wait for a drink right now . . ." Evans continued talking, and Morton allowed himself to be led out of the room.

". . . too late to fight," he sang, "too late to change me . . ."

Before they could get out of the room, there was a TV camera with lights shining in their faces, and two reporters shoving small tape recorders in front of Morton. Everybody was yelling questions. Evans put his head down and said, "Excuse us, sorry, coming through, excuse us . . ."

Morton never stopped singing. They made their way through the hotel lobby. The reporters were running in front of them, trying to get some distance ahead, so they could film them walking forward. Evans gripped Morton firmly by the elbow as Morton sang:

"I was only having fun, wasn't hurting anyone, and we all enjoyed the weekend for a change . . ."

"This way," Evans said, heading for the door.

"I was stranded in the combat zone . . ."

And then at last they were through the swinging doors, and outside in the night. Morton stopped singing abruptly when the cold air hit him. They waited for his limousine to pull around. Sarah came out, and stood beside Morton. She didn't say anything, she just put her hand on his arm.

Then the reporters came out, and the lights came on again. And then Drake burst through the doors, saying "God damn it, George—"

He broke off when he saw the cameras. He glared at Morton, turned, and went back inside. The cameras remained on, but the three of them just stood there. It was awkward, just waiting. After what seemed like an eternity, the limousine pulled up. Harry came around, and opened the door for George.

"Okay, George," Evans said.

"No, not tonight."

"Harry's waiting, George."

"I said, *not tonight.*"

There was a deep-throated growl in the darkness, and a silver Ferrari convertible pulled up alongside the limousine.

"My car," Morton said. He started down the stairs, lurching a bit.

Sarah said, "George, I don't think—"

But he was singing again: "And you told me not to drive, but I made it home alive, so you said that only proves that I'm in-sayyy-nnne."

One of the reporters muttered, "He's insane, all right."

Evans followed Morton, very concerned. Morton gave the parking attendant a hundred dollar bill, saying "A twenty for you, my good man." He fumbled with the Ferrari door. "These crummy Italian imports." Then he got behind the wheel of the convertible, gunned the engine, and smiled. "Ah, a manly sound."

Evans leaned over the car. "George, let Harry drive you. Besides," he added, "don't we need to talk about something?"

"We do not."

"But I thought—"

"Kid, get out of my way." The camera lights were still on them. But Morton moved so that he was in the shadow cast by Evans's body. "You know, the Buddhists have a saying."

"What saying?"

"Remember it, kid. Goes like this: 'All that matters is not remote from where the Buddha sits.'"

"George, I really think you should not be driving."

"Will you remember what I just said to you?"

"Yes."

"Wisdom of the ages. Good-bye, kid."

And he accelerated, roaring out of the parking lot as Evans jumped back. The Ferrari squealed around the corner, ignoring a stop sign, and was gone.

"Peter, come on."

Evans turned, and saw Sarah standing by the limousine. Harry was getting in behind the wheel. Evans got in the back seat with Sarah, and they drove off after Morton.

• • •

The Ferrari turned left at the bottom of the hill, disappearing around the corner. Harry accelerated, handling the huge limousine with skill.

Evans said, "Do you know where he's going?"

"No idea," she said.

"Who wrote his speech?"

"He did."

"Really?"

"He was working in the house all day yesterday, and he wouldn't let me see what he was doing . . ."

"Jesus," Evans said. "Montaigne?"

"He had a book of quotations out."

"Where'd he come up with Dorothy?"

She shook her head. "I have no idea."

They passed Golden Gate Park. Traffic was light; the Ferrari was moving fast, weaving among the cars. Ahead was the Golden Gate Bridge, brightly lit in the night. Morton accelerated. The Ferrari was going almost ninety miles an hour.

"He's going to Marin," Sarah said.

Evans's cell phone rang. It was Drake. "Will you tell me what the hell that was all about?"

"I'm sorry, Nick. I don't know."

"Was he serious? About withdrawing his support?"

"I think he was."

"That's unbelievable. He's obviously suffered a nervous breakdown."

"I couldn't say."

"I was afraid of this," Drake said. "I was afraid something like this might happen. You remember, on the plane coming back from Iceland? I said it to you, and you told me I shouldn't worry. Is that your opinion now? That I shouldn't worry?"

"I don't know what you're asking, Nick."

"Ann Garner said he signed some papers on the plane."

"That's right. He did."

"Are they related to this sudden and inexplicable withdrawal of support for the organization that he loved and cherished?"

"He seems to have changed his mind about that," Evans said.

"And why didn't you tell me?"

"He instructed me not to."

"Fuck you, Evans."

"I'm sorry," Evans said.

"Not as sorry as you will be."

The phone went dead. Drake had hung up. Evans flipped the phone shut.

Sarah said, "Drake is mad?"

"Furious."

Off the bridge, Morton headed west, away from the lights of the freeway, onto a dark road skirting the cliffs. He was driving faster than ever.

Evans said to Harry, "Do you know where we are?"

"I believe we're in a state park."

Harry was trying to keep up, but on this narrow, twisting road, the limousine was no match for the Ferrari. It moved farther and farther ahead. Soon they could see only the taillights, disappearing around curves a quarter mile ahead.

"We're going to lose him," Evans said.

"I doubt it, sir."

But the limousine fell steadily behind. After Harry took one turn too fast—the big rear end lost traction and swung wide toward a cliff's edge—they were obliged to slow down even more. They were in a desolate area now. The night was dark and the cliffs deserted. A rising moon put a streak of silver on the black water far below.

Up ahead, they no longer saw any taillights. It seemed they were alone on the dark road.

They came around a curve, and saw the next curve a hundred yards ahead—obscured by billowing gray smoke.

"Oh no," Sarah said, putting her hand to her mouth.

• • •

The Ferrari had spun out, struck a tree, and flipped over. It now lay upside down, a crumpled and smoking mass. It had very nearly gone off the cliff itself. The nose of the car was hanging over the edge.

Evans and Sarah ran forward. Evans got down on his hands and knees and crawled along the cliff's edge, trying to see into the driver's compartment. It was hard to see much of anything—the front windshield was flattened, and the Ferrari lay almost flush to the pavement. Harry came over with a flashlight, and Evans used it to peer inside.

The compartment was empty. Morton's black bow tie was dangling from the doorknob, but otherwise he was gone.

"He must have been thrown."

Evans shone the light down the cliff. It was crumbling yellow rock, descending steeply for eighty feet to the ocean below. He saw no sign of Morton.

Sarah was crying softly. Harry had gone back to get a fire extinguisher from the limousine. Evans swung his light back and forth over the rock face. He did not see George's body. In fact, he did not see any sign of George at all. No disturbance, no path, no bits of clothing. Nothing.

Behind him he heard the whoosh of the fire extinguisher. He crawled away from the cliff's edge.

"Did you see him, sir?" Harry said, his face full of pain.

"No. I didn't see anything."

"Perhaps . . . over there." Harry pointed toward the tree. And he was right; if Morton had been thrown from the car by the initial impact, he might be twenty yards back, on the road.

Evans walked back, and shone his flashlight down the cliff again. The battery was running down, the beam was weakening. But almost immediately, he saw a glint of light off a man's patent leather slipper, wedged among the rocks at the edge of the water.

He sat down in the road and put his head in his hands. And cried.

POINT MOODY
TUESDAY, OCTOBER 5
3:10 A.M.

By the time the police were finished talking with them, and a rescue team had rappelled down the cliff to recover the shoe, it was three o'clock in the morning. They found no other sign of the body, and the cops, talking among themselves, agreed that the prevailing currents would probably carry the body up the coast to Pismo Beach. "We'll find him," one said, "in about a week or so. Or at least, what's left by the great whites."

Now the wreck was being cleared away, and loaded onto a flatbed truck. Evans wanted to leave, but the highway patrolman who had taken Evans's statement kept coming back to ask for more details. He was a kid, in his early twenties. It seemed he had not filled out many of these forms before.

The first time he came back to Evans, he said, "How soon after the accident would you say you arrived on the scene?"

Evans said, "I'm not sure. The Ferrari was about half a mile ahead of us, maybe more. We were probably going forty miles an hour, so . . . maybe a minute later?"

The kid looked alarmed. "You were going forty in that limo? On this road?"

"Well. Don't hold me to it."

Then he came back and said, "You said you were the first on the scene. You told me you crawled around at the edge of the road?"

"That's right."

"So you would have stepped on broken glass, on the road?"

"Yes. The windshield was shattered. I had it on my hands, too, when I crouched down."

"So that explains why the glass was disturbed."

"Yes."

"Lucky you didn't cut your hands."

"Yes."

The third time he came back, he said, "In your estimation, what time did the accident occur?"

"What time?" Evans looked at his watch. "I have no idea. But let me see . . ." He tried to work backward. The speech must have started about eight-thirty. Morton would have left the hotel at nine. Through San Francisco, then over the bridge . . . "Maybe nine-forty-five, or ten at night."

"So, five hours ago? Roughly?"

"Yes."

The kid said, "Huh." As if he were surprised.

Evans looked over at the flatbed truck, which now held the crumpled remains of the Ferrari. One cop was standing on the flatbed, beside the car. Three other cops were on the street, talking with some animation. There was another man there, wearing a tuxedo. He was talking to the cops. When the man turned, Evans was surprised to see that it was John Kenner.

"What's going on?" Evans asked the kid.

"I don't know. They just asked me to check on the time of the accident."

Then the driver got into the flatbed truck, and started the engine. One of the cops yelled to the kid, "Forget it, Eddie!"

"Never mind, then," the kid said to Evans. "I guess everything's okay."

Evans looked over at Sarah, to see if she had noticed Kenner. She was leaning on the limousine, talking on the phone. Evans looked back in time to see Kenner get into a dark sedan driven by the Nepali guy, and drive off.

The cops were leaving. The flatbed turned around and headed up the road, toward the bridge.

Harry said, "Looks like it's time to go."

Evans got into the limousine. They drove back toward the lights of San Francisco.

TO LOS ANGELES
TUESDAY, OCTOBER 5
12:02 P.M.

Morton's jet flew back to Los Angeles at noon. The mood was somber. All the same people were on board, and a few more, but they sat quietly, saying little. The late-edition papers had printed the story that millionaire philanthropist George Morton, depressed by the death of his beloved wife, Dorothy, had given a disjointed speech (termed "rambling and illogical" by the *San Francisco Chronicle*) and a few hours later had died in a tragic automobile crash while test-driving his new Ferrari.

In the third paragraph, the reporter mentioned that single-car fatalities were frequently caused by undiagnosed depression and were often disguised suicides. And this, according to a quoted psychiatrist, was the likely explanation for Morton's death.

About ten minutes into the flight, the actor Ted Bradley said, "I think we should drink a toast in memory of George, and observe a minute of silence." And to a chorus of "Hear, hear," glasses of champagne were passed all around.

"To George Morton," Ted said. "A great American, a great friend, and a great supporter of the environment. We, and the planet, will miss him."

For the next ten minutes, the celebrities on board remained relatively subdued, but slowly the conversation picked up, and finally they began to talk and argue as usual. Evans was sitting in the back, in the same seat he had occupied when they flew up. He watched the action at the table in the center, where Bradley was now explaining that the US got only 2 percent of its energy from sustainable sources and that we needed a crash program to build thousands of offshore wind farms, like England and Denmark were doing. The talk moved on to fuel cells, hydrogen cars, and photovoltaic households running off the grid. Some talked about how much they loved their hybrid cars, which they had bought for their staff to drive.

Evans felt his spirits improve as he listened to them. Despite the loss of George Morton, there were still lots of people like these—famous, high-profile people committed to change—who would lead the next generation to a more enlightened future.

He was starting to drift off to sleep when Nicholas Drake dropped into the seat beside his. Drake leaned across the aisle. "Listen," he said. "I owe you an apology for last night."

"That's all right," Evans said.

"I was way out of line. And I want you to know I'm sorry for how I behaved. I was upset, and very worried. You know George has been acting weird as hell the last couple of weeks. Talking strangely, picking fights. I guess in retrospect he was beginning to have a nervous breakdown. But I didn't know. Did you?"

"I am not sure it was a nervous breakdown."

"It must have been," Drake said. "What else could it have been? My God, the man disowns his life's work, and then goes out and kills himself. By the way, you can forget about any documents that he signed yesterday. Under the circumstances, he obviously was not in his right mind. And I know," he added, "that you wouldn't argue the point differently. You're already conflicted enough, doing work both for him and for us. You really should have recused yourself and seen to it that any papers were drawn up by a neutral attorney. I'm not going to accuse you of malpractice, but you've shown highly questionable judgment."

Evans said nothing. The threat was plain enough.

"Well, anyway," Drake said, resting his hand on Evans's knee, "I just wanted to apologize. I know you did your best with a difficult situation, Peter. And . . . I think we're going to come out of this all right."

The plane landed in Van Nuys. A dozen black SUV limos, the latest fashion, were lined up on the runway, waiting for the passengers. All the celebrities hugged, kissed air, and departed.

Evans was the last to leave. He didn't rate a car and driver. He climbed into his little Prius hybrid, which he'd parked there the day before, and drove through the gates and onto the freeway. He thought he should go to the office, but unexpected tears came to his eyes as he negotiated the midday traffic. He wiped them away and decided he was too damned tired to go to the office. Instead, he would go back to his apartment to get some sleep.

He was almost home when his cell phone rang. It was Jennifer Haynes, at the Vanutu litigation team. "I'm sorry about George," she said. "It's just terrible. Everybody here is very upset, as you can imagine. He pulled the funding, didn't he?"

"Yes, but Nick will fight it. You'll get your funding."

"We need to have lunch," she said.

"Well, I think—"

"Today?"

Something in her voice made him say, "I'll try."

"Phone me when you're here."

He hung up. The phone rang again almost immediately. It was Margo Lane, Morton's mistress. She was angry. "What the fuck is going on?"

"How do you mean?" Evans said.

"Was anybody going to fucking call me?"

"I'm sorry, Margo—"

"I just saw it on TV. Missing in San Francisco and presumed dead. They had pictures of the car."

"I was going to call you," Evans said, "when I got to my office." The truth was, she had completely slipped his mind.

"And when would that have been, next week? You're as bad as that sick assistant of yours. You're his lawyer, Peter. Do your fucking job. Because, you know, let's face it, this is not a surprise. I knew this was going to happen. We all did. I want you to come over here."

"I have a busy day."

"Just for a minute."

"All right," he said. "Just for a minute."

Margo Lane lived on the fifteenth floor of a high-rise apartment building in the Wilshire Corridor. The doorman had to call up before Evans was allowed in the elevator. Margo knew he was coming up, but she still answered the door wrapped in a towel. "Oh! I didn't realize you'd be here so soon. Come in, I just got out of the shower." She frequently did something like this, flaunting her body. Evans came into the apartment and sat on the couch. She sat opposite him. The towel barely covered her torso.

"So," she said, "what's all this about George?"

"I'm sorry," Evans said, "but George crashed his Ferrari at very high speed and was thrown from the car. He fell down a cliff—they found a shoe at the bottom—and into the water. His body hasn't been recovered but they expect it to turn up in a week or so."

With her love of drama, he was sure Margo would start to cry, but she didn't. She just stared at him. "That's bullshit," she said.

"Why do you say that, Margo?"

"Because. He's hiding or something. You know it."

"Hiding? From what?"

"Probably nothing. He'd become completely paranoid. You know that."

As she said it, she crossed her legs. Evans was careful to keep his eyes on her face.

"Paranoid?" he asked.

"Don't act like you didn't know, Peter. It was obvious."

Evans shook his head. "Not to me."

"The last time he came here was a couple of days ago," she said. "He went right to the window and stood back behind the curtain, looking down onto the street. He was convinced he was being followed."

"Had he done that before?"

"I don't know. I hadn't seen him much lately; he was traveling. But whenever I called him and asked when he was coming over, he said it wasn't safe to come here."

Evans got up and walked to the window. He stood to one side and looked down at the street below.

"Are you being followed, too?" she said.

"I don't think so."

Traffic on Wilshire Boulevard was heavy, the start of afternoon rush hour. Three lanes of cars moving fast in each direction. He could hear the roar of the traffic, even up there. But there was no place to park, to pull out from the traffic. A blue Prius hybrid had pulled to the curb across the street, and traffic was backing up behind it, honking. After a moment, the Prius started up again.

No place to stop.

"Do you see anything suspicious?" she asked.

"No."

"I never did either. But George did—or thought he did."

"Did he say who was following him?"

"No." She shifted again. "I thought he should have medication. I told him."

"And what did he say to that?"

"He said I was in danger, too. He told me I should leave town for a while. Go visit my sister in Oregon. But I won't."

Her towel was coming loose. Margo tightened it, lowering it across her firm, enhanced breasts. "So I'm telling you, George went into

STATE OF FEAR ▷ 145

hiding," she said. "And I think you better find him fast, because the man needs help."

"I see," Evans said. "But I suppose it's possible he isn't in hiding, that he really crashed his car. . . . In which case, there are things you need to do now, Margo."

He explained to her that if George remained missing, his assets could be ordered frozen. Which meant that she ought to withdraw everything from the bank account into which he put money for her every month. So she would be sure to have money to live on.

"But that's silly," she protested. "I know he'll be back in a few days."

"Just in case," Evans said.

She frowned. "Do you know something you're not telling me?"

"No," Evans said. "I'm just saying, it could be a while before this thing gets cleared up."

"Look," she said. "He's sick. You're supposed to be his friend. Find him."

Evans said that he would try. When he left, Margo was flouncing off to the bedroom to get dressed before going to the bank.

Outside, in the milky afternoon sunlight, fatigue overwhelmed him. All he wanted to do was go home and go to sleep. He got in his car and started driving. He was within sight of his apartment when his phone rang again.

It was Jennifer, asking where he was.

"I'm sorry," he said. "I can't come today."

"It's important, Peter. Really."

He said he was sorry, and would call her later.

Then Lisa, Herb Lowenstein's secretary, called to say that Nicholas Drake had been trying to reach him all afternoon. "He really wants to talk to you."

"Okay," Evans said, "I'll call."

"He sounds pissed."

"Okay."

"But you better call Sarah first."

"Why?"

His phone went dead. It always did in the back alley of his apartment; it was a dead spot in the cellular net. He slipped the phone into his shirt pocket; he'd call in a few minutes. He drove down the alley, and pulled into his garage space.

He walked up the back stairs to his apartment and unlocked the door. And stared.

The apartment was a mess. Furniture torn apart, cushions slashed open, papers all over the place, books tumbled out of the bookshelves and lying scattered on the floor.

He stood in the entrance, stunned. After a moment he walked into the room, straightened one of the toppled chairs and sat down in it. It occurred to him that he had to call the police. He got up, found the phone on the floor, and dialed them. But almost immediately the cell phone in his pocket began to ring. He hung up on the police and answered the cell phone. "Yes."

It was Lisa. "We got cut off," she said. "You better call Sarah right away."

"Why?"

"She's over at Morton's house. There was a robbery there."

"*What?*"

"I know. You better call her," she said. "She sounded upset."

Evans flipped the phone shut. He stood and walked into the kitchen. Everything was a mess there, too. He glanced into the bedroom. Everything was a mess. All he could think was the maid wasn't coming until next Tuesday. How could he ever clean this up?

He dialed his phone.

"Sarah?"

"Is that you, Peter?"

"Yes. What happened?"

"Not on the phone. Have you gone home yet?"

• • •

"Just got here."

"So . . . did it happen to you too?"

"Yes. Me too."

"Can you come here?"

"Yes."

"How soon?" She sounded frightened.

"Ten minutes."

"Okay. See you." She hung up.

Evans turned the ignition of his Prius and it hummed to life. He was pleased to have the hybrid; the waiting list in Los Angeles to get one was now more than six months. He'd had to take a light gray one, which wasn't his preferred color, but he loved the car. And he took a quiet satisfaction in noticing how many of them there were on the streets these days.

He drove down the alley to Olympic. Across the street he saw a blue Prius, just like the one he had seen below Margo's apartment. It was electric blue, a garish color. He thought he liked his gray better. He turned right, and then left again, heading north through Beverly Hills. He knew there would be rush hour traffic starting at this time of day and he should get up to Sunset, where traffic moved a little better.

When he got to the traffic light at Wilshire, he saw another blue Prius behind him. That same ugly color. Two guys in the car, not young. When he made his way to the light at Sunset, the same car was still behind him. Two cars back.

He turned left, toward Holmby Hills.

The Prius turned left, too. Following him.

Evans pulled up to Morton's gate and pressed the buzzer. The security camera above the box blinked on. "Can I help you?"

"It's Peter Evans for Sarah Jones."

A momentary pause, and then a buzz. The gates swung open slowly, revealing a curving roadway. The house was still hidden from view.

While he waited, Evans glanced down the road to his left. A block away, he saw the blue Prius coming up the road toward him. It passed him without slowing down, and disappeared around a curve.

So. Perhaps he was not being followed after all.

He took a deep breath, and let it out slowly.

The gates swung wide, and he drove inside.

It was almost four o'clock as Evans drove up the driveway to Morton's house. The property was crawling with security men. There were several searching among the trees near the front gate, and more in the driveway, clustered around several vans marked ANDERSON SECURITY SERVICE.

Evans parked next to Sarah's Porsche. He went to the front door. A security man opened it. "Ms. Jones is in the living room."

He walked through the large entryway and past the staircase that curved up to the second floor. He looked into the living room, prepared to see the same disarray that he'd witnessed at his own apartment, but here everything seemed to be in its place. The room appeared exactly as Evans remembered it.

Morton's living room was arranged to display his extensive collection of Asian antiquities. Above the fireplace was a large Chinese screen with shimmering gilded clouds; a large stone head from the Angkor region of Cambodia, with thick lips and a half-smile, was mounted on a pedestal near the couch; against one wall stood a seventeenth-century Japanese *tansu*, its rich wood glowing. Extremely rare, two hundred-year-old wood-cuts by Hiroshige hung on the back wall. A standing Burmese Buddha, carved in faded wood, stood at the entrance to the media room, next door.

In the middle of the room, surrounded by these antiquities, Sarah sat slumped on the couch, staring blankly out the window. She looked over as Evans came in. "They got your apartment?"

"Yes. It's a mess."

"This house was broken into, too. It must have happened last night. All the security people here are trying to figure out how it could have happened. Look here."

She got up and pushed the pedestal that held the Cambodian head. Considering the weight of the head, the pedestal moved surprisingly easily, revealing a safe sunk in the floor. The safe door stood open. Evans saw neatly stacked manila folders inside.

"What was taken?" he said.

"As far as I can tell, nothing," she said. "Seems like everything is still in its place. But I don't know exactly what George had in these safes. They were his safes. I rarely went into them."

She moved to the *tansu*, sliding open a center panel, and then a false back panel, to expose a safe in the wall behind. It, too, was open. "There are six safes in the house," she said. "Three down here, one in the second-floor study, one in the basement, and one up in his bedroom closet. They opened every one."

"Cracked?"

"No. Someone knew the combinations."

Evans said, "Did you report this to the police?"

"No."

"Why not?"

"I wanted to talk to you first."

Her head was close to his. Evans could smell a faint perfume. He said, "Why?"

"Because," she said. "Someone knew the combinations, Peter."

"You mean it was an inside job."

"It had to be."

"Who stays in the house at night?"

"Two housekeepers sleep in the far wing. But last night was their night off, so they weren't here."

"So nobody was in the house?"

"That's right."

"What about the alarm?"

"I armed it myself, before I went to San Francisco yesterday."

"The alarm didn't go off?"

She shook her head.

"So somebody knew the code," Evans said. "Or knew how to bypass it. What about the security cameras?"

"They're all over the property," she said, "inside the house and out. They record onto a hard drive in the basement."

"You've played it back?"

She nodded. "Nothing but static. It was scrubbed. The security people are trying to recover something, but . . ." She shrugged. "I don't think they'll get anywhere."

It would take pretty sophisticated burglars to know how to wipe a hard drive. "Who has the alarm codes and safe combinations?"

"As far as I know, just George and me. But obviously somebody else does, too."

"I think you should call the police," he said.

"They're looking for something," she said. "Something that George had. Something they think one of us has now. They think George gave it to one of us."

Evans frowned. "But if that's true," he said, "why are they being so obvious? They smashed my place so I couldn't help notice. And even here, they left the safes wide open, to be sure you'd know you'd been robbed . . ."

"Exactly," she said. "They want us to know what they're doing." She bit her lip. "They want us to panic, and rush off to retrieve this thing, whatever it is. Then they'll follow us, and take it."

Evans thought it over. "Do you have any idea what it could be?"

"No," she said. "Do you?"

Evans was thinking of the list George had mentioned to him, on the airplane. The list he never got around to explaining, before he died. But certainly the implication was that Morton had paid a lot of money for some sort of list. But something made Evans hesitate to mention it now.

"No," he said.

"Did George give you anything?"

"No," he said.

"Me neither." She bit her lip again. "I think we should leave."

"Leave?"

"Get out of town for a while."

"It's natural to feel that way after a robbery," he said. "But I think the proper thing to do right now is to call the police."

"George wouldn't like it."

"George is no longer with us, Sarah."

"George hated the Beverly Hills police."

"Sarah . . ."

"He never called them. He always used private security."

"That may be, but . . ."

"They won't do anything but file a report."

"Perhaps, but . . ."

"Did you call the police, about your place?"

"Not yet. But I will."

"Okay, well you call them. See how it goes. It's a waste of time."

His phone beeped. There was a text message. He looked at the screen. It said: N. DRAKE COME TO OFFICE IMMED. URGENT.

"Listen," he said. "I have to go see Nick for a bit."

"I'll be fine."

"I'll come back," he said, "as soon as I can."

"I'll be fine," she repeated.

He stood, and she stood, too. On a sudden impulse he gave her a hug. She was so tall they were almost shoulder to shoulder. "It's going to be okay," he said. "Don't worry. It'll be okay."

She returned the hug, but when he released her, she said, "Don't ever do that again, Peter. I'm not hysterical. I'll see you when you get back."

He left hastily, feeling foolish. At the door, she said, "By the way, Peter: Do you have a gun?"

"No," he said. "Do you?"

"Just a 9-millimeter Beretta, but it's better than nothing."

"Oh, okay." As he went out the front door, he thought, so much for manly reassurances for the modern woman.

He got in the car, and drove to Drake's office.

It was not until he had parked his car and was walking in the front door to the office that he noticed the blue Prius parked at the end of the block, with two men sitting inside it.

Watching him.

BEVERLY HILLS
TUESDAY, OCTOBER 5
4:45 P.M.

"No, no, *no!*" Nicholas Drake stood in the NERF media room, surrounded by a half-dozen stunned-looking graphic designers. On the walls and tables were posters, banners, flyers, coffee mugs, and stacks of press releases, and media kits. All were emblazoned with a banner that went from green to red, with the superimposed words: "Abrupt Climate Change: The Dangers Ahead."

"I hate it," Drake said. "I just fucking *hate* it."

"Why?"

"Because it's *boring*. It sounds like a damn PBS special. We need some punch here, some pizzazz."

"Well, sir," one of the designers said, "if you remember, you originally wanted to avoid anything that looked like overstatement."

"I did? No, I didn't. Henley wanted to avoid overstatement. Henley thought it should be made to look exactly like a normal academic conference. But if we do that, the media will tune us out. I mean, shit, do you know how many climate change conferences there are every year? All around the world?"

"No sir, how many?"

"Well, um, forty-seven. Anyway, that's not the point." Drake rapped the banner with his knuckles. "I mean look at this, 'Dangers.' It's so vague; it could refer to anything."

"I thought that's what you wanted—that it could refer to anything."

"No, I want 'Crisis' or 'Catastrophe.' 'The Crisis Ahead.' 'The Catastrophe Ahead.' That's better. 'Catastrophe' is much better."

"You used 'Catastrophe' for the last conference, the one on species extinction."

"I don't care. We use it because it works. This conference must point to a catastrophe."

"Uh, sir," one said, "with all due respect, is it really accurate that abrupt climate change will lead to catastrophe? Because the background materials we were given—"

"Yes, God damn it," Drake snapped, "it'll lead to a catastrophe. Believe me, it will! Now make the damn changes!"

The graphic artists surveyed the assembled materials on the table. "Mr. Drake, the conference starts in four days."

"You think I don't know it?" Drake said. "You think I fucking don't know it?"

"I'm not sure how much we can accomplish—"

"Catastrophe! Lose 'Danger,' add 'Catastrophe'! That's all I'm asking for. How difficult can it be?"

"Mr. Drake, we can redo the visual materials and the banners for the media kits, but the coffee mugs are a problem."

"Why are they a problem?"

"They're made for us in China, and—"

"*Made in China?* Land of pollution? Whose idea was that?"

"We always have the coffee mugs made in China for—"

"Well, we definitely can't use them. This is NERF, for Christ's sake. How many cups do we have?"

"Three hundred. They're given to the media in attendance, along with the press kit."

"Well get some damn eco-acceptable mugs," Drake said. "Doesn't Canada make mugs? Nobody ever complains about anything Canada does. Get some Canadian mugs and print 'Catastrophe' on them. That's all."

The artists were looking at one another. One said, "There's that supply house in Vancouver . . ."

"But their mugs are cream-colored . . ."

"I don't care if they're chartreuse," Drake said, his voice rising. "Just do it! Now what about the press releases?"

Another designer held up a sheet. "They're four-color banners printed in biodegradable inks on recycled bond paper."

Drake picked up a sheet. "This is recycled? It looks damn good."

"Actually, it's fresh paper." The designer looked nervous. "But no one will know."

"You didn't tell me that," Drake said. "It's essential that recycled materials look good."

"And they do, sir. Don't worry."

"Then let's move on." He turned to the PR people. "What's the timeline of the campaign?"

"It's a standard starburst launch to bring public awareness to abrupt climate change," the first rep said, standing up. "We have our initial press break on Sunday-morning talk shows and in the Sunday newspaper supplements. They'll be talking about the start of the conference Wednesday and interviewing major photogenic principals. Stanford, Levine, the other people who show well on TV. We've given enough lead time to get into all the major weekly newsbooks around the world, *Time*, *Newsweek*, *Der Spiegel*, *Paris Match*, *Oggi*, *The Economist*. All together, fifty news magazines to inform lead opinion makers. We've asked for cover stories, accepting banner folds with a graphic. Anything less and they didn't get us. We expect covers on at least twenty."

"Okay," Drake said, nodding.

"We start the conference on Wednesday. Well-known, charismatic environmentalists and major politicians from industrialized nations are scheduled to appear. We have delegates from around the world, so B-roll reaction shots of the audience will be satisfactorily color-mixed. Industrialized countries now include India and Korea and Japan, of course. The Chinese delegation will participate but there will be no speakers.

"Our two hundred invited television journalists will stay at the Hilton, and we will have interview facilities there as well as in the conference halls, so our speakers can spread the message to video audiences around the world. We will also have a number of print media people to carry the word to elite opinion makers, the ones that read but do not watch TV."

"Good," Drake said. He appeared pleased.

"Each day's theme will be identified by a distinctive graphic icon, emphasizing flood, fire, rising sea levels, drought, icebergs, typhoons, and hurricanes, and so on. Each day we have a fresh contingent of politicians from around the world coming to attend and give interviews explaining the high level of their dedication and concern about this newly emerging problem."

"Good, good." Drake nodded.

"The politicians will stay for only a day—some only a few hours—and they will not have time to attend the conferences beyond a brief photo-op showing them in the audience, but they are briefed and will be effective. Then we have local schoolchildren, grades four to seven, coming each day to learn about the dangers—sorry, the catastrophe—in their futures, and we have educational kits for grade-school teachers, so they can teach their kids about the crisis of abrupt climate change."

"When do those kits go out?"

"They were going out today, but now we'll hold them for re-bannering."

"Okay," Drake said. "And for high schools?"

"We have some trouble there," the PR guy said. "We showed the kits to a sample of high school science teachers and, uh . . ."

"And what?" Drake said.

"The feedback we got was they might not go over so well."

Drake's expression turned dark. "And why not?"

"Well, the high school curriculum is very college oriented, and there isn't a lot of room for electives . . ."

"This is hardly an *elective* . . ."

"And, uh, they felt it was all speculative and unsubstantiated. They kept saying things like, 'Where's the hard science here?' Just reporting, sir."

"God damn it," Drake said, "it is *not* speculative. It is *happening!*"

"Uh, perhaps we didn't get the right materials that show what you are saying . . ."

"Ah fuck. Never mind now," Drake said. "Just trust me, it's happening. Count on it." He turned, and said in a surprised voice, "Evans, how long have you been here?"

Peter Evans had been standing in the doorway for at least two minutes and had overheard a good deal of the conversation. "Just got here, Mr. Drake."

"All right." Drake turned to the others. "I think we've gone through this. Evans, you come with me."

Drake shut the door to his office. "I need your counsel, Peter," he said quietly. He walked around to his desk, picked up some papers, and slid them toward Evans. "What the fuck is this?"

Evans looked. "That is George's withdrawal of support."

"Did you draw it up?"

"I did."

"Whose idea was paragraph 3a?"

"Paragraph 3a?"

"Yes. Did you add that little bit of wisdom?"

"I don't really remember—"

"Then let me refresh your memory," Drake said. He picked up the document and started to read. " 'In the event of any claim that I am not of sound mind, there may be an attempt to obtain injunctive relief from the terms of this document. Therefore this document authorizes the payment of fifty thousand dollars per week to NERF while awaiting the judgment of a full trial. Said monies shall be deemed sufficient to pay ongoing costs incurred by NERF and shall by said payment deny injunctive relief.' Did you write this, Evans?"

"I did."

"Whose idea was it?"

"George's."

"George is not a lawyer. He had help."

"Not from me," Evans said. "He more or less dictated that clause. I wouldn't have thought of it."

Drake snorted in disgust. "Fifty thousand a week," he said. "At that rate, it will take us four years to receive the ten-million-dollar grant."

"That's what George wanted the document to say," Evans said.

"But whose idea was it?" Drake said. "If it wasn't you, who was it?"

"I don't know."

"Find out."

"I don't know if I can," Evans said. "I mean, George is dead now, and I don't know who he might have consulted—"

Drake glared at Evans. "Are you with us here, Peter, or not?" He started pacing back and forth. "Because this Vanutu litigation is undoubtedly the most significant lawsuit we have ever filed." He lapsed into his speech-making mode. "The stakes are enormous, Peter. Global warming is the greatest crisis facing mankind. You know that. I know that. Most of the civilized world knows that. We *must* act to save the planet, before it is too late."

"Yes," Evans said. "I know that."

"Do you?" Drake said. "We have a lawsuit, a very important lawsuit, that needs our help. And fifty thousand dollars a week will strangle it."

Evans was sure that was not true. "Fifty thousand is a lot of money," he said, "I don't see why it should strangle—"

"*Because it will!*" Drake snapped. "*Because I am telling you it will!*" He seemed surprised by his own outburst. He gripped the desk, got control of himself. "Look," he said. "We can never forget about our opponents here. The forces of industry are strong, phenomenally strong. And industry wants to be left alone to pollute. It wants to pollute here, and in Mexico, and in China, and wherever else it does its business. The stakes are huge."

"I understand," Evans said.

"Many powerful forces are taking an interest in this case, Peter."

"Yes, I'm sure."

"Forces that will stop at nothing to be sure that we lose it."

Evans frowned. What was Drake telling him?

"Their influence is everywhere, Peter. They may have influence with members of your law firm. Or other people you know. People whom you believe you can trust—but you can't. Because they are on the other side, and they don't even know it."

Evans said nothing. He was just looking at Drake.

"Be prudent, Peter. Watch your back. Don't discuss what you are doing with anyone—with *anyone*—except me. Try not to use your cell phone. Avoid e-mail. And keep an eye out in case you are followed."

"Okay. . . . But actually I've already been followed," Evans said. "There's a blue Prius—"

"Those were our guys. I don't know what they are doing. I called them off days ago."

"Your guys?"

"Yes. It's a new security firm we've been trying out. They're obviously not very competent."

"I'm confused," Evans said. "NERF has a security firm?"

"Absolutely. For years, now. Because of the danger we face. Please understand me: *We are all in danger*, Peter. Don't you understand what this lawsuit means if we win? Trillions of dollars that industry must pay in the coming years, to halt their emissions that are causing global warming. *Trillions*. With those stakes, a few lives don't matter. So: Be very damn careful."

Evans said that he would. Drake shook his hand.

"I want to know who told George about the paragraph," Drake said. "And I want that money freed up for us to use it as we see fit. This is all riding on you now," he said. "Good luck, Peter."

On his way out of the building, Evans ran into a young man who was sprinting up the stairs. They collided so hard that Evans was almost knocked down. The young man apologized hastily, and continued on his way. He looked like one of the kids working on the conference. Evans wondered what the crisis could be, now.

When he got back outside, he looked down the street. The blue Prius was gone.

He got into the car and drove back to Morton's, to see Sarah.

Traffic was heavy. He crept slowly along Sunset; he had plenty of time to think. The conversation with Drake left him feeling odd. There had been a funny quality to the actual meeting. As if it didn't really need to happen, as if Drake just wanted to make sure he was able to call Evans in, and Evans would come. As if he were asserting his authority. Or something like that.

Anyway, Evans felt, something was off.

And Evans also felt a little strange about the security firm. That just didn't seem right. After all, NERF was one of the good guys. They shouldn't be sneaking around and following people. And Drake's paranoid warnings were somehow not persuasive. Drake was overreacting, as he so often did.

Drake was dramatic by nature. He couldn't help it. Everything was a crisis, everything was desperate, everything was vitally important. He lived in a world of extreme urgency, but it wasn't necessarily the real world.

Evans called his office, but Heather had gone for the day. He called Lowenstein's office and spoke to Lisa. "Listen," he said, "I need your help."

Her voice was lower, conspiratorial. "Of course, Peter."

"My apartment was robbed."

"No—you, too?"

"Yes, me, too. And I really need to talk to the police—"

"Well, yes, you certainly do—my goodness—did they take anything?"

"I don't think so," he said, "but just to file a report, all that—I'm kind of busy right now, dealing with Sarah . . . it may go later into the night . . ."

"Well, of course, do you need me to deal with the police about your robbery?"

"Could you?" he said. "It would help so much."

"Why of course, Peter," she said. "Leave it to me." She paused. When she spoke again, it was almost a whisper. "Is there, ah, anything you don't want the police to find?"

"No," he said.

"I mean, it's all right with me, everybody in LA has a few bad habits, otherwise we wouldn't be here—"

"No, Lisa," he said. "Actually, I don't have any drugs, if that's what you mean."

"Oh, no," she said quickly. "I wasn't assuming anything. No pictures or anything like that?"

"No, Lisa."

"Nothing, you know, underage?"

"Afraid not."

"Okay, I just wanted to be sure."

"Well, thanks for doing this. Now to get in through the door—"

"I know," she said, "the key is under the back mat."

"Yes." He paused. "How'd you know that?"

"Peter," she said, sounding a little offended. "You can count on me to know things."

"All right. Well, thanks."

"Don't mention it. Now, what about Margo? How's she doing?" Lisa said.

"She's fine."

"You went to see her?"

"This morning, yes, and—"

"No, I mean at the hospital. Didn't you hear? Margo was coming back from the bank today and walked in while her apartment was being robbed. Three robberies in one day! You, Margo, Sarah! What is going on? Do you know?"

"No," Evans said. "It's very mysterious."

"It *is*."

"But about Margo . . . ?"

"Oh yes. So I guess she decided to fight these guys, which was the wrong thing to do, and they beat her up, maybe knocked her unconscious. She had a black eye, I heard, and while the cops were there interviewing her, she passed out. Got completely paralyzed and couldn't move. And she even stopped breathing."

"You're kidding."

"No. I had a long conversation with the detective who was there. He told me it just came over her, and she was unable to move and was dark blue before the paramedics showed up and took her to UCLA. She's been in intensive care all afternoon. The doctors are waiting to ask her about the blue ring."

"What blue ring?"

"Just before she became paralyzed, she was slurring her words but she said something about the blue ring, or the blue ring of death."

"The blue ring of death," Evans said. "What does that mean?"

"They don't know. She isn't able to talk yet. Does she take drugs?"

"No, she's a health nut," Evans said.

"Well, I hear the doctors say she'll be okay. It was some temporary paralysis."

"I'll go see her later," he said.

"When you do, will you call me afterward? And I'll handle your apartment, don't worry."

It was dark when he got to Morton's house. The security people were gone; the only car parked in front was Sarah's Porsche. She opened the front door when he rang. She had changed into a tracksuit. "Everything all right?" he said.

"Yes," she said. They came into the hallway, and they crossed to the living room. The lights were on, and the room was warm and inviting.

"Where are the security people?"

"They left for dinner. They'll be back."

"They *all* left?"

"They'll be back. I want to show you something," she said. She pulled out a wand with an electronic meter attached to it. She ran it over his body, like an airport security check. She tapped his left pocket. "Empty it."

The only thing in his pocket were his car keys. He dropped them on the coffee table. Sarah was running the wand over his chest, his jacket. She touched his right jacket pocket, gestured for him to empty it out.

"What's this about?" he said.

She shook her head, and didn't speak.

He pulled out a penny. Set it on the counter.

She waved her hand: more?

He felt again. Nothing.

She ran the wand over his car keys. There was a plastic rectangle on the chain, which unlocked his car door. She pried it open with a pocket-knife.

"Hey, listen . . ."

The rectangle popped open. Evans saw electronic circuits inside, a watch battery. Sarah pulled out a tiny bit of electronics hardly bigger than the tip of a lead pencil. "Bingo."

"Is that what I think it is?"

She took the electronic unit and dropped it into a glass of water. Then she turned to the penny. She examined it minutely, then twisted it in her fingers. To Evans's surprise, it broke in half, revealing a small electronic center.

She dropped that in the glass of water, too. "Where's your car?" she said.

"Out in front."

"We can check it later."

He said, "What's this about?"

"The security guys found bugs on me," she said. "And all over the house. The best guess is that was the reason for the robbery—to plant bugs. And guess what? You have bugs, too."

He looked around. "Is the house okay?"

"The house has been electronically swept and cleared. The guys found about a dozen bugs. Supposedly it's clean now."

They sat together on the couch. "Whoever is doing all this, they think we know something," she said. "And I'm beginning to believe they're right."

Evans told her about Morton's comments about the list.

"He bought a list?" she said.

Evans nodded. "That's what he said."

"Did he say what kind of a list?"

"No. He was going to tell me more, but he never got around to it."

"He didn't say anything more to you, when you were alone with him?"

"Not that I remember."

"Going up on the plane?"

"No . . ."

"At the table, at dinner?"

"I don't think so, no."

"When you walked him to his car?"

"No, he was singing all that time. It was sort of embarrassing, to tell you the truth. And then he got in his car . . . Wait a minute." Evans sat up. "He did say one funny thing."

"What was that?"

"It was some Buddhist philosophical saying. He told me to remember it."

"What was it?"

"I don't remember," Evans said. "At least not exactly. It was something like 'Everything that matters is near where the Buddha sits.'"

"George wasn't interested in Buddhism," Sarah said. "Why would he say that to you?"

"Everything that matters is near where the Buddha sits," Evans said, repeating it again.

He was staring forward, into the media room adjacent to the living room.

"Sarah . . ."

Directly facing them, under dramatic overhead lighting, was a large wooden sculpture of a seated Buddha. Burmese, fourteenth century.

Evans got up and walked into the media room. Sarah followed him. The sculpture was four feet high, and mounted on a high pedestal. Evans walked around behind the statue.

"You think?" Sarah said.

"Maybe."

He ran his fingers around the base of the statue. There was a narrow space there, beneath the crossed legs, but he could feel nothing. He crouched, looked: nothing. There were some wide cracks in the wood of the statue, but nothing was there.

"Maybe move the base?" Evans said.

"It's on rollers," Sarah said.

They slid it to one side, exposing nothing but white carpet. Evans sighed.

"Any other Buddhas around here?" he said, looking around the room.

Sarah was down on her hands and knees. "Peter," she said.

"What?"

"Look."

He crouched down. There was a roughly one-inch gap between the base of the pedestal and the floor. Barely visible in that gap was the corner of an envelope, attached to the inside of the pedestal.

"I'll be damned."

"It's an envelope."

She slid her fingers in.

"Can you reach it?"

"I . . . think so . . . got it!"

She pulled it out. It was a business-size envelope, sealed and unmarked.

"This could be it," she said, excited. "Peter, I think we may have found it!"

The lights went out, and the house was plunged into darkness.

They scrambled to their feet.

"What happened?" Evans said.

"It's okay," she said. "The emergency generator will cut in at any second."

"Actually, it won't," a voice in the darkness said.

Two powerful flashlights shone directly in their faces. Evans squinted in the harsh light; Sarah raised her hand to cover her eyes.

"May I have the envelope, please," the voice said.

Sarah said, "No."

There was a mechanical click, like the cocking of a gun.

"We'll take the envelope," the voice said. "One way or another."

"No you won't," Sarah said.

Standing beside her, Evans whispered, "*Sar-ah . . .*"

"Shut up, Peter. They can't have it."

"We'll shoot if we have to," the voice said.

"Sarah, give them the fucking envelope," Evans said.

"Let them take it," Sarah said defiantly.

"*Sar-ah . . .*"

"Bitch!" the voice screamed, and a gunshot sounded. Evans was embroiled in chaos and blackness. There was another scream. One of the flashlights bounced on the floor and rolled, pointing in a corner. In the shadows Evans saw a large dark figure attack Sarah, who screamed and kicked. Without thinking, Evans threw himself against the attacker, grabbing an arm in a leather jacket. He could smell the man's beery breath, hear him grunting. Then someone else pulled him off, slamming him to the ground, and he was kicked in the ribs.

He rolled away, banging against the furniture, and then a new, deep voice held up a flashlight and said "Move away *now*." Immediately the attacker stopped fighting with them, and turned to this new voice. Evans looked back to see Sarah, who was on the floor. Another man got up and turned toward the flashlight.

There was a crackling sound and the man screamed and fell backward. The flashlight swung to the man who had been kicking Peter.

"You. Down."

The man immediately lay on the carpet.

"Face down."

The man rolled over.

"That's better," the new voice said. "Are you two all right?"

"I'm fine," Sarah said, panting, staring into the light. "Who the hell are you?"

"Sarah," the voice said. "I'm disappointed you don't recognize me."

Just then, the lights came back up in the room.

Sarah said, "John!"

And to Evans's astonishment, she stepped across the body of the fallen attacker to give a grateful hug to John Kenner, professor of Geoenvironmental Engineering at MIT.

"I think I deserve an explanation," Evans said. Kenner had crouched down and was handcuffing the two men lying on the floor. The first man was still unconscious.

"It's a modulated taser," Kenner said. "Shoots a five-hundred-megahertz dart that delivers a four-millisecond jolt that inactivates cerebellar functioning. Down you go. Unconsciousness is immediate. But it only lasts a few minutes."

"No," Evans said. "I meant—"

"Why am I here?" Kenner said, looking up with a faint smile.

"Yes," Evans said.

"He's a good friend of George's," Sarah said.

"He is?" Evans said. "Since when?"

"Since we all met, a while back," Kenner said. "And I believe you remember my associate, Sanjong Thapa, as well."

A compact, muscular young man with dark skin and a crew cut came into the room. As before, Evans was struck by his vaguely military bearing, and British accent. "Lights are all back on, Professor," Sanjong Thapa said. "Should I call the police?"

"Not just yet," Kenner said. "Give me a hand here, Sanjong." Together, Kenner and his friend went through the pockets of the handcuffed men. "As I thought," Kenner said, straightening at last. "No identification on them."

"Who are they?"

"That'll be a question for the police," he said. The men were beginning to cough, and wake up. "Sanjong, let's get them to the front door." They hauled the intruders to their feet, and half-led, half-dragged them out of the room.

Evans was alone with Sarah. "How did Kenner get in the house?"

"He was in the basement. He's been searching the house most of the afternoon."

"And why didn't you tell me?"

"I asked her not to," Kenner said, walking back into the room. "I wasn't sure about you. This is a complicated business." He rubbed his hands together. "Now then, shall we have a look at that envelope?"

"Yes." Sarah sat down on the couch, and tore it open. A single sheet of paper, neatly folded, was inside. She stared at it in disbelief. Her face fell.

"What is it?" Evans said.

Without a word, she handed it to him.

It was a bill from the Edwards Fine Art Display Company of Torrance, California, for construction of a wooden pedestal to support a statue of a Buddha. Dated three years ago.

Feeling dejected, Evans sat down on the couch next to Sarah.

"What?" Kenner said. "Giving up already?"

"I don't know what else to do."

"You can begin by telling me exactly what George Morton said to you."

"I don't remember exactly."

"Tell me what you do remember."

"He said it was a philosophical saying. And it was something like, 'Everything that matters is near where the Buddha sits.'"

"No. That's impossible," Kenner said, in a definite tone.

STATE OF FEAR ▶ 171

"Why?"

"He wouldn't have said that."

"Why?"

Kenner sighed. "I should think it's self-evident. If he was giving instructions—which we presume he was—he wouldn't be so inexact. So he must have said something else."

"That's all I remember," Evans said, defensively. Evans found Kenner's quick manner to be brusque, almost insulting. He was beginning not to like this man.

"That's all you remember?" Kenner said. "Let's try again. *Where* did George make this statement to you? It must have been after you left the lobby."

At first Evans was puzzled. Then he remembered: "Were you there?"

"Yes, I was. I was in the parking lot, off to one side."

"Why?" Evans said.

"We'll discuss that later," Kenner said. "You were telling me, you and George went outside . . ."

"Yes," Evans said. "We went outside. It was cold, and George stopped singing when he felt the cold. We were standing on the steps of the hotel, waiting for the car."

"Uh-huh . . ."

"And when it came, he got into the Ferrari, and I was worried he shouldn't be driving, and I asked him about that, and George said, 'This reminds me of a philosophical saying.' And I said, 'What is it?' And he said. 'Everything that matters is not far from where the Buddha sits.'"

"Not far?" Kenner said.

"That's what he said."

"All right," Kenner said. "And at this moment, you were . . ."

"Leaning over the car."

"The Ferrari."

"Yes."

"Leaning over. And when George told you this philosophical saying, what did you answer back?"

"I just asked him not to drive."

"Did you repeat the phrase?"

"No," Evans said.

"Why not?"

"Because I was worried about him. He shouldn't be driving. Anyway, I remember thinking it was sort of awkwardly phrased. 'Not remote from where the Buddha sits.'"

"Not remote?" Kenner said.

"Yes," Evans said.

"He said to you, 'not remote?'"

"Yes."

"*Much* better," Kenner said. He was moving restlessly around the room, his eyes flicking from object to object. Touching things, dropping them, moving on.

"Why is it much better?" Evans said irritably.

Kenner gestured around the room. "Look around you, Peter. What do you see?"

"I see a media room."

"Exactly."

"Well, I don't understand—"

"Sit down on the couch, Peter."

Evans sat down, still furious. He crossed his arms over his chest and glowered at Kenner.

The doorbell rang. They were interrupted by the arrival of the police. Kenner said, "Let me handle this. It's easier if they don't see you," and he again walked out of the room. From the hallway, they heard several low voices discussing the two captured intruders. It sounded all very chummy.

Evans said, "Does Kenner have something to do with law enforcement?"

"Not exactly."

"What does that mean?"

"He just seems to know people."

Evans stared at her. "He knows people," he repeated.

"Different sorts of people. Yes. He sent George off to see a lot of them. Kenner has a tremendously wide range of contacts. Particularly in the environmental area."

"Is that what the Center for Risk Analysis does? Environmental risks?"

"I'm not sure."

"Why is he on sabbatical?"

"You should ask him these things."

"Okay."

"You don't like him, do you?" she said.

"I like him fine. I just think he's a conceited asshole."

"He's very sure of himself," she said.

"Assholes usually are."

Evans got up, and walked to where he could see into the hallway. Kenner was talking to the policemen, signing some documents, and turning over the intruders. The police were joking with him. Standing to one side was the dark man, Sanjong.

"And what about the little guy with him?"

"Sanjong Thapa," she said. "Kenner met him in Nepal when he was climbing a mountain there. Sanjong was a Nepali military officer assigned to help a team of scientists studying soil erosion in the Himalaya. Kenner invited him back to the States to work with him."

"I remember now. Kenner's a mountain climber, too. And he was almost on the Olympic ski team." Evans couldn't conceal his annoyance.

Sarah said, "He's a remarkable man, Peter. Even if you don't like him."

Evans returned to the couch, sat down again, folded his arms. "Well, you're right about that," he said. "I don't."

"I have the feeling you're not alone there," she said. "The list of people who dislike John Kenner is a long one."

Evans snorted, and said nothing.

They were still sitting on the couch when Kenner came bounding back into the room. He was again rubbing his hands. "All right," he said. "All the two boys have to say is that they want to talk to a lawyer, and they seem to know one. Imagine that. But we'll know more in a few hours." He turned to Peter. "So: mystery solved? Concerning the Buddha?"

Evans glared at him. "No."

"Really? It's quite straightforward."

"Why don't you just tell us," Evans said.

"Reach your right hand out to the end table," Kenner said.

Evans put his hand out. There were five remote controls on the table. "Yes?" he said. "And?"

"What are they for?"

"It's a media room," Evans said. "I think we've established that."

"Yes," Kenner said. "But *what are they for?*"

"Obviously," Evans said, "to control the television, the satellite, the DVD, the VHS, all that."

"Which one does which?" Kenner said.

Evans stared at the table. And suddenly he got it. "Oh my God," he said. "You're absolutely right."

He was flipping them over, one after another.

"This one's the flat panel . . . DVD . . . satellite . . . high def . . ." He stopped. There was one more. "Looks like there are two DVD controllers." The second one was stubby and black and had all the usual buttons, but it was slightly lighter than the other.

Evans pulled open the battery compartment. Only one battery was there. In place of the other was a tightly rolled piece of paper.

"Bingo," he said.

He took the paper out.

All that matters is not remote from where the Buddha sits. That's what George had said. Which meant that this paper was all that matters.

Carefully, Evans unrolled the tiny sheet and pressed it flat on the coffee table with the heel of his hand, smoothing out the wrinkles.

And then he stared.

The paper contained nothing but columns of numbers and words:

662262	3982293	24FXE 62262 82293	TERROR
882320	4898432	12FXE 82232 54393	SNAKE
774548	9080799	02FXE 67533 43433	LAUGHER
482320	5898432	22FXE 72232 04393	SCORPION

ALT

662262	3982293	24FXE 62262 82293	TERROR
382320	4898432	12FXE 82232 54393	SEVER
244548	9080799	02FXE 67533 43433	CONCH
482320	5898432	22FXE 72232 04393	SCORPION

ALT

662262	3982293	24FXE 62262 82293	TERROR
382320	4898432	12FXE 82232 54393	BUZZARD
444548	7080799	02FXE 67533 43433	OLD MAN
482320	5898432	22FXE 72232 04393	SCORPION

ALT

662262	3982293	24FXE 62262 82293	TERROR
382320	4898432	12FXE 82232 54393	BLACK MESA
344548	9080799	02FXE 67533 43433	SNARL
482320	5898432	22FXE 72232 04393	SCORPION

Evans said, "Is *this* what everybody's after?"

Sarah was looking at the paper over his shoulder. "I don't get it. What does it mean?"

Evans passed the paper to Kenner. He hardly glanced at it before he said, "No wonder they were so desperate to get this back."

"You know what it is?"

"There's no doubt about what it is," Kenner said, handing the paper to Sanjong. "It's a list of geographic locations."

"Locations? Where?"

"We'll have to calculate that," Sanjong said. "They're recorded in UTM, which may mean the listing was intended for pilots." Kenner saw the blank looks on the others' faces. "The world is a globe," he said, "and maps are flat. Therefore all maps are projections of a sphere onto a flat surface. One projection is the Universal Transverse Mercator grid, which divides the globe into six-degree grids. It was originally a military projection, but some pilot charts use it."

Evans said, "So these numbers are latitude and longitude in a different form?"

"Correct. A military form." Kenner ran his finger down the page. "It appears to be several alternate sets of four locations. But in every instance the first and last locations are the same. For whatever reason . . ." He frowned, and stared off into space.

"Is that bad?" Sarah said.

"I'm not sure," Kenner said. "But it might be, yes." He looked at Sanjong.

Sanjong nodded gravely. "What is today?" he said.

"Tuesday."

"Then . . . time is very short."

Kenner said, "Sarah, we're going to need George's plane. How many pilots does he have?"

"Two, usually."

"We'll need at least four. How soon can you get them?"

"I don't know. Where do you want to go?" she said.

"Chile."

"Chile! And leave when?"

"As soon as possible. Not later than midnight."

"It'll take me some time to arrange—"

"Then get started now," Kenner said. "Time is short, Sarah. Very short."

Evans watched Sarah go out of the room. He turned back to Kenner. "Okay," he said. "I give up. What's in Chile?"

"A suitable airfield, I presume. With adequate jet fuel." Kenner snapped his fingers. "Good point, Peter. Sarah," he called into the next room, "what kind of a plane is it?"

"G-five!" she called back.

Kenner turned to Sanjong Thapa, who had taken out a small handheld computer and was tapping away at it. "Are you connected to Akamai?"

"Yes."

"Was I right?"

"I've only checked the first location so far," Sanjong said. "But yes. We need to go to Chile."

"Then Terror is Terror?" Kenner said.

"I think so, yes."

Evans looked from one man to the other. "Terror is Terror?" he said, puzzled.

"That's right," Kenner said.

Sanjong said, "You know, Peter's got a point."

Evans said, "Are you guys ever going to tell me what's going on?"

"Yes," Kenner said. "But first, you have your passport?"

"I always carry it."

"Good man." Kenner turned back to Sanjong. "What point?"

"It's UTM, Professor. It's a six-degree grid."

"Of course!" Kenner said, snapping his fingers again. "What's the matter with me?"

"I give up," Evans said. "What's the matter with you?"

But Kenner didn't answer; he now seemed almost hyperactive, his fingers twitching nervously as he picked up the remote control from the table beside Peter and peered at it closely, turning it in the light. Finally, he spoke.

"A six-degree grid," Kenner said, "means that these locations are only accurate to a thousand meters. Roughly half a mile. That's simply not good enough."

"Why? How accurate should it be?"

"Three meters," Sanjong said. "About ten feet."

"Assuming they are using PPS," Kenner said, still squinting at the remote control. "In which case . . . Ah. I thought so. It's the oldest trick in the book."

He pulled the entire back of the remote off, exposing the circuit board. He lifted that away to reveal a second folded sheet of paper. It was thin, hardly more than tissue paper. It contained rows of numbers and symbols.

```
-2147483640,8,0*x°%ÁgKÀ__^O#_QÀ__cÁ«ᵃᵃᵃᵃᵃÚ?_ ___ÿÿÿ__å
-2147483640,8,0%h° â#KÀ_O,__@BÀ__cÁ«ᵃᵃᵃᵃᵃÚ?ÿÿÿÿ___ÿÿÿ__
-2147483640,8,0ã'»^$PNÀ_N__éxFÀ__cÁ¬ᵃᵃᵃᵃᵃÚ¿___ÿÿÿ__Å
-2147483640,8,06W»1/4_OÀ     ò°q_IMÀ__cÁ«ᵃᵃᵃᵃᵃÚ?ÿÿÿÿ___ÿÿÿ__¥
-2147483640,8,0‰œ°/Ñ_LÀøø_8_ÔPÀ__cÁ«ᵃᵃᵃᵃᵃÚ?____ÿÿÿ__

-2147483640,8,0*x°%ÁgKÀ__^O#_QÀ__cÁ«ᵃᵃᵃᵃᵃÚ?_ ___ÿÿÿ__å
-2147483640,8,0%h° â#KÀ_O,__@BÀ__cÁ«ᵃᵃᵃᵃᵃÚ?ÿÿÿÿ___ÿÿÿ__
-2147483640,8,06W»1/4_OÀ     ò°q_IMÀ__cÁ«ᵃᵃᵃᵃᵃÚ?ÿÿÿÿ___ÿÿÿ__¥
-2147483640,8,0ë{»I_´OÀã°°"d,LÀ__cÁ¬ᵃᵃᵃᵃᵃÚ¿___ÿÿÿ
-2147483640,8,0‰œ°/Ñ_LÀøø_8_ÔPÀ__cÁ«ᵃᵃᵃᵃᵃÚ?____ÿÿÿ__

-2147483640,8,0*x°%ÁgKÀ__^O#_QÀ__cÁ«ᵃᵃᵃᵃᵃÚ?_ ___ÿÿÿ__å
-2147483640,8,0%h° â#KÀ_O,__@BÀ__cÁ«ᵃᵃᵃᵃᵃÚ?ÿÿÿÿ___ÿÿÿ__
-2147483640,8,06W»1/4_OÀ     ò°q_IMÀ__cÁ«ᵃᵃᵃᵃᵃÚ?ÿÿÿÿ___ÿÿÿ__¥
-2147483640,8,0ë{»I_´OÀã°°"d,LÀ__cÁ¬ᵃᵃᵃᵃᵃÚ¿___ÿÿÿ
-2147483640,8,0‰œ°/Ñ_LÀøø_8_ÔPÀ__cÁ«ᵃᵃᵃᵃᵃÚ?____ÿÿÿ__
```

"All right," Kenner said. "This is more like it."

"And these are?" Evans said.

"True coordinates. Presumably for the same locations."

"Terror is Terror?" Evans said. He was starting to feel foolish.

Kenner said, "Yes. We're talking about Mount Terror, Peter. An inactive volcano. You have heard of it?"

"No."

"Well, we're going there."

"Where is it?"

"I thought you'd have guessed that by now," Kenner said. "It's in Antarctica, Peter."

II

TERROR

TO PUNTA ARENAS
TUESDAY, OCTOBER 5
9:44 P.M.

Van Nuys Airport sank beneath them. The jet turned south, crossing the flat, glowing expanse of the Los Angeles Basin. The flight attendant brought Evans coffee. On the little screen, it said 6,204 miles to destination. Flying time was nearly twelve hours.

The flight attendant asked them if they wanted dinner, and went off to prepare it.

"All right," Evans said. "Three hours ago, I'm coming to help Sarah deal with a robbery. Now I'm flying to Antarctica. Isn't it time somebody told me what this is about?"

Kenner nodded. "Have you heard of the Environmental Liberation Front? ELF?"

"No," Evans said, shaking his head.

"Not me," Sarah said.

"It's an underground extremist group. Supposedly made up of ex-Greenpeace and Earth First! types who thought those organizations had gone soft. ELF engages in violence on behalf of environmental causes. They've burned hotels in Colorado, houses on Long Island, spiked trees in Michigan, torched cars in California."

Evans nodded. "I read about them. . . . The FBI and other law enforcement agencies can't infiltrate them because the organization consists of separate cells that never communicate with one another."

"Yes," Kenner said. "Supposedly. But cell phone conversations have been recorded. We've known for some time that the group was going global, planning a series of major events around the world, starting a few days from now."

"What kind of events?"

Kenner shook his head. "That, we don't know. But we have reason to think they'll be big—and destructive."

Sarah said, "What does this have to do with George Morton?"

"Funding," Kenner said. "If ELF is preparing actions around the world, they need a lot of money. The question is, where are they getting it?"

"Are you saying George has funded an extremist group?"

"Not intentionally. ELF is a criminal organization, but even so, radical groups like PETA fund them. Frankly, it's a disgrace. But the question became whether better-known environmental groups were funding them, too."

"Better-known groups? Like who?"

"Any of them," Kenner said.

"Wait a minute," Sarah said. "Are you suggesting that the Audubon Society and the Sierra Club fund terrorist groups?"

"No," Kenner said. "But I'm telling you that nobody knows exactly what any of these groups do with their money. Because government oversight of foundations and charities is extraordinarily lax. They don't get audited. The books don't get inspected. Environmental groups in the US generate half a billion dollars a year. What they do with it is unsupervised."

Evans frowned. "And George knew this?"

"When I met him," Kenner said, "he was already worrying about NERF. What it was doing with its money. It dispenses forty-four million dollars a year."

Evans said, "You're not going to tell me that NERF—"

"Not directly," Kenner said. "But NERF spends nearly sixty percent of its money on fund-raising. It can't admit that, of course. It'd look bad. It gets around the numbers by contracting nearly all of its work to outside direct-mail advertisers and telephone solicitation groups. These groups have misleading names, like the International Wildlife Preservation Fund—that's an Omaha-based direct-mail organization, that in turn outsources the work to Costa Rica."

"You're kidding," Evans said.

"No. I am not. And last year the IWPF spent six hundred fifty thousand dollars to gather information on environmental issues, including three hundred thousand dollars to something called the Rainforest Action and Support Coalition, RASC. Which turns out to be a drop box in Elmira, New York. And an equal sum to Seismic Services in Calgary, another drop box."

"You mean . . ."

"A drop box. A dead end. That was the true basis of the disagreement between Morton and Drake. Morton felt that Drake wasn't minding the store. That's why he wanted an external audit of the organization, and when Drake refused, Morton got really worried. Morton is on the NERF board; he has liability. So he hired a team of private investigators to investigate NERF."

"He did?" Evans said.

Kenner nodded. "Two weeks ago."

Evans turned to Sarah. "Did you know this?"

She looked away, then back. "He told me I couldn't tell anyone."

"George did?"

"I did," Kenner said.

"So you were behind this?"

"No, I merely consulted with George. It was his ball game. But the point is, once you outsource the money, you no longer control how it is spent. Or, you have deniability about how it is spent."

"Jesus," Evans said. "All this time, I just thought George was worried about the Vanutu lawsuit."

"No," Kenner said. "The lawsuit is probably hopeless. It is very unlikely it will ever go to trial."

"But Balder said when he gets good sea-level data—"

"Balder already has the good data. He has had it for months."

"What?"

"The data show no rise in South Pacific sea levels for the last thirty years."

"*What?*"

Kenner turned to Sarah. "Is he always like this?"

The flight attendant set out placemats, napkins, and silverware. "I've got fusilli pasta with chicken, asparagus, and sun-dried tomatoes," she said, "and a mixed green salad to follow. Would anyone like wine?"

"White wine," Evans said.

"I have Puligny-Montrachet. I'm not sure of the year, I think it's '98. Mr. Morton usually kept '98 on board."

"Just give me the whole bottle," Evans said, trying to make a joke. Kenner had unnerved him. Earlier in the evening, Kenner had been excited, almost twitchy-nervous. But now, sitting on the airplane, he was very still. Implacable. He had the manner of a man who was telling obvious truths, even though none of it was obvious to Peter. "I had it all wrong," Evans said finally. "If what you're saying is true . . ."

Kenner just nodded slowly.

Evans thought: He's letting me put it together. He turned to Sarah. "Did you know this, too?"

"No," she said. "But I knew something was wrong. George was very upset for the last two weeks."

"You think that's why he gave that speech, and then killed himself?"

"He wanted to embarrass NERF," Kenner said. "He wanted intense media scrutiny of that organization. Because he wanted to stop what is about to happen."

The wine came in cut glass crystal. Evans gulped it, held out his glass for more. "And what is about to happen?" he said.

"According to that list, there will be four events," Kenner said. "In four locations in the world. Roughly one day apart."

"What kind of events?"

Kenner shook his head. "We now have three good clues."

Sanjong fingered his napkin. "This is real linen," he said, in an awestruck tone. "And real crystal."

"Nice, huh?" Evans said, draining his glass again.

Sarah said, "What are the clues?"

"The first is the fact that the timing is not exact. You might think a terrorist event would be precisely planned, down to the minute. These events are not."

"Maybe the group isn't that well organized."

"I doubt that's the explanation. The second clue we got tonight, and it's very important," Kenner said. "As you saw from the list, there are several alternate locations for these events. Again, you'd think a terrorist organization would pick one location and stick to it. But this group hasn't done that."

"Why not?"

"I assume it reflects the kind of events that are planned. There must be some uncertainty inherent in the event itself, or in the conditions needed for it to take place."

"Pretty vague."

"It's more than we knew twelve hours ago."

"And the third clue?" Evans said, gesturing to the flight attendant to refill his glass.

"The third clue we have had for some time. Certain government agencies track the sale of restricted high technologies that might be useful to terrorists. For example, they track everything that can be used in nuclear weapons production—centrifuges, certain metals, and so on. They track the sale of all conventional high explosives. They track certain critical biotechnologies. And they track equipment that might be used to disrupt communications networks—that generate electromagnetic impulses, for example, or high-intensity radio frequencies."

"Yes . . ."

"They do this work with neural network pattern-recognition computers that search for regularities in great masses of data—in this case, basically thousands of sales invoices. About eight months ago, the computers detected a very faint pattern that seemed to indicate a common origin for the widely scattered sale of certain field and electronic equipment."

"How did the computer decide that?"

"The computer doesn't tell you that. It just reports the pattern, which is then investigated by agents on the ground."

"And?"

"The pattern was confirmed. ELF was buying very sophisticated high technology from companies in Vancouver, London, Osaka, Helsinki, and Seoul."

"What kind of equipment?" Evans said.

Kenner ticked them off on his fingers. "Fermentation tanks for AOB primers—that's ammonia-oxidizing bacteria. Mid-level particle-dispersal units, military grade. Tectonic impulse generators. Transportable MHD units. Hypersonic cavitation generators. Resonant impact processor assemblies."

"I don't know what any of that is," Evans said.

"Few people do," Kenner said. "Some of it's fairly standard environmental technology, like the AOB primer tanks. They're used in industrial wastewater treatment. Some of it's military but sold on the open market. And some of it's highly experimental. But it's all expensive."

Sarah said, "But how is it going to be used?"

Kenner shook his head. "Nobody knows. That's what we're going to find out."

"How do you *think* it's going to be used?"

"I hate to speculate," Kenner said. He picked up a basket of rolls. "Bread, anyone?"

TO PUNTA ARENAS
WEDNESDAY, OCTOBER 6
3:01 A.M.

The jet flew through the night.

The front of the cabin was darkened; Sarah and Sanjong were sleeping on makeshift beds, but Evans couldn't sleep. He sat in the back, staring out the window at the carpet of clouds glowing silver in the moonlight.

Kenner sat opposite him. "It's a beautiful world, isn't it?" he said. "Water vapor is one of the distinctive features of our planet. Makes such beauty. It's surprising there is so little scientific understanding of how water vapor behaves."

"Really?"

"The atmosphere is a bigger mystery than anyone will admit. Simple example: No one can say for sure if global warming will result in more clouds, or fewer clouds."

"Wait a minute," Evans said. "Global warming is going to raise the temperature, so more moisture will evaporate from the ocean, and more moisture means more clouds."

"That's one idea. But higher temperature also means more water vapor in the air and therefore fewer clouds."

"So which is it?"

"Nobody knows."

"Then how do they make computer models of climate?" Evans said.

Kenner smiled. "As far as cloud cover is concerned, they guess."

"They *guess?*"

"Well, they don't call it a guess. They call it an estimate, or parameterization, or an approximation. But if you don't understand something, you can't approximate it. You're really just guessing."

Evans felt the beginnings of a headache. He said, "I think it's time for me to get some sleep."

"Good idea," Kenner said, glancing at his watch. "We still have another eight hours before we land."

The flight attendant gave Evans some pajamas. He went into the bathroom to change. When he came out, Kenner was still sitting there, staring out the window at the moonlit clouds. Against his better judgment, Evans said, "By the way. You said earlier that the Vanutu lawsuit won't go to trial."

"That's right."

"Why not? Because of the sea-level data?"

"In part, yes. It's hard to claim global warming is flooding your country if sea levels aren't rising."

"It's hard to believe sea levels aren't rising," Evans said. "Everything you read says that they are. All the television reports . . ."

Kenner said, "Remember African killer bees? There was talk of them for years. They're here now, and apparently there's no problem. Remember Y2K? Everything you read back then said disaster was imminent. Went on for months. But in the end, it just wasn't true."

Evans thought that Y2K didn't prove anything about sea levels. He felt an urge to argue that point, but found himself suppressing a yawn.

"It's late," Kenner said. "We can talk about all this in the morning."

"You're not going to sleep?"

"Not yet. I have work to do."

Evans went forward to where the others were sleeping. He lay down across the aisle from Sarah, and pulled the covers up to his chin. Now his feet were exposed. He sat up, wrapped the blanket around his toes, and then lay down again. The blanket only came to mid-shoulder. He thought about getting up and asking the flight attendant for another.

And then he slept.

He awoke to harsh, glaring sunlight. He heard the clink of silverware, and smelled coffee. Evans rubbed his eyes, and sat up. In the back of the plane, the others were eating breakfast.

He looked at his watch. He'd slept for more than six hours.

He walked to the back of the plane.

"Better eat," Sarah said, "we land in an hour."

They stepped out onto the runway of Marso del Mar, shivering in the chill wind that whipped in off the ocean. The land around them was low, green, marshy, and cold. In the distance Evans saw the jagged, snow-covered spires of the El Fogara range of southern Chile.

"I thought this was summer," he said.

"It is," Kenner said. "Late spring, anyway."

The airfield consisted of a small wooden terminal, and a row of corrugated steel hangars, like oversize Quonset huts. There were seven or eight other aircraft on the field, all four-engine prop planes. Some had skis that were retracted above the landing wheels.

"Right on time," Kenner said, pointing to the hills beyond the airport. A Land Rover was bouncing toward them. "Let's go."

Inside the little terminal, which was little more than a single large room, its walls covered with faded, stained air charts, the group tried on parkas, boots, and other gear brought by the Land Rover. The parkas were all bright red or orange. "I tried to get everybody's size right," Kenner said. "Make sure you take long johns and microfleece, too."

Evans glanced at Sarah. She was sitting on the floor, pulling on heavy socks and boots. Then she unselfconsciously stripped down to her bra, and pulled a fleece top over her head. Her movements were quick, businesslike. She didn't look at any of the men.

Sanjong was staring at the charts on the wall, and seemed particularly interested in one. Evans went over. "What is it?"

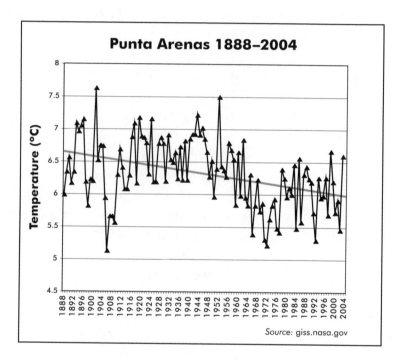

"It's the record from the weather station at Punta Arenas, near here. It's the closest city to Antarctica in the world." He tapped the chart and laughed. "There's your global warming."

Evans frowned at the chart.

"Finish up, everybody," Kenner said, glancing at his watch. "Our plane leaves in ten minutes."

Evans said, "Where exactly are we going?"

"To the base nearest Mount Terror. It's called Weddell Station. Run by New Zealanders."

"What's there?"

"Not much, mate," the Land Rover driver said, and he laughed. "But the way the weather's been lately, you'll be lucky if you can get there at all."

Evans stared out the narrow window of the Hercules. The vibration of the props made him sleepy, but he was fascinated by what he saw beneath him—mile after mile of gray ice, a vista broken by intermittent fog, and the occasional outcrop of black rock. It was a monochromatic, sunless world. And it was huge.

"Enormous," Kenner said. "People have no perspective on Antarctica, because it appears as a fringe at the bottom of most maps. But in fact, Antarctica is a major feature on the Earth's surface, and a major factor in our climate. It's a big continent, one and a half times the size of either Europe or the United States, and it holds ninety percent of all the ice on the planet."

"Ninety percent?" Sarah said. "You mean there's only ten percent in the rest of the world?"

"Actually, since Greenland has four percent, all the other glaciers in the world—Kilimanjaro, the Alps, the Himalaya, Sweden, Norway, Canada, Siberia—they all account for six percent of the planet's ice. The overwhelming majority of the frozen water of our planet is in the continent of Antarctica. In many places the ice is five or six miles thick."

"No wonder they're concerned that the ice here is melting," Evans said.

Kenner said nothing.

Sanjong was shaking his head.

Evans said, "Come on, guys. Antarctica *is* melting."

"Actually, it's not," Sanjong said. "I can give you the references, if you like."

Kenner said, "While you were asleep, Sanjong and I were talking about how to clarify things for you, since you seem to be so ill-informed."

"Ill-informed?" Evans said, stiffening.

"I don't know what else one would call it," Kenner said. "Your heart may be in the right place, Peter, but you simply don't know what you're talking about."

"Hey," he said, controlling his anger. "Antarctica *is* melting."

"You think repetition makes something true? The data show that one relatively small area called the Antarctic Peninsula is melting and calving huge icebergs. That's what gets reported year after year. But the continent as a whole is getting colder, and the ice is getting thicker."

"Antarctica is getting *colder?*"

Sanjong had taken out a laptop and was hooking it up to a small portable bubble jet printer. He flipped open his laptop screen.

"What we decided," Kenner said, "is that we're going to give you references from now on. Because it's too boring to try and explain everything to you."

A sheet of paper began to buzz out of the printer. Sanjong passed it to Evans.

Doran, P. T., Priscu, J. C., Lyons, W. B., Walsh, J. E., Fountain, A. G., McKnight, D. M., Moorhead, D. L., Virginia, R. A., Wall, D. H., Clow, G. D., Fritsen, C. H., McKay, C. P., and Parsons, A. N., 2002, "Antarctic climate cooling and terrestrial ecosystem response," *Nature* **415**: 517–20.

From 1986 to 2000 central Antarctic valleys cooled .7° C per decade with serious ecosystem damage from cold.

Comiso, J. C., 2000, "Variability and trends in Antarctic surface temperatures from *in situ* and satellite infrared measurements," *Journal of Climate* **13:** 1674–96.

Both satellite data and ground stations show slight cooling over the last 20 years.

Joughin, I., and Tulaczyk, S., 2002, "Positive mass balance of the Ross Ice Streams, West Antarctica," *Science* **295:** 476–80.

Side-looking radar measurements show West Antarctic ice is increasing at 26.8 gigatons/yr. Reversing the melting trend of the last 6,000 years.

Thompson, D. W. J., and Solomon, S., 2002, "Interpretation of recent Southern Hemisphere climate change," *Science* **296:** 895–99.

Antarctic peninsula has warmed several degrees while interior has cooled somewhat. Ice shelves have retreated but sea ice has increased.

Petit, J. R., Jouzel, J., Raynaud, D., Barkov, N. I., Barnola, J.-M., Basile, I., Bender, M., Chappellaz, J., Davis, M., Delaygue, G., Delmotte, M., Kotlyakov, V. M., Legrand, M., Lipenkov, V. Y., Lorius, C., Pepin, L., Ritz, C., Saltzman, E., and Stievenard, M., 1999, "Climate and atmospheric history of the past 420,000 years from the Vostok ice core, Antarctica," *Nature* **399:** 429–36.

During the last four interglacials, going back 420,000 years, the Earth was warmer than it is today.

Anderson, J. B., and Andrews, J. T., 1999, "Radiocarbon constraints on ice sheet advance and retreat in the Weddell Sea, Antarctica," *Geology* **27:** 179–82.

Less Antarctic ice has melted today than occurred during the last interglacial.

Liu, J., Curry, J. A., and Martinson, D. G., 2004, "Interpretation of recent Antarctic sea ice variability," *Geophysical Research Letters* **31:** 10.1029/2003 GL018732.

Antarctic sea ice has increased since 1979.

Vyas, N. K., Dash, M. K., Bhandari, S. M., Khare, N., Mitra, A., and Pandey, P. C., 2003, "On the secular trends in sea ice extent over the antarctic region based on OCEANSAT-1 MSMR observations," *International Journal of Remote Sensing* **24:** 2277–87.

Trend toward more sea ice may be accelerating.

Parkinson, C. L., 2002, "Trends in the length of the southern Ocean sea-ice season, 1979–99," *Annals of Glaciology* **34:** 435–40.

The greater part of Antarctica experiences a longer sea-ice season, lasting 21 days longer than it did in 1979.

"Okay, well, I see *slight* cooling referred to here," Evans said. "I also see warming of the peninsula of *several degrees*. That certainly seems more significant. And that peninsula's a pretty big part of the continent, isn't it?" He tossed the paper aside. "Frankly, I'm not impressed."

Sanjong said, "The peninsula is two percent of the continent. And frankly, I am surprised that you did not comment on the most significant fact in the data you were given."

"Which is?"

"When you said earlier that the Antarctic is melting," Sanjong said, "were you aware that it has been melting for the last *six thousand years?*"

"Not specifically, no."

"But generally, you knew that?"

"No," Evans said. "I wasn't aware of that."

"You thought that the Antarctic melting was something new?"

"I thought it was melting faster than previously," Evans said.

"Maybe we won't bother anymore," Kenner said.

Sanjong nodded, and started to put the computer away.

"No, no," Evans said. "I'm interested in what you have to say. I'm not closed-minded about this. I'm ready to hear new information."

"You just did," Kenner said.

Evans picked up the sheet of paper again, and folded it carefully. He slipped it into his pocket. "These studies are probably financed by the coal industry," he said.

"Probably," Kenner said. "I'm sure that explains it. But then, everybody's paid by somebody. Who pays your salary?"

"My law firm."

"And who pays them?"

"The clients. We have several hundred clients."

"You do work for all of them?"

"Me, personally? No."

"In fact, you do most of your work for environmental clients," Kenner said. "Isn't that true?"

"Mostly. Yes."

"Would it be fair to say that the environmental clients pay your salary?" Kenner said.

"You could make that argument."

"I'm just asking, Peter. Would it be fair to say environmentalists pay your salary?"

"Yes."

"Okay. Then would it be fair to say the opinions you hold are because you work for environmentalists?"

"Of course not—"

"You mean you're not a paid flunky for the environmental movement?"

"No. The fact is—"

"You're not an environmental stooge? A mouthpiece for a great fundraising and media machine—a multi-billion-dollar industry in its own right—with its own private agenda that's not necessarily in the public interest?"

"God damn it—"

"Is this pissing you off?" Kenner said.

"You're damn right it is!"

"Good," Kenner said. "Now you know how legitimate scientists feel when their integrity is impugned by slimy characterizations such as the one you just made. Sanjong and I gave you a careful, peer-reviewed interpretation of data. Made by several groups of scientists from several different countries. And your response was first to ignore it, and then to make an ad hominem attack. You didn't answer the data. You didn't provide counter evidence. You just smeared with innuendo."

"Oh, fuck you," Evans said. "You think you have an answer for everything. But there's only one problem: Nobody agrees with you. Nobody in the world thinks that Antarctica is getting colder."

"These scientists do," Kenner said. "They published the data."

Evans threw up his hands. "The hell with it," he said. "I don't want to talk about this anymore."

He walked to the front of the plane and sat down, crossed his arms, and stared out the window.

Kenner looked at Sanjong and Sarah. "Anyone feel like coffee?"

• • •

Sarah had watched Kenner and Evans with a certain amount of uneasiness. Even though she had worked for the past two years for Morton, she had never shared her employer's passion for environmental issues. All during that time, Sarah had been in a tempestuous, exciting relationship with a handsome young actor. Their time together consisted of an unending series of passionate evenings, angry confrontations, slammed doors, tearful reconciliations, jealousies, and infidelities—and it had consumed her more than she cared to admit. The truth was that she had paid no more attention to NERF or Morton's other environmental interests than the job required. At least, until the son-of-a-bitch actor appeared in the pages of *People* magazine with a young actress from his TV show, and Sarah finally decided she had had enough, erased the guy from her cell phone, and threw herself into her work.

But she certainly held the same general view about the state of the world as Evans did. Perhaps Evans was more aggressive in stating his views, and more trusting of his assumptions, but she basically agreed with him. And here was Kenner, casting doubt after doubt.

It left her wondering whether Kenner was really correct about everything he was saying. And it also made her wonder just how he and Morton had become friends.

She asked Kenner, "Did you have these same discussions with George?"

"In the last weeks of his life, yes."

"And did he argue with you the way Evans is?"

"No." Kenner shook his head. "Because by then, he knew."

"Knew what?"

They were interrupted by the pilot's voice on the intercom. "Good news," he said. "The weather's broken over Weddell, and we will land in ten minutes. For those of you who have never made a landing on ice, seat belts should be low and tight, and all your gear safely stowed. And we really mean it."

The plane began a slow, curving descent. Sarah looked out the window at a crusty expanse of white, snow-covered ice. In the distance she saw a series of brightly colored buildings—red, blue, green—built on a cliff, overlooking the gray and choppy ocean.

"That's Weddell Station," Kenner said.

WEDDELL STATION
WEDNESDAY, OCTOBER 6
11:04 A.M.

Trudging toward structures that looked like oversize children's building blocks, Evans kicked a clump of ice out of his path. He was in a grumpy mood. He felt relentlessly bullied by Kenner, whom he now recognized as one of those perpetual contrarians who argued against all conventional wisdom, simply because it was conventional.

But since Evans was stuck with this lunatic—at least for the next few days—he decided to avoid Kenner as much as possible. And certainly not engage him in any more conversations. There was no point in arguing with extremists.

He looked at Sarah, walking across the ice airfield beside him. Her cheeks were flushed in the cold air. She looked very beautiful. "I think the guy is a nut," Evans said.

"Kenner?"

"Yeah. What do you think?"

She shrugged. "Maybe."

"I bet those references he gave me are fake," he said.

"They'll be easy enough to check," she said. They stamped their feet and entered the first building.

• • •

Weddell Research Station turned out to be home to thirty-odd scientists, graduate students, technicians, and support staff. Evans was pleasantly surprised to find it was quite comfortable inside, with a cheerful cafeteria, a game room, and a large gym with a row of treadmills. There were big picture windows with views of the choppy, restless ocean. Other windows looked out over the vast, white expanse of the Ross Ice Shelf, stretching away to the west.

The head of the station greeted them warmly. He was a heavyset, bearded scientist named MacGregor who looked like Santa Claus in a Patagonia vest. Evans was annoyed that MacGregor seemed to know Kenner, at least by reputation. The two men immediately struck up a friendly conversation.

Evans excused himself, saying he wanted to check his e-mail. He was shown to a room with several computer terminals. He signed on to one, and went directly to the site for *Science* magazine.

It took him only a few moments to determine that the references Sanjong had given him were genuine. Evans read the online abstracts, and then the full text. He began to feel a little better. Kenner had summarized the raw data correctly, but he had drawn a different interpretation from that of the authors. The authors of those papers were firmly committed to the idea of global warming—and said so in the text.

Or at least, most of them did.

It was a bit complicated. In one paper, it was clear that even though the authors gave lip service to the threat of global warming, their data seemed to suggest the opposite of what they were saying in the text. But that apparent confusion, Evans suspected, was probably just the result of drawing up a paper with half a dozen authors. What they *said* was they supported the idea of global warming. And that was what counted.

More disturbing was the paper on the increase in ice thickness in the Ross Ice Shelf. Here Evans found some troubling points. First, the author did say that the shelf had been melting for the last six thousand years, ever since the Holocene era. (Though Evans could not remember reading, in any article about melting Antarctic ice, that it had been going on for the last six thousand years.) If that were true, it wasn't exactly news. On the contrary, the author suggested that the real news was the end of this long-term melting trend, and the first evidence of ice thickening. The author was hinting that this might be the first sign of the start of the next Ice Age.

Jesus!

The next *Ice Age?*

There was a knock on the door behind him. Sarah stuck her head in. "Kenner wants us," she said. "He's discovered something. Looks like we're going out on the ice."

The map covered the entire wall, showing the enormous, star-shaped continent. In the lower right-hand corner was Weddell Station, and the curving arc of the Ross Ice Shelf.

"We've learned," Kenner said, "that a supply ship docked five days ago bringing boxes of field material for an American scientist named James Brewster, from the University of Michigan. Brewster is a very recent arrival who was permitted to come at the last minute because the terms of his research grant were unusually generous in their allowance for overhead—meaning the station would get some much-needed money for operations."

"So he bought his way in?" Evans said.

"In effect."

"When did he get here?"

"Last week."

"Where is he now?"

"Out in the field." Kenner pointed to the map. "Somewhere south of the slopes of Mount Terror. And that's where we're going."

"You say this guy's a scientist from Michigan?" Sarah said.

"No," Kenner said. "We just checked with the university. They have a Professor James Brewster, all right. He's a geophysicist at the University of Michigan, and right now he's in Ann Arbor waiting for his wife to deliver a baby."

"So who is this guy?"

"Nobody knows."

"And what was his offloaded equipment?" Evans said.

"Nobody knows that, either. It was helicoptered out to the field, still in the original crates. The guy's been out there a week with two so-called graduate students. Whatever he's doing, he's apparently working across a large area, so he moves his base camp frequently. Nobody here knows precisely where he is." Kenner lowered his voice. "One of the graduate students came back yesterday to do some computer work. But we won't use him to lead us out there, for obvious reasons. We'll use one of the staff people at Weddell, Jimmy Bolden. He's very knowledgeable.

"The weather's too dicey for helicopters, so we have to take snow-tracks. It's seventeen miles to the camp. The snowtracks should get us there in two hours. The outside temperature's perfect for springtime in Antarctica—minus twenty-five degrees Fahrenheit. So, bundle up. Any questions?"

Evans glanced at his watch. "Won't it get dark soon?"

"We have much less nighttime now that spring is here. We'll have daylight all the time we're out there. The only problem we face is right here," Kenner said, pointing to the map. "We have to cross the shear zone."

THE SHEAR ZONE
WEDNESDAY, OCTOBER 6
12:09 P.M.

"The shear zone?" Jimmy Bolden said, as they trudged toward the vehicle shed. "There's nothing to it. You just have to be careful, that's all."

"But what is it?" Sarah said.

"It's a zone where the ice is subjected to lateral forces, shear forces, a bit like the land in California. But instead of having earthquakes, you get crevasses. Lots of 'em. Deep ones."

"We have to cross that?"

"It's not a problem," Bolden said. "Two years ago they built a road that crosses the zone safely. They filled in all the crevasses along the road."

They went into the corrugated steel shed. Evans saw a row of boxy vehicles with red cabs and tractor treads. "These are the snowtracks," Bolden said. "You and Sarah'll go in one, Dr. Kenner in one, and I'll be in the third, leading you."

"Why can't we all go in one?"

"Standard precaution. Keep the weight down. You don't want your vehicle to fall through into a crevasse."

"I thought you said there was a road where the crevasses were filled in?"

"There is. But the road is on an ice field, and the ice moves a couple of inches a day. Which means the road moves. Don't worry, it's clearly marked with flags." Bolden climbed up onto the tread. "Here, let me show you the features of the snowtrack. You drive it like a regular car:

clutch there, handbrake, accelerator, steering wheel. You run your heater on this switch here—" he pointed to a switch "—and keep it on at all times. It will maintain the cab at around ten above zero. This bulgey orange beacon on the dashboard is your transponder. It turns on when you push this button here. It also turns on automatically if the vehicle shifts more than thirty degrees from horizontal."

"You mean if we fall into a crevasse," Sarah said.

"Trust me; that isn't going to happen," Bolden said. "I'm just showing you the features. Transponder broadcasts a unique vehicle code, so we can come and find you. If for any reason you need to be rescued, you should know the average time to rescue is two hours. Your food is here; water here; you have enough for ten days. Medical kit here, including morphine and antibiotics. Fire extinguisher here. Expedition equipment in this box—crampons, ropes, carabiners, all that. Space blankets here, equipped with mini heaters; they'll keep you above freezing for a week, if you crawl inside 'em. That's about it. We communicate by radio. Speaker in the cab. Microphone above the windshield. Voice-activated— just talk. Got it?"

"Got it," Sarah said, climbing up.

"Then let's get started. Professor, you clear on everything?"

"I am," Kenner said, climbing up into the adjacent cab.

"Okay," Bolden said. "Just remember that whenever you are outside your vehicle, it is going to be thirty below zero. Keep your hands and face covered. Any exposed skin will get frostbite in less than a minute. Five minutes, and you're in danger of losing anatomy. We don't want you folks going home without all your fingers and toes. Or noses."

Bolden went to the third cab. "We proceed single file," he said. "Three cab-lengths apart. No closer under any circumstances, and no farther. If a storm comes up and visibility drops, we maintain the same distance but reduce our speed. Got it?"

They all nodded.

"Then let's go."

At the far end of the shed, a corrugated door rolled up, the icy metal screeching. Bright sunlight outside.

"Looks like a beautiful day in the neighborhood," Bolden said. And with a sputter of diesel exhaust, he drove the first snowtrack out through the door.

It was a bouncing, bone-jolting ride. The ice field that had looked so flat and featureless from a distance was surprisingly rugged when experienced up close, with long troughs and steep hillocks. Evans felt like he was in a boat, crashing through choppy seas, except of course this sea was frozen, and they were moving slowly through it.

Sarah drove, her hands confident on the wheel. Evans sat in the passenger seat beside her, clutching the dashboard to keep his balance.

"How fast are we going?"

"Looks like fourteen miles an hour."

Evans grunted as they nosed down a short trench, then up again. "We've got two hours of this?"

"That's what he said. By the way, did you check Kenner's references?"

"Yes," Evans said, in a sulky voice.

"Were they made up?"

"No."

Their vehicle was third in the row. Ahead was Kenner's snowtrack, following behind Bolden's in the lead.

The radio hissed. "Okay," they heard Bolden say, over the speaker. "Now we're coming into the shear zone. Maintain your distance and stay within the flags."

Evans could see nothing different—it just looked like more ice field, glistening in the sun—but here there were red flags on both sides of the route. The flags were mounted on six-foot-high posts.

As they moved deeper into the field, he looked beyond the road to the openings of crevasses in the ice. They had a deep blue color, and seemed to glow.

"How deep are they?" Evans said.

"The deepest we've found is a kilometer," Bolden said, over the radio. "Some of them are a thousand feet. Most are a few hundred feet or less."

"They all have that color?"

"They do, yes. But you don't want a closer look."

Despite the dire warnings, they crossed the field in safety, leaving the flags behind. Now they saw to the left a sloping mountain, with white clouds.

"That's Erebus," Bolden said. "It's an active volcano. That's steam coming from the summit. Sometimes it lobs chunks of lava, but never this far out. Mount Terror is inactive. You see it ahead. That little slope."

Evans was disappointed. The name, Mount Terror, had suggested something fearsome to him—not this gentle hill with a rocky outcrop at the top. If the mountain hadn't been pointed out to him, he might not have noticed it at all.

"Why is it called Mount Terror?" he said. "It's not terrifying."

"Has nothing to do with that. The first Antarctic landmarks were named after the ships that discovered them," Bolden said. "Terror was apparently the name of a ship in the nineteenth century."

"Where's the Brewster camp?" Sarah said.

"Should be visible any minute now," Bolden said. "So, you people are some kind of inspectors?"

"We're from the IADG," Kenner said. "The international inspection agency. We're required to make sure that no US research project violates the international agreements on Antarctica."

"Uh-huh . . ."

"Dr. Brewster showed up so quickly," Kenner went on, "he never submitted his research grant proposal for IADG approval. So we'll check in the field. It's just routine."

They bounced and crunched onward for several minutes in silence. They still did not see a camp.

"Huh," Bolden said. "Maybe he moved it."

"What type of research is he doing?" Kenner said.

"I'm not sure," Bolden said, "but I heard he's studying the mechanics of ice calving. You know, how the ice flows to the edge, and then breaks off the shelf. Brewster's been planting GPS units in the ice to record how it moves toward the sea."

"Are we close to the sea?" Evans said.

"About ten or eleven miles away," Bolden said. "To the north."

Sarah said, "If he's studying iceberg formation, why is he working so far from the coast?"

"Actually, this isn't so far," Kenner said. "Two years ago an iceberg broke off the Ross Shelf that was four miles wide and forty miles long. It was as big as Rhode Island. One of the biggest ever seen."

"Not because of global warming, though," Evans said to Sarah, with a disgusted snort. "Global warming couldn't be responsible for that. Oh no."

"Actually, it wasn't responsible," Kenner said. "It was caused by local conditions."

Evans sighed. "Why am I not surprised?"

Kenner said, "There's nothing wrong with the idea of local conditions, Peter. This is a *continent*. It would be surprising if it didn't have its own distinctive weather patterns, irrespective of global trends that may or may not exist."

"And that's very true," Bolden said. "There are definitely local patterns here. Like the katabatic winds."

"The what?"

"Katabatic winds. They're gravitational winds. You've probably noticed that it's a lot windier here than in the interior. The interior of the continent is relatively calm."

"What's a gravitational wind?" Evans said.

"Antarctica's basically one big ice dome," Bolden said. "The interior is higher than the coast. And colder. Cold air flows downhill, and gathers speed as it goes. It can be blowing fifty, eighty miles an hour when it reaches the coast. Today is not a bad day, though."

"That's a relief," Evans said.

And then Bolden said, "See there, dead ahead. That's Professor Brewster's research camp."

BREWSTER CAMP
WEDNESDAY, OCTOBER 6
2:04 P.M.

It wasn't much to look at: a pair of orange domed tents, one small, one large, flapping in the wind. It looked like the large one was for equipment; they could see the edges of boxes pressing against the tent fabric. From the camp, Evans could see orange-flagged units stuck into the ice every few hundred yards, in a line stretching away into the distance.

"We'll stop now," Bolden said. "I'm afraid Dr. Brewster's not here at the moment; his snowtrack is gone."

"I'll just have a look," Kenner said.

They shut the engines and climbed out. Evans had thought it was chilly in the cab, but it was a shock to feel the cold air hit him as he stepped out onto the ice. He gasped and coughed. Kenner appeared to have no reaction; he went straight for the supply tent and disappeared inside.

Bolden pointed down the line of flags. "You see his vehicle tracks there, parallel to the sensor units? Dr. Brewster must have gone out to check his line. It runs almost a hundred miles to the west."

Sarah said, "A hundred miles?"

"That's right. He has installed GPS radio units all along that distance. They transmit back to him, and he records how they move with the ice."

"But there wouldn't be much movement . . ."

"Not in the course of a few days, no. But these sensors will remain in place for a year or more. Sending back the data by radio to Weddell."

"Dr. Brewster is staying that long?"

"Oh no, he'll go back, I'm sure. It's too expensive to keep him here. His grant allows an initial twenty-one-day stay only, and then monitoring visits of a week every few months. But we'll be forwarding his data to him. Actually, we just put it up on the Internet; he takes it wherever he happens to be."

"So you assign him a secure web page?"

"Exactly."

Evans stamped his feet in the cold. "So, is Brewster coming back, or what?"

"Should be coming back. But I couldn't tell you when."

From within the tent, Kenner shouted, "Evans!"

"I guess he wants me."

Evans went to the tent. Bolden said to Sarah, "Go ahead with him, if you want to." He pointed off to the south, where clouds were darkening. "We don't want to be staying here too long. Looks like weather coming up. We have two hours ahead of us, and it won't be any fun if it socks in. Visibility drops to ten feet or less. We'd have to stay put until it cleared. And that might be two or three days."

"I'll tell them," she said.

Evans pushed the tent flap aside. The interior glowed orange from the fabric. There were the remains of wooden crates, broken down and stacked on the ground. On top of them were dozens of cardboard boxes, all stenciled identically. They each had the University of Michigan logo, and then green lettering:

University of Michigan
Dept. of Environmental Science
Contents: Research Materials
Extremely Sensitive
HANDLE WITH CARE
This Side Up

"Looks official," Evans was saying. "You sure this guy isn't an actual research scientist?"

"See for yourself," Kenner said, opening one cardboard carton. Within it, Evans saw a stack of plastic cones, roughly the size of highway cones. Except they were black, not orange. "You know what these are?"

"No." Evans shook his head.

Sarah came into the tent. "Bolden says bad weather coming, and we shouldn't stay here."

"Don't worry, we won't," Kenner said. "Sarah, I need you to go into the other tent. See if you can find a computer there. Any kind of computer—laptop, lab controller, PDA—anything with a microprocessor in it. And see if you can find any radio equipment."

"You mean transmitters, or radios for listening?"

"Anything with an antenna."

"Okay." She turned and went outside again.

Evans was still going through the cartons. He opened three, then a fourth. They all contained the same black cones. "I don't get it."

Kenner took one cone, turned it to the light. In raised lettering it said: "Unit PTBC-XX-904/8776-AW203 US DOD."

Evans said, "These are military?"

"Correct," Kenner said.

"But what are they?"

"They're the protective containers for coned PTBs."

"PTBs?"

"Precision-timed blasts. They're explosives detonated with millisecond timing by computer in order to induce resonant effects. The individual blasts are not particularly destructive, but the timing sets up standing waves in the surrounding material. That's where the destructive power comes from—the standing wave."

"What's a standing wave?" Evans said.

"You ever watch girls play jump rope? Yes? Well, if instead of spinning the rope, they shake it up and down, they generate loopy waves that travel along the length of the rope, back and forth."

"Okay . . ."

"But if the girls shake it just right, the waves appear to stop moving back and forth. The rope takes on a single curved shape and holds it.

You've seen that? Well, that's a standing wave. It reflects back and forth in perfect synchronization so it doesn't seem to move."

"And these explosives do that?"

"Yes. In nature, standing waves are incredibly powerful. They can shake a suspension bridge to pieces. They can shatter a skyscraper. The most destructive effects of earthquakes are caused by standing waves generated in the crust."

"So Brewster's got these explosives . . . set in a row . . . for a hundred miles? Isn't that what Bolden said? A hundred miles?"

"Right. And I think there's no question what he intends. Our friend Brewster is hoping to fracture the ice for a hundred miles, and break off the biggest iceberg in the history of the planet."

Sarah stuck her head in.

Kenner said, "Did you find a computer?"

"No," she said. "There's nothing there. Nothing at all. No sleeping bag, no food, no personal effects. Nothing but a bare tent. The guy's gone."

Kenner swore. "All right," he said. "Now, listen carefully. Here's what we are going to do."

TO WEDDELL STATION
WEDNESDAY, OCTOBER 6
2:22 P.M.

"Oh no," Jimmy Bolden said, shaking his head. "I'm sorry, but I can't allow that, Dr. Kenner. It's too dangerous."

"Why is it dangerous?" Kenner said. "You take these two back to the station, and I'll follow Brewster's snowtracks until I meet up with him."

"No, sir, we all stay together, sir."

"Jimmy," Kenner said firmly, "we're not going to do that."

"With all due respect, sir, you don't know your way around this part of the world . . ."

"You forget, I am an IADG inspector," Kenner said. "I was resident in Vostok Station for six months in the winter of '99. And I was resident in Morval for three months in '91. I know exactly what I'm doing."

"Gee, I don't know . . ."

"Call back to Weddell. The station chief will confirm it."

"Well, sir, if you put it that way . . ."

"I do," Kenner said firmly. "Now get these two people back to base. Time is wasting."

"Okay, if you'll be all right . . ." Bolden turned to Evans and Sarah. "Then I guess we go. Mount up, folks, and we'll head out."

Within minutes, Evans and Sarah were jouncing along on the ice, following behind Bolden's snowtrack. Behind them, Kenner was driving parallel to the line of flags, heading east. Evans looked back just in time to see Kenner stop, get out, check one of the flags briefly, then get back in again and drive on.

Bolden saw it, too. "What is he doing?" he said in an anxious tone.

"Just looking at the unit, I guess."

"He shouldn't be getting out of his vehicle," Bolden said. "And he shouldn't be alone on the shelf. It's against regulations."

Sarah had the feeling Bolden was about to turn back. She said, "I can tell you something about Dr. Kenner, Jimmy."

"What's that?"

"You don't want to make him mad."

"Really?"

"No, Jimmy. You don't."

"Well . . . okay then."

They drove on, climbing a long rise, descending on the other side. Brewster's camp was gone, and so was Kenner's snowtrack. Ahead lay the vast white field of the Ross Ice Shelf, stretching away to the gray horizon.

"Two hours, folks," Bolden said. "And then a hot shower."

The first hour passed uneventfully. Evans started to fall asleep, only to be jolted awake by the sharp movements of the vehicle. Then he would drift off again, his head nodding until the next shock.

Sarah was driving. He said to her, "Aren't you tired?"

"No, not at all," she said.

The sun was now low on the horizon, and obscured by fog. The landscape was shades of pale gray, with almost no separation between land and sky. Evans yawned. "Want me to take over?"

"I've got it, thanks."

"I'm a good driver."

"I know you are."

He was thinking she had a definite bossy side, despite her charm and her beauty. She was the kind of woman who would want to control the remote.

"I bet you want the remote," he said.

"You think so?" She smiled.

It was irritating in a certain way, he thought, that she did not take him seriously as a man. At least, not as a man she could be interested in. In truth, she was a little too cool for his taste. A little too ice blond. A little too controlled, beneath that beautiful exterior.

The radio clicked. Bolden said, "I don't like this weather coming in. We better take a shortcut."

"What shortcut?"

"It's only half a mile, but it'll save twenty minutes on our time. Follow me." He turned his snowtrack left, leaving the packed snow road, and heading off onto the ice fields.

"Okay," Sarah said. "Right behind you."

"Good work," Bolden said. "We're still an hour from Weddell. I know this route, it's a piece of cake. Just stay directly behind me. Not to the left or right, but directly behind, you understand?"

"Got it," Sarah said.

"Good."

In a matter of minutes, they had moved several hundred yards from the road. The ice there was bare and hard, the treads of the snowtracks scratching and squeaking as they crossed it.

"You're on ice now," Bolden said.

"I noticed."

"Won't be long now."

Evans was looking out the window. He could no longer see the road. In fact, he wasn't sure anymore in which direction it lay. Everything now looked the same. He felt anxious suddenly. "We're really in the middle of nowhere."

The snowtrack slid laterally a little, across the ice. He grabbed for the dashboard. Sarah immediately brought the vehicle back under control.

"Jeez," Evans said, clinging to the dashboard.

"Are you a nervous passenger?" she said.

"Maybe a little."

"Too bad we can't get some music. Is there any way to get music?" she asked Bolden.

"You should," Bolden said. "Weddell broadcasts twenty-four hours. Just a minute." He stopped his snowtrack, and walked back to their stopped vehicle. He climbed up on the tread and opened the door, in a blast of freezing air. "Sometimes you get interference from this," he said, and unclipped the transponder from the dash. "Okay. Try your radio now."

Sarah fiddled with the receiver, twisting the knob. Bolden walked back to his red cab, carrying the transponder. His diesel engine spit a cloud of black exhaust as he put the snowtrack in gear.

"You think they'd be a little more ecologically minded," Evans said, looking at the exhaust as Bolden's snowtrack chugged forward.

"I'm not getting any music," Sarah said.

"Never mind," Evans said. "I don't care that much."

They drove another hundred yards. Then Bolden stopped again.

"Now what?" Evans said.

Bolden climbed out of his vehicle, walked to the back of it, and looked at his own treads.

Sarah was still fiddling with the radio. Punching the buttons for the different transmission frequencies, she got bursts of static for each.

"I'm not sure this is an improvement," Evans said. "Just let it go. Why have we stopped, anyway?"

"I don't know," Sarah said. "He seems to be checking something."

Now Bolden turned and looked back at them. He didn't move. He just stood there and stared.

"Should we get out?" Evans said.

The radio crackled and they heard "—is Weddell CM to—401. Are you there, Dr. Kenner? Weddell CM to—Kenner. Can you hear—?"

"Hey," Sarah said, smiling. "I think we finally got something."

The radio hissed and sputtered.

"—just found Jimmy Bolden unconscious in—maintenance room. We don't know who is—out there with—but it's not—"

"Oh shit," Evans said, staring at the man in front of them. "That guy's not Bolden? Who is he?"

"I don't know, but he's blocking the way," Sarah said. "And he's waiting."

"Waiting for what?"

There was a loud *crack!* from beneath them. Inside the cab, the sound echoed like a gunshot. Their vehicle shifted slightly.

"Screw this," Sarah said. "We're getting out of here, even if I have to ram the bastard." She put the snowtrack in gear, and started to back away from the vehicle in front of them. She shifted, starting the snowtrack forward again.

Another *crack!*

"Let's go!" Evans said. "Let's *go!*"

Crack! Crack! Their vehicle lurched beneath them, tilted sideways at an angle. Evans looked out at the guy pretending to be Bolden.

"It's the ice," Sarah said. "He's waiting for our weight to break through."

"Ram him!" Evans said, pointing ahead. The bastard was making some hand gesture to them. It took him a moment for Evans to understand what it meant. Then he got it.

The man was waving goodbye.

Sarah stomped on the accelerator and the engine rumbled forward, but in the next moment the ground gave way completely beneath them, and their vehicle nosed down. Evans saw the blue-ice wall of a crevasse. Then the vehicle began to tumble forward, and they were encased for an instant in a world of eerie blue before they plunged onward into the blackness below.

Sarah opened her eyes and saw a huge blue starburst, streaks radiating outward in all directions. Her forehead was icy cold, and she had terrible pain in her neck. Tentatively, she shifted her body, checking each of her limbs. They hurt, but she could move all of them except her right leg, which was pinned under something. She coughed and paused, taking stock. She was lying on her side, her face shoved up against the windshield, which she had shattered with her forehead. Her eyes were just inches from the fractured glass. She eased away, and slowly looked around.

It was dark, a kind of twilight. Faint light coming from somewhere to her left. But she could see that the whole cab of the snowtrack was lying on its side, the treads up against the ice wall. They must have landed on a ledge of some kind. She looked upward—the mouth of the crevasse was surprisingly close, maybe thirty or forty yards above her. It was near enough to give her a burst of encouragement.

Next she looked down, trying to see Evans. But it was dark everywhere beneath her. She couldn't see him at all. Her eyes slowly adjusted. She gasped. She saw her true situation.

There was no ledge.

The snowtrack had tumbled into the narrowing crevasse, and wedged itself sideways within the crevasse walls. The treads were against one wall, the roof of the cab against the other, and the cab itself was suspended over the inky downward gash. The door on Evans's side hung open.

Evans was not in the cab.

He had fallen out.

Into the blackness.

"Peter?"

No answer.

"Peter, can you hear me?"

She listened. There was nothing. No sound or movement.

Nothing at all.

And then the realization hit her: *She was alone down there*. A hundred feet down in a freezing crevasse, in the middle of a trackless ice field, far off the road, miles from anywhere.

And she realized, with a chill, that this was going to be her tomb.

Bolden—or whoever he was—had planned it very well, Sarah thought. He had taken their transponder. He could drive a few miles, drop it down the deepest crevasse he could find, and then go back to the base. When the rescue parties set out, they would head for the transponder. It would be nowhere near where she was. The party might search for days in a deep crevasse before giving up.

And if they widened the search? They still wouldn't find the snow-track. Even though it was only about forty yards below the surface, it might as well be four hundred yards below. It was too deep to be seen by a passing helicopter, or even a vehicle as it drove by. Not that any vehicle would. They would think the snowtrack had gone off the marked road, and they would search along the edge of the road. Not way out here, in the middle of the ice field. The road was seventeen miles long. They would spend days searching.

No, Sarah thought. They would never find her.

And even if she could get herself to the surface, what then? She had no compass, no map, no GPS. No radio—it lay smashed beneath her knee.

She didn't even know in what direction Weddell Station might be from her present location.

Of course, she thought, she had a bright red parka that would be visible from a distance, and she had supplies, food, equipment—all the equipment that guy had talked about, before they set out. What was it, exactly? She vaguely remembered something about climbing supplies. Crampons and ropes.

Sarah bent down, managed to free herself from a toolbox that had pinned her foot to the floor, and then crawled to the rear of the cab, balancing carefully to avoid the gaping, wide-open door beneath her. In the perpetual twilight of the crevasse, she saw the supply locker. It was crumpled slightly from the impact, and she couldn't get it open.

She went back to the toolbox, opened it, took out a hammer and a screwdriver, and spent the better part of the next half hour trying to pry the locker open. At last, with a metallic screech, the door swung wide. She peered inside.

The locker was empty.

No food, no water, no climbing supplies. No space blankets, no heaters.

Nothing at all.

Sarah took a deep breath, let it out slowly. She remained calm, refusing to panic. She considered her options. Without ropes and crampons, she could not get to the surface. What could she use instead? She had a toolbox. Could she use the screwdriver as an ice axe? Probably too small. Perhaps she could disassemble the gearshift and make an ice axe out of the parts. Or perhaps she could take apart some of the tread and find parts to use.

She had no crampons, but if she could find sharp pointed things, screws or something like that, she could push them through the soles of her boots and then climb. And for a rope? Some sort of cloth perhaps . . . She looked around the interior. Maybe she could tear the fabric off the seats? Or cut it off in strips? That might work.

In this way, she kept her spirits up. She kept herself moving forward. Even if her chance of success was small, there was still a chance. A *chance*.

She focused on that.

Where was Kenner? What would he do when he heard the radio message? He probably had, already. Would he come back to Weddell? Almost certainly. And he would look for that guy, the one they thought of as Bolden. But Sarah was pretty sure that guy had disappeared.

And with his disappearance, her hopes for rescue.

The crystal of her watch was smashed. She didn't know how long she had been down there, but she noticed that it was darker than before. The gap above her was not as bright. Either the weather on the surface was changing, or the sun was low on the horizon. That would mean she had been down there for two or three hours already.

She was aware of a stiffening in her body—not just from the fall, but also, she realized, because she was cold. The cab had lost its heat.

It occurred to her that perhaps she could start the motor, and get heat going. It was worth a try. She flicked on the headlights, and one of them worked, glaring off the ice wall. So there was still electricity from the battery.

She turned the key. The generator made a grinding sound. The engine did not kick on.

And she heard a voice yell, "Hey!"

Sarah looked up, toward the surface. She saw nothing but the gap and the strip of gray sky beyond.

"Hey!"

She squinted. Was somebody really up there? She yelled back: "Hey! I'm down here!"

"I know where you are," the voice said.

And then she realized the voice was coming from *below* her.

She looked down, into the depths of the crevasse.

"Peter?" she said.

"I'm fucking freezing," he said. His voice floated up from the darkness.

"Are you hurt?"

"No, I don't think so. I don't know. I can't move. I'm wedged in some kind of cleft or something."

"How far down are you?"

"I don't know. I can't turn my head to look up. I'm stuck, Sarah." His voice trembled. He sounded frightened.

"Can you move at all?" she said.

"Just one arm."

"Can you see anything?"

"Ice. I see a blue wall. It's about two feet away."

Sarah was straddling the open door, peering down into the crevasse, straining to see. It was very dark down there. But it seemed as if the crevasse narrowed quickly, farther down. If so, he might not be that far beneath her.

"Peter. Move your arm. Can you move your arm?"

"Yes."

"Wave it."

"I am."

She didn't see anything. Just darkness.

"Okay," she said. "Stop."

"Did you see me?"

"No."

"Shit." He coughed. "It's really cold, Sarah."

"I know. Hang on."

She had to find a way to see down into the cleft. She looked under the dashboard, near where the fire extinguisher was clipped to the car wall. If there was a fire extinguisher, there was probably a flashlight there, too. They would be sure to have a flashlight . . . someplace.

Not under the dashboard.

Maybe the glove compartment. She opened it, shoved her hand in, feeling in the darkness. Crunching paper. Her fingers closed around a thick cylinder. She brought it out.

It was a flashlight.

She flicked it on. It worked. She shone it down into the depths of the crevasse.

"I see that," Peter said. "I see the light."

"Good," she said. "Now swing your arm again."

"I am."

"Now?"

"I'm doing it now."

She stared. "Peter, I don't see—wait a minute." She *did* see him—just the tips of his fingers in their red gloves, protruding briefly beyond the tractor treads, and the ice below.

"Peter."

"What."

"You're very near me," she said. "Just five or six feet below me."

"Great. Can you get me out?"

"I could, if I had a rope."

"There's no rope?" he said.

"No. I opened the supply chest. There's nothing at all."

"But it's not in the supply chest," he said. "It's under the seat."

"What?"

"Yeah, I saw it. The ropes and stuff are under the passenger seat."

She looked. The seat was on a steel base anchored firmly to the floor of the snowtrack. There were no doors or compartments in the base. It was difficult to maneuver around the seat to see, but she was sure: no doors. On a sudden impulse, she lifted up the seat cushion, and saw a compartment beneath it. The light of her flashlight revealed ropes, hooks, snow axes, crampons . . .

"Got it," she said. "You were right. It's all here."

"Whew," he said.

She brought the equipment out carefully, making sure none of it fell through the open door. Already her fingers were growing numb, and she felt clumsy as she held a fifty-foot length of nylon rope with a three-pronged ice hook at one end.

"Peter," she said. "If I lower a rope, can you grab it?"

"Maybe. I think so."

"Can you hold the rope tight, so I can pull you out?"

"I don't know. I just have the one arm free. The other one's pinned under me."

"Are you strong enough to hold the rope with one arm?"

"I don't know. I don't think so. I mean, if I got my body partway out, and lost my grip . . ." His voice broke off. He sounded on the verge of tears.

"Okay," she said. "Don't worry."

"I'm *trapped*, Sarah!"

"No, you're not."

"I am, I'm trapped, I'm fucking trapped!" Now there was panic. "I'm going to die here!"

"Peter. Stop." She was coiling the rope around her waist as she spoke. "It's going to be all right. I have a plan."

"What plan?"

"I'm going to lower an ice hook on the rope," she said. "Can you hook it onto something? Like your belt?"

"Not my belt . . . No. I'm wedged in here, Sarah. I can't move. I can't reach my belt."

She was trying to visualize his situation. He must be wedged in some sort of cleft in the ice. It was frightening just to imagine it. No wonder he was scared. "Peter," she said, "can you hook it onto anything?"

"I'll try."

"Okay, here it comes," she said, lowering the rope. The hook disappeared into the darkness. "Do you see it?"

"I see it."

"Can you reach it?"

"No."

"Okay, I'll swing it toward you." She turned her wrist gently, starting the rope in a lateral swing. The hook vanished out of sight, then swung back, then out of sight again.

"I can't . . . keep doing it, Sarah."

"I am."

"I can't get it, Sarah."

"Keep trying."

"It has to be lower."

"Okay. How much lower?"

"About a foot."

"Okay." She lowered it a foot. "How's that?"

"Good, now swing it."

She did. She heard him grunting, but each time the hook swung back into view.

"I can't do it, Sarah."

"Yes you can. Keep trying."

"I can't. My fingers are too cold."

"Keep trying," she said. "Here it is again."

"I can't, Sarah, I can't . . . Hey!"

"What?"

"I almost got it."

Looking down, she saw the hook spinning when it came back into view. He'd touched it.

"Once more," she said. "You'll do it, Peter."

"I'm trying, it's just I have so little—I got it, Sarah. *I got it!*"

She gave a long sigh of relief.

He was coughing in the darkness. She waited.

"Okay," he said. "I got it hooked on my jacket."

"Where?"

"Right on the front. Just on my chest."

She was visualizing that if the hook ripped free, it would tear right into his chin. "No, Peter. Hook it on the armpit."

"I can't, unless you pull me out a couple of feet."

"Okay. Say when."

He coughed. "Listen, Sarah. Are you strong enough to pull me out?"

She had avoided thinking about that. She just assumed that somehow she could. Of course she didn't know how hard he was wedged in, but . . . "Yes," she said. "I can do it."

"Are you sure? I weigh a hundred and sixty." He coughed again. "Maybe a little more. Maybe ten more."

"I've got you tied off on the steering wheel."

"Okay, but . . . don't drop me."

"I won't drop you, Peter."

There was a pause. "How much do you weigh?"

"Peter, you never ask a lady that question. Especially in LA."

"We're not in LA."

"I don't know how much I weigh," she said. Of course she knew exactly. She weighed a hundred and thirty-seven pounds. He weighed over thirty pounds more than that. "But I know I can pull you up," she said. "Are you ready?"

"Shit."

"Peter, are you ready or not?"

"Yeah. Go."

She drew the rope tight, then crouched down, planting her feet firmly on either side of the open door. She felt like a sumo wrestler at the start of a match. But she knew her legs were much stronger than her arms. This was the only way she could do it. She took a deep breath.

"Ready?" she said.

"I guess."

Sarah began to stand upright, her legs burning with effort. The rope stretched taut, then moved upward—slowly at first, just a few inches. But it was moving.

It was moving.

. . .

"Okay, stop. Stop!"

"What?"

"*Stop!*"

"Okay." She was in mid-crouch. "But I can't hold this for long."

"Don't hold it at all. Let it out. Slowly. About three feet."

She realized that she must have already pulled him part of the way out of the cleft. His voice sounded better, much less frightened, though he was coughing almost continuously.

"Peter?"

"Minute. I'm hooking it on my belt."

"Okay . . ."

"I can see up now," he said. "I can see the tread. The tread is about six feet above my head."

"Okay."

"But when you pull me up, the rope's going to rub on the edge of the tread."

"It'll be okay," she said.

"And I'll be hanging right over the, uh . . ."

"I won't let you go, Peter."

He coughed for a while. She waited. He said, "Tell me when you're ready."

"I'm ready."

"Then let's get this over with," he said, "before I get scared."

There was only one bad moment. She had pulled him up about four feet, and he came free of the cleft, and she suddenly took the full weight of his body. It shocked her; the rope slid three feet down. He howled.

"*Sar-ah!*"

She gripped the rope, stopped it. "Sorry."

"Fuck!"

"Sorry." She adjusted to the added weight, started pulling again. She was groaning with the effort but it was not long before she saw his hand appear above the tread, and he gripped it, and began to haul himself over. Then two hands, and his head appeared.

That shocked her, too. His face was covered in thick blood, his hair matted red. But he was smiling.

"Keep pulling, sister."

"I am, Peter. I am."

Only after he finally had scrambled into the cab did Sarah sink to the floor. Her legs began to shake violently. Her body trembled all over. Evans, lying on his side, coughing and wheezing beside her, hardly noticed. Eventually the trembling passed. She found the first-aid kit and began to clean his face up.

"It's only a superficial cut," she said, "but you'll need stitches."

"If we ever get out of here . . ."

"We'll get out, all right."

"I'm glad you're confident." He looked out the window at the ice above. "You done much ice climbing?"

She shook her head. "But I've done plenty of rock climbing. How different can it be?"

"More slippery? And what happens when we get up there?" he said.

"I don't know."

"We have no idea where to go."

"We'll follow the guy's snowtracks."

"If they're still there. If they haven't blown away. And you know it's at least seven or eight miles to Weddell."

"Peter," she said.

"If a storm comes up, maybe we're better off down here."

"I'm not staying here," she said. "If I'm going to die, I'll die in daylight."

• • •

The actual climb up the crevasse wall was not so bad, once Sarah got used to the way she had to kick her boots with the crampons, and how hard she had to swing the axe to make it bite into the ice. It took her only seven or eight minutes to cover the distance, and clamber onto the surface.

The surface looked exactly the same as before. The same dim sunlight, the same gray horizon that blended with the ground. The same gray, featureless world.

She helped Evans up. His cut was bleeding again, and his mask was red, frozen stiff against his face.

"Shit it's cold," he said. "Which way, do you think?"

Sarah was looking at the sun. It was low on the horizon, but was it sinking, or rising? And which direction did the sun indicate, anyway, when you were at the South Pole? She frowned: She couldn't work it out, and she didn't dare make a mistake.

"We'll follow the tracks," she said at last. She took off her crampons and started walking.

She had to admit, Peter was right about one thing: It was much colder here on the surface. After half an hour, the wind came up, blowing strongly; they had to lean into it as they trudged forward. Worse, the snow began to blow across the ground beneath their feet. Which meant—

"We're losing the tracks," Evans said.

"I know."

"They're getting blown away."

"I *know*." Sometimes he was such a baby. What did he expect her to do about the wind?

"What do we do?" he said.

"I don't *know*, Peter. I've never been lost in Antarctica before."

"Well, me neither."

They trudged onward.

"But it was your idea to come up here."

"Peter. Pull yourself together."

"Pull myself together? It's fucking freezing, Sarah. I can't feel my nose or my ears or my fingers or my toes or—"

"Peter." She grabbed him by the shoulders and shook him. "*Shut up!*"

He was silent. Through slots in his facemask, he stared out at her. His eyelashes were white with ice.

"I can't feel my nose either," Sarah said. "We have to keep a grip."

She looked around, turning a full circle, trying to conceal her own growing desperation. The wind was blowing more snow now. It was becoming harder to see. The world was flatter and grayer, with almost no sense of depth. If this weather continued, they would soon not be able to see the ground well enough to avoid the crevasses.

Then they would have to stop where they were.

In the middle of nowhere.

He said, "You're beautiful when you're angry, you know that?"

"Peter, for Christ's sake."

"Well, you are."

She started walking, looking down at the ground, trying to see the tread marks. "Come on, Peter." Perhaps the tracks would return soon to the road. If they did, the road would be easier to follow in a storm. And safer for walking.

"I think I'm falling in love, Sarah."

"Peter . . ."

"I had to tell you. This may be my last chance." He started coughing again.

"Save your breath, Peter."

"Fucking freezing."

They stumbled on, no longer speaking. The wind howled. Sarah's parka was pressed flat against her body. It became harder and harder to move forward. But she pressed on. She did not know how much longer she continued in that way before she raised a hand, and stopped. Evans must not have been able to see her, because he walked into her back, grunted, and stopped.

They had to put their heads together and shout to hear each other above the wind.

"We have to stop!" she yelled.

"I know!"

And then, because she didn't know what else to do, she sat down on the ground and pulled her legs up and lowered her head to her knees, and tried not to cry. The wind grew louder and louder. Now it was shrieking. The air was thick with flying snow.

Evans sat down beside her. "We're going to fucking die," he said.

SHEAR ZONE
WEDNESDAY, OCTOBER 6
5:02 P.M.

She started shivering, little tremulous bursts at first, and then almost continuously. She felt as if she were having a seizure. From skiing, she knew what that meant. Her core temperature had dropped dangerously, and the shivering was an automatic physiological attempt to warm her body up.

Her teeth chattered. It was hard to speak. But her mind was still working, still looking for a way out. "Isn't there a way to build a snow house?"

Evans said something. The wind whipped his words away.

"Do you know how?" she said.

He didn't answer her.

But it was too late, anyway, she thought. She was losing control of her body. She could hardly even keep her arms wrapped around her knees, the shaking was so bad.

And she was starting to feel sleepy.

She looked over at Evans. He was lying on his side on the ice.

She nudged him to get up. She kicked him. He didn't move. She wanted to yell at him but she couldn't, because her teeth were chattering so badly.

Sarah fought to retain consciousness, but the desire to sleep was becoming overpowering. She struggled to keep her eyes open and, to her astonishment, began to see swift scenes from her life—her childhood, her mother, her kindergarten class, ballet lessons, the high school prom . . .

Her whole life was passing before her. Just like the books said happened, right before you died. And when she looked up, she saw a light in the distance, just like they said happened. A light at the end of a long, dark tunnel . . .

She couldn't fight it any longer. She lay down. She couldn't feel the ground anyway. She was lost in her own, private world of pain and exhaustion. And the light before her was growing brighter and brighter, and now there were two other lights, blinking yellow and green . . .

Yellow and green?

She fought the sleepiness. She tried to push herself upright again, but she couldn't. Her muscles were too weak, her arms blocks of frozen ice. She couldn't move.

Yellow and green lights, growing larger. And a white light in the center. Very white, like halogen. She was starting to see details through the swirling snow. There was a silver dome, and wheels, and large glowing letters. The letters said—

NASA.

She coughed. The thing emerged from the snow. It was some kind of small vehicle—about three feet high, no larger than those Sunday lawnmowers that people drove around on. It had big wheels and a flattened dome, and it was beeping as it came directly toward her.

In fact, it was going to drive right over her. She realized it without concern. She could do nothing to prevent it. She lay on the ground, dazed, indifferent. The wheels grew larger and larger. The last thing she remembered was a mechanical voice saying, "Hello. Hello. Please move out of the way. Thank you very much for your cooperation. Hello. Hello. Please move out of the way . . ."

And then nothing.

WEDDELL STATION
WEDNESDAY, OCTOBER 6
8:22 P.M.

Darkness. Pain. Harsh voices.

Pain.

Rubbing. All over her body, arms and legs. Like fire rubbed on her body.

She groaned.

A voice spoke, rasping and distant. It sounded like "Coffee grounds."

The rubbing continued, brisk and harsh and excruciating. And a sound like sandpaper—scratching, rough, terrible.

Something struck her in the face, on the mouth. She licked her lips. It was snow. Freezing snow.

"Cousins set?" a voice said.

"Nod eely."

It was a foreign language, Chinese or something. Sarah heard several voices now. She tried to open her eyes but could not. Her eyes were held shut by something heavy over her face, like a mask, or—

She tried to reach up, but couldn't. All her limbs were held down. And the rubbing continued, rubbing, rubbing . . .

She groaned. She tried to speak.

"Thin song now whore nod?"

"Don thin song."

"Kee pub yar wok."

Pain.

They rubbed her, whoever they were, while she lay immobilized in darkness, and gradually more sensation returned to her limbs and to her face. She was not glad for it. The pain grew worse and worse. She felt as if she were burned everywhere on her body.

The voices seemed to float around her, disembodied. There were more of them now. Four, five—she was not sure anymore. All women, it sounded like.

And now they were doing something else, she realized. Violating her. Sticking something in her body. Dull and cold. Not painful. Cold.

The voices floated, slithered all around her. At her head, at her feet. Touching her roughly.

It was a dream. Or death. Maybe she was dead, she thought. She felt oddly detached about it. The pain made her detached. And then she heard a woman's voice in her ear, very close to her ear, and very distinct. The voice said:

"Sarah."

She moved her mouth.

"Sarah, are you awake?"

She nodded slightly.

"I am going to take the icepack off your face, all right?"

She nodded. The weight, the mask was lifted.

"Open your eyes. Slowly."

She did. She was in a dimly lit room with white walls. A monitor to one side, a tangle of green lines. It was like a hospital room. A woman looked down at her with concern. The woman wore a white nurse's uniform and a down vest. The room was cold. Sarah could see her breath.

She said, "Don't try to speak."

Sarah didn't.

"You're dehydrated. It'll be a few hours yet. We're bringing your temperature up slowly. You're very lucky, Sarah. You're not going to lose anything."

Not lose anything.

She felt alarmed. Her mouth moved. Her tongue was dry, thick feeling. A sort of hissing sound came from her throat.

"Don't speak," the woman said. "It's too soon. Is your pain bad? Yes? I'll give you something for it." She raised a syringe. "Your friend saved your life, you know. He managed to get to his feet, and open the radio-phone on the NASA robot. That's how we knew where to find you."

Her lips moved.

"He's in the next room. We think he'll be all right, too. Now just rest."

She felt something cold in her veins.

Her eyes closed.

The nurses left Peter Evans alone to get dressed. He put on his clothes slowly, taking stock of himself. He was all right, he decided, though his ribs hurt when he breathed. He had a big bruise on the left side of his chest, another big bruise on his thigh, and an ugly purple welt on his shoulder. A line of stitches on his scalp. His whole body was stiff and aching. It was excruciating to put on his socks and shoes.

But he was all right. In fact, better than that—he felt new somehow, almost reborn. Out there on the ice, he had been certain he was going to die. How he found the strength to get to his feet, he did not know. He had felt Sarah kicking him, but he did not respond to her. Then he'd heard the beeping sound. And when he looked up, he saw the letters "NASA."

He'd realized vaguely that it was some kind of vehicle. So there must be a driver. The front tires had stopped just inches from his body. He managed to get to his knees, and haul himself up over the tires, grabbing onto the struts. He hadn't understood why the driver hadn't climbed out and helped him. Finally, he managed to get to his knees in the howling wind. He realized that the vehicle was low and bulbous, barely four feet off the ground. It was too small for any human operator—it was some kind of robot. He scraped snow away from the dome-like shell. The lettering read, "NASA Remote Vehicle Meteorite Survey."

The vehicle was talking, repeating a taped voice over and over. Evans couldn't understand what it was saying because of the wind. He brushed away the snow, thinking there must be some method of communication, some antenna, some—

Then his fingers had touched a panel with a finger hole. He pulled it open. Inside he saw a telephone—a regular telephone handset, bright red. He held it to his frozen mask. He could not hear anything from it, but he said, "Hello? Hello?"

Nothing more.

He collapsed again.

But the nurses told him what he had done was enough to send a signal to the NASA station at Patriot Hills. NASA had notified Weddell, who sent out a search party, and found them in ten minutes. They were both still alive, barely.

That had been more than twenty-four hours ago.

It had taken the medical team twelve hours to bring their body temperatures back to normal, because, the nurse said, it had to be done slowly. They told Evans he was going to be fine, but he might lose a couple of his toes. They would have to wait and see. It would be a few days.

His feet were bandaged with some kind of protective splints around the toes. He couldn't fit into his regular shoes, but they had found him an oversized pair of sneakers. They looked like they belonged to a basketball player. On Evans, they made huge clown feet. But he could wear them, and there wasn't much pain.

Tentatively, he stood. He was tremulous, but he was all right.

The nurse came back. "Hungry?"

He shook his head. "Not yet."

"Pain?"

He shook his head. "Just, you know, everywhere."

"That'll get worse," she said. She gave him a small bottle of pills. "Take one of these every four hours if you need it. And you'll probably need it to sleep, for the next few days."

"And Sarah?"

"Sarah will be another half hour or so."

"Where's Kenner?"

"I think he's in the computer room."

"Which way is that?"

She said, "Maybe you better lean on my shoulder . . ."

"I'm fine," he said. "Just tell me the way."

She pointed, and he started walking. But he was more unsteady than he realized. His muscles weren't working right; he felt shaky all over. He started to fall. The nurse quickly ducked, sliding her shoulder under his arm.

"Tell you what," she said. "I'll just show you the way."

This time he did not object.

Kenner sat in the computer room with the bearded station chief, Mac-Gregor, and Sanjong Thapa. Everybody was looking grim.

"We found him," Kenner said, pointing to a computer monitor. "Recognize your friend?"

Evans looked at the screen. "Yeah," he said. "That's the bastard."

On the screen was a photo of the man Evans knew as Bolden. But the ID form onscreen gave his name as David R. Kane. Twenty-six years old. Born Minneapolis. BA, Notre Dame; MA, University of Michigan. Current Status: PhD candidate in oceanography, University of Michigan, Ann Arbor. Research Project: Dynamics of Ross Shelf Flow as measured by GPS sensors. Thesis Advisor/Project Supervisor: James Brewster, University of Michigan.

"His name's Kane," the Weddell chief said. "He's been here for a week, along with Brewster."

"Where is he now?" Evans said darkly.

"No idea. He didn't come back to the Station today. Neither did Brewster. We think they may have gone to McMurdo and hopped the morning transport out. We have a call in to McMurdo to do a vehicle count, but they haven't gotten back to us yet."

"You're sure he's not still here?" Evans said.

"Quite sure. You need an ID tag to open the exterior doors here, so we always know who's where. Neither Kane nor Brewster opened any doors in the last twelve hours. They aren't here."

"So you think they may be on the plane?"

"McMurdo Tower wasn't sure. They're pretty casual about the daily transport—if somebody wants to go, they just hop on and leave. It's a C-130, so there's always plenty of room. You see, a lot of the research grants don't permit you to leave during the period of your research, but people have birthdays and family events back on the mainland. So they just go, and come back. It's unrecorded."

"If I recall," Kenner said, "Brewster came here with two graduate students. Where's the other one?"

"Interesting. He left from McMurdo yesterday, the day you arrived."

"So they all got out," Kenner said. "Got to give them credit: They're smart." He looked at his watch. "Now let's see what, if anything, they left behind."

The name on the door said "Dave Kane, U. Mich." Evans pushed it open, and saw a small room, an unmade bed, a small desk with a messy stack of papers, and four cans of Diet Coke. There was a suitcase lying open in the corner.

"Let's get started," Kenner said. "I'll take the bed and the suitcase. You check the desk."

Evans began to go through the papers on the desk. They all seemed to be reprints of research articles. Some were stampe U MICH GEO LIB followed by a number.

"Window dressing," Kenner said, when he was shown the papers. "He brought those papers with him. Anything else? Anything personal?"

Evans didn't see anything of interest. Some of the papers were highlighted in yellow marker. There was a stack of 3-by-5 notecards, with some notes written on them, but they seemed to be genuine, and related to the stack of papers.

"You don't suppose this guy is really a graduate student?"

"Could be, though I doubt it. Eco-terrorists aren't usually well educated."

There were pictures of glacier flows, and satellite images of various sorts. Evans shuffled through them quickly. Then he paused at one:

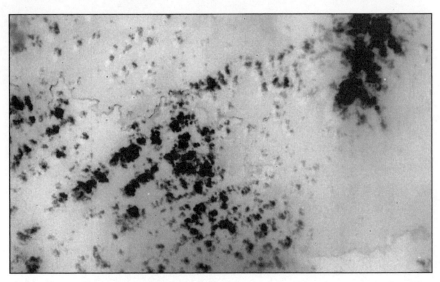

ISS006.ESC1.03003375 SCORPION B

What caught his eye was the caption. "Listen," he said, "on that list of four locations, wasn't one of them called 'Scorpion'?"

"Yes . . ."

"It's right here, in Antarctica," Evans said. "Look at this."

Kenner started to say, "But it can't be—" and abruptly broke off. "This is extremely interesting, Peter. Well done. It was in that stack? Good. Anything else?"

Despite himself, Evans felt pleased by Kenner's approval. He searched quickly. A moment later he said, "Yes. There's another one."

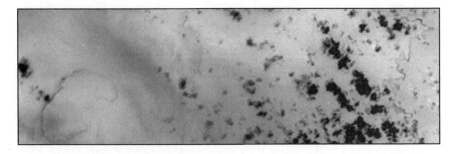

ISS006.ESC1.03003375 SCORPION B

"It's the same basic pattern of rock outcrops in the snow," Evans said, excitedly. "And, I don't know about these faint lines . . . roads? Rocks covered in snow?"

"Yes," Kenner said. "I think that's almost certainly correct."

"And if they're aerial photographs, there must be a way to trace them. Do you think these numbers are references of some kind?"

"There's no question." Kenner pulled out a small pocket magnifying glass, and scanned the image, peering closely. "Yes, Peter. Very well done."

Evans beamed.

From the doorway, MacGregor said, "You found something? Can I help?"

"I don't think so," Kenner said. "We'll deal with this ourselves."

Evans said, "But maybe he will recognize—"

"No," Kenner said. "We'll get the ID off the NASA image files. Let's continue."

They searched in silence for several minutes more. Kenner took out a pocketknife and began cutting the lining of the suitcase lying open in the corner of Brewster's office. "Ah." He straightened. In his fingers, he held two curved arcs of pale rubber.

"What are those?" Evans said. "Silicon?"

"Or something very similar. A kind of soft plastic, at any rate." Kenner seemed very pleased.

"What're they for?" Evans said.

"I have no idea," Kenner said. He resumed his search of the suitcase. Privately, Evans wondered why Kenner was so pleased. Probably he was not saying what he knew in front of MacGregor. But what could two bits of rubber mean, anyway? What could they be used for?

Evans went through the documents on the desk a second time, but found nothing more. He lifted the desk lamp and looked under the base. He crouched down and looked under the desk, in case something was taped there. He found nothing.

Kenner closed the suitcase. "As I thought, nothing more. We were very lucky to find what we did." He turned to MacGregor. "Where's Sanjong?"

"In the server room, doing what you requested—cutting Brewster and his team out of the system."

The "server room" was hardly larger than a closet. There were twin racks of processors running floor to ceiling, and the usual mesh ceiling for cabling. There was a master terminal in the room, on a small steel table. Sanjong was crowded in there with a Weddell technician at his side, looking frustrated.

Kenner and Evans stood outside, in the hallway. Evans was pleased that he felt steady enough to stand. His strength was coming back quickly.

"It hasn't been easy," Sanjong said to Kenner. "The procedure here is to give each Weddell researcher private storage space and also direct radio and Internet connections. And these three guys knew how to take advantage of it. Apparently the third man with Brewster was the computer guy. Within a day of his arrival, he got into the system as root, and installed back doors and trojans all over the place. We're not sure how many. We're trying to get them out."

"He also added a few dummy user accounts," the technician said.

"Like about twenty," Sanjong said. "But I'm not worried about those. They're probably just that—dummies. If this guy was smart—and he was—he'd have given himself access to the system through an existing user, so he'd go undetected. We're looking now for any users who have added a new secondary password in the last week. But this system doesn't have a lot of maintenance utilities. It's slow going."

"What about the trojans?" Kenner said. "How are they timed?" In computer slang, a trojan was an innocent-looking program installed in the system. It was designed to wake up at a later time and carry out some action. It derived its name from the way the Greeks won the Trojan war—by making a huge horse and presenting it to the Trojans as a gift. Once the horse was within the walls of Troy, the Greek soliders who had been hiding inside it came out and attacked the city.

The classic trojan was one installed by a disgruntled employee. It erased all the hard drives in a business three months after the employee was fired. But there were many variations.

"Timing on all of the ones I found here is short," Sanjong said. "One day, two days from now. We found one that is three days from now. Nothing after that."

"So. Just as we suspected," Kenner said.

"Exactly," Sanjong said, nodding. "They intended it to happen soon."

"Intended what?" Evans said.

"The calving of the big iceberg," Kenner said.

"Why soon? They would still have been here."

"I'm not sure they would have. But in any case the timing was determined by something else."

"Yes? What?" Evans said.

Kenner gave him a look. "We can go into it later." He turned back to Sanjong. "And what about the radio connects?"

"We disabled all the direct connects right away," he said. "And I assume you did work on the ground at the location itself."

"I did," Kenner said.

"What did you do on the ground?" Evans said.

"Random disconnects."

"Of what?"

"Tell you later."

"So we're redundant," Sanjong said.

"No. Because we can't be sure there's not someone else embedded in this place who will undo our work."

"I wish," Evans said, "I knew what the hell you guys were talking about . . ."

"*Later*," Kenner said. This time the look was sharp.

Evans was silent. He felt a little wounded.

MacGregor said, "Ms. Jones is awake, and getting dressed."

"All right," Kenner said. "I believe our work here is done. Wheels up in an hour."

"To go where?" Evans said.

"I thought that was obvious," Kenner said. "Helsinki, Finland."

The plane flew back through the dazzling morning light. Sarah was sleeping. Sanjong was working on his laptop. Kenner stared out the window.

Evans said, "All right, what did you disconnect randomly?"

"The cone charges," Kenner said. "They were laid out in a precise pattern, four hundred meters apart. I disconnected fifty at random, mostly along the eastern end of the line. That will suffice to prevent the standing wave from being generated."

"So, no iceberg?"

"That's the idea."

"And why are we going to Helsinki?"

"We're not. I only said that for the benefit of the technician. We're going to Los Angeles."

"Okay. And why are we going to Los Angeles?"

"Because that's where the NERF Conference on Abrupt Climate Change is being held."

"This is all related to the conference?"

Kenner nodded.

"These guys are trying to break off an iceberg to coincide with the conference?"

"Exactly. All part of any good starburst media plan. You arrange an event with good visuals that reinforces the point of the conference."

"You seem awfully calm about it," Evans said.

"It's the way things are done, Peter." Kenner shrugged. "Environmental concerns don't come to the public's attention by accident, you know."

"What do you mean?"

"Well, take your favorite fear, global warming. The arrival of global warming was announced dramatically by a prominent climatologist, James Hansen, in 1988. He gave testimony before a joint House and Senate committee headed by Senator Wirth of Colorado. Hearings were scheduled for June, so Hansen could deliver his testimony during a blistering heat wave. It was a setup from the beginning."

"That doesn't bother me," Evans said. "It's legitimate to use a government hearing as a way to make the public aware—"

"Really? So you're saying that in your mind, there's no difference between a government hearing and a press conference?"

"I'm saying hearings have been used that way many times before."

"True. But it is unquestionably manipulative. And Hansen's testimony wasn't the only instance of media manipulation that's occurred in the course of the global warming sales campaign. Don't forget the last-minute changes in the 1995 IPCC report."

"IPCC? What last-minute changes?"

"The UN formed the Intergovernmental Panel on Climate Change in the late 1980s. That's the IPCC, as you know—a huge group of bureaucrats, and scientists under the thumb of bureaucrats. The idea was that since this was a global problem, the UN would track climate research and issue reports every few years. The first assessment report in 1990 said it would be very difficult to detect a human influence on climate, although everybody was concerned that one might exist. But the 1995 report announced with conviction that there was now 'a discernable human influence' on climate. You remember that?"

"Vaguely."

"Well, the claim of 'a discernable human influence' was written into the 1995 summary report after the scientists themselves had gone home.

Originally, the document said scientists couldn't detect a human influence on climate for sure, and they didn't know when they would. They said explicitly, 'we don't know.' That statement was deleted, and replaced with a new statement that a discernable human influence did indeed exist. It was a major change."

"Is that true?" Evans said.

"Yes. Changing the document caused a stir among scientists at the time, with opponents and defendants of the change coming forward. If you read their claims and counter-claims, you can't be sure who's telling the truth. But this is the Internet age. You can find the original documents and the list of changes online and decide for yourself. A review of the actual text changes makes it crystal clear that the IPCC is a political organization, not a scientific one."

Evans frowned. He wasn't sure how to answer. He'd heard of the IPCC, of course, although he didn't know much about it. . . .

"But my question is simpler, Peter. If something is real, if it is a genuine problem that requires action, why does anybody have to exaggerate their claims? Why do there have to be carefully executed media campaigns?"

"I can give you a simple answer," Evans said. "The media is a crowded marketplace. People are bombarded by thousands of messages every minute. You have to speak loudly—and yes, maybe exaggerate a little—if you want to get their attention. And try to mobilize the entire world to sign the Kyoto treaty."

"Well, let's consider that. When Hansen announced in the summer of 1988 that global warming was here, he predicted temperatures would increase .35 degrees Celsius over the next ten years. Do you know what the actual increase was?"

"I'm sure you'll tell me it was less than that."

"*Much* less, Peter. Dr. Hansen overestimated by three hundred percent. The actual increase was .11 degrees."

"Okay. But it *did* increase."

And ten years after his testimony, he said that the forces that govern climate change are so poorly understood that long-term prediction is impossible."

"He did not say that."

Kenner sighed. "Sanjong?"

Sanjong pecked at his laptop. "Proceedings of the National Academy of Sciences, October 1998."*

"Hansen didn't say that prediction was *impossible*."

"He said quote 'The forcings that drive long-term climate change are not known with an accuracy sufficient to define future climate change' endquote. And he argued that, in the future, scientists should use multiple scenarios to define a range of possible climate outcomes."

"Well that isn't exactly—"

"Stop quibbling," Kenner said. "He said it. Why do you think Balder is worried about his witnesses in the Vanutu case? It's because of statements like these. However you attempt to reframe it, it's a clear statement of limited knowledge. And it's hardly the only one. The IPCC itself made many limiting statements."†

"But Hansen still believes in global warming."

"Yes, he does. And his 1988 prediction," Kenner said, "was wrong by three hundred percent."

"So what?"

"You are ignoring the implication of an error that large," Kenner said. "Compare it to other fields. For example, when NASA launched the rocket carrying the Mars Rover, they announced that in two hundred and fifty three days, the Rover would land on the surface of Mars at 8:11 P.M., California time. In fact, it landed at 8:35 P.M. That is an error of a few *thousandths* of a percent. The NASA people knew what they were talking about."

---

* James E. Hansen, Makiko Sato, Andrew Lacis, Reto Ruedy, Ina Tegen, and Elaine Matthews, "Climate Forcings in the Industrial Era," *Proceedings of the National Academy of Sciences* 95 (October 1998): 12753–58.
† IPCC. *Climate Change 2001: The Scientific Basis.* Cambridge, UK: Cambridge University Press, 2001, p. 774: "In climate research and modelling [*sic*], we should recognize that we are dealing with a coupled non-linear chaotic system, and therefore that the long-term prediction of future climate states is not possible." See also: IPCC. *Climate Change 1995: The Science of Climate Change*, p. 330. "Natural climate variability on long time-scales will continue to be problematic for CO2 climate change analysis and detection."

"Okay, fine. But there are some things you have to estimate."

"You're absolutely right," Kenner said. "People estimate all the time. They estimate sales, they estimate profits, they estimate delivery dates, they estimate—by the way, do you estimate your taxes for the government?"

"Yes. Quarterly."

"How accurate does that estimate have to be?"

"Well, there's no fixed rule—"

"Peter. How accurate, without penalty?"

"Maybe fifteen percent."

"So if you were off by three hundred percent, you'd pay a penalty?"

"Yes."

"Hansen was off by three hundred percent."

"Climate is not a tax return."

"In the real world of human knowledge," Kenner said, "to be wrong by three hundred percent is taken as an indication you don't have a good grasp on what you are estimating. If you got on an airplane and the pilot said it was a three-hour flight, but you arrived in one hour, would you think that pilot was knowledgeable or not?"

Evans sighed. "Climate is more complicated than that."

"Yes, Peter. Climate *is* more complicated. It is so complicated that no one has been able to predict future climate with accuracy. Even though billons of dollars are being spent, and hundreds of people are trying all around the world. Why do you resist that uncomfortable truth?"

"Weather prediction is much better," Evans said. "And that's because of computers."

"Yes, weather prediction has improved. But nobody tries to predict weather more than ten days in advance. Whereas computer modelers are predicting what the temperature will be one hundred years in advance. Sometimes a thousand years, three thousand years."

"And they are doing better."

"Arguably they aren't. Look," Kenner said. "The biggest events in global climate are the El Niños. They happen roughly every four years. But climate models can't predict them—not their timing, their duration, or their intensity. And if you can't predict El Niños, the predictive value of your model in other areas is suspect."

"I heard they can predict El Niños."

"That was claimed in 1998. But it is not true."* Kenner shook his head. "Climate science simply isn't there yet, Peter. One day it will be. But not now."

---

* C. Landsea, et al., 2000, "How Much Skill Was There in Forecasting the Very Strong 1997–98 El Niño?" *Bulletin of the American Meteorological Society* 81: 2107-19. ". . . one could have even less confidence in anthropogenic global warming studies because of the lack of skill in predicting El Niño . . . the successes in ENSO forecasting have been overstated (sometimes drastically) and misapplied in other arenas."

TO LOS ANGELES
FRIDAY, OCTOBER 8
2:22 P.M.

Another hour passed. Sanjong was working continuously on the laptop. Kenner sat motionless, staring out the window. Sanjong was accustomed to this. He knew that Kenner could stay silent and immobile for several hours. He only turned away from the window when Sanjong swore.

"What's the matter?" Kenner said.

"I lost our satellite connection to the Internet. It's been in and out for a while."

"Were you able to trace the images?"

"Yes, that was no problem. I have the location fixed. Did Evans really think these were images from Antarctica?"

"Yes. He thought they showed black outcrops against snow. I didn't disagree with him."

"The actual location," Sanjong said, "is a place called Resolution Bay. It's in northeast Gareda."

"How far from Los Angeles?"

"Roughly six thousand nautical miles."

"So the propagation time is twelve or thirteen hours."

"Yes."

"We'll worry about it later," Kenner said. "We have other problems first."

. . .

Peter Evans slept fitfully. His bed consisted of a padded airplane seat laid flat, with a seam in the middle, right where his hip rested. He tossed and turned, waking briefly, hearing snatches of conversation between Kenner and Sanjong at the back of the plane. He couldn't hear the whole conversation over the drone of the engines. But he heard enough.

Because of what I need him to do.

He'll refuse, John.

. . . he likes it or not . . . Evans is at the center of everything.

Peter Evans was suddenly awake. He strained to hear now. He raised his head off the pillow so he could hear better.

Didn't disagree with him.

Actual location . . . Resolution Bay . . . Gareda.

How far . . . ?

. . . thousand miles . . .

. . . the propagation time . . . thirteen hours . . .

He thought: *Propagation time? What the hell were they talking about?* On impulse he jumped up, strode back there, and confronted them.

Kenner didn't blink. "Sleep well?"

"No," Evans said, "I did not sleep well. I think you owe me some explanations."

"About what?"

"The satellite pictures, for one."

"I couldn't very well tell you right there in the room, in front of the others," Kenner said. "And I hated to interrupt your enthusiasm."

Evans went and poured himself a cup of coffee. "Okay. What do the pictures really show?"

Sanjong flipped his laptop around to show Evans the screen. "Don't feel bad. You would never have had any reason to suspect. The images were negatives. They're often used that way, to increase contrast."

"Negatives . . ."

"The black rocks are actually white. They're clouds."

Evans sighed.

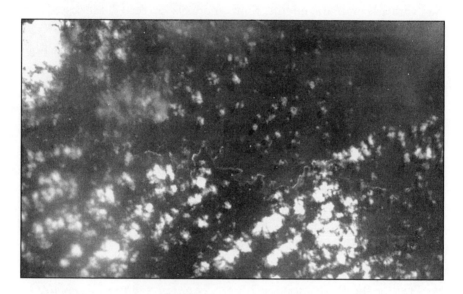

"And what is the land mass?"

"It's an island called Gareda, in the southern part of the Solomon chain."

"Which is . . ."

"Off the coast of New Guinea. North of Australia."

"So this is an island in the South Pacific," Evans said. "This guy in Antarctica had a picture of a Pacific island."

"Correct."

"And the SCORPION reference is . . ."

"We don't know," Sanjong said. "The actual location is called Resolution Bay on the charts. But it may be known locally as Scorpion Bay."

"And what are they planning down there?"

Kenner said, "We don't know that, either."

"I heard you talking about propagation times. Propagation times for what?"

"Actually, you misheard me," Kenner said smoothly. "I was talking about interrogation times."

"Interrogation times?" Evans said.

"Yes. We were hoping we'd be able to identify at least one of the three men in Antarctica, since we have good photographs of all three. And we know the photographs are accurate because people on the base saw them. But, I'm afraid we're out of luck."

Sanjong explained that they had transmitted photos of Brewster and the two graduate students to several databases in Washington, where pattern-recognition computers checked them against individuals with known criminal records. Sometimes you got lucky, and the computer found a match. But this time, no match had come back.

"It's been several hours, so I think we're out of luck."

"As we expected," Kenner said.

"Yes," Sanjong said. "As we expected."

"Because these guys don't have criminal records?" Evans said.

"No. They very well may."

"Then why didn't you get a match?"

"Because this is a netwar," Kenner said. "And at the moment, we are losing it."

TO LOS ANGELES
FRIDAY, OCTOBER 8
3:27 P.M.

In media accounts, Kenner explained, the Environmental Liberation Front was usually characterized as a loose association of eco-terrorists, operating in small groups on their own initiative, and employing relatively unsophisticated means to create havoc—starting fires, trashing SUVs in car lots, and so on.

The truth was quite different. Only one member of ELF had ever been apprehended—a twenty-nine-year-old graduate student at the University of California at Santa Cruz. He was caught sabotaging an oil rig in El Segundo, California. He denied any association with the group, and insisted he was acting alone.

But what troubled authorities was the fact that he was wearing an appliance on his forehead that changed the shape of his skull and made his eyebrows jut out prominently. He was also wearing false ears. It wasn't much of a disguise. But it was troubling, because it suggested that he knew quite a lot about the pattern-matching programs used by the government.

Those programs were tuned to look past changes in facial hair—wigs, beards, and mustaches—since that was the most common method of disguise. They were also designed to compensate for changes in age, such as increased heaviness in the face, drooping features, receding hairlines.

But ears didn't change. The shape of the forehead didn't change. So the programs were therefore weighted to rely on the configuration of ears, and the shape of the forehead. Changing these parts of the face would result in a "no-match" outcome on a computer.

The guy from Santa Cruz knew that. He knew security cameras would photograph him when he got near the rig. So he changed his appearance in a way that would prevent identification by computer.

Similarly, the three extremists at Weddell clearly had formidable backing to carry out their high-tech terrorist act. It took months of planning. Costs were high. And they obviously had in-depth support to obtain academic credentials, university stencils on their shipping boxes, shell companies for their Antarctic shipments, false websites, and dozens of other details necessary for the undertaking. There was nothing unsophisticated about their plan or the way they had executed it.

"And they would have succeeded," Kenner said, "except for that list George Morton obtained shortly before his death."

All of which suggested that if ELF was once a loose association of amateurs, it was no longer. Now it was a highly organized network—one that employed so many channels of communication among its members (e-mail, cell phones, radio, text messaging) that the network as a whole eluded detection. The governments of the world had long worried about how to deal with such networks, and the "netwars" that would result from trying to fight them.

"For a long time, the concept of a netwar was theoretical," Kenner said. "There were studies coming out of RAND, but nobody in the military was really focusing on it. The notion of a networked enemy, or terrorists, or even criminals was too amorphous to bother with."

But it was the amorphous quality of the network—fluid, rapidly evolving—that made it so difficult to combat. You couldn't infiltrate it. You couldn't listen in on it, except by accident. You couldn't locate it geographically because it wasn't in any one place. In truth, the network represented a radically new kind of opponent, and one that required radically new techniques to combat it.

"The military just didn't get it," Kenner said. "But like it or not, we're in a netwar right now."

"And how do you fight a netwar?" Evans said.

"The only way to oppose a network is with another network. You expand your listening posts. You decrypt around the clock. You employ techniques of networked deception and entrapment."

"Such as what?"

"It's technical," Kenner said vaguely. "We rely on the Japanese to spearhead that effort. They are the best at it in the world. And of course we extend our feelers in multiple directions at the same time. Based on what we've just learned at Weddell, we have lots of irons in the fire." Kenner had databases being searched. He had state organizations mobilized. He had inquiries into where the terrorists had obtained their academic credentials, their encrypted radio transmitters, their explosive charges, their computerized detonation timers. None of this was commonplace stuff and it could be traced, given enough time.

"Is there enough time?" Evans said.

"I'm not sure."

Evans could see that Kenner was worried. "So: What is it you want me to do?"

"Just one very simple thing," Kenner said.

"What's that?"

Kenner smiled.

III

ANGEL

LOS ANGELES
SATURDAY, OCTOBER 9
7:04 A.M.

"Is this really necessary?" Peter Evans said, with a worried look.

"It is," Kenner said.

"But it's illegal," Evans said.

"It's not," Kenner said firmly.

"Because you are a law-enforcement officer?" Evans said.

"Of course. Don't worry about it."

They were flying in over Los Angeles, approaching the runway at Van Nuys. The California sun shone through the windows. Sanjong was hunched over the dining table in the middle of the plane. In front of him lay Evans's cell phone, the back removed. Sanjong was attaching a thin gray plate the size of his thumbnail right on top of the battery.

"But what exactly is it?" Evans said.

"Flash memory," Sanjong said. "It'll record four hours of conversation in a compressed format."

"I see," Evans said. "And what am I supposed to do?"

"Just carry the phone in your hand, and go about your business."

"And if I get caught?" he said.

"You won't get caught," Kenner said. "You can take it anywhere. You'll go right through any security, no problem."

"But if they have bug sweepers . . ."

"They won't detect you, because you're not transmitting anything. It's got a burst transmitter. For two seconds every hour, it transmits. The rest of the time, nothing." Kenner sighed. "Look, Peter. It's just a cell phone. Everyone has them."

"I don't know," Evans said. "I feel bad about this. I mean, I'm not a stool pigeon."

Sarah came to the back, yawning, clearing her ears. "Who's a stool pigeon?"

"It's how I feel," Evans said.

"That's not the issue," Kenner said. "Sanjong?"

Sanjong took out a printed list, passed it to Evans. It was Morton's original sheet, now with additions to it:

662262	3982293	24FXE 62262 82293	TERROR	Mt. Terror, Antarctica
882320	4898432	12FXE 82232 54393	SNAKE	Snake Butte, Arizona
774548	9080799	02FXE 67533 43433	LAUGHER	Laugher Cay, Bahamas
482320	5898432	22FXE 72232 04393	SCORPION	Resolution, Solomon Is.
ALT				
662262	3982293	24FXE 62262 82293	TERROR	Mt. Terror, Antarctica
382320	4898432	12FXE 82232 54393	SEVER	Sever City, Arizona
244548	9080799	02FXE 67533 43433	CONCH	Conch Cay, Bahamas
482320	5898432	22FXE 72232 04393	SCORPION	Resolution, Solomon Is.
ALT				
662262	3982293	24FXE 62262 82293	TERROR	Mt. Terror, Antarctica
382320	4898432	12FXE 82232 54393	BUZZARD	Buzzard Gulch, Utah
444548	7080799	02FXE 67533 43433	OLD MAN	Old Man Is., Turks & Caicos
482320	5898432	22FXE 72232 04393	SCORPION	Resolution, Solomon Is.
ALT				
662262	3982293	24FXE 62262 82293	TERROR	Mt. Terror, Antarctica
382320	4898432	12FXE 82232 54393	BLACK MESA	Black Mesa, New Mexico
344548	9080799	02FXE 67533 43433	SNARL	Snarl Cay, BWI
482320	5898432	22FXE 72232 04393	SCORPION	Resolution, Solomon Is.

"As you see, Sanjong has identified the precise GPS locations," Kenner said. "You've undoubtedly noticed a pattern in the list. The first incident we know about. The second incident will take place somewhere in the American desert—either Utah, Arizona, or New Mexico. The third incident will be somewhere in the Caribbean, east of Cuba. And the fourth incident will be in the Solomon Islands."

"Yes? So?"

"Our concern right now is for the second incident," Kenner said. "And the problem is that from Utah to Arizona to New Mexico there are fifty thousand square miles of desert. Unless we can get additional information, we'll never find these guys."

"But you have exact GPS locations . . ."

"Which they will undoubtedly change, now that they know of the trouble in Antarctica."

"You think they have already changed plans?"

"Of course. Their network knew something was wrong as soon as we arrived at Weddell yesterday. I think that's why the first guy left. I think he's actually the leader of the three. The other two were just foot soldiers."

"So you want me to go see Drake," Evans said.

"Right. And find out whatever you can."

"I hate this," Evans said.

"I understand," Kenner said. "But we need you to do it."

Evans looked at Sarah, who was rubbing her eyes, still sleepy. He was annoyed to see that she had arisen from her bed perfectly composed, her face uncreased, beautiful as ever. "How are you?" he said to her.

"I need to brush my teeth," she said. "How long until we land?"

"Ten minutes."

She got up, and walked to the back of the plane.

Evans looked out the window. The sunlight was glaring, harsh. He hadn't had enough sleep. The line of stitches in his scalp pinched. His body ached from being wedged in the damned crevasse for so long. Just to rest his elbow on the armrest of the seat was painful.

He sighed.

"Peter," Kenner said, "those guys tried to kill you. I wouldn't be too careful about the niceties when you fight back."

"Maybe so, but I'm a lawyer."

"And you could be a dead lawyer," Kenner said. "I don't advise it."

• • •

It was with a sense of unreality that Peter Evans merged his hybrid car onto the San Diego freeway, twelve lanes of roaring traffic on an expanse of concrete as wide as half a football field. Sixty-five percent of the surface area of Los Angeles was devoted to cars. People had to wedge themselves in what little was left. It was an inhuman design and it was environmentally absurd. Everything was so far apart, you couldn't walk anywhere, the pollution was incredible.

And people like Kenner did nothing but criticize the good work of environmental organizations, without whose efforts the environment of a place like Los Angeles would be much, much worse.

Face it, he thought. The world needed help. It desperately needed an environmental perspective. And nothing in Kenner's smooth manipulation of facts would change that truth.

His thoughts rambled on in this way for another ten minutes, until he crossed Mulholland Pass and came down toward Beverly Hills.

He looked at the passenger seat beside him. The doctored cell phone glinted in the sunlight. He decided to take it to Drake's office right away. Get this whole thing over with.

He telephoned Drake's office and asked to talk to him; he was told Drake was at the dentist and would return later in the day. The secretary wasn't sure exactly when.

Evans decided to go to his apartment and take a shower.

He parked in the garage and walked through the little garden to his apartment. The sun was shining down between the buildings; the roses were in bloom, beautiful. The only thing that marred it, he thought, was the lingering odor of cigar smoke in the air. It was offensive to think that somebody had smoked a cigar and that what remained was—

"Sssst! Evans!"

He paused. He looked around. He could see nothing.

Evans heard an intense whisper, like a hiss: "Turn right. Pick a damn rose."

"What?"

"Don't talk, you idiot. And stop looking around. Come over here and pick a rose."

Evans moved toward the voice. The cigar smell was stronger. Behind the tangle of the bushes, he saw an old stone bench that he had never noticed before. It was crusted with algae. Hunched down on the bench was a man in a sportcoat. Smoking a cigar.

"Who are—"

"Don't talk," the man whispered. "How many times do I have to tell you. Take the rose, and smell it. That'll give you a reason to stay a minute. Now listen to me. I'm a private investigator. I was hired by George Morton."

Evans smelled the rose. Inhaling cigar smoke.

"I have something important for you," the guy said. "I'll bring it to your apartment in two hours. But I want you to leave again, so they'll follow you. Leave your door unlocked."

Evans turned the rose in his fingers, pretending to examine it. In fact, he was looking past the rose at the man on the bench. The man's face was familiar, somehow. Evans was sure he had seen him before . . .

"Yeah, yeah," the man said, as if reading his thoughts. He turned his lapel, to show a badge. "AV Network Systems. I was working in the NERF building. Now you remember, right? Don't *nod*. For Christ's sake. Just go upstairs, change your clothes, and leave for a while. Go to the gym or whatever. Just go. These assholes—" he jerked his head toward the street "have been waitin' for you. So don't disappoint them. Now *go*."

His apartment had been put back together very well. Lisa had done a good job—the slashed cushions had been flipped over; the books were back in the bookcase. They were out of order, but he would deal with that later.

From the large windows in his living room, Evans looked out toward the street. He could see nothing except the green expanse of Roxbury Park. The kids playing at midday. The clusters of gossiping nannies. There was no sign of surveillance.

It looked perfectly normal.

Self-consciously, he started unbuttoning his shirt, and turned away. He went to the shower, letting the hot spray sting his body. He looked at his toes, which were dark purple, a worrisome, unnatural color. He wiggled them. He didn't have much sensation, but other than that, they seemed to be all right.

He toweled off, and checked his messages. There was a call from Janis, asking if he was free tonight. Then another, nervous one from her, saying her boyfriend had just come back into town and she was busy (which meant, don't call her back). There was a call from Lisa, Herb Lowenstein's assistant, asking where he was. Lowenstein wanted to go over some documents with him; it was important. A call from Heather, saying that Lowenstein was looking for him. A call from Margo Lane, saying she was still in the hospital and why hadn't he called her back? A call from his client the BMW dealer, asking when he was coming to the showroom.

And about ten hang-ups. Far more than he usually had.

The hang-ups gave him a creepy feeling.

Evans dressed quickly, putting on a suit and tie. He came back into the living room and, feeling uneasy, clicked on the television set, just in time for the local noon news. He was heading for the door when he heard: "Two new developments emphasize once again the dangers of global warming. The first study, out of England, says global warming is literally changing the rotation of the Earth, shortening the length of our day."

Evans turned back to look. He saw two co-anchors, a man and a woman. The man was explaining that even more dramatic was a study that showed that the Greenland ice cap was going to melt entirely away. That would cause sea levels to rise twenty feet.

"So, I guess it's good-bye Malibu!" the anchor said cheerfully. Of course, that wouldn't happen for a few years yet. "But it's coming . . . unless we all change our ways."

Evans turned away from the television and headed for the door. He wondered what Kenner would have to say about this latest news. Changing the rotation speed of the Earth? He shook his head at the sheer enormity of it. And melting all the ice in Greenland? Evans could imagine Kenner's discomfiture.

But then, he'd probably just deny it all, the way he usually did.

Evans opened the door, carefully ensured that it would remain unlocked, closed it behind him, and headed for his office.

CENTURY CITY
SATURDAY, OCTOBER 9
9:08 A.M.

He ran into Herb Lowenstein in the hall, walking toward a conference room. "Jesus," Lowenstein said, "where the hell have you been, Peter? Nobody could find you."

"I've been doing a confidential job for a client."

"Well next time tell your damn secretary how to reach you. You look like shit. What happened, you get in a fight or something? And what's that above your ear? Jesus, are those stitches?"

"I fell."

"Uh-huh. What client were you doing this confidential job for?"

"Nick Drake, actually."

"Funny. He didn't mention it."

"No?"

"No, and he just left. I spent the whole morning with him. He's very unhappy about the document rescinding the ten-million-dollar grant from the Morton Foundation. Especially that clause."

"I know," Evans said.

"He wants to know where the clause came from."

"I know."

"Where did it come from?"

"George asked me not to divulge that."

"George is dead."

"Not officially."

"This is bullshit, Peter. Where did the clause come from?"

Evans shook his head. "I'm sorry, Herb. I have specific instructions from the client."

"We're in the same firm. And he's my client, too."

"He instructed me in writing, Herb."

"In *writing?* Horseshit. George didn't write anything."

"Handwritten note," Evans said.

"Nick wants the terms of the document broken."

"I'm sure he does."

"And I told him we'd do that for him," Lowenstein said.

"I don't see how."

"Morton was not in his right mind."

"But he was, Herb," Evans said. "You'll be taking ten million out of his estate and if anybody whispers in the ear of his daughter—"

"She's a total cokehead—"

"—who goes through cash like a monkey through bananas. And if anybody whispers in her ear, this firm will be liable for the ten million, and for punitive damages for conspiracy to defraud. Have you talked to the other senior partners about this course of action?"

"You're being obstructive."

"I'm being cautious. Maybe I should express my concerns in an e-mail to you."

"This is not how you advance in this firm, Peter."

Evans said, "I think I am acting in the firm's best interest. I certainly don't see how you can abrogate this document without, at the very least, first obtaining written opinions from attorneys outside the firm."

"But no outside attorney would countenance—" He broke off. He glared at Evans. "Drake is going to want to talk to you about this."

"I'll be happy to do that."

"I'll tell him you'll call."

"Fine."

Lowenstein stalked off. Then he turned back. "And what was all that business about the police and your apartment?"

"My apartment was robbed."

"For what? Drugs?"

"No, Herb."

"My assistant had to leave the office to help you with a police matter."

"That's true. As a personal favor. And it was after hours, if I recall."

Lowenstein snorted, and stomped off down the hall.

Evans made a mental note to call Drake. And get this entire business behind him.

In the hot midday sun, Kenner parked his car in the downtown lot and walked with Sarah out onto the street. Heat shimmered off the pavement. The signs there were all in Spanish, except for a few English phrases—"Checks Cashed" and "Money Loaned." From scratchy loudspeakers, mariachi music blared out.

Kenner said, "All set?"

Sarah checked the small sports bag on her shoulder. It had nylon mesh at either end. The mesh concealed the video lens. "Yes," she said. "I'm ready."

Together, they walked toward the large store on the corner, "Brader's Army/Navy Surplus."

Sarah said, "What're we doing here?"

"ELF purchased a large quantity of rockets," Kenner said.

She frowned. "Rockets?"

"Small ones. Lightweight. About two feet long. They're outdated versions of an '80s Warsaw Pact device called Hotfire. Handheld, wire-guided, solid propellant, range of about a thousand yards."

Sarah wasn't sure what all that meant. "So, these are weapons?"

"I doubt that's why they bought them."

"How many did they buy?"

"Five hundred. With launchers."

"Wow."

"Let's just say they're probably not hobbyists."

Above the doors, a banner in flaking yellow and green paint read, Camping Gear Paintball Paratrooper Jackets Compass Sleeping Bags Much, Much More!

The front door chimed as they went in.

The store was large and disorderly, filled with military stuff on racks and piled in untidy heaps on the floor. The air smelled musty, like old canvas. There were few people inside at this hour. Kenner walked directly to the kid at the cash register, flashed his wallet, and asked for Mr. Brader.

"In the back."

The kid smiled at Sarah. Kenner went to the back of the store. Sarah stayed at the front.

"So," she said. "I need a little help."

"Do my best." He grinned. He was a crew-cut kid, maybe nineteen or twenty. He had a black T-shirt that said "The Crow." His arms looked like he worked out.

"I'm trying to find a guy," Sarah said, and slid a sheet of paper toward him.

"You think any guy would be trying to find you," the kid said. He picked up the paper. It showed a photograph of the man they knew as Brewster, who had set up camp in Antarctica.

"Oh yeah," the kid said immediately. "Sure, I know him. He comes in sometimes."

"What's his name?"

"I don't know, but he's in the store now."

"Now?" She glanced around for Kenner, but he was in the back, huddled with the owner. She didn't want to call to him or do anything to cause attention.

The kid was standing on tiptoes, looking around. "Yeah, he's here. I mean, he was in here a few minutes ago. Came in to buy some timers."

"Where are your timers?"

"I'll show you." He came around the counter, and led her through the stacks of green clothing and the boxes piled seven feet high. She couldn't see over them. She could no longer see Kenner.

The kid glanced over his shoulder at her. "What are you, like a detective?"

"Sort of."

"You want to go out?"

They were moving deeper into the store when they heard the chime of the front door. She turned to look. Over stacks of flak jackets, she had a glimpse of a brown head, a white shirt with a red collar, and the door closing.

"He's leaving . . ."

She didn't think. She just turned and sprinted for the door. The bag banged against her hip. She jumped over stacked canteens, running hard.

"Hey," the kid yelled behind her. "You coming back?"

She banged through the door.

She was out on the street. Glaring hot sun and shoving crowds. She looked left and right. She didn't see the white shirt and red collar anywhere. There hadn't been time for him to cross the street. She looked around the corner, and saw him strolling casually away from her, toward Fifth Street. She followed him.

He was a man of about thirty-five, dressed in cheap golf-type clothes. His pants were rumpled. He wore dirty hiking boots. He had tinted glasses and a small, trim moustache. He looked like a guy who spent a lot of time outdoors, but not a construction guy—more of a supervisor. Maybe a building contractor. Building inspector. Something like that.

She tried to notice the details, to remember them. She gained on him, then decided that was a bad idea, and dropped back. "Brewster" stopped in front of one window and looked at it intently for a few moments, then went on.

She came to the window. It was a crockery store, displaying cheap plates. She wondered, then, if he already knew he was being followed.

• • •

To trail a terrorist on a downtown street felt like something out of a movie, but it was more frightening than she anticipated. The surplus store seemed very far behind her. She didn't know where Kenner was. She wished he were here. Also, she was hardly inconspicuous; the crowd on the sidewalk was largely Hispanic, and Sarah's blond head stuck up above most people's.

She stepped off the curb, and walked along the street gutter, hanging at the edge of the crowd. That way she lost six inches of height. But still, she was uncomfortably aware that her hair was distinctively blonde. But there was nothing she could do about that.

She let Brewster get twenty yards ahead of her. She didn't want to allow more distance than that because she was afraid she'd lose him.

Brewster crossed Fifth Street, and continued on. He went another half a block, and then turned left, down an alley. Sarah got to the alley entrance, and paused. There were garbage bags stacked at intervals. She could smell the rotten odor from where she was. A big delivery truck blocked the far end of the alley.

And no Brewster.

He had vanished.

It wasn't possible, unless he had walked through one of the back doors that opened onto the alley. There were doors every twenty feet or so, many of them recessed into the brick wall.

She bit her lip. She didn't like the idea that she couldn't see him. But there were delivery men down at the truck. . . .

She started down the alley.

She looked at each door as she passed it. Some were boarded shut, some were locked. A few had grimy signs giving the name of the firm, and saying USE FRONT ENTRANCE or PRESS BELL FOR SERVICE.

No Brewster.

She had gotten halfway down the alley when something made her look back. She was just in time to see Brewster step out of a doorway and head back to the street, moving quickly away from her.

She ran.

As she passed the doorway, she saw an elderly woman standing in the door. The sign on the door said, Munro Silk and Fabrics.

"Who is he?" she shouted.

The old woman shrugged, shaking her head. "Wrong door. They all do—" She said something more, but by then Sarah couldn't hear.

She was back on the sidewalk, still running. Heading toward Fourth. She could see Brewster half a block ahead. He was walking quickly, almost a jog.

He crossed Fourth. A pickup truck pulled over to the side, a few yards ahead. It was battered blue, with Arizona license plates. Brewster jumped in the passenger side, and the truck roared off.

Sarah was scribbling down the license plate when Kenner's car screeched to a stop alongside her. "Get in."

She did, and he accelerated forward.

"Where were you?" she said.

"Getting the car. I saw you leave. Did you film him?"

She had forgotten all about the bag on her shoulder. "Yes, I think so."

"Good. I got a name for this guy, from the store owner."

"Yes?"

"But it's probably an alias. David Poulson. And a shipping address."

"For the rockets?"

"No, for the launch stands."

"Where?"

Kenner said, "Flagstaff, Arizona."

Ahead, they saw the blue pickup.

They followed the pickup down Second, past the *Los Angeles Times* building, past the criminal courts, and then onto the freeway. Kenner was skilled; he managed to stay well back, but always kept the truck in sight.

"You've done this before," Sarah said.

"Not really."

"What is that little card you show everybody?"

Kenner pulled out his wallet, and handed it to her. There was a silver badge, looking roughly like a police badge, except it said "NSIA" on it. And there was an official license for "National Security Intelligence Agency," with his photograph.

"I've never heard of the National Security Intelligence Agency."

Kenner nodded, took the wallet back.

"What does it do?"

"Stays below the radar," Kenner said. "Have you heard from Evans?"

"You don't want to tell me?"

"Nothing to tell," Kenner said. "Domestic terrorism makes domestic agencies uncomfortable. They're either too harsh or too lenient. Everyone in NSIA is specially trained. Now, call Sanjong and read him the license plate on that pickup, see if he can trace it."

"So you do domestic terrorism?"

"Sometimes."

Ahead, the pickup truck moved onto the Interstate 5 freeway, heading east, past the clustered yellowing buildings of County General Hospital.

"Where are they going?" she said.

"I don't know," he said. "But this is the road to Arizona."

She picked up the phone and called Sanjong.

Sanjong wrote down the license, and called back in less than five minutes. "It's registered to the Lazy-Bar Ranch, outside Sedona," he told Kenner. "It's apparently a guest ranch and spa. The truck hasn't been reported stolen."

"Okay. Who owns the ranch?"

"It's a holding company: Great Western Environmental Associates. They own a string of guest ranches in Arizona and New Mexico."

"Who owns the holding company?"

"I'm checking on that, but it'll take some time."

Sanjong hung up.

Ahead, the pickup truck moved into the right lane, and turned on its blinker.

"It's pulling off the road," Kenner said.

They followed the truck through an area of seedy industrial parks. Sometimes the signs said SHEET WORKS or MACHINE TOOLING, but most of the buildings were blocky and unrevealing. The air was hazy, almost a light fog.

After two miles, the truck turned right again, just past a sign that said LTSI CORP. And beneath that, a small picture of an airport, with an arrow.

"It must be a private airfield," Kenner said.

"What's LTSI?" she said.

He shook his head. "I don't know."

Farther down the road, they could see the little airfield, with several small prop planes, Cessnas and Pipers, parked to one side. The truck drove up and parked alongside a twin-engine plane.

"Twin Otter," Kenner said.

"Is that significant?"

"Short takeoff, large payload. It's a workhorse aircraft. Used for firefighting, all sorts of things."

Brewster got out of the truck, and walked to the cockpit of the plane. He spoke briefly to the pilot. Then he got back in the truck, and drove a hundred yards down the road, pulling up in front of a huge rectangular shed of corrugated steel. There were two other trucks parked alongside it. The sign on the shed said LTSI, in big blue letters.

Brewster got out of the truck, and came around the back as the driver of the truck got out.

"Son of a bitch," Sarah said.

The driver was the man they knew as Bolden. He was now wearing jeans, a baseball cap, and sunglasses, but there was no doubt about his identity.

"Easy," Kenner said.

They watched as Brewster and Bolden walked into the shed through a narrow door. The door closed behind them with a metallic clang.

Kenner turned to Sarah. "You stay here."

He got out of the car, walked quickly to the shed, and went inside.

She sat in the passenger seat, shading her eyes against the sun, and waited. The minutes dragged. She squinted at the sign on the side of the shed, because she could detect small white lettering beneath the large LTSI initials. But she was too far away to make out what it said.

She thought of calling Sanjong, but didn't. She worried about what would happen if Brewster and Bolden came out, but Kenner remained inside. She would have to follow them alone. She couldn't let them get away. . . .

That thought led her to slide over into the driver's seat. She rested her hands on the wheel. She looked at her watch. Surely nine or ten minutes had already passed. She scanned the shed for any sign of activity, but the building was clearly made to be as unobtrusive and as unrevealing as possible.

She looked at her watch again.

She began to feel like a coward, just sitting there. All her life, she had confronted the things that frightened her. That was why she had learned to ski black diamond ice, to rock climb (even though she was too tall), to scuba dive wrecks.

Now, she was just sitting in a hot car, waiting as the minutes ticked by.

The hell with it, she thought. And she got out of the car.

At the door to the shed, there were two small signs. One said LTSI LIGHTNING TEST SYSTEMS INTERNATIONAL. The second said WARNING: DO NOT ENTER TEST BED DURING DISCHARGE INTERVALS.

Whatever that meant.

Sarah opened the door cautiously. There was a reception area, but it was deserted. On a plain wooden desk was a handwritten sign and a buzzer. PRESS BUZZER FOR ASSISTANCE.

She ignored the buzzer, and opened the inner door, which was ominously marked:

NO TRESPASSING
HIGH VOLTAGE DISCHARGE
AUTHORIZED PERSONNEL ONLY

She went through the door and came into an open, dimly lit industrial space—pipes on the ceiling, a catwalk, rubber-tile floor underfoot. It was all quite dark except for a two-story glass-walled chamber in the center, which was brightly lit. It was a fairly large space, roughly the size of her living room. Inside the chamber she saw what looked like an airplane jet engine, mounted on a small section of wing. At the side of the room was a large metal plate, set against the wall. And outside the room was a control panel. A man was sitting in front of the panel. Brewster and Bolden were nowhere to be seen.

Inside the room, a recessed monitor screen flashed CLEAR AREA NOW. A computer voice said, "Please clear the test area. Testing begins in . . . thirty seconds." Sarah heard a slowly building whine, and the chugging of a pump. But nothing was happening that she could see.

Curious, she moved forward.

"Ssst!"

She looked around, but could not see where the sound was coming from.

"Ssst!"

She looked up. Kenner was above her, on the catwalk. He gestured for her to join him, pointing to a set of stairs at the corner of the room.

The computer voice said, "Testing begins in . . . twenty seconds."

She climbed the stairs and crouched beside Kenner. The whine had now built to a shriek, and the chugging was rapid, almost a continuous sound. Kenner pointed to the jet engine, and whispered, "They're testing airplane parts." He explained quickly that airplanes were frequently struck by lightning, and all their components had to be lightning proof.

He said something else, too, but she couldn't really hear him over the increasing noise.

Inside the center room, the lights went off, leaving just a faint blue glow over the jet engine and its smoothly curved cowling. The computer voice was counting backward from ten.

"Testing begins . . . now."

There was a *snap!* so loud it sounded like a gunshot, and a bolt of lightning snaked out from the wall and struck the engine. It was immediately followed by more bolts from the other walls, striking the engine from all sides. The lightning crackled over the cowling in jagged white-hot fingers, then abruptly shot down to the floor, where Sarah saw a dome-shaped piece of metal about a foot in diameter.

She noticed a few of the lightning bolts seemed to shoot directly to this dome, missing the engine entirely.

As the test continued, the lightning bolts grew thicker, brighter. They made a long *crack!* as they shot through the air, and etched black streaks over the metal cowl. The fan blades were struck by one bolt, causing the fan to spin silently.

As Sarah watched, it seemed as if more and more of the bolts did not strike the engine, but instead struck the small dome on the floor until finally there was a white spiderweb of lightning strikes, coming from all sides, going directly to the dome.

And then, abruptly, the test ended. The whining sound stopped, and the room lights came on. Faint, hazy smoke rose from the engine cowling. Sarah looked over at the console, and saw Brewster and Bolden standing behind the seated technician. All three men walked into the central room, where they crouched beneath the engine and inspected the metal dome.

"What is it?" Sarah whispered.

Kenner put a finger to his lips, and shook his head. He looked unhappy.

Inside the room, the men upended the dome, and Sarah had a glimpse of its complexity—green circuit boards and shiny metal attachments. But the men were clustered around it, talking excitedly, and it was hard for her to see. Then they put the dome back down on the floor again, and walked out of the room.

They were laughing and slapping each other on the back, apparently very pleased with the test. She heard one of them say something about buying a round of beer, and there was more laughter, and they walked out through the front door. The test area was silent.

They heard the outer door slam shut.

She and Kenner waited.

She looked at Kenner. He waited, motionless for a full minute, just listening. Then, when they still heard nothing, he said, "Let's have a look at that thing."

They climbed down from the catwalk.

On the ground level, they saw and heard nothing. The facility was apparently deserted. Kenner pointed to the inner chamber. They opened the door, and went inside.

The interior of the chamber was bright. There was a sharp smell in the air.

"Ozone," Kenner said. "From the strikes."

He walked directly to the dome on the floor.

"What do you think it is?" Sarah said.

"I don't know, but it must be a portable charge generator." He crouched, turned the dome over. "You see, if you can generate a strong enough negative charge—"

He broke off. The dome was empty. Its electronic innards had been removed.

With a *clang*, the door behind them slammed shut.

Sarah whirled. Bolden was on the other side of the door, calmly locking it with a padlock.

"Oh shit," she said. Over at the console she saw Brewster, turning knobs, flipping switches. He flicked an intercom.

"There's no trespassing in this facility, folks. It's clearly marked. Guess you didn't read the signs . . ."

Brewster stepped away from the console. The room lights went dark blue. Sarah heard the start of the whine, beginning to build. The screen flashed CLEAR AREA NOW. And she heard a computer voice say, "Please clear the test area. Testing begins in . . . thirty seconds."

Brewster and Bolden walked out, without looking back.

Sarah heard Bolden say, "I hate the smell of burning flesh."

And they were gone, slamming the door.

The computer voice said, "Testing begins in . . . fifteen seconds."

Sarah turned to Kenner. "What do we do?"

Outside the facility, Bolden and Brewster got into their car. Bolden started the engine. Brewster put a hand on the other man's shoulder.

"Let's just wait a minute."

They watched the door. A red light began to flash, slowly at first, then faster and faster.

"Test has started," Brewster said.

"Damn shame," Bolden said. "How long you figure they can survive?"

"One bolt, maybe two. But by the third one, they're definitely dead. And probably on fire."

"Damn shame," Bolden said again. He put the car in gear, and drove toward the waiting airplane.

IV

FLASH

Inside the test chamber, the air took on a sizzly, electric quality, like the atmosphere before a storm. Sarah saw the hairs on her arm standing up. Her clothing was sticking to her body, flattened by the electric charge.

"Got a belt?" Kenner said.

"No . . ."

"Hairclip?"

"No."

"Anything metal?"

"No! Damn it, no!"

Kenner flung himself against the glass wall, but just bounced off. He kicked it with his heel; nothing happened. He slammed his weight against the door, but the lock was strong.

"Ten seconds to test," the computer voice said.

"What are we going to do?" Sarah said, panicked.

"Take your clothes off."

"What?"

"Now. Do it." He was stripping off his shirt, ripping it off, buttons flying. "Come on, Sarah. Especially the sweater."

She had a fluffy angora sweater, and bizarrely, she recalled it had been a present from her boyfriend, one of the first things he ever bought her. She tore it off, and the T-shirt beneath.

"Skirt," Kenner said. He was down to his shorts, pulling off his shoes.

"What is this—"

"It's got a zipper!"

She fumbled, getting the skirt off. She was down to her sports bra and panties. She shivered. The computer voice was counting backward. "Ten . . . nine . . . eight . . ."

Kenner was draping the clothes over the engine. He took her skirt, draped it over, too. He arranged the angora sweater to lie on the top.

"What are you doing?"

"Lie down," he said. "Lie flat on the floor—make yourself as flat as you can—and *don't move.*"

She pressed her body against the cold concrete. Her heart was pounding. The air was bristling. She felt a shiver down the back of her neck.

"Three . . . two . . . one . . ."

Kenner threw himself on the ground next to her and the first lightning bolt crashed through the room. She was shocked by the violence of it, the blast of air rushing over her body. Her hair was rising into the air, she could feel the weight of it lift off her neck. There were more bolts— the crashing sound was terrifying—blasting blue light, so bright she saw it even though she squeezed her eyes shut. She pressed herself against the ground, willing herself to be even flatter, exhaling, thinking *Now is a time for prayer.*

But suddenly there was another kind of light in the room, yellower, flickering, and a sharp acrid smell.

Fire.

A piece of her flaming sweater fell on her bare shoulder. She felt searing pain.

"It's a fire—"

"Don't move!" Kenner snarled.

The bolts were still blasting, coming faster and faster, crackling over the room, but she could see out of the corner of her eye that the clothes heaped on the engine were aflame, the room was filling with smoke.

She thought, *My hair is burning.* And she could feel it suddenly hot at the base of her neck, along her scalp . . .

And suddenly the room was filled with blasting water, and the lightning had stopped, and the sprinkler nozzles hissed overhead. She felt cold; the fires went out; the concrete was wet.

"Can I get up now?"

"Yes," Kenner said. "You can get up now."

He spent several more minutes trying to break the glass without success. Finally he stopped and stared, his hair matted by the sizzling water. "I don't get it," he said. "You can't have a room like this without a safety mechanism to enable someone to get out."

"They locked the door, you saw it yourself."

"Right. Locking it from the outside with a padlock. That padlock must be there to make sure nobody can enter the room from the outside while the facility is closed. But there still has to be some way to get out *from the inside.*"

"If there is, I don't see it." She was shivering. Her shoulder hurt where she was burned. Her underwear was soaked through. She wasn't modest, but she was cold, and he was nattering on . . .

"There just has to be a way," he said, turning slowly, looking.

"You can't break the glass . . ."

"No," he said. "You can't." But that seemed to suggest something to him. He bent and carefully examined the glass frame, looking at the seam where the glass met the wall. Running his finger along it.

She shivered while she watched him. The sprinklers were still on, still spraying. She was standing in three inches of water. She could not understand how he could be so focused, so intent on—

"I'll be damned," he said. His fingers had closed on a small latch, flush with the mounting. He found another on the opposite side of the window, flicked it open. And then he pushed the window, which was hinged in the center, and rotated it open.

He stepped through into the outer room.

"Nothing to it," he said. He extended his hand. "Can I offer you some dry clothes?"

"Thank you," she said, and took his hand.

The LTSI washrooms weren't anything to write home about, but Sarah and Kenner dried off with paper towels and found some warm coveralls, and Sarah began to feel better. Staring in the mirror, she saw that she'd lost two inches of hair around her left side. The ends were ragged, black, twisted.

"Could have been worse," she said, thinking *Ponytails for a while.*

Kenner tended to her shoulder, which he said was just a first-degree burn with a few blisters. He put ice on it, telling her that burns were not a thermal injury but were actually a nerve response within the body, and that ice in the first ten minutes reduced the severity of the burn by numbing the nerve, and preventing the response. So, if you were going to blister, ice prevented it from happening.

She tuned out his voice. She couldn't actually see the burned area, so she had to take his word for it. It was starting to hurt. He found a first-aid kit, brought back aspirin.

"Aspirin?" Sarah said.

"Better than nothing." He dropped two tablets in her hand. "Actually, most people don't know it, but aspirin's a true wonder drug, it has more pain-killing power than morphine, and it is anti-inflammatory, anti-fever—"

"Not right now," she said. "Please." She just couldn't take another of his lectures.

He said nothing. He just put on the bandage. He seemed to be good at that, too.

"Is there anything you're not good at?" she said.

"Oh sure."

"Like what? Dancing?"

"No, I can dance. But I'm terrible at languages."

"That's a relief." She herself was good at languages. She'd spent her junior year in Italy, and was reasonably fluent in Italian and French. And she'd studied Chinese.

"And what about you?" he said. "What are you bad at?"

"Relationships," she said. Staring in the mirror and pulling at the blackened strands of her hair.

As Evans climbed the steps to his apartment, he could hear the television blaring. It seemed louder than before. He heard cheers and laughter. Some sort of show with a live studio audience.

He opened the door, and went into the living room. The private investigator from the courtyard was sitting on the couch, his back to Evans while he watched television. His jacket was off and flung over a nearby chair. He had his arm draped across the back of the sofa. His fingers drummed impatiently.

"I see you've made yourself at home," Evans said. "Pretty loud, don't you think? Would you mind turning it down?"

The man didn't answer, he just continued to stare at the TV.

"Did you hear me?" Evans said. "Turn it down, would you?"

The man did not move. Just his fingers, moving restlessly on the back of the couch.

Evans walked around to face the man. "I'm sorry, I don't know your name but—"

He broke off. The investigator hadn't turned to look at him but continued to stare fixedly at the TV. In fact, no part of his body moved. He was immobile, rigid. His eyes didn't move. They didn't even blink. The only part of his body that moved was his fingers, on the top of the couch. They almost seemed to be twitching. In spasm.

Evans stepped directly in front of the man. "Are you all right?"

The man's face was expressionless. His eyes stared forward, seeming to look straight through Evans.

"Sir?"

The investigator was breathing shallowly, his chest hardly moving. His skin was tinged with gray.

"Can you move at all? What happened to you?"

Nothing. The man was rigid.

Just like the way they described Margo, Evans thought. The same rigidity, the same blankness. Evans picked up the phone and dialed 911, called for an ambulance to his address.

"Okay, help is coming," he said to the man. The private detective gave no visible response, but even so, Evans had the impression that the man could hear, that he was fully aware inside his frozen body. But there was no way to be sure.

Evans looked around the room, hoping to find clues as to what had happened to this man. But the apartment seemed undisturbed. One chair in the corner seemed to have been moved. The guy's smelly cigar was on the floor in the corner, as if it had rolled there. It had burned the edge of the rug slightly.

Evans picked up the cigar.

He brought it back to the kitchen, ran it under the faucet, and tossed it in the wastebasket. Then he had an idea. He went back to the man. "You were going to bring me something . . ."

There was no movement. Just the fingers on the couch.

"Is it here?"

The fingers stopped. Or almost stopped. They still moved slightly. But there was clearly an effort being made.

"Can you control your fingers?" Evans said.

They started, then stopped again.

"So you can. Okay. Now: is the thing you wanted me to see here?"

Fingers moved.

Then stopped.

"I take that as a yes. Okay." Evans stepped back. In the distance, he heard an approaching siren. The ambulance would be here in a few minutes. He said, "I am going to move in one direction, and if it is the right direction, move your fingers."

The fingers started, then stopped, as if to signal "yes."

"Okay," Evans said. He turned and took several steps to his right, heading toward the kitchen. He looked back.

The fingers did not move.

"So it's not that way." He now moved toward the television, directly in front of the man.

The fingers did not move.

"All right, then." Evans turned left, walking toward the picture windows. Still the fingers did not move. There was only one direction remaining: he moved behind the investigator, heading toward the door. Since the man could not see him, Evans said, "Now I am walking away from you, toward the front door . . ."

The fingers did not move.

"Maybe you didn't understand," Evans said. "I wanted you to move your fingers if I was heading in the right direction . . ."

Fingers moved. Scratching the couch.

"Yeah, okay, but which direction? I went in all four directions and—"

The doorbell rang. Evans opened it, and two paramedics rushed in, bringing a stretcher. And now there was pandemonium, they were asking him rapid-fire questions, and loading the guy onto the stretcher. The police arrived a few moments later, with still more questions. They were the Beverly Hills police, so they were polite, but they were insistent. This man was paralyzed in Evans's apartment, and Evans did not seem to know anything about it.

Finally, a detective came through the door. He wore a brown suit and introduced himself as Ron Perry. He gave Evans his card. Evans gave him his own card. Perry looked at it, then looked at Evans and said, "Haven't I seen this card before? It looks familiar. Oh yeah, I remember. It was at that apartment on Wilshire where the lady was paralyzed."

"She was my client."

"And now it's happened again, the same paralysis," Perry said. "Is that a coincidence or what?"

"I don't know," Evans said, "because I wasn't here. I don't know what happened."

"Somehow people just become paralyzed wherever you go?"

"No," Evans said. "I told you, I don't know what happened."

"Is this guy a client, too?"

"No."

"Then who is he?"

"I have no idea who he is."

"No? How'd he get in here?"

Evans was about to say he had left the door open for him, but he realized that was going to be a long explanation, and a difficult one.

"I don't know. I, uh . . . Sometimes I don't lock my door."

"You should always lock your door, Mr. Evans. That's just common sense."

"Of course, you're right."

"Doesn't your door lock automatically, when you leave?"

"I told you, I don't know how he got in my apartment," Evans said, looking directly into the detective's eyes.

The detective returned the stare. "How'd you get those stitches in your head?"

"I fell."

"Looks like quite a fall."

"It was."

The detective nodded slowly. "You could save us a lot of trouble if you'd just tell me who this guy is, Mr. Evans. You've got a man in your apartment, you don't know who he is, you don't know how he got here. Forgive me if I feel you're maybe leaving something out."

"I am."

"Okay." Perry took out his notebook. "Go ahead."

"The guy's a private detective."

"I know that."

"You do?" Evans said.

"The paramedics checked his pockets, found a license in his wallet. Go on."

"He told me he had been hired by a client of mine."

"Uh-huh. Which client is that?" Perry was writing.

"I can't tell you that," Evans said.

He looked up from his pad. "Mr. Evans—"

"I'm sorry. That's privileged."

The detective gave a long sigh. "Okay, so this guy is a private investigator hired by a client of yours."

"Right," Evans said. "The investigator contacted me and said he wanted to see me, to give me something."

"To give you something?"

"Right."

"He didn't want to give it to the client?"

"He couldn't."

"Because?"

"The client is, uh, unavailable."

"I see. So he came to you instead?"

"Yes. And he was a bit paranoid, and wanted to meet me in my apartment."

"So you left the door to your apartment open for him."

"Yes."

"Some guy you'd never seen before?"

"Yes, well, I knew he was working for my client."

"How did you know that?"

Evans shook his head. "Privileged."

"Okay. So this guy comes into your apartment. Where are you?"

"I was at my office."

Evans quickly recounted his movements during the intervening two hours.

"People saw you at the office?"

"Yes."

"Conversations?"

"Yes."

"More than one person?"

"Yes."

"You see anybody else besides people in the law firm?"

"I stopped to get gas."

"Attendant will recognize you?"

"Yes. I had to go in to use my credit card."

"Which station?"

"Shell on Pico."

"Okay. So you were gone two hours, you come back here, and the guy is . . ."

"As you saw him. Paralyzed."

"And what was he going to give you?"

"I have no idea."

"You didn't find anything in the apartment?"

"No."

"Anything else you want to tell me?"

"No."

Another long sigh. "Look, Mr. Evans. If two people I knew were mysteriously paralyzed, I'd be a little worried. But you don't seem worried."

"Believe me, I'm worried," Evans said.

The detective frowned at him. "Okay," he said finally. "You have a client privilege you're invoking. I have to tell you that I've gotten calls from UCLA and from the CDC on this paralysis thing. Now that there's a second case, there are going to be more calls." He flipped his notebook shut. "I'm going to need you to come by the station and give us a signed statement. Can you do that later today?"

"I think so."

"Four o'clock?"

"Yes. Fine."

"The address is on the card. Just ask for me at the desk. Parking is under the building."

"Okay," Evans said.

"See you then," the detective said, and turned to leave.

. . .

Evans shut the door behind him and leaned against it. He was glad to finally be alone. He walked around the apartment slowly, trying to focus his thoughts. The television was still on, but the sound was turned off. He looked at the couch where the private investigator had been sitting. The indentation of his body was still visible.

He still had half an hour before he was supposed to meet with Drake. But he wanted to know what the PI had brought to him. Where was it? Evans had moved in every direction of the compass, and each time the man had indicated with his fingertips that it was the wrong direction.

Which meant what? He hadn't brought the thing? It was somewhere else? Or that whoever paralyzed him had taken it, so it was no longer there?

Evans sighed. The critical question—is it here?—was one he hadn't asked the detective. Evans just assumed it was there.

And suppose it was? Where would it be?

North, south, east, west. All wrong.

Which meant . . .

What?

He shook his head. He was having trouble concentrating. The truth was, the private investigator's paralysis had unnerved him more than he wanted to admit. He looked at the couch, and the indentation. The guy couldn't move. It must have been terrifying. And the paramedics had lifted him up bodily, like a sack of potatoes, and put him on the stretcher. The cushions on the couch were in disarray, a reminder of their efforts.

Idly, Evans straightened up the couch, putting the cushions in place, fluffing them . . .

He felt something. Inside a slit in one cushion. He stuck his hand deeper into the padding.

"Damn," he said.

• • •

Of course it was obvious in retrospect. Moving away in every direction was wrong, because the investigator wanted Evans to move *toward* him. The guy was sitting on the thing, which he had slipped inside the couch cushion.

It turned out to be a shiny DVD.

Evans dropped it in the DVD player, and watched as a menu came up, a list of dates. They were all in the last few weeks.

Evans clicked on the first date.

He saw a view of the NERF conference room. It was a side angle, from the corner of the room, waist high. It must have been from a camera hidden in the speaker's podium or something, Evans thought. Undoubtedly the investigator had installed the camera the day Evans had seen him in the NERF conference room.

At the bottom of the screen was a running time code, numbers flickering. But Evans stared at the image itself, which showed Nicholas Drake talking to John Henley, the PR guy. Drake was upset, throwing up his hands.

"I *hate* global warming," Drake said, almost shouting. "I fucking *hate* it. It's a goddamn disaster."

"It's been established," Henley said calmly. "Over many years. It's what we have to work with."

"To work with? But *it doesn't work*," Drake said. "That's my point. You can't raise a dime with it, especially in winter. Every time it snows people forget all about global warming. Or else they decide some warming might be a good thing after all. They're trudging through the snow, *hoping* for a little global warming. It's not like pollution, John. Pollution *worked*. It still works. Pollution scares the shit out of people. You tell 'em they'll get cancer, and the money rolls in. But nobody is scared of a little warming. Especially if it won't happen for a hundred years."

"You have ways to play it," Henley said.

"Not anymore," Drake said. "We've tried them all. Species extinction from global warming—nobody gives a shit. They've heard that most of the species that will become extinct are insects. You can't raise money on insect extinctions, John. Exotic diseases from global warming—nobody cares. Hasn't happened. We ran that huge campaign last year connecting global warming to the Ebola and Hanta viruses. Nobody went for it. Sea-level rise from global warming—we all know where that'll end up. The Vanutu lawsuit is a fucking disaster. Everybody'll assume the sea level isn't rising anywhere. And that Scandinavian guy, that sea level expert. He's becoming a pest. He's even attacking the IPCC for incompetence."

"Yes," Henley said patiently. "That's all true . . ."

"So you tell me," Drake said, "how the hell I'm supposed to *play* global warming. Because you know what I have to raise to keep this organization going, John. I need forty-two million dollars a year. The foundations will only give me a quarter of that this year. The celebrities show up at the fund-raisers, but they don't give us shit. They're so egotistical they think showing up should be payment enough. Of course we sue the EPA every year, and they may cough up three, four million. With EPA grants, maybe five total. That still leaves a big gap, John. Global warming isn't going to cut it. I need a fucking *cause*. A cause that *works!*"

"I understand," Henley said, still very calm. "But you are forgetting the conference."

"Oh, Christ, the conference," Drake said. "These assholes can't even get the posters right. Bendix is our best speaker; he's got a family problem. Wife is having chemo. Gordon was scheduled, but he's got some lawsuit about his research . . . Seems his notebooks were faked . . ."

"Those are details, Nicholas," Henley said. "I'm asking you to stay with the big picture—"

At that moment, the phone rang. Drake answered it, listened briefly. Then he put his hand over the phone and turned to Henley.

"We have to continue this later, John. I've got an emergency here."

Henley got up, and left the room.

The clip ended.

The screen went black.

Evans stared at the blank screen. He felt as if he were going to be ill. A wave of dizziness passed over him. His stomach churned. He held the remote in his hand, but he did not press the buttons.

The moment passed. He took a breath. On reflection, he realized that what he had seen wasn't really surprising. Perhaps Drake was more explicit in private—everyone was—and obviously he felt under pressure to raise money. But the frustration he expressed was perfectly understandable. From the beginning, the movement had had to fight apathy in the broader society. Human beings didn't think in the long term. They didn't see the slow degradation of the environment. It had always been an uphill battle to rouse the public to do what was really in its own best interest.

That fight was far from over. In fact, it was just beginning.

And it was probably true that it wasn't easy to raise money for global warming. So Nicholas Drake had his work cut out for him.

And environmental organizations were really working with very small funds. Forty-four million for NERF, the same for the NRDC, maybe fifty for the Sierra Club. The big one was the Nature Conservancy, they had three quarters of a billion. But what was that compared with the zillions of dollars that could be mobilized by corporations? It was David and Goliath. And Drake was David. As he had said himself, on every occasion.

Evans glanced at his watch. In any case, it was time to go see Drake.

He took the DVD out of the player, slipped it into his pocket, and left the apartment. On his way, he reviewed what he was going to say. He went over it, again and again, trying to make it perfect. He had to do it carefully, because everything Kenner had told him to say was a lie.

BEVERLY HILLS
SATURDAY, OCTOBER 9
11:12 A.M.

"Peter, Peter," Nicholas Drake said, shaking his hand warmly. "I am very pleased to see you. You've been away."

"Yes."

"But you haven't forgotten my request."

"No, Nick."

"Have a seat."

Evans sat down and Drake sat behind the desk. "Go ahead."

"I traced the origin of that clause."

"Yes?"

"Yes. You were right. George did get the idea from a lawyer."

"I knew it! Who?"

"An outside attorney, not in our firm." Evans spoke carefully, saying just what Kenner had instructed him to say.

"Who?"

"Unfortunately, Nick, there's documentation. Red-lined drafts with George's handwritten comments."

"Ah, shit. From when?"

"Six months ago."

"Six months!"

"Apparently George has been concerned for some time about . . . things. The groups he supports."

"He never told me."

"Nor me," Evans said. "He chose an outside attorney."

"I want to see this correspondence," Drake said.

Evans shook his head. "The attorney will never permit it."

"George is dead."

"Privilege continues after death. *Swidler and Berlin v. United States.*"

"This is bullshit, Peter, and you know it."

Evans shrugged. "But this attorney plays by the book. And I have arguably overstepped proper bounds by saying as much as I have."

Drake drummed his fingers on the desk top. "Peter, the Vanutu lawsuit is desperately in need of that money."

"I keep hearing," Evans said, "that that lawsuit may be dropped."

"Nonsense."

"Because the data sets don't show any rise in Pacific sea level."

"I'd be careful about saying things like that," Drake said. "Where did you hear that? Because that has to be disinformation from industry, Peter. There is *no question* sea levels are rising around the world. It's been scientifically demonstrated time and again. Why, just the other day I was looking at the satellite measurements of sea level, which are a relatively new way to make those measurements. The satellites show a rise of several millimeters, just in the last year."

"Was that published data?" Evans said.

"I don't remember offhand," Drake said, giving him an odd look. "It was in one of the briefing summaries I get."

Evans hadn't planned to ask questions like these. They had just somehow come out of his mouth, unbidden. And he was uncomfortably aware that his tone was skeptical. No wonder Drake was giving him an odd look.

"I don't mean anything," Evans said quickly. "It's just that I heard these rumors . . ."

"And you wanted to get to the bottom of it," Drake said, nodding. "As is only natural. I'm glad you brought this to my attention, Peter. I'll get on the horn with Henley and find out what's being disseminated. Of course it's an endless battle. You know we have those Neanderthals at the Competitive Enterprise Institute, and the Hoover Foundation, and the

Marshall Institute to deal with. Groups financed by right-wing radicals and brain-dead fundamentalists. But, unfortunately, they have a tremendous amount of money at their disposal."

"Yes, I understand," Evans said. He turned to go. "Do you need me for anything else?"

"I'll be frank," Drake said, "I'm not happy. Are we back to fifty thousand a week?"

"Under the circumstances, I think we have no option."

"Then we will have to manage," Drake said. "The lawsuit's going fine, by the way. But I have to focus my energies on the conference."

"Oh, right. When does that start?"

"Wednesday," Drake said. "Four days from now. Now, if you'll excuse me . . ."

"Of course," Evans said. He walked out of the office, leaving his cell phone on the side table across from the desk.

Evans had gone all the way down the stairs to the ground floor before he realized Drake hadn't asked him about his stitches. Everyone else he had seen that day had made some comment about them, but not Drake.

Of course, Drake had a lot on his mind, with the preparations for the conference. Directly ahead, Evans saw the ground-floor conference room bustling with activity. The banner on the wall read, ABRUPT CLIMATE CHANGE—THE CATASTROPHE AHEAD. Twenty young people clustered around a large table, on which stood a scale model of the interior of an auditorium, and the surrounding parking lot. Evans paused to watch for a moment.

One of the young people was putting wooden blocks in the parking lot, to simulate cars.

"He won't like that," another one said. "He wants the slots nearest the building reserved for news vans, not buses."

"I left three spaces over here for news," the first kid said. "Isn't that enough?"

"He wants ten."

"Ten spaces? How many news crews does he think are going to show up for this thing?"

"I don't know, but he wants ten spaces and he's told us to arrange extra power and phone lines."

"For an academic conference on abrupt climate change? I don't get it. How much can you say about hurricanes and droughts? He'll be lucky to have three crews."

"Hey, he's the boss. Mark off the ten slots and be done with it."

"That means the buses have to go way in the back."

"Ten slots, Jake."

"Okay, okay."

"Next to the building, because the line feeds are very expensive. The auditorium's charging us an arm and a leg for the extra utilities."

At the other end of the table, a girl was saying, "How dark will it be in the exhibition spaces? Will it be dark enough to project video?"

"No, they're limited to flat panels."

"Some of the exhibitors have all-in-one projectors."

"Oh, that should be all right."

A young woman came up to Evans as he was standing looking into the room. "Can I help you, sir?" She looked like a receptionist. She had that bland prettiness.

"Yes," he said, nodding toward the conference room. "I was wondering how I arrange to attend this conference."

"It's by invitation only, I'm afraid," she said. "It's an academic conference, not really open to the public."

"I've just left Nick Drake's office," Evans said, "and I forgot to ask him—"

"Oh. Well, actually, I have some comp tickets at the reception desk. Do you know which day you'll be attending?"

"All of them," Evans said.

"That's quite a commitment," she said, smiling. "If you'll come this way, sir . . ."

• • •

It was only a short drive from NERF to the conference headquarters, in downtown Santa Monica. Workmen on a cherry picker were placing letters on the large sign: so far it said, ABRUPT CLIMATE CHA, and beneath, THE CATASTR.

His car was hot in the midday sun. Evans called Sarah on the car phone. "It's done. I left my phone in his office."

"Okay. I was hoping you'd call earlier. I don't think that matters anymore."

"No? Why?"

"I think Kenner already found out what he needed."

"He did?"

"Here, talk to him."

Evans thought, she's with him?

"Kenner speaking."

"It's Peter," he said.

"Where are you?"

"In Santa Monica."

"Go back to your apartment and pack some hiking clothes. Then wait there."

"For what?"

"Change all the clothes you are wearing now. Take nothing with you that you are wearing right now."

"Why?"

"Later."

Click. The phone was dead.

Back in his apartment, he hastily packed a bag. Then he went back to the living room. While he waited, he put the DVD back into the player and waited for the menu of dates.

He chose the second date on the list.

On the screen, he once again saw Drake and Henley. It must have been the same day, because they were dressed in the same clothes. But now it was later. Drake had his jacket off, hung over a chair.

"I've listened to you before," Drake was saying. He sounded resentful. "And your advice didn't work."

"Think structurally," Henley said, leaning back in his chair, staring up at the ceiling, fingertips tented.

"What the hell does that mean?" Drake said.

"Think structurally, Nicholas. In terms of how information functions. What it holds up, what holds it up."

"This is just PR bullshit."

"Nicholas," Henley said, sharply. "I am trying to help you."

"Sorry." Drake looked chastened. He hung his head a little.

Watching the video, Evans thought: *Is Henley in charge here?* For a moment, it certainly appeared that way.

"Now then," Henley said. "Let me explain how you are going to solve your problem. The solution is simple. You have already told me—"

There was a loud pounding on Evans's door. Evans stopped the DVD, and just to be safe, removed it from the player and slipped it into his pocket. The pounding continued, impatient, as he went to the door.

It was Sanjong Thapa. He looked grim.

"We have to leave," he said. "Right now."

V

SNAKE

DIABLO
SUNDAY, OCTOBER 10
2:43 P.M.

The helicopter thumped over the Arizona desert, twenty miles east of Flagstaff, not far from Canyon Diablo. In the back seat, Sanjong handed Evans pictures and computer printouts. Speaking of the Environmental Liberation Front, he said, "We assume their networks are up, but so are ours. All our networks are running," he said, "and we picked up an unexpected clue from one of them. Of all things, the Southwestern Parks Management Association."

"Which is?"

"It's an organization of state park managers from all the western states. And they discovered that something very odd had happened." A large percentage of the state parks in Utah, Arizona, and New Mexico were booked in advance, and paid for, to reserve them for company picnics, school celebrations, institutional birthday parties, and so on, for this weekend. In each case they were family affairs, involving parents and kids, sometimes grandparents, too.

True, this was a long three-day weekend. But nearly all the advance bookings were for Monday. Only a handful had been for Saturday or Sunday. None of the park superintendents could remember such a thing happening before.

"I don't get it," Evans said.

"They didn't either," Sanjong said. "They thought it might be some cult thing, and because the parks can't be used for religious purposes, they got on the phone and called some of the organizations. And they found in every case that the organization had received a special donation to fund the function on this particular weekend."

"Donation from whom?"

"Charitable organizations. In every case the situation was the same. They'd receive a letter saying 'Thank you for your recent request for funding. We are pleased to say we can support your get-together at such-and-such park on Monday, October eleventh. The check has already been sent in your name. Enjoy your gathering.' "

"But the groups never requested the booking?"

"No. So they'd call the charity, and someone would tell them it must have been a mixup, but since the checks were already sent out, they might as well go ahead and use the park that day. And a lot of the groups decided they would."

"And these charitable organizations were?"

"None you ever heard of. The Amy Rossiter Fund. The Fund for a New America. The Roger V. and Eleanor T. Malkin Foundation. The Joiner Memorial Foundation. All together, about a dozen charities."

"Real charities?"

Sanjong shrugged. "We assume not. But we're checking that now."

Evans said, "I still don't get it."

"Somebody wants those parks used this weekend."

"Yes, but why?"

Sanjong handed him a photograph. It was an aerial shot in false colors, and it showed a forest, the trees bright red against a dark blue ground. Sanjong tapped the center of the picture. There, in a clearing in the forest, Evans saw what looked like a spiderweb on the ground—a series of concentric lines connecting fixed points. Like a spiderweb.

"And that is?"

"It's a rocket array. The launchers are the fixed points. The lines are the power cables to control the launch." His finger moved across the picture. "And you see, there's another array here. And a third one here. The three arrays form a triangle, approximately five miles on each side."

Evans could see it. Three separate spiderwebs, set in clearings in the forest.

"Three rocket arrays . . ."

"Yes. We know they have purchased five hundred solid-state rockets. The rockets themselves are quite small. Close analysis of the picture elements indicates that the launchers are four to six inches in diameter, which means the rockets are capable of going up about a thousand feet or so. Not more than that. Each array has about fifty rockets, wired together. Probably not set to fire at the same time. And you notice the launchers are placed quite far apart . . ."

"But for what purpose?" Evans said. "These things are out in the middle of nowhere. They shoot up a thousand feet, and then fall back down? Is that it? What's the point of that?"

"We don't know," Sanjong said. "But we have another clue. The picture you're holding in your hands was taken yesterday. But here is a picture from a flyby this morning." He handed Evans a second picture, showing the same terrain.

The spiderwebs were gone.

"What happened?" Evans said.

"They packed up and left. You see in the first picture, there are vans parked at the edge of the clearings. Apparently, they just put everything in the vans and moved."

"Because they were spotted?"

"It's unlikely they know they were spotted."

"Then what?"

"We think they had to move to a more favorable setting."

"More favorable for what?" Evans said. "What's going on?"

"It may be significant," Sanjong said, "that at the time they purchased the rockets, they also purchased a hundred and fifty kilometers of microfilament wire."

He was nodding to Evans, as if that was supposed to explain everything.

"A hundred and fifty kilometers . . ."

Sanjong flicked his eyes toward the helicopter pilot, and shook his head. "We can go into it in greater detail later on, Peter."

And then he looked out the window.

Evans stared out the opposite window. He saw mile after mile of eroded desert landscape, cliffs brown with streaks of orange and red. The helicopter rumbled northward. He could see the helicopter's shadow racing over the sand. Distorted, twisted, then recognizable again.

Rockets, he thought. Sanjong had given him this information as if he were supposed to figure it out on his own. Five hundred rockets. Groups of fifty launchers, set widely apart. One hundred and fifty kilometers of microfilament wire.

Perhaps that was supposed to mean something, but Peter Evans didn't have the faintest idea what it could possibly be. Groups of small rockets, for what?

Microfilament, for what?

In his head, it was easy enough to calculate that if this microfilament was attached to the rockets, each rocket would have about a third of a kilometer of wire. And a third of a kilometer was . . . roughly a thousand feet.

Which was how high Sanjong said the rockets could go, anyway.

So these rockets were flying a thousand feet into the air, dragging a microfilament wire behind them? What was the point of that? Or was the wire intended to be used to retrieve them, later on? But no, he thought, that couldn't be. The rockets would fall back into the forest, and any microfilament would snap.

And why were the rockets spaced widely apart? If they were only a few inches in diameter, couldn't they be packed closer together?

He seemed to recall that the military had rocket launchers where the rockets were so close together the fins almost touched. So why should these rockets be far apart?

A rocket flies up . . . dragging a thin wire . . . and it gets to a thousand feet . . . and . . .

And what?

Perhaps, he thought, there was some instrumentation in the nose of each rocket. The wire was a way to transmit information back to the ground. But what instrumentation?

What was the point of all this?

He glanced back at Sanjong, who was now hunched over another photograph.

"What're you doing?"

"Trying to figure out where they've gone."

Evans frowned as he saw the picture in Sanjong's hand. It was a satellite weather map.

Sanjong was holding a weather map.

Did all this have to do with weather?

"Yes," Kenner said, leaning forward in the booth of the restaurant. They were in the back of a steakhouse in Flagstaff. The jukebox at the bar was playing old Elvis Presley: "Don't Be Cruel." Kenner and Sarah had showed up just a few minutes before. Sarah, Evans thought, looked drawn and worried. Not her usual cheerful self.

"We think this is all about the weather," Kenner was saying. "In fact, we're sure it is." He paused while a waitress brought salads, then continued. "There are two reasons to think so. First, ELF has bought a considerable amount of expensive technology that seems to have no use in common, except perhaps attempts to influence the weather. And second, the—"

"Hold on, hold on," Evans said. "You said attempts to influence the weather?"

"Exactly."

"Influence how?"

"Control it," Sanjong said.

Evans leaned back in the booth. "This is crazy," he said. "I mean, you're telling me these guys think they can control the weather?"

"They can," Sarah said.

"But how?" Evans said. "How could they do it?"

"Most of the research is classified."

"Then how do they get it?"

"Good question," Kenner said. "And we'd like to know that answer. But the point is, we assume that these rocket arrays are designed to produce major storms, or to amplify the power of existing storms."

"By doing what?"

"They cause a change in the electric potentials of the infra-cumulus strata."

"I'm glad I asked," Evans said. "That's very clear."

"We don't really know the details," Kenner said, "although I'm sure we'll find out soon enough."

"The strongest evidence," Sanjong said, "comes from the pattern of park rentals. These guys have arranged for lots of picnics over a large area—three states, in point of fact. Which means they are probably going to decide at the last minute where to act, based on existing weather conditions."

"Decide what?" Evans said. "What are they going to do?"

Nobody spoke.

Evans looked from one to another.

"Well?"

"We know one thing," Kenner said. "They want it documented. Because if there's one thing you can count on at a school picnic or a company outing with families and kids, it's lots of cameras. Lots of video, lots of stills."

"And then of course the news crews will come," Sanjong said.

"They will? Why?"

"Blood draws cameras," Kenner said.

"You mean they're going to hurt people?"

"I think it's clear," Kenner said, "that they're going to try."

An hour later they all sat on lumpy motel beds while Sanjong hooked a portable DVD player to the television set in the room. They were in a crappy motel room in Shoshone, Arizona, twenty miles north of Flagstaff.

On the screen, Evans once again saw Henley talking to Drake.

"I've listened to you before," Drake said resentfully. "And it didn't work."

"Think structurally," Henley answered. He was leaning back in his chair, staring up at the ceiling, fingertips tented.

"What the hell does that mean?" Drake said.

"Think structurally, Nicholas. In terms of how information functions. What it holds up, what holds it up."

"This is just PR bullshit."

"Nicholas," Henley said, sharply. "I am trying to help you."

"Sorry." Drake looked chastened. He hung his head a little.

Watching the screen, Evans said, "Does it look like Henley is in charge here?"

"He's always been in charge," Kenner said. "Didn't you know that?"

On the screen, Henley was saying, "Let me explain how you are going to solve your problem, Nicholas. The solution is simple. You have already told me that global warming is unsatisfactory because whenever there is a cold snap, people forget about it."

"Yes, I told you—"

"So what you need," Henley said, "is to structure the information so that whatever kind of weather occurs, it always confirms your message. That's the virtue of shifting the focus to abrupt climate change. It enables you to use everything that happens. There will always be floods, and freezing storms, and cyclones, and hurricanes. These events will always get headlines and airtime. And in every instance, you can claim it is an example of abrupt climate change caused by global warming. So the message gets reinforced. The urgency is increased."

"I don't know," Drake said doubtfully. "That's been tried, the last couple of years."

"Yes, on a scattered, individual basis. Isolated politicians, making claims about isolated storms or floods. Clinton did it, Gore did it, that blithering science minister in England did it. But we're not talking about isolated politicians, Nicholas. We are talking about an organized campaign throughout the world to make people understand that global warming is responsible for abrupt and extreme weather events."

Drake was shaking his head. "You know," he said, "how many studies show no increase in extreme weather events."

"Please." Henley snorted. "Disinformation from skeptics."

"That's hard to sell. There are too many studies . . ."

"What are you talking about, Nicholas? It's a snap to sell. The public already believes that industry is behind any contrary view." He sighed. "In any case, I promise you there will soon be more computer models showing that extreme weather *is* increasing. The scientists will get behind this and deliver what is needed. You know that."

Drake paced. He looked unhappy. "But it just doesn't make sense," he said. "It's not logical to say that freezing weather is caused by global warming."

"What's logic got to do with it?" Henley said. "All we need is for the media to report it. After all, most Americans believe that crime in their country is increasing, when it has actually been declining *for twelve years.* The US murder rate is as low as it was in the early 1970s, but Americans are more frightened than ever, because so much more airtime is devoted to crime, they naturally assume there is more in real life, too." Henley sat up in his chair. "Think about what I am saying to you, Nicholas. A twelve-year trend, and they still don't believe it. There is no greater proof that all reality is media reality."

"The Europeans are more sophisticated—"

"Trust me—it'll be even easier to sell abrupt climate change in Europe than in the US. You just do it out of Brussels. Because bureaucrats *get it*, Nicholas. They'll see the advantages of this shift in emphasis."

Drake did not reply. He walked back and forth, hands in his pockets, staring at the floor.

"Just think how far we have come!" Henley said. "Back in the 1970s, all the climate scientists believed an ice age was coming. They thought the world was getting colder. But once the notion of global *warming* was raised, they immediately recognized the advantages. Global warming creates a crisis, a call to action. A crisis needs to be studied, it needs to be funded, it needs political and bureaucratic structures around the world. And in no time at all, a huge number of meteorologists, geologists, oceanographers suddenly became 'climate scientists' engaged in the management of this crisis. This will be the same, Nicholas."

"Abrupt climate change has been discussed before, and it hasn't caught on."

"That's why you are holding a conference," Henley said patiently. "You hold a well-publicized conference and it happens to coincide with some dramatic evidence for the dangers of abrupt climate. And by the end of the conference, you will have established abrupt climate change as a genuine problem."

"I don't know . . ."

"Stop whining. Don't you remember how long it took to establish the global threat of nuclear winter, Nicholas? It took *five days*. On one Saturday in 1983, nobody in the world had ever heard of nuclear winter. Then a big media conference was held and by the following Wednesday the entire world was worried about nuclear winter. It was established as a bona fide threat to the planet. Without a single published scientific paper."

Drake gave a long sigh.

"Five days, Nicholas," Henley said. "They did it. You'll do it. Your conference is going to change the ground rules for climate."

The screen went black.

"My God," Sarah said.

Evans said nothing. He just stared at the screen.

Sanjong had stopped listening some minutes before. He was working with his laptop.

Kenner turned to Evans. "When was that segment recorded?"

"I don't know." Evans slowly came out of his fog. He looked around the room in a daze. "I have no idea when it was recorded. Why?"

"You've got the remote in your hand," Kenner said.

"Oh, sorry." Evans pressed the buttons, brought the menu up, saw the date. "It was two weeks ago."

"So Morton's been bugging Drake's offices for two weeks," Kenner said.

"Looks like it."

Evans watched as the recording ran again, this time with the sound off. He stared at the two men, Drake pacing and worried, Henley just sitting there, sure of himself. Evans was struggling to assimilate what he had heard. The first recording had seemed reasonable enough to him. There, Drake was complaining about the problems of publicizing a genuine environmental threat, global warming, when everybody naturally ceased to care about the topic in the middle of a snowstorm. All that made sense to Evans.

But this conversation . . . He shook his head. This one worried him.

Sanjong clapped his hands together and said, "I got it! I have the location!" He turned his laptop so everyone could see the screen. "This is NEXRAD radar from Flagstaff-Pulliam. You can see the precipitation center forming northeast of Payson. There should be a storm there by midday tomorrow."

"How far is that from us?" Sarah said.

"About ninety miles."

Kenner said, "I think we better get in the helicopter."

"And do what?" Evans said. "It's ten o'clock at night, for God's sake."

"Dress warmly," Kenner said.

The world was green and black, the trees slightly fuzzy through the lenses. The night-vision goggles pressed heavily against his forehead. There was something wrong with the straps: they cut into his ears and were painful. But everybody was wearing them, looking out the windows of the helicopter at the miles of forest below.

They were looking for clearings, and had already passed a dozen or more. Some were inhabited, the houses dark rectangles with glowing windows. In a couple of clearings, the buildings were completely black—ghost towns, abandoned mining communities.

But they hadn't yet found what they were looking for.

"There's one," Sanjong said, pointing.

Evans looked off to his left, and saw a large clearing. The familiar spiderweb pattern of launchers and cables was partially obscured in tall grass. To one side stood a large trailer truck of the size used to deliver groceries to supermarkets. And indeed, in black lettering, he saw "A&P" printed on the side panels.

"Food terrorists," Sarah said. But no one laughed.

And then the clearing had flashed past, the helicopter continuing onward. The pilot had explicit instructions not to slow down or to circle any clearing.

"That was definitely one," Evans said. "Where are we now?"

"Tonto Forest, west of Prescott," the pilot said. "I've marked the coordinates."

Sanjong said, "We should find two more, in a five-mile triangle."

The helicopter thumped onward into the night. It was another hour before they located the remaining spiderwebs, and the helicopter headed home.

The morning was warm and sunny, although dark clouds threatened to the north. At McKinley State Park, the Lincoln Middle School was having its annual outing. There were balloons attached to the picnic tables, the barbecue grills were smoking, and about three hundred kids and their families were playing on the grassy field beside the waterfall, throwing Frisbees and baseballs. More were playing along the banks of the nearby Cavender River, which meandered peacefully through the park. The river was low at the moment, with sandy banks on either side, and small rocky pools where the younger children played.

Kenner and the others were parked to one side, watching.

"When that river overflows," Kenner said, "it'll take out the entire park and everyone in it."

"It's a pretty big park," Evans said. "Will it really overflow that much?"

"Doesn't take much. The water will be muddy and fast moving. Six inches of fast water is enough to knock a person off his feet. Then they slide; it's slippery, they won't be able to get back up again. There're rocks and debris in the water; mud blinds them, they hit things, lose consciousness. Most drownings occur because people try to move across very low water."

"But six inches . . ."

"Muddy water has power," Kenner said. "Six inches of mud will take a car, no problem. Lose traction, sweep it right off the road. Happens all the time."

Evans found this hard to believe, but Kenner was now talking about some famous flood in Colorado, the Big Thompson, where a hundred and forty people died in a matter of minutes. "Cars crushed like beer cans," he said. "People with clothes ripped off their bodies by mud. Don't kid yourself."

"But here," Evans said, pointing to the park. "If the water starts to rise, there will be enough time to get out. . . ."

"Not if it's a flash flood. Nobody here will know until it's too late. That's why we're going to make sure they don't have a flash flood."

He checked his watch, looked up at the darkening sky, and then walked back to the cars. They had three SUVs in a row. Kenner would drive one; Sanjong would drive one; Peter and Sarah would drive the third.

Kenner opened the back door to his car. He said to Peter, "Do you have a gun?"

"No."

"You want one?"

"You think I need one?"

"You might. When was the last time you were on a range?"

"Uh, it's been a while." In truth, Evans had never fired a gun in his life. And until this moment, he was proud of it. He shook his head. "I'm not much of a gun guy."

Kenner had a revolver in his hands. He had opened the round barrel-thing and was checking it. Sanjong was over by his own car, checking an evil-looking rifle, matte black stock with a telescopic sight. His manner was quick, practiced. A soldier. Uneasily, Evans thought: *What is this, the O.K. Corral?*

"We'll be all right," Sarah said to Kenner. "I have a gun."

"You know how to use it?"

"I do."

"What is it?"

"A 9-millimeter Beretta."

Kenner shook his head. "Can you handle a .38?"

"Sure."

He gave her a gun and a holster. She clipped the holster to the waist-band of her jeans. She seemed to know what she was doing.

Evans said, "Do you really expect us to shoot somebody?"

"Not unless you have to," Kenner said. "But you may need to defend yourself."

"You think they'll have guns?"

"They might. Yes."

"Jesus."

"It's okay," Sarah said. "Personally, I'll be happy to shoot the bastards." Her voice was hard, angry.

"All right, then," Kenner said. "That about does it. Let's mount up."

Evans thought, *Mount up*. Jesus. This *was* the O.K. Corral.

Kenner drove to the other side of the park and spoke briefly to a state trooper, whose black-and-white patrol car stood at the edge of a clearing. Kenner had arranged radio contact with the trooper. In fact, they were all going to be in radio contact, because the plan required a high degree of coordination. They would have to hit the three spiderweb sites at the same time.

As Kenner explained it, the rockets were intended to do something called "charge amplification" of the storm. It was an idea from the last ten years, when people first began to study lightning in the field, in actual storms. The old idea was that each lightning strike decreased the storm's intensity, because it reduced the difference in electrical charge between the clouds and the ground. But some researchers had concluded that lightning strikes had the opposite effect—they increased the power of storms dramatically. The mechanism for this was not known, but was presumed to be related to the sudden heat of the lightning bolt, or the shock-wave it created, adding turbulence to the already turbulent storm center. In any case, there was now a theory that if you could make more lightning, the storm would get worse.

"And the spiderwebs?" Evans said.

"They're little rockets with microfilaments attached. They go up a thousand feet into the cloud layer, where the wire provides a low-resistance conduction pathway and creates a lightning strike."

"So the rockets cause more lightning? That's what they're for?"

"Yes. That's the idea."

Evans remained doubtful. "Who pays for all this research?" he said. "The insurance companies?"

Kenner shook his head. "It's all classified," he said.

"You mean it's military?"

"Correct."

"The military pays for weather research?"

"Think about it," Kenner said.

Evans was not inclined to do so. He was deeply skeptical of all things military. The notion that they were paying for weather research struck him as the same sort of ludicrous excess as the six-hundred-dollar toilet seats and thousand-dollar wrenches that had become so notorious. "If you ask me, it's all a waste of money."

"ELF doesn't think so," Kenner said.

It was then that Sanjong spoke, with considerable intensity. Evans had forgotten that he was a soldier. Sanjong said that whoever could control the weather would control the battlefield. It was an age-old military dream. Of course the military would spend money on it.

"You're saying it actually works."

"Yes," Sanjong said. "Why do you think we are here?"

The SUV wound up into the wooded hills north of McKinley Park. This was an area of intermittent dense forest and open grassy fields. In the passenger seat, Sarah looked at Peter. He was good-looking, and he had the strong physique of an athlete. But sometimes he behaved like such a wimp.

"You ever do any sports?" she said.

"Sure."

"What?"

"Squash. A little soccer."

"Oh."

"Hey," he said. "Just because I don't shoot guns . . . I'm a lawyer, for Christ's sake."

She was disappointed with him and not even sure why. Probably, she thought, because she was nervous and wanted somebody competent to be with her. She liked being around Kenner. He was so knowledgeable, so skilled. He knew what was going on. He was quick to respond to any situation.

Whereas Peter was a nice guy, but . . .

She watched his hands on the wheel. He drove well. And that was important today.

It was no longer sunny. They were close to the storm clouds. The day was dark, gloomy, threatening. The road ahead was deserted as it wound through the forests. They hadn't seen a car since they left the park.

"How much farther?" Evans said.

Sarah consulted the GPS. "Looks like another five miles."

He nodded. Sarah shifted in her seat, moving so the holstered gun would not press against her hip. She glanced at the passenger-side mirror.

"Oh shit."

"What?"

Behind them was a battered blue pickup truck. With Arizona plates.

AURORAVILLE
MONDAY, OCTOBER 11
10:22 A.M.

"We've got trouble," Sarah said.

"Why?" Evans said. He glanced in the rearview mirror, saw the truck. "What is it?"

Sarah had the radio in her hand. "Kenner. They spotted us."

"Who did?" Evans said. "Who are they?"

The radio clicked. "Where are you?" Kenner said.

"On Highway 95. We're about four miles away."

"Okay," Kenner said. "Stick with the plan. Do your best."

"Who is it?" Evans said, looking in the mirror.

The blue pickup was advancing fast. Very fast. In the next instant, it banged into the back of their car. Evans was startled, swerved, got control again. "What the *fuck?*" he said.

"Just drive, Peter."

Sarah took the revolver from its holster. She held the gun on her lap, looked out the side mirror.

The blue truck had dropped back for a moment, but now raced forward again.

"Here he comes—"

Perhaps because Peter stepped on the gas, the impact was surprisingly gentle. It was hardly more than a nudge. Peter careened around the curves, glancing at the rearview mirror.

Again, the blue truck dropped back. It followed them for the next half mile, but it was never closer than five or six car lengths.

"I don't get it," Evans said. "Are they going to ram us or not?"

"Guess not," she said. "See what happens if you slow down."

He slowed the SUV, dropping their speed to forty.

The blue truck slowed too, falling back farther.

"They're just following us," she said.

Why?

The first scattered drops of rain spattered the windshield. The road ahead was spotted. But they weren't yet in full rain.

The blue truck dropped even farther back now.

They came around a curve, and immediately ahead of them saw a big silver eighteen-wheeler, with a big trailer. It was rumbling slowly along the road, not going more than thirty miles an hour. On its back doors it said, "A&P."

"Oh shit," Evans said. In the back mirror, they saw the blue truck, still following. "They've got us front and back."

He swerved out, trying to pass the big trailer, but as soon as he did, the driver moved toward the center of the road. Evans immediately fell back.

"We're trapped," he said.

"I don't know," she said. "I don't get it."

The trailer blocked them at the front, but behind them the blue truck was farther back than ever, several hundred yards down the road.

She was still puzzling over this situation when a bolt of lightning crashed down at the side of the road as they drove past. It couldn't have been more than ten yards away, a white-hot, dazzling blast of light and sound. They both jumped.

"Jesus, that was close," Evans said.

"Yes . . ."

"I've never seen one that close."

Before she could answer, a second bolt crashed down, directly in front of them. The sound was explosive; Evans swerved involuntarily, even though the bolt was gone.

"Holy shit."

By then Sarah had a suspicion, just as the third bolt hit the car itself, a deafening crash and a sudden pressure that made knife pains in her ears and a blast of white that enveloped the car. Evans screamed in fear and let go of the wheel; Sarah grabbed it and straightened the car in the road.

A fourth bolt smashed down by the driver's side, just inches from the car. The driver's-side window cracked and splintered.

"Holy shit," Evans was saying. "Holy shit! What is this?"

To Sarah, it was only too obvious.

They were attracting lightning.

The next bolt cracked down, and was immediately followed by another, which smashed into the hood and spread burning white, jagged fingers over the car, and then was gone. There was a huge black indentation in the hood.

"I can't do this," Evans was saying. "I can't, I can't do this."

"Drive, Peter," Sarah said, grabbing his arm and squeezing hard. *"Drive."*

Two more bolts hit them, in rapid succession. Sarah smelled the odor of something burning—she wasn't sure what. But now she understood why they had been so gently rammed.

The blue pickup had stuck something onto their car. Some kind of electronic thing. And it was drawing the lightning to them.

"What do we do? What do we do?" Evans was whimpering. He howled as each new bolt struck.

But they were trapped, driving on a narrow road, hemmed in by dense pine forest on both sides of the road . . .

Something she should know.

Forest . . . What about the forest?

A lightning bolt cracked the rear window with explosive force. Another bolt struck them so hard it bounced the car on the macadam, as if it had been hit by a hammer.

"The hell with this," Evans said, and spun the wheel, turning off the highway and onto a dirt track in the forest. Sarah saw a sign flash by, the name of a town on a battered post. They were plunged into near darkness under the huge, green pines. But the lightning immediately stopped.

Of course, she thought. *The trees.*

Even if their car was attracting lightning, it would strike the taller trees first.

A moment later, it did. They heard a sharp crack just behind them, and lightning flashed down the side of a tall pine, splitting the trunk open with what looked like steam and bursting the tree into flames.

"We're going to start a forest fire."

"I don't care," Evans said. He was driving fast. The vehicle was bouncing over the dirt road, but it was an SUV and it rode high so Sarah knew they would be all right.

Looking back, she saw the tree burning, and the fire spreading laterally in fingers along the ground.

Kenner on the radio: "Sarah, what's happening?"

"We had to leave the road. We're being struck by lightning."

"A lot!" Evans yelled. "All the time!"

"Find the attractor," Kenner said.

"I think it's attached to the car," Sarah said. As she spoke, a bolt smashed down on the road just ahead of them. The glare was so bright she saw green streaks before her eyes.

"Then dump the car," Kenner said. "Go out as low as you can."

He clicked off. Evans continued to race forward, the SUV bouncing on the ruts. "I don't want to leave," he said. "I think we're safer inside. They always say don't leave your car because you're safer inside. The rubber tires insulate you."

"But something's on fire," she said, sniffing.

The car jolted and bounced. Sarah tried to keep her balance, just holding onto her seat, not touching the metal of the doors.

"I don't care, I think we should stay," Evans said.

"The gas tank might explode . . ."

"I don't want to leave," he said. "I'm not leaving." His knuckles were white, gripping the wheel. Ahead, Sarah saw a clearing in the forest. It was a large clearing, with high, yellow grass.

A lightning bolt smashed down with a fearsome crack, shattering the side mirror, which blew apart like a bomb. A moment later, they heard a soft *whump*. The car tilted to one side. "Oh shit," Evans said. "It blew a tire."

"So much for the insulation," she said.

The car was now grinding, the underside scraping over a dirt rut, metal squealing.

"Peter," she said.

"All right, all right, just let me get to the clearing."

"I don't think we can wait."

But the rut ended, the road flattened, and Evans drove forward, creaking on the rim, into the clearing. Raindrops spattered the windshield. Above the grass, Sarah saw the roofs of wooden buildings bleached by the sun. It took her a moment to realize that this was a ghost town. Or a mining town.

Directly ahead was a sign, AURORAVILLE, POP. 82. Another lightning bolt crashed down, and Evans hit the sign, knocking it over.

"Peter, I think we're here."

"Okay, yeah, let me get a little closer—"

"*Now, Peter!*"

He stopped the car, and they flung open their doors in unison. Sarah threw herself bodily onto the ground, and another bolt crashed so close to her that the blast of hot air knocked her sideways and sent her rolling on the ground. The roar of the lightning was deafening.

She got up on hands and knees, and scrambled around to the back of the vehicle. Evans was on the other side of the SUV, yelling something, but she couldn't hear him. She examined the rear bumper. There was no attachment, no device.

There was nothing there.

But she had no time to think, because another bolt struck the back of the SUV, rocking it, and the rear window shattered, sprinkling her with shards of glass. She fought panic and scrambled forward, staying low as she moved around the SUV and through the grass toward the nearest building.

Evans was somewhere ahead, yelling to her. But she couldn't hear him over the rumbling thunder. She just didn't want another bolt, not now, if she could just go a few more seconds . . .

Her hands touched wood. A board.

A step.

She crawled forward quickly, pushing aside the grass, and now she saw a porch, a dilapidated building, and swinging from the roof a sign bleached so gray she couldn't see what it said. Evans was inside, and she scrambled forward, ignoring the splinters in her hands, and he was yelling, yelling.

And she finally heard what he was saying:

"Look out for the scorpions!"

They were all over the wooden porch—tiny, pale yellow, with their stingers in the air. There must have been two dozen. They moved surprisingly fast, scampering sideways, like crabs.

"Stand up!"

She got to her feet, and ran, feeling the arachnids crunch under her feet. Another lightning bolt smashed into the building's roof, knocking down the sign, which fell in a cloud of dust onto the porch.

But then she was inside the building. And Evans was standing there, fists raised, yelling, "Yes! Yes! We did it!"

She was gasping for breath. "At least they weren't snakes," she said, chest heaving.

Evans said, "What?"

"There're always rattlers in these old buildings."

"Oh Jesus."

Outside, thunder rumbled.

And the lightning started again.

Through the shattered, grimy window Sarah was looking at the SUV, and thinking that now that they had left the car, there were no more lightning strikes on the SUV . . . thinking . . . nothing on the bumper . . . then why had the pickup nudged the SUV? What was the point? She turned to ask Evans if he had noticed—

And a lightning bolt blasted straight down through the roof, smashing it open to the dark sky, sending boards flying in all directions, and blasting into the ground right where she had been standing. The lightning left a blackened pattern of jagged streaks, like the shadow of a thorn bush on the floor. The ozone smell was strong. Wisps of smoke drifted up from the dry floorboards.

"This whole building could go," Evans said. He was already flinging a side door open, heading outside.

"Stay low," Sarah said, and followed him out.

The rain was coming down harder, big splattering drops that struck her back and shoulders as she ran to the next building. It had a brick chimney, and looked generally better built. But the windows were the same, broken and thickly coated with dust and grime.

They tried the nearest door, but it was jammed shut, so they ran around to the front, and found that door wide open. Sarah ran inside. A lightning bolt smashed down behind her, sagging the roof over the porch, splintering one of the side posts as it streaked down into the ground. The shockwave blasted the front windows in a shower of dirty glass. Sarah turned away, covering her face, and when she looked out again, she realized she was in a blacksmith's shop. There was a large firepit in the center of the room, and above it all sorts of iron implements hanging from the ceiling.

And on the walls, she saw horseshoes, tongs, metal of all sorts.

This room was full of metal.

The thunder rumbled ominously. "We have to get out of here," Evans shouted. "This is the wrong place to—"

He never finished. The next bolt knocked him off his feet as it came crashing down through the ceiling, spinning the iron implements, then smashing into the firepit, blasting the bricks outward in all directions. Sarah ducked, covering her head and ears, felt bricks striking her shoulders, back, legs—knocking her over—and then there was a burst of pain in her forehead, and she saw brief stars before blackness settled over her and the rumble of thunder faded to endless silence.

FOREST
MONDAY, OCTOBER 11
11:11 A.M.

Kenner was fifteen miles away, driving east on Route 47, listening to Sarah's radio. Her transmitter was still on, clipped to her belt. It was hard to be sure what was happening because each lightning strike produced a burst of static that lasted for the next fifteen seconds. Nevertheless he understood the most important point—Evans and Sarah had gotten away from the SUV, but the lightning hadn't stopped. In fact it seemed that the lightning was following them.

Kenner had been yelling into his handset, trying to get Sarah's attention, but apparently she had turned her volume down, or was too busy dealing with what was happening in the ghost town. He kept saying, "It's following you!" over and over.

But she never answered.

Now there was a long burst of static, followed by silence. Kenner switched channels.

"Sanjong?"

"Yes, Professor."

"Have you been listening?"

"Yes."

"Where are you?" Kenner said.

"I am on Route 190, going north. I estimate I am three miles from the web."

"Any lightning yet?"

"No. But the rain has just started here. First drops on the windshield."

"Okay. Hang on."

He went back to Sarah's channel. There was still static, but it was fading.

"Sarah! Are you there? Sarah! Sarah!"

Kenner heard a cough, a distant cough.

"Sarah!"

A click. A bang. Someone fumbling with the radio. A cough. "This is Peter. Evans."

"What's happening there?"

"—dead."

"What?"

"She's dead. Sarah's dead. She got hit with a brick, and she fell and then there was a lightning strike that hit her full on the body and she's dead. I'm right here beside her. She's dead, oh shit, she's dead . . ."

"Try mouth-to-mouth."

"I'm telling you, she's dead."

"Peter. *Mouth-to-mouth.*"

"Oh God . . . She's *blue* . . ."

"That means she's alive, Peter."

"—like a corpse, a—corpse—"

"Peter, listen to me."

But Evans wasn't hearing anything. The idiot had his finger on the radio button. Kenner swore in frustration. And then suddenly a new blast of static. Kenner knew what it meant.

There had been another lightning strike. A bad one.

"Sanjong?"

Now, Kenner heard nothing but static on Sanjong's channel, too. It lasted ten seconds, fifteen seconds. So Sanjong had a strike, too. Only then did Kenner realize what must be causing it.

Sanjong came back, coughing.

"Are you all right?"

"I had a lightning strike. Very near the car. I cannot imagine, so close."

"Sanjong," Kenner said. "I think it's the radios."

"You think?"

"Where'd we get them?"

"I had them FedExed from DC."

"Package delivered to you personally?"

"No. To the motel. The owner gave it to me when I checked in . . . But the box was sealed . . ."

"Throw your radio away," Kenner said.

"There's no cellular net, we won't be in communic—"

Nothing more. Just a blast of static.

"Peter."

There was no answer. Only silence on the radio. Not even static now.

"Peter. Answer me. Peter. Are you there?"

Nothing. Dead.

Kenner waited a few moments. There was no answer from Evans.

The first drops of rain splashed on Kenner's windshield. He rolled down his window, and threw his radio away. It bounced on the pavement, and went into the grass on the other side of the road.

Kenner had gone another hundred yards down the road when a bolt of lightning crashed down behind him on the opposite side of the road.

It was the radios, all right.

Somebody had gotten to the radios. In DC? Or in Arizona? It was hard to know for sure, and at this point it didn't matter. Their carefully coordinated plan was now impossible to carry out. The situation was suddenly very dangerous. They had planned to hit all three rocket arrays at the same time. That would not happen now. Of course Kenner could still hit his array. If Sanjong was still alive, he might get to the second array, but their attack would not be coordinated. If one of them were later than the other, the second rocket team would have been informed by radio, and would be waiting with guns ready. Kenner had no doubt about that.

And Sarah and Evans were either dead or unable to function. Their car was broken down. Certainly they would never make it to the third array.

So. Just one rocket array taken out. Maybe two.

Would that be enough?

Maybe, he thought.

Kenner looked at the road ahead, a pale strip under dark skies. He did not think about whether his friends were alive or not. Perhaps all three were dead. But if Kenner did not stop the storm, there would be hundreds dead. Children, families. Paper plates in the mud, while the searchers dug out the bodies.

Somehow he had to stop it.

He drove forward, into the storm.

MCKINLEY
MONDAY, OCTOBER 11
11:29 A.M.

"Mommy! Mommy! Brad hit me! Mommy! Make him stop!"

"All right, kids . . ."

"Bradley? How many times do I have to tell you? Leave your sister alone!"

Standing to one side of McKinley Park, Trooper Miguel Rodriguez of the Arizona Highway Patrol stood by his car and watched the picnic in progress. It was now eleven-thirty in the morning, and the kids were getting hungry. They were starting to fight. All around the park, barbecues were going, the smoke rising into an ever-darkening sky. Some of the parents looked upward with concern, but nobody was leaving the park. And the rain hadn't started here, even though they had heard the crack of lightning and the rumble of thunder a few miles to the north.

Rodriguez glanced at the bullhorn resting on the seat of his car. For the last half hour, he had waited impatiently for the radio call from Agent Kenner, telling him to clear the park.

But the call hadn't yet come.

And Agent Kenner had given him explicit instructions. Do not clear McKinley Park before he was given the word.

Trooper Rodriguez didn't understand why it was necessary to wait, but Kenner had been insistent. He said it was a matter of national security. Rodriguez didn't understand that either. How was a damn picnic in a park a matter of national security?

But he knew an order when he heard one. So Rodriguez waited, impatient and uneasy, and watched the sky. Even when he heard the weather service announce a flash flood advisory for the eastern counties from Kayenta to Two Guns and Camp Payson—an area that included McKinley—Rodriguez still waited.

He could not know that the radio call he was waiting for would never come.

In retrospect, what saved Peter Evans was the slight tingling he had felt, holding the radio in his sweating palm. In the minutes before, Evans had realized that something was causing the lightning to follow them wherever they went. He didn't know any science, but assumed it must be something metallic or electronic. Talking to Kenner, he had felt the faint electric tingle from the handset—and on an impulse he had flung it across the room. It landed against a large iron viselike contraption that looked like a bear trap.

The lightning crashed down a moment later, glaring white and roaring, and Evans threw himself flat, across Sarah's dead body. Lying there, dizzy with fear, his ears ringing from the blast, he thought for a moment that he felt some movement from her body beneath him.

He got up quickly and began to cough. The room was full of smoke. The opposite wall was on fire, the flames still small, but already licking up the wall. He looked back at Sarah, blue and cold. There was no question in his mind that she was dead. He must have imagined her movement, but—

He pinched her nose and began to give her mouth-to-mouth. Her lips were cold. It frightened him. He was sure she was dead. He saw hot embers and ash floating in the smoky air. He would have to leave before the entire building came down around him. He was losing his count, blowing into her lungs.

There was no point anyway. He heard the flames crackling around him. He looked up and saw that the ceiling timbers were starting to burn.

He felt panic. He jumped to his feet, ran to the door, and threw it open and went outside.

He was stunned to feel hard rain coming down—pelting him, soaking him instantly. It shocked him to his senses. He looked back and saw Sarah lying on the floor. He couldn't leave her.

He ran back, grabbed both her arms, and dragged her out of the house. Her inert body was surprisingly heavy. Her head sagged back, eyes closed, her mouth hanging open. She was dead, all right.

Out in the rain once more, he dropped her in the yellow grass, got down on his knees, and gave her more mouth-to-mouth. He was not sure how long he kept up his steady rhythm. One minute, two minutes. Maybe five. It was clearly pointless, but he continued long past any reason, because in a strange way the rhythm relieved his own sense of panic, it gave him something to concentrate on. He was out there in the middle of a pelting downpour with a ghost town in flames around him anyway, and—

Sarah retched. Her body rose up suddenly, and he released her in astonishment. She had a spasm of dry heaves, and then fell into a fit of coughing.

"Sarah . . ."

She groaned. She rolled over. He grabbed her in his arms, and held her. She was breathing. But her eyes fluttered wildly. She didn't seem to be conscious.

"Sarah, come on . . ."

She was coughing, her body shaking. He wondered if she was choking to death.

"Sarah . . ."

She shook her head, as if to clear it. She opened her eyes and stared at him. "Oh man," she said. "Do I have a *headache*."

He thought he was going to cry.

. . .

Sanjong glanced at his watch. The rain was coming down harder now, the wipers flicking back and forth. It was very dark, and he had turned on his headlights.

He had thrown his radio away many minutes before, and the lightning had stopped around his car. But it was continuing elsewhere—he heard the rumble of distant thunder. Checking the GPS, he realized he was only a few hundred yards from the spiderweb he was meant to disrupt.

He scanned the road ahead, looking for the turnoff. That was when he saw the first cluster of rockets firing skyward, like black birds streaking straight up into the dark and roiling clouds.

And in a moment, a cluster of lightning bolts came blasting downward, carried on the wires.

Ten miles to the north, Kenner saw the rocket array fire upward from the third spiderweb. He guessed there were only about fifty rockets in that array, which meant there were another hundred still on the ground.

He came to the side road, turned right, and came instantly into a clearing. There was a large eighteen-wheeler parked to one side. There were two men in yellow rain slickers standing beside the cab. One of them held a box in his hands—the firing device.

Kenner didn't hesitate. He spun the wheel of the SUV and drove right for the cab. The men were stunned for a moment, and at the last moment jumped aside just as Kenner scraped along the side of the cab, screeching metal, and then turned into the rocket field itself.

In his rearview mirror he saw the men scrambling up, but by now he was within the spiderweb array, driving along the line of wires, trying to crush the launch tubes under his wheels. As he hit them he could hear: *Thunk! Thunk! Thunk!* He hoped that would disrupt the firing pattern, but he was wrong.

Directly ahead, he saw another fifty rockets spout flames, and rush upward into the sky.

• • •

Sanjong was inside the second clearing. He saw a wooden cabin off to the right, and a large truck parked beside it. There were lights in the cabin, and he saw shapes moving in the windows. There were men in there. Wires came out from the front door of the cabin and disappeared in the grass.

He drove straight for the cabin, and he pushed the cruise control on the steering wheel.

From the front door he saw one man come out, cradling a machine gun. Flame spurted from the barrel and Sanjong's windshield shattered. He threw open his door and jumped out of the SUV, holding his rifle away from his body, then landing and rolling in the grass.

He looked up just in time to see the SUV smash into the cabin. There was a lot of smoke and shouting. Sanjong was only about twenty yards away. He waited. After a moment, the man with the machine gun came running around to the side of the SUV, to look for the driver. He was shouting excitedly.

Sanjong fired once. The man fell backward.

He waited. A second man came out, yelling in the rain. He saw the fallen man, and jumped back, huddling behind the front bumper of the SUV. He leaned forward and called to the fallen man.

Sanjong shot at him. The man disappeared, but Sanjong was not certain he had hit him.

He had to change position now. The rain had matted down the grass, so there was not as much cover as he would have liked. He rolled quickly, moving laterally about ten yards, and then crawled forward cautiously, trying to get a view into the cabin. But the car had smashed in the front door, and the lights inside were now out. He was sure there were more men in the cabin but he did not see anyone now. The shouting had stopped. There was just the rumble of thunder and the patter of rain.

He strained, listening. He heard the crackle of radios. And voices.

There were still men in the cabin.

He waited in the grass.

• • •

Rain dripped in Evans's eyes as he spun the wrench, tightening the lug nuts on the front wheel of the SUV. The spare tire was now securely in place. He wiped his eyes, and then briefly tightened each lug nut in turn. Just to be sure. It was a rough road going back to the main highway, and now with this rain it would be muddy. He didn't want the wheel coming loose.

Sarah was waiting for him in the passenger seat. He had half-dragged, half-carried her back to the vehicle. She was still dazed, out of it, so he was surprised to hear her shouting something over the sound of the rain.

Evans looked up.

He saw headlights, in the distance. On the far side of the clearing.

He squinted.

It was the blue pickup truck.

"Peter!"

He dropped the lug wrench and ran for the driver's side. Sarah had already started the engine. He got behind the wheel and put the SUV in gear. The blue truck was gaining on them, coming across the clearing.

"Let's go," Sarah said.

Evans stepped on the gas, turned, and drove into the forest— heading back the way they had come. Behind them, the burning building had been put out by the rain. It was now a smoldering wreck, hissing clouds of steam.

The blue pickup drove past the building without a pause. And came down the road after them.

Kenner turned, and came back toward the eighteen-wheeler. The men were standing there, holding the firing box. One had a pistol out, and began firing at Kenner. Kenner accelerated hard, driving straight at them. He hit the man with the pistol. His body was thrown into the air, over the top of the SUV. The second man had somehow gotten away. Kenner spun the wheel.

As he came back he saw the man he had hit staggering to his feet in the grass. The other man was nowhere to be seen. The staggering man raised his gun just as Kenner hit him again. He went down, and the SUV bounced over his body. Kenner was looking for the other man—the man with the firing box.

He didn't see him anywhere.

He spun the wheel. There was only one place the man could have gone.

Kenner drove straight for the truck.

Sanjong was waiting in the grass when he heard the sound of a truck engine. His view was blocked by his own crashed SUV. The truck was behind the SUV. He heard someone put it into gear, backing up.

Sanjong got to his feet and began to run. A bullet whined past him. He dropped to the ground again.

They had left someone in the house.

He stayed low in the grass, and crawled forward, heading for the truck. Bullets snapped in the grass all around him. Somehow they had his position, even in the grass. That meant . . .

He twisted, turning to face the house. He wiped the rain out of his eyes and looked through the sights of his rifle.

The guy was on the roof of the cabin. Barely visible, except when he rose up to fire.

Sanjong fired just below the roofline. He knew the bullet would pass right through the wood. He didn't see the man again. But the man's rifle slid down the roof as Sanjong watched.

He got to his feet and ran toward the truck, but it was already driving away, heading out from the clearing, a pair of red taillights in the rain, disappearing onto the main road.

Kenner was out of his SUV, and on the ground. He could see the last guy, a silhouette under the big eighteen-wheeler.

"Don't shoot me, don't shoot me!" the guy was yelling.

"Come out slowly, with your hands empty," Kenner shouted. "I want to see your hands."

"Just don't shoot . . ."

"Come out. Real slow and—"

A sudden burst of machine gun fire. The wet grass around him snapped.

Kenner pressed his face into the wet earth, and waited.

"Go faster!" Sarah said, looking over her shoulder.

Their SUV bounced in the mud, headlights jumping wildly.

"I don't think I can . . ." Evans said.

"They're gaining!" she said. "You have to go faster!"

They were almost out of the forest. Evans could see the highway just a few dozen yards ahead. He remembered that the last section of the dirt track was less eroded, and he accelerated, heading there.

And came out onto the highway, going south.

"What are you doing?" Sarah said. "We have to go to the rocket field."

"It's too late now," he said. "We're going back to the park."

"But we promised Kenner—"

"It's too late," he said. "Look at the storm. It's already full blown. We have to get back to help those families in the park."

He turned the windshield wipers on full force, and raced down the road in the storm.

Behind them, the pickup truck turned and followed them.

Trooper Miguel Rodriguez had been watching the waterfall. An hour ago, it had been a clear mist, coming over the cliff's edge. Now it was tinged with brown, and it had more volume. The river, too, was starting to rise. It was flowing faster, and beginning to turn a muddy brown.

But it was still not raining at the park. The air had turned distinctly humid, and there had been scattered raindrops for a few minutes, but then the rain had stopped. A few families had abandoned their barbecues. A half-dozen more were packing up their cars in anticipation of the coming storm. But most had chosen to ignore it. The school principal was walking among the picnickers, telling people the weather would pass, urging everyone to stay.

Rodriguez was edgy. He tugged at his uniform collar, uncomfortable in the dampness. He paced back and forth beside his open car door. He heard the police radio announce flash flood warnings for Clayton County, which was where McKinley Park was located. He didn't want to wait any longer, but still he hesitated.

He couldn't understand why Kenner hadn't called him. The park was located in a canyon, and there was every sign of a potential flash flood. Rodriguez had lived in northern Arizona his whole life. He knew he should clear the park now.

Why hadn't Kenner called?

He drummed his fingers on the door of the car.

He decided to give it five more minutes.

Five minutes. No more.

What worried him most at the moment was the waterfall. The brown tinge had put people off, and most of the crowd had moved away. But a few teenagers were still playing in the pool at the base of the fall. Rodriguez knew that rocks could come over the cliff any minute now. Even small rocks would have enough force to kill a person at the bottom.

Rodriguez was thinking about clearing the waterfall area when he noticed something strange. Up at the top of the cliff, where the water came over the lip, he saw a van with an antenna. It looked like a TV station van. There was no lettering on the side, but there was a logo of some kind. Still he couldn't make it out from this distance. He saw a cameraman get out of the van and take a position by the waterfall, crouching down with a camera mounted on his shoulder and looking down into the park. A woman in a skirt and blouse stood by his side, pointing in this direction and that. Apparently telling him where to film, because he was turning the camera where she pointed.

It was definitely a news crew.

He thought: *A news crew for a school picnic?*

Rodriguez squinted, trying to identify the van's logo. It was yellow and blue, sort of swirly interlocking circles. He didn't recognize it as one of the local stations. But there was something distinctly creepy about this crew, coming here right as the storm was descending on the park. He decided he'd better walk over and have a talk with them.

Kenner didn't want to kill the guy now huddled beneath the semi. No member of ELF had ever been captured, and this one seemed a likely candidate. Kenner could tell from the sound of the guy's voice that he was scared. And he sounded young, maybe in his twenties. Probably he was shaken by the death of his friend. Certainly he couldn't handle a machine gun very well.

Now this guy was afraid he was going to die, too. Maybe he was having second thoughts about his cause.

"Come out now," Kenner yelled to him. "Come out, and everything will be all right."

"Fuck you," the guy said. "Who the fuck are you, anyway? What is your fucking problem? Don't you get it, man? We're trying to save the planet."

"You're breaking the law," Kenner said.

"The *law*," the guy said contemptuously. "The law's owned by the corporations that pollute the environment and destroy human life."

"The only one killing people is you," Kenner said. Thunder was rumbling and lightning flickered dimly behind the inky clouds. It was absurd to be having this conversation in the middle of a storm.

But it was worth it to get the guy alive.

"Hey, I'm not killing anyone," the guy said. "Not even you."

"You're killing little kids," Kenner said, "in the park. You're killing families on a picnic."

"Casualties are inevitable in accomplishing social change. History tells us that."

Kenner wasn't sure whether the guy believed what he was saying, had been fed it at college, or was just distracted by fear. Then again, maybe it was meant to be a distraction . . .

He looked to his right, beneath his own vehicle. And he saw a pair of feet moving around the SUV and heading toward him.

Ah hell, he thought. It was disappointing. He aimed carefully and shot once, hitting the man behind the SUV in the ankle. The guy screamed in pain and went down on his back. Kenner could see him under the car. He wasn't young, maybe forty or forty-five. Bearded. He carried a machine gun, and he was rolling over to shoot—

Kenner fired twice. The man's head jerked back. He dropped the machine gun and did not move, his body sprawled awkwardly in the grass.

The man under the semi began to fire his own machine gun. The bullets were flying wildly. Kenner heard several *thunk* into his SUV. Kenner lay in the grass, head down.

When the shooting stopped, he yelled, "Last chance!"

"Fuck you!"

Kenner waited. There was a long pause. He listened to the sound of the rain. It was coming down very hard, now.

He waited.

The guy yelled, "Did you hear me, you fucking asshole?"

"I heard you," Kenner said, and shot once.

It was a real desert downpour, Evans thought, gripping the steering wheel. The rain was coming down in dense sheets. Even with the windshield wipers going as fast as they could, he found it almost impossible to see the road ahead. He had dropped his speed to fifty, then forty. Now he was down to thirty. The pickup truck behind them had slowed, too. There was no real choice.

He passed one or two other cars, but they were all pulled over to the side of the road. It was the sensible thing to do.

The pavement was awash in water, and whenever the pavement dipped a little, it formed a lake, or a rushing rivulet. Sometimes he could not tell how deep the water was, and he didn't want to soak his ignition. He gunned the engine to keep it dry.

He didn't see any road signs. It was almost as dark as night out there, and he had his headlights on, but they seemed to make no difference. He could see only a few yards ahead through the rain.

He looked over at Sarah, but she was just staring forward. Not moving, not speaking. He wondered if she was all right.

Looking in the rearview mirror, he could sometimes see the lights of the pickup truck following him, and sometimes not. There was that much rain.

"I think we're almost to the park," he said. "But I can't be sure."

The interior of the windshield was starting to fog up. He rubbed it with the back of his arm and his elbow, making a squeaking sound on the glass. Now he could see a little better. They were at the top of a gentle hill, heading down toward—

"Oh shit."

"What?" Sarah said.

"Look."

At the bottom of the hill was a fifteen-foot culvert, the road passing over a series of large pipes carrying water from a small stream. Earlier, the stream had been little more than a silvery trickle in a rocky bed. But it had broadened and risen so that it now flowed over the surface of the road, the water moving swiftly.

Evans couldn't tell how deep it was. Probably not very deep.

"Peter," Sarah said. "You've stopped the car."

"I know."

"You can't stop."

"I don't know if I can go through this," he said. "I don't know how deep—"

Six inches of water is enough to carry away a car.

"You've got no choice."

In his rearview mirror, he saw the lights of the pickup truck. He headed down the hill, toward the culvert. He kept his eyes on the mirror, waiting to see what the truck did. It had slowed as well, but it was still following as he drove the SUV down the hill.

"Keep your fingers crossed," Evans said.

"I've got everything crossed."

He entered the water. It was whooshing up on the sides of the car, spraying up as high as the windows, and gurgling under the floorboards. He was terrified that he would lose the ignition, but so far, so good.

He gave a sigh. He was approaching the middle now, and it wasn't that deep. No more than two, two and a half feet. He would make it okay.

"Peter . . ." Sarah pointed ahead.

There was a large eighteen-wheeler coming down the road toward them. Its lights were flaring. It wasn't slowing down at all.

"He's an idiot," Evans said.

Moving slowly in the water, he turned right, moving farther toward his side of the road, to make room.

In response, the truck moved directly into his lane.

It did not slow down.

Then he saw the logo above the cab.

It said in red letters, "A&P."

"Peter, *do something!*"

"Like *what?*"

"*Do something!*"

Several tons of roaring steel were coming right at him. He glanced in the rearview mirror. The blue pickup truck was still behind him, closing in.

They had him front and back.

They were going to drive him off the road.

The semi was in deeper water now, roaring forward. The water plumed high on both sides.

"*Peterrrrr!*"

There wasn't any choice.

He spun the wheel and drove off the road, plunging into the water of the rushing stream.

The SUV nosed down, and water came over the hood, up to the windshield, and for a moment he thought they were going to sink right there. Then the bumper crunched against the rocks of the streambed, and the wheels gained purchase, and the car straightened.

For a thrilling moment he thought he was going to be able to drive the car along the streambed—the river wasn't that deep, not really—but almost at once, the engine died, and he felt the rear end pull loose and spin around.

And they were carried helplessly along in the river.

Evans turned the ignition, trying to start the engine again, but it wasn't working. The SUV moved gently, rocking and bumping against rocks. Occasionally it would stop, and he considered getting out, but then it would begin to float downstream again.

He looked over his shoulder. The road was surprisingly far back. Now that the engine was out, the car was fogging up quickly. He had to rub all the windows, to see out.

Sarah was silent. Gripping the arms of her seat.

The car came to a stop again, against a rock. "Should we get out?" she said.

"I don't think so," he said. He could feel the car shuddering in the moving water.

"I think we should," she said.

The car started to move again. He tried the ignition, but it would not start up. The alternator whirred and sputtered. Then he remembered.

"Sarah," he said. "Open your window."

"What?"

"Open your window."

"Oh." She flicked the switch. "It doesn't work."

Evans tried his own window on the driver's side. It didn't work, either. The electrical systems were shot.

On a chance, he tried the rear windows. The left window opened smoothly.

"Hey! Success."

Sarah said nothing. She was looking forward. The stream was moving faster, the car picking up speed.

He kept rubbing the fogged windows, trying to see, but it was difficult and suddenly the car gave a sharp jolt, and afterward the movement was different. It went swiftly ahead, turning slowly in circles. The wheels no longer touched rock.

"Where are we? What happened?" Together, they rubbed the windshield frantically to get it clean.

"Oh Jesus," Sarah said, when she saw.

They were in the middle of a rushing river. Muddy brown, and moving fast, standing waves of churning water. There were big tree branches and debris moving swiftly along. The car was going faster and faster every second.

And water was coming in through the floor now. Their feet were wet. Evans knew what that meant.

They were sinking.

"I think we should get out, Peter."

"No." He was looking at the standing waves of churning water. There were rapids, big boulders, sinkholes. Maybe if they had helmets and body protection, they might try to go into the current. But without helmets they would die.

The car tilted to the right, then came back up. But he had the feeling that sooner or later it would roll onto its side and sink. And he had the feeling it would sink fast.

He looked out the window and said, "Does this look familiar? What river is this?"

"Who cares?" Sarah yelled.

And then Evans said, "Look!"

• • •

Trooper Rodriguez saw the SUV bouncing and spinning down the river and immediately hit his car siren. He grabbed the bullhorn and turned to the picnickers.

"Folks, please clear the area! We have a flash flood *now*. Everybody move to higher ground, and do it now!"

He hit the siren again.

"Now, folks! Leave your things for later. *Go now!*"

He looked back at the SUV, but it was already almost out of sight, headed down the river toward the McKinley overpass. And right beyond McKinley overpass was the cliff's edge, a ninety-foot drop.

The car and its occupants wouldn't survive it.

And there was nothing they could do about it.

Evans couldn't think, couldn't plan—it was all he could do to hang on. The SUV rolled and turned in the churning water. The vehicle was sinking lower, and the water now sloshing at knee height was freezing cold, and seemed to make the car more unstable, its movements more unpredictable.

At one point he banged heads with Sarah, who grunted, but she was not saying anything either. Then he banged his head on the door post, saw stars briefly.

Ahead, he saw an overpass, a roadway held up with big concrete stanchions. Each stanchion had caught debris floating downriver; the pylons were now wrapped with a tangled mat of tree branches, burned trunks, old boards, and floating junk, so that there was little room to pass by.

"Sarah," he yelled, "unbuckle your seat belt." His own belt was now under the chilly water. He fumbled with it, as the car rolled.

"I can't," she said. "I can't get it."

He bent to help her.

"What are we going to do?'

"We're going to get out," he said.

The car raced forward, then slammed into a mass of branches. It shuddered in the current, but held position. It clanged against an old refrigerator (*a refrigerator?* Evans thought) that bobbed in the water nearby. The pylon loomed above them. The river was so high, the road overpass was only about ten feet above them.

"We have to get out, Sarah," he said.

"My belt is stuck; I can't."

He bent to help her, plunging his hands into the water, fumbling for the belt. He couldn't see it in the mud. He had to do it by feel.

And he felt the car begin to move.

It was going to break free.

Sanjong was driving furiously along the upper road. He saw Peter and Sarah in their SUV, riding the current toward the bridge. He saw them crash against the pylon, and hold precariously there.

The traffic on the bridge was swarming away from the park, passengers panicking, honking horns, confusion. Sanjong drove across the bridge, and jumped out of his car. He began to run across the bridge, toward the car in the water below.

Evans hung on desperately as the SUV rolled and spun in the churning water. The refrigerator clanged against them, again and again. Branches stuck through the shattered windows, the tips quivering like fingers. Sarah's seat belt was jammed, the latch was crumpled or something. Evans's fingers were numb in the cold. He knew that the car wouldn't stay in position very long. He could feel the current pulling at it, dragging it laterally.

"I can't get it open, Sarah," he said.

The water had risen; it was now almost chest high.

"What do we do?" she said. Her eyes were panicky.

For an instant he didn't know, and then he thought *I'm an idiot* and he threw himself bodily across her, plunged his head underwater, and felt for the door post on her side of the car. He dragged a three-foot length of the seat belt away from the post, and brought his head back up, gasping for air.

"Slide out!" he yelled. "Slide out!"

She understood immediately, putting her hands on his shoulder and shoving as she slithered out from the belt. His head went back under the water, but he could feel her getting free. She moved into the backseat, kicking him in the head as she went.

He was back up above the water, gasping.

"Now climb out!" he yelled.

The car was starting to move. The branches creaking. The refrigerator clanging.

Sarah's athleticism stood her in good stead. She slipped through the rear window, and hung onto the car.

"Go for the branches! Climb!" He was afraid the current would take her if she held onto the car. He was scrambling back into the rear seat, then squeezing himself through the window. The car was pulling loose, trembling at first, then distinctly moving, rolling around the debris pile, and he was still half out the window.

"Peter!" Sarah shouted.

He lunged, throwing himself forward into the branches, scratching his face but feeling his hands close around large branches and he pulled his body clear of the car just as the current ripped it away, dragging it under the bridge.

The car was gone.

He saw Sarah climbing up the debris stack, reaching up for the concrete railing of the roadway. He followed her, shivering from cold and fear. In a few moments, he felt a strong hand reach down and pull him up the rest of the way. He looked up and saw Sanjong grinning at him.

"My friend. You are a lucky one."

Evans came over the railing and toppled onto the ground, gasping, exhausted.

Distantly, he heard the sound of a police siren, and a bullhorn barking orders. He became aware of the traffic on the bridge, the honking horns, the panic.

"Come on," Sarah said, helping him up. "Somebody's going to run over you if you stay here."

Trooper Rodriguez was still getting everybody into their cars, but there was pandemonium in the parking lot and a traffic jam on the bridge. The rain was starting to come down hard. That was making people move faster.

Rodriguez cast a worried eye at the waterfall, noting that it was a darker brown, and flowing more heavily than before. He saw then that the TV crew had gone. The van was no longer atop the cliff. That was odd, he thought. You'd think they'd have stayed to film the emergency exit.

Cars were honking on the bridge, where traffic was stalled. He saw a number of people standing there, looking over the other side. Which could only mean that the SUV had gone over the cliff.

Rodriguez slipped behind the wheel to radio for an ambulance. That was when he heard that an ambulance had already been called to Dos Cabezas, fifteen miles to the north. Apparently a group of hunters had gotten into a drunken argument, and there had been some shooting. Two men were dead and a third was injured. Rodriguez shook his head. Damn guys went out with a rifle and a bottle of bourbon each, and then had to sit around drinking because of the rain, and before you knew it, couple of them were dead. Happened every year. Especially around the holidays.

"I don't see why this is necessary," Sarah said, sitting up in bed. She had electrodes stuck to her chest and legs.

"Please don't move," the nurse said. "We're trying to get a record."

They were in a small, screened-off cubicle in the Flagstaff hospital emergency room. Kenner, Evans, and Sanjong had insisted she come there. They were waiting outside. She could hear them talking softly.

"But I'm twenty-eight years old," Sarah said. "I'm not going to have a heart attack."

"The doctor wants to check your conduction pathways."

"My conduction pathways?" Sarah said. "There's nothing wrong with my conduction pathways."

"Ma'am? Please lie down and don't move."

"But this is—"

"And don't talk."

She lay down. She sighed. She glanced at the monitor, which showed squiggly white lines. "This is ridiculous. There's nothing wrong with my heart."

"No, there doesn't seem to be," the nurse said, nodding to the monitor. "You're very lucky."

Sarah sighed. "So, can I get up now?"

"Yes. And don't you worry yourself about those burn marks," the nurse said. "They'll fade over time."

Sarah said, "What burn marks?"

The nurse pointed to her chest. "They're very superficial."

Sarah sat up and looked down her blouse. She saw the white adhesive tags of the electrodes. But she also saw pale brown streaks, jagged marks that ran across her chest and abdomen. Like zigzags or something—

"What is this?" she said.

"It's from the lightning."

She said, "What?"

"You were struck by lightning," the nurse said.

"What are you talking about?"

The doctor came in, an absurdly young man, prematurely balding. He seemed very busy and preoccupied. He said, "Don't worry about those burn marks, they'll fade in no time at all."

"It's from lightning?"

"Pretty common, actually. Do you know where you are?"

"In Flagstaff hospital."

"Do you know what day it is?"

"Monday."

"That's right. Very good. Look at my finger, please." He held his finger up in front of her face, moved it left and right, up and down. "Follow it. That's good. Thank you. You have a headache?"

"I did," she said. "Not anymore. Are you telling me I was struck by lightning?"

"You sure as heck were," he said, bending to hit her knees with a rubber hammer. "But you're not showing any signs of hypoxia."

"Hypoxia . . ."

"Lack of oxygen. We see that when there's a cardiac arrest."

She said, "What are you talking about?"

"It's normal not to remember," the doctor said. "But according to your friends out there, you arrested and one of them resuscitated you. Said it took four or five minutes."

"You mean I was dead?"

"Would have been, if you hadn't gotten CPR."

"*Peter* resuscitated me?" It had to be Peter, she thought.

"I don't know which one." Now he was tapping her elbows with the hammer. "But you're a very lucky young woman. Around here, we get three, four deaths a year from strikes. And sometimes very serious burns. You're just fine."

"Was it the young guy?" she said. "Peter Evans? Him?"

The doctor shrugged. He said, "When was your last tetanus?"

"I don't understand," Evans said. "On the news report it said they were hunters. A hunting accident or an argument of some kind."

"That's right," Kenner said.

"But you're telling me you guys shot them?" Evans looked from Kenner to Sanjong.

"They shot first," Kenner said.

"Jesus," Evans said. "Three deaths?" He bit his lip.

But in truth, he was feeling a contradictory reaction. He would have expected his native caution to take over—a series of killings, possibly murders, he was an accomplice or at the very least a material witness, he could be tied up in court, disgraced, disbarred. . . . That was the path his mind usually followed. That was what his legal training had emphasized.

But at this moment he felt no anxiety at all. Extremists had been discovered and they had been killed. He was neither surprised nor disturbed by the news. On the contrary, he felt quite satisfied to hear it.

He realized then that his experience in the crevasse had changed him—and changed him permanently. Someone had tried to kill him. He could never have imagined such a thing growing up in suburban Cleveland, or in college, or in law school. He could never have imagined such a thing while living his daily life, going to work at his firm in Los Angeles.

And so he could not have predicted the way that he felt changed by it now. He felt as if he had been physically moved—as if someone had picked him up and shifted him ten feet to one side. He was no longer standing in the same place. But he had also been changed internally. He felt a kind of solid impassivity he had not known before. There were unpleasant realities in the world, and previously he had averted his eyes from them, or changed the subject, or made excuses for what had occurred. He had imagined that this was an acceptable strategy in life—in fact, that it was a more humane strategy. He no longer believed that.

If someone tried to kill you, you did not have the option of averting your eyes or changing the subject. You were forced to deal with that person's behavior. The experience was, in the end, a loss of certain illusions.

The world was not how you wanted it to be.

The world was how it was.

There were bad people in the world. They had to be stopped.

"That's right," Kenner was saying, nodding slowly. "Three deaths. Isn't that right, Sanjong?"

"That's right," Sanjong said.

"Screw 'em," Evans said.

Sanjong nodded.

Kenner said nothing.

The jet flew back to Los Angeles at six o'clock. Sarah sat in the front, staring out the window. She listened to the men in the back. Kenner was talking about what would happen next. The dead men were being ID'd. Their guns and trucks and clothes were being traced. And the television film crew had already been found: it was a truck from KBBD, a cable station in Sedona. They'd gotten an anonymous call saying that the highway patrol had been derelict and had allowed a picnic to proceed despite flash flood warnings, and disaster was probable. That was why they had gone to the park.

Apparently it never occurred to anyone to question why they'd got an anonymous call half an hour before a flash flood warning had been issued from the NEXRAD center. The call had been traced, however. It had been placed from a pay phone in Calgary, Canada.

"That's organization," Kenner said. "They knew the phone number of the station in Arizona before they ever started this thing."

"Why Calgary?" Evans said. "Why from there?"

"That seems to be one primary location for this group," Kenner said.

Sarah looked at the clouds. The jet was above the weather. The sun was setting, a golden band in the west. The view was serene. The events of the day seemed to have occurred months before, years before.

She looked down at her chest and saw the faint brownish markings from the lightning. She'd taken an aspirin, but it was still beginning to hurt slightly, to burn. She felt marked. A marked woman.

She no longer listened to what the men were saying, only to the sound of their voices. She noticed that Evans's voice had lost its boyish hesitancy. He was no longer protesting everything Kenner said. He sounded older somehow, more mature, more solid.

After a while, he came up to sit with her. "You mind company?"

"No." She gestured to a seat.

He dropped into it, wincing slightly. He said, "You feel okay?"

"I'm okay. You?"

"A little sore. Well. Very sore. I think I got banged around in the car."

She nodded, and looked out the window for a while. Then she turned back. "When were you going to tell me?" she said.

"Tell you what?"

"That you saved my life. For the second time."

He shrugged. "I thought you knew."

"I didn't."

She felt angry when she said it. She didn't know why it should make her angry, but it did. Maybe because now she felt a sense of obligation, or . . . or . . . she didn't know what. She just felt angry.

"Sorry," he said.

"Thanks," she said.

"Glad to be of service." He smiled, got up, and went to the back of the plane again.

It was odd, she thought. There was something about him. Some surprising quality she hadn't noticed before.

When she looked out the window again, the sun had set. The golden band was turning richer, and darker.

TO LOS ANGELES
MONDAY, OCTOBER 11
6:25 P.M.

In the back of the plane, Evans drank a martini and stared at the monitor mounted on the wall. They had the satellite linkup of the news station in Phoenix. There were three anchors, two men and a woman, at a curved table. The graphic behind their heads read "Killings in Canyon Country" and apparently referred to the deaths of the men in Flagstaff, but Evans had come in too late to hear the news.

"There's other news from McKinley State Park, where a flash flood warning saved the lives of three hundred schoolchildren on a school picnic. Officer Mike Rodriguez told our own Shelly Stone what happened."

There followed a brief interview with the highway patrol officer, who was suitably laconic. Neither Kenner nor his team was mentioned.

Then there was footage of Evans's overturned SUV, smashed at the bottom of the cliff. Rodriguez explained that fortunately no one was in the car when it was carried away by the floodwater.

Evans gulped his martini.

Then the anchors came back onscreen, and one of the men said, "Flood advisories remain in effect, even though it is unseasonable for this time of year."

"Looks like the weather's changing," the anchorwoman said, tossing her hair.

"Yes, Marla, there is no question the weather is changing. And here, with that story, is our own Johnny Rivera."

They cut to a younger man, apparently the weatherman. "Thanks, Terry. Hi, everybody. If you're a longtime resident of the Grand Canyon State, you've probably noticed that our weather is changing, and scientists have confirmed that what's behind it is our old culprit, global warming. Today's flash flood is just one example of the trouble ahead—more extreme weather conditions, like floods and tornadoes and droughts—all as a result of global warming."

Sanjong nudged Evans, and handed him a sheet of paper. It was a printout of a press release from the NERF website. Sanjong pointed to the text: ". . . scientists agree there will be trouble ahead: more extreme weather events, like floods and tornadoes and drought, all as a result of global warming."

Evans said, "This guy's just reading a press release?"

"That's how they do it, these days," Kenner said. "They don't even bother to change a phrase here and there. They just read the copy outright. And of course, what he's saying is not true."

"Then what's causing the increase in extreme weather around the world?" Evans said.

"There is no increase in extreme weather."

"That's been studied?"

"Repeatedly. The studies show no increase in extreme weather events over the past century. Or in the last fifteen years. And the GCMs don't predict more extreme weather. If anything, global warming theory predicts *less* extreme weather."

"So he's just full of shit?" Evans said.

"Right. And so is the press release."

Onscreen, the weatherman was saying, "—is becoming so bad, that the latest news is—get this—glaciers on Greenland are melting away and will soon vanish entirely. Those glaciers are three miles thick, folks. That's a lotta ice. A new study estimates sea levels will rise twenty feet or more. So, sell that beach property now."

Evans said, "What about that one? It was on the news in LA yesterday."

"I wouldn't call it news," Kenner said. "Scientists at Reading ran computer simulations that suggested that Greenland *might* lose its ice pack in the next thousand years."

"Thousand years?" Evans said.

"*Might.*"

Evans pointed to the television. "He didn't say it could happen a thousand years from now."

"Imagine that," Kenner said. "He left that out."

"But you said it isn't news . . ."

"You tell me," Kenner said. "Do you spend much time worrying about what might happen a thousand years from now?"

"No."

"Think anybody should?"

"No."

"There you are."

When he had finished his drink he suddenly felt sleepy. His body ached; however he shifted in his seat, something hurt—his back, his legs, his hips. He was bruised and exhausted. And a little tipsy.

He closed his eyes, thinking of news reports of events a thousand years in the future.

All reported as if it were up-to-the-minute, important life-and-death news.

A thousand years from now.

His eyes were heavy. His head fell to his chest, then jerked up abruptly as the intercom came on.

"Fasten your seat belts," the captain said. "We are landing in Van Nuys."

All he wanted to do was sleep. But when he landed, he checked his cell phone messages and discovered that he had been missed, to put it mildly:

"Mr. Evans, this is Eleanor in Nicholas Drake's office. You left your cell phone. I have it for you. And Mr. Drake would like to speak to you."

"Peter, it's Jennifer Haynes at John Balder's office. We'd like you to come to the office no later than ten o'clock tomorrow please. It's quite important. Call me if for some reason you can't make it. See you then."

"Peter, call me. It's Margo. I'm out of the hospital."

"Mr. Evans, this is Ron Perry at the Beverly Hills police department. You've missed your four o'clock appointment to dictate a statement. I don't want to issue a warrant for your arrest. Call me. You have the number."

"This is Herb Lowenstein. Where the hell are you? We don't hire junior associates to have them disappear day after day. There is work to be done here. Balder's office has been calling. They want you at the Culver City office tomorrow morning by ten A.M. sharp. My advice is, be there, or start looking for another job."

"Mr. Evans, this is Ron Perry from Beverly Hills police. Please return my call ASAP."

"Peter, call me. Margo."

"Peter, want to get together tonight? It's Janis. Call me."

"Mr. Evans, I have Mr. Drake for you, at the NERF office."

"Peter, it's Lisa in Mr. Lowenstein's office. The police have been calling for you. I thought you would want to know."

"Peter, it's Margo. When I call my lawyer I expect to get a call back. Don't be an asshole. Call me."

"This is Ron Perry from the Beverly Hills police department. If I do not hear from you I will have to ask the judge to issue a warrant for your arrest."

"Evans, it's Herb Lowenstein. You really are a dumb shit. The police are going to issue a warrant for your arrest. Deal with it at once. Members of this firm do not get arrested."

Evans sighed, and hung up.

Sarah said, "Trouble?"

"No. But it doesn't look like I will be getting any sleep for a while."

He called the detective, Ron Perry, and was told that Perry was gone for the day, and would be in court in the morning. His cell phone would be off. Evans left a number for him to call back.

He called Drake, but he was gone for the day.

He called Lowenstein, but he was not in the office.

He called Margo, but she did not answer.

He called Jennifer Haynes and said that he would be there tomorrow, at ten o'clock.

"Dress professionally," she said.

"Why?"

"You're going to be on television."

There were two white camera trucks parked outside the offices of the Vanutu litigation team. Evans went inside and found workmen setting up lights and changing fluorescent light bulbs in the ceiling. Four different video crews were walking around, inspecting different angles. But nobody was shooting yet.

The offices themselves, he noticed, had been considerably transformed. The graphs and charts on the walls were now much more complicated and technical looking. There were huge, blowup photographs of the Pacific nation of Vanutu, as seen from the air and from the ground. Several featured the erosion of the beaches, and houses leaning at an angle, ready to slide into the water. There was a school picture from the Vanutu school, beautiful brown-skinned kids with smiling faces. In the center of the room, there was a three-dimensional model of the main island, specially lit for cameras.

Jennifer was wearing a skirt and blouse and heels. She looked startlingly beautiful in a dark, mysterious way. Evans noticed that everyone was better dressed than at his first visit; all the researchers were now in jackets and ties. The jeans and T-shirts were gone. And there seemed to be a lot more researchers.

"So," Evans said, "what is this about?"

"B-roll," Jennifer said. "We're shooting B-roll for the stations to use as background and cutaways. And of course we're making a video press kit as well."

"But you haven't announced the lawsuit yet."

"That happens this afternoon, here outside the warehouse. Press conference at one P.M. You'll be there, of course?"

"Well, I didn't—"

"I know John Balder wants you there. Representing George Morton."

Evans felt uneasy. This could create a political problem for him at the firm. "There are several attorneys more senior than I who handled George's—"

"Drake specifically asked for you."

"He did?"

"Something about your involvement in getting the papers signed to finance this suit."

So that was it, Evans thought. They were putting him on television so he would not be able later to say anything about the gift of ten million dollars to NERF. No doubt they would stick him in the background for the announcement ceremony, maybe make a brief acknowledgment of his presence. Then Drake would say that the ten million was coming, and unless Evans stood up and contradicted him, his silence would be taken as acquiescence. Later, if he developed any qualms, they could say, But you were there, Evans. Why didn't you speak up then?

"I see," Evans said.

"You look worried."

"I am . . ."

"Let me tell you something," she said. "Don't worry about it."

"But you don't even know—"

"Just listen to me. Don't worry about it." She was looking directly into his eyes.

"Okay . . ."

Of course she meant well, but despite her words, Evans was experiencing an unpleasant, sinking feeling. The police were threatening to issue a warrant for his arrest. The firm was complaining about his absences. Now this effort to force him into silence—by putting him on television.

He said, "Why did you want me here so early?"

"We need you to sit in the hot seat again, as part of our test for jury selection."

"I'm sorry, I can't—"

"Yes. You have to. Same thing as before. Want some coffee?"

"Sure."

"You look tired. Let's get you to hair and makeup."

Half an hour later he was back in the deposition room, at the end of the long table. There was again a crew of eager young scientific types looking down at him.

"Today," Jennifer said, "we would like to consider issues of global warming and land use. Are you familiar with this?"

"Only slightly," Evans said.

Jennifer nodded to one of the researchers at the far end. "Raimundo? Will you give him the background?"

The researcher had a heavy accent, but Evans could follow him. "It is well known," he said, "that changes in land use will cause changes in average ground temperature. Cities are hotter than the surrounding countryside—what is called the 'urban heat island' effect. Croplands are warmer than forested lands, and so on."

"Uh-huh," Evans said. Nodding. He hadn't heard about these land use concepts, but it certainly stood to reason.

Raimundo continued, "A high percentage of weather stations that were out in the countryside forty years ago are now surrounded by concrete and skyscrapers and asphalt and so on. Which makes them register warmer."

"I understand," Evans said. He glanced away, through the glass wall. He saw film crews moving around the warehouse, shooting various things. He hoped the crews wouldn't come in. He didn't want to sound stupid in front of them.

"These facts," Raimundo said, "are well known within the field. So researchers take the raw temperature data from stations near cities and reduce them by some amount to compensate for the urban heat island effect."

Evans said, "And how is this reduction calculated?"

"Different ways, depending on who does it. But most algorithms are based on population size. The larger the population, the greater the reduction."

Evans shrugged. "That sounds like the right way to do it."

"Unfortunately," he said, "it probably isn't. Do you know about Vienna? It was studied by Bohm a few years back. Vienna has had no increase in population since 1950, but it has more than doubled its energy use and increased living space substantially. The urban heat island effect has increased, but the calculated reduction is unchanged, because it only looks at population change."[*]

"So the heating from cities is being underestimated?" Evans said.

"It's worse than that," Jennifer said. "It used to be assumed that urban heating was unimportant because the urban heat island effect was only a fraction of total warming. The planet warmed about .3 degrees Celsius in the last thirty years. Cities are typically assumed to have heated by around .1 degree Celsius."

"Yes? So?"

"So those assumptions are wrong. The Chinese report that Shanghai warmed 1 degree Celsius in the last twenty years alone.[†] That's more than the total global warming of the planet in the last hundred years. And Shanghai is not unique. Houston increased .8 degrees Celsius in the last twelve years.[‡] Cities in South Korea are heating

---

[*] R. Bohm, "Urban bias in temperature time series—a case study for the city of Vienna, Austria," *Climatic Change* 38, (1998): 113–1128. Ian G. McKendry, "Applied Climatology," *Progress in Physical Geography* 27, 4 (2003): 597–606. "Population-based adjustments for the UHI in the USA may be underestimating the urban effect."

[†] L. Chen, et al., 2003, "Characteristics of the heat island effect in Shanghai and its possible mechanism," *Advances in Atmospheric Sciences* 20: 991–1001.

[‡] D. R. Streutker, "Satellite-measured growth of the urban heat island of Houston, Texas," *Remote Sensing of Environment* 85 (2003): 282–289. "Between 1987 and 1999, the mean nighttime surface temperature heat island of Houston increased 0.82 ± 0.10 °C."

rapidly.* Manchester, England, is now 8 degrees warmer than the surrounding countryside.† Even small towns are much hotter than the surrounding areas."

Jennifer reached for her charts. "Anyway," she said, "the point is that the graphs you see are not raw data. They have already been adjusted with fudge factors to compensate for urban heating. But probably not enough."

At that moment, the door opened and one of the four video crews came in, their camera light shining. Without hesitation, Jennifer reached for some charts, and brought them up. She whispered, "B-roll is silent, so we need to be active and provide visuals."

She turned toward the camera and said, "Let me show you some examples of weather station data. Here, for instance, is a record of the average temperature for Pasadena since 1930."‡

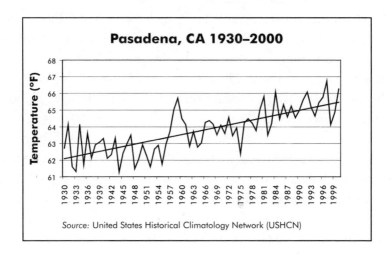

Pasadena, CA 1930–2000

Source: United States Historical Climatology Network (USHCN)

"As you see," Jennifer said, "a dramatic rise in temperature. And here is Berkeley since 1930."

* Y. Choi, H.-S. Jung, K.-Y. Nam, and W.-T. Kwon, "Adjusting urban bias in the regional mean surface temperature series of South Korea, 1968–99," *International Journal of Climatology* 23 (2003): 577–91.
† http://news.bbc.co.uk/1/hi/in_depth/sci_tech/2002/leicester_2002/2253636.stm. The BBC gives no scientific reference for the eight-degree claim.
‡ LA population is 14,531,000; Berkeley is 6,250,000; New York is 19,345,000.

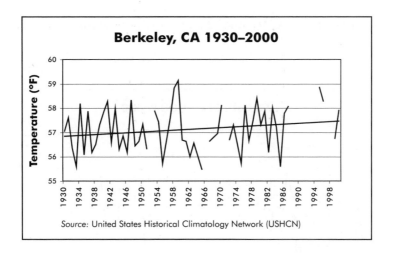

Berkeley, CA 1930–2000

Source: United States Historical Climatology Network (USHCN)

"A surprisingly incomplete record. But we are using raw data, so you can see missing years. And you see a clear warming trend. Indisputable, wouldn't you agree?"

"I would," Evans said, thinking that it wasn't much of a trend—less than a degree.

"Now, here is Death Valley, one of the hottest, driest places on Earth. No urbanization has occurred here. Again, missing years."

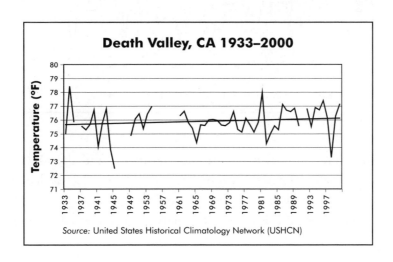

Death Valley, CA 1933–2000

Source: United States Historical Climatology Network (USHCN)

Evans said nothing. It must be an anomaly, he thought. Jennifer put up more graphs:

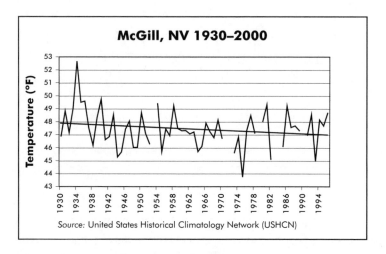

McGill, NV 1930–2000

Source: United States Historical Climatology Network (USHCN)

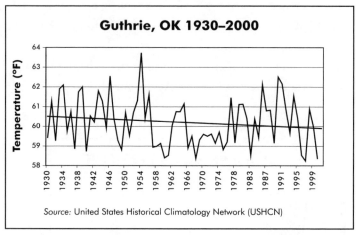

Guthrie, OK 1930–2000

Source: United States Historical Climatology Network (USHCN)

"These are stations from the Nevada desert and the Oklahoma plains," she said. "They show temperatures that are flat, or declining. And not only rural areas. Here is Boulder, Colorado. It's only of interest because NCAR is located there—the National Center for

Atmospheric Research, where so much global warming research is done."

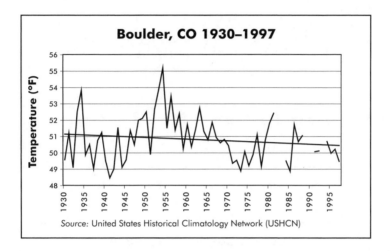

"Here are some more small cities. Truman, Missouri, where the buck stops . . ."

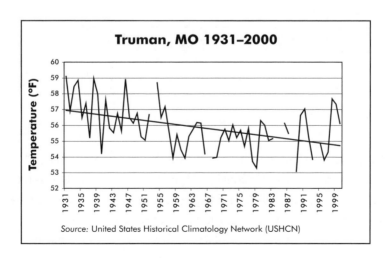

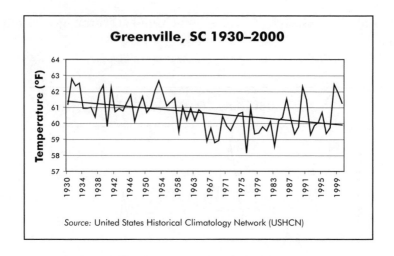

Greenville, SC 1930–2000

Source: United States Historical Climatology Network (USHCN)

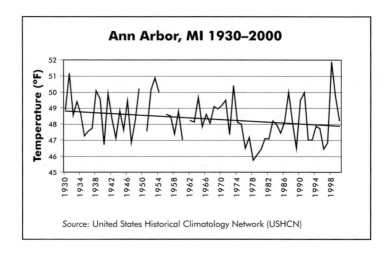

Ann Arbor, MI 1930–2000

Source: United States Historical Climatology Network (USHCN)

Evans said, "Well, you have to admit, it's not very dramatic."

"I'm not sure what you consider dramatic. Truman has gotten colder by 2.5 degrees, Greenville by 1.5 degrees, Ann Arbor by one degree since 1930. If the globe is warming, these places have been left out."

"Let's look at some bigger places," Evans said, "like Charleston."

"I happen to have Charleston." She thumbed through her graphs.

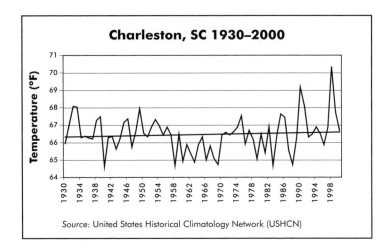

Evans said, "So, a bigger city gets warmer. What about New York?"
"I have several records from New York, city and state."

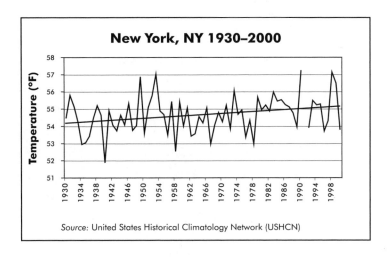

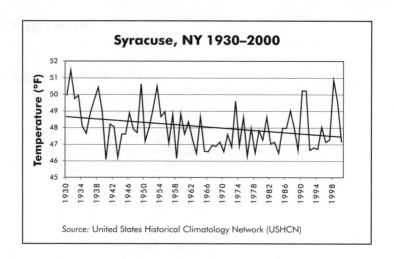

Source: United States Historical Climatology Network (USHCN)

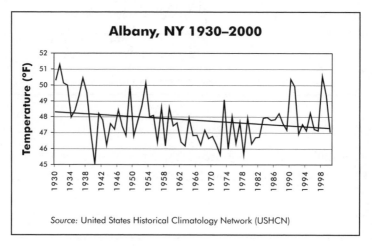

Source: United States Historical Climatology Network (USHCN)

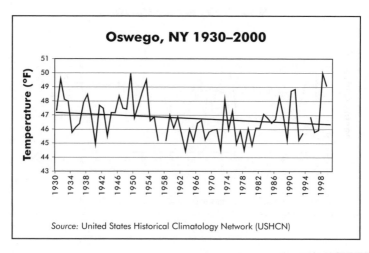

Source: United States Historical Climatology Network (USHCN)

"As you see," Jennifer said, "New York City is warmer, but many other parts of the state, from Oswego to Albany, have become colder since 1930."

Evans was acutely aware of the cameras on him. He nodded in what he hoped was a judicious, thoughtful manner and said, "And where does this data come from?"

"From the Historical Climatology Network data set," she said. "It's a government dataset, maintained at Oak Ridge National Laboratories."

"Well," Evans said. "It's quite interesting. However, I'd like to see the data from Europe and Asia. This is, after all, a global phenomenon."

"Certainly," Jennifer said. She, too, was playing to the cameras. "But before we do that, I'd like your reaction to the data so far. As you can see, many places in the United States do not seem to have become warmer since 1930."

"I'm sure you cherry-picked your data," Evans said.

"To some degree. As we can be sure the defense will do."

"But the results do not surprise me," Evans said. "Weather varies locally. It always has and always will." A thought occurred to him. "By the way, why are all these graphs since 1930? Temperature records go much further back than that."

"Your point is well taken," Jennifer said, nodding. "It definitely makes a difference how far back you go. For example . . ."

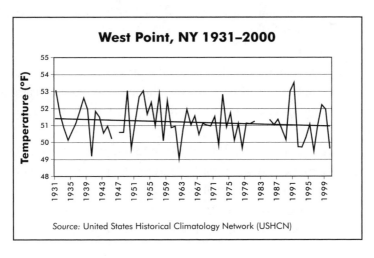

Source: United States Historical Climatology Network (USHCN)

"Here is West Point, New York, from 1931 to 2000. Trending down. And . . ."

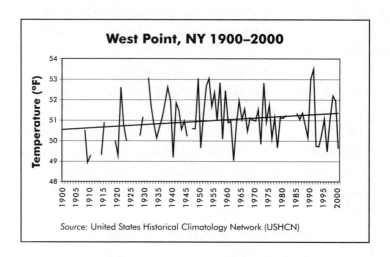

West Point, NY 1900–2000

Source: United States Historical Climatology Network (USHCN)

"Here is West Point from 1900 to 2000. This time the trend is up, not down."

"Ah-ha," Evans said. "So you *were* massaging the data. You picked the interval of years that made you look good!"

"Absolutely," Jennifer said, nodding. "But the trick only works because temperatures in many parts of the US were warmer in the 1930s than they are today."

"It's still a trick."

"Yes, it is. The defense will not miss the opportunity to show the jury numerous examples of this trick from environmental fund-raising literature. Selecting specific years that appear to show things are getting worse."

Evans registered her insult to environmental groups. "In that case," he said, "let's not permit any tricks at all. Use the full and complete temperature record. How far back does it go?"

"At West Point, back to 1826."

"Okay. Then suppose you use that?" Evans felt confident proposing this, because it was well known that a worldwide warming trend had begun at about 1850. Every place in the world had gotten warmer since then, and the graph from West Point would reflect that.

Jennifer seemed to know it too, because she suddenly appeared very hesitant, turning away, thumbing through her stack of graphs, frowning as if she couldn't find it.

"You don't have that particular graph, do you?" Evans said.

"No, no. Believe me, I have it. Yes. Here." And then she pulled it out.

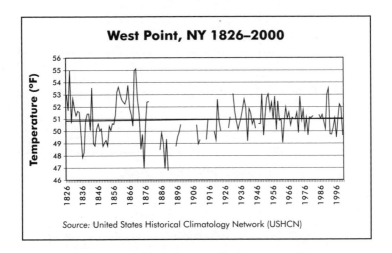

Source: United States Historical Climatology Network (USHCN)

Evans took one look and saw that she had sandbagged him.

"As you predicted, this graph is quite telling," she said. "For the last one hundred seventy-four years, there has been no change in the average temperature at West Point. It was 51 degrees Fahrenheit in 1826, and it is 51 degrees in 2000."

"But that's just one record," Evans said, recovering quickly. "One of many. One of hundreds. Thousands."

"You're saying that other records will show other trends?"

"I'm sure they will. Especially using the *full* record from 1826."

"And you are correct," she said. "Different records do show different trends."

Evans sat back, satisfied with himself. Hands crossed over his chest.

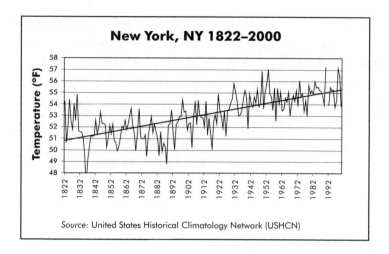

New York, NY 1822–2000

Source: United States Historical Climatology Network (USHCN)

"New York City, a rise of 5 degrees Fahrenheit in a hundred seventy-eight years."

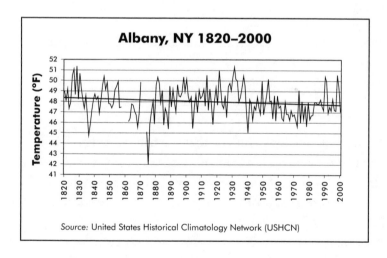

Albany, NY 1820–2000

Source: United States Historical Climatology Network (USHCN)

"Albany, a decline of half a degree in a hundred eighty years."

Evans shrugged. "Local variations, as I said before."

"But I wonder," Jennifer said, "how these local variations fit into a theory of *global* warming. As I understand it, global warming is caused by an increase in so-called greenhouse gases, such as carbon dioxide, that trap heat in the Earth's atmosphere and prevent it from escaping into space. Is that your understanding?"

"Yes," Evans said, grateful he did not have to summon a definition on his own.

"So, according to the theory," Jennifer said, "the atmosphere itself gets warmer, just as it would inside a greenhouse?"

"Yes."

"And these greenhouse gases affect the entire planet."

"Yes."

"And we know that carbon dioxide—the gas we all worry about—has increased the same amount everywhere in the world . . ." She pulled out another graph:*

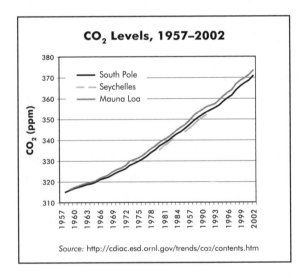

"Yes . . ."

"And its effect is presumably the same everywhere in the world. That's why it's called *global* warming."

* South Pole, Mauna Loa: C. D. Keeling, T. P. Whorf, and the Carbon Dioxide Research Group, Scripps Institute of Oceanography (SIO), University of California, La Jolla, CA 92093, U.S.A.; Seychelles: Thomas J. Conway, Pieter Tans, Lee S. Waterman, National Oceanic and Atmospheric Administration, Climate Monitoring and Diagnostics Laboratory, 325 Broadway, Boulder CO 80303. See http://cdiac.esd.ornl.gov/trends/co2/contents.htm.

"Yes . . ."

"But New York and Albany are only a hundred forty miles apart. You can drive between them in three hours. Their carbon dioxide levels are identical. Yet one got a lot warmer and the other got slightly colder. Is that evidence for *global* warming?"

"Weather is local," Evans said. "Some places are warmer or colder than others. And always will be."

"But we are talking about climate, not weather. Climate is weather over a long time period."

"Yes . . ."

"So I would agree with you if both locations got warmer, albeit by different amounts. But here, one got warmer and one got colder. And as we saw, West Point—which is midway between them—remained unchanged."

Evans said, "I think the theory of global warming predicts that some places will get colder."

"Really? Why is that?"

"I'm not sure, but I read it somewhere."

"The Earth's entire atmosphere warms, and as a result some places get colder?"

"I believe so."

"As you think about it now, does that claim make sense to you?"

"No," Evans said, "but you know, climate is a complex system."

"Which means what, to you?"

"It means it's, uh, complicated. It doesn't always behave the way you think it will."

"That's certainly true," Jennifer said. "But going back to New York and Albany. The fact that these two locations are so close, yet their temperature records are so different, could lead a jury to wonder whether we're really measuring something other than a *global* effect. You would agree that in the last hundred eighty-five years, New York has grown to a city of eight million, whereas Albany has grown much less?"

"Yes," Evans said.

"And we know that the urban heat island effect makes cities hotter than the surrounding countryside."

"Yes . . ."

"And this urban heat effect is a local effect, unrelated to global warming?"

"Yes . . ."

"So, tell me: how do you know that the dramatic increase in temperature in New York is caused by global warming, and not just from an excess of concrete and skyscrapers?"

"Well." Evans hesitated. "I don't know the answer to that. But I assume it is known."

"Because if cities like New York become larger and hotter than they were before, they will raise the average global temperature, will they not?"

"I assume they will."

"In which case, as cities expand all around the world, we might see an increase in average ground temperature simply because of urbanization. Without any global atmospheric effect at all."

"I am sure the scientists have thought of that already," Evans said. "I'm sure they can answer that."

"Yes, they can. Their answer is that they have subtracted a factor from the raw data to compensate for the urban heat effect."

"Well, there you are."

"Excuse me? Mr. Evans, you're a lawyer. Surely you are aware of the extraordinary efforts that are made in a lawsuit to be certain the evidence is untainted."

"Yes, but—"

"You don't want anybody to be able to change it."

"Yes . . ."

"But in this case, the evidence is the raw temperature data. And it is tainted by the very scientists who claim global warming is a worldwide crisis."

"Tainted? It's adjusted *downward*."

"But the question the defense will ask is, have they adjusted downward *enough?*"

"I don't know," Evans said, "this is getting very specialized and nitpicky."

"Hardly. It's a core issue. Urbanization versus greenhouse gases as the cause of the increased average surface temperature. And the defense will have a good argument on their side," Jennifer said. "As I said before, several recent studies suggest the reduction for urban bias has, in fact, been too small.* At least one study suggests that half of the observed temperature change comes from land use alone. If that's true, then global warming in the past century is less than three tenths of a degree. Not exactly a crisis."

Evans said nothing. He tried to look intelligent for the cameras.

"Of course," Jennifer continued, "that study can be debated, too. But the point remains: as soon as anybody adjusts the data, they open themselves to the claim that their adjustment was incorrect. That's better ground for the defense. And the larger point the defense will make is that we have allowed the data to be adjusted by the very people who have the most to gain from that adjustment."

"You're saying that climate scientists are unethical?"

"I'm saying it is never a good policy for the fox to guard the hen house. Such procedures are never allowed in medicine, for example, where double-blind experimental designs are required."

"So you're saying climate scientists *are* unethical."

"No, I'm saying that there are good reasons why double-blind procedures are instituted. Look: Every scientist has some idea of how his experiment is going to turn out. Otherwise he wouldn't do the experiment in the first place. He has an expectation. But expectation works in mysterious ways—and totally unconsciously. Do you know any of the studies of scientific bias?"

"No." Evans shook his head.

"Okay. Simple example. A group of genetically identical rats are sent to two different labs for testing. One lab is told that the rats were bred for intelligence and will run a maze faster than normal. The other lab is told that the rats are dumb and will run a maze slowly. Results come

---

* For a summary, see Ian G. McKendry, 2003, "Applied climatology," *Progress in Physical Geography* 27, 4:597–606. "Recent studies suggest that attempts to remove the 'urban bias' from long-term climate records (and hence identify the magnitude of the enhanced greenhouse effect) may be overly simplistic."

back—faster in one lab, slower in the other. Yet the rats are genetically identical."

"Okay, so they fudged."

"They said they didn't. Anyway, there's much more," she said. "Next example. A group of survey takers are told, Look, we know that pollsters can influence results in subtle ways. We want to avoid that. So you knock on the door, and the minute someone answers you start reading only what is on this card: 'Hello, I am doing a survey, and I am reading from this card in order not to influence you . . . et cetera.' The poll takers say nothing except what is on the card. One group of pollsters is told, this questionnaire will get seventy percent positive answers. They tell another group, you can expect thirty percent positive answers. Identical questionnaires. The results come back—seventy and thirty."

"How?" Evans said.

"It doesn't matter," she said. "All that matters is that hundreds of studies prove again and again that expectations determine outcome. People find what they think they'll find. That's the reason for 'double-blind' experiments. To eliminate bias, the experiment is divided up among different people *who do not know each other.* The people who prepare the experiment do not know the people who conduct the experiment or the people who analyze the results. These groups never communicate in any way. Their spouses and children never meet. The groups are in different universities and preferably in different countries. That's how new drugs are tested. Because that's the only way to prevent bias from creeping in."

"Okay . . ."

"So now we're talking about temperature data. It has to be adjusted in all kinds of ways. Not just for urban heat bias. Lots of other things. Stations move. They upgrade, and the new equipment may read hotter or colder than before. The equipment malfunctions and you have to decide whether to throw out certain data. You deal with lots of judgment calls in putting together the temperature record. And that's where the bias creeps in. Possibly."

"Possibly?"

"You don't know," Jennifer said, "but whenever you have one team doing all the jobs, then you're at risk for bias. If one team makes a model and also tests it and also analyzes the results, those results are at risk. They just are."

"So the temperature data are no good?"

"The temperature data are *suspect*. A decent attorney will tear them apart. To defend them, what we intend to do is—"

Abruptly, the camera crew got up and left the room. Jennifer rested her hand on his arm. "Don't worry about any of that, the footage they shot was without sound. I just wanted it to look like a lively discussion."

"I feel foolish."

"You looked good. That's all that matters for TV."

"No," he said, leaning closer to her. "I mean, when I gave those answers, I wasn't saying what I really think. I'm, uh . . . I'm asking some— I'm changing my mind about a lot of this stuff."

"Really?"

"Yes," he said, speaking quietly. "Those graphs of temperature, for instance. They raise obvious questions about the validity of global warming."

She nodded slowly. Looking at him closely.

He said, "You, too?"

She continued to nod.

They lunched at the same Mexican restaurant as before. It was almost empty, as before; the same Sony film editors laughing at the corner table. They must come here every day, Evans thought.

But somehow everything was different, and not just because his body ached and he was on the verge of falling asleep any moment. Evans felt as if he had become a different person. And their relationship was different, too.

Jennifer ate quietly, not saying much. Evans had the sense she was waiting for him.

After a while, he said, "You know, it would be crazy to imagine that global warming wasn't a real phenomenon."

"Crazy," she said, nodding.

"I mean, the whole world believes it."

"Yes," she said. "The whole world does. But in that war room, we think only about the jury. And the defense will have a field day with the jury."

"You mean, the example you told me?"

"Oh, it's much worse than that. We expect the defense to argue like this: Ladies and gentlemen of the jury, you've all heard the claim that something called 'global warming' is occurring because of an increase in carbon dioxide and other greenhouse gases in the atmosphere. But what you haven't been told is that carbon dioxide has increased by only a tiny amount. They'll show you a graph of increasing carbon dioxide that looks like the slope of Mount Everest. But here's the reality. Carbon dioxide has increased from 316 parts per million to 376 parts per million. *Sixty parts per million* is the total increase. Now, that's such a small change in our entire atmosphere that it is hard to imagine. How can we visualize that?"

Jennifer sat back, swung her hand wide. "Next, they'll bring out a chart showing a football field. And they'll say, Imagine the composition of the Earth's atmosphere as a football field. Most of the atmosphere is nitrogen. So, starting from the goal line, nitrogen takes you all the way to the seventy-eight-yard line. And most of what's left is oxygen. Oxygen takes you to the ninety-nine-yard line. Only one yard to go. But most of what remains is the inert gas argon. Argon brings you within three and a half inches of the goal line. That's pretty much the thickness of the chalk stripe, folks. And how much of that remaining three inches is carbon dioxide? One inch. That's how much CO_2 we have in our atmosphere. One inch in a hundred-yard football field."

She paused dramatically, then continued. "Now, ladies and gentlemen of the jury," she said, "you are told that carbon dioxide has increased in the last fifty years. Do you know how much it has increased, on our football field? It has increased by three-eighths of an inch—less than the thickness of a pencil. It's a lot more carbon dioxide, but it's a minuscule change in our total atmosphere. Yet you are asked to believe that this tiny change has driven the entire planet into a dangerous warming pattern."

Evans said, "But that's easily answered—"

"Wait," she said. "They're not done. First, raise doubts. Then, offer alternative explanations. So, now they take out that temperature chart for New York City that you saw before. A five-degree increase since 1815. And they say, back in 1815 the population of New York was a hundred twenty thousand. Today it's eight million. The city has grown by *six thousand percent.* To say nothing of all those skyscrapers and air-conditioning and concrete. Now, I ask you. Is it reasonable to believe that a city that has grown by six thousand percent is hotter because of a *tiny* increase in little old carbon dioxide around the world? Or is it hotter because it is now much, much bigger?"

She sat back in her chair.

"But it's easy to counter that argument," Evans said. "There are many examples of small things that produce big effects. A trigger represents a small part of a gun, but it's enough to fire it. And anyway, the preponderance of the evidence—"

"Peter," she said, shaking her head. "If you were on the jury and you were asked that question about New York City, what would you conclude? Global warming or too much concrete? What *do* you think, anyway?"

"I think it's probably hotter because it's a big city."

"Right."

"But you still have the sea-level argument."

"Unfortunately," she said, "the sea levels at Vanutu are not significantly elevated. Depending on the database, either they're flat or they've increased by forty millimeters. Half an inch in thirty years. Almost nothing."

"Then you can't possibly win this case," Evans said.

"Exactly," she said. "Although I have to say your trigger argument is a nice one."

"If you can't win," Evans said, "then what is this press conference about?"

• • •

"Thank you all for coming," John Balder said, stepping up to a cluster of microphones outside the offices. Photographers' strobes flashed. "I am John Balder, and standing with me is Nicholas Drake, the president of the National Environmental Resource Fund. Here also is Jennifer Haynes, my lead counsel, and Peter Evans, of the law firm of Hassle and Black. Together we are announcing that we will be filing a lawsuit against the Environmental Protection Agency of the United States on behalf of the island nation of Vanutu, in the Pacific."

Standing in the back, Peter Evans started to bite his lip, then thought better of it. No reason to make a facial expression that might be construed as nervous.

"The impoverished people of Vanutu," Balder said, "stand to become even more impoverished by the greatest environmental threat of our times, global warming, and the danger of abrupt climate changes that will surely follow."

Evans recalled that just a few days before, Drake had called abrupt climate change a possibility on the horizon. Now it had been transformed into a certainty in less than a week.

Balder spoke in vivid terms about how the people of Vanutu were being flooded out of their ancestral homeland, emphasizing the tragedy of young children whose heritage was washing away in raging surf caused by a callous industrial giant to the north.

"It is a matter of justice for the people of Vanutu, and of the future of the entire world now threatened by abrupt weather, that we're announcing this lawsuit today."

Then he opened the floor to questions.

The first one was, "When exactly are you filing this lawsuit?"

"The issue is technically complex," Balder said. "Right now, we have in our offices forty research scientists working on our behalf day and night. When they have finished their labors, we will make our filing for injunctive relief."

"Where will you file?"

"In Los Angeles federal district court."

"What damages are you asking?" another said.

"What is the administration's response?"

"Will the court hear it?"

The questions were coming quickly now, and Balder was in his element. Evans glanced over at Jennifer, standing on the other side of the podium. She tapped her watch. Evans nodded, then looked at his own watch, made a face, and exited the podium. Jennifer was right behind him.

They went inside the warehouse and past the guards.

And Evans stared in amazement.

CULVER CITY
TUESDAY, OCTOBER 12
1:20 P.M.

The lights were turned down. Most of the people Evans had seen earlier were gone. The rooms were being stripped, the furniture stacked up, the documents packed into legal storage boxes. Movers were carrying out stacks of boxes on rolling dollies. Evans said, "What's going on?"

"Our lease is up," Jennifer said.

"So you're moving?"

She shook her head. "No. We're leaving."

"What do you mean?"

"I mean, we're leaving, Peter. Looking for new jobs. This litigation is no longer being actively pursued."

Over a loudspeaker, they heard Balder say, "We fully expect to seek an injunction within the next three months. I have complete confidence in the forty brilliant men and women who are assisting us in this groundbreaking case."

Evans stepped back as movers carried a table past him. It was the same table he had been interviewed at just three hours before. Another mover followed, lugging boxes of video equipment.

"How is this going to work?" Evans said, hearing Balder over the loudspeaker. "I mean, people are going to know what's happening . . ."

"What's happening is perfectly logical," Jennifer said. "We will file a request for a preliminary injunction. Our pleading has to work its way through the system. We expect it will be rejected by the district court for jurisdiction, so we will take it to the Ninth Circuit, and then we expect to go to the Supreme Court. The litigation cannot proceed until the issue of injunction is resolved, which could take several years. Therefore we sensibly put our large research staff on hold and close our expensive offices while we wait with a skeleton legal team in place."

"Is there a skeleton team in place?"

"No. But you asked how it would be handled."

Evans watched as the boxes rolled out the back door. "Nobody ever intended to file this lawsuit, did they?"

"Let's put it this way," she said. "Balder has a remarkable winning record in the courtroom. There's only one way to build a record like that—you dump the losers long before you ever get to trial."

"So he's dumping this one?"

"Yeah. Because I guarantee you, no court is going to grant injunctive relief for excess carbon dioxide production by the American economy." She pointed to the loudspeaker. "Drake got him to emphasize abrupt climate change. That nicely dovetails with Drake's conference, which starts tomorrow."

"Yes, but—"

"Look," she said. "You know as well as I do that the whole purpose of this case was to generate publicity. They've got their press conference. There's no need to pursue it further."

She was asked by movers where to put things. Evans wandered back into the interrogation room and saw the stack of foam core graphs in the corner. He had wanted to see the ones she *hadn't* shown him, so he pulled a few out. They showed foreign weather stations around the world.

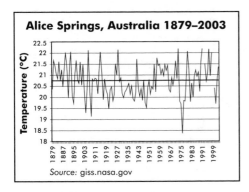

Alice Springs, Australia 1879–2003

Source: giss.nasa.gov

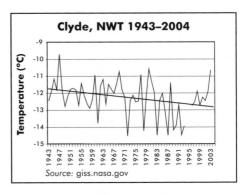

Clyde, NWT 1943–2004

Source: giss.nasa.gov

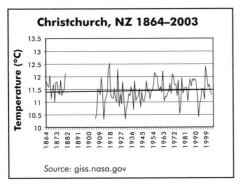

Christchurch, NZ 1864–2003

Source: giss.nasa.gov

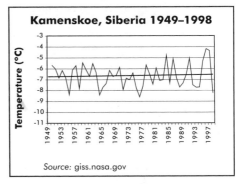

Kamenskoe, Siberia 1949–1998

Source: giss.nasa.gov

Of course, he knew that these particular charts had been chosen to prove the opposition's point. So they showed little or no warming. But still, it troubled him that there should be so many like these, from all around the world.

He saw a stack marked "Europe" and shuffled through them quickly:

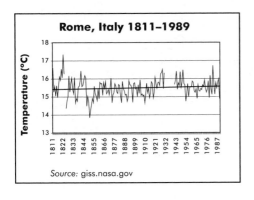

Rome, Italy 1811–1989

Source: giss.nasa.gov

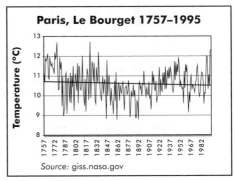

Paris, Le Bourget 1757–1995

Source: giss.nasa.gov

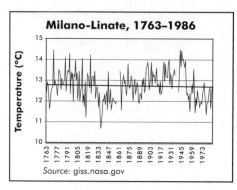

Milano-Linate, 1763–1986

Source: giss.nasa.gov

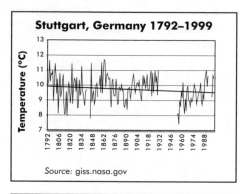

Stuttgart, Germany 1792–1999

Source: giss.nasa.gov

Navacerrada, Spain 1941–2004

Source: giss.nasa.gov

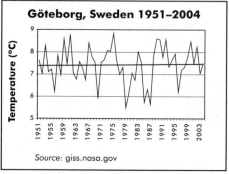

Göteborg, Sweden 1951–2004

Source: giss.nasa.gov

There was another stack marked "Asia." He flipped through it.

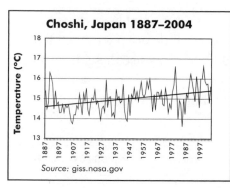

Choshi, Japan 1887–2004

Source: giss.nasa.gov

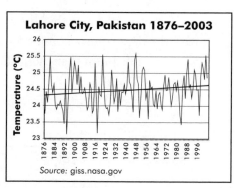

Lahore City, Pakistan 1876–2003

Source: giss.nasa.gov

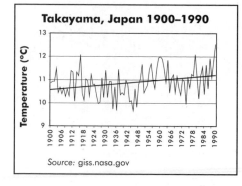

Takayama, Japan 1900–1990

Source: giss.nasa.gov

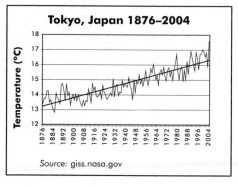

Tokyo, Japan 1876–2004

Source: giss.nasa.gov

"Peter?"

She was calling him.

Her own office was already packed up. She had only a few boxes of things. He helped her carry them out to her car.

"So," he said, "what're you doing now? Going back to DC and your boyfriend?"

"I don't think so," she said.

"Then what?"

"Actually, I thought I'd go with you."

"With me?"

"You're working with John Kenner, aren't you?"

Evans said, "How did you know that?"

She just smiled.

Heading out the back door, they heard the loudspeaker from the conference. Drake was talking now, thanking the press for coming, urging them to attend his forthcoming conference, and saying that the real danger from global warming was its potential for abrupt climate change.

And then he said, "Excuse me, but I regret to say, I have an extremely sad announcement to make. I have just been handed a note that says the body of my dear friend George Morton has just been found."

CULVER CITY
TUESDAY, OCTOBER 12
2:15 P.M.

The full story was on the news that afternoon. The body of millionaire financier George Morton had washed up on the shore near Pismo Beach. The identification was made from clothing and from a watch on the victim's wrist. The body itself was mutilated, the result of shark attacks, the newscaster said.

The family of the philanthropist had been notified, but no date for the memorial service had been set. There was a statement from Morton's close friend Nicholas Drake, director of NERF. Drake said that Morton had devoted his life to the environmental movement and to the work of organizations like NERF, which had just recently named him their Concerned Citizen of the Year.

"If anyone was concerned about the terrible changes that are taking place around our globe, it was George Morton," Drake said. "Ever since we learned he was missing, we have been hoping against hope that he would be found in good spirits and good health. I am saddened to learn that this is not the case. I mourn the loss of my dear and dedicated friend. The world is poorer without him."

Evans was driving when Lowenstein called him on the car phone. "What're you doing?"

"Coming back from the press conference I was ordered to attend."

"Well, you're going to San Francisco."

"Why?"

"Morton's been found. Somebody has to identify the body."

"What about his daughter?"

"She's in rehab."

"What about his ex-wife? What about—"

"Evans, you're officially assigned. Make your arrangements. The forensic guys don't want to delay the autopsy so they need him ID'd before dinner."

"But—"

"Get your ass up there. I don't know what you're bitching about. Take the guy's plane, for Christ's sake. You've certainly been helping yourself to it lately, from what I hear. Now that he's dead you'd better be more careful. Oh, one more thing. Since you're not family, they'll need two people to ID him."

"Well, I can take Sarah, his secretary—"

"No. Drake wants you to take Ted Bradley."

"Why?"

"How the hell do I know? Bradley wants to go. Drake wants to indulge him, keep him happy. Bradley probably thinks there'll be news cameras there. He is an actor, after all. And he was George's close friend."

"Sort of."

"He was at the banquet table with you."

"But Sarah would be—"

"Evans, what part of this do you not understand? You're going to San Francisco and you are taking Bradley with you. Period."

Evans sighed. "Where is he?"

"He's in Sequoia. You have to stop and get him."

"Sequoia?"

"National Park. It's on the way."

"But—"

"Bradley's already been notified. My secretary will give you the number for the San Francisco morgue. Good-bye, Evans. Don't screw up."

Click.

Jennifer said, "Problem?"

"No. But I have to go to San Francisco."

"I'll come with you," she said. "Who is Sarah?"

"Morton's personal secretary. His old assistant."

"I've seen pictures of her," Jennifer said. "She doesn't look very old."

"Where did you see pictures?"

"In a magazine. They were at a tennis tournament. She's a championship tennis player, something like that?"

"I guess."

"I would have thought that since you spent so much time with Morton, you'd know her well."

"Not really," he said, shrugging. "I mean, we've spent a little time in the last few days."

"Uh-huh." She looked at him, amused. "Peter," she said. "I don't care. She's very pretty. It's only natural."

"No, no," he said, reaching for the phone. "It's nothing like that." Desperate to put an end to this conversation, he dialed the Beverly Hills police and asked for Detective Perry. The detective was not yet back from court. Evans left a message and hung up. He turned to Jennifer. "How does it work if they issue a warrant for your arrest?"

"Criminal," she said. "Not my area. Sorry."

"Me neither."

"Somebody going to arrest you?"

"I hope not."

Then Lisa, Herb Lowenstein's chatty assistant, called. "Hi, Peter. I have the numbers for Mr. Bradley and for the San Francisco morgue. They close at eight. Can you make it by then? Herb wants to know. He's very upset."

"About what?"

"I've never seen him this way. I mean, not for a few weeks."

"What's the matter?"

"I think he's upset about George. Such a shock. And then Drake is giving him fits. He must have called five times today. And I think they were discussing you."

"Me?"

"Yes." Lisa lowered her voice, taking on a conspiratorial tone. "Herb had his door closed while he was talking, but I, uh, I heard a few things."

"Like what?" Evans said.

"Don't say anything."

"I won't."

"I mean I wasn't—I just thought that you would want to know."

"I do."

"Because there's a lot of talk here," she said, dropping her voice even lower, "about whether you have to leave."

"Leave the firm?"

"Be, uh, let go. I thought you would want to know."

"I do. Thanks. Who's talking?"

"Well, Herb. And Don Blandings, and a couple of other senior partners. Bob and Louise. Because for some reason Nick Drake is furious with you. And somebody you are spending time with, a person named Kanner or Connor?"

"I see."

"Mr. Drake is very upset about Mr. Connor."

"Why is that?"

"He says he is a spy. For industry. For *polluters*."

"I see."

"Anyway, the feeling is Mr. Drake is an important client and you've pissed him off. Even so, they would never dare fire you if Morton were alive. But he's not, anymore. And you're gone all the time. And the police are calling here for you, which I have to tell you is *not good*. It makes everybody nervous. And then they—what are you doing with this Mr. Connor, anyway?"

"It's a long story."

"Peter. I told *you*." She sounded sulky. He knew he would have to trade information.

"Okay," he said, trying to sound reluctant. "I'm carrying out an assignment that Morton gave me, before he died."

"Really? What is it?"

"It's a secret, I can't tell you yet."

"George Morton gave you an assignment?"

"In writing," he said. Thinking: That will cool their jets.

"Wow. Really. They don't dare fire you if you're on the business of the firm."

"Lisa, I have to go."

"And if they did, you would have *such* a wrongful termination action."

"Lisa . . ."

"Okay, okay. I know you can't talk. But just . . . good luck!"

He hung up. Jennifer was smiling. "That was very skillfully done," she said.

"Thank you."

But he wasn't smiling back. As far as he was concerned, the world was closing in around him. It didn't feel good. And he was still very, very tired.

He called Sarah to arrange for the plane, but got her voice mail. He called the pilot and was told that he was in the air.

"What do you mean?"

"He's flying, right now."

"Where?"

"I can't tell you that, sir. Would you like his voice mail?"

"No," Evans said. "I need to charter a plane."

"When would you like it?"

"In half an hour. To go to San Francisco, with a stop at whatever the airport is nearest Sequoia. Returning tonight."

"I'll see what I can do."

And then fatigue overcame him. He pulled over to the side of the road and got out of the car.

Jennifer said, "What's the matter?"

"You know the way to Van Nuys?"

"Sure."

"Then you drive."

He dropped into the passenger seat and fastened his seat belt. He watched her pull into traffic, and then closed his eyes and slept.

SEQUOIA
TUESDAY, OCTOBER 12
4:30 P.M.

The forest floor was dark and cool. Shafts of sunlight filtered down from the magnificent trees rising all around them. The air smelled of pine. The ground was soft underfoot.

It was a pleasant spot, with sunlight dappling the forest floor, but even so the television cameras had to turn on their lights to film the third-grade schoolchildren who sat in concentric circles around the famous actor and activist Ted Bradley. Bradley was wearing a black T-shirt that set off his makeup and his dark good looks.

"These glorious trees are your birthright," he said, gesturing all around him. "They have been standing here for centuries. Long before you were born, before your parents or your grandparents or your great-grandparents were born. Some of them, before Columbus came to America! Before the Indians came! Before anything! These trees are the oldest living things on the planet; they are the guardians of the Earth; they are wise; and they have a message for us: *Leave the planet alone*. Don't mess with it, or with us. And we must listen to them."

The kids stared open-mouthed, transfixed. The cameras were trained on Bradley.

"But now these magnificent trees—having survived the threat of fire, the threat of logging, the threat of soil erosion, the threat of acid rain—

now face their greatest threat ever. Global warming. You kids know what global warming is, don't you?"

Hands went up all around the circle. "I know, I know!"

"I'm glad you do," Bradley said, gesturing for the kids to put their hands down. The only person talking today would be Ted Bradley. "But you may not know that global warming is going to cause a very sudden change in our climate. Maybe just a few months or years, and it will suddenly be much hotter or much colder. And there will be hordes of insects and diseases that will take down these wonderful trees."

"What kind of insects?" one kid asked.

"Bad ones," Bradley said. "The ones that eat trees, that worm inside them and chew them up." He wiggled his hands, suggesting the worming in progress.

"It would take an insect a long time to eat a whole tree," a girl offered.

"No, it wouldn't!" Bradley said. "That's the trouble. Because global warming means lots and lots of insects will come—a plague of insects— and they'll eat the trees fast!"

Standing to one side, Jennifer leaned close to Evans. "Do you believe this shit?"

Evans yawned. He had slept on the flight up, and had dozed off again in the ride from the airport to this grove in Sequoia National Park. He felt groggy now, looking at Bradley. Groggy and bored.

By now the kids were fidgeting, and Bradley turned squarely to the cameras. He spoke with the easy authority he had mastered while playing the president for so many years on television. "The threat of abrupt climate change," he said, "is so devastating for mankind, and for all life on this planet, that conferences are being convened all around the world to deal with it. There is a conference in Los Angeles starting tomorrow, where scientists will discuss what we can do to mitigate this terrible threat. But if we do nothing, catastrophe looms. And these mighty, magnificent trees will be a memory, a postcard from the past, a snapshot of man's inhumanity to the natural world. We're responsible for catastrophic climate change. And only we can stop it."

He finished, with a slight turn to favor his good side, and a piercing stare from his baby blues, right into the lens.

"I have to pee-pee," one girl said.

The plane lifted off the runway and rose over the forest.

"Sorry to rush you," Evans said. "But we have to get to the morgue before six."

"No problem, no problem." Bradley smiled indulgently. After his talk, he had taken a few minutes to sign autographs for the kids. The cameras filmed that as well. He turned to Jennifer, giving her his best smile. "And what do you do, Miss Hadley?"

"I'm on the global warming legal team."

"Good, so you're one of us. How's the lawsuit going?"

"Just fine," she said, glancing at Evans.

"I get the feeling you're as brilliant as you are beautiful," Bradley said.

"Actually, no," she said. Evans could see that the actor was annoying her.

"You're being modest. It's very charming."

"I'm being honest," she said, "and telling you I don't like flattery."

"Hardly flattery, in your case," he said.

"And hardly honest, in yours," she replied.

"Believe me when I say that I genuinely admire what you're doing," Bradley said. "I can't wait for you people to stick it to the EPA. We have to keep the pressure on. That's why I did this thing with the kids. It's a sure-fire television segment for abrupt climate change. And I thought it went extremely well, didn't you?"

"Reasonably well, considering."

"Considering?"

"That it was all bullshit," Jennifer said.

Bradley's smile remained fixed, but his eyes narrowed. "I'm not sure what you're referring to," he said.

"I'm referring to all of it, Ted. The whole speech. Sequoias are sentinels and guardians of the planet? They have a message for us?"

"Well, they do—"

"They're *trees*, Ted. Big *trees*. They have about as much of a message for mankind as an eggplant."

"I think you are missing—"

"And they've managed to survive forest fires? Hardly—they're *dependent* on fires, because that's how they reproduce. Redwoods have tough seeds that only burst open in the heat of a fire. Fires are essential for the health of the redwood forest."

"I think," Bradley said rather stiffly, "that you may have missed my point."

"Really? What did I miss?"

"I was trying to convey—perhaps a bit lyrically—the timeless quality of these great primeval forests, and—"

"Timeless? Primeval? Do you know anything about these forests?"

"Yes. I think I do." His voice was tight. He was visibly angry now.

"Look out the window," Jennifer said, pointing to the forest as they flew above it. "How long do you think your primeval forest has looked the way it does now?"

"Obviously, for hundreds of thousands of years—"

"Not true, Ted. Human beings were here for many thousands of years before these forests ever appeared. Did you know that?"

He was clenching his jaw. He did not answer.

"Then let me lay it out for you," she said.

Twenty thousand years ago, the Ice Age glaciers receded from California, gouging out Yosemite Valley and other beauty spots as they left. As the ice walls withdrew, they left behind a gunky, damp plain with lots of lakes fed by the melting glaciers, but no vegetation at all. It was basically wet sand.

After a few thousand years, the land dried as the glaciers continued to move farther north. This region of California became arctic tundra, with tall grasses supporting little animals, like mice and squirrels. Human beings had arrived here by then, hunting the small animals and setting fires. "Okay so far?" Jennifer said. "No primeval forests yet."

"I'm listening," Ted growled. He was clearly trying to control his temper.

She continued. "At first, arctic grasses and shrubs were the only plants that could take hold in the barren glacial soil. But when they died they decomposed, and over thousands of years a layer of topsoil built up. And that initiated a sequence of plant colonization that was basically the same everywhere in post-glacial North America.

"First, lodgepole pine comes in. That's around fourteen thousand years ago. Later it's joined by spruce, hemlock, and alder—trees that are hardy but can't be first. These trees constitute the real 'primary' forest, and they dominated this landscape for the next four thousand years. Then the climate changed. It got much warmer, and all the glaciers in California melted. There were no glaciers at all in California back then. It was warm and dry, there were lots of fires, and the primary forest burned. It was replaced by a plains-type vegetation of oak trees and prairie herbs. And a few Douglas fir trees, but not many, because the climate was too dry for fir trees.

"Then, around six thousand years ago, the climate changed again. It became wetter, and the Douglas fir, hemlock, and cedar moved in and took over the land, creating the great closed-canopy forests that you see now. But someone might refer to these fir trees as a pest plant—an oversized weed—that invaded the landscape, crowding out the native plants that had been there before them. Because these big canopy forests made the ground too dark for other trees to survive. And since there were frequent fires, the closed-canopy forests were able to spread like mad. So they're not timeless, Ted. They're merely the last in line."

Bradley snorted. "They're still six thousand years old, for God's sake."

But Jennifer was relentless. "Not true," she said. "Scientists have shown that the forests continuously changed their composition. Each thousand-year period was different from the one before it. The forests changed constantly, Ted. And then, of course, there were the Indians."

"What about them?"

"The Indians were expert observers of the natural world, so they realized that old-growth forests sucked. Those forests may look impressive, but they're dead landscapes for game. So the Indians set fires, making sure the forests burned down periodically. They made sure there were only islands of old-growth forest in the midst of plains and meadows. The forests that the first Europeans saw were hardly primeval. They were *cultivated*, Ted. And it's not surprising that one hundred fifty years ago, there was less old-growth forest than there is today. The Indians were realists. Today, it's all romantic mythology."*

She sat back in her chair.

"Well, that's a very nice speech," Bradley said. "But those are technical objections. People aren't interested. And it's a good thing, because you're saying that these forests aren't really old and therefore aren't worth preserving. Whereas I say they are reminders of the beauty and power of the natural world and should be preserved at all costs. Especially from the dire threat of global warming."

Jennifer blinked. She said, "I need a drink."

"I'll join you there," Bradley said.

For Evans—who had intermittently been attempting to call Detective Perry while this discussion was taking place—the most disturbing aspect was the implication of constant change. Evans had never really focused on the idea that Indians had lived at the same time as the glaciers. Of course, he knew that this was true. He knew that early Indians had hunted the mammoth and other large mammals to extinction. But he had never considered the possibility that they would also have burned forests and changed the environment to suit their purposes.

But of course they had.

Equally disturbing was the image of so many different forests taking over, one after another. Evans had never wondered what had existed before the redwood forests. He, too, had considered them primeval.

---

* Alston Chase, *In a Dark Wood*, p. 157ff. See also p. 404ff.

Nor had he ever thought about the landscape that the glaciers would have left behind. Thinking about it now, he realized that it probably looked like the land he had recently seen in Iceland—cold, wet, rocky, and barren. It stood to reason that generations of plants would have to grow there, building up a layer of topsoil.

But in his mind, he had always imagined a sort of animated movie in which the glaciers receded and redwood trees popped up immediately along the receding edge. The glaciers pulled away leaving redwood forest behind.

He realized now how silly that view had been.

And Evans had also noticed, in passing, how frequently Jennifer had spoken of a changing climate. First it was cold and wet, then it was warm and dry and the glaciers melted, then it was wetter again, and the glaciers came back. Changing, and changing again.

Constant change.

After a while, Bradley excused himself and went to the front of the plane to call his agent. Evans said to Jennifer, "How did you know all that stuff?"

"For the reason Bradley himself mentioned. The 'dire threat of global warming.' We had a whole team researching dire threats. Because we wanted to find everything we could to make our case as impressive as possible."

"And?"

She shook her head. "The threat of global warming," she said, "is essentially nonexistent. Even if it were a real phenomenon, it would probably result in a net benefit to most of the world."

The pilot clicked on the intercom, telling them to take their seats because they were on their final approach to San Francisco.

The anteroom was gray, cold, and smelled of disinfectant. The man behind the desk wore a lab coat. He typed at his keyboard. "Morton . . . Morton . . . Yes. George Morton. Okay. And you are . . ."

"Peter Evans. I'm Mr. Morton's attorney," Evans said.

"And I'm Ted Bradley," Ted said. He started to extend his hand, then thought better of it, pulled it back.

"Oh. Hey," the technician said. "I thought you looked familiar. You're the secretary of state."

"Actually, I'm the president."

"Right, right, the president. I knew I'd seen you before. Your wife is a drunk."

"No, actually, the secretary of state's wife is a drunk."

"Oh. I don't get to see the show that often."

"It's off the air now."

"That explains it."

"But it's in syndication in all the major markets."

Evans said, "If we could make the identification now . . ."

"Okay. Sign here, and I'll get you visitor tags."

Jennifer remained in the anteroom. Evans and Bradley walked into the morgue. Bradley looked back. "Who is she anyway?"

"She's an attorney working on the global warming team."

"I think she's a plant for industry. She's obviously some kind of extremist."

"She works right under Balder, Ted."

"Well, I can understand *that*," Bradley said, snickering. "I'd like her working under me, too. But did you listen to her, for God's sake? Old-growth forests 'suck?' That's industry talking." He leaned closer to Evans. "I think you should get rid of her."

"Get rid of her?"

"She's up to no good. Why is she with us now anyway?"

"I don't know. She wanted to come. Why are you with us, Ted?"

"I have a job to do."

The sheet draping the body was spotted with gray stains. The technician lifted it back.

"Oh Jesus," Ted Bradley said, turning quickly away.

Evans forced himself to gaze at the body. Morton had been a large man in life, and now he was even larger, his torso purple gray and bloated. The odor of decay was strong. Indenting the puffy flesh was an inch-wide ring around one wrist. Evans said, "The watch?"

"Yeah, we took it off," the technician said. "Barely got it over the hand. You need to see it?"

"Yes, I do." Evans leaned closer and stiffened his body against the smell. He wanted to look at the hands and the nails. Morton had had a childhood injury to the fourth nail on his right hand, leaving the nail dented, deformed. But one of the hands of this body was missing, and the other was gnawed and mangled. There was no way he could be sure of what he was seeing.

Behind him, Bradley said, "Are you done yet?"

"Not quite."

"Je-sus, man."

The technician said, "So, will the show go back on the air?"

"No, it's been canceled."

"Why? I liked that show."

"They should have consulted you," Bradley said.

Evans was looking at the chest now, trying to recall the pattern of chest hair that Morton had had. He'd seen him often enough in a bathing suit. But the bloating, the stretching of the skin made it difficult. He shook his head. He could not be sure it was Morton.

"Are you done yet?" Bradley said.

"Yes," Evans said.

The drape went back on, and they walked out. The technician said, "Lifeguards in Pismo made the discovery, called the police. The police ID'd him from the clothes."

"He still had clothes on?"

"Uh-huh. One leg of the pants and most of the jacket. Custom made. They called the tailor in New York and he confirmed that they had been made for George Morton. Will you be taking his effects with you?"

"I don't know," Evans said.

"Well, you're his lawyer . . ."

"Yes, I guess I will."

"You have to sign for them."

They went back outside, where Jennifer was waiting. She was talking on her cell phone. She said, "Yes, I understand. Yes. Okay, we can do that." She flipped the phone shut when she saw them. "Finished?"

"Yes."

"And was it . . ."

"Yes," Ted said. "It was George."

Evans said nothing. He went down the hall and signed for the personal effects. The technician brought out a bag and handed it to Evans. Evans fished in it and pulled out the shreds of the tuxedo. There was a small NERF pin on the inside pocket of the jacket. He reached in and came out with the watch, a Rolex Submariner. It was the same watch Morton wore. Evans looked at the back. It was engraved GM 12–31–89. Evans nodded, put it back in the bag.

All these things belonged to George. Just touching them now made him feel inexpressibly sad.

"I guess that does it," he said. "Time to go."

They all walked back to the waiting car. After they got in, Jennifer said, "We have to make another stop."

"Oh?" Evans said.

"Yes. We have to go to the Oakland Municipal Garage."

"Why?"

"The police are waiting for us."

OAKLAND
TUESDAY, OCTOBER 12
7:22 P.M.

It was an enormous concrete structure, adjacent to a vast parking lot on the outskirts of Oakland. It was lit by harsh halogen lights. Behind the cyclone fence, most of the cars in the lot were junkers, but a few Cadillacs and Bentleys were there, too. Their limousine pulled up to the curb.

"Why are we here?" Bradley said. "I don't understand."

A policeman came to the window. "Mr. Evans? Peter Evans?"

"That's me."

"Come this way, please."

They all started to get out of the car. The cop said, "Just Mr. Evans."

Bradley sputtered, "But we are—"

"Sorry, sir. They just want Mr. Evans. You'll have to wait here."

Jennifer smiled at Bradley. "I'll keep you company."

"Great."

Evans got out of the car and followed the policeman through the metal door into the garage itself. The interior space was divided into long bays, where cars were worked on in a row. Most of the bays seemed to be given over to the repair of police cars. Evans smelled the sharp odor of acetylene torches. He sidestepped patches of motor oil and gobs of grease on the floor. He said to the cop accompanying him, "What's this about?"

"They're waiting for you, sir."

They were heading for the rear of the garage. They passed several crushed and blood-covered wrecks. Seats drenched in blood, shattered windows dark red. Some wrecks had pieces of string that stretched out from them in various directions. One wreck was being measured by a pair of technicians in blue lab coats. Another crash was being photographed by a man with a camera on a tripod.

"Is he a policeman?" Evans said.

"Nah. Lawyer. We have to let 'em in."

"So you deal with car wrecks here?"

"When it's appropriate."

They came around the corner and Evans saw Kenner standing with three plainclothes policemen, and two workers in blue lab coats. They were all standing around the crushed body of Morton's Ferrari Spyder, now raised on a hydraulic lift, with bright lights shining up at it.

"Ah, Peter," Kenner said. "Did you make the identification of George?"

"Yes."

"Good man."

Evans came forward to stand beneath the car. Various sections of the underside had been marked with yellow cloth tags. Evans said, "Okay, what's up?"

The plainclothesmen looked at one another. Then one of them began to speak. "We've been examining this Ferrari, Mr. Evans."

"I see that."

"This is the car that Mr. Morton recently bought in Monterey?"

"I believe so."

"When was that purchase made?"

"I don't know exactly." Evans tried to think back. "Not long ago. Last month or so. His assistant, Sarah, told me George had bought it."

"Who bought it?"

"She did."

"What was your involvement?"

"I had none. She merely informed me that George had bought a car."

"You didn't make the purchase or arrange insurance, anything like that?"

"No. All that would have been done by George's accountants."

"You never saw paperwork on the car?"

"No."

"And when did you first see the actual car itself?"

"The night George drove it away from the Mark Hopkins Hotel," Evans said. "The night he died."

"Did you ever see the car prior to that evening?"

"No."

"Did you hire anyone to work on the car?"

"No."

"The car was transported from Monterey to a private garage in Sonoma, where it remained for two weeks, before being taken to San Francisco. Did you arrange the private garage?"

"No."

"The rental was in your name."

Evans shook his head. "I don't know anything about that," he said. "But Morton often put rentals and leases in the name of his accountants or attorneys, if he didn't want the owner or lessee to be publicly known."

"But if he did that, he would inform you?"

"Not necessarily."

"So you didn't know your name was being used?"

"No."

"Who worked on the car, in San Jose?"

"I have no idea."

"Because, Mr. Evans, somebody did rather extensive work on this Ferrari before Morton ever got into it. The frame was weakened at the places you see marked by the yellow tags. Anti-skid—primitive, in a vehicle this old—was disabled, and the discs were cross-loosened on the left front, right rear. Are you following me, here?"

Evans frowned.

"This car was a death trap, Mr. Evans. Someone used it to kill your client. Lethal changes were made in a garage in Sonoma. And your name is on the lease."

• • •

Downstairs in the car, Ted Bradley was grilling Jennifer Haynes. She might be pretty, but everything about her was wrong—her manner, her tough-guy attitude, and most of all her opinions. She had said she was working on the lawsuit, and that her salary was paid by NERF, but Ted didn't think it was possible. For one thing, Ted Bradley was very publicly associated with NERF, and as a hired employee she should have known that, and she should have treated his opinions with respect.

To call the information he had shared with those kids "bullshit"—a talk he didn't have to give, a moment he had offered out of the goodness of his heart and his dedication to the environmental cause—to call that "bullshit" was outrageous. It was confrontational in the extreme. And it showed absolutely no respect. Plus, Ted knew that what he had said was true. Because, as always, NERF had given him a talking points memo listing the various things to be emphasized. And NERF would not have told him to say anything that was untrue. And the talking points said nothing about the fucking Ice Age. Everything Jennifer had said was irrelevant.

Those trees *were* magnificent. They *were* sentinels of the environment, just as the talking points claimed. In fact, he pulled the talking points out of his jacket pocket to be sure.

"I'd like to see that," Jennifer said.

"I bet you would."

"What is your problem?" she said.

See? he thought. That kind of attitude. Aggressive and confrontational.

She said, "You're one of those television stars who thinks everyone wants to touch your dick. Well, guess what, oh Big Swinging One, I don't. I think you're just an actor."

"And I think you're a plant. You're a corporate spy."

"I must not be a very good one," she said, "because you found me out."

"Because you shot your mouth off, that's why."

"It's always been my problem."

All during this conversation, Bradley felt a peculiar tension building in his chest. Women did not argue with Ted Bradley. Sometimes they were hostile for a while, but that was only because they were intimidated by him, his good looks, and his star power. They wanted to screw him, and often he'd let them. But they did not *argue* with him. This one was arguing, and it excited him and angered him in equal proportions. The tension building up inside him was almost unbearable. Her calmness, just sitting there, the direct way she looked into his eyes, the complete lack of intimidation—it was an indifference to his fame that drove him wild. All right, hell, she was beautiful.

He grabbed her face in both hands and kissed her hard on the mouth.

He could tell she liked it. To complete his dominance he stuck his tongue down her throat.

Then there was a blinding flash of pain—in his neck, his head—and he must have lost consciousness for a moment. Because the next thing he knew he was sitting on the floor of the limousine, gasping and watching blood drip all over his shirt. Ted was not sure how he had gotten there. He was not sure why he was bleeding or why his head was throbbing. Then he realized that his tongue was bleeding.

He looked up at her. She crossed her legs coolly, giving him a glimpse up her skirt, but he didn't care. He was resentful. "You bit my tongue!"

"No, asshole, you bit your own tongue."

"You assaulted me!"

She raised an eyebrow.

"You did! You assaulted me!" He looked down. "Jesus, this was a new shirt, too. From Maxfield's."

She stared at him.

"You assaulted me," he repeated.

"So sue me."

"I think I will."

"Better consult your lawyer first."

"Why?"

She nodded her head toward the front of the car. "You're forgetting the driver."

"What about him?"

"He saw it all."

"So what? You encouraged me," he said, hissing. "You were being seductive. Any guy knows the signs."

"Apparently you didn't."

"Hostile ballbreaker?" He turned and took the vodka bottle from the rack. He needed it to rinse out his mouth. He poured himself a glass, and looked back.

She was reading the talking points. She held the paper in her hands. He lunged for it. "That's not yours."

She was quick, holding the paper away from him. She raised her other hand, edge on, like a chopping knife.

"Care to try your luck again, Ted?"

"Fuck you," he said, and took a big gulp of the vodka. His tongue was on fire. What a bitch, he thought. What a goddamned bitch. Well, she'd be looking for a new job tomorrow. He'd see to that. This bimbo lawyer couldn't fuck around with Ted Bradley and get away with it.

Standing beneath the crashed Ferrari, Evans endured another ten minutes of grilling by the plainclothesmen who encircled him. Fundamentally, the story didn't make sense to him.

Evans said, "George was a good driver. If all these changes were made to the car, wouldn't he have noticed something was wrong?"

"Perhaps. But not if he was drinking heavily."

"Well, he was drinking, that's for sure."

"And who got him the drinks, Mr. Evans?"

"George got his own drinks."

"The waiter at the banquet said you were pushing drinks at Morton."

"That's not true. I was trying to limit his drinking."

Abruptly, they changed course. "Who worked on the Ferrari, Mr. Evans?"

"I have no idea."

"We know you rented a private garage outside Sonoma on Route 54.

It was fairly quiet and out of the way. Any person or persons who worked on the car would have been able to come and go as they wished, without being seen. Why would you choose such a garage?"

"I didn't choose it."

"Your name is on the lease."

"How was the lease arranged?"

"By phone."

"Who paid for it?"

"It was paid in cash."

"By whom?"

"Delivered by messenger."

"You have my signature on anything? Fingerprints?"

"No. Just your name."

Evans shrugged. "Then I'm sorry, but I don't know anything about this. It's well known that I'm George Morton's attorney. Anybody could have used my name. If anything was done to this car, it was done without my knowledge."

He was thinking that they should have been asking Sarah about all this, but then, if they were good at their jobs, they'd already have talked to her.

And sure enough, she appeared from around the corner, talking on a cell phone and nodding to Kenner.

That was when Kenner stepped forward. "Okay, gentlemen. Unless you have further questions, I'll take Mr. Evans into custody on my recognizance. I don't believe he is a flight risk. He will be safe enough with me."

The cops grumbled, but in the end they agreed. Kenner handed out his card, and then he headed back toward the entrance, his arm firmly on Evans's shoulder.

Sarah followed some distance behind. The cops stayed with the Ferrari.

As they neared the door, Kenner said, "Sorry about all that. But the police didn't tell you everything. The fact is, they photographed the car from various angles and fed the shots into a computer that simulates crashes. And the computer-generated simulation didn't match the photos of the actual crash."

"I didn't know you could do that."

"Oh yes. Everybody uses computer models these days. They are *de rigueur* for the modern organization. Armed with their computer simulation, the police went back to the wreck itself, where they now decided that it had been monkeyed with. They never imagined this during their previous examinations of the wreck, but now they do. Clear example of using a computer simulation to alter your version of reality. They trusted the simulation and not the data from the ground."

"Uh-huh."

"And of course their simulation was optimized for the most common vehicle types on American roads. The computer had no ability to model the behavior of a forty-year-old, limited-production Italian racing car. They ran the simulation anyway."

Evans said, "But what's all this about a garage in Sonoma?"

Kenner shrugged. "You don't know. Sarah doesn't know. Nobody can even verify if the car was ever there. But the garage was rented—I'd guess by George himself. Though we'll never know for sure."

Back outside, Evans threw open the door to his limo and climbed in. He was astonished to see Ted Bradley covered in blood, all down his chin and shirt front.

"What happened?"

"He slipped," Jennifer said. "And hurt himself."

TO LOS ANGELES
TUESDAY, OCTOBER 12
10:31 P.M.

On the flight back, Sarah Jones was overcome with confused feelings. First of all, she was profoundly distressed by the fact that George Morton's body had been recovered; in some part of her mind, she had been hoping against hope that he would turn up alive. Then there was the question of Peter Evans. Just as she was starting to like him—starting to see a side of him that was not wimpy, but rather tough and resilient in his own bumbling way—just as she was beginning, in fact, to have the first stirrings of feelings toward the man who had saved her life, suddenly there was this new woman, Jennifer somebody, and Peter was obviously taken with her.

And in addition, there was the arrival of Ted Bradley. Sarah had no illusions about Ted; she had seen him in action at innumerable NERF gatherings, and she had even once allowed him to work his charms on her—she was a sucker for actors—but at the last moment decided he reminded her too much of her ex. What was it about actors, anyway? They were so engaging, so personal in their approach, so intense in their feelings. It was hard to realize that they were just self-absorbed people who would do anything to get you to like them.

At least, Ted was.

And how had he been injured? Bitten his own tongue? Sarah had the feeling it had to do with this Jennifer. Undoubtedly, Ted had made a pass at her. The woman was pretty enough in a street-smart kind of way;

dark hair, toughish face, compact body, muscular but skinny. A typical speeded-up New York type—in every way Sarah's opposite.

And Peter Evans was fawning over her.

Fawning.

It was sort of disgusting, but she had to admit she was disappointed personally as well. Just as she had started to like him. She sighed.

As for Bradley, he was talking to Kenner about environmental issues, showing off his extensive knowledge. And Kenner was looking at Bradley the way a python looks at a rat.

"So," Kenner said, "global warming represents a threat to the world?"

"Absolutely," Bradley said. "A threat to the whole world."

"What sort of threat are we talking about?"

"Crop failures, spreading deserts, new diseases, species extinction, all the glaciers melting, Kilimanjaro, sea-level rise, extreme weather, tornadoes, hurricanes, El Niño events—"

"That sounds extremely serious," Kenner said.

"It is," Bradley said. "It really is."

"Are you sure of your facts?"

"Of course."

"You can back your claims with references to the scientific literature?"

"Well, I can't personally, but scientists can."

"Actually, scientific studies do not support your claims. For example, crop failure—if anything, increased carbon dioxide *stimulates* plant growth. There is some evidence that this is happening. And the most recent satellite studies show the Sahara has shrunk since 1980.* As for new diseases—not true. The rate of emergence of new diseases has not changed since 1960."

"But we'll have diseases like malaria coming back to the US and Europe."

---

* Fred Pearce, "Africans go back to the land as plants reclaim the desert," *New Scientist* 175, 21 September 2002, pp. 4–5. "Africa's deserts are in retreat . . . Analysis of satellite images . . . reveals that dunes are retreating right across the Sahel region . . . Vegetation is ousting sand across a swathe of land stretching . . . 6000 kilometers. . . . Analysts say the gradual greening has been happening since the mid 1980s, though has gone largely unnoticed."

"Not according to malaria experts."*

Bradley snorted and folded his hands across his chest.

"Species extinction hasn't been demonstrated either. In the 1970s, Norman Myers predicted a million species would be extinct by the year 2000. Paul Ehrlich predicted that fifty percent of all species would be extinct by the year 2000. But those were just opinions.† Do you know what we call opinion in the absence of evidence? We call it prejudice. Do you know how many species there are on the planet?"

"No."

"Neither does anybody else. Estimates range from three million to one hundred million. Quite a range, wouldn't you say? Nobody really has any idea."‡

"Your point being?"

"It's hard to know how many species are becoming extinct if you don't know how many there are in the first place. How could you tell if you were robbed if you didn't know how much money you had in your wallet to begin with? And fifteen thousand new species are described every year. By the way, do you know what the known rate of species extinction is?"

"No."

"That's because there is no known rate. Do you know how they measure numbers of species and species extinctions? Some poor bastard marks off a hectare or an acre of land and then tries to count all the bugs and animals and plants inside it. Then he comes back in ten years and counts again. But maybe the bugs have moved to an adjacent acre in the meantime. Anyway, can you imagine trying to count all the bugs in an acre of land?"

---

* Paul Reiter, et al., "Global warming and malaria: a call for accuracy," *Lancet*, 4, no. 1 (June 2004). "Many of these much-publicized predictions are ill informed and misleading."

† Discussion in Lomborg, p. 252.

‡ Morjorie L. Reaka-Kudia, et al., *Biodiversity II, Understanding and Protecting our Biological Resources*, Washington: National Academies Press, 1997. "Biologists have come to recognize just how little we know about the organisms with which we share the planet Earth. In particular, attempts to determine how many species there are in total have been surprisingly fruitless." Myers: "We have no way of knowing the actual extinction rate in the tropical forests, let alone an approximate guess." In Lomborg, p. 254.

"It would be difficult."

"To put it mildly. And very inaccurate," Kenner said, "which is the point. Now, about all the glaciers melting—not true. Some are, some aren't."*

"Nearly all of them are."

Kenner smiled thinly. "How many glaciers are we talking about?"

"Dozens."

"How many glaciers are there in the world, Ted?"

"I don't know."

"Guess."

"Maybe, uh, two hundred."

"There are more than that in California.† There are one hundred sixty thousand glaciers in the world, Ted. About sixty-seven thousand have been inventoried, but only a few have been studied with any care. There is mass balance data extending five years or more for only seventy-nine glaciers in the entire world. So, how can you say they're all melting? Nobody knows whether they are or not."‡

"Kilimanjaro is melting."

"Why is that?"

"Global warming."

"Actually, Kilimanjaro has been rapidly melting since the 1800s— long before global warming. The loss of the glacier has been a topic of scholarly concern for over a hundred years. And it has always been something of a mystery because, as you know, Kilimanjaro is an equatorial volcano, so it exists in a warm region. Satellite measurements of that region show no warming trend at the altitude of the Kilimanjaro glacier. So why is it melting?"

---

* Roger J. Braithwaite, "Glacier mass balance, the first 50 years of international monitoring," *Progress in Physical Geography* 26, no. 1 (2002): 76–95. "There is no obvious common global trend of increasing glacier melt in recent years."

† California has 497 glaciers; Raub, et al., 1980; Guyton: 108 glaciers and 401 glacierets, *Glaciers of California*, p. 115.

‡ H. Kieffer, et al., 2000, "New eyes in the sky measure glaciers and ice sheets," *EOS, Transactions, American Geophysical Union* 81: 265, 270–71. See also R. J. Braithwaite and Y. Zhang, "Relationships between interannual variability of glacier mass balance and climate," *Journal of Glaciology* 45 (2000): 456–62.

Sulking: "You tell me."

"Because of deforestation, Ted. The rain forest at the base of the mountain has been cut down, so the air blowing upward is no longer moist. Experts think that if the forest is replanted the glacier will grow again."

"That's bullshit."

"I'll give you the journal references.* Now then—sea-level rise? Was that the next threat you mentioned?"

"Yes."

"Sea level is indeed rising."

"Ah-hah!"

"As it has been for the last six thousand years, ever since the start of the Holocene. Sea level has been rising at the rate of ten to twenty centimeters—that's four to eight inches—every hundred years."[†]

"But it's rising faster now."

"Actually, not."

"Satellites prove it."

"Actually, they don't."[‡]

"Computer models prove it's rising faster."[§]

"Computer models can't *prove* anything, Ted. A prediction can't ever be proof—it hasn't happened yet. And computer models have failed to accurately predict the last ten or fifteen years. But if you want to believe in them anyway, there is no arguing with faith. Now, what was next on

---

* Betsy Mason, "African Ice Under Wraps," *Nature*, 24, November 2003. "Although it's tempting to blame the ice loss on global warming, researchers think that deforestation of the mountain's foothills is the more likely culprit," http://www.nature.com/nsu/031117/031117–8.html.

Kaser, et al., "Modern glacier retreat on Kilimanjaro as evidence of climate change: Observations and facts," *International Journal of Climatology* 24: (2004): 329–39. "In recent years, Kilimanjaro and its vanishing glaciers have become an 'icon' of global warming . . . [but] processes other than air temperature control the ice recession . . . A drastic drop in atmospheric moisture at the end of the 19th century and the ensuing drier climate conditions are likely forcing glacier retreat."

† See, for example, http://www.csr.utexas.edu/gmsl/main.html. "Over the last century, global sea-level change has typically been estimated from tide gauge measurements by long-term averaging. Most recent estimates of global mean sea-level rise from tide gauge measurements range from 1.7 to 2.4 mm/yr" [that is, 6″ to 9″ every hundred years—MC].

‡ Op. cit. Global mean sea-level rise as measured by satellite is 3.1 mm/yr for the last decade or slightly more than 12″ a century. However, satellites show considerable variation. Thus the northern Pacific has risen, but the southern Pacific has fallen by several millimeters in recent years.

§ Lomborg, pp. 289–90 on inadequacy of IPCC sea-level models.

your list? Extreme weather—again, not true. Numerous studies show there is no increase."*

"Look," Ted said, "you may enjoy putting me down, but the fact is, lots of people think there will be more extreme weather, including more hurricanes and tornadoes and cyclones, in the future."

"Yes, indeed, lots of people think so. But scientific studies do not bear them out.† That's why we *do* science, Ted, to see if our opinions can be verified in the real world, or whether we are just having fantasies."

"All these hurricanes are not fantasies."

Kenner sighed. He flipped open his laptop.

"What are you doing?"

"One moment," Kenner said. "Let me bring it up."

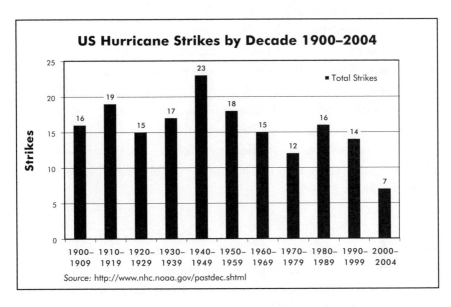

US Hurricane Strikes by Decade 1900–2004

Source: http://www.nhc.noaa.gov/pastdec.shtml

* See Henderson-Sellers, et al., 1997, "Tropical Cyclones and Global Climate Change: a post-IPCC assessment," *Bulletin of the American Meteorological Society* 79:9–38. C. Nicholls Landsea, et al. "Downward Trend in the Frequency of Intense Atlantic Hurricanes during the past five decades," *Geophysical Research Letters* 23:527–30. 1996. According to the United Nations Intergovernmental Panel on Climate Change, "Examination of meteorological data fails to support the perception [of increased frequency and severity of extreme climate events] in the context of a long-term climate change." IPCC 1995, p. 11. "Overall, there is no evidence that extreme weather events, or climate variability, has increased, in a global sense, throughout the twentieth century . . ." IPCC, *Climate Change 1995*. In the 2001 IPCC report, "No long-term trends evident" for tropical and extratropical storms, and no systematic changes in the "frequency of tornadoes, thunder days, or hail." *Executive summary*, p.2. For fuller discussion, see Lomborg, p. 292ff.
† Richard Feynman: "Science is what we have learned about how not to fool ourselves."

"Here is the actual data, Ted," Kenner said. "US hurricane strikes over the last hundred years are clearly not increasing. And similarly, extreme weather is not more frequent globally. The data simply do not agree with you. Now, you also mentioned El Niño events."

"Yes . . ."

"As you know, El Niño is a global weather pattern that begins when ocean temperatures along the west coast of South America remain above normal for several months. Once it's triggered, El Niño lasts about a year and a half, affecting weather around the world. El Niño occurs roughly every four years—twenty-three times in the last century. And it has been occurring for thousands of years. So it long precedes any claim of global warming.* But what threat does El Niño represent to the US, Ted? There was a major El Niño in 1998."

"Floods, crops ruined, like that."

"All that happened. But the net economic effect of the last El Niño was a gain of fifteen billion dollars because of a longer growing season and less use of winter heating oil. That's after deducting $1.5 billion for flooding and excess rain in California. Still a net benefit."

"I'd like to see that study," Bradley said.

"I'll make sure you get it.† Because of course it also suggests that if global warming really does occur, it will probably benefit most nations of the world."

"But not *all*."

"No, Ted. Not all."

"So what exactly is your point?" Bradley said. "You're saying that we don't need to pay any attention to the environment, that we can just leave it alone and let industry pollute and everything will be hunky-dory?"

---

* Lomborg, p. 292.
† Stanley A. Changnon, 1999: "Impacts of 1997–98 El Niño–Generated Weather in the United States," *Bulletin of the American Meteorological Society* 80, no. 9: pp. 1819–28. ("The net economic benefit was surprisingly positive . . . direct losses nationally were about $4 billion and the benefits were approximately $19 billion.")

• • •

For a moment, it looked to Sarah as if Kenner would get angry, but he did not. He said, "If you oppose the death penalty, does it also mean you are in favor of doing nothing at all about crime?"

"No," Ted said.

"You can oppose the death penalty but still favor punishing criminals."

"Yes. Of course."

"Then I can say that global warming is not a threat but still favor environmental controls, can't I?"

"But it doesn't sound like you are saying that."

Kenner sighed.

Sarah was listening to this exchange, thinking Bradley wasn't really hearing what Kenner had to say. As if to prove her thoughts, Bradley continued: "Well? Aren't you saying that the environment needs no protection from us? Isn't that what you are *really* saying?"

Kenner said, "No," in a way that suggested that the conversation was over.

Sarah thought: Ted really is a fool. He has a severely limited understanding of what he is talking about. Ted was an actor with a script, at a loss if the conversation moved away from scripted lines.

She turned away and looked toward the front of the cabin. She saw Peter talking to Jennifer, their heads together. There was a sort of intimacy in their gestures that was instantly recognizable.

She was glad when the pilot announced they were landing in Los Angeles.

VAN NUYS
TUESDAY, OCTOBER 12
11:22 P.M.

Sanjong Thapa was waiting at the airport, looking worried. He and Kenner got immediately into a car and drove off. Sarah went home to her apartment. Bradley climbed into an SUV limo and left with an irritable wave. He was already on his cell phone. Peter Evans drove Jennifer to her car, which was back in Culver City. There was an awkward moment saying good-bye. He wanted to kiss her but sensed some reserve, and didn't. She promised she would call him in the morning.

He drove home, thinking of her. Sarah did not enter his mind.

It was almost midnight when Evans got back to his apartment. He was very tired and was stripping off his shirt when the phone rang. It was Janis, the exercise instructor. "Where have you *been*, you cute thing?"

"Traveling," he said.

"I have called you *every single day*," she said. "Sometimes more. Sometimes every hour."

"Uh-huh. What's up?"

"My boyfriend broke up with me."

"I'm sorry to hear that," Evans said. "Was it very—"

"Can I come over?" she said.

He sighed. "You know, Janis, I'm really tired . . ."

"I need to talk to you. I promise I won't stay, if you don't want me to. I'm only about a block away. Five minutes?"

He sighed again, louder this time. "Janis, tonight is not—"

"Okay, good, see you in five."

Click.

He sighed. He took his shirt off and tossed it in the hamper. She never listened, that was the trouble. He decided that when she got to his apartment, he would just tell her to leave. That's all. Just go.

Or then again, maybe he wouldn't.

Janis was uncomplicated. He was ready for an uncomplicated exchange. He pulled off his shoes and dropped them on the floor. On the other hand, he didn't want Janis around in the morning if Jennifer called. Would Jennifer call? She said she would. Did Jennifer know his home number? He wasn't sure. Maybe not.

He decided to take a shower. He might not hear Janis in the shower, so he unlocked the front door for her and headed for the bathroom. The hallway was dark and he had just a fleeting glimpse of a dark shadow before something hit him on the head, very hard. Evans yelled. The pain was intense, making him gasp, and he fell to his knees. He groaned. Someone hit him again, this time in the ear, and he fell over on his side.

Disoriented, he found himself staring at a pair of feet in dirty socks. He was being dragged into the living room. He was dropped unceremoniously on the floor. There were three men, moving around him. They had dark masks over their faces, like ski masks. One of them stepped on both his arms, pinning him down, flat on his back. Another one sat on his legs and said, "Don't talk. Don't move." A growly menacing voice.

Evans couldn't move anyway. He still felt disoriented. He looked around for the third man. He heard sloshing water. He glimpsed what looked like a plastic baggie.

"Hold him good." The third man spoke in a whisper. He crouched by Evans's shoulder, pulled up the shirtsleeve, exposing the flesh of his arm. He was wheezing softly behind the black mask. In the same whisper, he said, "You know what this is?"

He held up the baggie. The water was cloudy. Evans saw what looked like a fleshy ball, and in a panic he thought, *Oh God, they cut somebody's balls off.* But then he saw the ball moving, undulating. It was brown with white spots, about the size of a golf ball.

"You know?" the man said.

Evans shook his head.

"You will," the man whispered, and unzipped the baggie. He pushed it against the underside of Evans's arm. Evans felt wetness. The man was manipulating the baggie, squeezing the ball. Evans was trying to see, but it was hard to see exactly what was—

The ball moved. It spread, extended what looked like wings. No, not wings. It was a tiny octopus! Tiny! It could not have weighed more than a few ounces. Brownish with white rings. The man was squeezing the baggie, compressing it, pushing the little octopus toward the flesh of Evans's arm.

And then he understood.

Evans moaned and began to struggle, trying to move against his captors, but they had him firmly, and he felt the touch of the octopus, a kind of sticky sensation, like cellophane or Sticky Putty or something. He lifted his head in horror and saw that the man was snapping the baggie with his finger, trying to goad the octopus, which had wrapped itself against the skin of Evans's arm, and in a flash the rings on the octopus changed from white to blue.

The blue ring of death.

"That means he's mad." The third man holding the baggie said, "You won't feel it," but Evans did. It was a bite from the tiny beak, a single sting, almost like the sting of a needle. Evans jerked his arm and the man withdrew the baggie and sealed it again. He whispered, "Hold him good."

He went away a moment, then came back with a kitchen rag. He wiped the underside of Evans's arm, wiped the water off the floor. Still whispering, he said, "You won't feel anything for a few minutes." He walked over to the phone. "Don't try to call anybody," he said, and ripped the phone off the wall, smashing it on the floor.

The men released him. They moved quickly to the door, opened it, and were gone.

• • •

He coughed, and got to his hands and knees. He looked at his underarm; the bite looked like a dimple in the flesh, a small pink spot just at the edge of the hairs of his armpit. Nobody would ever see it.

He did not feel anything except a sort of dull tingling at the spot where the bite had occurred. His mouth was dry, but that was probably from fear. His head hurt. He reached up, felt blood, realized that they had torn open some of his stitches.

Jesus. He tried to get to his feet but his arm gave way, and he fell down again, rolling on the floor. He was still disoriented. He stared into the lights in the ceiling. His apartment had that cottage-cheese kind of ceiling. He hated that ceiling. He wanted to do something about it but it was too expensive. Anyway, he had always thought he would be moving soon. He was still disoriented. He got onto his elbows. His mouth was very dry now. It was the effect of the poison.

Some kind of a toad. No, he thought, that wasn't right. It wasn't a toad. It was a . . .

He couldn't remember.

Octopus.

That's right. It was a little octopus, hardly bigger than a thumbnail. Cute little thing.

The Indians in the Amazon used them for poison for their arrowheads. No, he thought, that was toads. No octopus in the Amazon. Or were there?

He was confused. Becoming more confused. He broke into a cold sweat. Was that part of it, too? He had to get to a phone. He might only have a few minutes of consciousness left.

He crawled to the nearest object, which was an easy chair . . . he'd had it in law school, it was pretty ratty, he had intended to get rid of it when he moved here but he hadn't gotten around to it yet . . . the living room needed a chair right in this spot . . . he'd had it re-covered in fabric his second year in law school . . . pretty dirty now . . . who had time to go shopping? With his mind racing, he pulled himself up until his chin was resting on the seat of the chair. He was gasping for breath, it felt as if he had climbed a mountain. He thought, Why am I here? Why is my chin on the chair? Then he remembered that he was trying to climb up, to sit in it.

Sit in the chair.

He got the elbow of his good arm up onto the seat and began to press himself up. Finally he was able to heave his chest onto the chair, then the rest of his body. His limbs were getting numb, and cold, and heavier by the minute. They were becoming too heavy to move. His whole body was getting heavy. He managed to get himself almost upright in the chair. There was a phone on the table beside him, but his arm was too heavy to reach for it. He tried, but he could not reach out at all now. His fingers moved slightly, but that was all. His body was very cold and very heavy.

He began to lose his balance, slowly at first and then sliding over sideways, until his chest rested on the arm of the chair and his head hung over the side. And there he stayed, unable to move. He could not lift his head. He could not move his arms. He could not even move his eyes. He stared at the fabric of the chair and the carpet on the floor and he thought, *This is the last thing I will see before I die.*

VI

BLUE

How long Peter Evans stared at the carpet he did not know. The arm of the chair pressing against his chest impeded his breathing, but it was becoming more difficult to breathe in any case. Images from his life flashed into consciousness—the basement where he played with his first computer, the blue bicycle that was stolen the same day he got it, the boxed corsage for his senior prom date, standing up in Professor Whitson's con law class, his legs shaking, while old Whitson took him apart—

"Peter? Hel-*lo?* Peter?"

—and terrorized him, they were all terrorized by Whitson, and the dinner that was the final interview for his LA job, where he spilled soup all over his shirt and the partners pretended not to notice, and—

"Peter? *Peter!* What are you doing there? Peter? Get up, Peter."

He felt hands on his shoulders, burning hot hands, and with a grunt he was hauled back into sitting position. "There, that's better." Janis peered at him, her face inches from his. "What's the matter with you? What did you take? Talk to me."

But he could not talk. He could not move at all. She was wearing a leotard top and jeans and sandals. If she moved to one side, she was out of his field of view.

"Peter?" A puzzled tone. "I think something is really wrong. Have you been doing ecstasy? Did you have a stroke? You're too young for a stroke. But it could happen, I guess. Especially with your diet. I told you no more than sixty-five grams of fat a day. If you were a vegetarian you would never have a stroke. Why don't you answer me?"

She touched his jaw, a questioning look on her face. Evans was feeling distinctly lightheaded because he could hardly breathe anymore. It was as if he had a twenty-ton stone on his chest. Even though he was sitting up, the great stone weighed on him.

He thought, *Call the hospital!*

"I don't know what to do, Peter," she said. "I just wanted to talk to you tonight, and now you're like this. I mean, I guess it's a bad time. But it's kind of scary, too. I have to be honest. I wish you would answer me. Can you answer me?"

Call the hospital!

"Maybe you'll hate me for this, but I don't know what you took that makes you this way, so I'm going to call 911 and get an ambulance. I'm really sorry and I don't want to get you into trouble, but this is freaking me out, Peter."

She went out of his field of view but he heard her picking up the phone on the table next to his chair. He thought, *Good. Hurry.*

She said, "Something is wrong with your phone."

Oh Jesus.

She stepped back into his field of view. "Your phone is not working, did you know that?"

Use your cell phone.

"Do you have your cell phone? I left mine in the car."

Go get it.

"Maybe one of the other phones in your apartment is working. You need to call your service provider, Peter. It's not safe to be without phones—what's this? Somebody tore the phone out of the wall? Have we been having a fit of pique?"

Knocking on the door. It sounded like the front door. "Hell-lo? Anybody here? Hello? Peter?" A woman's voice. He couldn't see who it was.

He heard Janis say, "Who are you?"

"Who are *you?*"

"I'm Janis. I'm Peter's friend."

"I'm Sarah. I work with Peter."

"You're tall."

"Where is Peter?" Sarah said.

"He's over there," Janis said. "Something's wrong with him."

Evans could see none of this, because he could not move his eyes. And now he saw the first gray spots that signaled the impending loss of consciousness. It took every ounce of energy he possessed to move his chest and fill his lungs the tiniest bit.

"Peter?" Sarah said.

She moved into his field of view. She looked at him.

"Are you paralyzed?" she said.

Yes! Call the hospital!

"He's sweating," Sarah said. "Cold sweats."

"He was that way when I found him," Janis said. She turned to Sarah. "What are you doing here anyway? How well do you know Peter?"

"Did you call an ambulance?" Sarah said.

"No, because my phone is in my car, and—"

"I'll do it."

Sarah flipped open her cell phone. It was the last thing Evans remembered.

It was late. The house was dark all around him. Nicholas Drake was sitting at his desk in his home in Brentwood, near Santa Monica. He was precisely 2.9 miles from the beach (he had recently measured it in his car), so he felt secure there. It was a good thing, too, because NERF had bought this house for him only one year before. There had been some discussion about that, because they had also bought him a townhouse in Georgetown. But Drake had pointed out that he needed a residence on the West Coast in which to entertain celebrities and important contributors.

California was, after all, the most environmentally conscious state in the nation. It had been the first to pass anti-smoking laws, almost ten years before New York or any other Eastern state did. And even when a Federal Court overturned the EPA on the issue of secondhand smoke in 1998, saying that the EPA had violated its own rules of evidence and banned a substance they had failed to prove caused any harm at all—the Federal Judge was from a tobacco state, *obviously*—even then, California did not budge. The anti-smoking laws stayed. In fact, Santa Monica was about to ban all smoking outdoors, even at the beach! Now *that* was progress!

It was easy here.

But as for getting *major* funds . . . well, that was another matter. There were some rich people in the entertainment industry who could be counted on, but for the real money in California—the investment bankers, portfolio managers, CEOs, real estate, trust funders, people with five hundred million to a couple billion, *serious* money—well, those people weren't so easy. Those people inhabited a different California. Those people belonged to golf courses that didn't allow actors to join. The big money was in the hands of pioneers and tech entrepreneurs, and they were very smart and very tough. A lot of them knew their science. Christ, a lot of them *were* scientists.

Which was why they presented such a challenge to Drake, if he wanted that bonus for making his numbers for the year. He was staring at the screen, thinking it was time for a Scotch, when a new window opened and the cursor blinked:

SCORPIO_L: Can you talk?

Speaking of dimwits, he thought. He typed:

Yes I can.

Drake shifted in his seat, adjusting the light over his desk so it would illuminate his face. He looked at the camera lens mounted just above his screen.

The window opened up. He saw Ted Bradley, sitting at his desk in his house in the San Fernando Valley.

"Well?"

"It was just as you said," Bradley said. "Evans has gone over to the dark side."

"And?"

"He was with that girl, Jennifer, who works on the lawsuit . . ."

"Jennifer Haynes?"

"Yeah. She's a wise-ass bitch."

Drake said nothing. He was listening to the sound of the voice. Bradley had been drinking again. He said, "Ted, we've talked about this before. Not everybody likes it when you come on to them."

"Yeah, they do. I mean, mostly they do."

"Ted, this is not the impression we want to make."

"Well, she insulted me."

"All right. So Jennifer Haynes was there . . ."

"She's a stooge for big oil and coal. Gotta be."

"And who else was there?"

"Sarah Jones."

"Uh-huh. She flew up to see the body?"

"I don't know why she was there. She was with a guy named Kenner, a real asshole. Another know-it-all."

"Describe him."

"Forties, dark, kind of butch. Looks military to me."

"Uh-huh. Anyone else?"

"No."

"Nobody foreign? No other people?"

"No, just the ones I described."

"Would you say that Peter Evans knew Kenner?"

"Yeah. Pretty well, I would say."

"So, it was your impression they were working together?"

"Yes. I would say very much together."

"All right, Ted," Drake said. "I like your instincts here." He watched as Bradley preened on the monitor. "I think you may be on to something. Evans could prove a problem to us."

"I'll say."

"He's been one of our trusted attorneys. Why, he was in my office just the other day, getting an assignment from me. If he's turned on us, he could do damage."

"Damn turncoat," Ted said. "He's another Bennett Arnold."

"I want you to stick close to him for the next week or so."

"My pleasure."

"Hang out with him, stay by his side. Buddy-buddy. You know."

"I got you, Nick. I'll be on him like glue."

"I'm sure he'll be at the opening of the conference later this morning," Drake said. And he thought, *Or then again, he might not make it.*

WESTWOOD
WEDNESDAY, OCTOBER 13
3:40 A.M.

Kenner said, "I must say, it was an excellent choice. *Hapalochlaena fasciata*, the most deadly of the three species of blue-ringed octopus. So named because when it is threatened it changes color and produces bright blue rings on its skin. It's found everywhere in the coastal waters of Australia. The animal is very tiny, the bite is small and almost undetectable, and envenomation is often deadly. There is no antivenom. And a bite's not likely to be quickly recognized at a hospital in Los Angeles. Really, a masterful choice."*

Evans, who was lying in the emergency room at UCLA with a respirator on his face, just stared. He was still unable to speak. But he was no longer so frightened. Janis had gone home in a huff, mentioning something about teaching an early class. Sarah was sitting by his bed, rubbing his hand gently and looking beautiful. "Where would they have gotten one?"

"I imagine they have several," Kenner said. "They're delicate, and don't live very long anyway. But they are captured in fairly large numbers because the Aussies are trying to make an antivenin. You probably know the Australians lead the world in deadly poisonous animals. The most

---

* See S. K. Sutherland, et al., "Toxins and mode of envenomation of the common ringed or blue-banded octopus," *Med. J.Aust.* 1 (1969): 893–98. Also H. Flecker, et al., "Fatal bite from octopus," *Med. J.Aust.* 2 (1955): 329–31.

poisonous snake, the most poisonous mollusk, the most poisonous fish—all from Australia or found there."

Evans thought, *Great.*

"But now of course UCLA has seen three cases. They're on it."

"Yes, we are," an intern said, coming into the room. He checked Evans's IV and his respirator. He said, "We have your preliminary blood work. It's a tetrodotoxin, like the others. You should be up and around in about three more hours. Lucky guy." He smiled winningly at Sarah, then walked out again.

"Anyway, I'm glad you're all right," Kenner said. "It would have been embarrassing to lose you."

Evans thought, *What is he talking about?* He was increasingly able to use his eye muscles, and he glanced over at Sarah. But she just smiled.

"Oh yes," Kenner said. "I need you alive, Peter. At least for a while."

Sitting in a corner of the room on his cell phone, Sanjong said, "Okay, we have some action."

Kenner said, "Is it where we thought?"

"Yes."

"What happened?"

"We just got the receipt notice. They rented an aircraft last month. A C-57 transport."

"Whew," Kenner said.

"What does that mean?" Sarah said.

"Big aircraft. They probably need it to spray."

She looked puzzled. "Spray?"

Sanjong said, "It's pretty clear they're going to disseminate AOB, ammonia-oxidizing bacteria, in large quantities. And perhaps some hydrophilic nanoparticles as well."

"To do what?"

"Control the path of a storm," Kenner said. "There's some evidence that disseminated AOB at altitude can shift a hurricane or cyclone track. Hydrophilic nanoparticles potentiate the effect. At least in theory. I don't know if it's been tried on a large system."

"They're going to control a hurricane?"

444 ▶ MICHAEL CRICHTON

"They're going to try."

"Maybe not," Sanjong said. "Tokyo says some recent cellular and Internet traffic suggests that the project may be canceled."

"Then they don't have the initial conditions?"

"Looks like they don't, no."

Evans coughed. "Oh good," Kenner said. "You're coming around." He patted his arm. "Just rest now, Peter. Try and sleep if you can. Because, as you know, today is the big day."

"The big day?" Sarah said.

"The conference begins in about five and a half hours," Kenner said. He stood to go, then turned back to Evans. "I'm going to have Sanjong stay with you the rest of the night," he said. "I think you'll be all right here, but they've already made one attempt on your life, and I don't want them to try another."

Sanjong smiled and sat on the chair beside the bed, a stack of magazines beside him. He opened the latest issue of *Time* magazine. The cover story was "Climate Change Doomsday Ahead." He also had *Newsweek:* "Abrupt Climate Change—A New Scandal for the Administration?" And *The Economist:* "Climate Change Rears Its Ugly Head." And *Paris-Match:* "Climat: Le Nouveau Péril Américain."

Sanjong smiled cheerfully. "Just rest now," he said.

Evans closed his eyes.

At nine o'clock that morning, the invited attendees to the conference were milling around on the floor, not taking their seats. Evans was standing near the entrance, drinking coffee. He felt incredibly tired, but he was all right. He'd been a little shaky in his legs earlier, but that had passed.

The delegates were clearly academic types, many dressed casually in a manner to suggest an outdoorsy lifestyle—khakis and L.L.Bean shirts, hiking boots, Patagonia vests. "It looks like a lumberjack convention, doesn't it?" Jennifer said, standing beside Evans. "You'd never know these guys spend most of their time in front of computer monitors."

"Is that true?" Evans said.

"A lot of them, yes."

"And the hiking shoes?"

She shrugged. "The rugged look is in, at the moment."

At the podium, Nicholas Drake tapped the microphone. "Good morning, everyone," he said. "We will begin in ten minutes." Then he stepped away, and huddled with Henley.

"Waiting for the TV cameras," Jennifer said. "They had some electrical problems this morning. Crews are still setting up."

"So, of course, everything waits for television."

At the entrance to the convention hall, there was a commotion and shouting. Evans looked over and saw an elderly man in a tweed coat and tie struggling with two security guards. "But I have been invited!" he said. "I am supposed to be here."

"Sorry, sir," the guards were saying, "your name is not on the sheet."

"But, I tell you, I have been invited!"

"Oh boy," Jennifer said, shaking her head.

"Who's that?"

"That is Professor Norman Hoffman. Ever heard of him?"

"No, why?"

"The ecology of thought? He's a famous sociologist, or should I say a notorious one. Extremely critical of environmental beliefs. A bit of a mad dog. We had him over to the war room to ask him his views. That was a mistake. The guy never shuts up. He talks a mile a minute and goes off on tangents—in every direction—and you can't turn him off. It's like a TV set that changes channels every few seconds, and there's no remote."

"No wonder they don't want him here."

"Oh yes, he would cause trouble. He already is."

Over by the entrance, the old man was struggling with the security guards. "Let go of me! How dare you! I was invited! By George Morton himself. He and I are personal friends. George Morton invited me!"

The mention of George Morton sparked something. Evans went over to the old man.

Jennifer said, "You'll be sor-ry . . ."

He shrugged. "Excuse me," he said, coming up to the guards. "I'm Mr. Morton's attorney. Can I help you?"

The old man writhed in the grip of the guards. "I'm Professor Norman Hoffman and George Morton invited me!" Up close, Evans saw that the old man was messily shaven, unkempt, his hair wild. "Why do you think I would come to this horrible convocation? For one reason only: George asked me to. He wanted my *impression* of it. Although I could have told him weeks ago: There are no surprises to be had here, I can assure you. It will unfold with all the stately ceremony of any cheap funeral."

Evans was thinking Jennifer had been right to warn him about this guy. He said politely, "Do you have a ticket, sir?"

"No, I don't have a *ticket*. I don't *need* a ticket. What don't you understand, young man? I am Professor Norman Hoffman and I am a personal friend of George Morton's. Anyway," he said, "they took my ticket."

"Who did?"

"One of those guards."

Evans said to the guards, "Did you take his ticket?"

"He didn't have a ticket."

"Do you have a stub?" Evans said to Hoffman.

"No, damn it, I do not have a *stub*. I do not need a *stub*. I do not need any of this, frankly."

"I'm sorry, Professor, but—"

"However, I managed to hold on to *this*." He gave Evans the torn corner of a ticket. It was a genuine ticket.

"Where is the rest?"

"I told you, they took it."

A guard standing to one side beckoned to Evans. Evans went over to him. The guard turned his cupped hand, revealing the rest of the ticket in his palm. "I'm sorry, sir," he said, "but Mr. Drake gave specific orders this gentleman was not to be allowed in."

"But he has a ticket," Evans said.

"Perhaps you'd like to take it up with Mr. Drake."

By now, a television crew had wandered over, drawn by the commotion. Hoffman immediately played to the cameras, struggling anew.

"Don't bother with Drake!" Hoffman yelled to Evans. "Drake won't let truth into these proceedings!" He turned to the camera. "Nicholas Drake is an immoral fraud, and these proceedings are a travesty to the poor of the world. I bear witness to the dying children of Africa and Asia! Breathing their last because of conferences like this! Fearmongers! Immoral fearmongers!" He struggled maniacally. His eyes were wild. There was spittle on his lips. He certainly appeared crazy, and the cameras switched off; the crews turned away, seemingly embarrassed. At once, Hoffman stopped his struggle. "Never mind. I've said my piece.

No one is interested, as usual." He turned to his guards. "You can let me go. I have had enough of this chicanery. I cannot bear to be here another minute. Let me go!"

Evans said, "Let him go."

The guards released Hoffman. He immediately dashed into the center of the room, where a crew was now interviewing Ted Bradley. Hoffman stepped in front of Bradley and said, "This man is a pimp! He is an eco-pimp for a corrupt establishment that makes its living by spreading false fears! Don't you understand? False fears are a plague, a modern plague!"

Then the guards were on Hoffman again, dragging him bodily out of the hall. He didn't struggle this time. He just went limp, his heels scraping on the ground as he was carried out. All he said was, "Be careful, I have a bad back. You hurt me and I'll sue you for assault."

They set him outside on the curb, dusted him off, released him.

"Have a good day, sir."

"I intend to. My days are numbered."

Evans hung back with Jennifer, watching Hoffman. "I won't say I told you," Jennifer said.

"Just who is he, anyway?"

"He's a professor *emeritus* at USC. He was one of the first people to study in a rigorous statistical fashion the media and its effect on society. He's quite interesting, but as you see he has developed, uh, strong opinions."

"You think Morton really invited him here?"

"Peter, I need your help," a voice said. Evans turned and saw Drake striding toward him.

"What is it?"

"That *nut*," Drake said, nodding to Hoffman, "is probably going to go straight to the police and claim he was assaulted. We don't need that this morning. Go talk to him. See if you can calm him down."

Cautiously, Evans said, "I don't know what I can do . . ."

"Get him to explain his nutty theories," Drake said. "That'll keep him busy for *hours*."

"But then I'll miss the conf—"

"We don't need you here. We need you *there*. With the cuckoo."

There was a large crowd outside the conference center. The overflow was watching the proceedings on a big TV screen, with subtitles running underneath the speaker. Evans pushed through the gathering. "I know why you are following me," Hoffman said, when he saw Evans. "And it won't work."

"Professor—"

"You're the bright young *poseur* Nick Drake sent to put me off my purpose."

"Not at all, sir."

"Yes, you are. Don't lie to me. I don't like to be lied to."

"All right," Evans said, "it's true. I was sent by Drake."

Hoffman stopped. He seemed startled by the honesty. "I knew it. And what did he tell you to do?"

"Stop you from going to the police."

"All right then, you've succeeded. Go and tell him, I am not going to the police."

"It looks like you are."

"Oh. It *looks like* I am. You're one of those people who care what it *looks like*."

"No, sir, but you—"

"I don't care what it *looks like*. I care what *is*. Do you have any idea what is?"

"I'm not sure I follow you."

"What is your line of work?"

"I'm a lawyer."

"I should have known. Everybody is a lawyer these days. Extrapolating the statistical growth of the legal profession, by the year 2035 every single person in the United States will be a lawyer, including newborn infants. They will be *born* lawyers. What do you suppose it will be like to live in such a society?"

"Professor," Evans said, "you made some interesting comments in the hall—"

"*Interesting?* I accused them of flagrant immorality, and you call that *interesting?*"

"I'm sorry," Evans said, trying to move the discussion toward Hoffman's views. "You didn't explain why you think—"

"I do not *think* anything, young man. I *know.* That is the purpose of my research—to know things, not to surmise them. Not to theorize. Not to hypothesize. But to *know* from direct research in the field. It's a lost art in academia these days, young man—you are not *that* young—what is your name, anyway?"

"Peter Evans."

"And you work for Drake, Mr. Evans?"

"No, for George Morton."

"Well, *why didn't you say so!*" Hoffman said. "George Morton was a great, *great* man. Come along, Mr. Evans, and I will buy you some coffee and we can talk. Do you know what I do?"

"I'm afraid I don't, sir."

"I study the ecology of thought," Hoffman said. "And how it has led to a State of Fear."

SANTA MONICA
WEDNESDAY, OCTOBER 13
9:33 A.M.

They were sitting on a bench across the street from the conference hall, just beyond the milling crowds near the entrance. It was a busy scene, but Hoffman ignored everything around him. He spoke rapidly, with great animation, moving his hands so wildly that he often slapped Evans in the chest, but he never seemed to notice.

"Ten years ago, I began with fashion and slang," he said, "the latter being of course a kind of verbal fashion. I wanted to know the determinants of change in fashion and speech. What I quickly found is that there are no identifiable determinants. Fashions change for arbitrary reasons and although there are regularities—cycles, periodicities, and correlations— these are merely descriptive, not explanatory. Are you following me?"

"I think so," Evans said.

"In any case, I realized that these periodicities and correlations could be regarded as systems in themselves. Or if you will, ecosystems. I tested that hypothesis and found it heuristically valuable. Just as there is an ecology of the natural world, in the forests and mountains and oceans, so too there is an ecology of the man-made world of mental abstractions, ideas, and thought. That is what I have studied."

"I see."

"Within modern culture, ideas constantly rise and fall. For a while everybody believes something, and then, bit by bit, they stop believing it. Eventually, no one can remember the old idea, the way no one can remember the old slang. Ideas are themselves a kind of fad, you see."

"I understand, Professor, but why—"

"Why do ideas fall out of favor, you are wondering?" Hoffman said. He was talking to himself. "The answer is simply—they do. In fashion, as in natural ecology, there are disruptions. Sharp revisions of the established order. A lightning fire burns down a forest. A different species springs up in the charred acreage. Accidental, haphazard, unexpected, abrupt change. That is what the world shows us on every side."

"Professor . . ."

"But just as ideas can change abruptly, so, too, can they hang on past their time. Some ideas continue to be embraced by the public long after scientists have abandoned them. Left brain, right brain is a perfect example. In the 1970s, it gains popularity from the work of Sperry at Caltech, who studies a specific group of brain-surgery patients. His findings have no broader meaning beyond these patients. Sperry denies any broader meaning. By 1980, it is clear that the left and right brain notion is just wrong—the two sides of the brain do not work separately in a healthy person. But in the popular culture, the concept does not die for another twenty years. People talk about it, believe it, write books about it for decades after scientists have set it aside."

"Yes, all very interesting—"

"Similarly, in environmental thought, it was widely accepted in 1960 that there is something called 'the balance of nature.' If you just left nature alone it would come into a self-maintaining state of balance. Lovely idea with a long pedigree. The Greeks believed it three thousand years ago, on the basis of nothing. Just seemed nice. "However, by 1990, no scientist believes in the balance of nature anymore. The ecologists have all given it up as simply wrong. Untrue. A fantasy. They speak now of dynamic disequilibrium, of multiple equilibrium states. But they now understand that nature is *never* in balance. Never has been, never will be. On the contrary, nature is always *out of* balance, and that means—"

"Professor," Evans said, "I'd like to ask you—"

"That means that mankind, which was formerly defined as the great disrupter of the natural order, is nothing of the sort. The whole environment is being constantly disrupted all the time anyway."

"But George Morton . . ."

"Yes, yes, you wonder what I discussed with George Morton. I am coming to that. We are not off topic. Because of course, Morton wanted to know about environmental ideas. And particularly the idea of environmental crisis."

"What did you tell him?"

"If you study the media, as my graduate students and I do, seeking to find shifts in normative conceptualization, you discover something extremely interesting. We looked at transcripts of news programs of the major networks—NBC, ABC, CBS. We also looked at stories in the newspapers of New York, Washington, Miami, Los Angeles, and Seattle. We counted the frequency of certain concepts and terms used by the media. The results were very striking." He paused.

"What did you find?" Evans said, taking his cue.

"There was a major shift in the fall of 1989. Before that time, the media did not make excessive use of terms such as *crisis, catastrophe, cataclysm, plague,* or *disaster.* For example, during the 1980s, the word *crisis* appeared in news reports about as often as the word *budget.* In addition, prior to 1989, adjectives such as *dire, unprecedented, dreaded* were not common in television reports or newspaper headlines. But then it all changed."

"In what way?"

"These terms started to become more and more common. The word *catastrophe* was used five times more often in 1995 than it was in 1985. Its use doubled again by the year 2000. And the stories changed, too. There was a heightened emphasis on fear, worry, danger, uncertainty, panic."

"Why should it have changed in 1989?"

"Ah. A good question. *Critical* question. In most respects 1989 seemed like a normal year: a Soviet sub sank in Norway; Tiananmen Square in China; the *Exxon Valdez;* Salmon Rushdie sentenced to death; Jane Fonda, Mike Tyson, and Bruce Springsteen all got divorced; the Episcopal Church hired a female bishop; Poland allowed striking unions;

Voyager went to Neptune; a San Francisco earthquake flattened highways; and Russia, the US, France, and England all conducted nuclear tests. A year like any other. But in fact the rise in the use of the term *crisis* can be located with some precision in the autumn of 1989. And it seemed suspicious that it should coincide so closely with the fall of the Berlin Wall. Which happened on November ninth of that year."

Hoffman fell silent again, looking at Evans in a significant way. Very pleased with himself.

Evans said, "I'm sorry, Professor. I don't get it."

"Neither did we. At first we thought the association was spurious. But it wasn't. The Berlin Wall marks the collapse of the Soviet empire. And the end of the Cold War that had lasted for half a century in the West."

Another silence. Another pleased look.

"I'm sorry," Evans said finally. "I was thirteen years old then, and . . ." He shrugged. "I don't see where you are leading."

"I am leading to the notion of social control, Peter. To the requirement of every sovereign state to exert control over the behavior of its citizens, to keep them orderly and reasonably docile. To keep them driving on the right side of the road—or the left, as the case may be. To keep them paying taxes. And of course we know that social control is best managed through fear."

"Fear," Evans said.

"Exactly. For fifty years, Western nations had maintained their citizens in a state of perpetual fear. Fear of the other side. Fear of nuclear war. The Communist menace. The Iron Curtain. The Evil Empire. And within the Communist countries, the same in reverse. Fear of us. Then, suddenly, in the fall of 1989, it was all finished. Gone, vanished. *Over.* The fall of the Berlin Wall created a vacuum of fear. Nature abhors a vacuum. Something had to fill it."

Evans frowned. "You're saying that environmental crises took the place of the Cold War?"

"That is what the evidence shows. Of course, now we have radical fundamentalism and post–9/11 terrorism to make us afraid, and those are certainly real reasons for fear, but that is not my point. My point is, there is always a cause for fear. The cause may change over time, but the fear is always with us. Before terrorism we feared the toxic environment. Before that we had the Communist menace. The point is, although the specific cause of our fear may change, we are never without the fear itself. Fear pervades society in all its aspects. Perpetually."

He shifted on the concrete bench, turning away from the crowds.

"Has it ever occurred to you how astonishing the culture of Western society really is? Industrialized nations provide their citizens with unprecedented safety, health, and comfort. Average life spans increased fifty percent in the last century. Yet modern people live in abject fear. They are afraid of strangers, of disease, of crime, of the environment. They are afraid of the homes they live in, the food they eat, the technology that surrounds them. They are in a particular panic over things they can't even see—germs, chemicals, additives, pollutants. They are timid, nervous, fretful, and depressed. And even more amazingly, they are convinced that the environment of the entire planet is being destroyed around them. Remarkable! Like the belief in witchcraft, it's an extraordinary delusion—a global fantasy worthy of the Middle Ages. Everything is going to hell, and we must all live in fear. Amazing.

"How has this world view been instilled in everybody? Because although we imagine we live in different nations—France, Germany, Japan, the US—in fact, we inhabit exactly the same state, the State of Fear. How has that been accomplished?"

Evans said nothing. He knew it wasn't necessary.

"Well, I shall tell you how," he said. "In the old days—before your time, Peter—citizens of the West believed their nation-states were dominated by something called the military-industrial complex. Eisenhower warned Americans against it in the 1960s, and after two world wars Europeans knew very well what it meant in their own countries. But the military-industrial complex is no longer the primary driver of society. In reality, for the last fifteen years we have been under the control of an entirely new complex, far more powerful and far more pervasive. I call it the politico-legal-media complex. The PLM. And it is dedicated to promoting fear in the population—under the guise of promoting safety."

"Safety is important."

"Please. Western nations are fabulously safe. Yet people do not feel they are, because of the PLM. And the PLM is powerful and stable, precisely because it unites so many institutions of society. Politicians need fears to control the population. Lawyers need dangers to litigate, and make money. The media need scare stories to capture an audience. Together, these three estates are so compelling that they can go about their business even if the scare is totally groundless. If it has no basis in fact at all. For instance, consider silicon breast implants."

Evans sighed, shaking his head. "Breast implants?"

"Yes. You will recall that breast implants were claimed to cause cancer and autoimmune diseases. Despite statistical evidence that this was not true, we saw high-profile news stories, high-profile lawsuits, high-profile political hearings. The manufacturer, Dow Corning, was hounded out of the business after paying $3.2 billion, and juries awarded huge cash payments to plaintiffs and their lawyers.

"Four years later, definitive epidemiological studies showed beyond a doubt that breast implants did not cause disease. But by then the crisis had already served its purpose, and the PLM had moved on, a ravenous machine seeking new fears, new terrors. I'm telling you, *this is the way modern society works*—by the constant creation of fear. And there is no countervailing force. There is no system of checks and balances, no restraint on the perpetual promotion of fear after fear after fear. . . ."

"Because we have freedom of speech, freedom of the press."

"That is the classic PLM answer. That's how they stay in business," Hoffman said. "But think. If it is not all right to falsely shout 'Fire!' in a crowded theater, why is it all right to shout 'Cancer!' in the pages of *The New Yorker?* When that statement is not true? We've spent more than twenty-five billion dollars to clear up the phony power-line cancer claim.* 'So what?' you say. I can see it in your face. You're thinking, we're rich, we can afford it. It's only twenty-five billion dollars. But the fact is that twenty-five billion dollars is more than the total GDP of the poorest fifty nations of the world *combined*. Half the world's population lives on two dollars a day. So that twenty-five billion would be enough to support thirty-four million people for a year. Or we could have helped all the people dying of AIDS in Africa. Instead, we piss it away on a fantasy published by a magazine whose readers take it very seriously. Trust it. It is a *stupendous* waste of money. In another world, it would be a criminal waste. One could easily imagine another Nuremberg trial—this time for the relentless squandering of Western wealth on trivialities—and complete with pictures of the dead babies in Africa and Asia that result."

He hardly paused for breath. "At the very least, we are talking about a moral outrage. Thus we can expect our religious leaders and our great humanitarian figures to cry out against this waste and the needless deaths around the world that result. But do any religious leaders speak out? No. Quite the contrary, *they join the chorus.* They promote 'What Would Jesus Drive?' As if they have forgotten that what Jesus would drive is the false prophets and fearmongers out of the temple."

He was getting quite heated now.

"We are talking about a situation that is *profoundly* immoral. It is *disgusting*, if truth be told. The PLM callously ignores the plight of the poorest and most desperate human beings on our planet in order to keep fat politicians in office, rich news anchors on the air, and conniving lawyers in Mercedes-Benz convertibles. Oh, and university professors in Volvos. Let's not forget *them*."

"How's that?" Evans said. "What does this have to do with university professors?"

"Well, that's another discussion."

"Is there a short version?" Evans said.

"Not really. That's why headlines aren't news, Peter. But I will try to

---

* Estimate from the White House Science Office for all costs of the scare, including property devaluation and relocation of power lines. Cited in Park, *Voodoo Science*, p. 161. (Park was a participant in the controversy.)

be succinct," he said. "The point is this: the world has changed in the last fifty years. We now live in the knowledge society, the information society, whatever you want to call it. And it has had enormous impact on our universities.

"Fifty years ago, if you wanted to lead what was then called 'the life of the mind,' meaning to be an intellectual, to live by your wits, you had to work in a university. The society at large had no place for you. A few newspaper reporters, a few magazine journalists could be considered as living by their wits, but that was about it. Universities attracted those who willingly gave up worldly goods to live a cloistered intellectual life, teaching timeless values to the younger generation. Intellectual work was the exclusive province of the university.

"But today, whole sectors of society live the life of the mind. Our entire economy is based on intellectual work, now. Thirty-six percent of workers are knowledge workers. That's more than are employed in manufacturing. And when professors decided they would no longer teach young people, but leave that task to their graduate students who knew much less than they did and spoke English poorly—when that happened, the universities were thrown into crisis. What good were they anymore? They had lost their exclusive hold on the life of the mind. They no longer taught the young. Only so many theoretical texts on the semiotics of Foucault could be published in any single year. What was to become of our universities? What relevance did they have in the modern era?"

He stood up, as if energized by this question. Then abruptly, he sat down again.

"What happened," he continued, "is the universities transformed themselves in the 1980s. Formerly bastions of intellectual freedom in a world of Babbittry, formerly the locus of sexual freedom and experimentation, they now became the most restrictive environments in modern society. Because they had a new role to play. They became the creators of new fears for the PLM. Universities today are factories of fear. They invent all the new terrors and all the new social anxieties. All the new restrictive codes. Words you can't say. Thoughts you can't think. They produce a steady stream of new anxieties, dangers, and social terrors to be used by politicians, lawyers, and reporters. Foods that are bad for you. Behaviors that are unacceptable. Can't smoke, can't swear, can't screw, can't *think*. These institutions have been stood on their heads in a generation. It is really quite extraordinary.

"The modern State of Fear could never exist without universities feeding it. There is a peculiar neo-Stalinist mode of thought that is required to support all this, and it can thrive only in a restrictive setting, behind closed doors, without due process. In our society, only universities have created that—so far. The notion that these institutions are *liberal* is a cruel joke. They are fascist to the core, I'm telling you."

He broke off and pointed down the walkway. "Who is this fellow pushing toward us through the crowd? He looks oddly familiar."

Evans said, "That's Ted Bradley, the actor."

"Where have I seen him?"

"He plays the president on television."

"Oh yes. *Him.*"

Ted came to a halt in front of them, panting. "Peter," he said, "I've been looking everywhere for you. Is your cell phone on?"

"No, because—"

"Sarah has been trying to reach you. She says it's important. We have to leave town right away. And bring your passport."

Evans said, "We? What does this have to do with you?"

"I'm coming with you," Ted said.

As they started to walk away, Hoffman clutched at Evans's sleeve, holding him back. He had a new thought. "We haven't talked about *involution*," he said.

"Professor—"

"It is the next step in the development of nation-states. Indeed it is already happening. You must see the irony. After all, twenty-five billion dollars and ten years later the same rich elitists who were terrified of power-line cancer are buying magnets to strap to their ankles or put on their mattresses—imported Japanese magnets are the best, the most expensive—in order to enjoy the *healthful effects of magnetic fields*. The same magnetic fields—only now they can't get enough of them!"

"Professor," Evans said, "I have to go."

"Why don't these people just lie back against a TV screen? Snuggle up to a kitchen appliance? All the things that terrified them before."

"We'll talk later," Evans said, pulling his arm away.

"They even sell magnets in the *health* magazines! Healthy living through magnetic fields! Insanity! No one remembers even a few years ago! George Orwell. No memory!"

"Who is that guy?" Bradley said, as they headed off. "He seems a little wound up, doesn't he?"

"The record of catastrophe is contained within the ice cores," the speaker said, droning on at the podium. He was Russian and spoke with a heavy accent. "These ice cores from Greenland show that, in the last one hundred thousand years, there have been four abrupt climate change events. Some have occurred very quickly, in a few years. While the mechanisms by which these events occurred are still being studied, they demonstrate that there can be 'trigger' effects in climate, whereby small changes—including man-made changes—can produce catastrophically large effects. We have seen a foretaste of such effects in recent days with the calving of the world's largest iceberg, and the terrible loss of life from the flash flood in the American Southwest. And it is no difficulty to predict we will see more—"

He paused, as Drake hurried up onto the stage, whispered in his ear, then stepped down again, looking at his watch.

"Uh, I must beg the forgiveness of you," the speaker said. "I seem to have brought up an outdated version of my remarks. Word processors! That was a part from an old talk from 2001. What I wanted to say was that the calving of the iceberg in 2001—larger than many American states—and the dangerously unseasonal weather around the world, including the sunny Southwest, portends further climate instability. It is just beginning."

Sarah Jones, standing in the back, was talking with Ann Garner, the wife of a prominent Hollywood lawyer and a major contributor to NERF. Ann was emphatic as always, and talking nonstop.

"I'll tell you what I heard," Ann was saying. "I heard there is an industry-sponsored campaign to discredit NGOs. Industry is afraid of the growing power of the environmental movement and they are desperate, *desperate* to stop it. We have had our modest successes in recent years, and it is driving them crazy, and—"

"I'm sorry," Sarah said. "Just a minute, Ann." She turned to look at the Russian speaker at the podium. *What did he say?* she thought.

She walked quickly to the press table, where reporters were lined up with their laptops open. They were getting real-time transcripts of the conference.

She looked over the shoulder of Ben Lopez, the reporter for the *Los Angeles Times.* Ben didn't mind; he had been after her for months.

"Hi ya, sweet thing."

"Hi, Ben. Mind if I look at something?"

She touched the mouse, scrolling up the screen.

"Sure, be my guest. Nice perfume."

She read:

CAN BE TRIGGER EFFECTS IN CLIMATE, WHEREBY SMALL CHANGES INCLUDING MAN-MADE CHANGES CAN PRODUCE CATASTROPHICALLY LARGE EFFECTS. WE HAVE HAD A FORETASTE OF SUCH EFFECTS ~~IN RECENT DAYS WITH THE CALVING OF THE WORLD'S LARGEST ICEBERG AND THE TERRIBLE LOSS OF LIFE FROM THE FLASH FLOOD IN THE AMERICAN SOUTHWEST. AND IT IS NO DIFFICULTY TO PREDICT WE WILL SEE MORE~~

While she watched, the text changed, the strikeout disappearing, and replaced with new text:

CAN BE TRIGGER EFFECTS IN CLIMATE, WHEREBY SMALL CHANGES INCLUDING MAN-MADE CHANGES CAN PRODUCE CATASTROPHICALLY LARGE EFFECTS. WE HAVE HAD A FORETASTE OF SUCH EFFECTS WITH THE CALVING OF THE ICEBERG IN 2001 LARGER THAN MANY AMERICAN STATES AND THE DANGEROUSLY UNSEASONAL WEATHER AROUND THE WORLD INCLUDING THE SUNNY SOUTHWEST PORTENDS FURTHER CLIMATE INSTABILITY

"Holy shit," she said.

"Something wrong?" Ben said.

"Did you see what he said?"

"Yeah. Poor guy. Probably has jet lag to beat hell. And obviously, he's struggling with English . . ."

The original remarks were gone. The record was corrected. But there was no doubt about it: *the Russian had known in advance about the iceberg and the flash flood.* It was written into his speech. And somebody had forgotten to tell him, when he got off the plane, that it never happened.

He knew in advance.

But now the record was corrected, the remarks stricken. She glanced at the video camera in the back, recording the proceedings. No doubt the remarks would disappear from the video record as well.

The son of a bitch knew in advance.

"Hey," Ben said, "I don't know what you're so upset about. Clue me in, will you?"

"Later," she said. "I promise." She patted his shoulder, and went back to Ann.

"So," Ann said, "what we are facing is an industry-promoted campaign, well orchestrated, well financed, pervasive and ultra right-wing, that is intent on destroying the environmental movement that stands in its way."

After what she had just seen, Sarah was in no mood to put up with this blather. "Ann," she said. "Did it ever cross your mind you might be paranoid?"

"No. Anyway, even paranoids have enemies."

"How many industry executives serve on the NERF board right now?" Sarah said.

"Uh, not that many."

Sarah knew that there were thirty board members, of whom twelve were industry figures. This was the case with all modern environmental groups. They had all had industry representatives over the last twenty years.

"Did you ask your corporate board members about this secret industry campaign?"

"No," she said. She was looking at Sarah oddly.

"Do you think," Sarah said, "that it is possible that NGOs like NERF could be the ones who are engaged in a secret campaign?"

"What are you talking about?" Ann said, stiffening. "Sarah. We're the good guys."

"Are we?"

"Yes. We are," Ann said. "What's going on with you, Sarah?"

In the parking lot outside the convention hall, Sanjong Thapa sat in the car with his laptop on his knees. He had easily hacked the WiFi network used by the journalists and was receiving the conference transcript, which was instantaneously saved. He had done it that way because he was afraid he might be discovered and locked out at any moment, but now it meant that he had the complete transcript, including the revisions. Kenner, he thought, was going to love this.

On another screen, Sanjong was monitoring the satellite images from the western Atlantic, off the coast of Florida. A large high-pressure mass was beginning to rotate, forming the ragged beginnings of a hurricane. Clearly an event was scheduled around a hurricane, but for some reason it had been abandoned.

And now he was tracking other investigative leads. In particular, Kenner was concerned about a small research submarine known as DOEV/2, and the tender ship *AV Scorpio*. That submarine and its tender ship had been leased by CanuCo, a natural gas corporation based in Calgary, to conduct research in the South Pacific, looking for undersea gas deposits. The tender had sailed to Port Moresby, New Guinea, some two months before, and had subsequently left that harbor and had been spotted near Bougainville, in the Solomon Islands.

Nothing of great interest there, until it became known that CanuCo was not a registered Canadian corporation, and that it had no assets other than a website and web address. The owner of the site was CanuCo Leasing Corp, another nonexistent company. The lease payments had been made from a Cayman Island account and paid in euros. The name of the account was Seismic Services, also in Calgary, and sharing the same postal address as CanuCo.

They were obviously the same entity. And it was Seismic Services that had originally attempted to lease a submarine. And presumably had later caused the death of Nat Damon in Vancouver.

Now there were agencies in Washington searching satellite maps, trying to find the *AV Scorpio*, somewhere in the Solomon Island chain. But the Solomons had scattered cloud cover, and the satellite passes had not yet revealed the ship's location.

That in itself was worrisome. It suggested that the ship had already hidden itself in some way, perhaps by going into a covered dock.

Somewhere in the South Pacific.

And it was a big ocean.

Equally worrisome was the fact that the tender had sailed first to Vancouver, where it had taken on thirty tons of "industrial equipment," in five-ton cartons. The Canadian government had thought the company was illegally transporting automobiles in the cartons, so they opened one. The customs officers instead found some complex equipment that they listed as "diesel generators."

Generators!

Sanjong didn't know what was in those cartons, but he was sure they weren't diesel generators. Because you didn't have to go to Vancouver to get a bunch of generators. So it was worrisome—

"Hey! You!"

He looked up and saw two security guards walking across the parking lot toward his car. Obviously his WiFi hack had been detected. It was time to go. He turned the key in the ignition and drove away, waving cheerfully to the security guards as he passed them.

"Sarah? What's going on? You're just staring into space."

"Nothing, Ann." Sarah shook her head. "Just thinking."

"About what? And what do you mean about my being paranoid?" Ann put her hand on Sarah's arm. "Really. I'm a little concerned about you."

Sarah thought, *And I'm concerned about you.*

In truth, it was Sarah who was feeling a distinct paranoid chill. She looked around the room, and her eyes met Drake's. He was staring at her, studying her from across the room. For how long? Had he seen her quick dash to the reporters' desk? Had he deduced the meaning of it? Did he know she knew?

"Sarah," Ann said, shaking her arm.

"Listen," Sarah said. "I'm really sorry, but I have to go."

"Sarah. I'm worried about you."

"I'll be fine." She started to leave the room.

"I'll just come with you," Ann said, falling into step with her.

"I'd rather you didn't."

"I'm concerned for your welfare."

"I think I need to be alone for a while," Sarah said.

"Is that any way to treat a friend?" Ann said. "I insist, darling. You need a little mothering, I can see that. And I'm here for you."

Sarah sighed.

Nicholas Drake watched as Sarah left the room. Ann was sticking with her, just as he had asked. Ann was dedicated and tenacious. Sarah would be no match for her, unless she elected to turn and literally run. But if she did that . . . well, they would have to take stronger action. These were critical times, and sometimes strong action was essential. Just as in wartime.

But Drake suspected dire action would not prove necessary. True, Kenner had managed to disrupt the first two events, but only because ELF was a bunch of amateurs. Their brand of do-it-yourself schoolboy spontaneity was unsuited to the demands of modern media. Drake had said that to Henley a dozen times. Henley shrugged it off; he was concerned about deniability. Well, NERF could certainly deny they knew these clowns. What a bunch of fuckups!

But this last event was different. It had been planned far more carefully—it had to be—and it was in professional hands. Kenner would never be able to disrupt it. He could not even get there in time, Drake thought. And between Ted Bradley and Ann, Drake had lots of eyes and ears on that team as they progressed. And just to be sure, he had other surprises in store for Kenner as well.

He flipped open his phone and dialed Henley. "We've got them covered," he said.

"Good."

"Where are you?"

"I am about to deliver the news to V.," Henley said. "I am pulling up to his house now."

Through binoculars, Kenner watched as the silver Porsche convertible pulled into the driveway of the beach house. A tall, dark man in a blue golf shirt and tan slacks got out. He wore a baseball cap and dark glasses, but Kenner recognized him at once as Henley, the head of PR for NERF.

That closed the circle, he thought. He put the binoculars down on the fence and paused to consider the implications.

"Do you know who he is, sir?" the young FBI agent said, standing by his side. He was just a kid, no more than twenty-five.

"Yes," Kenner said. "I know who he is."

They were standing on the cliffs of Santa Monica, overlooking the beach and the ocean. The beach here was several hundred yards wide, from the shore to the bike path. Then a line of houses, packed close together along the coast highway. Then six lanes of roaring traffic.

Even though they abutted the highway, the houses were phenomenally expensive—twenty or thirty million dollars each, it was said, and perhaps much more. They were inhabited by some of the wealthiest people in California.

Henley was putting up the cloth top on his Porsche. He moved in a precise, almost fussy way. Then he went to the gate and buzzed it. The house he was entering was ultra-modern, curving shapes of glass. It glistened like a jewel in the morning sun.

Henley went inside. The gate closed behind him.

"But you don't care about people *entering* the house," the FBI agent said.

"That's right," Kenner said. "I don't."

"You don't want a list, or a record of who—"

"No."

"But it might prove—"

"No," Kenner said. The kid was trying to be helpful, but it was annoying. "I don't care about any of that. I just want to know when they all leave."

"Like, if they go on vacation or something?"

"Yes," Kenner said.

"What if they leave a maid behind?"

"They won't," Kenner said.

"Actually, sir, I'm pretty sure they will. These guys always leave somebody to watch the house."

"No," Kenner said. "This house will clear out. Everybody will go."

The kid frowned. "Whose house is it, anyway?"

"It belongs to a man named V. Allen Willy," Kenner said. He might as well tell him. "He's a philanthropist."

"Uh-huh. What is he, mixed up in the mob or something?"

"You might say," Kenner said. "Sort of a protection racket."

"It figures," the kid said. "Nobody makes that much money without a story behind it, you know what I mean?"

Kenner said he did. In fact, V. Allen Willy's story was as typically American as Horatio Alger's. Al Willy had started a chain of inexpensive clothing stores, taking clothes sewn in Third-World sweatshops and selling them in Western cities for thirty times the cost. After ten years, he sold his company for $400 million. Soon after, he became (by his own definition) a radical socialist, a crusader for a sustainable world, and an advocate for environmental justice.

The exploitations he had found so profitable he now attacked with the money he had made from them. He was fiery and righteous, and with the V. added to his name, memorable too. However, his attacks often led companies to pull out of their Third World factories, which were then taken over by Chinese corporations that paid local workers even less than before. Thus, by any sensible account, V. Allen Willy was exploiting workers twice—once to make his fortune, and a second time to assuage his guilty conscience at their expense. He was a strikingly handsome man and not stupid, just an egotistical and impractical do-gooder. Currently, he was said to be writing a book on the precautionary principle.

He had also started the V. Allen Willy Foundation, which supported the cause of environmental justice through dozens of organizations, including NERF. And he was important enough to rate a personal visit from Henley himself.

"So he's a rich environmentalist?" the FBI kid said.

"That's right," Kenner said.

The kid nodded. "Okay," he said. "But I still don't get it. What makes you think a rich guy would leave his house empty?"

"I can't tell you that," Kenner said. "But he will. And I want to know the minute it happens." He handed the agent a card. "Call this number."

The kid looked at the card. "That's it?"

"That's it," Kenner said.

"And when is this going to happen?"

"Soon," Kenner said.

His phone buzzed. He flipped it open. It was a text message from Sanjong.

THEY FOUND AV SCORPIO.

"I have to go," Kenner said.

"Nonsense," Ted Bradley said, sitting back in the passenger seat as Evans drove to Van Nuys. "You can't have all the fun, Pietro. I know you've been going on these secret excursions for the last week. I'm coming, too."

"You can't come, Ted," Evans said. "They won't allow it."

"Let me worry about that, okay?" he said, grinning.

Evans thought: What's going on? Bradley was staying so close, he was practically holding his hand. He refused to leave him alone.

Evans's cell phone rang. It was Sarah.

"Where are you?" she said.

"Almost to the airport. I have Ted with me."

"Uh-huh," she said, in the vague tone that meant she couldn't talk. "Well, we just got to the airport, and there seems to be a problem."

"What kind of a problem?"

"Legal," she said.

"What does that mean?" Evans said. But even as he spoke, he was turning off the road toward the gate leading to the runway, and he could see for himself.

Herb Lowenstein was standing there with eight security guards. And it looked like they were sealing the doors to Morton's jet.

Evans went through the gate and got out of the car. "What's going on, Herb?"

"The aircraft is being sealed," Herb said, "as required by law."

"What law?"

"George Morton's estate is now in probate, in case you've forgotten, and the contents of said estate, including all bank accounts and real property, must be sealed pending federal evaluation and assessing of death taxes. This aircraft will remain sealed until the conclusion of that evaluation. Six to nine months from now."

At that moment, Kenner pulled up in a town car. He introduced himself, shook hands with Lowenstein. "So it's a matter of probate," he said.

"That's right," Lowenstein said.

Kenner said, "I'm surprised to hear you say that."

"Why? George Morton is deceased."

"Is he? I hadn't heard."

"They found his body yesterday. Evans and Bradley went up and made the identification."

"And the medical examiner concurred?"

Lowenstein hesitated fractionally. "I presume so."

"You presume? Surely you've received documentation from the medical examiner to that effect. The autopsy was performed last night."

"I presume—I believe that we have the documentation."

"May I see it?"

"I believe it is at the office."

Kenner said, "May I see it?"

"That would merely cause unnecessary delay of my work here." Lowenstein turned to Evans. "Did you or did you not make a positive identification of Morton's body?"

"I did," Evans said.

"And you, Ted?"

"Yeah," Bradley said. "I did. It was him, all right. It was George. Poor guy."

Kenner said to Lowenstein, "I'd still like to see the medical examiner's notification."

Lowenstein snorted. "You have no basis for such a request, and I formally deny it. I am the senior attorney in charge of the estate. I am his designated executor, and I have already told you that my office has the documentation in hand."

"I heard you," Kenner said. "But I seem to remember that to falsely declare probate is fraud. That could be quite serious for an officer of the court such as you."

"Look," Lowenstein said, "I don't know what your game is—"

"I merely want to see the document," Kenner said calmly. "There's a fax machine in the flight office, right there." He pointed to the building, near the airplane. "You can have the document sent over in a few seconds and resolve this matter without difficulty. Or, barring that, you can call the medical examiner's office in San Francisco and confirm that they have, in fact, made a positive identification."

"But we are in the presence of two eyewitnesses who—"

"These are the days of DNA testing," Kenner said, looking at his watch. "I recommend that you make the calls." He turned to the security officers. "You can open the aircraft."

The security officers looked nonplussed. "Mr. Lowenstein?"

"Just a minute, just a goddamned minute," Lowenstein said, and stalked off toward the office, putting his cell phone to his ear as he went.

"Open the plane," Kenner said. He flipped open his wallet and showed the guards his badge.

"Yes, sir," they said.

Another car pulled up, and Sarah got out with Ann Garner. Ann said, "What's the fuss?"

"Just a little misunderstanding," Kenner said. He introduced himself to her.

"I know who you are," she said, with barely concealed hostility.

"I thought you might," Kenner said, smiling.

"And I have to say," she continued, "it's guys like you—smart and unscrupulous and immoral—who have made our environment the polluted mess that it now is. So let's just get that on the table right away. I don't like you, Mr. Kenner. I don't like you personally, and I don't like what you do in the world, and I don't like anything you stand for."

"Interesting," Kenner said. "Perhaps some day you and I could have a detailed and specific conversation about exactly what is wrong with our environment, and exactly who is responsible for making it a polluted mess."

"Whenever you want," she said, angrily.

"Good. You have legal training?"

"No."

"Scientific training?"

"No."

"What is your background?"

"I worked as a documentary film producer. Before I quit to raise my family."

"Ah."

"But I am very dedicated to the environment, and I have been all my life," she said. "I read everything. I read the 'Science' section of the *New York Times* every Tuesday *cover to cover*, of course *The New Yorker*, and the *New York Review*. I am extremely well informed."

"Well then," Kenner said, "I look forward to our conversation."

The pilots were driving up to the gate; they waited while it opened. "I think we can leave in a few minutes," Kenner said. He turned to Evans. "Why don't you confirm that that is all right with Mr. Lowenstein."

"Okay," Evans said, and headed toward the flight office.

"Just so you know," Ann said, "we're going with you. I am, and so is Ted."

"That will be delightful," Kenner said.

Inside the flight office, Evans found Lowenstein hunched over a phone in the back room reserved for pilots. "But I'm telling you, the guy isn't going for it, he wants documentation," Lowenstein said. And then after a pause, "Look, Nick, I'm not going to lose my license over this one. The guy's got a law degree from Harvard."

Evans knocked on the door. "Everything okay for us to leave?"

"Just a minute," Lowenstein said into the phone. He put his hand over the receiver. "You're going to leave now?"

"That's right. Unless you have the document . . ."

"It seems there is some confusion about the exact status of Morton's estate."

"Then we're going, Herb."

"Okay, okay."

He turned back to the phone. "They're leaving, Nick," he said. "You want to stop them, do it yourself."

In the cabin, everyone was sitting down. Kenner went around passing out sheets of paper. "What's this?" Bradley said, with a glance to Ann.

"It's a release," Kenner said.

Ann was reading aloud, "'. . . not liable in the event of death, serious bodily injury, disability, dismemberment'—*dismemberment?*"

"That's right," Kenner said. "You need to understand that where we are going is extremely dangerous. I strongly advise both of you not to come. But if you insist on ignoring my advice, you need to sign that."

"Where are we going?" Bradley said.

"I can't tell you that until the plane is in the air."

"Why is it dangerous?"

"Do you have a problem signing the form?" Kenner said.

"No. Hell." Bradley scrawled his signature.

"Ann?"

Ann hesitated, bit her lip, and signed.

The pilot closed the doors. The engines whined as they taxied up the runway. The flight attendant asked what they would like to drink.

"Puligny-Montrachet," Evans said.

Ann said, "Where are we going?"

"To an island off the coast of New Guinea."

"Why?"

"There is a problem," Kenner said, "that has to be dealt with."

"You want to be any more specific?"

"Not right now."

The plane rose above the cloud layer in Los Angeles, and turned west, over the Pacific.

Sarah felt relieved when Jennifer Haynes went to the front of the cabin to take a nap, falling instantly asleep. But she found it awkward to have Ann and Ted onboard. Conversation in the cabin was stilted; Kenner was not saying much. Ted was drinking heavily. He said to Ann, "Just so you know, Mr. Kenner doesn't believe in anything that normal people believe in. Not even global warming. Or Kyoto."

"Of course he doesn't believe in Kyoto," Ann said. "He's an industry hit man. Representing coal and oil interests."

Kenner said nothing. He just handed her his card.

"Institute for Risk Analysis," Ann read aloud. "That's a new one. I'll add it to the list of phony right-wing fronts."

Kenner said nothing.

"Because it's *all* disinformation," Ann said. "The studies, the press releases, the flyers, websites, the organized campaigns, the big-money smears. Let me tell you, industry was *thrilled* when the US didn't sign Kyoto."

Kenner rubbed his chin, and said nothing.

Ann said, "We're the world's largest polluter, and our government doesn't give a damn."

Kenner smiled blandly.

"So now the United States is an international pariah, isolated from the rest of the world and justifiably despised because we failed to sign the Kyoto Protocol to attack a global problem."

She continued to goad him in this way, and finally, it seemed, he had had enough. "Tell me about Kyoto, Ann," he said. "Why should we have signed it?"

"Why? Because we have a moral obligation to join the rest of the civilized world in reducing carbon emissions to below 1990 levels."

"What effect would that treaty have?"

"The whole world knows that. It would reduce global temperatures in the year 2100."

"By how much?"

"I don't know what you're driving at."

"Don't you? The answer is well known. The effect of Kyoto would be to reduce warming by .04 degrees Celsius in the year 2100. Four hundredths of a degree. Do you dispute that outcome?"

"I certainly do. Four what? Hundredths of a degree? That's ridiculous."

"So you don't believe that would be the effect of the Kyoto Protocol?"

"Well, maybe because the United States didn't sign it—"

"No, that would be the effect if we *did* sign it. Four hundredths of a degree."

"No," she said, shaking her head. "I don't believe that's true."

"The figure has been published a number of times in scientific journals. I can give you the references."*

Raising his glass, Bradley said to Ann, "This guy is real big on references."

"As opposed to rhetoric," Kenner said, nodding. "Yes. I am."

Bradley belched. "Four hundredths of a degree? In a hundred years? What a bunch of bullshit."

"One could say so."

---

* Most recently, *Nature* 22 (October 2003): 395–741, stated, with Russia signed on, temperature affected by Kyoto would be −.02 degrees C by 2050. IPCC models estimate more, but none exceed .15 C. Lomborg, p. 302. Wigley, 1998: "Global warming reductions are small, .08–.28 C."

"I just did," Bradley said.

"But Kyoto's a first step," Ann said, "that's the point. Because if you believe in the precautionary principle, as I do—"

"I didn't think the purpose of Kyoto was to take a first step," Kenner said. "I thought the purpose was to reduce global warming."

"Well, it is."

"Then why make a treaty that won't accomplish that? That won't, in effect, do anything at all?"

"It's a first step, as I said."

"Tell me: do you think it's *possible* to reduce carbon dioxide?"

"Of course. There are a host of alternative energy sources just waiting to be adopted. Wind power, solar, waste, geothermal—"

"Tom Wigley and a panel of seventeen scientists and engineers from around the world made a careful study and concluded it is not possible. Their paper was published in *Science*. They said there is no known technology capable of reducing carbon emissions, or even holding them to levels many times higher than today. They conclude that wind, solar, and even nuclear power will not be sufficient to solve the problem. They say totally new and undiscovered technology is required."*

"That's crazy," Ann said. "Amory Lovins laid it all out twenty years ago. Wind and solar, conservation, energy efficiency. There's no problem."

"Apparently there is. Lovins predicted that thirty-five percent of US power would come from alternative energy by the year 2000. The actual figure turned out to be six percent."

"Not enough subsidies."

"No country in the world produces thirty-five percent renewable energy, Ann."

"But countries like Japan do much better than we do."

Kenner said, "Japan is five percent renewable. Germany is five percent. England two percent."

---

* Martin Hoffert, et al., "Advanced Technology Paths to Global Climate Stability: Energy for a Greenhouse Planet," *Science* 298 (Nov. 1, 2002): 981–87. "Energy sources that can produce 100 to 300% of present world power consumption without greenhouse emissions do not exist."

"Denmark."

"Eight percent."

"Well," she said, "it just means we have more work to do."

"No question about that. Wind farms chop birds to pieces, so they might not be so popular. But solar panels would work. Silent, efficient . . ."

"Solar is great," she said.

"Yes," Kenner said. "And all we need is about twenty-seven thousand square kilometers of panels to do the job. Just cover the state of Massachusetts with solar panels and we'd be done. Of course by 2050 our energy needs will triple, so maybe New York would be a better choice."

"Or Texas. Nobody I know cares about Texas," Ann said.

"Well, there you are," Kenner said. "Cover ten percent of Texas, and you're in business. Although," he added, "Texans would probably prefer to cover Los Angeles first."

"You're making a joke."

"Not at all. Let's settle on Nevada. It's all desert anyway. But I'm curious to hear about your personal experience with alternative energy. What about you yourself, Ann? Have you adopted alternative sources?"

"Yes. I have solar heating for my swimming pool. The maid drives a hybrid."

"What do you drive?"

"Well, I need a bigger car for the kids."

"How big?"

"Well, I drive an SUV. Sometimes."

"What about your residence? You have solar panels for your electricity?"

"Well, I had consultants come to the house. Only, Jerry—my husband—says it's too expensive to install. But I'm working on him."

"And your appliances . . ."

"Every single one is Energystar. Every one."

"That's good. And how large is your family?"

"I have two boys. Seven and nine."

"Wonderful. How big is your house?"

"I don't know exactly."

"How many square feet?"

She hesitated.

"Ah hell, tell him, Ann," Bradley said. "She has a *huge* fucking house. Must be ten, fifteen thousand square feet. Absolutely *beautiful*. And the grounds! Got to be an acre, acre and a half. Sprinklers going day and night. And such gorgeous landscaping—she has fund-raisers there all the time. Always wonderful events."

Kenner looked at her.

"Twelve thousand," Ann said. "Square feet."

"For four people?" Kenner said.

"Well, my mother-in-law lives with us, sometimes. And of course the maid in the back."

"And do you have a second home?" Kenner said.

"Shit, she's got *two*," Bradley said. "Got a *fabulous* place in Aspen, and a great house in Maine as well."

"That we inherited," Ann said. "My husband—"

"And that apartment in London," Bradley said, "is that yours or your husband's company or what?"

"The company."

Kenner said, "How about travel? You use private jets?"

"Well, I mean we don't *own* one, but we catch rides, whatever. We go when people are going anyway. We fill the plane up. Which is a *good* thing."

"Of course," Kenner said. "But I must admit I'm a little confused about the philosophy—"

"Hey," she said, suddenly angry. "I live in a milieu where I have to keep up a certain standard. It's necessary for my husband's business, and—anyway, where do you live?"

"I have an apartment in Cambridge."

"How big?"

"Nine hundred square feet. I do not own a car. I fly coach."

"I don't believe you," she said.

"I think you'd better," Bradley said. "This guy knows what he's—"

"Shut up, Ted," Ann said. "You're drunk."

"Not yet, I'm not," he said, looking wounded.

"I'm not judging you, Ann," Kenner said quietly. "I know you're a dedicated advocate. I'm just trying to figure out what your real position is on the environment."

"My position is human beings are heating the planet and poisoning the planet and we have a moral obligation to the biosphere—to all the plants and animals that are being destroyed, and to the unborn generations of human beings—to keep these catastrophic changes from taking place." She sat back, nodding her head.

"So our moral obligation is to others—other plants, animals, and other people."

"Exactly."

"We need to do what is in their interest?"

"What is in the interest of all of us."

"Conceivably their interest is not the same as ours. Conflict of interest is the usual case."

"Every creature has a right to live on the planet."

"Surely you don't believe that," Kenner said.

"I do. I'm not speciesist. Every living creature."

"Even the malaria parasite?"

"Well, it *is* part of nature."

"Then do you oppose the elimination of polio and smallpox? They were part of nature, too."

"Well, I would have to say it's part of the arrogant pattern of mankind, changing the world to suit his purposes. A testosterone-driven impulse, not shared by women—"

"You didn't answer me," Kenner said. "Do you oppose the elimination of polio and smallpox?"

"You're playing with words."

"Hardly. Is changing the world to suit one's purposes unnatural?"

"Of course. It is interfering with nature."

"Ever seen a termite mound? A beaver dam? Those creatures change the environment dramatically, affecting many other creatures. Are they interfering with nature?"

"The world is not in danger," she said, "from termite mounds."

"Arguably it is. The total weight of termites exceeds the total weight of all the humans in the world. A thousand times greater, in fact. Do you know how much methane termites produce? And methane is a more potent greenhouse gas than carbon dioxide."

"I can't continue this," Ann said. "You enjoy arguing. I don't. I just want to make the world a better place. I'm going to go read a magazine now." She went to the front of the plane and sat down, her back to Kenner.

Sarah stayed where she was. "Her intentions are good," she said.

"And her information is bad," Kenner said. "A prescription for disaster."

Ted Bradley roused himself. He had watched the debate between Kenner and Ann. He liked Ann. He was pretty sure he had gone to bed with her; when he was drinking, he sometimes couldn't remember, but he had a vaguely fond memory of Ann, and he assumed that was the reason for it.

"I think you're being harsh," Bradley said, in his presidential tone. "Why should you call someone like Ann 'a prescription for disaster?' She cares very much about these issues. She has devoted her life to them, really. She cares."

"So what?" Kenner said. "*Caring* is irrelevant. Desire to do good is irrelevant. All that counts is *knowledge* and *results*. She doesn't have the knowledge—and, worse, she doesn't know it. Human beings don't know how to do the things she believes ought to be done."

"Like what?"

"Like managing the environment. We don't know how to do that."

"What are you talking about?" Bradley said, throwing his hands in the air. "This is nonsense. Of course we can manage the environment."

"Really? Do you know anything about the history of Yellowstone Park? The first national park?"

"I've been there."

"That's not what I asked."

"Could you just get to the point?" Bradley said. "It's pretty late for Q-and-A, Professor. You know what I mean?"

"All right, then," Kenner said. "I'll tell you."

Yellowstone Park, he explained, was the first wilderness to be set aside as a natural preserve anywhere in the world. The region around the Yellowstone River in Wyoming had long been recognized for its wondrous scenic beauty. Lewis and Clark sang its praises. Artists like Bierstadt and Moran painted it. And the new Northern Pacific Railroad wanted a scenic attraction to draw tourists west. So in 1872, in part because of railroad pressure, President Ulysses Grant set aside two million acres and created Yellowstone National Park.

There was only one problem, unacknowledged then and later. No one had any experience trying to preserve wilderness. There had never been any need to do it before. And it was assumed to be much easier than it proved to be.

When Theodore Roosevelt visited the park in 1903, he saw a landscape teeming with game. There were thousands of elk, buffalo, black bear, deer, mountain lions, grizzlies, coyotes, wolves, and bighorn sheep. By that time there were rules in place to keep things as they were. Soon after that, the Park Service was formed, a new bureaucracy whose sole job was to maintain the park in its original condition.

Yet within ten years, the teeming landscape that Roosevelt saw was gone forever. And the reason for this was the park managers—charged with keeping the park in pristine condition—had taken a series of steps that they thought were in the best interest of preserving the park and its animals. But they were wrong.

"Well," Bradley said, "our knowledge has increased with time . . ."

"No, it hasn't," Kenner said. "That's my point. It's a perpetual claim that we know more today, and it's not borne out by what actually happened."

Which was this: the early park managers mistakenly believed that elk were about to become extinct. So they tried to increase the elk herds within the park by eliminating predators. To that end, they shot and poisoned all the wolves in the park. And they prohibited Indians from hunting in the park, though Yellowstone was a traditional hunting ground.

Protected, the elk herds exploded, and ate so much of certain trees and grasses that the ecology of the area began to change. The elk ate the trees that the beavers used to make dams, so the beavers vanished. That was when the managers discovered beavers were vital to the overall water management of the region.

When the beavers disappeared, the meadows dried up; the trout and otter vanished; soil erosion increased; and the park ecology changed even further.

By the 1920s it had become abundantly clear there were too many elk, so the rangers began to shoot them by the thousands. But the change in plant ecology seemed to be permanent; the old mix of trees and grasses did not return.

It also became increasingly clear that the Indian hunters of old had exerted a valuable ecological influence on the park lands by keeping down the numbers of elk, moose, and bison. This belated recognition came as part of a more general understanding that native Americans had strongly shaped the "untouched wilderness" that the first white men saw—or thought they were seeing—when they first arrived in the New World. The "untouched wilderness" was nothing of the sort. Human beings on the North American continent had exerted a huge influence on the environment for thousands of years—burning plains grasses, modifying forests, thinning specific animal populations, and hunting others to extinction.

In retrospect, the rule forbidding Indians from hunting was seen as a mistake. But it was just one of many mistakes that continued to be made in an unbroken stream by park managers. Grizzlies were protected, then killed off. Wolves were killed off, then brought back. Animal research involving field study and radio collars was halted, then resumed after certain species were declared endangered. A policy of fire prevention was instituted, with no understanding of the regenerative effects of fire. When the policy was finally reversed, thousands of acres burned so hotly that the ground was sterilized, and the forests did not grow back without reseeding. Rainbow trout were introduced in the 1970s, soon killing off the native cutthroat species.

And on and on.

And on.

"So what you have," Kenner said, "is a history of ignorant, incompetent, and disastrously intrusive intervention, followed by attempts to repair the intervention, followed by attempts to repair the damage caused by the repairs, as dramatic as any oil spill or toxic dump. Except in this case there is no evil corporation or fossil fuel economy to blame. This disaster was caused by environmentalists charged with protecting the wilderness, who made one dreadful mistake after another—and, along the way, proved how little they understood the environment they intended to protect."

"This is absurd," Bradley said. "To preserve a wilderness, you just preserve it. You leave it alone and let the balance of nature take over. That's all that is required."

"Absolutely wrong," Kenner said. "Passive protection—leaving things alone—doesn't preserve the status quo in a wilderness, any more than it does in your backyard. The world is alive, Ted. Things are constantly in flux. Species are winning, losing, rising, falling, taking over, being pushed back. Merely setting aside wilderness doesn't freeze it in its present state, any more than locking your children in a room will prevent them from growing up. Ours is a changing world, and if you want to preserve a piece of land in a particular state, you have to decide what that state is, and then actively, even aggressively, manage it."

"But you said we don't know how to do that."

"Correct. We don't. Because any action you take causes change in the environment, Ted. And any change hurts some plant or animal. It's inevitable. Preserving old-growth forest to help the spotted owl means Kirtland's warbler and other species are deprived of the new-growth forest they prefer. There is no free lunch."

"But—"

"No buts, Ted. Name an action that had only positive consequences."

"Okay, I will. Banning CFCs for the ozone layer."

"That harmed Third World people by eliminating cheap refrigerants so that their food spoiled more often and more of them died of food poisoning."

"But the ozone layer is more important—"

"Perhaps to you. They might disagree. But we're talking about whether you can take an action that does not have harmful consequences."

"Okay. Solar panels. Water recycling systems for houses."

"Enables people to put houses in remote wilderness areas where formerly they could not because of lack of water and power. Invades wilderness and thus endangers species that were previously unmolested."

"Banning DDT."

"Arguably the greatest tragedy of the twentieth century. DDT was the best agent against mosquitoes, and despite the rhetoric there was nothing anywhere near as good or as safe. Since the ban, two million people a year have died unnecessarily from malaria, mostly children. All together, the ban has caused more than fifty million needless deaths.* Banning DDT killed more people than Hitler, Ted. And the environmental movement pushed hard for it."†

"But DDT was a carcinogen."

"No, it wasn't. And everybody knew it at the time of the ban."‡

"It was unsafe."

"Actually, it was so safe you could eat it. People did just that for two

---

* Some estimates put the number at 30 million deaths.
† Full discussion of DDT in Wildavsky, 1994, pp. 55–80.
‡ Sweeney Committee, 25 April 1972, "DDT is not a carcinogenic hazard to man." Ruckelshaus banned it two months later, saying, DDT "poses a carcinogenic risk" to man. He never read the Sweeney report.

years, in one experiment.* After the ban, it was replaced by parathion, which is *really* unsafe. More than a hundred farm workers died in the months after the DDT ban, because they were unaccustomed to handling really toxic pesticides."[†]

"We disagree about all this."

"Only because you lack the relevant facts, or are unwilling to face up to the consequences of the actions of organizations you support. Banning DDT will someday be seen as a scandalous blunder."

"DDT was never banned."

"You're right. Countries were just told that if they used it, they wouldn't get foreign aid." Kenner shook his head. "But the unarguable point, based on UN statistics, is that before the DDT ban, malaria had become almost a minor illness. Fifty thousand deaths a year worldwide. A few years later, it was once again a global scourge. Fifty million people have died since the ban, Ted. Once again, there can be no action without harm."

A long silence followed. Ted shifted in his seat, started to speak, then closed his mouth again. Finally he said, "Okay. Fine." He adopted his most lofty, presidential manner. "You have persuaded me. I grant you the point. So?"

"So the real question with any environmental action is, do the benefits outweigh the harm? Because there is always harm."

"Okay, okay. So?"

"When do you hear any environmental group speak that way? Never. They're all absolutists. They go before judges arguing that regulations should be imposed with no consideration of costs at all.[‡] The requirement that regulations show a cost-benefit was imposed on them by the courts after a period of wretched excess. Environmentalists screamed bloody murder about cost-benefit requirements and they're still screaming. They don't want people to know how much their forays into regulation actually cost society and the world. The most egregious

---

* Hayes, 1969.
† John Noble Wilford, "Deaths from DDT Successor Stir Concern," *New York Times*, 21 August 1970, p. 1; Wildavsky, 1996, p. 73.
‡ Case references in Sunstein, pp. 200–1.

example was the benzene regulations in the late 1980s that were so expensive for so little benefit that they ended up costing twenty billion dollars for every year of life saved.* Do you agree with that regulation?"

"Well, when you put it in those terms, no."

"What other terms are there, Ted, besides the truth? Twenty billion dollars *to save one year of life*. That was the cost of the regulation. Should you support organizations that push for such wasteful regulation?"

"No."

"The lead benzene lobbying group in Congress was NERF. Are you going to resign from its board?"

"Of course not."

Kenner just nodded slowly. "And there we have it."

Sanjong was pointing to the computer screen, and Kenner came over, sliding into the seat next to him. The screen showed an aerial image of a tropical island, heavily forested, and a broad curving bay of blue water. The photo seemed to be taken from a low-flying airplane. Around the bay were four weathered wood shacks.

"Those are new," Sanjong said. "They went up in the last twenty-four hours."

"They look old."

"Yes, but they're not. Close inspection suggests that they are artificial. They may be made out of plastic instead of wood. The largest one appears to be a residence, and the other three house equipment."

"What kind of equipment?" Kenner said.

"Nothing has been visible in the photographs. The equipment was probably offloaded at night. But I went back and got a decent description from Hong Kong customs. The equipment consists of three hypersonic

---

* See the Harvard Center for Risk Analysis study: Tengs, et al., 1995. For full discussion, see Lomborg, p. 338ff. He concludes: "When we ignore the cost of our environmental decisions . . . on other areas . . . we are in reality committing statistical murder." He puts the number of unnecessary dead at 60,000 per year in the US alone.

cavitation generators. Mounted in carbon matrix resonant impact assembly frames."

"Hypersonic cavitation equipment is for sale?"

"They got it. I don't know how."

Kenner and Sanjong were huddled together, speaking in low tones. Evans drifted over, leaned in close. "What's a hypersonic whatever-it-is?" he said quietly.

"Cavitation generator," Kenner said. "It's a high-energy acoustic device the size of a small truck that produces a radially symmetric cavitation field."

Evans looked blank.

"Cavitation," Sanjong explained, "refers to the formation of bubbles in a substance. When you boil water, that's cavitation. You can boil water with sound, too, but in this case the generators are designed to induce cavitation fields in a solid."

Evans said, "What solid?"

"The earth," Kenner said.

"I don't get it," Evans said. "They're going to make bubbles in the ground, like boiling water?"

"Something like that, yes."

"Why?"

They were interrupted by the arrival of Ann Garner. "Is this a boys-only meeting?" she said. "Or can anyone sit in?"

"Of course," Sanjong said, tapping the keyboard. The screen showed a dense array of graphs. "We were just reviewing the carbon dioxide levels of ice cores taken from Vostok and from North GRIP in Greenland."

"You guys can't keep me in the dark forever, you know," Ann said. "Sooner or later we will land this plane. And then I'm going to find out what you're really up to."

"That's true," Kenner said.

"Why not tell me now?"

Kenner just shook his head.

The pilot clicked the radio. "Check your seat belts, please," he said. "Prepare for landing in Honolulu."

Ann said, "Honolulu!"

"Where did you think we were going?"

"I thought—"

And then she broke off.

Sarah thought: *She knows where we are going.*

While they refueled at Honolulu, a customs inspector came onboard and asked to see their passports. He seemed amused by the presence of Ted Bradley, whom he referred to as "Mr. President"; Bradley in turn was pleased by the attention from a man in uniform.

After the customs officer checked their passports, he said to the group, "Your destination is filed as Gareda in the Solomon Islands. I just want to make sure you're aware of the travel advisory for Gareda. Most embassies have warned visitors against going there in view of the current conditions."

"What current conditions?" Ann said.

"There are rebels active on the island. There have been a number of murders. The Australian army went in last year and captured most of the rebels, but not all. There have been three murders in the last week, including two foreigners. One of the corpses was, uh, mutilated. And the head was taken."

"What?"

"The head was taken. Not while he was alive."

Ann turned to Kenner. "That's where we are going? Gareda?"

Kenner nodded slowly.

"What do you mean, the head was taken?"

"Presumably, it was for the skull."

"The skull," she repeated. "So . . . you're talking about head-hunters . . ."

Kenner nodded.

"I'm getting off this plane," she said, and gathering up her hand bag, walked down the stairs.

Jennifer was just waking up. "What's her problem?"

"She doesn't like good-byes," Sanjong said.

Ted Bradley was stroking his chin in what he imagined was a thoughtful manner. He said, "A foreigner had his head cut off?"

"Apparently, it was worse than that," the customs officer said.

"Jesus. What's worse than that?" Bradley said, laughing.

The customs officer said, "The situation on the ground is not entirely clear. The reports are conflicting."

Bradley stopped laughing. "No. Seriously: I want to know. What's worse than beheading?"

There was a brief silence.

"They ate him," Sanjong said.

Bradley rocked back in his chair. "They *ate* him?"

The customs officer nodded. "Parts of him," he said. "At least, that's the report."

"Holy shit," Bradley said. "Which parts? Never mind, I don't want to know. Jesus Christ. They *ate* the guy."

Kenner looked at him. "You don't have to go, Ted," he said. "You can leave, too."

"I have to admit, I'm thinking about it," he said, in his judicious, pres- idential tone. "Getting eaten is not a distinguished end to a career. Think of any of the greats. Think of Elvis—eaten. John Lennon—eaten. I mean, it's not how we want to be remembered." He fell silent, lowering his chin to his chest, sunk deep in thought, then raising it again. It was a gesture he'd done a hundred times on television. "But, no," he said finally. "I'll accept the danger. If you're going, I'm going."

"We're going," Kenner said.

TO GAREDA
WEDNESDAY, OCTOBER 13
9:30 P.M.

It was nine hours flight time to Kontag Airport in Gareda. The cabin was dark; most of them slept. Kenner as usual stayed awake, sitting in the back with Sanjong, talking quietly.

Peter Evans woke up about four hours into the flight. His toes still burned from the Antarctic episode and his back was very sore from his being bounced around in the flash flood. But the pain in his toes reminded him that he was supposed to check them daily, to see if they were becoming infected. He got up and went to the back of the plane, where Kenner was sitting. He pulled off his socks and inspected his toes.

"Sniff 'em," Kenner said.

"What?"

"Smell them. You have any gangrene, you'll smell it first. They hurt?"

"Burn. Mostly just at night."

Kenner nodded. "You'll be all right. I think you'll keep them all."

Evans sat back, thinking how strange it was to have a conversation about losing his toes. Somehow it made his back hurt more. He went into the bathroom at the back of the plane and rummaged through the drawers looking for painkillers. All they had was Advil, so he took that, then came back.

"That was a clever story you arranged in Honolulu," he said. "Too bad it didn't work on Ted."

Kenner just stared.

"It's not a story," Sanjong said. "There were three murders yesterday."

"Oh. And they ate somebody?"

"That was the report."

"Oh," Evans said.

Going forward into the dark cabin, Evans saw Sarah sitting up. She whispered, "Can't sleep?"

"No. A little achy. You?"

"Yeah. Toes hurt. From the frostbite."

"Me, too."

She nodded toward the galley. "Any food back there?"

"I think so."

She got up, headed back. He trailed after her. She said, "The tops of my ears hurt, too."

"Mine are okay," he said.

She rummaged around, found some cold pasta. She held a plate out to him. He shook his head. She spooned out a plate for herself and began to eat. "So, how long have you known Jennifer?"

"I don't really know her," he said. "I just met her recently, at the law office."

"Why is she coming with us?"

"I think she knows Kenner."

"She does," Kenner said, from his chair.

"How?"

"She's my niece."

"Really?" Sarah said. "How long has she been your nie—never mind. I'm sorry. It's late."

"She's my sister's kid. Her parents died in a plane crash when she was eleven."

"Oh."

"She's been on her own a lot."

"Oh."

Evans looked at Sarah and thought once again that it was a kind of trick, how she could get up from sleeping and appear beautiful, and perfect. And she had on that perfume that had driven him quietly crazy from the moment he first smelled it.

"Well," Sarah said. "She seems very nice."

"I don't, uh, there's nothing . . ."

"It's fine," she said. "You don't have to pretend with me, Peter."

"I'm not pretending," he said, leaning slightly closer, smelling her perfume.

"Yes, you are." She moved away from him, and sat down opposite Kenner. "What happens when we get to Gareda?" she said.

The thing about her, Evans thought, was that she had the most chilling ability to instantly behave as if he did not exist. Right now she was not looking at him; she was focusing all her attention on Kenner, talking with apparent concentration to Kenner and behaving as if no one else were there.

Was that supposed to be provocative? he thought. Was that supposed to be a turn-on, to get him excited and start the chase? Because it didn't make him feel that way at all. It pissed him off.

He wanted to slap his hand down on the counter, make a big noise, and say, "Hel-lo! Earth to Sarah!" Or something like that.

But somehow he thought that that would make things worse. He could imagine her annoyed glance. *You're such a baby*. Something like that. It made him long for somebody uncomplicated, the way Janis was uncomplicated. Just a great body and a voice you could tune out. That was exactly what he needed now.

He gave a long sigh.

She heard it, glanced up at him, and then patted the seat beside her. "Come sit here, Peter," she said, "and join the conversation." And she gave him a big, dazzling smile.

He thought: *I am very confused.*

• • •

"This is Resolution Bay," Sanjong said, holding out his computer screen. It showed the bay, then zoomed back to show a map of the entire island. "It's on the northeast side of the island. The airport is on the west coast. It's about twenty-five miles away."

The island of Gareda looked like a big avocado immersed in the water, with jagged edges along the shore. "There is a mountain spine running along the center of the island," Sanjong said. "In places, it's three thousand feet high. The jungle in the interior of the island is very dense, essentially impenetrable, unless you follow the roads or one of the footpaths through the jungle. But we can't make our way cross country."

"So we take a road," Sarah said.

"Maybe," Sanjong said. "But the rebels are known to be in this area here—" he circled the center of the island with his finger "—and they have split up in two or possibly three groups. Their exact locations are not known. They have taken over this small village here, Pavutu, near the north coast. That seems to be their headquarters. And they presumably have roadblocks up, and probably patrols on the jungle paths."

"Then how do we get to Resolution Bay?"

Kenner said, "By helicopter, if we can. I've arranged for one, but this is not the most reliable part of the world. If we can't do that, we'll head out by car. See how far we can get. But at this point we just don't know how we're going to do it."

Evans said, "And when we get to Resolution Bay?"

"There are four new structures on the beach. We have to take them down and dismantle the machinery inside. Make them inoperable. We also have to find their submarine tender and dismantle the submarine."

"What submarine?" Sarah said.

"They leased a small two-man research sub. It's been in the region for the last two weeks."

"Doing what?"

"We're pretty sure we know now. The whole Solomon Island chain

of more than nine hundred islands is located within a very active geological part of the world in terms of plate tectonics. The Solomons are
a part of the world where plates crunch together. That's why they have
many volcanoes there, and so many earthquakes. It's a very unstable
region. The Pacific Plate collides and slides under the Oldowan Java
Plateau. The result is the Solomon Trench, a huge undersea feature that
curves in an arc all along the northern side of the island chain. It's very
deep, between two thousand and six thousand feet. The trench is just
north of Resolution Bay, too."

"So it's an active geological region with a deep trench," Evans said. "I
still don't see the game."

"Lot of undersea volcanoes, lot of slope debris, and therefore the
potential for landslides," Kenner said.

"Landslides." Evans rubbed his eyes. It was late.

"Undersea landslides," Kenner said.

Sarah said, "They're trying to cause an undersea landslide?"

"We think so. Somewhere along the slope of the Solomon Trench.
Probably at the five-hundred- to one-thousand-foot depth."

Evans said, "And what would that do? An undersea landslide?"

Kenner said to Sanjong, "Show them the big map." Sanjong brought
up a map of the entire Pacific basin, from Siberia to Chile, Australia to
Alaska.

"Okay," Kenner said. "Now draw a straight line out from Resolution
Bay and see where it takes you."

"California!"

"Right. In about eleven hours."

Evans frowned. "An undersea landslide . . ."

"Displaces an enormous volume of water very quickly. That is the
most common way a tsunami is formed. Once propagated, the wave front
will travel right across the Pacific at five hundred miles an hour."

"Holy shit," Evans said. "How big a wave are we talking?"

"Actually, it's a series, what's called a wave train. The undersea landslide in Alaska in 1952 generated a wave forty-seven feet high. But the

height of this one is impossible to anticipate because wave height is a function of the shoreline it hits. In parts of California it could be up to sixty feet high. A six-story building."

"Oh boy," Sarah said.

"And how much time do we have before they do this?" Evans said.

"The conference runs two more days. The wave will take a day to cross the Pacific. So . . ."

"We have one day."

"At most, yes. One day to land, make our way to Resolution Bay, and stop them."

"Stop who?" Ted Bradley said, yawning and coming back toward them. "Je-sus! Do I have a headache or what! How about a little hair of the dog?" He paused, stared at the group, looking from face to face. "Hey, what's going on here? You guys look like I interrupted a funeral."

TO GAREDA
THURSDAY, OCTOBER 14
5:30 A.M.

Three hours later, the sun came up and the plane began its descent. Now it was flying low, passing over green forested islands fringed in an unearthly pale blue. They saw few roads and few towns, mostly small villages.

Ted Bradley looked out the window. "Isn't it beautiful?" he said. "Truly unspoiled paradise. This is what is vanishing in our world."

Seated opposite him, Kenner said nothing. He, too, was staring out the window.

"Don't you think the problem," Bradley said, "is that we have lost contact with nature?"

"No," Kenner said. "I think the problem is I don't see many roads."

"Don't you think," Bradley said, "that's because it's the white man, not the natives, who wants to conquer nature, to beat it into submission?"

"No, I don't think that."

"I do," Bradley said. "I find that people who live closer to the earth, in their villages, surrounded by nature, that those people have a natural ecological sense and a feeling for the fitness of it all."

"Spent a lot of time in villages, Ted?" Kenner said.

"As a matter of fact, yes. I shot a picture in Zimbabwe and another one in Botswana. I know what I am talking about."

"Uh-huh. You stayed in villages all that time?"

"No, I stayed in hotels. I had to, for insurance. But I had a lot of experiences in villages. There is no question that village life is best and ecologically soundest. Frankly, I think everyone in the world should live that way. And certainly, we should not be encouraging village people to industrialize. That's the problem."

"I see. So you want to stay in a hotel, but you want everybody else to stay in a village."

"No, you're not hearing—"

"Where do you live now, Ted?" Kenner said.

"Sherman Oaks."

"Is that a village?"

"No. Well, it's a sort of a village, I suppose you could say . . . But I have to be in LA for my work," Bradley said. "I don't have a choice."

"Ted, have you ever stayed in a Third-World village? Even for one night?"

Bradley shifted in his seat. "As I said before, I spent a lot of time in the villages while we were shooting. I know what I'm talking about."

"If village life is so great, why do you think people want to leave?"

"They shouldn't leave. That's my point."

"You know better than they do?" Kenner said.

Bradley paused, then blurted: "Well, frankly, if you must know, yes. I do know better. I have the benefit of education and broader experience. And I know firsthand the dangers of industrial society and how it is making the whole world sick. So, yes, I think I do know what is best for them. Certainly I know what is ecologically best for the planet."

"I have a problem," Kenner said, "with other people deciding what is in my best interest when they don't live where I do, when they don't know the local conditions or the local problems I face, when they don't even live in the same country as I do, but they still feel—in some far-off Western city, at a desk in some glass skyscraper in Brussels or Berlin or New York—they still feel that they know the solution to all my problems and how I should live my life. I have a problem with that."

"What's your problem?" Bradley said. "I mean, look: You don't seriously believe everybody on the planet should do whatever they want, do you? That would be terrible. These people need help and guidance."

"And you're the one to give it? To 'these people?'"

"Okay, so it's not politically correct to talk this way. But do you want all these people to have the same horrific, wasteful living standard that we do in America and, to a lesser extent, Europe?"

"I don't see you giving it up."

"No," Ted said, "but I conserve where I can. I recycle. I support a carbon-neutral lifestyle. The point is, if all these other people industrialize, it will add a terrible, terrible burden of global pollution to the planet. That should not happen."

"I got mine, but you can't have yours?"

"It's a question of facing realities," Bradley said.

"Your realities. Not theirs."

At that point, Sanjong beckoned to Kenner. "Excuse me," Kenner said, and got up.

"Walk away if you want," Bradley said, "but you know I speak truth!" He gestured to the flight attendant and held up his glass. "Just one more, sweetie. One more for the road."

Sanjong said, "The helicopter's not there yet."

"What's the matter?"

"It was coming over from another island. They've closed the air space because they're worried the rebels have surface-to-air missiles."

Kenner frowned. "How long until we land?"

"Ten minutes."

"Keep your fingers crossed."

Abandoned, Ted Bradley slid to the other side of the plane, to sit with Peter Evans. "Isn't it gorgeous?" he said. "Look at that water. Crystalline and pure. Look at the depth of that blue. Look at those beautiful villages, in the heart of nature."

Evans was staring out the window but saw only poverty. The villages were clusters of corrugated tin shacks, the roads red mud ruts. The people looked poorly dressed and moved slowly. There was a depressing, disconsolate feeling about them. He imagined sickness, disease, infant death . . .

"Gorgeous," Bradley said. "Pristine! I can't wait to get down there. This is as good as a vacation! Did anyone here know the Solomons were so beautiful?"

From the front, Jennifer said, "Inhabited by headhunters, for most of history."

"Yes, well, that's all in the past," Bradley said. "If it ever existed at all. I mean, all that talk about cannibalism. Everybody knows it is not true. I read a book by some professor.* There never were any cannibals, anywhere in the world. It's all a big myth. Another example of the way the white man demonizes people of color. When Columbus came to the West Indies, he thought they told him there were cannibals there, but it wasn't true. I forget the details. There are no cannibals anywhere. Just a myth. Why are you staring at me that way?"

Evans turned. Bradley was talking to Sanjong, who was indeed staring.

"Well?" Bradley said. "You're giving me a look. Okay, buddy boy. Does that mean you disagree with me?"

"You're truly a fool," Sanjong said, in an astonished voice. "Have you ever been to Sumatra?"

"Can't say that I have."

"New Guinea?"

"No. Always wanted to go, buy some tribal art. Great stuff."

"Borneo?"

"No, but I always wanted to go there, too. That Sultan What's his name, he did a great job remodeling the Dorchester in London—"

"Well," Sanjong said, "if you go to Borneo you will see the Dyak longhouses where they still display the skulls of the people they killed."

---

* William Arens, *The Man-Eating Myth*.

"Oh, that's just tourist-attraction stuff."

"In New Guinea, they had a disease called *kuru*, transmitted by eating the brains of their enemies."

"That's not true."

"Gajdusek won a Nobel Prize for it. They were eating brains, all right."

"But that was a long time ago."

"Sixties. Seventies."

"You guys just like to tell scare stories," Bradley said, "at the expense of the indigenous people of the world. Come on, face the facts, human beings are not cannibals."*

Sanjong blinked. He looked at Kenner. Kenner shrugged.

"Absolutely beautiful down there," Bradley said, looking out the window. "And it looks like we're going to land."

---

* Cannibalism in the American southwest: http://www.nature.com/nature/fow/000907.html; Richard A. Marlar, Leonard L. Banks, Brian R. Billman, Patricia M. Lambert, and Jennifer Marlar, "Biochemical evidence of cannibalism at a prehistoric Puebloan site in southwestern Colorado, *Nature* 407, 74078 (7 Sept. 2000). Among Celts in England: http://www.bris.ac.uk/Depts/Info-Office/news/archive/cannibal.htm. Among Neanderthals: http://news.bbc.co.uk/1/hi/sci/tech/462048.stm; same issue, Jared M. Diamond, "Archeology, talk of cannibalism" ("Incontrovertible evidence of cannibalism has been found at a 900-year-old site in the southwestern United States. Why do horrified critics deny that many societies have found cannibalism acceptable?").

VII

RESOLUTION

GAREDA
THURSDAY, OCTOBER 14
6:40 A.M.

Kotak Field was sticky with humid heat. They walked to the small open shack that was marked KASTOM in roughly painted letters. To one side of the building was a wooden fence and a gate marked with a red hand-print and a sign that said, NOGOT ROT.

"Ah, nougat rot," Bradley said. "Must be a local tooth problem."

"Actually," Sanjong said, "the red hand means *kapu*. 'Forbidden.' The sign says 'No Got Right,' which is Pidgin for 'You don't have permission to pass.'"

"Huh. I see."

Evans found the heat almost unbearable. He was tired after the long plane ride, and anxious about what lay ahead of them. Alongside him, Jennifer walked casually, seemingly fresh and energetic. "You're not tired?" Evans said to her.

"I slept on the plane."

He looked back at Sarah. She, too, seemed to have plenty of energy, striding forward.

"Well, I'm pretty tired."

"You can sleep in the car," Jennifer said. She didn't seem very interested in his condition. He found it a little irritating.

And it was certainly debilitatingly hot and humid. By the time they reached the customs house, Evans's shirt was soaked. His hair was wet.

Sweat was dripping off his nose and chin onto the papers he was supposed to fill out. The pen from the ink ran in the puddles of his sweat. He glanced up at the customs officer, a dark, muscular man with curly hair and wearing pressed white trousers and a white shirt. His skin was dry; he looked almost cool. He met Evans's eyes, and smiled. *"Oh, waitman, dis no taim bilong san. You tumas hotpela."*

Evans nodded. "Yes, true," he said. He had no idea what the man had said.

Sanjong translated. "It's not even the hot time of summer. But you're too much hot. You *tumas hot.* Ya?"

"He got that right. Where'd you learn Pidgin?"

"New Guinea. I worked there a year."

"Doing what?"

But Sanjong was hurrying on with Kenner, who was waving to a young man who had driven up in a Land Rover. The man jumped out. He was dark, wearing tan shorts and a T-shirt. His shoulders were covered in tattoos. His grin was infectious. "Hey, Jon Kanner! *Hamamas klok!"* He pounded his chest with his fist and hugged Kenner.

"He has a happy heart," Sanjong said. "They know each other."

The newcomer was introduced all around as Henry, with no other name. "Hanri!" he said, grinning broadly, pumping their hands. Then he turned to Kenner.

"I understand there is trouble with the helicopter," Kenner said.

"What? No *trabel. Me got klostu long."* He laughed. "It's just over there, my friend," he said, in perfectly accented British English.

"Good," Kenner said, "we were worried."

"Yas, but serious Jon. We better *hariyap. Mi yet harim planti yangpelas, krosim, pasim birua, got plenti masket, noken stap gut, ya?"*

Evans had the impression Henry was speaking Pidgin so the rest of them would not understand.

Kenner nodded. "I heard that, too," he said. "Lots of rebels here. They're mostly young boys? And angry? And well armed. Figures."

"I worry for the helicopter, my friend."

"Why? Do you know something about the pilot?"

"Yes, I do."

"Why? Who is the pilot?"

Henry giggled, and slapped Kenner on the back. "I am!"

"Well, then, we should go."

They all started down the road, away from the airfield. The jungle rose up on both sides of the road. The air buzzed with the sound of cicadas. Evans looked back with longing at the beautiful white Gulfstream jet, poised on the runway against a blue sky. The pilots in their white shirts and black trousers were checking the wheels. He wondered if he would ever see the airplane again.

Kenner was saying, "And we heard, Henry, some people were killed?"

Henry made a face. "No just killed, Jon. *Olpela*. Ya?"

"So we heard."

"Ya. *Distru*."

So it was true. "The rebels did it?"

Henry nodded. "Oh! this new *chif*, him name Sambuca, like a drink. Don't ask why this name. Him crazy man, Jon. *Longlong man tru*. Everything back to *olpela* for dis guy. Old ways are better. *Allatime allatime*."

"Well, the old ways are better," Ted Bradley said, trudging along behind, "if you ask me."

Henry turned. "You got cell phones, you got computers, you got antibiotics, medicines, hospitals. And you say the old ways are better?"

"Yes, because they are," Bradley said. "They were more human, they allowed more of the human texture to life. Believe me, if you ever had a chance to experience these so-called modern miracles yourself, you would know that they're not so great—"

"I got a degree at the University of Melbourne," Henry said. "So I have some familiarity."

"Oh, well, then," Bradley said. And under his breath, he muttered, "Might have told me. Asshole."

"By the way," Henry said, "take my advice, don't do that here. Don't talk under your breath."

"Why not?"

"In this country, some *pelas* think it means you've been possessed by a demon and they'll get scared. And they might kill you."

"I see. Charming."

"So, in this country, if you have something to say, you speak up!"

"I'll remember that."

Sarah walked alongside Bradley, but she was not listening to the conversation. Henry was a character, caught between worlds, sometimes speaking in an Oxbridge accent, sometimes dropping into Pidgin. It didn't bother her.

She was looking at the jungle. The air on the road was hot and still, trapped between the huge trees that rose up on both sides of the path. The trees were forty, fifty feet high, covered in twisted vines. And at ground level, in the darkness beneath the canopy above, huge ferns grew so thickly they presented an impenetrable barrier, a solid green wall.

She thought: You could walk five feet into that and get lost forever. You'd never find your way out again.

Along the road were the rusted hulks of long-abandoned cars, windshields smashed, chassis crumpled and corroded brown and yellow. As she walked past she saw ripped upholstery, old dashboards with clocks and speedometers ripped out, leaving gaping holes.

They turned right onto a side path and she saw the helicopter ahead. She gasped. It was beautiful, painted green with a crisp white stripe, the metal blades and struts gleaming. Everybody commented on it.

"Yes, the outside is good," Henry said. "But I think the inside, the engine, maybe is not so good." He wiggled his hand. "So so."

"Great," Bradley said. "Speaking for myself, I'd prefer it the other way around."

They opened the doors to get in. In the back were stacks of wooden crates, with sawdust. They smelled of grease. "I got the supplies you wanted," he said to Kenner.

"And enough ammunition?"

"Oh ya. All things you asked for."

"Then we can go," Kenner said.

In the back, Sarah buckled her belt. She put on headphones. The engines whined, and the blades spun faster. The helicopter shuddered as it started to lift off. "We have too many people," Henry said, "so we will have to hope for the best! Cross your fingers!"

And giggling maniacally, he lifted off into the blue sky.

The jungle slid beneath them, mile after mile of dense canopy forest. In places, wisps of mist clung to the trees, particularly at the higher altitudes. Sarah was surprised at how mountainous the island was, how rugged the terrain. She saw no roads at all. From time to time, they passed over a small village in a jungle clearing. Otherwise, nothing but miles of trees. Henry was flying due north, intending to drop them off along the coast a few miles west of Resolution Bay.

"Charming villages," Ted Bradley said, as they flew over another one. "What do the people grow here?"

"Nothing. Land's no good here. They work the copper mines," Henry said.

"Oh, that's too bad."

"Not if you live here. Biggest money they ever saw. People kill to work in the mines. What I mean to say is, they kill. Some murders occur every year."

Bradley was shaking his head. "Terrible. Just terrible. But look down there," he said, pointing. "There's a village has actual thatched huts. Is that the old style, the old way of doing things, still kept alive?"

"No man," Henry said. "That's a rebel village. That's *new* style. Big thatch *haus*, very impressive, big house for *chif*." He explained that Sambuca had instructed the people in every village to build these huge, three-story structures of thatch, complete with ladders going up to high walkways at the third level. The idea was to give rebels a view over the jungle, so they could see the arrival of Australian troops.

But in the old days, Henry said, the people never had such buildings in Gareda. The architecture was low and open, erected mostly to protect against rain and let smoke out. There was no need for high buildings, which were impractical since they would blow down in the next cyclone anyway. "But Sambuca, he wants them now, so he makes the *yangpelas*, the young fellows, build them. There may be six or eight on this island now, in rebel territory."

"So we're going over rebel territory now?" Bradley said.

"So far, so good," Henry said. And he giggled again. "Not so long now, we'll see the coast in four, five minutes and—Oh damn shit!"

"What?" They were skimming the forest canopy.

"I made a big mistake."

"What mistake?" Bradley said.

"*Tumas longwe es.*"

"You're too far east?" Kenner said.

"Damn shit. Damn damn shit. Hang on!" Henry banked the helicopter steeply, but not before they all glimpsed a huge clearing, with four of the enormous thatch structures interspersed with the more common houses of wood and corrugated tin. There were a half-dozen trucks clustered in the muddy center of the clearing. Some of the trucks had machine guns mounted on their backs.

"What is this?" Bradley said, looking down. "This is much bigger than the others—"

"This Pavutu! Rebel headquarters!"

And then the clearing was gone, the helicopter moving swiftly away. Henry was breathing hard. They could hear his breath over the earphones.

Kenner said nothing. He was staring intently at Henry.

"Well, I think we're all right," Bradley said. "It looks like they didn't see us."

"Oh yeah," Henry said. "Nice wish."

"Why?" Bradley said. "Even if they did see us—what can they do?"

"They have radios," Henry said. "They're not stupid, these *yangpelas.*"

"What do you mean?"

"They want this helicopter."

"Why? Can they fly it?"

"*Orait orait!* Yes! Because they want me, too." Henry explained that for months now, no helicopters had been allowed on the island. This one had been brought over only because Kenner had pulled some very important strings. But it was specifically not to fall into rebel hands.

"Well, they probably think we're going south," Bradley said. "I mean, we are, aren't we?"

"These boys know better," Henry said. "They know."

"They know what?" Bradley said.

Kenner said, "The ELF would have had to buy off the rebels in order to land on the island. So the rebels know there's something going on at Resolution Bay. When they saw this helicopter, they knew where it was going."

"These boys aren't stupid," Henry said again.

"I never said they were," Bradley protested.

"Ya. But you think it. I know you, *waitman.* This in the back of your tongue. You think it."

"I promise you, I did not," Bradley said. "Really. I have no such feelings at all. You simply didn't understand me."

"Ya," Henry said.

Sarah was sitting in the middle of the second seat, wedged between Ted and Jennifer. Peter and Sanjong were behind in the little backseat, with all the boxes. She couldn't really see out the windows, so she had trouble following the discussion. She wasn't sure what it was all about.

So she asked Jennifer. "Do you understand what's going on?"

Jennifer nodded. "As soon as the rebels saw the helicopter they knew it was going to Resolution. Now, whatever we do, they'll be expecting it to show up in that area. They have radios, and they're in different groups scattered around. They can keep an eye on us. And they'll be there when we land."

"I am very sorry," Henry said. "So very sorry."

"Never mind," Kenner said. His voice was neutral.

"What do we do now?" Henry said.

Kenner said, "Continue exactly as planned. Go north and put us down on the coast."

There was no mistaking the urgency in his voice.

In the backseat, pushed up against Sanjong, smelling the grease that coated the machine guns, Peter Evans wondered where this urgency came from. He looked at his watch. It was nine in the morning, which meant that of their original twenty-four hours, only twenty remained. But this was a small island, and it should allow plenty of time—

And then he had a thought. "Wait a minute," he said. "What time is it in Los Angeles?"

Sanjong said, "They're on the other side of the dateline. Twenty-seven hours behind."

"No, I mean elapsed time. Actual time difference."

"Six hours."

"And you calculated a transit time of what?"

"Thirteen hours," Sanjong said.

"I think we made a mistake," Evans said, biting his lip. He wasn't sure how much he should say in front of Henry. And indeed, Sanjong was shaking his head, indicating *not now*.

But they *had* made a mistake. There was no doubt about it. Assuming that Drake wanted the tidal wave to hit on the last day of the conference, he would surely want it to happen during the morning. That would provide the most visible disaster. And it would allow the whole afternoon for discussion and media interviews afterward. Every television camera in America would be at that conference, talking to the scientists who just happened to be there. It would create a gigantic media event.

So, Evans thought, assume the wave was to hit Los Angeles no later than noon tomorrow.

Subtract thirteen hours for the wave front to cross the Pacific.

That meant the wave had to be propagated at eleven P.M. Los Angeles time. Which meant that the local time in Gareda would be . . . five P.M.

Five P.M. *today.*

They didn't have a day to stop this thing from happening.

They had just eight hours.

So that was the reason for Kenner's urgency. That was why he was going ahead with his plan, despite the new problem. He had no choice, and he knew it. He had to land on the coast somewhere very near Resolution. There wasn't enough time to do anything else.

Even though it was possible they were heading right into a trap.

Leaving the forest behind, the helicopter burst out over blue water and turned around, going east. Evans saw a narrow sandy beach with patches of ragged lava rock, and mangrove swamps clinging to the water's edge. The helicopter swung low and followed the beach, heading east.

"How far from Resolution are we?" Kenner said.

"Five, six kilometers," Henry said.

"And how far from Pavutu?"

"Maybe ten kilometers, on a mud track."

"Okay," Kenner said. "Let's find a place to put down."

"There's a good place I know maybe one kilometer ahead."

"Fine. Go there."

Evans was thinking. Five kilometers walking on a beach, that was about three miles, should take them an hour and a half at most. They could make it to Resolution Bay well before noon. That would give them—

"This the spot," Henry said. A finger of rugged lava protruded into the ocean. Centuries of waves had smoothed it enough to make a landing possible.

"Do it," Kenner said.

The helicopter circled, prepared to descend. Evans was looking out over at the dense wall of jungle, where it met the beach. He saw tire tracks in the sand and a sort of gap in the trees that was probably a road. And those tire tracks—

"Say listen," Evans said. "I think—"

Sanjong jabbed him in the ribs. Hard.

Evans grunted.

"What is it, Peter?" Kenner said.

"Uh, nothing."

"We're going down," Henry said. The helicopter descended smoothly, slowly settling onto the lava. Waves lapped at the edge of the rock pad. It was peaceful. Kenner looked out the bubble canopy, scanning the area.

"Okay? This good spot?" Henry said. He seemed nervous now that they were down. "I don't want to stay so long, Jon. Because maybe they come soon . . ."

"Yeah, I understand."

Kenner cracked open the door, then paused.

"So, alla okay. Jon?"

"Just fine, Henry. Very nice spot. Get out and open this back door for us, will you?"

"Yeah, Jon, I think you can get it—"

"*Get out!*" And with astonishing swiftness there was a gun jammed against Henry's head. Henry sputtered and moaned in fear as he fumbled with his door. "But Jon, I need to stay inside, Jon—"

"You've been a bad boy, Henry," Kenner said.

"You going to shoot me now, Jon?"

"Not now," Kenner said, and abruptly he shoved him out. Henry tumbled onto the sharp lava, howling in pain. Kenner slid over to the pilot's seat and shut the door. Immediately Henry was up, pounding on the canopy, his eyes wild. He was terrified.

"Jon! Jon! Please, Jon!"

"Sorry, Henry." Kenner pushed the stick, and the helicopter began to rise into the air. They had not climbed twenty feet before a dozen men emerged from the jungle all along the beach and began firing at them with rifles. Kenner swung out over the ocean, going north, away from the island. Looking back, they could see Henry standing forlorn on the lava. Some of the men were running toward him. He threw up his hands.

"Little shit," Bradley said. "He would have gotten us killed."

"He may still," Kenner said.

They flew due north, over open water.

"So what do we do now," Sarah said, "land on the other side of the bay? Walk in from the other side?"

"No," Kenner said. "That's what they'll expect us to do."

"So, then . . ."

"We wait a few minutes and go back to the western side, same as before."

"They won't be expecting that?"

"They may. We'll go to a different spot."

"Farther away from the bay?"

"No. Closer."

"Won't ELF hear us?"

"Doesn't matter. By now, they know we're coming."

In the back, Sanjong was breaking open the wooden cases and reaching for the guns. He stopped abruptly.

"Bad news," he said.

"What?"

"No guns." He pushed a lid higher. "These crates contain ammunition. But no guns."

"That little bastard," Bradley said.

"What do we do now?" Sarah said.

"We go in anyway," Kenner said.

He turned the helicopter and, skimming the water, headed back to Gareda.

RESOLUTION
THURSDAY, OCTOBER 14
9:48 A.M.

The western arc of Resolution Bay consisted of a hilly, jungle-covered spine that jutted out into the water, terminating in a rocky point. The outer side of the spine flattened into a rocky plateau, some fifty feet above the beach, which curved off to the west. The plateau was protected by high overhanging trees.

That was where the helicopter now stood, covered in a camouflage tarp, overlooking the beach below. Evans glanced back at it, hoping that it would blend into the landscape, but instead it was only too obviously visible, especially when seen from above. The group was now already fifty feet above it, as they scrambled and clawed up the jungle slope that rose steeply from the beach. It was surprisingly tough going. They were climbing single file, and had to be careful because the ground underfoot was muddy. Bradley had already slipped, and slid some ten yards down. His whole left side was covered in black mud. And Evans could see that there was a fat leech on the back of his neck, but he decided not to point it out just then.

No one spoke. The team of six climbed in silence, trying to make as little noise as possible. Despite their best efforts, they were fairly noisy, the undergrowth crackling beneath their feet, small branches snapping as they reached to pull themselves up.

Kenner was somewhere farther ahead, leading the way. Evans couldn't see him. Sanjong was bringing up the rear. He had a rifle slung over his shoulder; he had brought it with him and assembled it from a small briefcase in the copter. Kenner carried a pistol. The rest of them were unarmed.

The air was still, wet, and stupefyingly hot. The jungle buzzed, an incessant background drone of insects. Halfway up the slope, it began to rain, lightly at first and then a stupendous tropical downpour. In a moment they were drenched. Water streamed down the hillside. It was slipperier than ever.

Now they were two hundred feet above the beach, and the prospect of losing footing was clearly nervous-making. Peter looked up at Sarah, who was just ahead of him. She moved with her usual agility and grace. She seemed to be dancing up the hillside.

There were times, he thought, huffing his way along, when he really resented her.

And Jennifer, who was ahead of Sarah, was climbing with equal ease. She hardly reached for the tree limbs, though Evans was grabbing for them constantly, feeling panic as his fingers slipped on the fungus-covered bark. Watching Jennifer, he had the sense that she was almost too good at this, too skilled. Going up this treacherous jungle hill, she radiated a kind of indifference, as if it were all to be expected. It was the attitude of an Army Ranger, or the member of some elite force, tough, experienced, conditioned. Unusual, he thought, for a lawyer. More than unusual. But then, she was Kenner's niece.

And farther up was Bradley, with the leech on his neck. He was muttering and cursing and grunting with every step. Finally Jennifer punched him, then held a finger to her lips: be quiet. Bradley nodded, and though he clearly disliked taking advice from her, he was silent from then on.

At around three hundred feet they felt the stirring of a breeze, and soon after, they climbed onto the crest of the ridge. The foliage was so thick they could not see down into Resolution Bay below, but they could hear the shouts of working men and the intermittent rumble of machinery.

Briefly, there was a kind of electronic hum, a sound that started softly, then built quickly until in a few moments it seemed literally to fill the air, and to make Evans's eardrums ache.

Then the sound was gone.

Evans looked at Kenner.

Kenner just nodded.

Sanjong climbed a tree, scaling it quickly. From his vantage point, he could look down on the valley. He came back down, and pointed to a hill leading down to the bay. He shook his head: too steep at this point. He indicated they should circle around, and descend on a more gentle slope.

So they started out, following the ridge around the bay. Most of the time they could see nothing but the six-foot-tall ferns dripping with water. After half an hour, there was a sudden break in the foliage, and they had a panoramic view of Resolution Bay spread out below them.

The bay was about a mile wide, and had structures set at intervals on the sand. The largest one was to the far right, at the eastern edge of the bay. Three others of equal size were arranged at intervals, making a sort of triangle in the western section of the bay.

Evans could see there was something funny about the houses, though. Something odd about the wood that was used. He squinted.

Sanjong nudged him. He wiggled his hand in the air.

Evans looked. Yes, it was true. The wooden structures were moving, fluttering in the air.

They were tents.

Tents made to look like wooden structures. And pretty good ones, too. It was no wonder they had fooled the aerial survey, Evans thought.

As they watched, men emerged from one or another of the tents and shouted to others down the beach. They were speaking English, but it was difficult to make out what they were saying at this distance. Most of it seemed to be technical.

Sanjong nudged Evans again. Evans saw him make a kind of pyramid with three fingers. Then he began to wiggle the fingers.

So, apparently they were tuning the generators in the tent. Or something like that.

The others in the group did not seem to be interested in the details. They were breathing hard, catching their breaths in the soft breeze, and staring down at the bay. And probably thinking, as Evans was, that there were a lot of men down there. At least eight or ten. All in jeans and work shirts.

"Christ, there's a lot of those bastards," Bradley muttered.

Jennifer nudged him hard in the ribs.

He mouthed: Oh, sorry.

She shook her head. She mouthed: You'll get us killed.

Bradley made a face. He clearly thought she was being melodramatic.

Then, from the jungle below them, they heard a cough.

They froze.

They waited in silence. They heard the buzz of cicadas, the occasional call of distant birds.

It came again, the same soft cough. As if the person was trying not to make noise.

Sanjong crouched down, listening hard. The cough came a third time, and to Evans there was the strangest sensation of familiarity about it. It reminded him of his grandfather, who had had heart failure when Evans was a kid. His grandfather used to cough like that, in the hospital. Weakly. Little coughs.

Now there was silence. They had not heard the cougher move away—if he had, he was truly noiseless—but the sound stopped.

Kenner looked at his watch. They waited five minutes, then he signaled for them to continue moving east, curving around the bay.

Just as they were leaving, they heard the cough once more. This time, there were three, in succession: *uh uh uh*. Then nothing.

Kenner signaled. Move out.

They had not gone a hundred yards when they came upon a path. It was a clear trail, even though the overhanging branches hung low. It must be an animal trail, Evans thought, wondering vaguely what kind of animals they might be. There were probably feral pigs here. There were pigs everywhere. He vaguely remembered stories of people being surprised by pigs, gored by the tusks of an aggressive boar that charged out of the underbrush—

The first thing he heard, however, was a mechanical *click*. He knew instantly what it was: the sound of a gun being cocked.

The entire group froze, strung out in single file. Nobody moved. Another *click*.

And another. *Click!*

Evans looked around quickly. He saw nobody. It seemed they were alone in the jungle.

Then he heard a voice: "*Dai. Nogot sok, waitman. Indai. Stopim!*"

Evans had no idea what it meant, but the meaning was clear enough to them all. Nobody moved.

From the bushes ahead, a young boy emerged. He was wearing boots without socks, green shorts, a "Madonna World Tour" T-shirt, and a baseball cap that said "Perth Glory." A half-smoked cigarette stub hung from his lips. He had an ammunition belt over one shoulder and a machine gun slung over the other shoulder. He was five feet tall and could not have been more than ten or eleven. He pointed his gun with casual insolence. "*Okay, waitman. You prisner biulong me, savve? Bookim dano!*" And he jerked his thumb, indicating they should move forward. "*Gohet!*"

For a moment, they were all too astonished to move. Then, from the jungle on both sides of the path, other boys emerged.

Bradley said, "What is this, the lost boys?"

Without expression, one of the kids slammed the butt of his rifle into Bradley's stomach. Bradley gasped and went down.

"*Stopim waitman bilong toktok.*"

"Oh, Jesus," Bradley said, rolling on the ground.

The kid hit him again, this time in the head, and kicked him hard. Bradley moaned.

"*Antap! Antap!*" the kid said, gesturing for him to get up. When Bradley didn't respond, the kid kicked him again. "*Antap!*"

Sarah went over and helped Bradley to his feet. Bradley was coughing. Sarah was smart enough not to say anything.

"*Oh, nais mari,*" the kid said. Then he pushed her away from Bradley. "*Antap!*"

But as they trudged forward, one of the kids went over to Bradley, and squeezed the back of his arm, the triceps. He laughed. "*Taiis gut!*"

Evans felt a chill, as the words sank in. These boys were speaking a version of English. He could decipher it, if he thought about it a little, and played the words back in his head. *Nais mari* was "Nice Mary." Maybe Mary was a word for woman. *Antap* was "And up."

And *taiis gut* was "Taste good."

They walked single file through the jungle, the kids at their side. Kenner was in the lead, then Ted, who was bleeding from his head, and Sarah, and Jennifer. Then Evans.

Evans glanced over his shoulder.

Sanjong was not behind him.

All he saw was another ragged kid with a rifle. "*Antap! Antap!*"

The kid made a threatening gesture with his rifle.

Evans turned, and hurried forward.

There was something chilling about being herded by children. Except these weren't children. He was only too aware of the cold look in their eyes. They had seen a lot in their lives. They lived in another world. It was not Evans's world.

But he was now in theirs.

Up ahead, he saw a pair of jeeps at the side of a muddy road.

He looked at his watch. It was ten o'clock.

Seven hours to go.

But somehow it didn't seem important anymore.

The kids pushed them into the jeeps, and then they drove off, down a muddy track, into the dark and trackless interior of the jungle.

PAVUTU
THURSDAY, OCTOBER 14
11:02 A.M.

There were times, Sarah thought, when she really did not want to be a woman. That was how she felt as she was driven into the muddy village of Pavutu, the rebel stronghold, in the back of an open jeep. The village seemed to be populated almost entirely by men, who came yelling into the clearing to see who had arrived. But there were women, too, including older women who stared at her height and her hair, and then came up and poked at her, as if she might not be real.

Jennifer, who was shorter and darker, stood beside her and attracted no attention at all. Nevertheless, they were herded together into one of the huge thatch houses. Inside the house was a large open space, a kind of central room, three stories high. There was a ladder made of wood leading up to a series of landings, going all the way to the top, where there was a kind of catwalk and a viewing area. In the center of the room was a fire, and at the fire sat a heavyset man with pale skin and a dark beard. He wore sunglasses and had a sort of beret with the Jamaican flag on it.

This, it seemed, was Sambuca. They were shoved in front of him, and he leered at them, but it was clear to Sarah—she had an instinct for these things—that he was not interested in them. He was interested in Ted, and in Peter. Kenner he inspected briefly, then looked away.

"Killim."

They pushed Kenner out the door, poking him with the butts of their rifles. They were clearly excited at the prospect of executing him.

"*No nau,*" Sambuca said, in a growl. "*Behain.*"

It took Sarah a moment to translate in her head. Not now. Behind. Which must mean later on, she thought. So Kenner had a reprieve, at least for a while.

Sambuca turned and stared at the others in the room.

"*Meris,*" he said, with a dismissive wave. "*Goapim meri behain.*"

Sarah had the distinct impression, from the grins on the faces of the boys, that they were being given the freedom to do with the two women what they wanted. Go up 'em. She and Jennifer were led off to a back room.

Sarah remained calm. Of course she knew things were bad. But they were not bad yet. She was noticing that Jennifer did not appear to be shaken in the least. She had the same flat, uninterested expression that she might have if she was walking toward a company cocktail party.

The boys took the two women into a thatched room at the back of the larger building. There were two posts sunk in the earthen floor. One of the kids took out a pair of handcuffs and cuffed Jennifer to one post, her hands behind her back. Then he cuffed Sarah to the other post in the same way. Then another kid reached up and squeezed Sarah's tit, smiled knowingly, and walked out of the room.

"Charming," Jennifer said, when they were alone. "You all right?"

"So far, yes." There were drums starting to beat from somewhere outside, in the courtyard between the thatch buildings.

"Good," Jennifer said. "It's not over yet."

"Sanjong is—"

"Right. He is."

"But we came a long way in the jeeps."

"Yes. At least two or three miles. I tried to see the odometer, but it was spattered with mud. But on foot, even running, it'll take him a while."

"He had a rifle."

"Yes."

"Can you get free?"

STATE OF FEAR ▶ 527

Jennifer shook her head. "It's too tight."

Through the open door, they saw Bradley and Evans being led away to another room. They glimpsed the two men only for a moment. Not long after, Kenner followed. He glanced into their room, giving what seemed to Sarah a meaningful look.

But she couldn't be sure.

Jennifer sat down on the bare earth, leaning back against the pole. She said, "Might as well sit down. It could be a long night." Sarah sat down, too.

A moment later, a young boy looked in and saw that they were sitting. He came into the room, looked at their handcuffs, and then walked out again.

Outside, the drums were louder. People must have been starting to gather, because the women could hear shouts and murmurs.

"Going to be a ceremony," Jennifer said. "And I'm afraid I know what it is."

In the next room, Evans and Kenner were also handcuffed around two posts. Because there was not a third post, Ted Bradley was handcuffed and left seated on the ground. His head was no longer bleeding, but he had a huge bruise over his left eye. And he looked distinctly frightened. But his eyelids were drooping, as if he might fall asleep.

"What's your impression of village life so far, Ted?" Kenner said. "Still think it's the best way to live?"

"This isn't village life. This is savagery."

"It's all part of it."

"No, it's not. These young kids, that fat creepy guy . . . this is lunacy. This is everything gone wrong."

"You just don't get it, do you?" Kenner said. "You think civilization is some horrible, polluting human invention that separates us from the state of nature. But civilization doesn't separate us from nature, Ted. Civilization *protects* us from nature. Because what you see right now, all around you—this *is* nature."

"Oh no. No, no. Humans are kind, cooperative . . ."

"Horseshit, Ted."

"There are genes for altruism."

"Wishful thinking, Ted."

"All cruelty springs from weakness."

"Some people *like* cruelty, Ted."

"Leave him alone," Evans said.

"Why should I? Come on, Ted. Aren't you going to answer me?"

"Oh, fuck you," Ted said. "Maybe we're all going to get killed here by these juvenile delinquent creeps, but I want you to know, if it's the last fucking thing I say in my life, that you are a major and unrelenting asshole, Kenner. You bring out the worst in everybody. You're a pessimist, you're an obstructionist, you're against all progress, against everything that is good and noble. You are a right-wing pig in . . . in . . . in whatever the fuck you are wearing. Whatever those clothes are. Where's your gun?"

"I dropped it."

"Where?"

"Back in the jungle."

"You think Sanjong has it?"

"I hope so."

"Is he coming to get us?"

Kenner shook his head. "He's doing the job we came to do."

"You mean he's going to the bay."

"Yes."

"So nobody is coming to get us?"

"No, Ted. Nobody."

"We're fucked," he said. "We're fucking *fucked*. I can't believe it." And he started to cry.

Two boys entered the room, carrying two heavy hemp ropes. They attached one rope to each of Bradley's wrists, tying them firmly. Then they walked out again.

The drums beat louder.

Out in the center of the village, people took up a rhythmic chant.

Jennifer said, "Can you see out the door from where you are?"

"Yes."

"Keep an eye out. Tell me if someone is coming."

"All right," Sarah said.

She glanced back and saw that Jennifer had arched her back and was gripping the pole between her hands. She had also bent her legs so her soles touched the wood, and proceeded to shimmy up the pole at a remarkable speed, like an acrobat. She got to the top, raised her cuffed hands clear of the top of the pole, and then jumped lightly to the ground.

"Anybody?" she said.

"No . . . How'd you learn to do that?"

"Keep looking out the door."

Jennifer slid back against her pole again, as if she were still handcuffed to it.

"Anybody yet?"

"No, not yet."

Jennifer sighed. "We need one of those kids to come in," she said. "Soon."

Outside, Sambuca was giving a speech, screaming brief phrases that were each answered by a shout from the crowd. Their leader was building them up, working them into a frenzy. Even in Ted's room, they could feel it building.

Bradley was curled in fetal position, crying softly.

Two men came in, much older than the boys. They unlocked his handcuffs. They lifted him to his feet. Each man took a rope. Together they led him outside.

A moment later, the crowd roared.

PAVUTU
THURSDAY, OCTOBER 14
12:02 P.M.

"Hey, cutie pie," Jennifer said, when a boy stuck his head in the door. She grinned. "You like what you see, cutie pie?" She shifted her pelvis suggestively.

The boy looked suspicious at first, but he came deeper into the room. He was older than the others, maybe fourteen or fifteen, and he was bigger. He was carrying a rifle and wore a knife on his belt.

"You want to have some fun? Want to let me go?" Jennifer said, smiling with a little pout. "You understand me? My arms hurt, baby. Want to have fun?"

He gave a laugh, sort of a gurgle from deep in his throat. He moved toward her and pushed her legs open, then crouched down in front of her.

"Oh, let me go first, please . . ."

"*No meri,*" he said, laughing and shaking his head. He knew he could have her while she remained cuffed to the pole. He was kneeling between her legs, fumbling with his shorts, but it was clumsy holding the gun, so he set the gun down.

What happened next was very fast. Jennifer arched her back and kicked her legs up, clipping the kid under the chin, snapping his head back. She continued the motion, crunching into a ball, swinging her arms under her hips and butt and then up her legs, so now her hands were in front of her instead of behind. As the kid staggered to his feet, she slammed him in the side of the head with both hands. He went down on his knees. She dove on him, knocking him over, and pounded his head into the ground. Then she pulled the knife off his belt and cut his throat.

She sat on his body while he shivered and spasmed and the blood poured from his throat and onto the bare earth. It seemed to take a long time. When the body was finally motionless, she got off him, and rifled through his pockets.

Sarah watched the whole thing, her mouth open.

"Damn it," Jennifer said. "Damn it."

"What's the matter?"

"He doesn't have the key!"

She rolled the body over, grunting with the effort. She got blood on her arms from the flowing throat. She paid no attention to it.

"Where are the damn keys?"

"Maybe the other kid has it."

"Which one cuffed us?"

"I don't remember," Sarah said. "I was confused." She was staring at the body, looking at all the blood.

"Hey," Jennifer said, "get over it. You know what these guys are going to do? They're going to beat us up, gang-bang us, and then kill us. Fuck 'em. We kill as many as we can and try to get out of here alive. But *I need the damn key!*"

Sarah struggled to her feet.

"Good idea," Jennifer said. She came over and crouched down in front of Sarah.

"What?"

"Stand on my back and shimmy up. Get yourself off the pole. And hurry."

Outside, the crowd was screaming and roaring, a constant and ugly sound.

Ted Bradley blinked in the bright sunlight. He was disoriented by pain and fear and by the sight that greeted his eyes: two lines of old women, forming a corridor for him to walk down, all applauding him wildly. In fact, beyond the old women was a sea of faces—dark-skinned men and young girls and kids hardly waist high. And they were all yelling and cheering. Dozens of people, crowded together.

They were cheering him!

Despite himself, Ted smiled. It was a weak smile, sort of a half-smile, because he was tired and hurt, but he knew from experience that it would convey just the right hint of subtle pleasure at their response. As he was carried forward by the two men, he nodded and smiled. He allowed his smile to become broader.

At the far end of the women was Sambuca himself—but he, too, was applauding wildly, his hands high in the air, a broad smile on his face.

Ted didn't know what was happening here, but obviously he had misunderstood the meaning of the whole thing. Either that or they had figured out who he was and now thought better of their original plan. It wouldn't be the first time. The women were cheering so loudly as he was carried forward, their mouths gaping with excitement, that he tried to shake off the men who were holding him, he tried to walk unaided. And he did!

But now that he was closer he noticed that the applauding women had heavy sticks resting against their hips as they cheered. Some had baseball bats and some lengths of metal pipe. And as he came closer they continued to shout, but they picked up their bats and sticks and began to strike him, heavy blows on the face and shoulders and body. The pain was instant and incredible, and he sank down to the ground, but immediately the men with the ropes hauled him up again, and dragged him while the women beat him and screamed and beat him. And the pain streaked through his body and he felt a vague detachment, an emptiness, but still the blows came, merciless, again and again.

And finally, barely conscious, he came to the end of the line of women and saw a pair of poles. The men quickly tied his arms to the two poles in a way that kept him upright. And now the crowd fell silent. His head was bowed, he saw blood dripping from his head onto the ground.

And he saw two naked feet appear in his line of vision, and the blood spattered on the feet, and someone lifted his head.

It was Sambuca, though Bradley could barely focus on his face. The world was gray and faint. But he saw that Sambuca was grinning at him, revealing a row of yellow pointed teeth. And then Sambuca held up a knife so Ted could see it, and smiled again, and with two fingers grabbed the flesh of Ted's cheek and sliced it off with the knife.

There was no pain, surprisingly no pain but it made him dizzy to see Sambuca hold up the bloody chunk of his cheek and, grinning, open his mouth and take a bite. The blood ran down Sambuca's chin as he chewed, grinning all the while. Bradley's head was spinning now. He was nauseated and terrified and revolted, and he felt a pain at his chest. He looked down to see a young boy of eight or nine cutting flesh from his underarm with a pocket knife. And a woman raced forward, screaming for the others to get out of the way, and she hacked a slice from the back of his forearm. And then the whole crowd was upon him, and the knives were everywhere, and they were cutting and yelling and cutting and yelling and he saw one knife move toward his eyes, and felt his trousers tugged down, and he knew nothing more.

Evans listened to the crowd cheering and yelling. Somehow he knew what was happening. He looked at Kenner. But Kenner just shook his head.

There was nothing to do. No help was coming. There was no way out.

The door opened, and two boys appeared. They carried two heavy hemp ropes, now visibly soaked in blood. They walked up to Evans and carefully knotted the ropes to his hands. Evans felt his heart start to pound.

The boys finished and left the room.

Outside, the crowd was roaring.

"Don't worry," Kenner said. "They'll let you wait a while. There's still hope."

"Hope for *what?*" Evans said in a burst of anger.

Kenner shook his head. "Just . . . hope."

Jennifer was waiting for the next kid to come in the room. He did, finally, and took one look at the fallen boy and began to bolt, but Jennifer had her arms around his neck. She yanked him back into the room with her hands over his mouth so he couldn't scream and she made a sudden, quick twist and let him fall to the ground. He wasn't dead, but he would be there a while.

But in that moment when she had looked outside, she had seen the keys. They were out in the thatch passageway, on a bench across the hall.

There were two guns in the room now, but there was no point in firing them. It would just bring everybody on them. Jennifer didn't want to look outside again. She heard murmuring voices. She couldn't be sure whether they were coming from the next room or from the hallway. She couldn't make a mistake.

She leaned back against the wall by the door and moaned. Softly at first, and then louder, because the crowd was still very noisy. She moaned and moaned.

Nobody came.

Did she dare to look out?

She took a breath and waited.

Evans was trembling. The blood-soaked ropes were cold on his wrists. He couldn't stand the waiting. He felt like he was going to pass out. Outside the crowd was slowly becoming quieter. They were settling down. He knew what that meant. Soon it would be time for the next victim.

Then he heard a quiet sound.

It was a man coughing. Softly, insistently.

Kenner understood first. "In here," he said loudly.

There was a whacking sound as a machete blade poked through the thatched wall. Evans turned. He saw the slash in the wall widen, and a thick, brown hand reached in to pull the slash wider open still. A heavily bearded face peered through the gash at them.

For a moment Evans did not recognize him, but then the man put his finger to his lips, and there was something in the gesture that was familiar, and Evans suddenly saw past the beard.

"George!"

It was George Morton.

Alive.

Morton stepped through into the room. "Keep it down," he hissed.

"You took your sweet time," Kenner said, turning so Morton could unlock his cuffs. Morton gave Kenner a pistol. Then it was Evans's turn. With a click, his hands were free. Evans tugged at the hemp ropes, trying to get them off his wrists. But they were securely tied.

Morton whispered, "Where are the others?"

Kenner pointed to the room next door. He took the machete from Morton. "You take Peter. I'll get the girls."

With the machete, Kenner stepped out into the hallway.

Morton grabbed Evans by the arm. Evans jerked his head.

"Let's go."

"But—"

"Do as he says, kid."

They stepped through the slash in the wall, and into the jungle beyond.

Kenner moved down the empty hallway. There were openings at both ends. He could be surprised at any moment. If the alarm went up, they were all dead. He saw the keys on the bench, picked them up, and went to the door of the women's room. Looking into the room, he saw that the poles were abandoned. He didn't see either of the women.

Staying outside, he tossed the keys into the room.

"It's me," he whispered.

A moment later, he saw Jennifer scramble from her hiding place behind the door to grab the keys. In a few seconds she and Sarah had both unlocked each other. They grabbed the boys' guns and started for the door.

Too late. From around the corner three heavyset young men were coming toward Kenner. They all carried machine guns. They were talking and laughing, not paying attention.

Kenner slipped into the women's room. He pressed back against the wall, gestured for the two women to go back to the poles. They made it just in time as the men entered the room. Jennifer said, "Hi, guys," with a big smile. At that moment, the men registered the two fallen boys and the blood-soaked earth, but it was too late. Kenner took one; Jennifer got the second with her knife. The third was almost out the door when Kenner hit him with the butt of the gun. There was the crack of skull. He went down hard.

It was time to go.

Out in the courtyard, the crowd was growing restless. Sambuca squinted. The first *waitman* was long dead, the body cooling at his feet, no longer as appetizing as he was before. And those in the crowd who had not tasted glory were clamoring for their piece, for the next opportunity. The women were resting their bats and pipes on their shoulders, talking in small clusters, waiting for the game to continue.

Where was the next man?

Sambuca barked an order, and three men ran toward the thatch building.

It was a long, muddy slide down the steep hill, but Evans didn't mind. He was following Morton, who seemed to know his way around the jungle very well. They fell to the bottom, landing in a shallow running stream, the water pale brown with peat. Morton signaled for him to follow, and ran splashing down the streambed. Morton had lost a lot of weight; his body was trim and fit, his face tight, hard looking.

Evans said, "We thought you were dead."

"Don't talk. Just go. They'll be after us in a minute."

And even as he spoke, Evans could hear someone sliding down the hillside after them. He turned and ran down the stream, slipping over wet rocks, falling, getting up and running again.

Kenner came down the hillside with the two women right behind him. They banged against gnarled roots and protruding brambles as they slid down, but it was still the fastest way to get away from the village. He could see from the streaks in the mud ahead of him that Morton had gone that way, too. And he was sure that he had no more than a minute's head start before the alarm was sounded.

They came crashing down through the last of the undergrowth to the streambed. They heard gunshots from the village above. So their escape had already been discovered.

The bay, Kenner knew, was off to the left. He told the others to go ahead, running in the streambed.

"What about you?" Evans said.

"I'll be with you in a minute."

The women headed off, moving surprisingly quickly. Kenner eased back to the muddy track, raised his gun, and waited. It was only a few seconds before the first of the rebels came down the slope. He fired three quick bursts. The bodies caught in the gnarled branches. One tumbled all the way to the streambed.

Kenner waited.

The men above would expect him to run now. So he waited. Sure enough, in a couple of minutes he heard them starting down again. They were noisy—frightened kids. He fired again, and heard screams. But he didn't think he'd hit anything. They were just screams of fear.

But from now on, he was sure they would take a different route down. And it would be slower.

Kenner turned and ran.

Sarah and Jennifer were moving fast through the water when a bullet whined past Sarah's ear. "Hey," she shouted. "It's us!"

"Oh, sorry," Morton said, as they caught up to him.

"Which way?" Jennifer said.

Morton pointed downstream.

They ran.

• • •

Evans looked for his watch, but one of the kids had taken it from him. His wrist was bare. But Morton had a watch. "What time is it?" Evans asked him.

"Three-fifteen."

They had less than two hours remaining.

"How far to the bay?"

"Maybe another hour," Morton said, "if we go cross jungle. And we must. Those boys are fearsome trackers. Many times they've almost gotten me. They know I'm here, but so far I've eluded them."

"How long have you been here?"

"Nine days. Seems like nine years."

Running down a streambed, they crouched low beneath overhanging branches. Evans's thighs burned. His knees ached. But somehow it didn't matter to him. For some reason, the pain felt like an affirmation. He didn't care about the heat or the bugs or the leeches that he knew were all over his ankles and legs. He was just glad to be alive.

"We turn here," Morton said. He left the streambed, dashing off to the right, scrambling over big boulders, and then crashing into dense, waist-high ferns.

"Any snakes in here?" Sarah said.

"Yeah, plenty," Morton said. "But I don't worry about them."

"What do you worry about?"

"*Plenti pukpuk.*"

"And they are?"

"Crocodiles."

And he plunged onward, vanishing into dense foliage.

"Great," Evans said.

Kenner stopped in the middle of the river. Something was wrong. Until now, he had seen signs of previous runners in the stream. Bits of mud on rocks, wet finger marks or shoe prints, or disturbed algae. But for the last few minutes, nothing.

The others had left the stream.

He'd missed where.

Morton would make sure of that, he thought. Morton would know a good place to leave the river where their exit wouldn't be noticed. Probably somewhere with ferns and swampy, marshy grass between boulders on riverbanks—grass that would be spongy underfoot and would spring back at once.

Kenner had missed it.

He turned around and headed upstream, moving slowly. He knew that if he didn't find their tracks, he couldn't leave the river. He would be sure to get lost. And if he stayed in the river too long, the kids would find him. And they'd kill him.

RESOLUTION
THURSDAY, OCTOBER 14
4:02 P.M.

There was one hour left, now. Morton crouched among the mangroves and rocks near the center of Resolution Bay. The others were clustered around him. The water lapped softly against the sand, a few feet away.

"This is what I know," he said, speaking low. "The submarine tender is hidden under a camouflage tarp at the east end of the bay. You can't see it from here. They have been sending the submarine down every day for a week. The sub has limited battery power, so it can stay at depth for only an hour at a time. But it seems pretty clear they are placing a kind of cone-shaped explosive that depends on accurately timed detonation—"

"They had them in Antarctica," Sarah said.

"All right, then you know. Here, they're intended to trigger an underwater avalanche. Judging how long the sub stays down, I figure they are placing them at about the ninety-meter level, which happens to be the most efficient level for tsunami-causing avalanches."

"What about the tents up here?" Evans said.

"It seems they're taking no chances. Either they don't have enough cone explosives or they don't trust them to do the job, because they have placed something called hypersonic cavitation generators in the tents. They're big pieces of equipment about the size of a small truck. Diesel powered, make a lot of noise when they fire them up to test them, which they've been doing for days. They moved the tents several times, just a foot or two each time, so I assume there's some critical issue about placement. Maybe they're focusing the beams, or whatever it is those things generate. I'm not entirely clear about what they do. But apparently they're important for creating the landslide."

Sarah said, "And what do we do?"

"There's no way we can stop them," Morton said. "We are only four—five, if Kenner makes it, which he doesn't seem to be doing. There are thirteen of them. Seven on the ship and six on shore. All armed with automatic weapons."

"But we have Sanjong," Evans said. "Don't forget him."

"That Nepali guy? I'm sure the rebels got him. There were gunshots about an hour ago along the ridge where they first found you. I was a few yards below, just before they picked you up. I tried to signal you by coughing, but . . ." He shrugged, turned back to the beach. "Anyway. Assuming the three cavitation generators are meant to work together to create some effect on the underwater slope, I figure our best chance is to take one of the generators out—or maybe two of them. That would disrupt their plan or at least weaken the effect."

Jennifer said, "Can we cut the power supply?"

Morton shook his head. "They're self-powered. Diesel attached to the main units."

"Battery ignition?"

"No. Solar panels. They're autonomous."

"Then we have to take out the guys running the units."

"Yes. And they've been alerted to our presence. As you can see, there's one standing outside each tent, guarding it, and they've got a sentry somewhere up on that ridge." He pointed to the western slope. "We can't see where he is, but I assume he is watching the whole bay."

"So? Big deal. Let him watch," Jennifer said. "I say we just take out all these guys in the tents, and trash the machines. We've got enough weapons here to do the job, and—" She paused. She had removed the magazine from her rifle; it was empty. "Better check your loads."

There was a moment of fumbling. They were all shaking their heads.

Evans had four rounds. Sarah had two. Morton's rifle had none. "Those guys had practically no ammo . . ."

"And we don't either." Jennifer took a long breath. "This is going to be a little tougher without weapons." She edged forward and looked out on the beach, squinting in the bright light. "There's ten yards between the jungle and those tents. Open beach, no cover. If we charge the tents we'll never make it."

"What about a distraction?"

"I don't know what it could be. There's one guy outside each tent and one guy inside. They both armed?"

Morton nodded. "Automatic weapons."

"Not good," she said. "Not good at all."

Kenner splashed down the river, looking hard left and right. He had not gone more than a hundred yards when he saw the faint imprint of a wet hand on a boulder. The damp print had almost dried. He looked more closely. He saw the grass at the edge of the stream had been trampled.

This was where they had left the stream.

He set out, heading toward the bay. Morton obviously knew his way around. This was another streambed, but much smaller. Kenner noticed with some unease that it sloped downward fairly steeply. That was a bad sign. But it was a passable route through the jungle. Somewhere up ahead, he heard the barking of a dog. It sounded like the dog was hoarse, or sick, or something.

Kenner hurried ahead, ducking beneath the branches.

He had to get to the others, before it was too late.

Morton heard the barking and frowned.

"What's the matter?" Jennifer said. "The rebels chasing us with dogs?"

"No. That's not a dog."

"It didn't really sound like a dog."

"It's not. They've learned a trick in this part of the world. They bark like a dog, and then when the dogs come out, they eat them."

"Who does?"

"Crocs. That's a crocodile you hear. Somewhere behind us."

Out on the beach, they heard the sudden rumbling of automobile engines. Peering forward through the mangroves, they saw three jeeps coming from the east side of the bay, rumbling across the sand toward them.

"What's this?" Evans said.

"They've been practicing this," Morton said. "All week. Watch. One stops at each tent. See? Tent one . . . tent two . . . tent three. They all stop. They all keep the motors running. All pointed west."

"What's west?"

"There's a dirt track, goes up the hill about a hundred yards and then dead-ends."

"Something used to be up there?"

"No. They cut the road themselves. First thing they did when they got here." Morton looked toward the eastern curve of the bay. "Usually by this time, the ship has pulled out, and moved into deep water. But it's not doing it yet."

"Uh-oh," Evans said.

"What is it?"

"I think we've forgotten something."

"What's that?"

"We've been worried about this tsunami wave heading toward the California coast. But a landslide would suck water downward, right? And then it would rise back up again. But that's kind of like dropping this pebble into this ditch." He dropped a pebble into a muddy puddle at their feet. "And the wave the pebble generates . . . is circular."

"It goes in all directions . . ."

"Oh no," Sarah said.

"Oh yes. All directions, including back to this coast. The tsunami will hit here, too. And fast. How far offshore is the Solomon Trench?"

Morton shrugged. "I don't know. Maybe two miles. I really don't know, Peter."

"If these waves travel five hundred miles an hour," Evans said, "then that means it gets to this coast in . . ."

"Twenty-four seconds," Sarah said.

"Right. That's how much time we have to get out of here, once the undersea landslide begins. Twenty-four seconds."

With a sudden chugging rumble, they heard the first diesel generator come to life. Then the second, then the third. All three were running.

Morton glanced at his watch. "This is it," he said. "They've started."

And now they heard an electronic whine, faint at first but rapidly building to a deep electronic hum. It filled the air.

"Those're the cavitators," Morton said. "Kicking in."

Jennifer slung her rifle over her shoulder. "Let's get ready."

Sanjong slid silently from the branches of the overhanging tree, onto the deck of the *AV Scorpion*. The forty-foot ship must have a very shallow draft, because it was pulled up close to the peninsula on the eastern side, so that the huge jungle trees overhung it. The ship couldn't really be seen from the beach; Sanjong had only realized that it was there when he heard the crackle of radios coming from the jungle.

He crouched in the stern, hiding behind the winch that raised the submarine, listening. He heard voices from all sides, it seemed like. He guessed that there were six or seven men onboard. But what he wanted was to find the timing detonators. He guessed that they were in the pilothouse, but he couldn't be sure. And between his hiding place and the pilothouse was a long expanse of open deck.

He looked at the mini-sub hanging above him. It was bright blue, about seven feet long, with a bubble canopy, now raised. The sub was raised and lowered into the water by the winch.

And the winch . . .

He looked for the control panel. He knew it had to be nearby because the operator would have to be able to see the submarine as it was lowered. Finally he saw it: a closed metal box on the other side of the ship. He crept over, opened the box, and looked at the buttons. There were six, marked with arrows in all directions. Like a big keypad.

He pressed the down arrow.

With a rumble, the winch began to lower the submarine into the water.

An alarm began to sound.

He heard running feet.

He ducked back into a doorway and waited.

From the beach, they faintly heard the sound of an alarm over the rumble of the generators and the cavitation hum. Evans looked around. "Where's it coming from?"

"It must be from the ship, over there."

Out on the beach, the men heard it, too. They were standing in pairs by the entrance to the tents, pointing. Wondering what to do.

And then, from the jungle behind them, a sudden burst of machine-gun fire opened up. The men on the beach were alarmed now, swinging their guns, looking this way and that.

"Screw it," Jennifer said, taking Evans's rifle. "This is it. It won't get any better."

And firing, she ran out onto the beach.

The crocodile had charged Kenner with frightening speed. He had little more than a glimpse of huge white jaws open wide and thrashing water before he fired with his machine gun. The jaw smashed down, just missing his leg; the animal writhed, twisted, and attacked again, jaws closing on a low-hanging branch.

The bullets hadn't done anything. Kenner turned and ran, sprinting down the streambed.

The croc roared behind him.

Jennifer was running across the sand, heading for the nearest tent. She went about ten yards before two bullets struck her left leg and knocked her down. She fell onto hot sand, still firing as she fell. She saw the guard at the entrance to the tent drop. She knew he was dead.

Evans came up behind her and started to crouch down. She shouted, "Keep going! Go!" Evans ran forward, toward the tent.

On the ship, the men halted the descent of the submarine, stopping the winch. Now they could hear the gunshots coming from the beach. They had all rushed to the starboard side of the ship, and now they were look-ing over the railing, trying to see what was going on.

Sanjong went down the deck on the port side. No one was there. He came to the cabin. There was a big board there, dense with electronics. A man in shorts and a T-shirt was crouched over it, making adjustments. At the top of the board were three rows of lights, marked with numerals.

The timing board.

For the undersea detonations.

Sarah and Morton were sprinting along the edge of the beach, staying close to the jungle, as they headed for the second tent. The man outside the tent saw them almost at once and was firing bursts of machine-gun fire at them, but he must have been very nervous, Sarah thought, because he wasn't hitting them. Branches and leaves snapped all around them from the bullets. And with every step, they were getting close enough for Sarah to fire back. She was carrying Morton's pistol. At twenty yards, she stopped and leaned against the nearest tree trunk. She held her arm stiffly and aimed. The first shot missed. The second one hit the man outside the tent in the right shoulder, and he dropped his gun in the sand. Morton saw it, and left the forest, running across the sand toward the tent. The man was struggling to get up. Sarah shot again.

And then Morton disappeared inside the tent. And she heard two quick gunshots and a scream of pain.

She ran.

Evans was inside the tent. He faced a wall of chugging machinery, a huge complex of twisting pipes and vents, ending in a flat, round plate eight feet wide, set about two feet above the surface of the sand. The generator was about seven feet high; all the metal was hot to the touch. The noise was deafening. He didn't see anybody there. Holding his rifle ready—painfully aware that the magazine was empty—he swung around the first corner, then the second.

And then he saw him.

It was Bolden. The guy from the Antarctic. He was working at a control panel, adjusting big knobs while he looked at a shaded LCD screen and a row of dials. He was so preoccupied, he didn't even notice Evans at first.

Evans felt a burst of pure rage. If his gun had been loaded he would have shot him. Bolden's gun was leaning against the wall of the tent. He needed both hands to adjust the controls.

Evans shouted. Bolden turned. Evans gestured for him to put up his hands.

Bolden charged.

Morton had just stepped into the tent when the first bullet struck his ear and the second hit his shoulder. He screamed in pain and fell to his knees. The movement saved his life because the next bullet whined past his forehead, ripping through the tent cloth. He was lying on the ground next to the chugging machinery when the gunman came around, holding his rifle ready. He was a twentyish man, bearded, grim, all business. He aimed at Morton.

And then he fell against the machine, blood hissing as it splattered on hot metal. Sarah was standing inside the tent, firing her pistol once, twice, three times, lowering her arm each time as the man fell. She turned to Morton.

"I forgot you were a good shot," he said.

"You okay?" she said. He nodded. "Then how do I turn this thing off?"

Evans grunted as Bolden smashed into his body. The two men stumbled back against the tent fabric, then forward again. Evans brought the butt of his gun down on Bolden's back, but it had no effect. He kept trying to hit him in the head, but only connected with his back. Bolden, for his part, seemed to be trying to drive Evans out of the tent.

The two men fell to the ground. The machinery was thumping above them. And now Evans realized what Bolden was trying to do.

He was trying to push Evans under the plate. Even by being near the edge, Evans could feel the air vibrating intensely. The air was much hotter here.

Bolden hit Evans in the head, and his sunglasses went flying across the ground, beneath the flat plate. Instantly, they shattered. Then the frames crumpled.

Then they pulverized.

Vanished into nothing.

Evans watched with horror. And little by little, Bolden was pushing him closer to the edge, closer, closer . . .

Evans struggled, with the sudden strength of desperation. Abruptly, he kicked up.

Bolden's face mashed against hot metal. He howled. His cheek was smoking and black. Evans kicked again, and got out from beneath him. Got to his feet. Standing over Bolden, he kicked him hard in the ribs, as hard as he could. He tried to kill him.

That's for Antarctica.

Bolden grabbed Evans's leg on the next kick, and Evans went down. But he kicked once more as he fell, hitting Bolden in the head, and with the impact, Bolden rolled once.

And rolled under the plate.

His body was half under, half out. It began to shake, to vibrate. Bolden opened his mouth to scream but there was no sound. Evans kicked him a final time, and the body went entirely under.

By the time Evans had dropped to his hands and knees, to look under the plate, nothing was there. Just a haze of acrid smoke.

He got to his feet, and went outside.

Glancing over her shoulder, Jennifer ripped her blouse with her teeth and tore a strip of cloth for a tourniquet. She didn't think an artery had been hit, but there was a lot of blood on one leg and a lot of blood in the sand, and she was feeling a little dizzy.

She had to keep watching because there was one more tent, and if the guys from that tent showed up . . .

She spun, raising her gun as a figure emerged from the forest.

It was John Kenner. She lowered the gun.

He ran toward her.

Sanjong fired into the glass in front of the control deck, but nothing happened. The glass didn't even shatter. Bulletproof glass, he thought in surprise. The technician inside looked up in shock. By then Sanjong was moving toward the door.

The technician reached for the control switches. Sanjong fired twice, once hitting the technician, once aiming for the control panel.

But it was too late. Across the top of the panel, red lights flashed, one after another. The undersea detonations were taking place.

Automatically, a loud alarm began to sound, like a submarine claxon. The men on the other side of the ship were shouting, terror in their voices, and with good reason, Sanjong thought.

The tsunami had been generated.

It was only a matter of seconds now before it would hit them.

RESOLUTION BAY
THURSDAY, OCTOBER 14
4:43 P.M.

The air was filled with sound.

Evans ran from the tent. Directly ahead he saw Kenner lifting Jennifer in his arms. Kenner was shouting something, but Evans couldn't hear. He could vaguely see that Jennifer was soaked in blood. Evans ran for the jeep, jumped in, and drove it over to Kenner.

Kenner put Jennifer in the back. She was breathing shallowly. Directly ahead, they saw Sarah helping Morton into the other jeep. Kenner had to shout over the noise. For a minute Evans couldn't understand.

Then he realized what Kenner was saying. "Sanjong! Where is Sanjong!"

Evans shook his head. "Morton says he's dead! Rebels!"

"Do you know for sure?"

"No!"

Kenner looked back down the beach.

"Drive!"

Sarah was in the car, trying to hold Morton upright and drive at the same time. But she had to let go of him to shift gears, and as soon as she did he'd flop over against her shoulder. He was wheezing, breathing with difficulty. She suspected that his lung was punctured. She was distracted, trying to count in her head. She thought it was already ten seconds since the landslide.

Which meant they had fifteen seconds to get up the hill.

Sanjong leapt from the ship to the trees on the shore. He grabbed a handful of leaves and branches. He scrambled down to the ground and began to climb the hill frantically. On the ship, the men saw him, and they jumped, too, trying to follow him.

Sanjong guessed that they all had half a minute before the first wave struck. It would be the smallest wave, but it would still probably be five meters high. The runup—the splash on the hillside—could be another five meters. That meant he had to scramble at least thirty feet up the muddy slope in the next thirty seconds.

He knew he would never make it.

He couldn't do it.

He climbed anyway.

Sarah drove up the muddy track, the jeep slipping precariously on the incline. Beside her, Morton was not saying anything and his skin had turned an ugly blue gray. She yelled, "Hold on, George! Hold on! Just a little!" The jeep fishtailed in the mud, and Sarah howled in panic. She downshifted, grinding gears, got control, and continued up. In the rearview mirror, she saw Evans behind her.

In her mind, she was counting:

Eighteen.

Nineteen.

Twenty.

From the third tent on the beach, two men with machine guns jumped into the last remaining jeep. They drove up the hill after Evans, firing at him as they drove. Kenner was firing back. The bullets shattered Evans's windshield. Evans slowed.

"Keep driving!" Kenner yelled. "Go!"

Evans couldn't really see. Where the windshield wasn't shattered it was spattered with mud. He kept moving his head, trying to see the route ahead.

"Go!" Kenner yelled.

The bullets were whizzing around them.

Kenner was shooting at the tires of the jeep behind them. He hit them, and the jeep lurched over onto its side. The two men fell out into the mud. They scrambled to their feet, limping. They were only about fifteen feet above the beach.

Not high enough.

Kenner looked back at the ocean.

He saw the wave coming toward the shore.

It was enormous, as wide as the eye could see, a foaming line of surf, a white arc spreading as it came toward the beach. It was not a very high wave, but it grew as it came ashore, rising up, rising higher . . .

The jeep lurched to a halt.

"Why did you stop?" Kenner yelled.

"It's the end of the damn road!" Evans shouted.

The wave was now about fifteen feet high.

With a roar of surf, the wave struck the beach and raced inland toward them.

To Evans, it seemed as if everything was happening in slow motion—the big wave churning white, boiling over the sand, and somehow keeping its crest all the way across the beach, and into the jungle, completely covering the green landscape in white as the water boiled up the slope toward them.

He couldn't take his eyes off it, because it seemed never to lose its power, but just kept coming. Farther down the muddy track the two men were scrambling away from their fallen jeep, and then they were covered in white water and gone from sight.

The wave rushed up the slope another four or five feet, then suddenly slowed, receded, sweeping back. It left behind no trace of the men or their jeep. The jungle trees were ragged, many uprooted.

The wave slid back into the ocean, farther and farther away, exposing the beach far out to sea, before it finally died away, and the ocean was gentle again.

"That's the first," Kenner said. "The next ones will be bigger."

Sarah was holding Morton upright, trying to keep him comfortable. His lips were a terrible blue color and his skin was cold, but he seemed to be alert. He wasn't talking, but he was watching the water.

"Hang on, George," she said.

He nodded. He was mouthing something.

"What is it? What are you saying?"

She read his lips. A weak grin.

Wouldn't miss it if it was the last thing I did.

The next wave came in.

From a distance, it looked exactly like the first, but as it neared the shore they could see that it was noticeably bigger, half again as large as the first, and the roar as it smashed into the beach was like an explosion. A vast sheet of water raced up the hill toward them, coming much higher than before.

They were almost a hundred feet away. The wave had come a good sixty feet up the slope.

"The next one will be bigger," Kenner said.

• • •

The sea was quiet for several minutes. Evans turned to Jennifer. "Listen," he said, "do you want me to—"

She wasn't there. For a moment he thought she had fallen out of the jeep. Then he saw she had fallen on the floor, where she lay curled in pain. Her face and shoulder were soaked in blood.

"Jennifer?"

Kenner grabbed Evans's hand, pushed it back gently. He shook his head. "Those guys in the jeep," he said. "She was okay until then." Evans was stunned. He felt dizzy. He looked at her. "Jennifer?"

Her eyes were closed. She was hardly breathing.

"Turn away," Kenner said. "She'll make it or she won't."

The next wave was coming in.

There was nowhere they could go. They had reached the end of the track. They were surrounded by jungle. They just waited, and watched the water rush up in a hissing, terrifying wall toward them. The wave had already broken. This was just surge rushing up the hillside, but it was still a wall of water nine or ten feet high.

Sarah was sure it was going to take them all, but the wave lost energy just a few yards away, thinning and slowing, and then sliding back down to the ocean.

Kenner looked at his watch. "We have a few minutes," he said. "Let's do what we can."

"What do you mean?" Sarah said.

"I mean, climb as high as we can."

"There's another wave?"

"At least."

"Bigger?"

"Yes."

. . .

Five minutes passed. They scrambled up the hillside another twenty yards. Kenner was carrying Jennifer's bleeding body. By now she had lost consciousness. Evans and Sarah were helping Morton, who was moving with great difficulty. Finally, Evans picked Morton up and carried him piggyback style.

"Glad you lost some weight," Evans said.

Morton, not speaking, just patted him on the shoulder.

Evans staggered up the hill.

The next wave came in.

When it receded, their jeeps had vanished. The spot where they had been parked was littered with the trunks of uprooted trees. They stared, very tired. They argued: Was that the fourth wave or the fifth? No one could remember. They decided it must have been the fourth.

"What do we do?" Sarah said to Kenner.

"We climb."

Eight minutes later, the next wave came in. It was smaller than the one before. Evans was too tired to do anything but stare at it. Kenner was trying to stop Jennifer's bleeding, but her skin was an ugly pale gray and her lips were blue. Down at the beach, there was no sign of human activity at all. The tents were gone. The generators were gone. There was nothing but piled-up debris, tree branches, pieces of wood, seaweed, foam.

"What's that?" Sarah said.

"What?"

"Someone is shouting."

They looked across to the opposite side of the bay. Someone was waving to them.

"It's Sanjong," Kenner said. "Son of a bitch." He grinned. "I hope he's smart enough to stay where he is. It'll take him a couple of hours to get across the debris. Let's go see if our helicopter is still there or if the wave took it. Then we'll go pick him up."

PACIFIC BASIN
FRIDAY, OCTOBER 15
5:04 P.M.

Eight thousand miles to the east, it was the middle of the night in Golden, Colorado, when the computers of the National Earthquake Information Center registered an atypical seismic disturbance originating from the Pacific basin, just north of the Solomon Islands, and measuring 6.3 Richter. That was a strong quake, but not unusually strong. The peculiar characteristics of the disturbance led the computer to categorize it as an "anomalous event," a fairly common designation for seismic events in that part of the world, where three tectonic plates met in strange overlapping patterns.

The NEIC computers assessed the earthquake as lacking the relatively slow movement associated with tsunamis, and thus did not classify it as a "tsunami-generating event." However, in the South Pacific, this designation was being reexamined, following the devastating New Guinea earthquake of 1998—the single most destructive tsunami of the century—which also did not have the classic slow tsunami profile. Thus, as a precaution, the computers flagged the earthquake to the sensors of the MORN, the Mid-Ocean Relay Network, operating out of Hilo, Hawaii.

Six hours later, mid-ocean buoys detected a nine-inch rise in the ocean level consistent with a tsunami wave train. Because of the great depth of the mid-ocean, tsunamis often raised the sea level only a few inches. On this particular evening, ships in the area felt nothing at all as the big wave front passed beneath them. Nevertheless, the buoys felt it, and triggered an alarm.

It was the middle of the night in Hawaii when the computers pinged and the screens came up. The network manager, Joe Ohiri, had been dozing. He got up, poured himself a cup of coffee and inspected the data. It was clearly a tsunami profile, though one that appeared to be losing force in its ocean passage. Hawaii was of course in its path, but this wave would strike the south shore of the islands, a relative rarity. Ohiri made a quick wave-force calculation, was unimpressed with the results, and so sent a routine notification to civil defense units on all the inhabited islands. It began "This is an information message . . ." and finished with the usual boilerplate about the alert being based on preliminary information. Ohiri knew that nobody would pay much attention to it. Ohiri also notified the West Coast and Alaska Warning Centers, because the wave train was due to strike the coast in early mid-morning of the following day.

Five hours later, the DART buoys off the coast of California and Alaska detected the passage of a tsunami train, now further weakened. Computers calculated the velocity and wave force and recommended no action. This meant that the message went out to the local stations as a tsunami information bulletin, not an alert:

BASED ON LOCATION AND MAGNITUDE THE EARTHQUAKE WAS NOT SUFFICIENT TO GENERATE A TSUNAMI DAMAGING TO CALIFORNIA–OREGON–WASHINGTON–BRITISH COLUMBIA OR ALASKA. SOME AREAS MAY EXPERIENCE SMALL SEA LEVEL CHANGES.

Kenner, who was monitoring the messages on his computer, shook his head when he saw this. "Nick Drake is not going to be a happy man today." It was Kenner's hypothesis that they had needed the cavitation generators to extend the effect of the underwater detonations, and to create the relatively long-lasting landslide that would have produced a truly powerful ocean-crossing tsunami. That had been thwarted.

Ninety minutes later, the much-weakened tsunami train struck the beaches of California. It consisted of a set of five waves averaging six feet in height that excited surfers briefly, but passed unnoticed by everyone else.

Belatedly, Kenner was notified that the FBI had been attempting to reach him for the past twelve hours. It turned out that V. Allen Willy had vacated his beach house at two A.M. local time. This was less than an hour after the events in Resolution Bay had taken place, and more than ten hours prior to the tsunami notification.

Kenner suspected that Willy had gotten cold feet, and had been unwilling to wait. But it was an important and telling mistake. Kenner called the agent and started proceedings to subpoena Willy's phone records.

None of them was allowed to leave the island for the next three days. There were formalities, forms, interrogations. There were problems with emergency care for Morton's collapsed lung and Jennifer's massive blood loss. Morton wanted to be taken to Sydney for surgery, but he was not allowed to leave because he had been reported as a missing person in America. Although he complained bitterly about witch doctors, a very good surgeon trained in Melbourne took care of his lung in Gareda Town. But Jennifer had not been able to wait for that surgeon; she had needed three transfusions during five hours of surgery to remove the bullets in her upper body, and then she was on a respirator, near death for the next forty-eight hours. But at the end of the second day she opened her eyes, pulled off her oxygen mask, and said to Evans, sitting at her bedside, "Stop looking so gloomy. I'm here, for God's sake." Her voice was weak, but she was smiling.

Then there were problems about their contact with the rebels. There were problems about the fact that one of their party had disappeared, the famous actor Ted Bradley. They all told the story of what had happened to Bradley, but there was no way to corroborate it. So the police made them tell it again.

And suddenly, abruptly, unaccountably, they were allowed to leave. Their papers were in order. Their passports were returned. There was no difficulty. They could leave whenever they wanted.

Evans slept most of the way to Honolulu. After the plane refueled and took off again, he sat up and talked to Morton and the others. Morton was explaining what had happened on the night of his car crash.

"There was obviously a problem with Nick and what he was doing with his money. NERF was not doing good things. Nick was very angry—dangerously angry. He threatened me, and I took him at his word. I had established the link between his organization and ELF, and he was threatened, to put it mildly. Kenner and I thought he would try to kill me. Well, he did try. With that girl at the coffee shop, that morning in Beverly Hills."

"Oh yes." Evans remembered. "But how did you stage that car crash? It was so incredibly dangerous—"

"What, do you think I'm crazy?" Morton said. "I never crashed."

"What do you mean?"

"I kept right on driving, that night."

"But." Evans fell silent, shaking his head. "I don't get it."

"Yes, you do," Sarah said. "Because I let it slip to you, by accident. Before George called me and told me to keep my mouth shut about it."

It came back to him then. The conversation from days ago. He hadn't paid much attention at the time. Sarah had said:

He told me to buy a new Ferrari from a guy in Monterey and have it shipped to San Francisco.

When Evans expressed surprise that George was buying another Ferrari:

I know. How many Ferraris can one man use? And this one doesn't seem up to his usual standard. From the e-mail pictures it looks kind of beat up.

And then she said:

The Ferrari he bought is a 1972 365 GTS Daytona Spyder. He already has one, Peter. It's like he doesn't know . . .

"Oh, I knew all right," Morton said. "What a waste of money. The car was a piece of crap. And then I had to fly a couple of Hollywood prop guys up to Sonoma to beat the hell out of it and make it look like a crash. Then they flat-bedded it out that night, set it on the road, fired up the smoke pots . . ."

"And you drove right past a wreck that was already in place," Evans said.

"Yes," Morton said, nodding. "Drove right around the corner. Pulled off the road, climbed up the hill, and watched you guys."

"You son of a bitch."

"I'm sorry," Morton said, "but we needed real emotion to distract the police from the problems."

"What problems?"

"Ice-cold engine block, for one," Kenner said. "That engine hadn't run for days. One of the cops noticed it was cold while the car was being put on the truck. He came back and asked you the time of the accident, all of that. I was concerned they would figure it out."

"But they didn't," Morton said.

"No. They knew something was wrong. But I don't think they ever guessed identical Ferraris."

"No one in his right mind," Morton said, "would intentionally destroy a 1972 365 GTS. Even a crappy one."

Morton was smiling, but Evans was angry. "Somebody could have told me—"

"No," Kenner said. "We needed you to work Drake. Like the cell phone."

"What about it?"

"The cell phone was a very low-quality bug. We needed Drake to suspect that you were part of the investigation. We needed him pressured."

"Well, it worked. That's why I got poisoned in my apartment, isn't it?" Evans said. "You guys were willing to take a lot of risks with my life."

"It turned out all right," Kenner said.

"You did this car crash to pressure Drake?"

"And to get me free," Morton said. "I needed to go down to the Solomons and find out what they were doing. I knew Nick would save the best for last. Although if they had been able to modify that hurricane—that was the third stunt they planned—so that it hit Miami, that would have been spectacular."

"Fuck you, George," Evans said.

"I'm sorry it had to be this way," Kenner said.

"And fuck you, too."

Then Evans got up and went to the front of the plane. Sarah was sitting alone. He was so angry he refused to speak to her. He spent the next hour staring out the window. Finally, she began talking quietly to him, and at the end of half an hour, they embraced.

Evans slept for a while, restless, his body sore. He couldn't find a comfortable position to rest. Intermittently, he would wake up, groggy. One time he thought he heard Kenner talking to Sarah.

Let's remember where we live, Kenner was saying. We live on the third planet from a medium-size sun. Our planet is five billion years old, and it has been changing constantly all during that time. The Earth is now on its third atmosphere.

The first atmosphere was helium and hydrogen. It dissipated early on, because the planet was so hot. Then, as the planet cooled, volcanic eruptions produced a second atmosphere of steam and carbon dioxide. Later the water vapor condensed, forming the oceans that cover most of the planet. Then, around three billion years ago, some bacteria evolved to consume carbon dioxide and excrete a highly toxic gas, oxygen. Other bacteria released nitrogen. The atmospheric concentration of these gases slowly increased. Organisms that could not adapt died out.

Meanwhile, the planet's land masses, floating on huge tectonic plates, eventually came together in a configuration that interfered with the circulation of ocean currents. It began to get cold for the first time. The first ice appeared two billion years ago.

And for the last seven hundred thousand years, our planet has been in a geological ice age, characterized by advancing and retreating glacial ice. No one is entirely sure why, but ice now covers the planet every hundred thousand years, with smaller advances every twenty thousand or so. The last advance was twenty thousand years ago, so we're due for the next one.

And even today, after five billion years, our planet remains amazingly active. We have five hundred volcanoes, and an eruption every two weeks. Earthquakes are continuous: a million and a half a year, a moderate Richter 5 quake every six hours, a big earthquake every ten days. Tsunamis race across the Pacific Ocean every three months.

Our atmosphere is as violent as the land beneath it. At any moment there are one thousand five hundred electrical storms across the planet. Eleven lightning bolts strike the ground each second. A tornado tears across the surface every six hours. And every four days, a giant cyclonic storm, hundreds of miles in diameter, spins over the ocean and wreaks havoc on the land.

The nasty little apes that call themselves human beings can do nothing except run and hide. For these same apes to imagine they can stabilize this atmosphere is arrogant beyond belief. They can't control the climate.

The reality is, they run from the storms.

"What do we do now?"

"I'll tell you what we do," Morton said. "You work for me. I'm starting a new environmental organization. I have to think of a name. I don't want one of these pretentious names with the words *world* and *resource* and *defense* and *wildlife* and *fund* and *preservation* and *wilderness* in them. You can string those words together in any combination. World Wildlife Preservation Fund. Wilderness Resource Defense Fund. Fund for the Defense of World Resources. Anyway, those fake names are all taken. I need something plain and new. Something honest. I was thinking of 'Study the Problem And Fix It.' Except the acronym doesn't work. But maybe that's a plus. We will have scientists and field researchers and economists and engineers—and one lawyer."

"What would this organization do?"

"There is so much to do! For example: Nobody knows how to manage wilderness. We would set aside a wide variety of wilderness tracts and run them under different management strategies. Then we'd ask outside teams to assess how we are doing, and modify the strategies. And then do it again. A true iterative process, externally assessed. Nobody's ever done that. And in the end we'll have a body of knowledge about how to manage different terrains. Not preserve them. You can't preserve them. They're going to change all the time, no matter what. But you could manage them—if you knew how to do it. Which nobody does. That's one big area. Management of complex environmental systems."

"Okay . . ."

"Then we'd do developing-world problems. The biggest cause of environmental destruction is poverty. Starving people can't worry about pollution. They worry about food. Half a billion people are starving in the world right now. More than half a billion without clean water. We need to design delivery systems that really work, test them, have them verified by outsiders, and once we know they work, replicate them."

"It sounds difficult."

"It's difficult if you are a government agency or an ideologue. But if you just want to study the problem and fix it, you can. And this would be entirely private. Private funding, private land. No bureaucrats. Administration is five percent of staff and resources. Everybody is out working. We'd run environmental research as a business. And cut the crap."

"Why hasn't somebody done it?"

"Are you kidding? Because it's radical. Face the facts, all these environmental organizations are thirty, forty, fifty years old. They have big buildings, big obligations, big staffs. They may trade on their youthful dreams, but the truth is, they're now part of the establishment. And the establishment works to preserve the status quo. It just does."

"Okay. What else?"

"Technology assessment. Third world countries can leapfrog. They skip telephone lines and go right to cellular. But nobody is doing decent technology assessment in terms of what works and how to balance the inevitable drawbacks. Wind power's great, unless you're a bird. Those things are giant bird guillotines. Maybe we should build them anyway. But people don't know how to think about this stuff. They just posture and pontificate. Nobody tests. Nobody does field research. Nobody dares to solve the problems—because the solution might contradict your philosophy, and for most people clinging to beliefs is more important than succeeding in the world."

"Really?"

"Trust me. When you're my age, you'll know it is true. Next, how about recreational land use—multipurpose land use. It's a rat's nest. Nobody has figured out how to do it, and it's so hot, so fierce that good people just give up and quit, or vanish in a blizzard of lawsuits. But that doesn't help. The answer probably lies in a range of solutions. It may be necessary to designate certain areas for one or another use. But everybody lives on the same planet. Some people like opera, some people like Vegas. And there's a lot of people that like Vegas."

"Anything else?"

"Yes. We need a new mechanism to fund research. Right now, scientists are in exactly the same position as Renaissance painters, commissioned to make the portrait the patron wants done. And if they are smart, they'll make sure their work subtly flatters the patron. Not overtly. Subtly. This is not a good system for research into those areas of science that affect policy. Even worse, the system works against problem solving. Because if you solve a problem, your funding ends. All that's got to change."

"How?"

"I have some ideas. Make scientists blind to their funding. Make assessment of research blind. We can have major policy-oriented research carried out by multiple teams doing the same work. Why not, if it's really important? We'll push to change how journals report research. Publish the article *and* the peer reviews in the same issue. That'll clean up everybody's act real fast. Get the journals out of politics. Their editors openly take sides on certain issues. Bad dogs."

Evans said, "Anything else?"

"New labels. If you read some authors who say, 'We find that anthropogenic greenhouse gases and sulphates have had a detectable influence on sea-level pressure' it sounds like they went into the world and measured something. Actually, they just ran a simulation. They talk as if simulations were real-world data. They're not. That's a problem that has to be fixed. I favor a stamp: WARNING: COMPUTER SIMULATION — MAY BE ERRONEOUS and UNVERIFIABLE. Like on cigarettes. Put the same stamp on newspaper articles, and in the corner of newscasts. WARNING: SPECULATION — MAY BE FACT-FREE. Can you see that peppered all over the front pages?"

"Anything else?" Evans was smiling now.

"There are a few more things," Morton said, "but those are the major points. It's going to be very difficult. It's going to be uphill all the way. We'll be opposed, sabotaged, denigrated. We'll be called terrible names. The establishment will not like it. Newspapers will sneer. But, eventually, money will start to flow to us because we'll show results. And then everybody will shut up. And then we will get lionized, which is the most dangerous time of all."

"And?"

"By then, I'm long dead. You and Sarah will have run the organization for twenty years. And your final job will be to disband it, before it becomes another tired old environmental organization spouting outmoded wisdom, wasting resources, and doing more harm than good."

"I see," Evans said. "And when it's disbanded?"

"You'll find a bright young person and try to excite him or her to do what really needs to be done in the next generation."

Evans looked at Sarah.

She shrugged. "Unless you have a better idea," she said.

Half an hour before they reached the California coast, they saw the spreading brown haze hanging over the ocean. It grew thicker and darker as they approached land. Soon they saw the lights of the city, stretching away for miles. It was blurred by the atmosphere above.

"It looks a bit like hell, doesn't it," Sarah said. "Hard to think we're going to land in that."

"We have a lot of work to do," Morton said.

The plane descended smoothly toward Los Angeles.

AUTHOR'S MESSAGE

A novel such as *State of Fear*, in which so many divergent views are expressed, may lead the reader to wonder where, exactly, the author stands on these issues. I have been reading environmental texts for three years, in itself a hazardous undertaking. But I have had an opportunity to look at a lot of data, and to consider many points of view. I conclude:

- We know astonishingly little about every aspect of the environment, from its past history, to its present state, to how to conserve and protect it. In every debate, all sides overstate the extent of existing knowledge and its degree of certainty.

- Atmospheric carbon dioxide is increasing, and human activity is the probable cause.

- We are also in the midst of a natural warming trend that began about 1850, as we emerged from a four-hundred-year cold spell known as the "Little Ice Age."

- Nobody knows how much of the present warming trend might be a natural phenomenon.

- Nobody knows how much of the present warming trend might be man-made.

- Nobody knows how much warming will occur in the next century. The computer models vary by 400 percent, de facto proof that nobody knows. But if I had to guess—the only thing anyone is doing, really—I would guess the increase will be 0.812436 degrees C. There is no evidence that my guess about the state of the world one hundred years from now is any better or worse than anyone else's. (We can't "assess" the future, nor can we "predict" it. These are euphemisms. We can only guess. An informed guess is just a guess.)

- I suspect that part of the observed surface warming will ultimately be attributable to human activity. I suspect that the principal human effect will come from land use, and that the atmospheric component will be minor.

- Before making expensive policy decisions on the basis of climate models, I think it is reasonable to require that those models predict future temperatures accurately for a period of ten years. Twenty would be better.

- I think for anyone to believe in impending resource scarcity, after two hundred years of such false alarms, is kind of weird. I don't know whether such a belief today is best ascribed to ignorance of history, sclerotic dogmatism, unhealthy love of Malthus, or simple pigheadedness, but it is evidently a hardy perennial in human calculation.

- There are many reasons to shift away from fossil fuels, and we will do so in the next century without legislation, financial incentives, carbon-conservation programs, or the interminable yammering of fearmongers. So far as I know, nobody had to ban horse transport in the early twentieth century.

- I suspect the people of 2100 will be much richer than we are, consume more energy, have a smaller global population, and enjoy more wilderness than we have today. I don't think we have to worry about them.

- The current near-hysterical preoccupation with safety is at best a waste of resources and a crimp on the human spirit, and at worst an invitation to totalitarianism. Public education is desperately needed.

- I conclude that most environmental "principles" (such as sustainable development or the precautionary principle) have the effect of preserving the economic advantages of the West and thus constitute modern imperialism toward the developing world. It is a nice way of saying, "We got ours and we don't want you to get yours, because you'll cause too much pollution."

- The "precautionary principle," properly applied, forbids the precautionary principle. It is self-contradictory. The precautionary principle therefore cannot be spoken of in terms that are too harsh.

- I believe people are well intentioned. But I have great respect for the corrosive influence of bias, systematic distortions of thought, the power of rationalization, the guises of self-interest, and the inevitability of unintended consequences.

- I have more respect for people who change their views after acquiring new information than for those who cling to views they held thirty years ago. The world changes. Ideologues and zealots don't.

- In the thirty-five-odd years since the environmental movement came into existence, science has undergone a major revolution. This revolution has brought new understanding of nonlinear dynamics, complex systems, chaos theory, catastrophe theory. It has transformed the way we think about evolution and ecology. Yet these no-longer-new ideas have hardly penetrated the thinking of environmental activists, which seems oddly fixed in the concepts and rhetoric of the 1970s.

- We haven't the foggiest notion how to preserve what we term "wilderness," and we had better study it in the field and learn how to do so. I see no evidence that we are conducting such research in a humble, rational, and systematic way. I therefore hold little hope for wilderness management in the twenty-first century. I blame environmental organizations every bit as much as developers and strip miners. There is no difference in outcomes between greed and incompetence.

- We need a new environmental movement, with new goals and new organizations. We need more people working in the field, in the actual environment, and fewer people behind computer screens. We need more scientists and many fewer lawyers.

- We cannot hope to manage a complex system such as the environment through litigation. We can only change its state temporarily— usually by preventing something—with eventual results that we cannot predict and ultimately cannot control.

- Nothing is more inherently political than our shared physical environment, and nothing is more ill served by allegiance to a single political party. Precisely because the environment is shared it cannot be managed by one faction according to its own economic or aesthetic preferences. Sooner or later, the opposing faction will take power, and previous policies will be reversed. Stable management of the environment requires recognition that all preferences have their place: snowmobilers and fly fishermen, dirt bikers and hikers, developers and preservationists. These preferences are at odds, and their incompatibility cannot be avoided. But resolving incompatible goals is a true function of politics.

- We desperately need a nonpartisan, blinded funding mechanism to conduct research to determine appropriate policy. Scientists are only too aware whom they are working for. Those who fund research— whether a drug company, a government agency, or an environmental organization—always have a particular outcome in mind. Research funding is almost never open-ended or open-minded.

Scientists know that continued funding depends on delivering the results the funders desire. As a result, environmental organization "studies" are every bit as biased and suspect as industry "studies." Government "studies" are similarly biased according to who is running the department or administration at the time. No faction should be given a free pass.

- I am certain there is too much certainty in the world.

- I personally experience a profound pleasure being in nature. My happiest days each year are those I spend in wilderness. I wish natural environments to be preserved for future generations. I am not satisfied they will be preserved in sufficient quantities, or with sufficient skill. I conclude that the "exploiters of the environment" include environmental organizations, government organizations, and big business. All have equally dismal track records.

- Everybody has an agenda. Except me.

APPENDIX I
Why Politicized Science Is Dangerous

Imagine that there is a new scientific theory that warns of an impending crisis, and points to a way out.

This theory quickly draws support from leading scientists, politicians, and celebrities around the world. Research is funded by distinguished philanthropies, and carried out at prestigious universities. The crisis is reported frequently in the media. The science is taught in college and high school classrooms.

I don't mean global warming. I'm talking about another theory, which rose to prominence a century ago.

Its supporters included Theodore Roosevelt, Woodrow Wilson, and Winston Churchill. It was approved by Supreme Court justices Oliver Wendell Holmes and Louis Brandeis, who ruled in its favor. The famous names who supported it included Alexander Graham Bell, inventor of the telephone; activist Margaret Sanger; botanist Luther Burbank; Leland Stanford, founder of Stanford University; the novelist H. G. Wells; the playwright George Bernard Shaw; and hundreds of others. Nobel Prize winners gave support. Research was backed by the Carnegie and Rockefeller Foundations. The Cold Springs Harbor Institute was built to carry out this research, but important work was also done at Harvard, Yale, Princeton, Stanford, and Johns Hopkins. Legislation to address the crisis was passed in states from New York to California.

These efforts had the support of the National Academy of Sciences, the American Medical Association, and the National Research Council. It was said that if Jesus were alive, he would have supported this effort.

All in all, the research, legislation, and molding of public opinion surrounding the theory went on for almost half a century. Those who opposed the theory were shouted down and called reactionary, blind to reality, or just plain ignorant. But in hindsight, what is surprising is that so few people objected.

Today, we know that this famous theory that gained so much support was actually pseudoscience. The crisis it claimed was nonexistent. And the actions taken in the name of this theory were morally and criminally wrong. Ultimately, they led to the deaths of millions of people.

The theory was eugenics, and its history is so dreadful—and, to those who were caught up in it, so embarrassing—that it is now rarely discussed. But it is a story that should be well known to every citizen, so that its horrors are not repeated.

The theory of eugenics postulated a crisis of the gene pool leading to the deterioration of the human race. The best human beings were not breeding as rapidly as the inferior ones—the foreigners, immigrants, Jews, degenerates, the unfit, and the "feeble minded." Francis Galton, a respected British scientist, first speculated about this area, but his ideas were taken far beyond anything he intended. They were adopted by science-minded Americans, as well as those who had no interest in science but who were worried about the immigration of inferior races early in the twentieth century— "dangerous human pests" who represented "the rising tide of imbeciles" and who were polluting the best of the human race.

The eugenicists and the immigrationists joined forces to put a stop to this. The plan was to identify individuals who were feeble-minded—Jews were agreed to be largely feeble-minded, but so were many foreigners, as well as blacks—and stop them from breeding by isolation in institutions or by sterilization.

As Margaret Sanger said, "Fostering the good-for-nothing at the expense of the good is an extreme cruelty . . . there is no greater curse to posterity than that of bequeathing them an increasing population of imbeciles." She spoke of the burden of caring for "this dead weight of human waste."

Such views were widely shared. H. G. Wells spoke against "ill-trained swarms of inferior citizens." Theodore Roosevelt said that "Society has no business to permit degenerates to reproduce their kind." Luther Burbank: "Stop permitting criminals and weaklings to reproduce." George Bernard Shaw said that only eugenics could save mankind.

There was overt racism in this movement, exemplified by texts such as

The Rising Tide of Color Against White World Supremacy, by American author Lothrop Stoddard. But, at the time, racism was considered an unremarkable aspect of the effort to attain a marvelous goal—the improvement of humankind in the future. It was this avant-garde notion that attracted the most liberal and progressive minds of a generation. California was one of twenty-nine American states to pass laws allowing sterilization, but it proved the most forward-looking and enthusiastic—more sterilizations were carried out in California than anywhere else in America.

Eugenics research was funded by the Carnegie Foundation, and later by the Rockefeller Foundation. The latter was so enthusiastic that even after the center of the eugenics effort moved to Germany, and involved the gassing of individuals from mental institutions, the Rockefeller Foundation continued to finance German researchers at a very high level. (The foundation was quiet about it, but they were still funding research in 1939, only months before the onset of World War II.)

Since the 1920s, American eugenicists had been jealous because the Germans had taken leadership of the movement away from them. The Germans were admirably progressive. They set up ordinary-looking houses where "mental defectives" were brought and interviewed one at a time, before being led into a back room, which was, in fact, a gas chamber. There, they were gassed with carbon monoxide, and their bodies disposed of in a crematorium located on the property.

Eventually, this program was expanded into a vast network of concentration camps located near railroad lines, enabling the efficient transport and killing of ten million undesirables.

After World War II, nobody was a eugenicist, and nobody had ever been a eugenicist. Biographers of the celebrated and the powerful did not dwell on the attractions of this philosphy to their subjects, and sometimes did not mention it at all. Eugenics ceased to be a subject for college classrooms, although some argue that its ideas continue to have currency in disguised form.

But in retrospect, three points stand out. First, despite the construction of Cold Springs Harbor Laboratory, despite the efforts at universities and the pleadings of lawyers, there was no scientific basis for eugenics. In fact, nobody at that time knew what a gene really was. The movement was able to proceed because it employed vague terms never rigorously defined. "Feeble-mindedness" could mean anything from poverty and illiteracy to epilepsy. Similarly, there was no clear definition of "degenerate" or "unfit."

Second, the eugenics movement was really a social program masquerading as a scientific one. What drove it was concern about immigration and racism and undesirable people moving into one's neighborhood or country. Once again, vague terminology helped conceal what was really going on.

Third, and most distressing, the scientific establishment in both the United States and Germany did not mount any sustained protest. Quite the contrary. In Germany scientists quickly fell into line with the program. Modern German researchers have gone back to review Nazi documents from the 1930s. They expected to find directives telling scientists what research should be done. But none were necessary. In the words of Ute Deichman, "Scientists, including those who were not members of the [Nazi] party, helped to get funding for their work through their modified behavior and direct cooperation with the state." Deichman speaks of the "active role of scientists themselves in regard to Nazi race policy . . . where [research] was aimed at confirming the racial doctrine . . . no external pressure can be documented." German scientists adjusted their research interests to the new policies. And those few who did not adjust disappeared.

A second example of politicized science is quite different in character, but it exemplifies the hazards of government ideology controlling the work of science, and of uncritical media promoting false concepts. Trofim Denisovich Lysenko was a self-promoting peasant who, it was said, "solved the problem of fertilizing the fields without fertilizers and minerals." In 1928 he claimed to have invented a procedure called vernalization, by which seeds were moistened and chilled to enhance the later growth of crops.

Lysenko's methods never faced a rigorous test, but his claim that his treated seeds passed on their characteristics to the next generation represented a revival of Lamarckian ideas at a time when the rest of the world was embracing Mendelian genetics. Josef Stalin was drawn to Lamarckian ideas, which implied a future unbounded by hereditary constraints; he also wanted improved agricultural production. Lysenko promised both, and became the darling of a Soviet media that was on the lookout for stories about clever peasants who had developed revolutionary procedures.

Lysenko was portrayed as a genius, and he milked his celebrity for all it was worth. He was especially skillful at denouncing his opponents. He used questionnaires from farmers to prove that vernalization increased crop yields, and thus avoided any direct tests. Carried on a wave of state-sponsored enthusiasm, his rise was rapid. By 1937, he was a member of the Supreme Soviet.

By then, Lysenko and his theories dominated Russian biology. The result was famines that killed millions, and purges that sent hundreds of dissenting Soviet scientists to the gulags or the firing squads. Lysenko was aggressive in attacking genetics, which was finally banned as "bourgeois pseudo-science" in 1948. There was never any basis for Lysenko's ideas, yet he controlled Soviet research for thirty years. Lysenkoism ended in the 1960s, but Russian biology still has not entirely recovered from that era.

Now we are engaged in a great new theory, that once again has drawn the support of politicians, scientists, and celebrities around the world. Once again, the theory is promoted by major foundations. Once again, the research is carried out at prestigious universities. Once again, legislation is passed and social programs are urged in its name. Once again, critics are few and harshly dealt with.

Once again, the measures being urged have little basis in fact or science. Once again, groups with other agendas are hiding behind a movement that appears high-minded. Once again, claims of moral superiority are used to justify extreme actions. Once again, the fact that some people are hurt is shrugged off because an abstract cause is said to be greater than any human consequences. Once again, vague terms like *sustainability* and *generational justice*—terms that have no agreed definition—are employed in the service of a new crisis.

I am not arguing that global warming is the same as eugenics. But the similarities are not superficial. And I do claim that open and frank discussion of the data, and of the issues, is being suppressed. Leading scientific journals have taken strong editorial positions on the side of global warming, which, I argue, they have no business doing. Under the circumstances, any scientist who has doubts understands clearly that they will be wise to mute their expression.

One proof of this suppression is the fact that so many of the outspoken critics of global warming are retired professors. These individuals are no longer seeking grants, and no longer have to face colleagues whose grant applications and career advancement may be jeopardized by their criticisms.

In science, the old men are usually wrong. But in politics, the old men are wise, counsel caution, and in the end are often right.

The past history of human belief is a cautionary tale. We have killed thousands of our fellow human beings because we believed they had signed a contract with the devil, and had become witches. We still kill more than a thousand people each year for witchcraft. In my view, there is only one hope for humankind to emerge from what Carl Sagan called "the demon-haunted world" of our past. That hope is science.

But as Alston Chase put it, "when the search for truth is confused with political advocacy, the pursuit of knowledge is reduced to the quest for power."

That is the danger we now face. And that is why the intermixing of science and politics is a bad combination, with a bad history. We must remember the history, and be certain that what we present to the world as knowledge is disinterested and honest.

APPENDIX II
Sources of Data for Graphs

World temperature data has been taken from the Goddard Institute for Space Studies, Columbia University, New York (GISS); the Jones, et al. data set from the Climate Research Unit, University of East Anglia, Norwich, UK (CRU); and the Global Historical Climatology Network (GHCN) maintained by the National Climatic Data Center (NCDC) and the Carbon Dioxide Information and Analysis Center (CDIAC) of Oak Ridge National Laboratory, Oak Ridge, Tennessee.

The GISS station page is not easy to find from their home page, but it is found at http://www.giss.nasa.gov/data/update/gistemp/station data/.

The Jones data set reference is P. D. Jones, D. E. Parker, T. J. Osborn, and K. R. Briffa, 1999. Global and hemispheric temperature anomalies—land and marine instrument records. In *Trends: A Compendium of Data on Global Change*. Carbon Dioxide Information Analysis Center, Oak Ridge National Laboratory, US Department of Energy, Oak Ridge, Tennessee.

Global Historical Climatology Network is maintained at NCDC and CDIAC of Oak Ridge National Laboratory. The home page is http://cdiac. esd.ornl.gov/ghcn/ghcn.html.

Temperature data for the United States comes from the United States Historical Climatology Network (USHCN) maintained at NCDC and CDIAC of Oak Ridge National Laboratory, which states: "We recommend using USHCN whenever possible for long-term climate analyses. . . ."

The USHCN home page is http://www.ncdc.noaa.gov/oa/climate/research/ushcn/ushcn.html.

The reference is D. R. Easterling, T. R. Karl, E. H. Mason, P. Y. Hughes, D. P. Bowman, R. C. Daniels, and T. A. Boden (eds.). 1996. *United States Historical Climatology Network (US HCN) Monthly Temperature and Precipitation Data*. ORNL/CDIAC-87, NDP-019/R3. Carbon Dioxide Information Analysis Center, Oak Ridge National Laboratory, Oak Ridge, Tennessee.

Graphs are generated in Microsoft Excel from tabular data provided on the websites.

The satellite images are from NASA (http://datasystem.earthkam.ucsd.edu). The rendering of the globe image on the title page and part-opener pages is adapted from NASA (http://earthobservatory.nasa.gov/Observatory/Datasets/tsurf.tovs.html).

BIBLIOGRAPHY

What follows is a list of books and journal articles I found most useful in preparing this novel. I found the texts by Beckerman, Chase, Huber, Lomborg, and Wildavsky to be particularly revealing.

Environmental science is a contentious and intensely politicized field. No reader should assume that any author listed below agrees with the views I express in this book. Quite the contrary: many of them disagree strongly. I am presenting these references to assist those readers who would like to review my thinking and arrive at their own conclusions.

Aber, John D., and Jerry M. Melillo. *Terrestrial Ecosystems*. San Francisco: Harcourt Academic Press, 2001. A standard textbook.

Abrupt Climate Change: Inevitable Surprises (Report of the Committee on Abrupt Climate Change, National Research Council). Washington, DC: National Academy Press, 2002. The text concludes that abrupt climate change might occur sometime in the future, triggered by mechanisms not yet understood, and that in the meantime more research is needed. Surely no one could object.

Adam, Barbara, Ulrich Beck, and Jost Van Loon. *The Risk Society and Beyond*. London: Sage Publications, 2000.

Altheide, David L. *Creating Fear, News and the Construction of Crisis*. New York: Aldine de Gruyter, 2002. A book about fear and its expanding place in public life. Overlong and repetitive, but addressing a highly significant subject. Some of the statistical analyses are quite amazing.

Anderson, J. B. and J. T. Andrews. "Radiocarbon Constraints on Ice Sheet Advance and Retreat in the Weddell Sea, Antarctica." *Geology* 27 (1999): 179–82.

Anderson, Terry L., and Donald R. Leal. *Free Market Environmentalism*. New York: Palgrave (St. Martin's Press), 2001. The authors argue government management of environmental resources has a poor track record in the former Soviet Union, and in the Western democracies as well. They make the case for the superiority of private and market-based management of environmental resources. Their case histories are particularly interesting.

Arens, William. *The Man-Eating Myth*. New York: Oxford, 1979.

Arquilla, John, and David Ronfeldt, eds. *In Athena's Camp: Preparing for Conflict in the Information Age*. Santa Monica, Calif.: RAND National Defense Research Institute, 1997. See particularly part III on the advent of netwar and its implications.

Aunger, Robert, ed. *Darwinizing Culture*. New York: Oxford University Press, 2000. See especially the last three chapters, which devastate the trendy concept of memes. There is no better example of the way that trendy quasi-scientific ideas can gain currency even in the face of preexisting evidence that they are baseless. And the text serves as a model for the expression of brisk disagreement without ad hominem characterization.

Beck, Ulrich. *Risk Society: Towards a New Modernity*. Trans. Mark Ritter. London: Sage, 1992. This highly influential text by a German sociologist presents a fascinating redefinition of the modern state as protector against industrial society, instead of merely the ground upon which it is built.

Beckerman, Wilfred. *A Poverty of Reason: Sustainable Development and Economic Growth*. Oakland, Calif.: Independent Institute, 2003. A short, witty, stinging review of sustainability, climate change, and the precautionary principle by an Oxford economist and former member of the Royal Commission on Environmental Pollution who cares more about the poor of the world than he does the elitist egos of Western environmentalists. Clearly argued and fun to read.

Bennett, W. Lance. *News: The Politics of Illusion*. New York: Addison-Wesley, 2003.

Black, Edwin. *War Against the Weak: Eugenics and America's Campaign to Create a Master Race*. New York: Four Walls, 2003. The history of the eugenics movement in America and Germany is an unpleasant story, and perhaps for that reason, most texts present it confusingly. This book is an admirably clear narrative.

Bohm, R. "Urban bias in temperature time series—a case study for the city of Vienna, Austria." *Climatic Change* 38 (1998): 113–28.

Braithwaite, Roger J. "Glacier mass balance: The first 50 years of international monitoring." *Progress in Physical Geography* 26, no. 1 (2002): 76–95.

Braithwaite, R. J., and Y. Zhang. "Relationships between interannual variability of glacier mass balance and climate." *Journal of Glaciology* 45 (2000): 456–62.

Briggs, Robin. *Witches and Neighbors: The Social and Cultural Context of European Witchcraft.* New York: HarperCollins, 1996.

Brint, Steven. "Professionals and the Knowledge Economy: Rethinking the Theory of the Postindustrial Society." *Current Sociology* 49, no. 1 (July 2001): 101–32.

Brower, Michael, and Warren Leon. *The Consumer's Guide to Effective Environmental Choices: Practical Advice from the Union of Concerned Scientists.* New York: Three Rivers Press, 1999. Of particular interest for its advice on mundane decisions: paper vs. plastic shopping bags (plastic), cloth vs. disposable diapers (disposable). On broader issues, the analysis is extremely vague and exemplifies the difficulties of determining "sustainable development" that are pointed out by Wilfred Beckerman.

Carson, Rachel. *Silent Spring.* Boston: Houghton Mifflin, 1962. I am old enough to remember reading this poetic persuasive text with alarm and excitement when it was first published; it was clear even then that it would change the world. With the passage of time Carson's text appears more flawed and more overtly polemical. It is, to be blunt, about one-third right and two-thirds wrong. Carson is particularly to be faulted for her specious promotion of the idea that most cancer is caused by the environment. This fear remains in general circulation decades later.

Castle, Terry. "Contagious Folly." In Chandler, Davidson, and Harootunian, *Questions of Evidence.*

Chandler, James, Arnold I. Davidson, and Harry Harootunian. *Questions of Evidence: Proof, Practice and Persuasion Across the Disciplines.* Chicago: University of Chicago Press, 1993.

Changnon, Stanley A. "Impacts of 1997–98 El Niño-Generated Weather in the United States." *Bulletin of the American Meteorological Society* 80, no. 9, (1999): 1819–28.

Chapin, F. Stuart, Pamela A. Matson, and Harold A. Mooney. *Principles of Terrestrial Ecosystems Ecology.* New York: Springer-Verlag, 2002. Clearer and with more technical detail than most ecology texts.

Chase, Alston. *In a Dark Wood: The Fight over Forests and the Myths of Nature.* New Brunswick, N.J.: Transaction Publishers, 2001. Essential reading. This book is a history of the conflict over the forests of the Northwest, a cheerless and distressing story. As a former professor of philosophy, the author is one of the few writers in the environmental field who shows the slightest interest in ideas—where they come from, what consequences have flowed from them in the historical past, and therefore what consequences are likely to flow from them now. Chase discusses such notions as the mystic vision of wilderness and the balance of nature from the standpoint of both science and philosophy. He is contemptuous of much conventional wisdom and the muddle-headed attitudes he calls "California cosmology." The book is long and sometimes rambling, but extremely rewarding.

―――. *Playing God in Yellowstone: The Destruction of America's First National Park.* New York: Atlantic, 1986. Essential reading. Arguably the first and clearest critique of ever-changing environmental beliefs and their practical consequences. Anyone who assumes we know how to manage wilderness areas needs to read this sobering history of the century-long mismanagement of Yellowstone, the first national park. Chase's text has been reviled in some quarters, but to my knowledge, never seriously disputed.

Chen, L., W. Zhu, X. Zhou, and Z. Zhou, "Characteristics of the heat island effect in Shanghai and its possible mechanism." *Advances in Atmospheric Sciences* 20 (2003): 991-1001.

Choi, Y., H.-S. Jung, K.-Y. Nam, and W.-T. Kwon, "Adjusting urban bias in the regional mean surface temperature series of South Korea, 1968–99." *International Journal of Climatology* 23 (2003): 577–91.

Christianson, Gale E. *Greenhouse: The 200-Year Story of Global Warming.* New York: Penguin, 1999.

Chylek, P., J. E. Box, and G. Lesins. "Global Warming and the Greenland Ice Sheet." *Climatic Change* 63 (2004): 201–21.

Comiso, J. C. "Variability and Trends in Antarctic Surface Temperatures From *in situ* and Satellite Infrared Measurements." *Journal of Climate* 13 (2000): 1674–96.

Cook, Timothy E. *Governing with the News: The News Media as a Political Institution.* Chicago: University of Chicago Press, 1998.

Cooke, Roger M. *Experts in Uncertainty.* New York: Oxford University Press, 1991.

Davis, Ray Jay, and Lewis Grant. *Weather Modification Technology and Law.* AAAS Selected Symposium. Boulder, Col.: Westview Press, Inc., 1978. Of historical interest only.

Deichmann, Ute. *Biologist Under Hitler,* tr. Thomas Dunlap. Cambridge, Mass.: Harvard University Press, 1996. Difficult in structure, disturbing in content.

Doran, P. T., J. C. Priscu, W. B. Lyons, J. E. Walsh, A. G. Fountain, D. M. McKnight, D. L. Moorhead, R. A. Virginia, D. H. Wall, G. D. Clow, C. H. Fritsen, C. P. McKay, and A. N. Parsons. "Antarctic Climate Cooling and Terrestrial Ecosystem Response." *Nature* 415 (2002): 517–20.

Dörner, Dietrich. *The Logic of Failure: Recognizing and Avoiding Error in Complex Situations.* Cambridge, Mass.: Perseus, 1998. What prevents human beings from successfully managing the natural environment and other complex systems? Dozens of pundits have weighed in with their unsubstantiated opinions. Dörner, a cognitive psychologist, performed experiments and found out. Using computer simulations of complex environments, he invited intellectuals to improve the situation. They often made it worse. Those who did well gathered information before acting, thought systemically, reviewed progress, and corrected their course often. Those who did badly clung to their theories, acted too quickly, did not correct course, and blamed others when things went wrong. Dörner concludes that our failures in managing complex systems do not represent any inherent lack of human capability. Rather they reflect bad habits of thought and lazy procedures.

Dowie, Mark. *Losing Ground: American Environmentalism at the Close of the Twentieth Century.* Cambridge, Mass.: MIT Press, 1995. A former editor of *Mother Jones* concludes that the American environmental movement has lost relevance through compromise and capitulation. Well written, but weakly documented, the book is most interesting for the frame of mind it conveys—an uncompromising posture that rarely specifies what solutions would be satisfactory. This makes the text essentially nonscientific in its outlook and its implications, and all the more interesting for that.

Drake, Frances. *Global Warming: The Science of Climate Change.* New York: Oxford University Press, 2000. This well-written overview for college students can be read by any interested reader.

Drucker, Peter. *Post-Capitalist Society.* New York: Harper Business, 1993.

Eagleton, Terry. *Ideology: An Introduction.* New York: Verso, 1991.

Edgerton, Robert B. *Sick Societies: Challenging the Myth of Primitive Harmony.* New York: Free Press, 1992. An excellent summary of the evidence disputing the notion of the noble savage that goes on to consider whether cultures adopt maladaptive beliefs and practices. The author concludes that all cultures do so. The text also attacks the currently trendy academic notion of "unconscious" problem-solving, in which primitive cultures are assumed to be acting in an ecologically sound fashion, even when they appear wasteful and destructive. Edgerton argues they aren't doing anything of the sort—they *are* wasteful and destructive.

Edwards, Paul. N., and Stephen Schneider. "The 1995 IPCC Report: Broad Consensus or 'Scientific Cleansing'?" *EcoFable/Ecoscience* 1, no. 1 (1997): 3–9. A spirited argument in defense of changes to the 1995 IPCC report by Ben Santer. However, the article focuses on the controversy that resulted and does not review in detail the changes to the text that were made. Thus the paper talks about the controversy without examining its substance.

Einarsson, Porleifur. *Geology of Iceland*. Trans. Georg Douglas. Reykjavík: Mal og menning, 1999. Surely one of the clearest geology textbooks ever written. The author is professor of geology at the University of Iceland.

Etheridge, D. M., et al. "Natural and anthropogenic changes in atmospheric CO_2 over the last 1000 years from air in Antarctic ice and firn." *Journal of Geophysical Research* 101 (1996): 4115–28.

Fagan, Brian. *The Little Ice Age: How Climate Made History 1300–1850*. New York: Basic Books, 2000. Our experience of climate is limited to the span of our lives. The degree to which climate has varied in the past, and even in historical times, is hard for anyone to conceive. This book, by an archaeologist who writes extremely well, makes clear through historical detail how much warmer—and colder—it has been during the last thousand years.

Feynman, Richard. *The Character of Physical Law*. Cambridge, Mass.: MIT Press, 1965. Feynman exemplifies the crispness of thought in physics as compared with the mushy subjectivity of fields such as ecology or climate research.

Finlayson-Pitts, Barbara J., and James N. Pitts, Jr. *Chemistry of the Upper and Lower Atmosphere: Theory, Experiments, and Applications*. New York: Academic Press, 2000. A clear text that can be read by anyone with a good general science background.

Fisher, Andy. *Radical Ecopsychology: Psychology in the Service of Life*. Albany, N.Y.: State University of New York Press, 2002. An astonishing text by a psychotherapist. In my opinion, the greatest problem for all observers of the world is to determine whether their perceptions are genuine and verifiable or whether they are merely the projections of inner feelings. This book says it doesn't matter. The text consists almost entirely of unsubstantiated opinions about human nature and our interaction with the natural world. Anecdotal, egotistical, and wholly tautological, it is a dazzling example of unbridled fantasy. It can stand in for a whole literature of related texts in which feeling-expression masquerades as fact.

Flecker, H., and B. C. Cotton. "Fatal bite from octopus." *Medical Journal of Australia* 2 (1955): 329–31.

Forrester, Jay W. *Principles of Systems*. Waltham, Mass.: Wright-Allen Press, 1971. Some day Forrester will be acknowledged as one of the most important scientists of the twentieth century. He is one of the first, and surely the most influential, researcher to model complex systems on the computer. He did groundbreaking studies of everything from high-tech corporate behavior to urban renewal, and he was the first to get any inkling of how difficult it is to manage complex systems. His work was an early inspiration for the attempts to model the world that ultimately became the Club of Rome's

Limits of Growth. But the Club didn't understand the most fundamental principles behind Forrester's work.

Forsyth, Tim. *Critical Political Ecology: The Politics of Environmental Science*. New York: Routledge, 2003. A careful but often critical examination of environmental orthodoxy by a lecturer in environment and development at the London School of Economics. The text contains many important insights I have not seen elsewhere, including the consequences of the IPCC emphasis on computer models (as opposed to other forms of data) and the question of how many environmental effects are usefully regarded as "global." However, the author adopts much of the postmodernist critique of science, and thus refers to certain "laws" of science, when few scientists would grant them such status.

Freeze, R. Allan. *The Environmental Pendulum: A Quest for the Truth about Toxic Chemicals, Human Health, and Environmental Protection*. Berkeley, Calif.: University of California Press, 2000. A university professor with on-the-ground experience dealing with toxic waste sites has written a cranky and highly informative book detailing his experiences and views. One of the few books by a person who is not only academically qualified but experienced in the field. His opinions are complex and sometimes seemingly contradictory. But that's reality.

Furedi, Frank. *Culture of Fear: Risk-taking and the Morality of Low Expectation*. New York: Continuum, 2002. As Western societies become more affluent and safer, as life expectancy has steadily increased, one might expect the populations to become relaxed and secure. The opposite has happened: Western societies have become panic-stricken and hysterically risk averse. The pattern is evident in everything from environmental issues to the vastly increased supervision of children. This text by a British sociologist discusses why.

Gelbspan, Ross. *The Heat Is On: The Climate Crisis, the Cover-Up, the Prescription*. Cambridge, Mass.: Perseus, 1998. A reporter who has written extensively on environmental matters presents the classic doomsday scenarios well. Penn and Teller characterize him in scatological terms.

Gilovitch, Thomas, Dale Griffin, and Daniel Kahneman, eds. *Heuristics and Biases: The Psychology of Intuitive Judgment*. Cambridge, UK: Cambridge University Press, 2002. Psychologists have created a substantial body of experimental data on human decision making since the 1950s. It has been well replicated and makes essential reading for anyone who wants to understand how people make decisions and how they think about the decisions that others make. The entire volume is compelling (though sometimes disheartening), and articles of particular interest are listed separately.

Glassner, Barry. *The Culture of Fear.* New York: Basic Books, 1999. Debunks fear-mongering with precision and calmness.

Glimcher, Paul W. *Decisions, Uncertainty, and the Brain.* Cambridge, Mass.: MIT Press, 2003.

Glynn, Kevin. *Tabloid Culture.* Durham, N.C.: Duke University Press, 2000.

Goldstein, William M., and Robin M. Hogarth, eds. *Research on Judgment and Decision Making.* Cambridge, UK: Cambridge University Press, 1997.

Gross, Paul R., and Norman Leavitt. *Higher Superstition: The Academic Left and Its Quarrels with Science.* Baltimore: Johns Hopkins University Press, 1994. See chapter 6, "The Gates of Eden" for a discussion of environmentalism in the context of current postmodern academic criticism.

Guyton, Bill. *Glaciers of California.* Berkeley, Calif.: University of California Press, 1998. An elegant gem of a book.

Hadley Center. "Climate Change, Observations and Predictions, Recent Research on Climate Change Science from the Hadley Center," December 2003. Obtainable at *www.metoffice.com.* In sixteen pages the Hadley Center presents the most important arguments relating to climate science and the predictions for future warming from computer models. Beautifully written, and illustrated with graphic sophistication, it easily surpasses other climate science websites and constitutes the best brief introduction for the interested reader.

Hansen, James E., Makiko Sato, Andrew Lacis, Reto Ruedy, Ina Tegen, and Elaine Matthews. "Climate Forcings in the Industrial Era." *Proceedings of the National Academy of Sciences* 95 (October 1998): 12753–58.

Hansen, James E. and Makiko Sato, "Trends of Measured Climate Forcing Agents." *Proceedings of the National Academy of Sciences* 98 (December 2001): 14778–83.

Hayes, Wayland Jackson. "Pesticides and Human Toxicity." *Annals of the New York Academy of Sciences* 160 (1969): 40–54.

Henderson-Sellers, et al. "Tropical cyclones and global climate change: A post-IPCC assessment." *Bulletin of the American Meteorological Society* 79 (1997): 9–38.

Hoffert, Martin, Ken Caldeira, Gregory Benford, David R. Criswell, Christopher Green, Howard Herzog, Atul K. Jain, Haroon S. Kheshgi, Klaus S. Lackner, John S. Lewis, H. Douglas Lightfoot, Wallace Manheimer, John C. Mankins, Michael E. Mauel, L. John Perkins, Michael E. Schlesinger, Tyler Volk, and Tom M. L. Wigley. "Advanced Technology Paths to Global Climate Stability: Energy for a Greenhouse Planet." *Science* 298 (1 November 2001): 981–87.

Horowitz, Daniel. *The Anxieties of Affluence.* Amherst, Mass.: University of Massachusetts Press, 2004.

Houghton, John. *Global Warming, the Complete Briefing*. Cambridge, UK: Cambridge University Press, 1997. Sir John is a leading figure in the IPCC and a world-renowned spokesperson for climate change. He presents a clear statement of the predictions of the global circulation models for future climate. He draws principally from IPCC reports, which this text summarizes and explains. Skip the first chapter, which is scattered and vague, unlike the rest of the book.

Huber, Peter, *Hard Green: Saving the Environment from the Environmentalists, a Conservative Manifesto*. New York: Basic Books, 1999. I read dozens of books on the environment, most quite similar in tone and content. This was the first one that made me sit up and pay serious attention. It's not like the others, to put it mildly. Huber holds an engineering degree from MIT and a law degree from Harvard; he has clerked for Ruth Bader Ginsburg and Sandra Day O'Connor; he is a fellow at the conservative Manhattan Institute. His book criticizes modern environmental thought in both its underlying attitudes and its scientific claims. The text is quick, funny, informed, and relentless. It can be difficult to follow and demands an informed reader. But anyone who clings to the environmental views that evolved in the 1980s and 1990s must answer the arguments of this book.

Inadvertent Climate Modification, Report of the Study of Man's Impact on Climate (SMIC). Cambridge, Mass.: MIT Press, 1971. A fascinating early attempt to model climate and predict human interaction with it.

IPCC. *Aviation and the Global Atmosphere*. Intergovernmental Panel on Climate Change. Cambridge, UK: Cambridge University Press, 1999.

————. *Climate Change 1992: The Supplementary Report to the IPCC Scientific Assessment*. Intergovernmental Panel of Climate Change. Cambridge, UK: Cambridge University Press, 1992.

————. *Climate Change 1995: Economic and Social Dimensions of Climate Change*. Intergovernmental Panel of Climate Change. Cambridge, UK: Cambridge University Press, 1996.

————. *Climate Change 1995: Impacts, Adaptation and Mitigation of Climate Change Scientific/Technical Analysis*. Contribution of Working Group II to the Second Assessment Report of the IPCC. Intergovernmental Panel of Climate Change. Cambridge, UK: Cambridge University Press, 1996.

————. *Climate Change 1995: The Science of Climate Change*. Intergovernmental Panel of Climate Change. Cambridge, UK: Cambridge University Press, 1996.

————. *Climate Change 2001: Impacts, Adaptation, and Vulnerability*. Intergovernmental Panel of Climate Change. Cambridge, UK: Cambridge University Press, 2001.

———. *Climate Change 2001: Synthesis Report.* Intergovernmental Panel of Climate Change. Cambridge, UK: Cambridge University Press, 2001.

———. *Climate Change 2001: The Scientific Basis.* Cambridge, UK: Cambridge University Press, 2001.

———. *Climate Change: The IPCC Response Strategies.* Intergovernmental Panel of Climate Change. Washington, DC: Island Press, 1991.

———. *Emissions Scenarios.* Intergovernmental Panel of Climate Change. Cambridge, UK: Cambridge University Press, 2000.

———. *Land Use, Land-Use Change, and Forestry.* Intergovernmental Panel of Climate Change. Cambridge, UK: Cambridge University Press, 2000.

———. *The Regional Impacts of Climate Change: An Assessment of Vulnerability.* Intergovernmental Panel on Climate Change. Cambridge, UK: Cambridge University Press, 1998.

Jacob, Daniel J. *Introduction to Atmospheric Chemistry.* Princeton, N.J.: Princeton University Press, 1999.

Joravsky, David. *The Lysenko Affair.* Chicago: University of Chicago Press, 1970. A readable account of this depressing episode.

Joughin, I., and S. Tulaczyk. "Positive Mass Balance of the Ross Ice Streams, West Antarctica." *Science* 295 (2002): 476–80.

Kahneman, Daniel, and Amos Tversky, eds. *Choices, Values and Frames.* Cambridge, UK: Cambridge University Press, 2000. The authors are responsible for a revolution in our understanding of the psychology behind human decision-making. The history of the environmental movement is characterized by some very positive decisions made on the basis of inadequate information, and some unfortunate decisions made despite good information that argued against the decision. This book sheds light on how such things happen.

Kalnay, Eugenia, and Ming Cai. "Impact of Urbanization and Land-Use on Climate." *Nature* 423 (29 May 2003): 528–31. "Our estimate of .27 C mean surface warming per century due to land use changes is at least twice as high as previous estimates based on urbanization alone." The authors later report a calculation error, raising their estimate [*Nature* 23 (4 September 2003): 102]. "The corrected estimate of the trend in daily mean temperture due to land use changes is .35 C per century."

Kaser, Georg, Douglas R. Hardy, Thomas Molg, Raymond S. Bradley, and Tharsis M. Hyera. "Modern Glacier Retreat on Kilimanjaro as Evidence of Climate Change: Observations and Facts." *International Journal of Climatology* 24 (2004): 329–39.

Kieffer, H., J. S. Kargel, R. Barry, R. Bindschadler, M. Bishop, D. MacKinnon, A. Ohmura, B. Raup, M. Antoninetti, J. Bamber, M. Braun, I. Brown, D.

Cohen, L. Copland, J. DueHagen, R. V. Engeset, B. Fitzharris, K. Fujita, W. Haeberli, J. O. Hagen, D. Hall, M. Hoelzle, M. Johansson, A. Kaab, M. Koenig, V. Konovalov, M. Maisch, F. Paul, F. Rau, N. Reeh, E. Rignot, A. Rivera, M. Ruyter de Wildt, T. Scambos, J. Schaper, G. Scharfen, J. Shroder, O. Solomina, D. Thompson, K. Van der Veen, T. Wohlleben, and N. Young. "New eyes in the sky measure glaciers and ice sheets." *EOS, Transactions, American Geophysical Union* 81, no. 265 (2000): 270–71.

Kline, Wendy. *Building a Better Race: Gender, Sexuality and Eugenics from the Turn of the Century to the Baby Boom.* Berkeley, Calif.: University of California Press, 2001.

Koshland, Daniel J. "Credibility in Science and the Press." *Science* 254 (1 Nov. 1991): 629. Bad science reporting takes its toll; the former head of the American Association for the Advancement of Science complains about it.

Kraus, Nancy, Trorbjorn Malmfors, and Paul Slovic. "Intuitive Toxicology: Expert and Lay Judgments of Chemical Risks." In *Slovic,* 2000. The extent to which uninformed opinion should be given a place in decision making is highlighted by the question of whether ordinary people have an intuitive sense of what in their environment is harmful—whether they are, in the words of these authors, intuitive toxicologists. As I read the data, they aren't.

Krech, Shepard. *The Ecological Indian: Myth and History.* New York: Norton, 1999. An anthropologist carefully reviews the data indicating that native Americans were not the exemplary ecologists of yore. Also reviews recent changes in ecological science.

Kuhl, Stevan. *The Nazi Connection: Eugenics, American Racism, and German National Socialism.* New York: Oxford University Press, 1994.

Kuran, Timur. *Private Truths, Public Lies: The Social Consequences of Preference Falsification.* Cambridge, Mass.: Harvard University Press, 1995.

Landsea, C., N. Nicholls, W. Gray, and L. Avila. "Downward Trend in the Frequency of Intense Atlantic Hurricanes During the Past Five Decades." *Geophysical Research Letters* 23 (1996): 527–30.

Landsea, Christopher W., and John A. Knaff. "How Much Skill Was There in Forecasting the Very Strong 1997–98 El Niño?" *Bulletin of the American Meteorological Society* 81, no. 9 (September 2000): 2017–19. Authors found the older, simpler models performed best. "The use of more complex, physically realistic dynamical models does not automatically provide more reliable forecasts. . . . [Our findings] may be surprising given the general perception that seasonal El Niño forecasts from dynamical models have been quite successful and may even be considered a solved problem." They discuss in detail that the models did not, in fact, predict well. Yet "others are using the supposed success in dynamical El Niño forecasting to support other agendas . . . one could even have less confidence in anthropogenic global studies because of the lack of skill in predicting El Niño. . . . The bottom line is that the successes in forecasting have been overstated (sometimes drastically) and misapplied in other areas."

Lave, Lester B. "Benefit-Cost Analysis: Do the Benefits Exceed the Costs?" In Robert W. Hahn, ed., *Risks, Costs, and Lives Saved: Getting Better Results from Regulation*. New York: Oxford University Press, 1996. A critical review of problems in cost-benefit analysis by an economist who supports the tool but acknowledges that opponents sometimes have a point.

Lean, Judith, and David Rind. "Climate Forcing by Changing Solar Radiation." *Journal of Climate* 11 (December 1988): 3069–94. How much does the sun affect climate? These authors suggest about half the observed surface warming since 1900 and one-third of the warming since 1970 may be attributed to the sun. But there are uncertainties here. "Present inability to adequately specify climate forcing by changing solar radiation has implications for policy making regarding anthropogenic global change, which must be detected against natural climate variability."

LeBlanc, Steven A., and Katherine E. Register. *Constant Battles*. New York: St. Martin's Press, 2003. The myth of the noble savage and the Edenic past dies hard. LeBlanc is one of the handful of archaeologists who have given close scrutiny to evidence for past warfare and has worked to revise an academic inclination to see a peaceful past. LeBlanc argues that primitive societies fought constantly and brutally.

Levack, Brian P. *The Witch-Hunt in Early Modern Europe*. Second Edition. London: Longman, 1995. In the sixteenth century, the educated elites of Europe believed that certain human beings had made contracts with the devil. They believed that witches gathered to perform horrific rites, and that they flew across the sky in the night. On the basis of these beliefs, these elites tortured countless people, and killed 50,000 to 60,000 of their countrymen, mostly old women. However, they also killed men and children, and sometimes (because it was thought unseemly to burn a child) they imprisoned the children until he or she was old enough to be executed. Most of the extensive literature on witchcraft (including the present volume) does not in my view fully come to grips with the truth of this period. The fact that so many people were executed for a fantasy—and despite the reservations of prominent skeptics—carries a lesson that we must always bear in mind. The consensus of the intelligentsia is not necessarily correct, no matter how many believe it, or for how many years the belief is held. It may still be wrong. In fact, it may be *very* wrong. And we must never forget it. Because it will happen again. And indeed it has.

Lilla, Mark. *The Reckless Mind: Intellectuals in Politics.* New York: New York Review of Books, 2001. This razor-sharp text focuses on twentieth-century philosophers but serves as a reminder of the intellectual's temptation "to succumb to the allure of an idea, to allow passion to blind us to its tyrannical potential."

Lindzen, Richard S. "Do Deep Ocean Temperature Records Verify Models?" *Geophysical Research Letters* 29, no. 0 (2002): 10.1029/2001GL014360. Changes in ocean temperature cannot be taken as a verification of GCMs, computer climate models.

———. "The Press Gets It Wrong: Our Report Doesn't Support the Kyoto Treaty." *Wall Street Journal,* 11 June 2001. This brief essay by a distinguished MIT professor summarizes one example of the way the media misinterprets scientific reports on climate. In this case, the National Academy of Sciences report on climate change, widely claimed to say what it did not. Lindzen was one of eleven authors of the report. http://opinionjournal.com/editorial/feature.html?id=95000606

Lindzen, R. S., and K. Emanuel. "The Greenhouse Effect." In *Encyclopedia of Global Change, Environmental Change and Human Society. Volume 1.* Andrew S. Goudie, ed., New York: Oxford University Press, 2002, pp. 562–66. What exactly is the greenhouse effect everybody talks about but nobody ever explains in any detail? A brief, clear summary.

Liu, J., J. A. Curry, and D. G. Martinson. "Interpretation of Recent Antarctic Sea Ice Variability." *Geophysical Research Letters* 31 (2004): 10.1029/2003 GL018732.

Lomborg, Bjorn. *The Skeptical Environmentalist.* Cambridge, UK: Cambridge University Press, 2002. By now, many people know the story behind this text: The author, a Danish statistician and Greenpeace activist, set out to disprove the views of the late Julian Simon, an economist who claimed that dire environmental fears were wrong and that the world was actually improving. To Lomborg's surprise, he found that Simon was mostly right. Lomborg's text is crisp, calm, clean, devastating to established dogma. Since publication, the author has been subjected to relentless ad hominem attacks, which can only mean his conclusions are unobjectionable in any serious scientific way. Throughout the long controversy, Lomborg has behaved in exemplary fashion. Sadly, his critics have not. Special mention must go to the *Scientific American,* which was particularly reprehensible. All in all, the treatment accorded Lomborg can be viewed as a confirmation of the postmodern critique of science as just another power struggle. A sad episode for science.

Lovins, Amory B. *Soft Energy Paths: Toward a Durable Peace.* New York: Harper and Row, 1977. Perhaps the most important advocate for alternative energy wrote this anti-nuclear energy text in the 1970s for Friends of the Earth, elaborating on an influential essay he wrote for *Foreign Affairs* the year before. The resulting text can be seen as a major link in the chain of events and thinking that set the US on a different energy path from the nations of Europe. Lovins is trained as a physicist and is a MacArthur Fellow.

McKendry, Ian G. "Applied Climatology." *Progress in Physical Geography* 27, no. 4 (2003): 597–606. "Recent studies suggest that attempts to remove the 'urban bias' from long-term climate records (and hence identify the magnitude of the enhanced greenhouse effect) may be overly simplistic. This will likely continue to be a contentious issue. . . ."

Manes, Christopher. *Green Rage: Radical Environmentalism and the Unmaking of Civilization.* Boston: Little Brown, 1990. Not to be missed.

Man's Impact on the Global Environment, Assessments and Recommendations for Action, Report of the Study of Critical Environmental Problems (SCEP). Cambridge, Mass.: MIT Press, 1970. The text predicts carbon dioxide levels of 370 ppm in the year 2000 and a surface-temperature increase of .5 C as a result. The actual figures were 360 ppm and .3 C—far more accurate than predictions made fifteen years later, using lots more computer power.

Marlar, Richard A., et al. "Biochemical evidence of cannibalism at a prehistoric Puebloan site in southwestern Colorado. *Nature* 407, 74078, 7 Sept. 2000.

Martin, Paul S. "Prehistoric Overkill: The Global Model." In *Quaternary Extinctions: A Prehistoric Revolution.* Paul S. Martin and Richard G. Klein, eds. Tucson, Ariz.: University of Arizona Press, 1984, 354–403.

Mason, Betsy. "African Ice Under Wraps." *Nature online publication,* 24 November 2003.

Matthews, Robert A. J. "Facts versus factions: The use and abuse of subjectivity in scientific research." In Morris, *Rethinking Risk,* pp. 247–82. A physicist argues "the failure of the scientific community to take decisive action over the flaws in standard statistical methods, and the resulting waste of resources spent on futile attempts to replicate claims based on them, constitute a major scientific scandal." The book also contains an impressive list of major scientific developments held back by the subjective prejudice of scientists. So much for the reliability of the "consensus" of scientists.

Meadows, Donella H., Dennis L. Meadows, Jorgen Randers, and William W. Behrens III. *The Limits to Growth: A Report for the Club of Rome's Project on the Predicament of Mankind.* New York: New American Library, 1972. It is a shame this book is out of print, because it was hugely influential in its day, and it set the tone ("the predicament of mankind") for much that followed. To read it now is to be astonished at how primitive were the techniques for assessing the state of the world, and how incautious the predictions of future trends. Many of the graphs have no axes, and are therefore just pictures of technical-looking curves. In retrospect, the text is notable not so much for its errors of prediction as for its consistent tone of urgent overstatement bordering on hysteria. The conclusion: "Concerted international measures and joint long-term planning will be necessary on a scale and scope without precedent. Such an effort calls for joint endeavor by all peoples, whatever their culture, economic system, or level of development. . . . This supreme effort is . . . founded on a basic change of values and goals at individual, national and world levels." And so forth.

Medvedev, Zhores A. *The Rise and Fall of T. D. Lysenko.* New York: Columbia University Press, 1969. Extremely difficult to read.

Michaels, Patrick J., and Robert C. Balling, Jr. *The Satanic Gases: Clearing the Air about Global Warming.* Washington, DC: Cato, 2000. These skeptical authors have a sense of humor and a clear style. Use of graphs is unusually good. The Cato Institute is a pro–free market organization with libertarian overtones.

Morris, Julian, ed. *Rethinking Risk and the Precautionary Principle.* Oxford, UK: Butterworth/Heinemann, 2000. A broad-ranging critique that discusses, for example, how precautionary thinking has harmed children's development.

Nye, David E. *Consuming Power.* Cambridge, Mass.: MIT Press, 1998. America consumes more power per capita than any other country, and Nye is the most knowledgeable scholar about the history of American technology. He draws markedly different conclusions from those less informed. This text is scathing about determinist views of technology. It has clear implications for the validity of IPCC "scenarios."

Oleary, Rosemary, Robert F. Durant, Daniel J. Fiorino, and Paul S. Weiland. *Managing for the Environment: Understanding the Legal, Organizational, and Policy Challenges.* New York: Wiley and Sons, 1999. A much-needed compendium that sometimes covers too much in too little detail.

Ordover, Nancy. *American Eugenics: Race, Queer Anatomy, and the Science of Nationalism.* Minneapolis, Minn.: University of Minnesota Press, 2003. Fascinating in content, confusing in structure, difficult to read, but uncompromising. The author insists on the culpability of both the left and right in the eugenics movement, both in the past and in the present day.

Pagels, Heinz R. *The Dreams of Reason: Computers and the Rise of the Sciences of Complexity.* New York: Simon and Schuster, 1988. The study of complexity represents a true revolution in science, albeit a rather old revolution. This delightful book is sixteen years old, written when the revolution was exciting and new. One would think sixteen years would be enough time for the understanding of complexity and nonlinear dynamics to revise the thinking of environmental activists. But evidently not.

Park, Robert. *Voodoo Science: The Road from Foolishness to Fraud*. New York: Oxford University Press, 2000. The author is a professor of physics and a director of the American Physical Society. His book is especially good on the "Currents of Death" EMF/powerline/cancer controversy, in which he was involved (as a skeptic).

Parkinson, C. L. "Trends in the Length of the Southern Ocean Sea-Ice Season, 1979–99." *Annals of Glaciology* 34 (2002): 435–40.

Parsons, Michael L. *Global Warming: The Truth Behind the Myth*, New York: Plenum, 1995. A skeptical review of data by a professor of health sciences (and therefore not a climate scientist). Outsider's analysis of data.

Pearce, Fred, "Africans go back to the land as plants reclaim the desert." *New Scientist* 175 (21 September 2002): 4–5.

Penn and Teller. *Bullshit!* Showtime series. Brisk, amusing attacks on conventional wisdom and sacred cows. The episode in which a young woman signs up environmentalists to ban "dihydrogen monoxide" (better known as water) is especially funny. "Dihydrogen monoxide," she explains, "is found in lakes and rivers, it remains on fruits and vegetables after they're washed, it makes you sweat . . ." And the people sign up. Another episode on recycling is the clearest brief explanation of what is right and wrong about this practice.

Pepper, David. *Modern Environmentalism: An Introduction*. London: Routledge, 1996. A detailed account of the multiple strands of environmental philosophy by a sympathetic observer. Along with the quite different work of Douglas and Wildavsky, this book considers why mutually incompatible views of nature are held by different groups, and why compromise among them is so unlikely. It also makes clear the extent to which environmental views encompass beliefs about how human society should be structured. The author is a professor of geography and writes well.

Petit, J. R., J. Jouzel, D. Raynaud, N. I. Barkov, J.-M. Barnola, I. Basile, M. Bender, J. Chappellaz, M. Davis, G. Delaygue, M. Delmotte, V. M. Kotlyakov, M. Legrand, V. Y. Lipenkov, C. Lorius, L. Pepin, C. Ritz, E. Saltzman, and M. Stievenard. "1999. Climate and atmospheric history of the past 420,000 years from the Vostok ice core, Antarctica." *Nature* 399: 429–36.

Pielou, E. C. *After the Ice Age: The Return of Life to Glaciated North America*. Chicago: University of Chicago Press, 1991. A wonderful book, a model of its kind. Explains how life returned as the glaciers receded twenty thousand years ago, and how scientists analyze the data to arrive at their conclusions. Along the way, an excellent reminder of how dramatically our planet has changed in the geologically recent past.

Ponte, Lowell. *The Cooling*. Englewood, N.J.: Prentice-Hall, 1972. The most highly praised of the books from the 1970s that warned of an impending ice age. (The cover asks: "Has the next ice age already begun? Can we survive it?") Contains a chapter on how we might modify the global climate to prevent excessive cooling. A typical quote: "We simply cannot afford to gamble against this possibility by ignoring it. We cannot risk inaction. Those scientists who say we are entering a period of climatic instability [i.e., unpredictability] are acting irresponsibly. The indications that our climate can soon change for the worse are too strong to be reasonably ignored" (p. 237).

Pritchard, James A. *Preserving Yellowstone's Natural Conditions: Science and the Perception of Nature*. Lincoln, Neb.: University of Nebraska Press, 1999. Balance of evidence that elk have changed habitat. Also the nonequilibrium paradigm.

Pronin, Emily, Carolyn Puccio, and Lee Rosh. "Understanding Misunderstanding: Social Psychological Perspectives." In Gilovitch, et al., pp. 636–65. A cool assessment of human disagreement.

Rasool, S. I., and S. H. Schneider. "Atmospheric Carbon Dioxide and Aerosols: Effects of Large Increases on Global Climate." *Science* (11 July 1971): 138–41. An example of the research in the 1970s that suggested that human influence on climate was leading to cooling, not warming. The authors state that increasing carbon dioxide in the atmosphere will not raise temperature as much as increasing aerosols will reduce it. "An increase by only a factor of 4 in global aerosol background concentration may be sufficient to reduce the surface temperature by as much as 3.5 K . . . believed to be sufficient to trigger an ice age."

Raub, W. D., A. Post, C. S. Brown, and M. F. Meier. "Perennial ice masses of the Sierra Nevada, California." *Proceedings of the International Assoc. of Hydrological Science*, no. 126 (1980): 33–34. Cited in Guyton, 1998.

Reference Manual on Scientific Evidence, Federal Judicial Center. Washington, DC: US Government Printing Office, 1994. After years of abuse, the Federal Courts in the US established detailed guidelines for the admissibility of various kinds of scientific testimony and scientific evidence. This volume runs 634 pages.

Reiter, Paul, Christopher J. Tomas, Peter M. Atkinson, Simon I. Hay, Sarah E. Randolph, David J. Rogers, G. Dennis Shanks, Robert W. Snow, and Andrew Spielman. "Global Warming and Malaria: A Call for Accuracy." *Lancet* 4, no. 1 (June 2004).

Rice, Glen E., and Steven A. LeBlanc, eds. *Deadly Landscape*. Salt Lake City, Utah: University of Utah Press, 2001. More evidence for a strife-filled human past.

Roberts, Leslie R. "Counting on Science at EPA." *Science* 249 (10 August 1990): 616–18. An important brief report on how the EPA ranks risks. Essentially it does what the public wants, not what the EPA experts advise. This is sometimes but not always a bad thing.

Roszak, Theodore. *The Voice of the Earth*. New York: Simon and Schuster, 1992. Roszak is often at the leading edge of emerging social movements, and here he gives an early insight into a blend of ecology and psychology that has since become widespread, even though it is essentially pure feeling without objective foundation. Nevertheless, ecopsychology has become a guiding light in the minds of many people, particularly those without scientific training. My own view is that the movement projects the dissatisfactions of contemporary society onto a natural world that is so seldom experienced that it serves as a perfect projection screen. One must also recall the blunt view of Richard Feynman: "We have learned from much experience that all philosophical intuitions about what nature is going to do fail."

Russell, Jeffrey B. *A History of Witchcraft, Sorcerers, Heretics and Pagans*. London: Thames and Hudson Ltd., 1980. Lest we forget.

Salzman, Jason. *Making the News: A Guide for Activists and Non-Profits*. Boulder, Col.: Westview Press, 2003.

Santer, B. D., K. E. Taylor, T. M. L. Wigley, T. C. Johns, P. D. Jones, D. J. Karoly, J. F. B. Mitchell, A. H. Oort, J. E. Penner, V. Ramaswamy, M. D. Schwarzkopf, R. J. Stouffer, and S. Tett. "A Search for Human Influences on the Thermal Structure of the Atmosphere." *Nature* 382 (4 July 1996): 39–46. "It is likely that [temperature change in the free atmosphere] is partially due to human activities, though many uncertainties remain, particularly relating to estimates of natural variability." One year after the 1995 IPCC statement that a human effect on climate had been discerned, this article by several IPCC scientists shows considerably more caution about such a claim.

Schullery, Paul. *Searching for Yellowstone: Ecology and Wonder in the Last Wilderness*. New York: Houghton Mifflin, 1997. The author was for many years an employee of the Forest Service and takes a more benign approach to events at Yellowstone than others do.

Scott, James C. *Seeing Like a State: How Certain Schemes to Improve the Human Condition Have Failed*. New Haven, Conn.: Yale University Press, 1998. An extraordinary and original book that reminds us how seldom academic thought is genuinely fresh.

Shrader-Frechette, K. S. *Risk and Rationality: Philosophical Foundations for Populist Reforms*. Berkeley, Calif.: University of California Press, 1991.

Singer, S. Fred. *Hot Talk, Cold Science: Global Warming's Unfinished Debate*. Oakland, Calif.: Independent Institute, 1998. Singer is among the most visible of global warming skeptics. A retired professor of environmental science who has held a number of government posts, including Director of Weather Satellite Service and Director for the Center for Atmospheric and Space Sciences, he is a far more qualified advocate for his views than his critics admit. They usually attempt to portray him as a sort of eccentric nutcase. This book is only seventy-two pages long, and the reader may judge for himself.

Slovic, Paul, ed. *The Perception of Risk.* London: Earthscan, 2000. Slovic has been influential in emphasizing that the concept of "risk" entails not only expert opinion but also the feelings and fears of the population at large. In a democracy, such popular opinions must be addressed in policy making. I take a tougher stance. I believe ignorance is best addressed by education, not by unneeded or wasteful regulation. Unfortunately, the evidence is that we spend far too much soothing false or minor fears.

Stott, Philip, and Sian Sullivan, eds. *Political Ecology: Science, Myth and Power.* London: Arnold, 2000. Focused on Africa. Stott is now retired, witty, and runs an amusing skeptical blog.

Streutker, D. R. "Satellite-measured growth of the urban heat island of Houston, Texas." *Remote Sensing of Environment* 85 (2003): 282–89. "Between 1987 and 1999, the mean nighttime surface temperature heat island of Houston increased 0.82 ± 0.10 °C."

Sunstein, Cass R. *Risk and Reason: Safety, Law, and the Environment.* New York: Cambridge University Press, 2002. A law professor examines major environmental issues from the standpoint of cost-benefit analysis and concludes that new mechanisms for assessing regulations are needed if we are to break free of the current pattern of "hysteria and neglect"—in which we aggressively regulate minor risks while ignoring more significant ones. The detailed chapter on arsenic levels is particularly revealing for anyone wishing to understand the difficulties that rational regulation faces in a highly politicized world.

Sutherland, S. K., and W. R. Lane. "Toxins and mode of envenomation of the common ringed or blue-banded octopus." *Medical Journal Australia* 1 (1969): 893–98.

Tengs, Tammo O., Miriam E. Adams, Joseph S. Plitskin, Dana Gelb Safran, Joanna E. Siegel, Milton C. Weinstein, and John D. Graham. "Five hundred life-saving interventions and their cost effectiveness." *Risk Analysis* 15, no. 3 (1995): 369–90. The Harvard School of Public Health is dismissed in some quarters as a right-wing institution. But this influential and disturbing study by the Harvard Center for Risk Analysis of the costs of regulation has not been disputed. It implies that a great deal of regulatory effort is wasted, and wasteful.

Thomas, Keith. *Man and the Natural World: Changing Attitudes in England 1500–1800.* New York: Oxford University Press, 1983. Are environmental attitudes a matter of fashion? Thomas's delightful book charts changing perceptions of nature from a locus of danger, to a subject of worshipful appreciation, and finally to the beloved wilderness of elite aesthetes.

Thompson, D. W. J., and S. Solomon. "Interpretation of Recent Southern Hemisphere Climate Change." *Science* 296 (2002): 895–99.

Tommasi, Mariano, and Kathryn Lerulli, eds. *The New Economics of Human Behavior.* Cambridge, UK: Cambridge University Press, 1995.

US Congress. *Final Report of the Advisory Committee on Weather Control.* United States Congress. Hawaii: University Press of the Pacific, 2003.

Victor, David G. "Climate of Doubt: The imminent collapse of the Kyoto Protocol on global warming may be a blessing in disguise. The treaty's architecture is fatally flawed." *The Sciences* (Spring 2001): 18–23. Victor is a fellow at the Council on Foreign Relations and an advocate of carbon emission controls who argues that "prudence demands action to check the rise in greenhouse gases, but the Kyoto Protocol is a road to nowhere."

Viscusi, Kip. *Fatal Tradeoffs: Public and Private Responsibilities for Risk.* New York: Oxford University Press, 1992. Start at section III.

———. *Rational Risk Policy.* Oxford: Clarendon, 1998. The author is a professor of law and economics at Harvard.

Vyas, N. K., M. K. Dash, S. M. Bhandari, N. Khare, A. Mitra, and P. C. Pandey. "On the Secular Trends in Sea Ice Extent over the Antarctic Region Based on OCEANSAT-1 MSMR Observations." *International Journal of Remote Sensing* 24 (2003): 2277–87.

Wallack, Lawrence, Katie Woodruff, Lori Dorfman, and Iris Diaz. *News for a Change: An Advocate's Guide to Working with the Media.* London: Sage Publications, 1999.

Weart, Spencer R. *The Discovery of Global Warming.* Cambridge, Mass.: Harvard University Press, 2003.

West, Darrell M. *The Rise and Fall of the Media Establishment.* New York: Bedford/St. Martin's Press, 2001.

White, Geoffrey M. *Identity Through History: Living Stories in a Solomon Islands Society.* Cambridge, UK: Cambridge University Press, 1991.

Wigley, Tom. "Global Warming Protocol: CO_2, CH_4 and climate implications." *Geophysical Research Letters* 25, no. 13 (1 July 1998): 2285–88.

Wildavsky, Aaron. *But Is It True? A Citizen's Guide to Environmental Health and Safety Issues.* Cambridge: Harvard University Press, 1995. A professor of political science and public policy at Berkeley turned his students loose to research both the history and the scientific status of major environmental issues: DDT, Alar, Love Canal, asbestos, the ozone hole, global warming, acid rain. The book is an excellent resource for a more complete discussion of these issues than is usually provided. For example, the author devotes twenty-five pages to the history of the DDT ban, twenty pages to Alar, and so on. Wildavsky concludes that nearly all environmental claims have been either untrue or wildly overstated.

———. *Searching for Safety*. New Brunswick, N.J.: Transaction, 1988. If we want a safe society and a safe life, how should we go about getting it? A good-humored exploration of strategies for safety in industrial society. Drawing on data from a wide range of disciplines, Wildavsky argues that resilience is a better strategy than anticipation, and that anticipatory strategies (such as the precautionary principle) favor the social elite over the mass of poorer people.

Winsor, P. "Arctic Sea Ice Thickness Remained Constant During the 1990s." *Geophysical Research Letters* 28, no. 6 (March 2001): 1039–41.

THE
RIVER CONGO

———◆◆◆———

The discovery, exploration and exploitation
of the world's most dramatic river

Peter Forbath

Harper & Row, Publishers
New York, Hagerstown, San Francisco, London

For Piry and John

THE RIVER CONGO. Copyright © 1977 by Peter Forbath. All rights reserved. Printed in the United States of America. No part of this book may be used or reproduced in any manner whatsoever without written permission except in the case of brief quotations embodied in critical articles and reviews. For information address Harper & Row, Publishers, Inc., 10 East 53rd Street, New York, N.Y. 10022. Published simultaneously in Canada by Fitzhenry & Whiteside Limited, Toronto.

FIRST EDITION

Designed by C. Linda Dingler

Library of Congress Cataloging in Publication Data

Forbath, Peter.
  The river Congo.
  Bibliography: p.
  Includes index.
  1. Congo River—Discovery and exploration.
2. Congo Valley—History. I. Title.
DT639.F65 1977   916.75/1′04   77-3749
ISBN 0-06-122490-1

77 78 79 80 81 10 9 8 7 6 5 4 3 2 1

CONTENTS

CONTENTS

Part Four: THE EXPLOITATION

ILLUSTRATIONS

PROLOGUE

———— ◆•●•◆ ————

Congo: the two sudden syllables beat on the imagination like the beat of a jungle drum, calling up nightmare visions of primeval darkness, unfathomable mystery, dreadful savagery. No other word has quite that power; no other symbol stands more vividly for the myth and magic of Africa than the fabulous river those two barbaric syllables name. And for hundreds and hundreds of years, from the time *Congo* first entered the geography and literature of Western civilization in the fifteenth century, this has been so.

For one age, it was the primitive splendor of the Kingdom of Kongo, which a Portuguese caravel captain discovered at the river's mouth, that charged the word and place with its awesome connotations. For another, it was the horrible cruelties of the European slave trade, which ravaged the river basin's forests for more than three hundred years. For still another, there were the terrifying tales the explorers told of their epic journeys on the river, and, for yet another, the unspeakable atrocities committed by sadistic adventurers in the service of an infamous Belgian king. For our age, and certainly for me, the chilling images the name and the river still have the power to evoke come from those ghastly years of tribal and civil wars that followed the Belgian Congo's independence in 1960.

I first saw the Congo during one of the bloodiest moments in those violent years. The place was Stanleyville (now called Kisangani) ; the time, the Simba uprising of 1964. For 110 days in the fall of that year, the Simbas (Swahili for *lions*) , a jungle army of cannibal warriors, doped up on *mira,* dressed out in monkey skins, armed with poisoned arrows, and in the thrall of a witchdoctor's *dawa,* had held Stanleyville in a reign of terror, which was finally broken by a lightning military strike of Belgian paratroopers and white mercenary soldiers. And by the time I got there, as a journalist covering the liberation, the city was a charnel house.

Thousands had been massacred. Mutilated corpses lay in the streets, some partially devoured. The stench of death and decay hung sickeningly in the oppressively hot and humid air. And fear was everywhere. The Simbas had fled but no one could be sure how far and for how long. They might still be lurking in the dark rain forests that surrounded the city, awaiting only their witch doctor's hissing signal to return. The population cowered in dread. The silence was uncanny.

I went down to the river then. The waterfront was deserted, the wrecked warehouses and sheds along the harbor abandoned. An old paddle-wheel steamer, some rusting barge hulks and derelict tugs creaked against the pier. Overhead, a fish eagle suddenly emitted its eerie cry, and from somewhere in the distance a woman, driven mad by terror, echoed the call. And the river flowed by unheedingly between its dark forested banks, silvery gray, glinting malevolently under the beating jungle sun, empty of all but its own implacable movement, moving agelessly down to the sea. In that atmosphere, the effect was hypnotic. In that moment, all the centuries of the West's trembling fascination with the Congo was there for me to understand, and it was then, I suppose, that I first began imagining this book.

The book I imagined, however, was not one I intended to write. It was one I wanted to read. When I had first come out to Africa I had read those two superb classics by Alan Moorehead, *The White Nile* and *The Blue Nile,* which had told me more about the myth and magic of *that* river than any I had read before or have read since, and it was for just that sort of book on the Congo that I began hunting after that astonishing day in Stanleyville. Now, there is, to be sure, a monumental literature on the Congo scattered in libraries and archives all over the world. There are books on the river's hydrography and the river basin's flora and fauna. There are monographs on the Kingdom of Kongo and the pygmies of the rain forest. There are chronicles of the earliest voyagers to the Congo, biographies of the later European explorers, accounts of their stupendous adventures, and volumes on various aspects of the river's recent politics. But oddly enough there is no book that tells the story of the Congo as Moorehead told the story of the Nile, the story of the river's discovery, exploration, and exploitation by Europe told as that seamless narrative of incredible adventure which more than anything else explains the

special place the Congo holds in the Western imagination. This then is meant to be that book.

In writing it, I had, at the outset, to face a nagging problem of nomenclature. For many, indeed most, of the place names involved have been changed—and not least of all the name of the river itself. Since 1971, as part of the *authenticité* campaign of a nationalistic African government intent on erasing the last traces of European colonial rule, the river has been called the Zaire. It is, of course, not difficult to understand and indeed sympathize with the sentiment behind the replacement of such obviously European names as Leopoldville, Stanleyville, and Elizabethville by such authentically African ones as Kinshasa, Kisangani, and Lubumbashi. But the change from *Congo,* a word so inarguably authentically African, to Zaire, which is not only not an authentic African word but no kind of real word at all—it is the clumsy Portuguese mispronunciation of the ancient Kikongo *nzadi* or *nzere,* meaning "the river that swallows all rivers"—is bound to make one wonder. Until one is reminded again, as I was reminded a few years ago, of the powerful connotations the word *Congo* still carries.

The occasion was while I was traveling on a *vedette* up the river's estuary from Banana Point to Matadi and had fallen into a conversation with a young Zairois official, a government veterinarian, who frequently made the trip to inspect the livestock of the tribal villages along the banks. At one point in our aimless, friendly chatter, I happened to refer to the river as the Congo. His expression stiffened and he corrected me pointedly, calling it the Zaire. I was surprised and apologized but took the opportunity to question him on what I regarded as the foolishness of the name change. No, it was not foolish, he replied firmly. "You will understand me, my friend, when I say that *Congo* is a very heavy word. It is a word far too heavy for a people like ourselves to bear in this modern age. When I was a student in Europe, I never liked to say I was Congolese. I pretended I was Guinean. Because there in Europe and also in your America and, yes, even here in Africa, *Congo* has come to stand for all the things we are now struggling so hard to leave behind, for all the savage and primitive things of our past."

There is no way in the world that I can quarrel with that sentiment. Indeed, it is one that I have no trouble at all subscribing to. But

as it is precisely that past, which Zaire is struggling to leave behind, that this book is about; as it is the story of the Congo when it was truly the Congo that I am writing here, I feel it will be understood that no insult is intended to present-day sensibilities that I have chosen to go on calling that marvelous river by its evocative ancient name.

Part One

THE VOYAGES

1

THE RIVER THAT SWALLOWS ALL RIVERS

The river rises in southeastern central Africa, more than 1000 miles south of the equator, more than 1000 miles from the continent's coasts, more than 5000 feet above the level of the sea. This is flat, open country, a highland savanna thinly covered in scrub and twisted thorn trees, solitary silver baobabs and yellow elephant grass, and spotted with those giant sandcastle-like structures that the driver ants build. The vast bowl of the sky, ablaze with the fierce white heat of the African sun during the day, a chilling star-washed velvet at night, falls in a dizzying arc here to immensely distant horizons, where rough brown hills, another 500 or 600 feet above the sea, seem to mark off the edge of the world.

This was once a land of great herds of wild game—zebra and giraffe, antelope and wildebeeste and elephant, and prides of lions hunting in the yellow grass—but it is no longer. For this plateau, which forms the southern rim of the 1.5-million-square-mile saucerlike depression in the heart of Africa that is the Congo River basin, lies in the continent's copper belt and contains astonishingly rich deposits of malachite ore. The Baluba and Balunda tribesmen of this region mined and smelted it, using the giant ant hills for their ovens, as long ago as the fourteenth century and founded a succession of rather wonderful savanna kingdoms on that industry. But in the twentieth century the European colonizers of the plateau, exploiting the ore on a mammoth scale, scarred the savanna into an ugly moonscape with their huge open-pit mines and killed or drove off the magnificent herds and the traveler now can count himself lucky to catch a glimpse of a lone gazelle, startled from the bush by a passing Land-Rover, or a

gang of angrily shrieking baboons scattering through a bamboo grove, or a few ostriches loping away with their dignified ladylike gait across the harshly monochromatic landscape.

The tribal villages are also by and large gone. Those lovely groupings of thatched-roof huts with their kraals and palisades and broom-swept avenues and their feathered, spear-bearing warriors, which David Livingstone visited in the nineteenth century as the first European to reach the Congo headwaters, have been displaced by dreary modern mining towns. The tribesmen now wear plastic hard hats and khaki shorts and carry lunch buckets, and row upon row of identical cinderblock houses and empty, sun-dazzled streets sprawl across the grassland. Railways follow the old game trails; mountains of waste tailings tower over the giant ant hills; power lines slice down from the river's earthenwork dams to the black metal sheds of the electrolytic copper refineries perched on the edges of the mines. And fires can be seen burning everywhere, burning through the grass, blackening the earth, destroying the land. Plumes of dust, whipped off the charred and cracked earth by sudden gusts of hot wind, blow hard against you in the dry season, tearing at your eyes and choking in your mouth. And, in the rainy season, ferocious thunderstorms lash across this ruined highland plain, flooding its lakes and rivers and turning huge tracts of it into swamp.

This is not the landscape one ordinarily associates with the Congo. It is not yet that region of gloom-haunted rain forests which Conrad called the heart of darkness and which do, in fact, dominate the greater part of the river's basin. Nor is the river we find here the one its name traditionally evokes. For here it has the appearance of a lively stream, crystal clear and emerald green, hardly ever much more than a hundred feet wide, splashing brightly over pebble-strewn rapids, tumbling through narrow gorges in bursts of brilliant white spray, rushing swiftly between sharply twisting and turning banks, marking a fertile green path through the austere yellow grassland. Here it is still a river on a human scale, an approachable river, a river you'd be tempted to swim in or fly-cast for fish in, a young river still free of the silent, lurking dangers to be found in its broad, deep, ominously slow-moving waters later on. And here, appropriately enough, it goes by other names.

The Congo begins its tremendous journey to the Atlantic Ocean— a journey of nearly 3000 miles, the fifth longest in the world (after the

Nile, the Mississippi-Missouri, Amazon, and Yangtze) —as the Chambezi. It originates just south of Lake Tanganyika in Zambia and meanders southwestward for a few hundred miles to vanish into Lake Bangweolo. Draining the marshes of the lake's southern shore, it reemerges as the Luapula, and then, turning northward, flows for over 300 miles along the frontier between Zambia and Zaire until it enters the southern end of Lake Mweru. As Mweru's outlet, now lying wholly in Zaire, it is called the Luvua and flows northwestward from the lake's northern end for another couple of hundred miles to join the Lualaba.

There is an argument over whether this circuitous riverine and lacustrine system is the Congo's true watershed and many geographers, bothered by its complexities, prefer to leave it aside altogether and assign the distinction straightaway to the Lualaba. To choose it, instead of the Chambezi, as the Congo's ultimate beginning is to shorten the river by about three hundred miles (and drop it in the world ranking to seventh or eighth place), but the choice does have the virtue of simplicity. For the Lualaba is a strong and straight stream. Its source lies about 250 miles south of the confluence with the Luvua, in those rough brown hills rimming the Shaba (formerly Katanga) Plateau near Zaire's southern border with Zambia, and once upon it the traveler has no trouble following its course. It flows almost directly due north, making none of those reversals in direction that the Chambezi and Luapula make, never vanishing into lakes as they do, and by the time it is joined by the Luvua it is a considerable river in its own right. Indeed, at this point, it is twice the river the Luvua is and anyone standing at their confluence would be hard pressed not to see the Lualaba as the mainstream and the Luvua as the tributary instead of the other way around.

But this is an academic argument and here the traveler can put it behind him, for at the confluence of the Lualaba and Luvua the headwaters of the Congo end and the river, under the name of the Lualaba, but in everything except name the Upper Congo, begins its long descent from the highland savanna toward the rain forests of its immense basin, a basin that encompasses more than one-tenth of the land surface of the African continent and includes all of the modern nations of Zaire and Congo-Brazzaville, most of the Central African Republic and parts of Zambia, Angola, Tanzania, Cameroon, and Gabon.

The Lualaba's course into this great basin continues as it began, almost directly due north, a course that it will now follow for nearly 1000 miles and follow so relentlessly that it appears to be journeying not to the Atlantic Ocean, which after all lies over 1000 miles to the west of it, but straight up the entire length of the continent to the Mediterranean Sea. Not until it crosses the equator will it at last turn away from this misleading course and, describing a remarkable counter-clockwise arc first to the west and then to the southwest, flow back across the equator and on down to the Atlantic.

In this the Congo is exceptional. No other major river in the world crosses the equator even once, let alone twice. Indeed, so astounding a geographical curiosity is this that for centuries no one could believe that even the Congo did. Until barely a hundred years ago, when Henry Morton Stanley proved otherwise, the idea that the relentlessly northbound Lualaba and the southwestward flowing stream that exits to the Atlantic over half a continent away had anything whatsoever to do with each other was inconceivable. They were perceived as two quite separate and distinct rivers, the former, for example, being taken for the mainstream of the Nile by no less an explorer than David Livingstone and the latter as the mouth of the Niger by Mungo Park, the discoverer of the Niger itself.

Something else needs to be mentioned about this astonishing course. The fact that the Congo flows in both the northern and southern hemispheres of the globe means that some part of it (and its network of tributaries) is always in a zone of rain, and thus it does not experience those great periodic rises and falls in its level which are characteristic of all other major rivers. It is, depending on how you choose to look at it, either always in flood or never in flood, because the flooding caused by the rainy season on one side of the equator is always compensated for by the drought caused by the dry season on the other. Thus, the Congo's flow is amazingly constant all the year round. And that flow is the second most powerful in the world (after the Amazon's), pouring almost 1.5 million cubic feet of water every second down to the sea.

The river's descent from the highland savanna to the rain forests occurs over a distance of some 500 miles. In places, it makes the descent in sudden, dramatic steps, plunging into a trough, rushing down a series of rapids, cutting through a gorge. But mostly it proceeds on its relentless northward course across open, gently sloping country,

growing always stronger and wider as tributaries feed into it on both banks, and the descent is perceptible mainly by the steadily increasing richness of the vegetation. The grass becomes thicker; stands of acacia trees form into shady woods, in which weaverbirds nest in great chattering flocks; the baobabs put out broad shiny leaves; and one begins to see palms and lotus and the mangos of the old slave trails. The copper belt is now far behind us, and the alert traveler is now likely to spot game: impala that have come down to the river to drink, a family of hippo bathing in the mud of its banks, just possibly a leopard or cheetah bolting through the high grass, or the carrion eaters that follow the game—hyenas and jackals, or vultures circling overhead. Far off to the east is Lake Tanganyika, and beyond, the Ruwenzoris, the legendary Mountains of the Moon, whose highest peaks, snow-capped the year round, soar to over 16,000 feet and form the Congo River basin's eastern rim just as the copper-belt plateau forms its southern.

The Lualaba in its course through these lower savannas is not yet the great riverine commercial highway that it will soon become, but in long stretches it is by now wide enough to be used by the people living along its banks. Here we begin to see the dugout canoes which become such a permanent feature of the Congo's life and scenery. They are long, narrow craft, carved from single tree trunks and gracefully river-worthy. The tribesmen paddle them standing up, with long-handled oars whose blades are shaped like gorgeous palm leaves, and one sees them here gliding swiftly along the river carrying bunches of green bananas or sugar cane to a market day at some village, or trailing fishing nets in the glassy waters of some quiet cove.

But at Kongolo the river suddenly funnels into the Portes d'Enfer, the Gates of Hell, a startling gorge in the floor of the savanna a half mile deep and barely one hundred yards wide, where the waters boil up alarmingly and turn into impassable rapids for nearly seventy-five miles. And, where they emerge from the gate, the jungle begins.

Strictly speaking, it is not a jungle. Botanists tell us that there is no such thing as a jungle in Africa, only in Asia and South America, and what the river now enters is properly called an equatorial rain forest. But there is a far more dramatic ring to the word *jungle* and no one who has been in the Congo forest would hesitate to use it to describe this incredible realm.

It is seemingly endless. It stretches east to west across the Congo basin, some 4 degrees of latitude to the north and 4 degrees to the

south of the equator, covering very nearly 1,000,000 square miles of the heart of Africa and enclosing very nearly 2000 miles of the river's course. The Congo's counter-clockwise journey twice across the equator occurs entirely within this jungle and this is the reason, above all others, why the river's remarkable course remained an insoluble mystery for so many centuries. For it is a killing place, a region so forbidding, a barrier so formidable that it blocked every attempt to unlock the Congo's geographical secret until a mere hundred years ago.

Traveling into it upon the river, Conrad wrote in *Heart of Darkness*,

was like travelling back to the earliest beginnings of the world, when vegetation rioted on the earth and the big trees were kings. An empty stream, a great silence, an impenetrable forest. The air was warm, thick, heavy, sluggish. There was no joy in the brilliance of sunshine. The long stretches of the waterway ran on, deserted, into the gloom of the overshadowed distances. On silvery sandbanks hippos and alligators sunned themselves side by side. The broadening waters flowed through a mob of wooded islands; you lost your way on the river as you would in a desert . . . this stillness of life did not in the least resemble a peace. It was the stillness of an implacable force brooding over an inscrutable intention. It looked at you with a vengeful aspect.

Moving into the brooding silence, downstream from the exit of the Gates of Hell, the river flows by Nyangwe. Today it is only a scattering of fishermen's mud huts on the Lualaba's right bank, but it was once a considerable town, the easternmost trading station of the Arab slavers and ivory hunters whose caravans penetrated Africa from Zanzibar and the Indian Ocean coast until a century ago, and the farthest any outsider—Arab or European—had ever dared go into the Congo forest until then.

We are here at an elevation of a little more than 2000 feet; the bright horizons of the savanna vanish and the heavy humid heat of the jungle closes down oppressively. It is true that the temperature rarely reaches much above 90 degrees Fahrenheit, but it never goes down much below it either. Between the height of the day and the depth of the night, the thermometer will show a drop of barely 10 degrees, and the mean temperature difference between the hottest and coldest months of the year is less than 5 degrees. Moreover, there is no clear distinction here between a rainy and a dry season; rain can fall in any

month, several times a day, nearly 100 inches of it a year. And in this climate oak, mahogany, ebony, red cedar, walnut, and rubber trees grow to heights of over 200 feet, forming dense canopies overhead that shut out the sky and plunge the forest into a perpetual twilight. A dozen varieties of fruit and palm trees proliferate, linked together in strangleholds of lianas and flowering vines. Giant orchids cling to the tree trunks, and lichens and mosses hang down from their branches like ghostly drapery. Rain and dew in the oppressive humidity of the suffocating air drip from everything.

There are pythons in those trees, and cobras and puff adders, and day and night you hear the hysterical screams of hordes of monkeys swinging through the upper branches, fleeing the deadly ambushes of the snakes. Elephants, of a breed smaller than those found on the savanna highlands, plod through the great stagnant pools made by the constant rainfall, and crocodiles slither in the marshes and ooze of the river's banks, their hooded eyes hypnotically watching the long-legged white water birds that step precariously around them—cranes and herons. There are bats and rats and civet cats. And dreadful diseases— malaria and sleeping sickness, bilharzia, river blindness, and black- water fever—breed invisibly in the silent, humid gloom.

Only the Pygmies live deep in the forest, but the traveler along the river is unlikely to see any of them. There are relatively few left (fewer than 300,000 scattered throughout the Congo basin) and they rarely come down to the river. They live in nomadic bands of ten or twenty families; their beehive-shaped huts, made of sticks and leaves and often set high in the trees, are built and abandoned from month to month as they keep on the move, hunting with bows and arrows, spears and nets, fearful of all other humanity. The people one does see along the river are of an entirely different race. They are Bantu speakers who migrated into the river basin from the surrounding grassland plateaus and, driving the Pygmies always deeper into the forest, settled along the banks of the Congo and its tributaries a thou- sand years ago. Very little has changed for them since.

When Stanley first came down the river these people were canni- bals, and they are known to indulge in the grisly practice occasionally still, for ritual reasons, out of hunger, simply for the taste of it. Theirs is an extremely primitive existence. The villages here are desperately poor places, four or five huts made of bamboo plastered with mud or covered with dried palm leaves, perched on the river's muddy shore.

Small patches of manioc and maize are cultivated in painfully hacked-out clearings, and here and there you'll see a few banana trees and pineapple plants. But because of the riot of vegetation and the lack of sunlight it is extremely difficult to raise anything more than a subsistence crop, and what little is raised is forever being destroyed by the elephants that trample through the forest. The tribesmen hunt the elephants; they dig pit traps, cover them with brush, and when an unlucky beast falls into one they pounce upon it with spears and tear it to pieces in a blood-spattering orgy. They also hunt the monkeys that chatter in the trees and the hairy forest pigs that root in the underbrush, amazingly accurate shots with their bows and arrows and slingshots, but their main source of life is the river, and they can be seen from dawn to dusk in their dugout canoes, fishing with immeasurable patience for the river's huge catfish and *capitaines*.

The river, fed by dozens of tributaries, has widened now to a half mile or more and, rolling ever northward, has taken on the glinting, greasy-gray color of the heavy, lowering sky. Islands, some quite large and heavily forested and with villages on them, begin appearing in the stream, but the channels around them are navigable, and, in fact, a steamer nowadays makes the 200-mile trip between Kindu and Ubundu from time to time. But at Ubundu (formerly called Ponthierville) the Stanley Falls begin, and the only sensible way downriver now is by the railroad the Belgians built around these falls early in the century.

Falls is a misnomer if the word calls to mind the magnificent plunge of the Zambezi over Victoria Falls or the Blue Nile's over the Tisisat Falls. What we have here rather is a series of seven cataracts and rapids, which in the course of some sixty miles drop the river to an elevation of about 1500 feet. They begin mildly enough. Just below Ubundu, reefs of slate and rose-colored granite jut out like fingers from the forested banks, breaking up the river's ponderous flow and creating eddies and whirlpools. But by the time we reach the last of them, the river is a roaring mass of white-water turbulence, rushing in several directions at once, throwing up waves five and ten feet high, boiling over boulders and reefs and crashing on the beaches of forested islands. It is called the Wagenia Cataract, after the tribe of fishermen who live along its banks, a tall, handsome, muscular people who have learned to negotiate the cataract in their long dugouts to set fish traps in its boiling waters. They paddle standing up in crews of ten, wearing

bright-colored sarongs and keeping the beat of their powerful strokes with wonderfully savage chants, like warriors setting out for battle. And, in the midst of the most turbulent rapids, hanging on with amazing grace, they erect elaborate structures of bamboo poles, and from these suspend conical raffia baskets, the mouths of which they face upstream to catch the hapless fish that come tumbling over the falls.

Wagenia lies just north of the equator and marks the end of the Lualaba or Upper Congo. Here the river, called now the Middle Congo, is turned away from its northbound course by the Cameroon Highlands, which form the river basin's northern rim, and begins its great sweeping arc to the west. And here we find the city of Kisangani.

Kisangani (formerly called Stanleyville) is the first real city one meets traveling down the river and, by African standards, it is a large one, with a population of around 200,000. It nevertheless retains much of the brooding, threatening atmosphere of the dark forests around it. For, since Stanley's passage around the river's great bend, it has suffered a history of almost ceaseless violence. The Zanzibari Arabs, who followed Stanley down the Lualaba, built a slaving depot on the site. The Belgians, whom Stanley brought back up the river, used it as a military garrison in their campaign to drive the Arabs out of the region. After that it became the main river port for shipping out the rubber and ivory that the Belgians harvested in the surrounding forests under the brutal conditions so vividly described in *Heart of Darkness*. In recent years, it was the scene of some of the most horrible atrocities committed during the tribal and civil wars following the Congo's independence in 1960.

The specter of that violence still seems to haunt the city. In the oppressive jungle heat, the thick, sweet scent of exotic flowers reminds one alarmingly of the stench of decaying flesh. The district along the waterfront, which was once the European quarter, is ruined; the large, luxurious villas are either abandoned or occupied by squatters, and their gardens are wildly overgrown as if the jungle were pressing in to reclaim them. There are very few whites in the city; in colonialism's heyday some 6000 lived here, but now there are no more than 200 or 300, mainly missionaries, contract technicians, a polyglot of traders and adventurers, who seem always vaguely on the alert for the recurrence of violence, ready on an instant's notice to flee.

The river here is almost a mile wide. Dugout canoes, fitted with

outboard motors, serve as ferries between the city's left- and right-bank settlements, and the riverfront harbor is a jumble of barge hulks, derelict paddle-wheel steamers, tugs tied up to creaking piers, rusting warehouses, and huge tripod cranes. A busy marketplace of kiosks operates just outside the harbor gate, and there large crowds, in bright-colored shirts and blouses, gather to wait for the boat that will take them downriver.

We are here at the beginning of the longest navigable stretch of the Congo, a 1000-mile journey around the river's great bend and back across the equator to Kinshasa (formerly Leopoldville), the capital of Zaire. This is the main stem of a great inland waterway system; the tributaries that feed the Middle Congo, some like the Ubangi as large as the Congo itself is here, form a network of some 8000 miles of navigable rivers, fanning out, like the veins of a leaf, throughout the Congo basin and the passenger boats, cargo barges, ferries, tugs, and canoes which ply these waterways often provide the only practical means of transport and communication in the equatorial rain forests. The steamer one takes from Kisangani is something called an "integrated tow boat." Its main unit is a four-deck pusher boat containing, besides the bridge, officers' and crew's quarters, and engine room, some first-class passenger cabins. To its squared-off prow, lower-class passenger and cargo barges, at least one but sometimes two or three, are lashed, and the assembled long-nosed, high-backed, rather cumbersome-looking vessel pushes out into the river, often with as many as 1000 people aboard.

The journey that took Stanley seven weeks now takes about seven days. Throughout it the river steadily widens. It is difficult to judge just how wide it is at any point because the Congo in this stretch is studded with thousands of sizable islands (4000 by some accounts), which sometimes appear to form the opposite bank and at others the confluence with tributaries, but at its widest it measures over nine miles across. The channels the boat follows form naturally under the force of the river's current (running here as much as six to eight knots), shifting with the shifting silt and mud of its bottom. Survey teams keep track of these changes and post channel markers—barrel buoys in the river, signals on the trees along its banks—to show the way. During the daylight hours, these are easy enough to see; at night the riverboat captain sweeps the water and shoreline with searchlight

beams in order to find them and if, for some reason, he can't, he stops.

The villages along the river now belong mostly to the Lokele. They are a relatively small tribe but they are settled in a thin line along the banks of this portion of the Congo and dominate the river's trade. They are famous for their "talking" drums, which one hears day and night sending messages of boats' progress downriver, so that at every village we pass the Lokele are expecting us and come out in their canoes loaded with goods to trade with the boat's passengers. They are quite relentless in this trade; throughout the journey, the riverboat is never without at least a dozen and often as many as a hundred dugout canoes tied up alongside, and what the Lokele bring aboard for sale or barter reflects the changing nature of the lands we pass through. First there are manioc and sugar cane, then bananas and avocados; pineapples and coconuts are replaced by tangerines and peanuts. At one point palm oil is brought aboard, at another baskets of live grubs; freshly caught fish give way to smoked fish and live eels, then smoked eels and fresh-killed monkeys, then smoked monkeys, live forest pigs, crocodile eggs, and dressed-out antelope.

This trade is the chief occupation and entertainment of the journey. The lower decks and cargo barges turn into thriving marketplaces, floating bazaars. Stalls are set up to barter or sell manufactured goods, barbers go into business, laundries materialize, butchers prepare the animals and fish brought aboard, restaurants serve meals from open fires, beer parlors spring into existence complete with brassy music from transistor radios, and the buying and selling goes on around the clock. And in this way the produce of the Congo rain forest makes its way to the outside world, and the manufactured goods of the outside world—salt, cigarettes, matches, cloth, wire, nails, tools, soap, razor blades—find their way into the forest.

Where the river recrosses the equator stands Mbandaka (formerly Coquilhatville), the only other sizable city on the river before Kinshasa. A few miles below it the Ubangi joins the Congo on the right, and from here the river marks the frontier between the Congo Republic on the right bank and Zaire on the left.

Rain, or the threat of rain, is always with us during the journey. The mornings dawn shrouded in fog, which never entirely burns off, and with the advance of the day the overcast sky lowers suffocatingly

until, toward afternoon, the light fades and there is the eerie gloom of a false night. A wind springs up, sweeping the decks with a fine drizzle, and up ahead you can see a luminous gray sheet of rain slanting down across the jungle. Then suddenly there will be a stunning flash of lightning, a crash of thunder, and the torrential downpour is upon us. The boat slows in the face of the furious onslaught. The captain switches on the searchlights and sweeps the beams into the curtain of rain, hunting for the channel markers. But it's no use; nothing can be seen, and, reversing the engines, the captain backs away as if from the pounding sheet of rain itself and eases the boat toward an island, there to anchor and wait out the storm.

It will last for perhaps an hour or two and then, as abruptly as it began, the rain lets up and the clouds clear away just in time for us to see the sun set. It is a great blood-orange sphere, painting a stripe of the same color across the rippling surface of the river; elsewhere the river is a pale purple under the smoky blue sky, and the forests have turned indigo. A glowing moon comes out and then the stars, and for a few hours the air seems fresh and washed. But then the steaming humidity emerges from the gleaming, dripping jungle, and the oppressive heat closes round again.

But one morning you wake up and go on deck and you discover that the jungle has thinned away and there are high, rugged yellow limestone hills rearing up on both banks. These are the Crystal Mountains, which form the western rim of the Congo basin. We are here at the entrance to the Stanley Pool (now called the Malebo Pool), a vast, lakelike expanse in the river, 15 miles across at its widest, more than 20 miles long, which marks the end of the Middle Congo. As we sail into it with the day's first light, the pool might be the river's mouth with the Atlantic Ocean lying just beyond, shrouded from view for the moment by the morning's lingering mists. But then in the distance you see the skyline of Kinshasa on the left bank and that of Brazzaville, the capital of the Congo Republic, on the right and slowly begin to make out the low distant roar of what Stanley named the Livingstone Falls. And you know you are still over 300 miles from the sea and nearly 1000 feet above it.

Kinshasa is a booming modern metropolis. It has a polyglot population of detribalized Africans and denationalized Europeans of close to 1.5 million. Downtown is a complex of towering skyscrapers; motor traffic rockets wildly along its broad boulevards. There are outdoor

cafés, rows of airline offices, apartment blocks, international hotels, fashionable boutiques, supermarkets, neon signs, expensive suburbs, and the outlying *cités* have the look and feel of urban slums. Its water-front is vibrantly alive, with tugs and ferries, barges and day liners, steamers and cargo boats, and miles of piers, cranes, petroleum tank farms, dry docks, shipyards, warehouses, chandleries. More than one million tons of cargo and ten times that many passengers pass through this port each year. It is the great Congo terminus. All the river's traffic ends or begins here. For the river has now reached the single most difficult obstacle, even including the rain forest, that its geography placed in the way of its discovery, exploration, and exploitation: the Livingstone Falls, by which the river cuts its way through the western rim of its basin, the Crystal Mountains, and rushes the last thousand feet down to the level of the sea.

Again, if what we are thinking of is some Victoria or Niagara, then Livingstone *Falls* is a misnomer. Like the Stanley Falls, what we have here is a series of rapids and cataracts, but with that all comparison must end. For the Livingstone Falls cover some 220 miles and include at least 32 cataracts, and their violence is a hundred times more terrible. They thunder through narrow gorges and ravines, boil up in vicious yellow waves 30 and 40 feet high, crash over giant boulders, rip giant trees and islands of sod from the river's banks, twist and turn and whirl around to create terrifying whirlpools and dreadful, fathomless holes. No tribesmen would dare, as the Wagenia do on the Stanley Falls, to venture into these cataracts in a dugout canoe. Indeed, no vessel of any design could hope to live in these waters. The force is so great that a hydroelectric power dam complex, currently being built on just one of the cataracts, Inga, will produce three times Italy's total annual electrical output, five times China's, twelve times Belgium's. All 32 cataracts have as much power potential as all the rivers and falls of the United States put together.

The only way down this stretch of the river is by the road or railway the Belgians built around it at the beginning of this century. Before that there was no way, in either direction. For 400 years after Europe discovered the Congo's mouth, every attempt to get up the river was defeated by these cataracts and by the mountains that enclose them. And when Stanley at last thought to come *down* the river, they very nearly killed him.

The last of the cataracts is called the Cauldron of Hell, and at this

point the river, emerging from the Crystal Mountains, flows into a coastal plain. It is still about 100 miles from the ocean, but in this, its final course, known as the Lower Congo, it is again wholly navigable, the only major African river to reach the sea via an estuary (the Nile and the Niger, for example, exit via unnavigable deltas). Just below the Cauldron of Hell stands Matadi, Zaire's seaport, which the largest ocean-going vessels are able to reach by sailing up this estuary. And ferries, which regularly make the trip to Banana Point at the river's mouth, take the traveler down it.

From Matadi to Banana, the river marks the border between Zaire on the right bank and Angola on the left. It steadily widens, in some places to as much as five miles, and once again we find sizable islands standing in its stream. Its banks are heavily forested, now mainly with palm trees and mangroves and jungles of giant water ferns. The people on this stretch of the river are the Bakongo, descendants of the inhabitants of that once great African kingdom that gave its name to the river. Their villages are larger than those we have seen until now, their houses more substantial, and they cultivate maize and manioc on a more ambitious scale. There are flocks of goats and pigs and chickens, and herds of cattle stand in the shallow water of the marsh-land of the river's edge. Naked children rush down to the bank to watch the ferry go by, and the tribesmen, dressed in mission shorts and colorful shirts, are everywhere in their canoes, trawling for fish with nylon nets.

Two sandy peninsulas, some 15 miles apart and arcing out into the Atlantic like the opposing jaws of a giant crab's claw, form the Congo's mouth. The river, now moving with a current of some nine knots and swollen to a flow of nearly 1.5 million cubic feet a second, rushes to it and through it and then well beyond it. For geologists tell us that this immensely powerful river has cut a submarine canyon in the ocean's floor, in some places 4000 feet deep, for another 100 miles out to sea. And we can see the river's waters, in their unrelenting flow, staining the ocean's surface for scores of miles offshore with the mud and vegetation carried down on the long journey from the savanna highlands.

That stained ocean—the muddy red sea offshore, the muddy yellow surf breaking on the coastline's beaches, the islands of vegetation riding the river's current far out in the Atlantic—was the first view that

Europeans ever had of the Congo. It was a sighting first made by a Portuguese caravel captain toward the end of the fifteenth century, a decade before Columbus discovered America, and it began an epoch of nearly 400 years of exploration by Europe, during which the rest of the great African river was ultimately found.

The history of that discovery and exploration is inextricably bound up in the geography which we've been following here. Indeed, it is a history so profoundly shaped by the astonishing direction of the river's course, by the forbidding nature of the land it passes through, by the murderous cataracts on its stream that it is virtually impossible to follow without a fair grasp of that geography. But the history begins with yet another geographical fact: the Congo's location in the heart of Africa, utterly remote from Europe and in no way ever touching upon it.

This was not true, for example, of the Nile or even the Niger, those two other great African rivers with whose histories the Congo's can best be compared. Europe had always been in contact with the Nile. The river's delta and lower valley had been visited by classical Greeks and conquered by Imperial Rome; its ancient civilizations had taught Europe how to be civilized; its history had been intertwined with Europe's since well before the Christian era. The Nile's great geographical mystery was the location of its source and, to be sure, it took centuries to find it. But Europe always knew it was there, always considered it vital to find, and searched for it for nearly 2000 years. The Niger too was a river of abiding fascination. Although no European actually laid eyes on it until the early nineteenth century, it was part of Europe's mythology from the earliest Middle Ages. For the Niger was the river of Timbuktoo, the fabled golden city from whence the Saharan caravans brought the precious merchandise of Bilad al-Sudan, the land of the blacks, to the Barbary Shore and the courts of the European kings. And for this, if for nothing else, it was a river to be sought, a lure compelling enough to have tempted adventurers on daring voyages of discovery for hundreds of years.

The Congo played no comparable role, offered no such tempting prizes, held no such place in Europe's literature. For, because of its remote geography, its very existence was unknown. No one could dream of setting out to find it because no one could dream that it was even there. Its discovery was an accident, the fruit of Europe's other

quests, its quests for the gold of the Niger and the secret of the Nile, for the silks of far Cathay and the spices of the Indies, for knowledge, for light in the darkness that lay beyond its circumscribed world, for allies against the dangerous mysteries of the unknown, but, in the first instance, for the legendary kingdom of Prester John.

2

THE QUEST FOR PRESTER JOHN

The first we hear of Prester John is in the twelfth century, a perilous time in medieval Christendom's history. The Pope, Eugenius II, had been driven from the Vatican by a popular revolt in Rome; the rift between the Roman and Byzantine branches of the Church had widened into open hostility and occasional warfare; and the conquests of the First Crusade, which had won for the Roman Church such strongholds in the Moslem world as Jerusalem, Tripoli, Antioch, and Edessa, were in the process of being reversed. Imad-al-Din Zengi, a Seljuk Turk general, had united the Moslem emirates of Syria and the Holy Land into a jihad against the Crusader states, and in 1144 his army of desert horsemen swept down on Edessa, captured it, and put all its defenders to the sword.

The news of this disastrous defeat was brought to the Pontifical Court, then in Viterbo, by Hugh, the Bishop of Jabala. Otto, the Bishop of Freising, was present, and it is in his *Historia de Duabus Civitatibus,* which includes an account of what transpired at the audience between Hugh and Eugenius, that we first read the name of the mysterious Christian priest-king of the Orient.

Hugh's main purpose at Viterbo was to persuade the Pope to call for a second crusade. There was already some enthusiasm for the idea—Conrad III of Germany and Louis VII of France had indicated that they were willing to take up the cross against the Saracens—and Hugh did all he could to inflame the passion. He described in grisly detail the atrocities committed by the Seljuk Turks at Edessa and warned that the capture of that city presaged the fall of all the other Latin states in the Holy Land, up to and including Jerusalem and the

Holy Sepulchre itself. Because of the enmity with Constantinople, the Latin knights could expect no help from the armies of Byzantium; only a great legion of Crusaders from Europe could stem the Moslem tide. Then, to further excite enthusiasm, Hugh, according to the account in the Bishop of Freising's *Historia,* told the following story:

Not many years ago a certain John, a king and priest who lives in the extreme Orient, beyond Persia and Armenia, and who like his people is a Christian . . . made war on the brothers known as the Samiardi, who are the kings of the Persians and the Medes, and stormed Ecbatana, the capital of their kingdoms. . . . When the aforesaid kings met him with Persian, Median and Assyrian troops, the ensuing battle lasted for three days. . . . At last Presbyter John, for so they customarily call him, put the Persians to flight. . . . He is said to be a direct descendant of the Magi, who are mentioned in the Gospel, and to rule over the same peoples they governed, enjoying such glory and prosperity that he uses no sceptre but one of emerald. Inspired by the example of his forefathers, who came to adore Christ in his cradle, he had planned to go to Jerusalem.

While this is the first *written* reference to Presbyter or Prester John that historians have managed to find, it is safe to presume that Bishop Hugh wasn't the inventor of this legendary figure. The belief that a Christian king and kingdom existed somewhere beyond Persia and Armenia, somewhere beyond the domains of the infidel Mohammedans, somewhere in the unknown realm of the extreme Orient, was in fairly wide circulation from at least the time of the First Crusade. Bishop Hugh, in raising the hope that this rich and powerful Christian monarch could prove a valuable ally in a second crusade, may have been quite deliberately seeking to exploit the belief for his own purposes, but he wasn't trying to gull the Pope with it. He himself surely believed the story he told at Viterbo, for there was, as is usually the case in matters like this, a basis in fact for it.

Because of the stupendous success of Mohammed and the incredible speed with which his faith spread out of Arabia, we think of Christianity as cut off from Africa and Asia from the eighth century onward, and therefore the idea that a Christian kingdom might have existed somewhere out in those remote parts in the Middle Ages seems utterly fanciful. What we tend to overlook is that in Christianity's first centuries, before the rise of Islam, Christian missionaries had wandered far and wide from the Holy Land. Indeed, at least apocryphally, Thomas the Apostle is believed to have gone to the land of the Magi,

there to baptize the kings of the Indies, Balthazar, Melchior, and Gaspar, and, similarly, Matthew is said to have traveled to Abyssinia to convert that kingdom to Christianity. Whatever the historical worth of such tales, it is certainly true that by the fifth century Christian missionaries, albeit heretical ones, had reached those lands, and beyond.

For example, the Council of Ephesus, in 431, in deposing Nestorius, the Patriarch of Constantinople, for teaching that Christ had a dual nature, equally human and divine, drove him and his followers, the Nestorians, into exile in Persia. From there they moved ever eastward, on through India, making converts and building churches along the way, and by the eighth century had reached and settled in Far Cathay. The Council of Chalcedon, in 451, pronouncing on yet another heresy, that of Monophysitism, which maintained a single nature of Christ, partly divine and partly human, as taught by the monk Eutyches, set loose another group of wandering heretical preachers, one of whom, St. Frumentius, is credited with establishing the Coptic Church (as the Monophysite sect is called today) in Abyssinia.

With the rise of Islam, these sects were cut off from European Christendom, but reports of their existence and activities, although in highly fragmentary and distorted forms, did manage to filter through to the Mediterranean world. The knights of the First Crusade, for example, surely saw Monophysite pilgrims from Abyssinia in Jerusalem, and we know, from contemporary documents, that someone who represented himself as the Patriarch of the Indies, a Nestorian, appeared in Rome in 1122 and lectured Pope Calixtus II on the miracles performed by the uncorrupted body of St. Thomas, which he claimed rested in a shrine of his church. Whatever else was made of this in Europe, there was certainly a realization that Christianity, in one form or another, existed in that unknown world beyond Islam. It is not hard to see how out of this realization the idea of a mighty Christian king of the extreme Orient might have arisen, especially at a time when the wish for such an ally against the infidel was most pressing.

It was against this background of belief that Bishop Hugh could speak of Prester John at the Pontifical Court in Viterbo and be listened to with complete credulity. But it was because of a specific event at the time that he could go beyond merely reiterating the existence of

Prester John and claim that the priest-king, having defeated a Mohammedan army, was now on the move to aid Jerusalem—and be listened to with equal credulity.

Just a few years before the fall of Edessa, in 1141 to be specific, a great battle had been fought at Samarkand between Sanjar, the Seljuk Turk ruler of Persia (of which Samarkand then was a vassal), and a certain Yeh-lu Ta-Shih, the prince of a Manchurian tribe called Khitai (which had once ruled China and from whose name Cathay derives), with the latter emerging victorious. Now this Yeh-lu Ta-Shih was anything but a Christian (he was, most probably, a Mongol Buddhist), but the fact that he had defeated the Persian army of the feared and hated Seljuk Turks qualified him as an enemy of Islam, and by the time the news of his victory had traveled out of the steppes of Central Asia from Samarkand and reached the beleaguered Crusader states in the Holy Land, this Manchurian enemy of Islam had been converted into the Christian king of Bishop Hugh's tale.

So, when the Second Crusade was launched, it was with the expectation that an army of a mysterious Christian ally from the Orient was then also on the march against the Saracens. But that army never materialized, Prester John did not come to the aid of the Crusaders, and the ill-conceived adventure ended in unmitigated disaster. The knights of Conrad III and Louis VII were defeated at the siege of Damascus and the advance of Islam continued unabated. Zengi was followed by Noureddin, and he in turn was succeeded by Saladin, whose fierce cavalry overran the Crusader states one by one, ultimately capturing Jerusalem and the Holy Sepulchre.

And then, at this moment of darkest despair and defeat, Europe once again heard of the fabulous priest-king of the Orient. This time, though, word came in a far more remarkable manner: a letter from Prester John himself arrived. This astonishing document was addressed to Manuel Comnenus, Emperor of Byzantium, but we know from contemporary chronicles that copies of it also reached the Pope, the Holy Roman Emperor Frederick Barbarossa, and other kings and princes of Europe around 1165.

John the Presbyter [it began], by the grace of God and the strength of our Lord Jesus Christ, king of kings, lord of lords, to his friend Manuel, Governor of the Byzantines, greetings, wishing him health and the continued enjoyment of the divine blessing. Our Majesty has been informed that you hold our Excellency in esteem, and that knowledge of our great-

ness has reached you. . . . If indeed you wish to know wherein consists our great power, then believe without doubting that I, Prester John, who reign supreme, exceed in riches, virtue and power all creatures who dwell under heaven. Seventy-two kings pay tribute to me. I am a devout Christian and everywhere protect the Christians of our empire, nourishing them with alms. We have made a vow to visit the sepulchre of our Lord with a great army, as befits the glory of our Majesty, to wage war against and chastise the enemies of the cross of Christ, and to exalt his sacred name.

Our magnificence dominates the Three Indias, and extends to Farther India, where the body of St. Thomas the Apostle rests. It reaches through the desert toward the place of the rising of the sun, and continues through the valley of deserted Babylon close by the Tower of Babel.

The letter then goes on to describe the wonders of this realm. We are told that "every kind of beast that is under heaven" can be found there, that milk and honey abound, that "no poison can do harm and no noisy frog croaks" in this kingdom. A river called the Physon, emerging from Paradise, winds through one province and is full of emeralds, sapphires, topazes, onyxes, beryls, and other precious stones.

Images of Africa: strange men (from an edition of Pliny's *Natural History,* Frankfurt, 1582)

There is a kind of worm there

which in our tongue are called salamanders. These worms can only live in
fire, and make a skin around them as the silkworm does. This skin is carefully spun by the ladies of our palace, and from it we have cloth for our
common use. When we wish to wash the garments made of this cloth, we
put them into fire, and they come forth fresh and clean.

The palace "in which our sublimity dwells" has a roof of ebony,
gables of gold, gates of sardonyx inlaid with the horn of a serpent,
windows of crystals, columns of ivory, a courtyard paved in onyx.

Our bed is of sapphire, because of its virtue of chastity. We possess the
most beautiful women, but they approach us only four times in the year
and then solely for the procreation of sons, and when they have been sancti-
fied by us, as Bathsheba was by David, each one returns to her place.

We feed daily at our table 30,000 men, besides casual guests. . . . .
This table is made of precious emerald, with four columns of amethyst
supporting it; the virtue of this stone is that no one sitting at the table can
fall into drunkedness. . . . During each month we are served at our table
by seven kings, each in his turn, by sixty-two dukes, and by three hundred
and sixty-five counts. . . . In our hall there dine daily, on our right hand,
twelve archbishops and on our left, twenty bishops and also the Patriarch
of St. Thomas, the Protopapas of Samarkand and the Archprotopapas of
Susa, in which city the throne of our glory and our imperial palace are
situated.

As for Prester John's military power, the letter informs us,

When we ride forth to war, our troops are preceded by thirteen huge and
lofty crosses made of gold and ornamented with precious stones, instead
of banners, and each of these is followed by ten thousand mounted soldiers
and one hundred thousand infantrymen, not counting those who have
charge of the baggage and provisions.

And finally, anticipating a question that must have been in the minds
of its readers, the letter says,

If you ask how it is that the Creator of all things, having made us the most
supreme and most glorious over all mortals, does not give us a higher title
than presbyter, priest, let not your wisdom be surprised on this account,
for here is the reason. At our court we have many ministers who are of
higher dignity than ourselves in the Church, and of greater standing in
divine office. For our household steward is a patriarch and a king, our
butler is an archbishop and a king, our chamberlain is a bishop and a king,

our marshal is a king and an archbishop, our chief cook is a king and an abbot. And therefor it does not seem proper to our Majesty to assume those names, or to be distinguished by those titles with which our palace overflows. Therefore to show our great humility, we choose to be called by a less name and to assume an inferior rank. If you can count the stars in the sky and the sands of the sea, you will be able to judge thereby the vastness of our realm and our power.

The letter was, of course, a forgery, albeit a wonderfully imaginative one. We don't know who the forger was or how the letter was delivered, but, no matter how preposterous it may seem to us 800 years later, it was taken for genuine, and the impact it had on medieval Europe was electrifying.

Almost surely the main purpose of the letter's author, as was Bishop Hugh's two decades before, was to bolster Europe's morale in a dark time and incite it to yet another crusade against the Saracens. (For this reason scholars tend to guess that the perpetrator of the forgery was Frederick Barbarossa, a keen champion of a Third Crusade.) In this it succeeded, providing much of the inspiration that sent the ill-fated Barbarossa, Richard the Lion-Hearted, and Philip Augustus of France to cross swords with Saladin at the gates of Jerusalem. But, inadvertently, at least for its author's original intent, the letter accomplished much more.

In one bold stroke, the existence of a Christian king and kingdom somewhere on the other side of the world seemed confirmed. Out of the cloudy swirl of rumor and fantasy and travelers' tales, which had circulated for almost a century, the legend of Prester John crystallized and took such hypnotic hold on the medieval imagination that it was to persist unshakably for nearly 500 years and set off a quest—as romantic and quixotic and rich in consequence as the search for the Golden Fleece or the Holy Grail or the Fountain of Youth—that was to be the great energizing force behind Europe's first great age of exploration and discovery. To find that shining and ever-elusive Kingdom of Prester John, with its fabulous wealth and magical powers, proved a sufficiently seductive goal to lure adventurous men of the Middle Ages out of the severely circumscribed limits of the known world into the dangerous enterprise of penetrating always farther into the unknown.

One is almost tempted to suggest that the legend arose expressly to serve this purpose, that some communal unconscious, mythic intelli-

gence within medieval Europe gave birth to the idea of a fabulous priest-king because of its need and desire at the time for knowledge of the world, knowledge to dispel the terrors of the geographical darkness that pressed all around, knowledge to promote its expansion. And the most cunning part of the idea was that the goal sought wasn't there to be found, so that the quest for it would have to go on for a long time and range in every conceivable direction. In time, other reasons would develop to promote European exploration, most of them far more material and practical. But throughout the greater part of the Middle Ages it was the quest for the legendary kingdom of Prester John that served as the preeminent motivation for Europe's geographical discoveries, including the Congo.

As no other piece of writing in that illiterate age, Prester John's letter was remarkably widely circulated. Thousands of copies were made, and it was translated out of the original Latin into most of the vernacular languages of medieval Europe. As it passed through the hands of the copyists and translators it was elaborated and distorted to become an anthology of all the myths and marvels and fables of the Middle Ages and the single most popular piece of literature of the times. Ants as big as foxes with the skins of panthers, the wings of sea locusts, and the tusks of forest boars, which burrowed in the ground and heaped up piles of gold, were said to be found in Prester John's kingdom. So too were unicorns that killed lions, serpents with "two heads and horns like rams and eyes which shine brightly as lamps," amazons and centaurs and "horned men, who have but one eye in front and three or four in back." In that realm was the nation of Gog and Magog, whose people were cannibals and whom the priest-king employed as soldiers, granting them permission "to eat our enemies, so that of a thousand foes not one remains who is not devoured and consumed, but later we send them home because, if we let them stay longer with us, they would eat us all."

We learn that Prester John made annual pilgrimages into the desert to pay homage at the tomb of the prophet Daniel, "accompanied by ten thousand priests and the same number of knights, and two hundred towers built on elephants which also carry a turret to protect us against the seven-headed dragons." Standing outside the priest-king's palace, we discover, is a tower thirteen stories high and at its top an enchanted mirror in which is reflected the whole of the world. There too is the Fountain of Youth. "A person who bathes in this

fountain," we're told, "whether he be of a hundred or a thousand years, will regain the age of thirty-two. Know that we were born and blessed in the womb of our mother 562 years ago and since then we have bathed in the fountain six times." Which helps to explain how it was that men would quest for Prester John for hundreds of years and continue to believe he was still there to be found.

But found where? In 1177, more or less in response to Prester John's letter, Pope Alexander III sent his personal physician, a Master Philip, on an embassy to the priest-king. He vanished without a trace; we don't know what happened to him or, for that matter, in which direction he traveled. The letter provided precious few clues where to look for the fabulous kingdom. Its mention of Babylon (a city of Mesopotamia near present-day Baghdad in Iraq), of Susa (several hundred miles farther east in present-day Iran), and of the Physon (cited in Genesis as one of the four rivers flowing out of Eden, which medieval geographers believed to be the Indus) only served to confirm the notion that Prester John's realm lay somewhere beyond Persia.

As for the reference to "the Three Indias," over which his magnificence dominated, that was of little more help. For twelfth-century Europe, real and practical knowledge of the world didn't extend much farther than the North African littoral, Asia Minor, and a portion of the Near East, and everything beyond was generally referred to as the Indies or the Orient. The geographers of the time often tried to make themselves seem more knowledgeable than they actually were, and on some maps of the twelfth century we find fanciful demarcations of the vast unknown into three parts. On one such map, we see an *India Ultima* comprising what might be today's Afghanistan and West Pakistan, and *India Inferior* marking out a region that would include today's India, and an *India Superior* ranging from the Ganges to the Caucasus across what today would be China. On another, Nearer India seems to cover the northern half of the Indian subcontinent, Farther India its southern half, and Middle India is roughly where Ethiopia and East Africa are today. On still another, *India Prima* is indicated as "the land of the pygmies," *India Secunda* "faces the land of the Medes," and *India Ultima* "occupies the ends of the earth with the ocean on one side and the realm of darkness on the other." Thus, anyone setting off to find Prester John had to be prepared to travel beyond Persia to the uttermost edge of the world.

Ironically, it was one of the deadliest perils that Christendom was ever to face that turned the quest for the priest-king initially in the direction of Far Cathay and so opened that unknown part of the world to Europe. In 1221, with the Fifth Crusade shattered in the defeat at Cairo, Jacques of Vitry, the Bishop of Acre, last of the Crusader states to survive, wrote to Pope Honorius III that "A new and mighty protector of Christianity has arisen. He is King David of India, who has taken the field of battle against the unbelievers at the head of an army of unparalleled size." This King David, who according to Bishop Jacques was commonly called Prester John, was believed to be the son or grandson of the Prester John who had been awaited at the time of the Second Crusade (giving rise to the sensible idea that "Prester John" was the title of a dynasty of Christian priest-kings in the Indies rather than a marvelously long-lived individual). But, whatever his lineage, ancestry, or relationships, one thing was certain: this Prester John was a mortal foe of Islam. For once again, out of the mysterious lands of the Indies where Nestorian Christians were known to reside, a great king was leading an invincible army of ferocious horsemen and scoring victory after victory over the Saracens. This king, it was to turn out, was Genghis Khan, lord of the Mongols, scourge of Asia.

It wasn't until the Golden Horde, under Genghis's successors, having routed the Moslems of Asia and Asia Minor, thundered down on the Christian kingdoms of Eastern Europe and massacred their populations that Europe suspected that it might be mistaken about this protector of Christianity. By then, though, the belief that Prester John's kingdom was to be found in Cathay had taken firm root and, under the Pax Mongolica of Kublai Khan, monks and friars and traders began venturing along the caravan routes deep into that exotic realm in search of it. It was quickly apparent to these travelers that the Great Khan himself, in his pleasure dome at Karakorum, wasn't Prester John. But they also realized that Kublai Khan wasn't the only king in the Indies; there were hundreds of lesser khans throughout the immense Mongol empire, and the Europeans, wandering about it endlessly, were very willing to believe that any one of these might be the Christian priest-king. What strengthened them in this hope was their discovery that Nestorian Christians served in the highest ranks of the Mongol courts, as generals and counselors, and often as wives of the Tatar chieftains. So it seemed likely that one day they would come upon a chieftain who was a Christian himself.

The most famous of the European travelers in Cathay was Marco Polo, a Venetian merchant who was employed by Kublai Khan. He roamed widely over the Mongol empire for 17 years and his wonderful account of his adventures, *Il Milione,* was Europe's most comprehensive and accurate report on the Orient for 250 years. In *Il Milione,* Marco Polo writes of Prester John as "that king most famous in the world" and identifies him as the monarch of a kingdom of the Indies which opposed the Mongols and which was defeated in battle against the Golden Horde. And then he reports that in this battle the long-sought Christian priest-king was killed. Other travelers in Cathay at roughly the same time, notably the Franciscans Giovanni de Piano Carpini and William of Rubruck and the Dominican Ascelin of Lombardy, reported very much the same shocking news. This was late in the thirteenth century, more than 100 years after Prester John's letter had arrived, and it would seem reasonable to conclude that this would be the end of the story. But it wasn't.

It is a measure of the hypnotic hold that his legend had on medieval Europe that, despite repeated "eyewitness'" accounts to the contrary, it would simply not let Prester John be killed. The will to believe in the Christian priest-king's fabulous realm and the need to quest after it were too compelling. Europe steadfastly refused to believe that Prester John was dead. The most that it would concede was that his kingdom, after all, might not be in Far Cathay. When the Pax Mongolica shattered with the rise of the Ming dynasty and, as a result, Europeans were expelled from Cathay, the caravan routes to that land were closed, and the eastern half of Asia was cut off from Europe for the next 200 years—when, in short, it was no longer feasible to search for Prester John in that part of the world—the quest turned to another mysterious realm: Africa.

This shift in geography seems to have occurred gradually. We see on what was called Fra Paolino's map, dated around 1320, Prester John's realm still situated in what we would consider Asia. But on the map of Angelino Dulcert of 1339 the mythical kingdom is placed in what we would regard as East Africa, in the vicinity of Ethiopia (or Abyssinia, as it was then called). In the 1330s, a Dominican friar, Jordanus of Severac, who had traveled in China and India and described his adventures in *Mirabilia Descripta,* identified the Emperor of Ethiopia as Prester John. And this idea is repeated and promoted in such accounts as *The Book of Knowledge of all the Kingdoms, Lands*

and Lordships that are in the World by an anonymous Spanish Fran-
ciscan published in the 1350s, which placed Prester John's realm in a
region beyond the Mountains of the Moon, and in the *Travels* of the
Florentine aristocrat Giovanni de' Marignolli, published in 1355.

That Prester John might be the Emperor of Ethiopia didn't vio-
late the fundamental beliefs that he was a Christian and that he was a
monarch of the Indies. For, as we have seen, in medieval geography, in
which there was only the vaguest realization that an ocean separated
the Indian subcontinent from the east coast of Africa, Ethiopia was
considered part of the Indies. And, as we also have seen, Europe had
known, since the time of the First Crusade, when Christian knights
had seen Monophysite pilgrims in Jerusalem, that the Coptic Church
was the religion of Ethiopia and her Emperor. So the only problem
now was to discover where Ethiopia was and how to get there.

For fourteenth-century Europe, Africa was totally unknown. Indeed, no European had so much as set foot on it since the days of the
Roman Empire. The North African littoral was occupied by the infidel Moors, the desert beyond was firmly in the control of warrior
Mohammedan Berber tribes, and what lay beyond that even the Moslems themselves had only the vaguest notion. In the geography of the
times—mainly the work of Arab geographers of the preceding three
centuries—a mighty river, flowing east to west, thought to be the western branch of the Nile but in reality the Niger, was said to mark the
end of the Sahara. The lands south of it, wherein the kingdom of
Prester John was assumed to lie, were referred to variously as Ethiopia
or Guinea or the Sudan. These were extremely imprecise, always shifting and often interchangeable terms, having nothing to do with the
nations that bear those names today but rather demarking a vast unknown into roughly eastern, central, and western parts, and all meaning, in the corruption of one vernacular or another, the land of the
men with burnt faces, the land of the blacks. To be sure, Arab traders
and travelers had made some contact with sub-Saharan Africa by this
time, sailing out of the Red Sea down the East African coast, pushing
up the Nile into the Sudan and trading with the black tribes on the
southern edge of the desert. But whatever useful geographical information they had gathered was hidden away in the libraries of Moslem
sultans and merchants, and what little filtered out to Europe only
served to feed its fantasies about Prester John's realm.

This was the land that Pliny, writing in the first century, had

called "the middle of the earth, where the Sunne hath his way and keepeth his course, scorched and burnt with flames." And there, he said, lived the mantichora, "which has a triple row of teeth, meeting like the teeth of a comb, the face and ears of a human being, grey eyes, a blood-red colour, a lion's body, inflicting stings with its tail in the manner of a scorpion, with a voice like the sound of a pan-pipe blended with a trumpet, of a great speed, with a special appetite for human flesh." Solinus, in the third century, had entitled a chapter of his geography "Of Aethyop, of the filthy fashion of the people of that Countrey, of their monstrous shape, of the Dragons and other wylde beastes of wonderful nature there," and then proceeded with great gusto to spin out fabulous stories altogether in keeping with this eye-popping rubric.

The tales of Arab travelers in the succeeding centuries further embroidered the fantastic nature of the realm in Europe's imagination. For example, al-Idrisi, writing in the twelfth century, told of a kingdom in the land of the blacks whose king was "the most just of all men" and in whose palace there was "an entire lump of Gold, not cast, nor wrought by any instrument, but perfectly formed by the Divine Providence only, of thirty Pounds Weight, which has been bored through and fitted for a Seat to the Royal Throne." Moreover, this king had an "abundance of rich ornaments, and Horses, with most sumptuous trappings, which on Solemn Days were led before him. He had many Troops who march each with their Colours, under his Royal Banner; Elephants, Camels and various kinds of animals, which are found in the Negroes Countries, precede him." Ibn-Batuta two centuries later described a city he had visited as made entirely out of gold; it was called Timbuktoo. And in the Catalan Atlas, prepared for Charles the Wise in 1375 by the Majorcan Jew Abraham Cresques and derived from Arab sources, we read of a certain Mansa Musa, who was "the richest and most noble lord because of the abundance of gold found in his country."

So the lure of Prester John remained and, as his kingdom was now said to lie in Africa, Europe was drawn to the continent in its enduring quest.

3

A HERO IN BARBARY

"I shall not find a better opening for this chapter than the recital of the remarkable conquest of the great city of Ceuta, a celebrated victory which glorified the heavens and favoured the earth."

In this way a fifteenth-century Portuguese chronicler, Gomes Eannes de Azurara, begins his account of the capture of the Moroccan citadel on the Barbary Shore by his countrymen in 1415. And it can serve equally well for the opening of this chapter because that celebrated Portuguese victory over the infidel forces of the Moorish Kingdom of Fez marked Europe's first step into Africa since Roman times and the start of its discovery of the mysterious "Ethiopia" beyond the Sahara where Prester John was thought to reside.

That it was Portugal, one of the smallest nations of medieval Europe (its population was much less than one million at the time), which showed Europe the way into Africa is not one of history's larger puzzles. We only have to remember that for nearly 700 years before that Portugal had been fighting the Moors in the great *Reconquista* by which it, along with Castile, Aragon, Navarre, and the other Christian Kingdoms of the Spains, drove the North African Mohammedans step by step out of the Iberian peninsula, which they had overrun in the eighth century. In addition, during much of the same period, Portugal had also been fighting Castile in order to retain the independence it was winning back from Islam. In 1385, with the Moors safely reduced to a single caliphate on the peninsula—Granada, Portugal under João of Aviz scored a stunning victory over Castile at the battle of Aljubarrota. During a pause in the hostilities, while the astonished Castile tried to decide whether to accept the defeat as the end of its ambitions against Portugal, João married Philippa, daughter of John of Gaunt,

and the alliance with England, which the marriage signified, settled the matter for Castile. In 1411, a peace treaty was signed between the two kingdoms, the new and vigorous Aviz dynasty was established on the Portuguese throne, and a confident, triumphant Portuguese army stood in the field spoiling for new worlds to conquer.

Azurara, in his chronicle, explains how it then came to passs that Portugal launched that army across the Straits of Gibraltar into Africa. It wasn't João's idea. We read in Azurara that, to commemorate the peace with Castile and occupy his restless soldiers, the new king planned a magnificent tournament in which all the *fidalgos* of the kingdom would participate and at which his three eldest sons—the Infantes Dom Duarte, Dom Pedro, and Dom Henrique—were to win their knighthoods. But, Azurara tells us, this scheme didn't appeal to the youngest of these princes, Dom Henrique. He felt that a fanciful joust in an arena for a fair maiden's favor was no way for a noble prince to gain his knighthood. For him, the only proper way was in a true test of arms, on the field of battle, at war against a worthy enemy. As he was only seventeen at the time, the hot-blooded prince had missed out on the fighting with Castile and, as Portugal had also made peace with Granada, the last Moorish stronghold in Iberia, the times seemed to offer no opportunity for such valorous display.

But Henrique had a solution. According to Azurara, it was the young prince who suggested the idea that, in place of a tournament, his father should attack Ceuta. King João, we read, was taken aback; the audacious idea had never occurred to him and, at the outset at least, he resisted it adamantly. Henrique, however, proved persuasive. Again and again he returned to his father with new arguments for the enterprise: As Ceuta was the port from which the Moors had originally invaded Iberia, its conquest would cripple Islam's ambitions against the Spains. As Ceuta was also the port from which the corsairs of the Barbary pirates sailed, its conquest would end their raids on European shipping and put Portugal in command of the western Mediterranean. And as Ceuta was known to be one of the wealthiest Moorish cities, its conquest would enrich the royal treasury, whereas the tournament would only deplete it. And, finally, Henrique argued, there could be no more glorious enterprise by which to celebrate the ascendancy of the Aviz dynasty and to employ its conquering army than by carrying Christendom's war against the Moor, so long fought on the soil of the Spains, into the infidel's own land.

At last, Azurara tells us, King João relented. In great secrecy, an armada of 33 galleys, 27 triremes, 32 biremes and 120 pinnaces, carrying 50,000 men-at-arms and 30,000 mariners was assembled on the Tagus before Lisbon and, sailing under a Papal Bull, which bestowed all the privileges and indulgences of a Crusade, assaulted the walled fortress of Ceuta in August of 1415.

You may imagine the ardour of the combatants on either side [Azurara writes]. The din of battle was so great that there were many persons who said afterwards that it was heard at Gibraltar . . . the rage of the Moors was such that at times, even without arms, they threw themselves upon the Christians; and their despair and their fury were so great that they did not surrender themselves, even if they found themselves alone before a multitude of enemies; and many of them, already lying on the ground, and with their souls half severed from their bodies, still made movements with their arms as though they would deal mortal blows to those who had vanquished them. . . . In this conquest the Infante Dom Henrique was the captain of a very great and powerful fleet, and, as a valiant knight, he fought all that day on which the city was taken from the Moors . . . the first royal captain who touched land near the walls of Ceuta was he of whom I write, and his square banner was the first to pass the gates of the city, the Infante himself being not far from its shadows. And the blows he dealt the enemy that day were noteworthy among all others, since for five hours he fought without respite, and neither the heat, which was great, nor the fatigue of such an effort could persuade him to depart and take some rest.

As initiator and hero of this victory over Islam, which gave Europe its first permanent possession in Africa in more than 700 years (and which Portugal kept for another 560 years), Dom Henrique was duly rewarded. Not only did he gain his knighthood in the bloody manner he coveted but he was also appointed Duke of Viseu (Portugal's premier duchy), Master of the Order of Christ (the Portuguese branch of the rich and famous Knights Templar), and Governor of Ceuta. In view of the profound impact it was to have on the young prince, the last must be judged the most valuable prize that he won.

In his role as governor, Dom Henrique returned again and again to the Moroccan citadel. In the first years after the conquest, his main interest was in employing the port as a base from which armed Portuguese *barinels* could patrol the western Mediterranean and clear it of the corsairs of the Barbary pirates. Later, he became involved in de-

fending the city against attacks by the Berber tribesmen of the Moroccan Atlas. And, still later, he entertained schemes for using this Portuguese stronghold in North Africa for further, more ambitious campaigns against the Kingdom of Fez. But, Azurara tells us, during all these visits, the prince also spent much of his time questioning the city's inhabitants, wandering in its streets and marketplaces, perusing the libraries and archives of its sultans and merchants, and developing an ever keener curiosity about the vast unknown continent that stretched away from the citadel's walls, across the forbidding wasteland of the desert, toward the mysterious realm of Prester John.

Ceuta at this time was at the height of its splendor, a gorgeous city built upon seven rolling hills (from which, Septa, its name derives), and sprawling in indolent luxury down to the glittering white beaches of the blue Mediterranean. It contained the flower of Moorish architecture; handsome watch towers, massive arches and gates, delicate minarets and gold-leafed domes of its mosques and palaces adorned the winding walled streets. Its bazaars overflowed with jewels and gold, silver and jade, ivory and amber, silks and spices, carpets and porcelain, incense and pearls, and its port bustled with the feluccas of Arabia and the galleys of Venice and Genoa. It was Islam's richest trading emporium on the western Mediterranean, terminus of the great Arab caravans.

Europe had long known, and always envied, the caravan routes from the Orient that the Moslems controlled—those that wound out of Cathay across the Central Asian steppes to the Black Sea, those that came from India to the Persian Gulf and on from there either through the Tigris and Euphrates valleys to Baghdad and Damascus or up the Red Sea to Cairo and Alexandria—all bringing their fabulous riches to the Moslem ports of Asia Minor and North Africa, such as Ceuta. But what Europe had not known, or at best had only heard vague rumors of, was that there was yet another set of caravan routes under Islam's control—those that crossed the burning wastes of the Sahara from the Negro lands of Ethiopia and Guinea and the Sudan, beyond the so-called Western Nile, which brought riches to the Moorish ports every bit as fabulous as those from the Orient. And Dom Henrique also discovered this in Ceuta.

Wandering in the caravanseries of the city, pushing through the exciting crush of camel trains and bearded Arab merchants on donkeys and white-robed tawny Moors called Azenegues from the

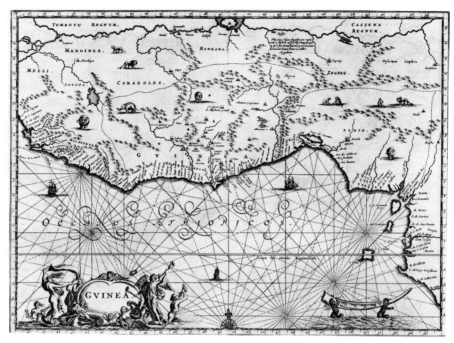

Ancient map of Guinea

farthest Sahara, his eyes darting from one wonder to another amid the tumble of stalls in the bazaars, the Portuguese prince could see for himself the precious goods that the trans-Saharan caravans brought. Bags of gold dust spilled open so as to glitter seductively under the desert sun; pyramids of elephant tusks and rhinoceros horns were stacked as tall as a man; there were ostrich feathers arranged in flowery bouquets, oryx skins stretched over warriors' shields; malaguetta peppers and civet furs; and huddles of mournful blacks waiting to be sold into slavery.

And, in his ceaseless questioning of Arab merchants and camel drivers and captive blacks and Berber traders, he heard of the kingdoms of Mali and Ghana and Songhai; the royal cities of Timbuktoo and Gao and Cantor, from whence those precious goods had come; the line of oases across the waterless desert by which trade to those distant places was made possible; and the way that trade was conducted once the caravans got there. He heard, for example, of the Silent Trade, which Herodotus was the first to mention, claiming that the Carthaginians had participated in it, and which Alvise da Cadamosto, a young Venetian merchant adventurer who was later to enlist in Dom Henrique's service, gives an account of in his fifteenth-century chronicle.

Deep in the Sahara, the prince was told, many weeks from Ceuta, there are rock-salt mines at an oasis called Taghaza. The Berber Moors of that region mine the salt, load it on camels, and take it for forty days southward, from oasis to oasis, across the desert to Timbuktoo, on the shores of the Western Nile, where they sell it to the Negro king for gold. But it is known that this king of Timbuktoo does not himself possess the gold which he exchanges for the salt. For he, in his turn, takes the salt and has it packed into blocks to be carried on men's heads, and they march with it still farther to the south, to the land of the Wangara. The Wangara, who are people said to have the heads and tails of dogs, are never seen. For the salt is laid down in their land, and the men who have brought it go far out of sight and light a fire. When the Wangara see the smoke of the fire, and when they are sure that the men from Timbuktoo are sufficiently distant, they come up to the salt and place by each block as much gold as they judge to be its equivalent. Then they go away out of sight too. Now the men from Timbuktoo return and look at the gold, and if they think it represents a fair price for their salt, they take the gold and go away for good. But if, on the other hand, the gold seems too little, they leave both the gold and the salt and go away to wait. Now the Wangara, coming up again, take away the salt where the gold for it has been accepted; but where it hasn't they add more gold. This process continues until both sides finally are satisfied that the amount of gold given is equal to the amount of salt taken away. "There is perfect honesty on both sides," Herodotus wrote of this Silent Trade. "The gold is never touched until it equals in value the salt that has been offered for it and the salt is never touched until the gold has been taken away."

Not everything Dom Henrique learned in Ceuta was accurate or even credible. Much of it, he realized, was wildly embroidered, but all of it so obviously contained a hard core of truth that, Azurara tells us, it fixed him in his determination to reach those lands beyond the Sahara, to take up the quest for the Kingdom of Prester John.

Throughout his life he never entirely gave up the idea of getting there by direct onslaught against Islam. That crusading zeal, that warrior temperament, that hatred of the infidel, which had led him to instigate the conquest of Ceuta, never completely left him, and from time to time he involved himself in Portuguese campaigns against the Kingdom of Fez in the hope of thus taking control of the Moor's trans-Saharan caravan routes and so opening the way to the Christian priest-

Prince Henry the Navigator

king in black Africa. But he must have realized early on that this would prove a futile course. The capture of Ceuta hadn't shaken the Moor's hold on North Africa, and the later attacks on Tangier and Arzila ended in total disaster. So it is likely that soon after the conquest of Ceuta, when he was still a regular visitor to the Moroccan citadel, Dom Henrique dreamed up his plan to turn Islam's flank by sailing down the Atlantic coast of Africa, bypassing the Moslem-controlled Sahara, and then striking inland from there to the Kingdom of Prester John—the audacious enterprise to which he would devote his life and for which historians of a later age would give him the title Prince Henry the Navigator.

This noble prince was of middle stature [Azurara tells us], a man thickset with limbs large and powerful, and bushy hair; the skin was white but the travail and the battles of life altered its hue as time went on. His aspect, to those who beheld him for the first time, was severe; when anger carried him away his countenance became terrifying. He had force of mind and acute intelligence in a high degree. His desire to accomplish great deeds was beyond all comparison.

There is some controversy over exactly what great deeds Henry desired to accomplish. Very much after the fact, historians have credited him with setting out not only to reach the Ethiopia of Prester John by sailing down the West African coast but also to go on and circumnavigate the African continent and so open a sea route to the Indies, break into the rich trade with the Orient, and found an overseas empire for Portugal. To be sure, these ultimately were to be direct consequences of the enterprise he launched. But Azurara, despite his desire to extol the virtues and accomplishments of his prince, doesn't mention any of them. He lists only these: (1) to find "the Christian king or seigneur, outside this kingdom, who, for the love of our Lord Jesus Christ, was willing to aid him" in the wars against the Moors; (2) to "increase the holy faith in Our Lord Jesus Christ, and to lead to His faith all souls desirous of being saved"; (3) to discover "the power of the Moors of this land of Africa . . . because every wise man is moved by the desire to know the strength of his enemy"; (4) to learn "if in these territories there should be . . . any harbours where men could enter without peril so that they could bring back to the realm many merchandises . . . and in like manner carry to these regions merchandise of the realm"; and (5) "to know what lands there were beyond the Canary Isles and a cape which was called Bojador."

For medieval Europe, these were stupendously daring goals. Indeed, the very idea of sailing into the Atlantic beyond Cape Bojador seemed utterly mad. For, if the heart of Africa was then a fantastic, unexplored mystery, it at least was believed to contain, for the brave adventurer, wonders as well as terrors. But the Atlantic Ocean, which was every bit as unknown as Africa at the time, contained in the medieval imagination nothing but terrors.

It is altogether likely that this wasn't always so. In the histories of Herodotus, for example, we find recounted the story of an expedition of Phoenician sailors, dispatched by Pharaoh Necho II of Egypt, which was said to have circumnavigated Africa around 600 B.C., sailing southward down the Red Sea and returning through the Pillars of Hercules three years later, having apparently passed through the Atlantic without incident. Herodotus also tells us of a certain Persian nobleman, Sataspes, who in order to escape execution for a crime against Xerxes, agreed to sail once around the continent, and though he didn't make it, the fact that he was willing to try suggests that the

Atlantic was not considered an impassable sea at the time. Similarly, Pliny records the exploits of Hanno, an admiral of Carthage, who in 450 B.C. sailed down the Atlantic coast of Africa to what appears to have been the Senegal, where "savages, bodies all over hairie" attacked his ships with stones. And in Strabo we can read of Eudoxus of Cyzicus, a Greek navigator who around 130 B.C. discovered the prow of a fishing boat from Cádiz on the East African coast and from this concluded that a vessel could sail from Spain clear around the continent without encountering any particular danger in the Atlantic.

But, by Prince Henry's time, the lore of the ancients was either lost or disbelieved. Even the notion that Africa was surrounded by oceans and thus could be circumnavigated at all, on which so much of this ancient lore was based, was wildly in doubt. Claudius Ptolemy's geography had been an overpowering and paralyzing influence on geographers since the second century, and in his elegantly symmetrical picture of the world, which was promoted by the Church because it placed Jerusalem at the center of the earth, Africa was not a continental island but a great land mass that extended southward to the ends of the earth, merging with what today we know as Antarctica.

Since the days of Necho's Phoenicians or of Hanno, Sataspes, or Eudoxus, if indeed even then, there had been no ocean-going expeditions ambitious enough to prove Ptolemy wrong. It is true that the Arabs had been sailing from the Red Sea around Cape Guardafui into the Indian Ocean and part way down the East African coast since at least the seventh century. But Europe didn't know about those voyages. And, besides, the Arabs themselves never ventured into the monsoon seas south of Madagascar, so even they didn't have any first-hand evidence that the Indian and Atlantic oceans flowed together at the southern tip of the continent.

On the other coast of Africa, geographical knowledge was even dimmer. The great European sailors of the time were those of the Italian city-states—Genoa, Venice, Pisa, Amalfi—who had gained their seamanship in the "carrying trade," that is, shipping the riches of the Orient from the Moslem ports of the Black Sea and the Barbary Shore across the Mediterranean to Europe. Their constant exposure to this wealth tempted many of them to try to short-circuit the Arab's overland caravan routes and get to the Orient via the Atlantic. We know, for example, of a certain Lancelot Malocello who is credited with sailing as far as the Canary Islands in 1270 (and, in a sense, rediscover-

ing them, for they are believed to be the Fortunate Isles of Greek mythology), but he lost his nerve in the face of the Atlantic and turned back. In 1281 (or possibly 1291), the Genoese galleys of Tedisio Doria and the brothers Vivaldi are said to have set off "to go by sea to the ports of India to trade there" and, apparently following Malocello's route, were never heard of again. Others may have tried in subsequent years—a Portuguese galley is supposed to have visited the Canaries in 1341, a Catalan ship from Majorca is said to have been lost in 1346 after passing Cape Bojador, a French vessel is said to have reached the cape in 1402—but there is no record of anyone getting any further. As Azurara tells us, "up to that time no one knew, whether by writing or the memory of man, what there might be beyond this cape."

What was commonly believed to be beyond this cape was the Mar Tenebroso, the Ocean of Darkness. In the medieval imagination, this was a region of uttermost dread. We see it pictured on the maps of the time as a place of monsters and monstrous occurrences, where the heavens fling down liquid sheets of flame and the waters boil, where ferocious tempests and mountainous waves and terrible whirlpools rage, where serpent rocks and ogre islands lie in wait for the mariner, where the giant hand of Satan reaches up from the fathomless depths to seize him, where he will turn black in face and body as a mark of God's vengeance for the insolence of his prying into this forbidden mystery. And even if he should be able to survive all these ghastly perils and sail on through, he would then arrive in the Sea of Obscurity and be lost forever in the vapors and slime at the edge of the world.

That, despite the terror with which the Atlantic was viewed, Prince Henry nevertheless proposed to sail beyond Cape Bojador is certainly a measure of the audaciousness of his enterprise. But that he should propose to do this in light of the primitive state of the art of seamanship at the time gives a far better sense of the magnificent daring of his conception.

For example, one only has to remember what sorts of vessels were available. There were the galleys, three-masted merchantmen propelled by banks of oars, used by the Venetians and other Italians in the carrying trade, which were far too frail to venture very far into the Mar Tenebroso and which besides, because they required such a large crew of oarsmen, couldn't carry enough provisions for a prolonged

ocean voyage. Then there were the *naos* and *barchas* of the Portuguese
fleet—the former, broad-beamed cargo vessels used in the trade with
England; the latter, fishing boats that worked the Atlantic shoals off
the Iberian coast. Both were single masted with square-rigged sails and
sturdy enough to ride out the rough weather and seas of the Atlantic.
Their trouble was their awkwardness except in a following wind; they
couldn't be tacked and were ill equipped to beat off a lee shore and
had to run for shelter in a storm or contrary wind. The Portuguese
had also developed the *barinel,* which combined the single square-
rigged sail of the *barcha* and the oarsmen of the galley, and as far as
long ocean voyages were concerned compounded the drawbacks of
both. Also available, though mainly in the eastern Mediterranean, was
the Arab felucca. It had a triangular, lateen-rigged sail and a raked
mast, copied from the Indian Ocean dhows, and could sail much closer
to the wind than any square-rigged vessel; but it too was far too lightly
built to take on the rigors of the Atlantic.

Moreover, and by whichever vessel, sailing in those days meant
coasting. Captains rarely, if ever—and then only for the shortest peri-
ods possible and in the most familiar waters—sailed out of sight of
land. Navigational knowledge and equipment just weren't up to it.
For example, there was no way of determining longitude. And, while
the astrolabe was available, which calculates latitude from the height
of the Polar Star above the horizon, the trouble here was that the
length of a degree of latitude was not known with any accuracy. The
compass was in use, having reached Europe from China via the Arabs,
but its value was limited to sea charts that indicated compass bearings
between visible landmarks and was of no value on the high seas, where
pilots had to rely on dead reckoning.

For vessels and navigational equipment of this sort, the Atlantic
coast of Africa posed formidable problems of seamanship. To be sure,
the currents, flowing southward from Portugal, and the prevailing
winds, northeast trades, favored the outbound leg of the voyage well
enough. The trouble was the nature of the shoreline along which the
craft were obliged to coast. This was, of course, the Sahara coast, a
burning waste which, as far as anyone knew at the time, might stretch
on forever, offering very few good anchorages and no food or water,
and made treacherous by shoals and unpredictable tides and winds
that no one had ever charted.

But these problems were minor compared with those that faced

the mariner who hoped to return from the journey. For now he would have to sail *into* the current and *against* the winds. The *naos* and *barchas,* which were sturdy enough in construction to venture out on the voyage in the first place, simply could not manage to beat against the winds and currents with their square-rigged sails and return home along the route they came. There was, in fact, only one way they could hope to get back to Portugal once they were beyond Cape Bojador and that was by sailing away from the African coast and describing a bold arc out into the mid-Atlantic, where they could pick up the westerlies and the eastward-running current. To do this would take incredible nerve. For it meant sailing out of sight of land for days, even weeks, at a time. And it meant sailing on an unknown sea without any reliable navigational aids.

So, even had the seamen not feared the legendary terrors of the Mar Tenebroso, they had reason enough to fear the real terrors the ocean posed. And yet, when Prince Henry called on them to go, they sailed out onto the Ocean of Darkness after all.

4

ON THE OCEAN OF DARKNESS

Sagres, "where endeth the land and beginneth the sea," as the medieval Portuguese epic poet Camões wrote, is a tiny peninsula, barely 500 yards wide and 1000 yards long, that juts southward into the Atlantic from Cape St. Vincent in Portugal's Algarve and points like a finger from Europe's extreme southwest corner down the west coast of Africa. A barren outcropping of jagged rock, spotted with stunted junipers, it is lashed by the Atlantic's thundering surf and, when the simoon sweeps the Sahara, by the sands of Africa as well. It was originally called the Sacred Promontory because legend has it that the guardians of the relics of St. Vincent, fleeing the Moslem conquest of the saint's place of martyrdom in Zaragoza, landed on this peninsula and buried the holy remains there. For centuries afterward the deep coves in the cliffs of its shoreline provided safe anchorage for ships coasting from the Mediterranean to the English channel ports.

The desolation and holiness of the place suited Prince Henry's temperament, and its geography was perfect for his Atlantic enterprise. In the early 1420s he set about establishing there his famous School of Navigation, which in the course of the next four decades was to become the Cape Canaveral of West African exploration. In time, the best of the world's mathematicians and astronomers, cartographers and cosmographers, pilots and ships' captains, makers of nautical instruments and shipwrights would be gathered at Sagres, and the finest available maps, atlases, sea charts, scientific treatises and travel literature would be collected in its libraries. Princes would come there eager to invest in the enterprise, and it would eventually win the official patronage of the crown and the Pope's blessing. A city would

grow up on the once-deserted promontory; a fortress, observatory, churches, and dockyards would be built. New maps would be drawn, unknown coastlines charted, currents and winds plotted, navigational instruments invented, and new ships designed that would overcome the problems posed by the Atlantic and step by step strip away its mysteries.

But, before any of this would happen, the first expeditions had to be launched into the terror of the Ocean of Darkness. As he enjoyed only token royal support for his enterprise at the outset, Prince Henry was required to finance the first voyages out of his own personal treasury. Moreover, he had to use the open, clumsy *naos, barchas,* and *barinels* as the vessels for those voyages, and as captains had to rely on the young, adventurous *fidalgos* of his own household, the knights and squires who had fought with him in North Africa and on whose courage he could count but who had little seafaring experience.

In the course of the next decade or so, Henry dispatched these *fidalgos* on expedition after expedition down the West African coast, each with instructions to sail beyond Cape Bojador. But none of them ever did. Most, on reaching the North African shore, spent their time attacking the pirate corsairs and raiding Barbary for booty. And, on their return to Sagres, Azurara, who lived there at the time, tells us, they explained their failure in this way:

How shall we pass beyond the limits established by our elders? What profit can the Infante win from the loss of our souls and our bodies? For plainly we should be like men taking their own lives. . . . This is clear; beyond this cape there is no one, there is no population; the land is no less sandy than the deserts of Libya, where is no water at all, neither trees nor green herbs; and the sea is so shallow that at a league from the shore its depth is hardly a fathom. The tides are so strong that the ships which pass the cape will never be able to return.

Azurara reports that the Prince dealt with these captains with great patience,

never showing them any resentment, listening graciously to the tale of their adventures, and rewarding them as those who were serving him well. And immediately he sent them back again to make the same voyage, them or others of his household, upon his armed ships, insisting more and more strongly upon the mission to be accomplished, and promising each time greater rewards.

In 1433, when his own squire Gil Eanes, "overcome by dread," also returned to Sagres without doubling the cape, Henry addressed him in this manner:

My son, you know that I have brought you up since you were a small boy and that I am confident you will serve me well. For this reason I have chosen you to be captain of this ship to go to Cape Bojador and discover what lies beyond. You can not meet there a peril so great that the hope of reward shall not be even greater.

This speech obviously made the necessary impression on the young squire. Azurara tells us that "having heard these words Gil Eanes promised himself resolutely that he would never again appear before his lord without having accomplished the mission with which he had been charged." And in 1434, "disdaining all peril," he became the first European to pass beyond the dreaded Cape Bojador. As we know that he made it back again, we can assume that he was also the first of Henry's captains daring enough to sail that bold arc out into the Atlantic, well out of sight of land, and, on a reach to the Azores, find the favoring currents and westerlies that sent his *barcha* home again.

With the jinx of the cape broken, with the terror of the unknown ocean somewhat diminished, and with the trick of getting home again learned, Henry and his young captains' hopes momentarily soared. Gil Eanes went out again and this time pressed 100 miles beyond Cape Bojador. Henry's cupbearer, Affonso Gonçalves Baldaya, took a *barinel* 50 miles further, and in the next couple of years four or five other voyages explored the West African coast still another some 50 miles southward. But progress was painfully slow, and, what was worse, the shore continued to be an unyielding, unpopulated, waterless desert. It seemed that there would never be any end to it, that the Sahara of Islam could never be bypassed. What's more, all that could be found of even the slightest value was herds of sea lions nesting on the arid, rocky outcroppings in the sea. These, from time to time, the captains hunted for their skins and oil, so that there might be some reward from the undertaking. But how paltry a reward this appeared when compared with the shining goal of reaching the fabulous kingdom of Prester John.

Henry grew impatient; the cost of the expeditions put an intolerable strain on his personal finances, which the occasional hauls of seal skin and seal oil did little to relieve. So, at this point, we find him

turning away from his West African enterprise and taking up that old scheme of penetrating to the legendary Ethiopia beyond the Sahara by direct onslaught against the Moors.

By this time, King João had died and Henry's eldest brother, Duarte, was on the throne, a rather weak figure, who was easily persuaded to renew the war against the Kingdom of Fez. Henry was given command of the Portuguese army and in 1438, with his youngest brother, Affonso (who forever after was to be known as the Unfortunate), as his second-in-command, he led an assault on Tangier. It was an unmitigated disaster. The Portuguese army was routed and Affonso was taken prisoner, to end his days in Moorish captivity. Blame for both catastrophes fell heavily on Henry's shoulders and he fled back to Sagres.

The Tangier debacle and the fate of his youngest brother had an even more devastating impact on Duarte; he died of a broken heart within a year of the Moroccan defeat. As his son, the heir apparent, was only six at the time, the second brother of the Aviz dynasty, Pedro, was named regent. The appointment was fortunate for Henry. Pedro had been a great traveler in his youth and had always taken a great interest in his brother's enterprise. And now as regent he did everything to promote royal support for it.

In 1441, this at last began to seem worthwhile. For in that year one of Henry's young *fidalgos*, Antao Gonçalves, commanding a *barcha*, sailed 120 leagues beyond Cape Bojador and, at Río de Oro in present-day Spanish Sahara, made contact with the first people ever encountered on the desert West African shore. They were Sanhaja Tuaregs, Arabic-speaking Moslem Berbers of the extreme Sahara, whom the Portuguese had seen in Ceuta and whom they called Azenegues.

At the sight of the Portuguese, the Azenegues fled, but the young *fidalgo* was ecstatic. "Oh how fair a thing it would be if we . . . would meet with the good fortune to bring the first captives before the face of our Prince for it would give great satisfaction to our Lord for from them he would learn much of the people who live in these parts." With this end in mind, Gonçalves landed a war party on the coast. Pressing inland, the Portuguese came upon two encampments of some twenty Azenegues, and "when our men had come nigh to them, they attacked very lustily, shouting at the tops of their voices St. James for Portugal, the fright of which so abashed the enemy that it threw

them all into disorder," and in the ensuing battle ten prisoners were taken.

At this point the *caravel* enters the picture. Dissatisfied all along with the *naos, barchas,* and *barinels* that he was forced to use and blaming their inadequacies for the slow progress of the coastal exploration, Henry had put his Sagres shipwrights to work experimenting with new hull constructions and sail riggings. In the early 1440s they came up with a ship design which for the next two centuries, in one variation or another, would carry Portuguese explorers to the ends of the earth and back again. In fact, the caravel was probably the single most important contribution made at Sagres to the discovery of the world.

By modern standards, it was a cockleshell. In its first version, the vessel had a draft of from 50 to 100 tons (and never much more than 200 tons even 100 years later), measuring some 20 to 25 feet in the beam and from 60 to 100 feet stem to stern. It was a round-bottomed ship with a hybrid hull adapted from fishing boats, strengthened to withstand ocean storms and rough seas, stout-decked, with a high poop and a castle in the stern, and fitted out with first two, then three, and finally four masts (when they were called *caravelas de armada*). But the key innovation in its design was its lateen-rigged triangular sails borrowed from the Arab feluccas of the eastern Mediterranean and the Indian Ocean dhows. With these, the ship could sail close to the wind and was capable of advancing in a side wind as well as tacking, and thus wasn't compelled to await a fair breeze to make headway. By the standards of the time, the caravel was extremely fast, developing speeds up to ten knots with the wind on the quarter or aft. Moreover, they were easy to handle—they carried crews of fewer than thirty and there's an account where only three sailors and two cabin boys sailed one 1000 miles home in an emergency—and were very well adapted for nosing in and out of the inlets and among the countless shoals of the West African coast.

The first caravel we hear of was commanded by Nuno Tristão. Sometime around 1443, unfurling the caravel's lateen sails like the wings of a great bird, he took his fast and maneuverable ship past the Río de Oro, across the Tropic of Cancer, around Cape Blanco and then 25 leagues beyond to discover the islands of the Arguin archipelago (off what is today Mauritania). The Arguin islands were then inhabited by Azenegues, and when Tristão first saw them they were

A port with caravels in harbor

paddling dugout canoes with their feet so that "our men, looking at them from a distance and quite unused to the sight, thought they were birds skimming over the water." The Portuguese, still full of the mythology of this unexplored region, apparently were perfectly prepared to come upon such marvelous creatures, and it wasn't until Tristão sailed the caravel closer that they realized what they were looking at was a reasonably natural scene. What the Azenegues thought of the caravel, in their turn, we have some idea from a report by Cadamosto a few years later:

This much is certain, that when they first saw the ships of Dom Henrique sailing past, they thought them to be birds coming from afar and cleaving the air with white wings. When the crews furled sail and drew into shore, the natives changed their minds and thought they were fishes. When they made out the men on board of them, it was much debated whether these men could be mortal; all stood, stupidly gazing at the new wonder.

In the case of Tristão's ship, that stupefaction cost them dearly. Using the same reasoning that had motivated Gonçalves at Río de Oro, Tristão ordered an attack on the astonished Azenegues and with comparative ease captured 29 to take back to Sagres for Henry's edification.

Tristão's return with his captives so soon after Gonçalves' similar success, coupled with the availability of the excellently seaworthy caravel, sparked a surge of interest in Henry's enterprise. Until then, the prince's voyages had been looked on with indifference,

and the worst of it was [Azurara informs us] that besides what the vulgar said among themselves, people of more importance talked about it in a mocking manner, declaring that no profit would result from all this toil and expense. But when they saw the first Moorish captives brought home and the second cargo that followed these [both by Gonçalves from the Río de Oro], they became already somewhat doubtful about the opinion they had at first expressed; and altogether renounced it when they saw the third consignment that Nuno Tristão brought home, captured in so short a time, and with so little trouble.

In renouncing their adverse opinion, these people of importance, merchants and nobles, became quite eager to get in on Henry's enterprise.

The first of these was Lancarote de Freitas, an officer of the Royal Customs at the port in Lagos, just up the Algarve coast from Sagres. He organized a private trading company with several Lagos merchants, and in 1444, with Henry's permission, he hired Gil Eanes and sent six caravels to the Arguin islands. While the ships stood off, five boats with some thirty soldiers were lowered into the waters at sunset. They rowed all that night until they reached an island village. At dawn, they attacked and

saw the Moors with their women and children coming out of their huts as fast as they could, when they caught sight of their enemy; and our men, crying out St. James, St. George and Portugal, fell upon them, killing and taking all they could. There you might have seen mothers catch up with their children, husbands, their wives, each one trying to flee as best he could. Some plunged into the sea, others thought to hide themselves in the corners of their hovels, others hid their children underneath the shrubs that grew about there, where our men found them. And at last our Lord God, who gives to all a due reward, to our men gave that day a victory over their enemies, in recompence for all their toil in His service, for they took, what of men, women and children, one hundred sixty-five, not counting the slain.

The Portuguese attacked several other villages and, when they returned to Lagos, they had 235 captives with them.

The Europeans trading with the Africans

On the next day, August 8, 1441, very early in the morning, the captives were disembarked from the caravels and marched to a meadow on the outskirts of town. And there was held Europe's first slave market. Azurara was present.

What heart [he tells us], even the hardest, would not be moved by the sentiment of pity on seeing such a flock; for some held their heads bowed down, and their faces were bathed with tears; others were groaning grievously, lifting their eyes to heaven, fixing them upon the heights, and raising an outcry as though imploring the Father of Nature to succour them; others beat upon their faces with their hands and cast themselves at length upon the ground; others raised their lamentations in the manner of a chant, according to the custom of their country; and although the words uttered in their language could not be understood by us, it was plain that they were consonant with the degree of their grief.

Then, as though the more to increase their suffering, came those who were commanded to make the division; and they began to part them one from another in order to form companies, in such manner that each should be of equal value; and for this it was necessary to separate children from their parents, and women from their husbands, and brothers from

brothers. There was no law in respect of kinship or affectation; each had perforce to go whither fate drove him . . . consider how they cling one to another, in such wise that they can hardly be parted! Who, without much travail, could have made such a division? So soon as they had been led to their place the sons, seeing themselves removed from their parents, ran hastily towards them; the mothers clasped their children in their arms, and holding them, cast themselves upon the ground, covering them with their bodies, without heeding the blows which they were given!

The market was an enormous success. And, as Azurara tells us, Henry without delay "made Lancarote knight, loading him with benefits according to his merits and valour. And he likewise granted benefits to all the other captains, so that over and above the gain they had of their captures they had others which rewarded them right well for all their fatigues." Predictably, this further promoted interest in the enterprise, and in the next year alone, four privately sponsored expeditions, forming an armada of 27 ships, headed back to the Arguin hunting grounds and attacked villages all along the Mauritanian coast, killing and capturing Africans for the Lagos slave market.

In that same year, 1445, a *fidalgo* named Dinis Dias, in a lone caravel, sailed past Cape Blanco and the Arguin islands down the coast to the mouth of the Sénégal River and then beyond to reach and double Cape Verde, the westernmost point of Africa (where Dakar stands today). In accomplishing this feat, he attained the goal that Prince Henry had set for his enterprise more than a quarter of a century before. Here at last was sub-Sahara Africa. The desert and Islam had been bypassed, the Moslem flank turned at last. The people Dias encountered were no longer Moorish Azenegues but Waloffs, pagan Negroes. Here, some 450 leagues (1350 miles) south of the once-dreaded Cape Bojador, began the grasslands and forests of the Guinea coast. And from here, Henry could believe, if one traveled far enough into the continent's interior, perhaps along the Sénégal River, which was taken to be the "Western Nile" of the Arab geographers, one would at last come to the Kingdom of Prester John.

But slaving fever had seized the coasting captains; the profit and adventure of it had become a more powerful lure than the search for geographical knowledge, than even the quest for the fabled Christian priest-king's realm. And by 1448 more than 50 ships had gone to Guinea and returned with nearly 1000 slaves.

Slaving, however, became increasingly dangerous. Word of what the Portuguese came for traveled swiftly, and soon enough the blacks all along the coast were up in arms. Gonçalo de Sintra, sent by Henry to explore beyond Cape Verde but unable to resist making a bit of profit on the way (as very few of his fellow captains could), stopped off to slave at the Sénégal mouth, was ambushed by a party of blacks, and so earned the distinction of being the first European to be killed in sub-Saharan Africa. Nuno Tristão, who in a way started it all with his slave raid in the Arguin islands, did sail beyond Cape Verde, past the mouth of the Gambia and on to discover the Río Grande. And, though it is unclear whether he had any slaving in mind, when he sailed into the mouth of that river, in what can be seen as a case of poetic justice, he and his party were also ambushed and killed.

The blacks realized, of course, that the white men in their strange boats came to kidnap them but, as none ever returned to tell the tale, they didn't know why. So they invented their own explanation, an explanation that Cadamosto, the Venetian merchant adventurer who joined in on the enterprise when it became so profitable, discovered. He and a Genoese merchantman had sailed their caravels to the mouth of the Gambia River. Before proceeding upstream, they decided to send a scout ahead to get the lay of the land, but "the poor wretch," Cadamosta tells us, "had no sooner swum ashore than he was seized and cut to pieces by armed savages." Then suddenly a war party in native canoes attacked the caravels. The blacks shot their arrows; the caravels, Cadamosta tells us, replied with their cannon. As the natives fled, Cadamosta had one of his interpreters shout after them: "Why have you greeted us in this unfriendly way? For we are men of peace and seek only to trade with you." And they replied: "We have heard of your visits to the Senegal and we know that you Christians eat human flesh and buy black men only to make a meal of them. We do not want peace on any terms. We hope only to make an end of you and give all you possess to our chief."

While it is true that the Portuguese started the West African slave trade, it has to be said that they didn't practice it, at least at this stage, with the despicable and degrading brutality that was employed in later centuries. They treated their captives with a measure of decency and humanity, converting them to Christianity, teaching them trades, occasionally granting some their freedom, and not infrequently marrying them off to their white servants. Moreover, and perhaps

more importantly, they did not conduct the traffic on the horrendous scale it was to attain a hundred years later. During Prince Henry's lifetime, the total number of slaves landed in Portugal could still be counted in the thousands. This was, of course, before the discovery of the New World, before the colonization of the Americas and the West Indies with their slave-run plantations, so the demand for slaves was not great. And, after the first flush of slaving fever subsided, the merchant sailors began seeking for other profit.

To be sure, slaving never ceased. But gradually slaves became only one, and not always the most valuable of several commodities that the Portuguese acquired along the West African coast. And gradually they began acquiring those products in a manner quite different from the initial slave raids. For they learned that the Azenegues of Cape Blanco and the Arguin islands and the Waloffs and other tribesmen of the Guinea coast were prepared to enter into peaceful trading relations given half a chance. So soon enough an orderly, profitable commerce developed, the caravels bringing out cloth, beads, brass wire, manufactured items, tin, coral, and bloodstone, and taking back slaves, ivory, and gold.

As commerce flourished, coastal exploration waned. A few intrepid caravel captains pushed south to what today would be Conakry, but the consuming interest in discovery now was less what lay further down the coast and what lay further inland from it. The Portuguese were aware that the people they traded with on the coast traded in their turn with peoples of the interior and that it was from there that the gold and ivory and slaves came. The temptation was great to try to circumvent the coastal middlemen and make direct contact with the black kingdoms of the interior. And the prospect that one of these might turn out to be the Kingdom of Prester John was always a lure to draw the Portuguese on. Several attempts were made. None, however, succeeded. Inland from Cape Blanco, for example, was the desert, and the Moslems controlled the caravan routes and oases there. Inland from the Guinea coast, fever-ridden swamps and jungles and deadly, unknown tropical diseases turned the Portuguese back.

Prince Henry doesn't seem to have been terribly disappointed. At the time of his death in 1460, he appears to have been quite satisfied with what he had wrought. And he had good reasons: Cape Bojador had been doubled, the desert of Islam had been bypassed by sea, some 2000 miles of previously unknown coastline had been

charted, Portugal had broken into the Moslem trade with black Africa, and the Christian faith had been extended if only to the poor slaves brought back to Portugal. In fact, of the five goals Azurara cites for Henry's enterprise, the Prince had failed to reach only one: the Kingdom of Prester John.

5

THE PERFECT PRINCE

Affonso V, son of King Duarte and nephew of Prince Henry, took the sobriquet *O Africano*. It was ill deserved and, certainly from the point of view of the daring Portuguese voyages of exploration under way during his reign, grossly misleading. The Africa to which it referred was North Africa, where Affonso conducted campaigns against the Moors of little consequence and less long-lasting significance. As for the Africa which his uncle's captains discovered and which was to be the cornerstone of an incredible Portuguese empire, Affonso expressed hardly any interest at all.

As a king and a human being, Affonso was rather a failure. There was something peculiarly unstable in his temperament, an impetuous witlessness, a callow dilettantism; he exhibited the delusionary boldness of the weakling, easily influenced and even more easily disloyal. When he reached his majority—at the tender age of fourteen—and formally ascended the throne in 1446, he turned against his regent, Dom Pedro, who had governed wisely in his stead since the death of Duarte in 1438, and put himself under the malevolent tutelage of the Duke of Braganza. The duke was the bastard son of João of Aviz, the offspring of a youthful romantic fling, who was never treated as the equal of his younger but legitimate half-brothers, Duarte, Pedro, and Henry, and who harbored bitter resentments against them throughout his life. One visualizes him as a dark, brooding man, hardening in his bitterness as he grew older, suffering what he fancied as insults, forever intriguing against the crown (and, indeed, passing his bitterness down through the generations until it ripened into the successful vengeance that put the House of Braganza on the Portuguese throne in the seventeenth century). From the moment of Duarte's death, the duke

plotted to secure power over the new boy-king, first clashing with Pedro in an attempt to win the regency for himself and then, when Affonso was crowned in his own right, provoking a bloody quarrel between the monarch and his regent. What character flaw Braganza recognized in the young Affonso, what weakness, what ambition, what vice he played to, it is hard to say, but the sour fruit of his work was a civil war and the murder of Dom Pedro by Affonso's soldiers at the castle of Affarrobeira in 1449. From this inauspicious beginning Affonso went on to torment his reign with other infamous adventures.

For example, a Crusade. It seemed just the thing to the foolish, vainglorious king. The Ottoman Turks were on the rampage in the East. In 1453, the army of Mohammed II conquered Constantinople, opening the way across the Dardenelles for the latest infidel scourge to strike into Europe. And once again the cry for a Crusade was heard in Christendom. But this time no one answered the call. Except Affonso. Eager to make a name for himself, thrilled by the prospect of grandeur, and ignorant of the uselessness of the venture, the young king assembled an armada and assaulted Alcazar on the Moroccan shore in 1458. Though the Portuguese were victorious, the conquest did nothing to stem the Turk's advance up the Danube half a world away. Nevertheless, the victory went to Affonso's head and, thirsting for more glory, he launched additional campaigns against the Kingdom of Fez, culminating with a victory at Tangier in 1471 for which he dubbed himself The African.

It was a title he retained for the rest of his life and with which he went into the history books, but even he eventually recognized its meaninglessness. As had been the case at Ceuta, these North African conquests did nothing to loosen the Moor's hold on the Barbary Shore, and the cost of defending the cities against ceaseless Moorish counterattacks came close to bankrupting the Royal Treasury. By 1475, Affonso the African had given up, if not his sobriquet, his ambitions in Africa and looked for new fields of glory and adventure. He found it in that other traditional enemy of Portugal: Castile.

Affonso had married Juana la Beltraneja, daughter of King Henry IV of Castile. In some circles she was considered the heiress to the Castilian throne, but it was more widely believed that she was an illegitimate child, and when the Castilian king died the crown went to her aunt Isabella. As usual, however, Affonso was not to be discouraged by rhyme or reason. He claimed the Castilian throne for himself

and plunged Portugal into a war with Castile (and with Aragon as
well, since Isabella was by then married to Ferdinand of that kingdom) which was to rage for five bloody years and end in 1479 with
Affonso's total defeat and humiliation.

Not surprisingly then, with O Africano so thoroughly preoccupied
with everything but West Africa, exploration along the continent's
Atlantic coast came to a virtual standstill in the years after Prince
Henry's death. Sagres itself, without the Navigator to serve as its mag-
netizing force, deteriorated. No more than two or three voyages of
discovery sailed from its harbor after Henry died; the last in 1462.
That caravel was captained by Pero de Sintra, son of the same Gonçalo
de Sintra who had been killed on a slave raid at the Sénégal River
some seventeen years before. Perhaps with the idea of avenging his
father's memory, the young *fidalgo* sailed beyond Cape Verde, beyond
the Gambia, and discovered the coast of Sierra Leone (so named because he was said to have heard the roar of lions atop the mountains
there). It was the final contribution to West African exploration by
the famed School of Navigation of Sagres. In the following years, the
astronomers and mathematicians, pilots and cartographers, whom
Henry had gathered together, drifted away. The city Henry had built
was abandoned, the dockyards fell into disrepair, the fortress and observatory crumbled. This isn't to say, of course, that ships no longer
sailed to West Africa. They did, and in increasing numbers. But they
were the ships of the private trading companies, little interested in
running the risks of further explorations southward when they could
traffic so profitably in slaves, ivory, and gold along the coast already
discovered. And they sailed now from Lagos and Lisbon, leaving
Sagres to the dusts of history.

Since 1454, when Pope Nicholas V recognized Portugal's claim to
all new lands on or near the West African coast and forbade all Christians to traffic there without Portugal's permission, the West African
trade had been a crown monopoly. And while Henry was alive, he
guarded that monopoly, as Cadamosta tells us, "with no small care."
Any merchant who wanted to partake in the trade had to get a royal
commission and strike a deal with the prince.

After Henry's death, however, with King Affonso so little interested in the enterprise, the guarding of the crown's West African trade
monopoly became increasingly lax. Most Portuguese merchants still
went through the formality of applying for a royal commission but

now, as there was no authority to check on the merchandise they brought back, they quite brazenly cheated the crown out of its share. Worse, foreign merchants, mainly from the Italian city-republics and the Spains, didn't bother even to go through the formality of applying for a royal commission. They sailed from their own Mediterranean ports, traded along the African coast, and returned without paying Portugal anything whatsoever for the privilege.

After nearly a decade of this abuse, someone finally called Affonso's attention to the vast sums in potential revenue that were being lost to the royal treasury. Affonso's response was characteristic: rather than take the responsibility of enforcing the crown's authority, he decided to turn the monopoly over to a private entrepreneur in return for a fixed annual payment. In this way, Affonso reckoned, he would be guaranteed at least some revenue from the trade without having to bother involving himself in it and distracting himself from his other adventures.

Fernão Gomes, a Lisbon merchant, was that lucky entrepreneur. In 1469, he contracted a five-year lease with Affonso for exclusive trading rights (pieces of which he could sell off, if he wished, to other merchants) along the Guinea coast and at Arguin for a rent of 300,000 *reis* per year. There was one condition, however. And it is to Affonso's everlasting credit—or to that of some unknown advisor—that he included this stipulation in the contract: Gomes had to explore 100 leagues (about 300 miles) of new coastline in every year of his lease. And it is to Gomes's credit that he fulfilled this condition most faithfully. In the five years the Lisbon merchant held the West African franchise, his captains discovered and charted nearly 2000 miles of the continent's Atlantic shore—as much as Prince Henry's captains had in the twenty years after Gil Eanes doubled Cape Bojador. They sailed from Sierra Leone into the Bight of Benin, through the full length of the Gulf of Guinea to the Bight of Biafra, and raised the richest part of West Africa in the process: the Ivory, Gold, and Malagueta coasts. And they raised another tantalizing prospect as well.

Whether or not Prince Henry had ever consciously aimed at finding a sea route to the Indies when he started sending his ships down the West African coast, the idea that Africa might after all be a circumnavigable island, no matter what Ptolemy said, had gained adherents in the years of exploration since. Now, thanks to Gomes's captains, the idea became more than wishful fancy. For, in their very

first push into unknown waters from Sierra Leone, they found that the West African coast, which had been followed steadily southward since Gil Eanes's day, turned to the east. Inevitably, this sparked the belief that the continent in fact had already been rounded, that the Ivory and Gold coasts were the bottom of Africa, and that by sailing far enough eastward now ships would enter the Indian Ocean and the seaway to the Indies. It was a belief that persisted for four years, and it wasn't until a caravel captain named Fernão Po in 1473 reached 9 degrees of longitude east, near the island in the Bight of Biafra which bears his name, that the coastline once again turned southward and the belief had to be abandoned. But this experience, the finding and rounding of Africa's great western bulge, fatally undermined the Ptolemaic picture of the continent and freed the Portuguese to seek the Indies by way of the Atlantic. So it was with a new eagerness that Gomes's captains pushed southward now, and by the time the Lisbon merchant's lease expired in 1474 one of them, Rui de Sequiera, had crossed the equator and sailed 2 degrees of latitude south of it to Cape St. Catherine on today's Gabon coast.

Gomes was well rewarded for his good work. He acquired great wealth exploiting the established and developing the new coastal trade and, into the bargain, was knighted for his discoveries of new lands. One would imagine that his franchise would have been renewed quite automatically. But it wasn't. Gomes himself didn't really want it. For, in point of fact, it had ceased being an exclusive franchise. Privateers, foreign merchantmen from the Spains and Flanders, Venice, and Genoa had, despite the Papal Bull expressly forbidding it, taken to openly poaching on the West African trade in ever-increasing numbers as soon as it was no longer even nominally under the direct supervision of the Portuguese crown. And there was nothing the Lisbon merchant could do about it. So when the time came to renegotiate the lease he refused to agree to the annual rental the king demanded, and Affonso passed the West African enterprise to his son and heir, the 19-year-old Prince John.

Utterly unlike his father in every trait of character and temperament, John seemed a throwback to the generation of his granduncle, Prince Henry. He was earnest and sensible, an astute politician and clever diplomat, intellectual, religious, visionary, physically strong, and ruthlessly determined; he came to be called the "Perfect Prince." Though still a child when Henry died, he grew up with a keen inter-

est in the Navigator's work (as king, he would add "Lord of Guinea" to his royal titles) , and when Gomes failed to renew his franchise John eagerly importuned his father for it. As the chronicler of his reign, Rui de Pina, wrote, "He was a good Catholic anxious for the propagation of the faith, and a man of inquiring spirit desirous of investigating the secrets of nature."

But at the moment he was put in charge of the West African enterprise there was little he could do with it. For it was just at this time that his father embarked on his ill-fated intrigues for the Castilian crown, and it fell to the Perfect Prince to save Affonso and the kingdom from this fiasco. Indeed, by the time of Affonso's humiliating defeat by Castile in 1479, and still two years before his death, *de facto* if not *de jure* rule of the realm had passed into John's far more capable hands.

When he formally ascended the throne in 1481 as King John II, the kingdom, thanks to Affonso's hare-brained adventures, was in a sorry mess. The royal treasury was virtually bankrupt and, what was worse, the feudal nobles, and most especially the Duke of Braganza, having won so much power under Affonso, were in a free-wheeling mood to defy the new king. A plot was already afoot, hatched by Braganza with Castile's connivance. Fearing John's strength of character and his ability to rule Portugal as Affonso never had, Braganza schemed to have the new king assassinated and his cousin Diogo, the Duke of Viseu, another pliant weakling like Affonso, put on the throne in his place. When John got wind of the plot, he moved with the decisive dispatch that was to characterize his reign. Unintimidated by the Duke's power, he had Braganza arrested, tried for treason, and executed, all in a matter of days. As for the co-conspirator, Diogo, this was slightly more complicated but no less directly taken care of. Since Diogo was of the blood royal, John could not have him arrested, so he invited his young cousin to his private apartment at the palace at Sintra. Present at the royal interview were three of John's most trusted *fidalgos*—and no one else. We do not know what John said to Diogo, whether he accused him or behaved as if nothing were amiss. Nor do we know how Diogo acted, whether he pleaded or was defiant, whether his eyes darted anxiously to the three *fidalgos* standing silently aside in the otherwise suspiciously empty royal chamber. But what we do know is that, not long after the interview began, John suddenly unsheathed a short dagger from his girdle and stabbed Diogo

King John II of Portugal

to death. Such then was the man who was now in charge of Portugal's West African enterprise.

As a king, John was able to bring far greater resources to the enterprise than Prince Henry ever could. More important, he also brought to it a far more ambitious vision, seeing a potential that his granduncle had, at best, only sensed. John, of course, had the benefit of the Navigator's pioneering work. Thanks to more than a half century of voyages, the Atlantic was no longer the Mar Tenebroso of legendary terror, the profit that could be gained by sailing upon it had been amply demonstrated, the seamanship it required was well advanced, the map of Africa was taking accurate shape, and the discovery of a sea route to the Indies seemed a realistic prospect. But because of his boldness and intelligence, John, as few men of his time could, was able to seize on these accomplishments and form them into a plan for Portugal's greatness. Virtually turning his back on Europe, he made the West African enterprise the top priority of his reign and set it the specific tasks of exploiting the Guinea trade to its fullest, circumnavigating the African continent and breaking into the Indies trade, establishing an overseas Portuguese empire, and finding Prester John.

Prester John? It was now over 300 years since Europe had received that marvelous letter from the legendary Christian monarch, and it would seem that, considering how much had been learned of the world since, Europeans, and especially one so estimable as King John II, would have given up the quest as rather old-fashioned and foolish. But the legend continued to exert its hypnotic hold and, as a matter of fact, on no one quite so obsessively as the Portuguese king.

It is true that by this time the vision of the priest-king was considerably less wonderful and the geography of his realm far more modest. Prester John now was quite specifically assumed to be the Emperor of Ethiopia, and his kingdom was fairly well understood to lie hidden somewhere in the mountains off the East African coast. But as yet no European had ever been there or, at least, no European who had ever returned to tell the tale. (In fact, as was later to be discovered, a handful of questers had managed to reach Ethiopia in the middle and late fifteenth century but, though they were treated with much honor, they were never allowed to leave again.) So Europe still hoped that Prester John, if no longer invested with quite the magical powers and magnificence he was once believed to possess, would nevertheless prove a potent Christian ally in the wars against the latest

infidel scourge, the Ottoman Turks. As a good Christian, John II shared fervently in this hope. But he had another, more self-serving reason for seeking Prester John. As he believed Prester John's kingdom extended to the East African coast, he hoped that the Ethiopian monarch, as a brother in Christ, would assist him in his ambition to circumnavigate Africa, by providing information on how and where the Indian and Atlantic oceans merged and by allowing Portuguese ports of call to be established in his realm for the long voyage from there to the Indies.

Perhaps the most famous of the Portuguese quests for Prester John was that of Pedro da Covilhã and Afonso de Paiva, two courtiers whom King John II dispatched by an overland route in the early years of his reign. They traveled together to Alexandria, where, disguised as Moorish traders, they joined a caravan of Muslim merchants. In this way they were able to pass through the domain of the Ottoman Turks to Cairo and from there on to the Red Sea, where they secured passage on an Arab dhow sailing to Aden. In Aden, they parted company. Covilhã was to attempt to reach India while Paiva was to go on to Ethiopia. They agreed that on their return each would wait for the other in Cairo.

Covilhã met with remarkable success. Traveling with Arab merchants who plied the Indies trade, he sailed from Aden across the Indian Ocean to the Malabar Coast of India, where Hindu traders brought the spices and other merchandise they collected throughout the Orient. These the Arab merchants bought and, with the dhows laden, Covilhã now sailed with them to the Persian Gulf and Arabia. Then, following the age-old caravan routes, he crossed the Arabian desert to the Red Sea, sailed back to Aden and returned to Cairo. By that time, Paiva had also returned to Cairo. But he was dead, of the plague. And, as Covilhã soon realized, he had died before he had had a chance to give anyone an account of his travels.

One must admire Covilhã's fidelity to his king at this point. He had a wife and children in Portugal, he had been traveling for more than two years under the most dangerous circumstances and must have been aching to get home. Yet he didn't. He realized that the most important part of the king's mission had been Paiva's, the discovery of Prester John's realm, and not his, the reaching of India. And, as there was no way of knowing whether Paiva had accomplished it, the faithful Covilhã took the task on himself. He had the presence of mind first

to send a detailed description of what he had discovered on his travels (and which doubtless proved of great value to the king's ambitions to break into the Indies trade), and then he set off for Ethiopia. We know that Covilhã, in fact, did succeed in reaching Axum. But the king never heard of it. For the same fate befell Covilhã that had befallen all Europeans who managed to reach Ethiopia in those days. He was treated with great esteem, given an honored place in the emperor's court, provided with a harem, a house, and servants, but never allowed to leave again. Thirty years later, when the Portuguese did at last establish relations with the Emperor of Ethiopia, Covilhã was found there, an old man but alive and well and living in the lap of luxury, no longer especially eager to return to Portugal.

Covilhã's disappearance didn't diminish the Portuguese king's zeal to find Prester John, and he set about trying to reach the African Christian kingdom by striking inland across the continent from the West African coast. For, if the continent's outline was becoming better known, its breadth was still very much underestimated, and it seemed likely that a few months' march into the interior would bring a traveler to Ethiopia. So John instituted a policy of having Christianized black slaves landed at various promising places along the coast, dressed in the best silks and bearing gifts of gold and silver, with instructions to go inland and proclaim the greatness of the Portuguese king and his desire to communicate with Prester John.

A flurry of excitement was generated when word was brought back from the Benin coast that a powerful monarch called Ogane lived 20 moons' march inland (reckoned to be about 900 miles, which, in the geography of the times, could put him in Ethiopia) and held sovereignty over all the other kings and chiefs of the region. In fact, before any of these other kings and chiefs could be crowned, it was said, they first had to send ambassadors to Ogane and gain his acceptance. João de Barros tells us in his chronicle *Decadas de Asia:*

As a sign of his approval Prince Ogane used to send to the kings of Benin, not a scepter and a crown, but a helmet of shining brass such as the Spaniards wear and a staff of the same metal. And he sent them also a cross of brass to wear on their hearts. And all the time the ambassadors were at the Court of Ogane they never caught sight of the Prince; they saw only silk curtains behind which he placed himself. And when the time came to say goodbye, he showed one foot beneath the curtain to satisfy them that he was there and to this foot they made reverence as to a holy thing. And when he

presented the insignia of office, the leader of the embassy received a small cross of the same kind sent to the king.

It was, of course, the cross that excited King John's hopes. But, alas, this Ogane (he probably was the Oni of Ife), as with all Prester Johns to date, was not found, and the Portuguese king at last concluded that if he ever was to be found it would be accomplished only by rounding Africa and approaching his realm from the continent's east coast. And so the voyages of exploration were resumed.

At that time, as we have seen, the most distant landfall in West Africa was Cape St. Catherine at 2 degrees of latitude south. From now on, ships would be sailing always further south of the equator, which raised some new seafaring problems. For example, the North Star vanishes in the southern skies, so the established practice of shooting it with a quadrant or astrolabe in order to determine latitude was no longer possible. What's more, south of the equator the coastal current sets to the north and the winds are southerlies, just the reverse of what they are north of the line, requiring entirely new sailing procedures. How John set about dealing with these new problems would have made Prince Henry proud. For the king gathered around him the best navigators, astronomers, mathematicians, and map makers of his time, assembling a sort of mini-Sagres at his palace in Sintra. And there men like Joseph Vizinho and Abraham Zacuto developed the new navigational and sailing techniques—such as the method for calculating the height of the sun above the horizon at noon and for preparing tables of declination so that latitude could be worked out without a North Star in the heavens—which made voyaging south of the equator a less risky adventure.

Then John clamped a vise of the closest secrecy on the enterprise. Not for him was Prince Henry's practice of swapping information and skills for a share of the profits with foreign merchantmen. Believing he was on his way to rounding the continent and breaking into the rich Indies trade, John didn't want other European vessels following in the wake of his caravels. They were not to know where to go or how to get there, and to throw them even further off course John not only wouldn't make accurate information available, he wasn't above putting about false information. In one case, the king deliberately caused a rumor to be circulated that "round ships," that is, those whose length measured only three or four times their breadth, could never

return from south of the equator, a breath-taking lie, since the caravel was itself a round ship. But John was prepared to go to any length to make the enterprise exclusively Portugal's. And to assure his claim to the discoveries, he outfitted his expeditions with stone pillars. Until now, the caravel captains had signified the discovery of new lands—if they signified them at all—by casually carving a marking on a tree or erecting a wooden cross. This was a far too informal and impermanent method for John. His captains were to erect a *padrão*, a shaft of lime- stone or marble some five feet high, topped with a stone cross and inscribed with the royal coat of arms, the king's name, and that of the commander of the expedition.

Part Two

THE DISCOVERY

6

THE STONE PILLARS

The first expedition commander to carry King John's stone pillars was Diogo Cão, a naval captain who had made a name for himself fighting privateers on the West African coast. Unlike Prince Henry, John did not count on amateur *fidalgos* for the captains of his expeditions. He could get the best and most experienced seamen of the time, and Cão was just that. He was later knighted for his discoveries, and genealogists then invented a noble pedigree for him, but there's every reason to believe that he was very much a commoner to begin with, descended from a bailiff at the Villa Real in Trás-os-Montes, Portugal's most primitive province, the son and grandson of ordinary soldiers. He probably enlisted in the Royal Fleet as a boy, made his way up through the ranks, and came to the king's attention with daring exploits against privateers. In any case, it was to him that John gave his first stone pillars, and commanded him to go further south down the Atlantic coast of Africa than anyone had ever gone before.

Cão set sail from the Tagus, in front of Lisbon, in May or June of 1482. We know little of his ship or, for that matter, ships—it would not have been unusual for John to fit out this expedition with more than one, considering the distances he hoped it would travel. One must have been a three-masted caravel, and if there was another it might have been a pinnace, serving as a store ship. We can assume that Cão followed what was by then a well-traveled route to West Africa, sailing with the winds and currents to the Canaries, then on to Arguin (where he may have called to revictual), then around Cape Verde to Beziquiche, where he certainly stopped to take on fresh water, before making the long haul past Sierra Leone into the Gulf of Guinea, there

to catch the eastward-running current that carried him to Elmina on the Gold Coast. This leg of the journey probably took about two months, and Cão may have spent a few more weeks at Elmina reprovisioning. Then came the run through the Bights of Benin and Biafra and across the equator to Cape St. Catherine, where he probably arrived in early August.

Now Cão's seamanship was tested. The current, setting to the north, and the prevailing winds were hard against him and the sailing was made all the more difficult by sudden squalls and thundershowers. Moreover, he couldn't run for the shore in case of trouble or even sail very close along it, for it was bound for the most part by high red clay cliffs, affording few safe anchorages, and the surf on its narrow beaches was rough and heavy while the beaches themselves sloped off so gradually that the offshore waters were very shallow for some distance out. Making judicious use of land and sea breezes, Cão had to inch his way along, standing off from the coast by as much as 15 miles at times and keeping his glass glued on the shoreline. For everything he saw now had never before been seen by a white man.

And then he spotted what appeared to be a bay or inlet. Squinting through the shimmering, humid haze of an August day, he made out the points of two spits of land, arcing out into the Atlantic like the opposing jaws of a giant crab's claw and forming what seemed a natural, safe deep-water harbor perhaps 12 to 15 miles across. The landfall was flat and featureless; the parapet of red clay cliffs had abruptly ended here and mangrove and palm trees stretched away from the shoreline's narrow beach of gleaming sand in a dark, unyielding forest to the horizon, where the vague blue outline of mountains could be seen.

But Cão's practiced seaman's eye would have immediately picked out the other, more startling features of this landfall. For the waves breaking on the beach here were an astonishing yellowish brown in color, and the ocean all around the ship was of a thick muddy-red hue as far as the eye could see. What's more, as he sailed toward this inlet, he found he was running against an amazingly powerful seaward current, four, six, or as much as nine knots the closer he got to shore. And dozens of floating islands, some of considerable size, came rushing past his ship, riding the strong muddy current far out to sea. We know that Cão had a sample of the ocean taken and tasted because on a map drawn by Cristoforo Soligo directly after Cão's voyage we see that the

ocean is indicated as being sweet, not salt, for scores of miles off the coast.

Cão must have instantly recognized the significance of these odd conditions. What lay ahead was not a bay or an inlet but the mouth of a great river,

so violent and so powerful from the quantity of its water, and the rapidity of its current [as a Portuguese chronicler recorded not long after], that it enters the sea on the western side of Africa, forcing a broad and free passage, in spite of the ocean, with so much violence, that for the space of 20 leagues it preserves its fresh water unbroken by the briny billows which encompass it on every side; as if this noble river had determined to try its strength in pitched battle with the ocean itself, and alone deny it the tribute which all other rivers in the world pay without resistance.

Diogo Cão had discovered the Congo.

We can be certain of the date of this discovery and confidently credit it to Cão because he erected one of John's stone pillars on the southern bank of the river's mouth; that *padrão* was found centuries later and its inscription deciphered:

In the year 6681 of the World and in that of 1482 since the birth of our Lord Jesus Christ, the most serene, the most excellent and potent prince, King John II of Portugal did order this land to be discovered and this pillar of stone to be erected by Diogo Cão, an esquire in his household.

That Cão chose to erect the very first of John's pillars here, though he had so far journeyed barely 6 degrees of latitude south of the equator and hardly 280 miles from Cape St. Catherine, when his instructions were to sail as far south as he possibly could, is a measure of the importance Cão attached to the discovery. For here was, far and away, the most powerful river any white man had ever set eyes upon until that time. And, what's more, it had an estuary that appeared to offer a way, the first practical way that had been found in over 60 years of exploration, into the interior of the continent.

Cão sailed slowly into the river's mouth, making use of the afternoon sea breeze, his leadsmen anxiously sounding the fathoms, finding the channels around the islands that spotted the estuary, staying close to the bank, aware of the flocks of parrots chattering in the palm trees, the fishing eagles and terns and herons, the crocodiles along the shore, aware too of the people emerging from the forests, silently watching the progress of the birdlike caravel. When the sea breeze dropped

toward dusk, Cão anchored in a mangrove-shaded cove a few miles upstream. Then he had the stone pillar offloaded from the ship and erected on the river's left bank while the local blacks gathered in great crowds around him. There may have been a few anxious moments. Cão had with him a few Christianized black slaves from the Guinea coast to serve as his interpreters, but though the people here looked much like the Guineans it turned out that they spoke a completely different language. Quickly enough, however, by means of signs and gestures and wide happy grins, the locals managed to make their friendly intentions known and their desire to become acquainted with the unusual newcomers. In the simple, direct and open way that strangers made friends in those far parts of the world in those distant times, the blacks and whites were soon trading with each other, lengths of wool and cotton cloth for elephant tusks, with Cão inviting aboard his ship those among the blacks whom he judged to be chiefs or headmen.

It makes a pretty picture to imagine the grizzled caravel captain attempting to parlay with the natives, squatting with them on the ship's deck while his sailors crowded around, no one quite understanding the other, everyone trying out various words in various languages, making signs and gestures, pointing at things, bringing out other things to show, grinning, touching. There must have been a lot of touching. These were the first white men the Bakongo had ever seen, and we know from the experiences of other voyagers that the blacks were always utterly baffled at the first sight of them. "The negroes came stupidly crowding around me," Cadamosta wrote, "wondering at our Christian symbols, our white color, our dress, our Damascenes, garments of black silk and robes of blue cloth or dyed wool all amazed them; some insisted that the white color of the strangers was not natural but put on." He goes on to tell us that the natives spat on his arm and tried to rub off the white paint, and then they wondered all the more when they found the skin itself was white.

Probably the first thing Cão wanted to find out was the name of the river he had discovered. The Bakongo called it *nzere* or *nzadi,* which in their language, Kikongo, meant "the river that swallows all rivers," a grandiose enough appellation to confirm Cão in his belief that he had made a major discovery. But he couldn't pronounce the Kikongo word and, with his tongue stumbling over it, it came out Zaire. And that was the name by which the river was to be known for

the next two centuries. It wasn't until the eighteenth century that it would be commonly called the Congo, from the name of the tribe that dominated its estuary.

But surely a far more exciting piece of information Cão gathered, amid all the gesturing, pointing, and grinning, was that these people were inhabitants of a great kingdom, the Kingdom of Kongo. Some unspecified distance into the interior, Cão learned, southeast from the river, through the rain forest, upon a high mountain, was a royal city called Mbanza Kongo, and there resided a most powerful king, known as the ManiKongo, Lord of the Kongo, to whom all other kings and chieftains paid homage and under whose rule all the people lived. We cannot doubt that Cão's first thought was of Prester John. And he immediately set about making arrangements to contact this monarch. He would not go himself or send any of his white crew, not at first; to march into the unknown of the steaming rain forest would be far too dangerous. He wanted first to have a better idea of who this Mani-Kongo was and what might be expected of him, so he selected four of his Christianized slaves to serve as his ambassadors. He had them dressed in Portuguese clothing, loaded them down with whatever impressive gifts he could find on board, and dispatched them to Mbanza in the company of local guides. The understanding—or at least the understanding Cão hoped he had managed to convey to the Bakongo—was that the ManiKongo would respond to Cão's ambassadors by returning them to the river in the company of his own emissaries, and in this way indicate his desire to enter into friendly relations with the Portuguese.

We don't know how long Cão remained in the river's estuary. His contacts with the natives probably developed over a number of weeks, beginning with a first tentative exchange of gifts, turning into a rather lively trade and culminating in the revelation of the ManiKongo's existence and the dispatch of emissaries to Mbanza. Cão realized that it might take them weeks, perhaps months, to reach the ManiKongo and return, and he was not willing to wait around that long. His own king had commanded him to sail as far south as he possibly could, and so, after perhaps a month at the Congo's mouth, he continued his journey of exploration. We know he sailed nearly 500 miles further along the West African coast to 13 degrees of latitude south and erected the second of King John's *padrões* at Cape St. Mary on what is today the Angola shore. It is probable that he went no further because he was

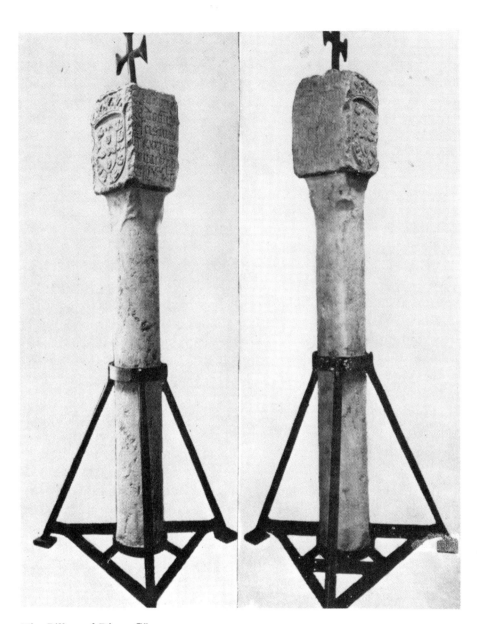

The Pillars of Diogo Cão

running low on provisions and was concerned about the long journey home that still faced him. But it also is possible that he was eager to discover what his emissaries had learned about the ManiKongo, and so we find him now speedily returning to the Congo's mouth.

But his emissaries were not there. Nor was there any word from them or the ManiKongo. Cão was enraged. He couldn't make head or tail of what the natives had to say about what had happened. They seemed to have forgotten about the whole thing and were only anxious to resume trading for the white men's wonderful merchandise, swarming out to the caravel in their dugout canoes, waving and smiling and holding up elephant tusks. Cão suddenly saw in all the happy, friendly faces a terrible duplicity. He was mistaken; as was to be learned later, his emissaries had been greeted with much delight and treated excellently by the ManiKongo and hadn't been returned with the monarch's own ambassadors only because of a misunderstanding due to a lack of a common language. But at that moment Cão feared the worst. He imagined that his emissaries had been imprisoned and, reverting to the old habits of a fighting naval captain, he had four of the Bakongo seized as hostages and had a message sent to the Mani-Kongo warning him that these people would be freed only in exchange for his own men. Then, promising to return, he sailed for Lisbon on the next favoring tide.

Cão arrived in Portugal in March or April of 1484. In making him a *cavalheiro,* awarding him a coat of arms charged with the two *padrões* he had erected and granting him a lifetime annuity of 10,000 *reis,* John expressed his extreme pleasure over Cão's accomplishments. He was ecstatic about the news of the Kingdom of Kongo. He seems to have been firmly convinced that the ManiKongo, if not himself the fabled Prester John, would know of him and prove a valuable ally in the endless quest for him. And, in a show of that innovative statesmanship that characterized his reign, John prepared for that alliance by treating the four hostages Cão had brought home as if they were, albeit unwitting and unwilling, ambassadors from the Kingdom of Kongo to the Portuguese court. It was an astonishing approach. For the first time, blacks seized on the West African coast were not automatically enslaved. Rather, they were provided with apartments at the palace, fitted out with the wardrobe of courtiers, set to studying Portuguese and Christianity, and given tours of the realm. John's intention was to return the quartet to Mbanza so bedazzled by Portugal

that the ManiKongo would be eager to enter an alliance and assist
John in his aims.

John was equally enthusiastic about the geographical discoveries
of Cão's voyage. He had every reason to believe that, in the Congo
River, his captain had found a great highway into the African interior,
a natural artery to lands never reached by Europeans before, promising access to untold riches. And in having traveled nearly 800 miles
further southward down the West African coast, Cão, by John's cal-
culations, had come close to rounding the continent and finding the
sea route to the Indies.

Yet, despite all the excitement, we find John delaying the dispatch
of Cão on a second expedition. Why, one can't help wondering. And
then we realize that it was just at this time that a young Genoese seaman turned up at the palace at Sintra. He was called in Portugal
Christovao Colom, and João de Barros describes him as "a man expert, eloquent and a good Latinist" who came to John with the request to "give him some vessels to go and discover the Isle Cypango by
the Western Ocean."

Christopher Columbus had been living in Lisbon for about eight
years at this time, in the Genoese community which had flocked there
to partake in the West African trade. He had married a Portuguese
noblewoman and had himself made a fair share of voyages in Portuguese and Genoese merchantmen to the Guinea coast. When exactly
he first conceived the idea of reaching Isle Cypango (as Marco Polo
had named Japan) and the Indies by sailing straight westward across
the Atlantic, instead of southward around Africa, as the captains with
whom he had sailed dreamed, we cannot say, but it was fully formed
when he presented it to King John in 1484.

John was the first person to whom Columbus brought his *Emprêsa
de las Índias*. As the only monarch of the time with the resources for
and commitment to this sort of daring ocean exploration, John was
the only one from whom the Genoese seaman could hope to get an
intelligent hearing. And an intelligent hearing he got. John turned
Columbus's amazing proposition over to his assembly of experts
(which now included Diogo Cão) for their consideration and advice.
But, as Barros tells us, "They all considered the words of Christovao
Colom as vain, simply founded on imagination or things like Marco
Polo's Isle Cypango." For his part, "the king," Barros reports, "as he
observed this Christovao Colom to be a big talker and boastful in

setting forth his accomplishments, and more puffed up with fancy and imagination about his Isle Cypango than certain of the things he told about, gave him small credit."

It is, of course, pure nonsense that, as popular histories would have it, Columbus was turned down because the Portuguese believed the earth was flat. After all their experience sailing the Atlantic, seeing ships hull-down over the horizon, no intelligent man among them, and certainly not King John or his experts, doubted for a moment that the world was a globe. The problem with Columbus's proposition lay elsewhere. He grossly underestimated the distance across the Atlantic and grossly overestimated the size of the Asian continent. Thus he made the trip from the Canaries to Japan one of only 2500 miles when in fact it is over 10,000 and that to the China coast only 3500 miles when it is in reality nearly 12,000. And somehow the Portuguese sensed the error. They simply would not believe that the voyage Columbus proposed could possibly be as short as Columbus said. Besides, as we've seen, John was satisfied that Diogo Cão had reached within a few days' voyaging of the Indian Ocean, so it made little sense for him to gamble the heavy investment of a westward expedition by the Genoese seaman when he felt he had a sure thing in hand by the southerly route. So Columbus was dismissed (to go on, of course, to John's father's old *bêtes noires,* Isabella and Ferdinand of Spain) and John set about outfitting Diogo Cão with a fleet for his second expedition.

Because of a lack of records, there is some confusion about Cão's second voyage. We know that he sailed from the Tagus sometime late in 1485 with at least three vessels. And, since he was again carrying John's stone pillars, we know how far he journeyed: one of the *padrões* was erected at what is today Cape Negro on the Angola coast, nearly 16 degrees latitude south of the equator, and a second was planted at nearly 22 degrees latitude south, just short of the Tropic of Capricorn, at what is today Cape Cross on the Namib Desert coast of South-West Africa. Thus, though he failed to make that "few days' journey" round the continent, he uncovered 700 miles more of African coastline, for a total of 1500 miles in just two voyages (as compared with the 2000 miles in the 5 years of Gomes's lease and in the 20 years of Prince Henry's enterprise).

What we also can be certain of is that Cão on this journey again called in at the Congo mouth. Aboard were the four hostages from the

first voyage, now speaking Portuguese, probably Christianized, and dressed like *fidalgos*. Cão landed them, according to Rui de Pina, to the great surprise and joy of the natives who had gathered to watch the return of the caravels. They were carried off to Mbanza, bearing sumptuous gifts from King John to the ManiKongo, with the request that the African monarch return Cão's four men along with envoys and ambassadors of his own. While waiting for this exchange of envoys to take place Cão decided to make a more thorough exploration of the river, to find how deep into the African interior it would take him. We know that he sailed up the full length of the estuary to a point just above today's Matadi, because we can find his name inscribed on a rock of an overhanging ledge there.

It was a trip of about 100 miles, across the coastal plain to the foothills of the Crystal Mountains. Though the river steadily narrowed and was studded with sizable islands, it remained completely navigable, and Cão had little difficulty finding his way. But at Matadi, where the river was barely one half mile wide, the Crystal Mountains abruptly and dramatically reared up on both banks, and the river, making a sudden sharp bend, was cut off from view. One can imagine Cão taking his little cockleshell of a vessel around that sharp bend into the narrow, spectacular mountain gorge—and encountering the Cauldron of Hell, the last of those 220 miles of thundering cataracts and rapids of the Livingstone Falls, over which the Congo roars through the Crystal Mountains before emerging into the coastal plain and flowing down to the sea. And this was the end of Cão's exploration of the Congo. For there was no possibility that his little caravel could sail through that ferocious white water. The disappointment for Cão must have been crushing, and it was surely with a heavy heart that he turned his caravel back toward the sea.

The confusion we have about this voyage concerns the sequence of the events. According to Rui de Pina, Cão called in at the Congo on the outbound leg of his journey, and it was then that he landed his hostages and discovered the Cauldron of Hell. After this, rather than wait until the hostages reached Mbanza and returned with his men and the ManiKongo's ambassadors, he went on to sail south and erected the *padrões* at Cape Negro and Cape Cross. In this account of the voyage, we have Cão calling in again at the Congo on the homeward leg, as he had on his first expedition; but this time he finds his men happily waiting for him on the riverbank along with a group of

envoys from the ManiKongo's court, and he gathers everyone up and sails home to Portugal with them.

The only trouble with this seemingly plausible sequence is that Diogo Cão, made so much of until now, abruptly vanishes from the chronicles, never to be heard of again. One explanation for his sudden disappearance is that, upon Cão's return to Lisbon, King John was so enraged at learning that his captain had failed to round the African continent, which he believed was merely a matter of a few days' voyaging, that he had Cão imprisoned and possibly executed. Given John's ruthless character and the bloody nature of the age, there is some merit in this explanation. But there's another which may be just a bit more plausible, and that is that Cão, after calling in at the Congo, landing his hostages, and discovering the Cauldron of Hell, went on to reach Cape Cross—and died there, shipwrecked on the barren, waterless wastes of the Namib Desert coast. How then, we must ask, did Cão's men and the ManiKongo's envoys reach Lisbon? For we know, as a matter of fact, that they did reach Lisbon, sometime in 1488. And the best answer is that Bartholomeu Dias de Novais took them there.

With Cão vanished without a trace, for whatever reason, Dias was the best sea captain around. So it was to him that John turned to accomplish what Cão had failed to do: round the continent and find the seaway to the Indies. Dias was put in command of two caravels and a store ship to carry sufficient water and provisions for the long voyage along the desert coast beyond Cape Cross, which may have been what defeated Cão. John put his experts to work on another problem Cão had encountered: that, beyond the Congo's mouth, the contrary winds and currents grew progressively stronger the further one sailed southward. Using the logic that had been applied successfully to the problem of beating against winds and currents north of the equator—but in reverse—the experts suggested that by sailing southwest in a wide enough arc away from the coast into the Atlantic, Dias might be able to pick up westerlies to carry him around the continent.

So, in the fall of 1487, Dias led his ships out of the Tagus roadstead. Following Cão's wake, he sailed beyond Cape Cross and put into a sheltered bay at 29 degrees latitude south, now called Alexander Bay near the mouth of the Orange River in present-day South Africa. By now the winds were blowing so strongly out of the south and southwest that his clumsy store ship could make no headway. Dias decided to leave it in the bay and for the next five days beat against the winds

along the coast. But this eventually proved impossible even for the handier caravels.

Then Dias made his daring move. Rather than give up in face of the adverse winds and current and return to Portugal a failure, he took the risk of sailing away from the coast and stood out on a tack into mid-ocean in hopes of finding the westerlies. For thirteen perilous days his ships scudded before a gale with shortened sails and then, at about 40 degrees latitude south, those winglike lateen sheets picked up the winds out of the west, driving the ships back toward Africa. Day after day, Dias watched for the continent's west coast to reappear, running north and south along the horizon. But it didn't. So Dias turned his vessels north and after several anxious days, he at last sighted a landfall. But, as the line of mountains rose along the horizon now, Dias had what must have been a heart-stopping revelation: the coastline was running not north and south but east and west. This was the bottom of Africa; he had turned the continent.

Dias's first landfall was what is today Mossel Bay, 200 miles beyond the Cape of Good Hope. To make dead certain that he had rounded the continent, he sailed along the shore some distance beyond today's Port Elizabeth, where the coast made a distinct turn to the north, revealing itself unquestionably as the east coast of Africa. We know that Dias wanted to press on still further, perhaps into the Indian Ocean and all the way to India, but his crew prevented him. The caravels were leaky, the rigging was in shreds, provisions were low; and there was a dreadfully long way to go before they would be home again. The seamen threatened to mutiny, so Dias turned back. Homeward bound, he stopped at Alexander Bay to recover his store ship. Then, by many accounts, he called in at the Congo mouth, where Cão's men and the ManiKongo's envoys were waiting and took them aboard for the journey to Lisbon. Sixteen months after departing, he crossed the Tagus roadstead with the emissaries from the Kingdom of Kongo in his ships.

Understandably, the great excitement in Lisbon on Dias's return focused mainly on the sea route he had found around the African continent (and which, in 1497, Vasco da Gama would follow to open Portugal's trade with the Indies). But the king had lost none of his enthusiasm for the quest for Prester John, and he took a great personal interest in the men who had been brought back from Mbanza Kongo. The envoys whom the ManiKongo had sent were the sons of

nobles of the Kongo court, led by a prince named Nsaku who had brought gifts of ivory and palm cloth to the Portuguese king and expressed his desire to learn the arts of the European kingdom. John was quick to seize the opportunity. As he had the four hostages Cão had brought to the palace, he treated this retinue of Kongo nobles with extraordinary extravagance. And, as Rui de Pina tells us, when it came time for their conversion to Christianity, John personally stood sponsor at Nsaku's baptism, where, amid great pomp and solemnity, he was christened Dom João da Silva (John of the Woods), and an unprecedented and honorable, though tragically brief, alliance between the European and African kingdoms was inaugurated.

7

KINGDOM OF KONGO

Sometime around the birth of Christ, give or take a few hundred years, a mysterious migration of peoples began in central Africa. It was comparable in extent and historical consequence to the "Indian" exodus from northern Asia that provided the American continents with their first populations, one of those not-quite-explicable but truly stupendous shifts of humanity that have periodically revolutionized the earth's demography. Here it was the Bantu-speaking blacks of the savanna highlands of the central Benue River valley, in what is today the frontier region between Cameroon and Nigeria, who embarked on the enigmatic journey away from their homeland and who, traveling south and southeast in the course of the first millennium A.D., fanned out and established themselves as the dominant people of the southern third of the African continent.

What exactly set them off is a matter of academic speculation, but a safe if rather simplistic guess is that it had to do with a drastic shortage of land. We know that in the preceding centuries these early Iron Age peoples had acquired the rudiments of agriculture, probably from the civilizations of the Upper Nile Valley, based on Sudanic millet or sorghum grain and employing the slash-and-burn technique of farming, at which they proved extremely proficient—in fact just a bit too proficient for their own good. For we know that not long afterward the Bantus experienced one of the most spectacular population explosions in human history. Coupling the profligate use made of land in slash-and-burn farming with the rapid rise in the numbers of people, it is not hard to see how the Bantus might have come under a terrific land pressure within a few generations.

Sub-tribes would have formed and hived off from the main tribal groupings and ventured always further afield in search of new lands, until eventually the homeland savanna had been overrun and the rain forests of the Congo River basin bordering the highlands on the south had been reached. Then, with land and population pressures still mounting relentlessly behind them, the Bantus would have had little choice but to press on into this alien landscape as well. No doubt some settled or attempted to settle in the forest, but, for all its riot of vegetation, they would have found it a very inhospitable place. Their Sudanic millets and sorghum grains, so fecund in the high, open grasslands, would not grow in that close, wet climate, and the forest's indigenous crops were inadequate to support the sizable populations. So the mainstream of the migration pushed on, instinctively following the streams and tributaries of the Congo drainage system, until at last one day they emerged from the forests and reached the Katanga (or Shaba) Plateau, there to discover a highland savanna remarkably like the one they had left behind.

We can assume there was then a hiatus in the migration while the Bantus settled this familiar grassland and reestablished their traditional slash-and-burn agricultural society. But the hiatus would have been relatively short-lived. Almost certainly within a century, and surely in less than two, the whole cycle of population boom and land shortage would have begun again, and again the Bantus would have been on the move, expanding now across the Shaba Plateau and down through what is today Zambia, Rhodesia, and Mozambique, all the way to the Indian Ocean coast.

And there something of a miracle occurred. In the vicinity of the mouth of the Zambezi River, the Bantus found food plants of southeast Asia, notably the banana, Asian yam, and taro (or coco yam). One theory explaining how these plants came to be there holds that they were brought by Indonesian mariners who had blown across the Indian Ocean on the monsoons and established settlements on the East African coast in the third or fourth century A.D. Whether the Bantus actually contacted these settlements or whether they simply found the plants proliferating in the wild we really don't know. What we do know is that the introduction of the Asian plants into African agriculture revolutionized the Bantu migration. The bananas and yams would thrive in the hot, moist climates where the Sudanic sorghum and millet were useless, and thus they allowed the Bantus to

expand into regions until then hostile to them, up the East African coast, into the areas of the great lakes of present-day Tanzania, Kenya, and Uganda, and then, in the tenth century A.D., back to the Congo River basin, through which they had passed a millennium before. By the twelfth and certainly no later than the thirteenth century, Bantus occupied virtually every part of the Congo forests and, having absorbed the indigenous aboriginal Pygmies or driven them into the most remote regions, settled into the tribal societies from one of which the Kingdom of Kongo arose.

There are no written records of this Bantu kingdom before the arrival of the Portuguese, and all we can know of its origins comes from its oral tradition, historical memory and myths. One of these, which the Portuguese heard on their arrival and which was later recorded by missionaries, concerns a certain Nimi a Lukeni, the son of a chief of a small Bantu tribe called the Vungu or Bungo, that had settled on the bank of the Congo near today's Stanley Pool. He was young, strong, ambitious, a fearless warrior, impatient for command but with little prospect of succeeding to the rule of his tribe, so, with a band of armed followers, he withdrew from his village and set himself up at a ford on the river, to collect tolls from all who wished to cross. One day, the legend relates, a sister of the chief, Nimi a Lukeni's aunt, came to the ford and sought to cross over. Nimi a Lukeni demanded the payment of a toll. She refused, invoking her privileges as the chief's sister, and when she set out to cross the river anyway, Nimi a Lukeni leapt upon her and disemboweled her.

It was an awesome, atrocious act and, in the legend's countless retellings, it echoes with all the symbolic horror that we find in so much of Greek mythology. For by this act, this killing of kin, we are told, Nimi a Lukeni violated all that was sacred, defied every tradition and broke irretrievably with the normal order of life. By his murder of the chief's sister he declared himself outside the restraints of tribal law, an exceptional being, godlike in his apartness, fearsome in his violence, incomparably courageous in his defiance, a figure of awe and power. He was, legend tells us, the founder-king of the Kingdom of Kongo, the first ManiKongo.

There is no way of knowing when or, for that matter, if this terrible event occurred. But there is evidence that sometime in the first decades of the fourteenth century a young outcast Bantu chieftain of towering, mythic authority—be he Nimi a Lukeni or someone else—

gathered a band of followers and, in the tradition of a millennium of
Bantu migration, led them southwestward away from the vicinity of
Stanley Pool in search of new lands. This was now no longer the
simple matter of finding and moving into unoccupied regions. By this
time the Bantus had pretty much taken over all the forest, so Nimi a
Lukeni had to acquire his new lands by conquest. In a series of wars,
he is said to have subdued the region of a people called the Mbundu
and Mbwela lying south of the Congo estuary (in present-day Angola)
and there, on a high hill about 100 miles from the river, built his
mbaji or *mbanza,* court of justice and palaver place. Legend, as tran-
scribed by a seventeenth-century Italian Capuchin missionary, Giovanni Antonio Cavazzi, says that "Such great respect the inhabitants of
the country had for this place in the forest . . . that those who passed
nearby dared not turn their eyes in that direction. They were
convinced that should they do so, they would die on the spot."

Nevertheless, we learn from the legends, the military conquest,
and the fear and respect inspired by that conquest, were not enough.
For Nimi a Lukeni was a stranger to this new land; it did not contain
the spirits of his ancestors, and so he could not truly control it. He had
no power over its fertility, or over the rains and the crops; he could
not regulate the sowing and the reaping or govern the hunt. This
control, this power, we are told, belonged still to the land's original
occupants, whose ancestors were buried there, and to ignore them, to
refuse to solicit their cooperation and their ritual mediation, was to
run the risk of catastrophe. Yet Nimi a Lukeni did ignore them. And
one day, legend says, he was struck down by *laukidi,* the convulsions of
a madman.

So his followers went to the priest of the conquered people. They
knelt down before him and said, "Lord, we know that you are the
elder, he who first occupied this region, who was first at the nostrils of
the universe. Our chief has fallen into convulsions; bring him peace
again." At first the priest looked angry and protested against what he
called an intrusion. At last, however, he consented to accompany them
to their chief. Nimi a Lukeni said to him, "You are the eldest among
us. Strike me with the *nsea,* the buffalo tail, that my convulsions may
cease." By this request he accepted the religious authority of the land's
original occupants, and he sealed the peace by taking for his first wife
the priest's daughter. And so the Kingdom of Kongo was born.

In the roughly 150 years between then and the arrival of the Por-

tuguese, at least five but perhaps as many as eight ManiKongos, all
presumably descendants of the mythic Nimi a Lukeni, ruled in
Mbanza. By a similar process of military conquest and religious alliance, they extended the boundaries of the realm to encompass more
than 200,000 square miles and upward of 4 or 5 million people. At its
height, it may have reached as far north as the Ogowe River in modern Gabon, eastward from the Atlantic beyond Stanley Pool to the
Bateke Plateau and the Kwango River in today's Zaire, and south
across the Kwanza River in today's Angola. By the time the Portuguese got there, however, the kingdom had somewhat diminished.
The peoples on the northern and southern peripheries had broken
away and formed rival kingdoms, and while some of these may have
still paid tribute as vassals to the ManiKongo, he exercised true sovereignty only over a realm bounded by the Congo River on the north,
the Kwango in the east, the Dande in the south, and the Atlantic
Ocean on the west.

We speak of this realm as a kingdom, rather than, say, a paramount chieftainship, which might seem more appropriate to Africa.
But, as long as we understand that what we are referring to here is a
state of feudal principalities owing allegiance to a central hereditary
authority, *kingdom* is a perfectly accurate description. For the Mani-
Kongo ruled as supremely as any European king in those Middle Ages.
He was regarded as a semi-divine, sacred personage surrounded by a
court of nobles, retainers, slaves, and wives and a royal protocol every
bit as elaborate as any in Europe at the time. Those who wanted to
approach him had to prostrate themselves and crawl forward on all
fours. He could not be observed eating or drinking, under pain of
death, and when he chose to do either a slave would strike two iron
staffs together and all present would fling themselves face down on the
ground. Whenever he traveled, no matter for how short a distance, he
was carried on a litter and escorted by a bodyguard, and whenever he
stopped, the ground was swept clean and mats strewn all about, for it
was regarded as a sacrilege for his feet to touch bare earth. He had a
palace and a throne and all the fabulous insignia of sovereignty. He
maintained a monopoly on the currency of the realm—cowrie shells,
called *nzimbu,* "mined" from the sea floor of the Atlantic coastline—
and extracted tribute from all his subjects. And it was from his loins,
and only his, that the successor ManiKongo could spring.

Nevertheless, for all his power and exalted standing, the Mani-

Kongo, as in any feudally organized state, had to take into account and contend with strong rival centers of power. The kingdom consisted of separate provinces or principalities—there were six at the time of the Portuguese arrival: Soyo, Mpemba (where the capital of Mbanza was located), Mbamba, Mpangu, Mbata, and Nsundi—each of which corresponded to a once independent state conquered by the ManiKongos and each of which was further divided into districts, and the districts, in turn, into villages and towns. Each of these political units had its own chief, enjoyed a large degree of autonomy, and retained a very real sense of separate tribal identity. The ManiKongo formally appointed the chiefs or lords (*manis*) of the provinces (who in turn appointed the district chiefs and so on down the political ladder) and they served at his pleasure, but undoubtedly he felt that prudence obliged him to honor regional traditions. Thus, the kingdom was a confederation of fiefdoms and the province chiefs feudal lords. They swore their fealty to the king, acknowledged his suzerainty, gathered tribute for his royal treasury, raised armies to fight his wars, and served as the nobles of his court and the ministers of his cabinet. At the same time, they had their own very real bases of power and it was not unknown for them to challenge or even rebel against a king.

One needs to be careful neither to overvalue nor to undervalue this kingdom. Certainly its political structure was remarkably sophisticated. Moreover, some arts and crafts were developed there to an impressive degree. For example, iron ore, which was found in the form of ferruginous rock, was mined, smelted, and, with well-designed hammer, anvil, and bellows, worked into a wide array of handsome and effective weapons, tools, ornaments, musical instruments, and other devices. The Bakongo also forged copper and apparently knew the lost-wax process, casting this metal into statuettes, fetishes, and jewelry.

In addition, they were brilliant weavers. They used vegetable fibers, stripped primarily from the leaves of the raffia palm tree, which they wove into fabrics with such fine skill and variety that on seeing them for the first time the Portuguese took them to be velvet and damask, brocade, satin, and taffeta. They also made a very usable cloth by beating the bark of trees; fashioned beautiful baskets, nets, and furniture from split vines and wicker; carved wood and ivory; made pottery; and cured hides with which to dress themselves and furnish their lives. Thus, in no sense can we imagine the Bakongo as a naked savage. He was handsomely dressed in his marvelous cloths, beauti-

A contemporary river scene

fully adorned with his skillfully crafted jewelry, outfitted with excellent tools and implements, and surrounded by the finest of artifacts.

But, for all this, he remained a member of an essentially primitive society, a society based on subsistence farming. The Bakongo cultivated the yams and bananas his ancestors had brought into the forest, gathered indigenous legumes and fruits, made excellent use of the native palm trees, from which he derived oil, wine, vinegar, and a kind of bread. He kept domesticated goats, pigs, and cattle and, using nets and baskets, harpoons and poisons, fished the Congo and its tributaries. But everything he caught or raised he ate. The concept of commodity farming, of a cash crop, of producing more than the immediate need for barter or sale, had not been developed. Indeed, the whole idea of trade outside the immediate neighborhood, which would involve a system of storage and transportation, had not yet caught hold on any extensive scale when the Portuguese arrived. And, without extensive trade, without the need for accounting records, storehouse inventories, and the like, there was no writing.

There also was no calendar, no means of telling time. And there was no wheel. A network of trails crisscrossed the forest, with bridges

of sturdy vines slung over the rivers and ravines, but there were no carts or carriages. What is perhaps more curious, the Bakongo never thought to use his domesticated animals to carry things or people, or even to pull the hoes with which he worked his fields. The only vehicles of transport available, if they can be called that, were the wooden horse and the litter, the first being a log fitted with a hide saddle for the traveler to straddle while being carried by slaves, the latter a skin slung between poles also carried by slaves, in which the nobles of the kingdom rode. Everyone else walked and carried their goods on their heads.

Yet, despite its limitations, the Kingdom of Kongo probably was the most highly advanced civilization on the west coast of Africa at the time. It certainly was the most highly advanced civilization that Europeans had come in contact with in sub-Sahara Africa up to that time, and the excitement generated by its discovery was immense, provoking a fabulous degree of exaggeration. The Portuguese imagined the kingdom as being far greater and more magnificent than it really was, and in the earliest chronicles we see its boundaries described as extending as far north as Benin (in modern Nigeria), as far south as the Cape of Good Hope, and reaching to the east all the way to Ethiopia, the realm of Prester John. And, if the ManiKongo was himself not the fabled Christian priest-king, the Portuguese were certain that he could show them the way to that long-sought kingdom. King John II quite specifically believed that the great river whose mouth Diogo Cão had discovered flowed from a huge lake in the highlands of Ethiopia and by following it upstream to its source one could cross Africa all the way to the Indian Ocean. So, even before dispatching Vasco da Gama to follow the sea route around the Cape of Good Hope that Bartholomeu Dias had found and so opened the seaway to the Indies, he first dispatched an expedition to the Congo.

Gonçalo de Sousa was given command of a fleet of three caravels. A dozen priests, a contingent of soldiers, masons, carpenters, printers, farmers, and various other artisans, even including a few women skilled in the domestic arts such as bread baking and sewing, along with the tools of their trades, sacerdotal objects, ornaments, gifts, and building materials were loaded aboard the vessels. And then, with Nsaku and the other Bakongo nobles who had been residing in Portugal for the past two years, the expedition set sail in December 1490 on the extraordinary mission of establishing diplomatic relations

with the Kingdom of Kongo and entering into an alliance of mutual
aid with it.

It proved a grim voyage. The plague, which was raging in Lisbon
at the time of the expedition's departure, had been carried aboard,
and before the journey was half done, it had taken a deathly toll,
killing among others Nsaku and Gonçalo de Sousa. Rui de Sousa, a
nephew of the expedition's leader, assumed command and reached the
mouth of the Congo at the end of March 1491. The ships anchored in
the lee of the south bank of the river's estuary, not far from where
Diogo Cão had erected his *padrão,* near the village of Mpinda. In
subsequent years, Mpinda became the first port of the Congo (it is
today Angola's Santo António do Zaire) and was at the time of the
arrival of de Sousa's expedition the capital city of the kingdom's province of Soyo and the residence of the chief of the province of Soyo, the
ManiSoyo.

"The ManiSoyo, with demonstrations of great joy, met the Portuguese with all his followers," a contemporary chronicler, Duarte
Lopes, tells us. Three thousand warriors, armed with bows and arrows,
naked to the waist, painted in various colors, and wearing headdresses
of parrot feathers, assembled to the sound of drums, ivory trumpets,
and stringed instruments. After three days of grand revelry, feasting,
and dancing, they took the Portuguese to Mbanza Kongo to meet their
king. It was a journey of a hundred miles along a footpath snaking
through dense forests, across streams and ravines, along precarious
ridges, through marshes and swamps, and always ascending to a plateau some 1700 feet above the sea in the Crystal Mountains. It took
very nearly three weeks, and throughout the journey, Duarte Lopes
tells us,

So great was the multitude who ran to see the Portuguese Christians, that
it seemed as if the whole country were covered with people, who loaded
them with kindness, singing and making sounds with cymbals and
trumpets, and other instruments . . . after three days on the road they
met the king's escort, who presented them with all manner of refreshments,
and paid them great honor, as did other nobles sent by the king to meet
the Christians.

When they came within three miles of Mbanza, at a place called
Mpangala, which was something of a suburb of the royal capital,

all the Court came to meet the Portuguese with great pomp, and with

music and singing . . . and so great was the crowd that not a tree or raised place but was covered with people running together to see these strangers.

Unfortunately, there are no contemporary descriptions of the kingdom's royal capital at the time of the Portuguese arrival. Duarte Lopes, unaccountably, fails us in this regard and all later descriptions of the city unavoidably include alterations made by the Portuguese. However, Monsignor Jean Cuvelier, the preeminent student of the ancient kingdom, has attempted to reconstruct what it must have looked like when Rui de Sousa became the first European to enter it. Because of its elevation, it was well up out of the worst of the jungle's humid heat and had a relatively mild and healthy climate for a population that must have numbered in the tens of thousands.

The streets were not laid out in straight lines [Cuvelier reckons]. Narrow paths ran in all directions through the tall grass. . . . The houses were of unadorned straw, except for their interiors, where there were mats with designs. . . . The dwellings of the notables were distinguished from those of ordinary people by a little more room and a greater number of painted mats. They were surrounded by walls of perennial trees. . . . To the north the mountain was crowned by a dark forest, a kind of sacred wood in which the sound of the axe was never heard. . . . It was in this wood that the former kings were buried. The founder of the kingdom, Nimi a Lukeni, was buried there. To the south lay a large square which was known as *mbasi a nkanu,* court of justice, because under the great wild fig tree . . . which shaded one corner of this square, the kings were accustomed to dispense justice. It provided a large open space where people assembled to receive the benediction of the king, or to attend dances and triumphal reviews of the troops. Not far from the public square was the residence or enclosure of the king. . . . This was made of stakes tied together with vines. . . . At the different gates of entry, the king's guard and a few trumpeters were stationed. Inside the enclosure there was a large yard; then there was another palisade which enclosed the dwelling of the king, which was approached through a maze.

At the end of this maze, Duarte Lopes tells us, the ManiKongo awaited the approach of the Portuguese embassy. His name was Nzinga a Nkuwu; he was perhaps sixty years old and was seated on a throne made of wood inlaid with ivory, which had been placed on a raised platform. He was draped in beautifully tanned, glossy hides and leopard and civet furs, and around his waist, affixed as a sort of apron

over his skirt of palm cloth, he wore a piece of European damask which Diogo Cão had sent him nearly ten years before. His arms were laden with bracelets of copper, the tail of a zebra hung from his shoulder, an ironwood baton and a bow and arrows lay across his lap, and on his head he wore a cap of palm cloth resembling velvet and embroidered with the figure of a snake. Assembled around him were his queen and lesser wives, the nobles of his court, the chiefs of the provinces—including his sons, Mbemba a Nzinga, chief of Nsundi and the heir apparent, and Mpanzu a Nzinga, chief of Mpemba province.

Rui de Sousa approached and, in the European custom, knelt before the monarch and kissed his hand. The ManiKongo responded by taking up a handful of dust, pressing it first against his heart and afterward against the Portuguese. Then Rui de Sousa called forward his porters and presented the gifts he had brought from the king of Portugal—lengths of satin, silk, and linen, brocade and velvet fabrics, silver and gold jewelry, trinkets and plate, and a flock of red pigeons. Duarte Lopes tells us,

After this the king rose from his seat, and showed by words and countenance the great joy he felt at the arrival of the Christians, and sat down again in presence of his people. These last, immediately after the speech of the king, with songs and music, and other signs of delight, also manifested their satisfaction with the embassy, and as an act of submission, prostrated themselves three times on the ground, and lifted their feet, according to the custom of those countries, praising and approving their king.

Then, using as his interpreter one of the Bakongo nobles who had returned from Lisbon, Rui de Sousa proceeded to explain his mission—the desire of King John II that the ManiKongo and his people accept the Christian faith and enter into an alliance with the kingdom of Portugal. We are told that this explanation occupied the rest of that day and most of the night. De Sousa described the virtues of Christianity and the wonders of Portuguese civilization, illustrating his lecture with the tools and equipment and sacerdotal objects he had brought—and by having his soldiers fire off a salute with their rifles. The ManiKongo, Duarte Lopes reports

listened with great attention. . . . Then the king retired and gave lodgings to the ambassadors in a palace set apart for them, and the rest were lodged in various houses of the nobles, with every provision for their comfort.

The ManiKongo couldn't have been anything but overwhelmingly impressed by Rui de Sousa's presentation. He obviously realized that he had come in contact with a superior civilization from which, as an ally, he and his kingdom could gain immense benefit and from which, as an enemy, they might suffer considerable harm. His, therefore, couldn't have been a difficult decision to make, and whether he made it with quite the alacrity the early Portuguese chroniclers would have us believe, there can be no doubt that he must have made it very soon after Rui de Sousa's arrival.

The next day, Duarte Lopes reports, the ManiKongo

sent privately for all the Portuguese, when they devised the manner in which the baptism of the king was to take place, and how to effect the conversion of these people to the Christian faith. After much discourse, it was decided first to build a church, in which to celebrate with great solemnity the rite of baptism and other services, and meanwhile to instruct the king and the people of the court in the truths of the Christian religion.

One thousand Bakongo, we are told, the ManiKongo himself included, joined the Portuguese masons and carpenters and artisans in the construction of the church, gathering rocks, lime and wood from as far as ten miles away, and by the first week of May the cornerstone was laid.

The church was built in the amazingly short time of two months but, as it turned out, before its completion an insurrection erupted within the realm. The ManiKongo's son and heir, the chief of Nsundi, Mbemba a Nzinga, was sent to deal with the rebels but soon returned to Mbanza in need of reinforcements. One might cynically suggest that part of the ManiKongo's eagerness to become a Christian and an ally of the Portuguese was connected with the impression their firearms had made on him. In any case, he insisted that the baptismal rites be performed before the church's completion.

A wooden hut was hastily raised and, according to some chroniclers, 100,000 people gathered in Mbanza to witness the historic event. The ManiKongo, in honor of the king of Portugal, took the Christian name John, his wife took that of the Portuguese Queen Eleanor, and his son and heir, Mbemba a Nzinga, that of the Portuguese heir to the throne, Affonso. Other lords of provinces and nobles were also baptized at the same ceremony, but it is important to note that a number were not. There were members of the ManiKongo's

court who disapproved of the king's hasty embrace of the newcomers and their religion, who feared the impact of the strangers on their traditional society, and who would have preferred to drive them out of the kingdom straight away while their numbers were still small. Among these was the ManiKongo's other son, the chief of Mpemba, Mpanzu a Nzinga. The Portuguese, however, were not disturbed by this. Everything was being done in haste anyway. The ManiKongo was eager to get on with the baptism so he could enlist the Portuguese in subduing the rebellion. Convincing and converting Mpanzu and other hostile nobles would have to wait. Now was a time for war. Here would be the practical proof of the power of Christianity. Rui de Sousa presented the ManiKongo with a banner with a cross embroidered on it, said to have been blessed by Pope Innocent VIII, and commanded his soldiers to fight in the black monarch's army as if on a crusade against infidels.

There is some confusion about who the rebels were and where the ManiKongo's battle against them took place. Duarte Lopes calls them Anzichi, living on islands in the Congo where "this great river, being restrained by falls, is greatly swollen and expands into a large and deep channel," and other chroniclers say the rebels lived on the banks of the Congo's "Great Lake." In both cases the reference seems to be to the Stanley Pool, the lakelike expanse above the Livingstone Falls, which would mean that the Anzichi rebels were probably the Bateke, then vassals of the ManiKongo. If it is true that the battle did occur at the Stanley Pool, it means that the Portuguese soldiers who fought in the battle accomplished, although surely unwittingly, the feat at which Diogo Cão ten years previously had failed, and that is to reach the Congo River further upstream than the Cauldron of Hell, a feat that would not formally be recognized as having been accomplished until Stanley did it nearly four hundred years later.

Born of conquest, the Kingdom of Kongo was a fiercely militaristic state at the time. Duarte Lopes tells us that the king's bodyguard consisted of some 20,000 warriors. Besides this, every able-bodied man in the realm considered himself a soldier of the king and, Lopes estimates, the ManiKongo could call up an army of more than 100,000 warriors virtually at a moment's notice. To assemble such a formidable army, the king needed but to order the war drums to be sounded. Hearing the signal, the men would take up their arms and run to the royal enclosure, where the king would appear and, flourishing his

weapons, leap about in a war dance of sham combat. His officers and nobles would join in, and then, as the mood would catch hold, the people would take up the ferocious war chants, working themselves into a blood lust, soon to be joined by the fetishers, banging wooden bells and rattles that were meant to obtain the assistance of the ancestors. After three days of this, the army was in a fit state to set off for battle—camouflaged in palm leaves; armed with bows and iron-tipped arrows, ironwood clubs, knives, lances, and assegais; wearing feathered headdresses, with iron-link chains hanging from their necks; and carrying shields of buffalo hide or bark.

Duarte Lopes tells us:

They fight only on foot; they divide their armies into several units, adapting themselves to the terrain and brandishing their emblems. . . . The movements of the combat are regulated . . . by different ways of beating the drum and sounding the trumpet. . . . In front of the fighters march valiant sturdy men who leap about, beating their bells with wooden sticks, firing the courage of the soldiers, and warning them of the weapons being launched against them and the dangers they face. When the fighting begins, the ordinary soldiers run into the fray in scattered formation, shooting their arrows from afar, turning and dodging this way and that, darting in all directions to avoid being hit. . . . When they have fought a certain length of time and the captain decides they are tired, the signal for retreat is given by the ringing of bells; when they hear this, they retrace their steps and other soldiers take their place in combat, until their armies are engaged with all their forces in the general melee.

A single battle usually was the war, for the army went into combat without provisions. They would fight for a couple of hours or so, and whichever side weakened first would then flee and the stronger side would give chase, killing the oldest men, taking the younger ones prisoners, pillaging the villages of the defeated, and shouting all the while, "We have won the war." In this way, the ManiKongo, fighting under the cross and with the help of Portuguese firearms, won his war against the rebels at Stanley Pool and marched triumphantly back to Mbanza with his prisoners and plunder.

Rui de Sousa departed for Lisbon with every reason to feel well-satisfied. A stone church stood in Mbanza Kongo, the ManiKongo and leading members of his entourage had accepted the Gospel, and the power of Portugal's arms had been demonstrated. What's more, he took back with him a number of young Bakongo nobles as ambassa-

dors to the Portuguese court and left behind a number of Portuguese
to promote the new alliance: four priests, several lay brothers and
artisans, a contingent of soldiers. "There also remained," Rui de Pina,
the official chronicler of King John II's reign, tells us, "other persons
of distinction ordered to go and discover other distant countries, with
India and Prester John as their objectives." Presumably this was to be
done by following the Congo River into the heart of Africa.

It is not unlikely that a party of soldiers and *fidalgos,* following the
route of the ManiKongo's army, did find their way once again overland through the forests and mountains around the Livingstone Falls
back to Stanley Pool. But almost certainly they didn't get much
farther than that. The jungle, the oppressive climate, fevers and unknown diseases, hostile tribes living outside the frontiers of the Kingdom of Kongo would have stopped them and they must have perished.
For they were never heard from again.

Meanwhile the Portuguese back in Mbanza were running into
troubles of their own. With the conversion of the ManiKongo and the
first military victory under the banner of the cross, the European
settlers had unquestionably made an auspicious beginning. The king
set aside a special quarter of the royal capital for the Portuguese,
directly across from his own enclosure, where they built themselves
comfortable houses, often of stone, and set about what they regarded
as their main civilizing mission in this primitive kingdom: the conversion of the people to Christianity. The priests and lay brothers pursued the task with zeal and, taking the lead from their king, the
Bakongo flocked to the missionaries. The mysterious rituals, the marvelous sacerdotal objects, the images and paintings of the Virgin and
the saints, the splendid processions, the solemn ceremonies in the
church excited and delighted the people, and they came to view the
religion, a chronicler wrote, "as a gay and pompous pageant, in
which it would be an amusement to join." But soon enough the zealous priests tried to get beyond the pretty formalities and teach the
faith's doctrines, precepts, duties, and obligations. And in that they
came into conflict with traditional Bakongo beliefs.

The Bakongo, as a matter of fact, did believe in a high god, a
supreme being called *Nzambi ampungu,* whom they perceived as the
creator of all things. But they also believed that, by virtue of this god's
very highness, he was exceedingly remote, quite beyond the influence
of men, and therefore, useless to worship. It was the lesser gods, gods

closer to men and earth, more intimately involved with the matters of daily life, who could be placated and bribed and who deserved the worshiper's attention. So it was nature spirits, ghosts of ancestors, and shades of every sort, along with the attendant witchcraft and sorcery, medicine men and diviners, fetishes, idols, and magical rituals, that constituted the Bakongo religion and which they, even after their ostensible conversion to Christianity, refused to give up.

The Portuguese felt obliged to try to force them to give it up, resorting to flogging individuals they couldn't otherwise convince, setting fire to fetishes, destroying idols and holy places. In one history we read of a priest who

having met one of the king's wives, and finding her inaccessible to all his instructions, determined to use sharper remedies and, seizing the whip, began to apply it to her majesty's person. The effect he describes as most auspicious; every successive blow opened her eyes more and more to the truth, and she at length declared herself wholly unable to resist such forcible argument in favour of the Catholic doctrine. She hastened to the king, however, with loud complaints respecting the mode of spiritual illumination, and the missionary henceforth lost all favour both with the king and the ladies of the court.

The Portuguese found other ways to fall from favor. As with missionaries in Africa ever since their time, these priests were appalled by the sexual behavior of the Bakongo. In fact, however, the Bakongo were hardly a licentious people. Rape, incest, and adultery were severely punished, sometimes by wrapping the culprits in dried banana leaves and setting them afire, sometimes by selling them into slavery. The defloration of a virgin required reparation payments to her family; the proper vocabulary for sexual matters was indirect and allusive; the courting procedure was complex and dignified; and the ultimate marriage ceremony was an elaborate and serious business.

Nevertheless, the Bakongo exhibited a refreshing candor about the realities and the pleasures of sex, and this is what seems to have incited the Portuguese priests. They would fly into rages at the sight of the Bakongo dances, which were often explicit pantomimes of sexual intercourse, at the fact that masturbation was considered quite normal, that young couples were allowed to live and sleep together in preparation for their marriages. But the practice the priests attacked most vehemently was polygamy. "Appalled by the host of wives that surrounded every prince or chief, and whom, as they fulfilled for him

all public as well as domestic services, it had been his constant study to multiply," a historian wrote, the Portuguese "called upon their converts to select one, and to make a sweeping dismissal of the rest." It proved the most unwise move of all. For polygamy was central to the political and social structure of the Kongo, and the attack on it "was considered an unwarrantable inroad on one of the most venerable institutions of the realm." To the ManiKongo and his nobles, a multiplicity of wives was a measure of their prestige, power, and wealth. It was also a vital political instrument; alliances were made through marriages, transforming rival feudal lords into in-laws. Moreover, it wasn't only the men who supported the practice. As the wives were the primary workers in households, performing a wide variety of domestic chores, they quite liked the idea of being part of a harem; indeed, the larger the harem the better, because this meant the work was shared out among more people.

So, as the Portuguese pressed uncompromisingly for observance of Church doctrine, disaffection with the new religion steadily grew, and so did the anti-Christian, anti-Portuguese faction led by Mpanzu a Nzinga, the ManiKongo's second son. Gathering always more closely around the ManiKongo, warning of the disorders and calamities that would befall the kingdom because of the abandonment of traditional customs, the betrayal of ancestors, the violation of powerful fetishes, this faction ultimately gained the upper hand in the kingdom. Mbemba a Nzinga, the heir apparent, baptized Affonso, remained faithful to the Church and led the Christian faction at the court, and, in the best tradition of court intrigue, Mpanzu set out to destroy his half-brother's influence with their father. Duarte Lopes tells us that Mpanzu "gave the king to understand that Affonso favoured the Christian religion in order to usurp his place." He claimed that Affonso came every night and slept with one of the king's wives, that he used the magic taught by the Portuguese priests to dry up the rivers and injure the fruits of the earth so that the king's territories might not yield their usual revenues.

At last the ManiKongo had had enough. Sometime around 1495 the king renounced the Christian faith and banished Affonso, along with all the Portuguese remaining in Mbanza, to Affonso's province of Nsundi on the banks of the Congo River. It seemed that the Portuguese experiment of alliance with an African kingdom had ended, and quickly, in failure.

We don't know exactly how many new Portuguese expeditions were dispatched to the Congo during this period of anti-Catholic reaction. The chronicles seem to suggest two or three, but in any case there were relatively few. The ManiKongo's apostasy was only partly responsible. For during this period, too, King John II, the great Congo enthusiast, died (in 1495) and his cousin, Manuel the Fortunate, on ascending the throne, sent Vasco da Gama on his successful voyage opening the sea route to India. Then, in 1500, Pedro Álvares Cabral, following da Gama, inadvertently discovered Brazil, and the Congo no longer seemed quite so important. Portuguese ships, money, men, ingenuity, and energy were now diverted to exploiting the rich Indies spice trade, establishing trading posts on the East African and Malabar coasts, and exploring the possibilities of the South American continent.

Affonso, however, even in his exile, remained unshakable in his attachment to Christianity and Portugal. He is said to have destroyed fetishes and driven the fetishers out of his province, observed the mass daily, and taken instruction from the handful of Portuguese priests, soldiers, and artisans who were left with him. Despite his isolation, he appears to have been convinced that his day would come. And it did.

In 1506 or thereabouts, the ManiKongo died. Though Affonso was the rightful heir to the throne, his exile had thrown the succession open to other pretenders, and there was no doubt that Affonso's half-brother, Mpanzu, as leader of the dominant anti-Christian faction, would attempt to seize the crown. A war of succession, between the Christian, modernist faction of Affonso and the pagan, traditionalist faction of Mpanzu, was inevitable as soon as the news of the old Mani-Kongo's death was out. And Affonso was at the disadvantage in this fight: he was far from the capital and he had fewer forces at his command.

But, when the day of reckoning arrived, Affonso found he had a powerful ally in Mbanza. Queen Eleanor, the ManiKongo's principal wife and Affonso's mother, is said to have remained a faithful, if secret, Catholic during the years of the pagan reaction. Be this as it may, it is obvious that she would have wanted her son, rather than the son of one of the ManiKongo's other wives, to inherit the crown. So she conspired to keep the death of the king secret for three days, long enough for Affonso to get to the capital. Duarte Lopes tells the story this way:

In a secret manner she informed her son by runners, who, placed at con-
venient distances, like posts, are always ready to carry the commands of
the king throughout the kingdom, of the death of his father, and that she
would keep it secret till he arrived, begging him to come without delay,
and with as great haste as possible to the court. Therefore, by means of
these same posts, and being carried by slaves, according to the custom of
the country, day and night, he accomplished with marvelous speed the
journey of two hundred miles, and suddenly appeared in the city.

Once there, he revealed the news of the ManiKongo's death and announced his own succession to the throne. And, with amazing aplomb,
he then arranged that his father, the old pagan monarch who had
exiled him for his Christianity, be given a Christian burial.

   Mpanzu, of course, did not accept this passively. Duarte Lopes tells
us that he "collected a great force, and came armed against his
brother, bringing with him the greater part of his subjects, to the
number of nearly 200,000 men." This army was positioned around the
royal city, cutting off all the roads leading to and from it. Then
Mpanzu sent word to Affonso and all who were with him that, if they
did not immediately surrender, recognize him as king, and abandon
Christianity, they would all be slain. Although Affonso, along with the
handful of Portuguese soldiers who still remained with him, had been
able to raise an army of barely 10,000 men to stand against Mpanzu's
hordes, the ultimatum was refused. And so the battle was joined.

   On the following dawn, we read in Duarte Lopes's account,
Mpanzu

led the assault with furious impetus on the side of the city that faces to
the north. . . . Here Dom Affonso, and his handful of men, were ranged
against the pagans and his brother; but before the latter had come face to
face with the king, he was suddenly and entirely routed, and put to flight.
Seeing himself conquered, Mpanzu was greatly amazed, not understanding
the cause of his defeat. Notwithstanding, he returned next day to the
assault in the same place, and again was discomfited in like manner. . . .
Therefore, the people in the city mocked the pagans, and taking heart
from such a victory, no longer feared, but became eager to attack their
adversaries, who told them that they had not won the day themselves, but
owed their victory to the presence of a lady in white, whose dazzling
splendour blinded the enemy, whilst a knight riding on a white palfrey,
and carrying a red cross on his breast, fought against them and put them
to flight. On hearing this, Dom Affonso sent to tell his brother that these

were the Virgin Mary, the mother of God, whose faith he had received, and St. James, who were sent from God to his aid.

Nonetheless, Duarte Lopes tells us, Mpanzu continued to fight, attempting to assault the city from two different positions. But the results were the same; the miracle of Christianity was unassailable, and finally,

being overcome by fright, Mpanzu rushed headlong into the ambush covered with stakes, which he had himself prepared for the Christians, and there, almost maddened with pain, the points of the stakes being covered with poison, and penetrating his flesh, ended his life.

This is, of course, a Portuguese Christian account of the event, written at a time of militant Catholicism, and obviously needs to be taken with a grain of salt. The miracle that allowed Affonso's inferior forces to prevail against the pagan hordes of his half-brother was more likely the presence of Portuguese firearms in his ranks than the visions of the Virgin and saint in the clouds. But no matter; Affonso's astonishing victory over his half-brother was perceived as a victory for Portuguese and Christian power, a power that the new ManiKongo, King Affonso, had allied to himself. And so, with his ascendancy to the throne, Europe got an unparalleled opportunity on the African continent.

8

THE FOREST OTHELLO

"A native of the Congo knows the name of only three kings; that of the present one, that of his predecessor and that of Affonso."

So wrote a Catholic missionary, Father Antonio Barroso, more than 300 years after the coronation of this ManiKongo. That long-lasting fame was well deserved, for Affonso was an extraordinary figure, not only in terms of his own kingdom or even of Africa, but, in a special way, on the world stage as well. He was as imposing and memorable as an Othello in his pride and ambition, and in his innocence and tragic betrayal as well, a man not merely years but literally centuries ahead of his time.

There is no way we can write a biography of this remarkable African monarch; the materials simply are not available from so remote a time and place. What we can safely assume, though, is that he was in his late twenties or early thirties when he ascended the Kongo throne. We can imagine him as tall and muscular, clean shaven, with his hair close cropped, noble in feature as befits the descendant of at least a half a dozen Bakongo kings. We can assume that he was physically strong, tempered as he was in jungle wars, and we know that he was intellectually brave, considering how fiercely he held to Christianity, suffering for his beliefs and persisting in them until he finally triumphed. We also know that, in a way no African would be until the European colonists of the twentieth century started sending their charges to Oxford and the Sorbonne, he was an educated and literate man in the strictest European sense.

Some fifteen years had passed between his baptism and his coronation, and throughout those years, especially during his exile, he studied with the Portuguese priests and artisans whom he had kept

close around him, learning everything he could of the civilization of Christian Europe. A Portuguese priest, Rui d'Aguiar, in the early years of Affonso's reign, described him in a letter to King Manuel of Portugal in this way:

May Your Highness be informed that his Christian life is such that he appears to me not as a man but as an angel sent by the Lord to this kingdom to convert it, especially when he speaks and when he preaches. For I assure Your Highness that it is he who instructs us; better than we he knows the prophets and the Gospel of Our Lord Jesus Christ and all the lives of the saints and all things regarding our Mother the Holy Church, so much so that if Your Highness could observe him yourself, you would be filled with admiration. He expresses things so well and with such accuracy that it seems to me that the Holy Spirit speaks always through his mouth. I must say, Lord, that he does nothing but study and that many times he falls asleep over his books; he forgets when it is time to dine, when he is speaking of the things of God.

It is impossible to gauge the true depth of Affonso's belief in the Catholic faith. Unquestionably he professed and practiced it with zeal, and equally unquestionably he understood it not only in its ceremonial and miraculous aspects but in its finest metaphysical nuances as well. But whether this means that he was convinced of its eternal truth we really don't know and, in fact, have some reason to doubt. But what cannot be doubted is that he recognized in a way that his predecessor had not—and as no African leader would until the twentieth century—that European knowledge, which was embodied then in the Catholic Church, was of immense potential value to himself and to his people. In his time and place, Affonso was a modernist, an apostle of new ideas, a bold innovator and reformer, and one can only wonder where he got that from. He believed in education, admired technology, wanted trade, and throughout his reign he remained steadfastly dedicated to bringing these benefits of European civilization to the Kongo. And he was convinced that the way to do it was by the evangelization of his kingdom.

His reign began auspiciously. To be sure, after the fratricidal war by which he won his throne, there was a brief bloody period during which Affonso's pagan enemies were put to death or driven into exile. But Affonso was anxious not to split his kingdom into warring factions, and he moved quickly to heal the wounds of the religious war. For example, he singled out the *ne vunda,* the chief earth priest and

witch doctor in the kingdom, who, in his natural opposition to Christianity, had been Mpanzu's major ally, and not only granted him a pardon but restored him to religious power in the capital by putting him in charge of the construction and maintenance of the churches and the furnishing of the holy water for the baptismal rites.

Moreover, in another effort to win over the pagan faction, he agreed to a particularly grisly ceremony, which traditionally confirmed the ascendance of a new ManiKongo. Harking back to the sacredly violent act of a Nimi a Lukeni, by which the legendary founder of the kingdom established his divine isolation, the rite required the new sovereign to bury alive one of his relatives and so demonstrate his position above the common law. That Affonso performed this ritual and participated in other pagan practices—he was, for example, almost surely polygamous throughout his life—may justify questioning just how deeply his Christian convictions ran. But it may be fairer to recognize even in this his remarkable modernism. For, as the Church itself was to do elsewhere in similar circumstances, he was sensible enough to bend the rules of Christianity to make it compatible with older sacred forms and thus give it a better chance of flourishing.

Central to Affonso's plans was restoration of relations with Portugal. The band of Portuguese who had been left behind by Rui de Sousa had dwindled to a mere handful; if Affonso was to realize his ambition of bringing European Christian civilization to the Kongo he needed to have more priests and artisans and teachers. And, as fate would have it, not long after his coronation—it appears to have been in 1507—one of those caravels which Portugal occasionally dispatched to the Congo, commanded by a certain Gonçalo Rodrigues Ribeiro, called at the river's mouth. Affonso seized the opportunity. He loaded Ribeiro's ship with gifts—copper jewelry, elephant tusks, parrots, civet cats, raffia cloth, and slaves—for King Manuel and sent to Lisbon aboard it the last remaining Portuguese priests in his kingdom along with his own son, baptized Henrique, and some other young Kongo nobles. The priests he charged with asking the Portuguese king for more missionaries and technicians; as for the youths, he asked the Portuguese king to provide them with a full education in Christianity and Portuguese civilization.

Portuguese enthusiasm for the alliance with the Kingdom of Kongo never revived to the level that had existed under King John II.

Manuel was far too busy with the burgeoning Indies trade and the development of Brazil, and the experience with the apostasy of the previous ManiKongo had been a souring one. Nonetheless, the arrival of Ribeiro's caravel with its rich cargo of gifts and the message from the long-lost Portuguese priests about Affonso's devout Christianity and zealous desire for Portuguese aid sparked a renewed interest to which Manuel couldn't help but respond. Affonso's son Henrique and the other Kongo nobles were enrolled in the college of the Santo Eloi cloister in Lisbon, and 15 priests from there, along with a company of artisans, craftsmen, soldiers, and teachers, were sent to Mbanza.

The Christianization of the Kongo was underway. Determined to create a literate class, Affonso concentrated on education. As early as 1509, we are told, mission schools for 400 students, including, remarkably enough, women, had been built in Mbanza, and by 1516, the priest Rui d'Aguiar reported the presence of more than 1000 students in the capital, "sons of noblemen" who were not only learning to read and write but were studying grammar, the humanities, and technology "as well as the things of faith." Moreover, in those first few years of Affonso's reign, every Portuguese ship that called at the Congo returned to Lisbon carrying Bakongo youths to be educated at Santo Eloi. At the same time, the conversion of the people grew apace. Duarte Lopes tells us that the priests "with much charity and zeal, disseminated the Catholic faith, which was received alike by everyone in the kingdom. The priests themselves were treated with as great reverence as if they were saints, being worshipped by the people on their knees, who kissed their hands and asked benediction every time they met them."

Using the technology of the Portuguese artisans, Affonso undertook something of an urban development program in the royal capital. The city was enclosed by a wall and both the Portuguese quarter and the king's enclosure were also walled off. Churches were built, the streets were straightened and lined with trees, houses were constructed of ironstone and came to cover an area of over 20 square miles, and the population there grew to more than 100,000. In addition, Affonso had the Portuguese introduce new food plants to improve his people's diet, including such fruit-bearing trees as the guava, lemon, and orange as well as maize, manioc, sugar cane, which Portuguese expeditions had brought back from Brazil and Asia. And they imported their tools and weapons, sabers and swords, muskets and mortars, and

taught the Bakongo how to manufacture and use them.

As for Affonso personally, he seems to have become more and more "Portuguese," at least in formal appearance and behavior, with every passing year. For example, he and his court adopted the Portuguese style of dress, wearing, as Duarte Lopes reports, "cloaks, capes, scarlet tabards, and silk robes. . . . They also wear hoods and capes, velvet and leather slippers, buskins, and rapiers at their sides. . . . The women also have adopted the Portuguese fashions, wearing veils over their heads, and above them black velvet caps, ornamented with jewels, and chains of gold around their necks." Portuguese titles were taken up: the king's sons became princes, the chiefs of the principal provinces dukes, while lesser nobles became marquises, counts, and barons. And Portuguese rules of etiquette and protocol were introduced. For example, Affonso abandoned the traditional rule that the ManiKongo could not be seen eating or drinking. Instead, imitating the Portuguese custom, he ate in public and, as Duarte Lopes notes,

Preparations for the coronation of the ManiKongo

"he always eats alone, no one ever sitting at the table with him, and the princes stand around with heads covered." He even adopted a royal coat of arms, prepared for him by the Portuguese, "for us to use as ensigns on our shields," we read in a letter Affonso wrote to the lords of his provinces around 1512, "as the Christian kings or princes of those lands generally carry so to show to whom they belong and whence they come."

One needs perhaps to step back for a moment and remind oneself what a really astonishing thing all this was. For here was the start of a genuine partnership, an alliance struck in peace and friendship, based on mutual respect between two nations an ocean apart, in which the two monarchs treated with each other as equals despite the difference in the color of their skins and in the character of their civilizations. One cannot help wondering what might have been, how Europe and America's relations with Africa would have been influenced in the centuries that followed, if this promising start, forged almost single-handedly by Affonso, had become what this remarkable African king's soaring vision dreamed it could be. But it didn't. It was doomed to fail almost at the outset. And what doomed it was the slave trade.

One must be very quick to say that neither Portugal nor any other European nation introduced slavery to Africa. African tribes and kingdoms, and not least among them the Kingdom of Kongo, slaved for as long ago as there is any record or memory. But one must be just as quick to point out that there was a vast difference between the slavery of Iron Age Africa and the slavery brought to Africa by Europe in the sixteenth century.

The African's slave was of course not a free man and his status certainly was inferior to that of a free man. But he was not a chattel slave as that term came to be understood in the subsequent centuries; he was not stripped of his property or human dignity or all his rights. He was rather what might more appropriately be called a serf or vassal or perhaps an indentured servant, a condition common enough to Christians during the Middle Ages. And it was a status to which he fell in much the same way Christians did in feudal Europe: in punishment for a crime—thieves, murderers, and adulterers were usually enslaved—by being taken prisoner in a war, or by being offered as tribute from a subjugated tribe to a dominant one. Once his status as a free man had been lost in some manner such as these, the slave or serf was required to perform work for his master (as a vassal peasant, for in-

stance, or artisan, soldier, or house servant) . But the amount of work
he performed and, more importantly, the duration of his enslavement
depended on the way he had become a slave in the first place. Africa
did not have the concept of perpetual enslavement. Slavery there was
almost always for a specified period of time, much like a prison sentence, commensurate with the nature of the crime, the circumstances
of capture, or the conditions agreed on between tribes. What's more,
every slave enjoyed the possibility of earning time off for good behavior or purchasing freedom outright with goods acquired during
that free time in which he was not required to work for his master.
Moreover, during his servitude the slave could not be abused; he was
regarded with respect and often became a confidant or trusted advisor of his master. And he was always free to marry, raise children,
and run his own household.

It is true that Islam introduced a much harsher form of slavery to
Africa. The Moslem traders, feeling no restraint in dealing with infidels, did take blacks into perpetual slavery, castrating the men and
totally denying them rights to property or anything else. But these
slavers had not yet succeeded in penetrating the forests of the Congo
River basin, and the Kingdom of Kongo was unaware of such cruel
practices. It was left to the Portuguese to teach it to them.

As we've seen, the Portuguese began slaving in Africa in a comparatively benign manner. After a brief, initial period of violent,
chaotic slave raids, the caravel captains settled down to a rather organized and peaceable trade, buying from African middlemen who
brought slaves—enslaved under the accepted rules and traditions of
Africa—down from the interior to the Portuguese posts on the coast.
The numbers remained limited; the greater trading interest still lay
in the gold dust, ivory, pepper, and other more seemly natural products of the continent. What's more, the slaves that were taken back to
Portugal were treated with a measure of human dignity. That they
were regarded as human beings and not as some highly developed
species of animal, as they would be later, is testified to by the fact that
the Portuguese always insisted on converting them to Christianity.

This was all to change from the beginning of the sixteenth
century onward, and what brought about the change was, of course,
the European discovery of new worlds. The opening of the rich Indies
trade sharply diminished Portuguese interest in Africa's comparable
natural products, making slaves the single most valuable commodity

the continent had to offer. And the settlement of the West Indies and the Americas, with their slave-worked mines and plantations, drastically escalated the demand for this valued commodity. No longer would the modest numbers of slaves taken from the coast be sufficient; therefore, no longer would the methods used to acquire these numbers be sufficient. Slaving was to become big business, the main business for Europe in Africa for the next four hundred years. Slaving fever, hyped by the huge profits to be made in the bloody business, was to seize white men everywhere near or on the continent, and the changed nature of slaving would doom Affonso's dream and destroy his kingdom.

It began on São Tomé, an island in the Gulf of Guinea some 600 miles northwest of the Congo's mouth off the coast of present-day Gabon. The Portuguese discovered it in the 1470s and, because it was uninhabitated and had a relatively healthy climate, attempted to settle it beginning in the 1490s. It was first used as a penal colony. Later, criminals were granted freedom if they accepted exile there, and they were soon followed voluntarily by adventurers and disreputable characters of every stripe who needed, for whatever reason, to flee Portugal. With the opening of the sea route to the Indies, São Tomé became a major port-of-call for the Indiamen and its economy boomed. The settlement grew to about 10,000. Sugar and coffee plantations were established, and to work them the São Tomistas began buying slaves along the Benin coast. Then, when the colonization of the Americas escalated the demand for slaves, the island's traders got into the business in a big way, moving always further southward down the coast, until by the early 1500s they were plying the trade in the Kingdom of Kongo.

In order to encourage the island's development at the outset, the Portuguese crown had leased it to a chartered trading company organized by a certain knight of the court named Fernão de Mello. As *donatário* (proprietor-general) of the company, de Mello was in effect governor of São Tomé. Formally, he was a subject of King Manuel, but Portugal was just too far away to exercise any real control over him. De Mello was the law on the island—indeed, very much a law unto himself. He ignored the crown with impunity and ruled his settlement of rogues and vagabonds with an iron hand, very much as he pleased.

By all accounts, he was a viciously avaricious and venal man. He

was determined to monopolize all the trade with the adjacent African coast and exploit the slave trade particularly to its fullest potential. Not for him was the traditional modest business of sending ships to the established slaving posts on the coast, such as the one that had developed at Mpinda at the Congo's mouth, there to buy the limited number of slaves that African middlemen had brought down from the interior for sale. De Mello's traders opened their own slaving depots and, bypassing the coastal middlemen, struck inland to do their business at the traditional slave markets of the interior. And they introduced new ways of doing that business. Since prisoners of war could be enslaved, they fomented wars. Since criminals could be enslaved, they promoted crime. They corrupted chiefs and headmen with gifts of firearms, cloth, and alcohol, developing in them a lust, almost an addiction, for these goods, and then used them as they chose. They led Africans on slave raids, induced rebellions against the vested authorities, and in short enough order began wreaking havoc in the Congo forests.

As early as 1511, we find Affonso appalled at what the São Tomé slavers were doing in his realm. In the first of what was to be a virtually endless stream of letters to reigning Portuguese monarchs, of which twenty-two have survived, the ManiKongo requested King Manuel to send a Portuguese ambassador to the Kongo with the power to control the atrocious behavior of the white men in his kingdom. Manuel responded to this request but he responded for reasons of his own, reasons which Affonso, in his noble innocence, never entirely grasped. For, with the boom in the demand for slaves, Manuel had taken a new interest in the Kongo. Slaving the kingdom, he realized, could prove an immensely profitable commercial proposition, which he did not enjoy seeing fall into the hands of the greedy, defiant *donatário* of São Tomé. He wanted it for himself. De Mello's activities were to be limited to the Guinea coast; the Kongo was to become a trade monopoly of the Portuguese crown. And the best way to accomplish that, Manuel decided, was by shoring up his alliance with the ManiKongo, an alliance which he still considered as one between equals.

"Most powerful and excellent king of Manycongo," Manuel wrote in reply to Affonso's request, "We send to you Simão da Silva, nobleman of our house, a person whom we most trust. . . . We beg you to listen to him and trust him with faith and belief in everything he says

from our part." Da Silva was sent out in command of an expedition of five ships, the largest ever dispatched to the Kongo, which carried to Affonso more missionaries, technicians, soldiers, books, tools, church furniture, and above all, a *regimento,* a fascinating document that Manuel had designed to formalize relations between the European and African kingdoms. It was cast in the form of instructions to da Silva, who was to serve as the Portuguese ambassador to the Kongo court. The first group of instructions outlined the kind of assistance Portugal was prepared to extend to the Kongo in such matters as education, missionary work, political, technical, and military affairs. The next group addressed itself directly to the abuses of which Affonso had complained. Saying "our plans can be carried out only with the best people," Manuel empowered da Silva to arrest and expel those Portuguese in the Kongo who did not lead exemplary lives.

But a group of instructions also dealt with the Kongo's obligations to Portugal in return for this assistance. "This expedition," Manuel wrote, "has cost us much; it would be unreasonable to send it home with empty hands. Although our principal wish is to serve God and the pleasure of the Manikongo, nonetheless you [da Silva] will make him [Affonso] understand—as though speaking in our own name— what he should do to fill the ships, whether with slaves or copper or ivory." In addition, da Silva was instructed to get Affonso to make regular annual payments of such commodities to Portugal in return for the aid. And finally da Silva was ordered to determine the present and potential value of the Kongo trade and set about organizing it as a royal monopoly between the Portuguese and Kongo kings, cutting de Mello and his São Tomistas out of it entirely.

The da Silva expedition reached the Congo's mouth in 1512. On the outbound journey, however, it called at São Tomé, as did all ships sailing these seas at that time, so de Mello, through his spies and informers, had learned the contents of Manuel's *regimento,* and by the time da Silva's first ship reached Mpinda the São Tomista slavers there were ready to stir up trouble. Exactly what kind of trouble it is hard to make out from the chronicles, but it was evidently so threatening that da Silva refused to leave his ship and instead sent the ship's physician to Mbanza to secure some protection from Affonso. But, by the time that protection could reach him, da Silva was dead of fever, and so it fell to the captain of the expedition's second ship, Álvaro Lopes, to deliver the *regimento* to Affonso, take up the office of ambassador at

the ManiKongo's court and set about trying to enforce its provisions.

It proved an impossible task. De Mello and the São Tomistas had defied the Portuguese king before and they were prepared to defy him now. Certain that Manuel was too far away to protect the crown's trading monopoly, their slaving gangs arrogantly ravaged the Kongo's forests, sowing violence, creating terror, inducing tribal chiefs and province lords, in their turn, to defy their king. What's more, taking advantage of São Tomé's geography astride the seaway to and from Portugal, they set about interposing themselves between Affonso and Manuel. De Mello had every ship bound from the Kongo to Lisbon searched, and he wasn't above delaying, turning back, or even imprisoning, enslaving, or killing messengers and ambassadors from the ManiKongo to the Portuguese king, ultimately cutting off the royal brothers of the alliance from each other.

The Portuguese in Mbanza were swiftly infected by São Tomé's defiance and slaving fever, and they split into bitterly contending factions on the issue of the crown's trading monopoly. There were some who remained loyal to Manuel and Affonso but the far larger number joined the São Tomistas, unable to resist the huge profits to be made in the freebooting slave trade. The masons, carpenters, teachers, and other artisans in the royal capital bought or took payment in slaves and assembled the coffles in caravans to be driven down to Mpinda for sale to the slaving caravels from the island that called there. Even the priests, men initially so revered by the Bakongo as to be treated as saints, soon followed the lead of their secular colleagues. They abandoned their cloister, set up housekeeping with black concubines and joined in the bloody business with zeal, not only neglecting but in fact enslaving their catechists.

The story is told that de Mello bribed one of these corrupt priests, who then, using the threat of excommunication, set about the evil work of sowing discord among the nobles of Affonso's court and luring them into the São Tomista camp. His activities so infuriated Álvaro Lopes, the Portuguese ambassador there, that, in a fit of rage, he killed the priest. The murder played right into the São Tomistas' hands. Expressing self-righteous indignation, they demanded the crime be punished, and Lopes was exiled to the penal colony on São Tomé, never to be heard from again. Then the São Tomistas contrived to have one of their own number installed as the Portuguese ambassador, and the ugly situation in the capital deteriorated even further.

One can visualize Mbanza turning into a sort of wide-open frontier boom town: The priests living with mistresses, their missionary work an utter sham, and every white man in the place neglecting his duties to make his fortune out of human flesh. Corrals were built in the main square, hard by the churches, in which slaves were assembled before being driven down to the coast. As the methods as well as the intensity of the trade got further beyond the pale, slave revolts became commonplace. We read of one slave caravan, organized by a priest and some masons, that rebelled and ran amok through the royal capital, setting fire to and pillaging the Portuguese quarter.

Although, at any one time, there probably were never more than 200 Portuguese in Mbanza, their impact was all out of proportion to their numbers, and the corruption they brought spread quickly to the Bakongo. The nobles of the court and the educated elite, aping the Portuguese in dress and manners, conspired with the contending white factions for or against Affonso, sold their servants and members of their households, and organized slave raids with Portuguese gunmen. The hundreds, and then thousands, of mulatto offspring of the loose-living whites who swarmed the capital became agents of the slave traders, bully-boy enforcers, petty officials, and lesser members of the corrupted clergy. From their female ranks, prostitutes were recruited for the Mbanza brothels, and with the introduction of that profession, until then unknown in the Kongo, was introduced what the Bakongo called *chitangas,* venereal diseases, which ravaged the black population as the tropical diseases ravaged the white, heightening the terrible mood of moral decay. "The climate is so unhealthy for the foreigner," a Portuguese trader in Mbanza wrote in 1515 (and by climate we can take him to mean the word in its broadest definition) ,

that of all those who go there few fail to sicken and of those who sicken few fail to die, and those who survive are obliged to withstand the intense heat of the torrid zone, suffering hunger, thirst, and many other miseries, for which there is no relief save patience, of which much is needed, not only to tolerate the discomforts of such a wretched place but what is more to fight the barbarity, ignorance, idolatry, and vices which seem scarcely human but rather those of irrational animals.

It was at this point that Portugal can be said to have betrayed Affonso. For, having issued his *regimento,* blueprinting the alliance of equals between the two kingdoms and the obligations each owed the other, Manuel failed to live up to his part of it. Neither he nor his

successor—King John III ascended the Portuguese throne in 1521— made any move to control the rapacious São Tomé slavers or discipline the defiant Portuguese in Mbanza. Rather, they stood aside and watched with cold, calculating eyes the havoc wreaked.

Once again one must note the increasing demands made on the Portuguese crown by its other overseas enterprises, its heavy expenditures in ships, men, and material for the development of the Indies, Brazil, and East Africa. But that serves as only a partial explanation for Portugal's betrayal of the bargain it struck with Affonso. Bluntly put, no sooner had the *regimento* been formulated than the Portuguese crown decided that to honor it was not really in its own best interest. The hard commercial truth of the matter, which quickly enough dawned on the Portuguese king, was that the chief value of the Kongo was as a source of slaves. The hope that the Congo River would prove a pathway to the kingdom of Prester John and the Indian Ocean was no longer operable; the Indian Ocean had been reached years before, and Ethiopia, the realm of the Christian African monarch, had by this time been entered from the East African coast. No, what the Kongo had of special and increasing worth was its population, and, to exploit it, the *regimento* was hardly necessary. Quite the contrary; the modernization of the Kongo, the evangelization and education of its peoples, could only make the slaving more difficult, both in practice and in conscience. The Portuguese king's only regret was that it was de Mello and the São Tomistas who were harvesting those slaves and not he. But that too could be changed—and in time it was. In 1522, the Portuguese king disenfranchised de Mello, and took over São Tomé as a crown colony. The ruthless slave trade continued unabated—by the 1530s at least 5000 slaves a year were being shipped from Mpinda alone—and, except for sporadic, empty gestures, Portugal abandoned Affonso.

It was at this point that Affonso revealed the tragic extent of his innocence. For he seemed unable or at least unwilling to grasp Portugal's motives and intentions; he refused to believe that the Portuguese kings could betray the Christian principles they professed. Again and again we find him, heartbreakingly and naïvely, appealing to his royal brother to heed those principles, to honor their alliance.

As early as 1515, Affonso asked the Portuguese king to simply hand over to him in fief the island of São Tomé so that he could control its abuses. When this request was ignored, he then asked for a ship of his

own. This was to be a recurring theme in his correspondence with the Portuguese crown. "Most powerful and most high prince and king my brother," a letter of 1517 begins, "I have already written to you how much I need a ship, and telling you how grateful I would be if you would let me buy one." He obviously believed that with his own ship he would be able to circumvent São Tomé and enter into direct communication with Portugal without the hated island's interference. "Most high and most powerful prince and king my brother, it is due to the need of several things for the church that I am importuning you. And this I would not probably do if I had a ship, since having it I would send for them at my own cost." But no matter how he couched his request for a vessel, or for the means of building one of his own, it was always refused or ignored.

Affonso sought to break out of his geographical confinement by trying to contact the only other European power he had any specific knowledge of—the Vatican. His son Henrique had been in Rome since 1513 and, with Manuel's agreement, the ManiKongo arranged to have the youth consecrated a bishop by Pope Leo X in 1518. It was a truly historic event; no black man would attain such an exalted rank in the Church for another four centuries. But Affonso's hope that this would open a new avenue for him to Christian Europe was quickly dashed. The Portuguese would allow Henrique to be named only an auxiliary to the Bishop of Madeira, who had his seat on São Tomé, so the Bishop of the Kongo, on returning to Mbanza in 1521, found himself taking his instructions from the hated island. Affonso's subsequent attempts to reach the Pope were also blocked. "We beg you to lend us five thousand *cruzados*," he wrote to John III at one point, "to provide for the expenses for our brother and ambassador . . . who on our behalf goes to see the Holy Father, accepting in exchange one hundred and fifty *cofos* of coins of our Kingdom with which slaves can be bought [in repayment for the loan]." It was refused.

But perhaps the clearest illustration of Portugal's betrayal of Affonso came with its steadily diminishing willingness to provide technical aid and material for the modernization and evangelization of the African realm. Affonso year after year wrote in vain requesting priests and missionaries, teachers and technicians, church artifacts and tools.

It happens that we have many and different diseases which put us very often in such a weakness that we reach almost the last extreme; and the same happens to our children, relatives and others owing to the lack in this

country of physicians and surgeons. . . . We have neither dispensaries nor drugs which might help us in our forlornness. . . . We beg you to be kind and agreeable enough to send two physicians and two apothecaries and one surgeon.

They were not sent. The grand experiment of Europeanizing the African kingdom ground to a halt and, because of the ravages of the slavers, the Kongo fell into a state far more chaotic and primitive than it had ever been before the Portuguese arrived.

By 1526 the situation was catastrophic. The Portuguese were totally out of hand but, worse yet, the Kongo nobles and chieftains, following the white man's example, were breaking loose from Affonso's control. Insubordination was rife in Mbanza, the Mani-Kongo's commands were defied throughout the realm, and wars between villages, tribes, provinces, and vassal kingdoms, incited to promote slaving, raged in the Congo forests.

The excessive freedom given by your factors and officials to the men and merchants who are allowed to come to this Kingdom . . . is such . . . that many of our vassals, whom we had in obedience, do not comply [Affonso wrote to King John III]. We can not reckon how great the damage is, since the above-mentioned merchants daily seize our subjects, sons of the land and sons of our noblemen and vassals and relatives. . . . Thieves and men of evil conscience take them because they wish to possess the things and wares of this Kingdom. . . . They grab them and cause them to be sold; and so great, Sir, is their corruption and licentiousness that our country is being utterly depopulated . . . to avoid this, we need from your Kingdoms no other than priests and people to teach in schools, and no other goods but wine and flour for the holy sacrament; that is why we beg your Highness to help and assist us in this matter, commanding the factors that they should send here neither merchants nor wares, because it is *our will that in these kingdoms there should not be any trade in slaves nor market for slaves.*

When this letter too went unanswered, Affonso issued an edict banning slaving in the Kongo and expelling all Portuguese who participated in the slave trade. It was an inflammatory and ultimately vain command. Both the black and white slavers not only ignored it; they seized upon it to stir up new intrigues against the ManiKongo and, within four months of the edict's promulgation, Affonso was forced to revoke it. He settled then instead for the creation of a sort of

slaving board, which was meant to inspect all coffles before they were shipped to São Tomé to make sure that the slaves had been taken by accepted African practices and not by kidnapping and other illegal means. How effective this was can be seen in one of the last letters Affonso was to write to King John III. The missive accompanied five of Affonso's nephews and one grandson who were going to Lisbon to be educated.

We beg of Your Highness to give them shelter and boarding and to treat them in accordance with their rank, as relatives of ours with the same blood . . . and if we are reminding you of this and begging of your attention it is because . . . we sent from this Kingdom to yours . . . with a certain Antonio Veira . . . more than twenty youngsters, our grandsons, nephews and relations who were the most gifted to learn the service of God. . . . The above-mentioned Antonio Veira left some of these youngsters in the land of Panzamlumbo, our enemy, and it gave us great trouble later to recover them; and only ten of these youngsters were taken to your Kingdom. But about them we do not know so far whether they are alive or dead, nor what happened to them, so that we have nothing to say to their fathers and mothers.

Subsequent records show what happened to those ten: they were seized and enslaved on São Tomé and shipped to Brazil.

Nonetheless, Affonso never could bring himself to give up his innocent trust in the Catholic rulers of Portugal. It is said that, with increasing age and repeated disappointments, he became something of an eccentric, exaggerating to the point of grotesqueness the Portuguese style and manners at his court. On Easter Day, 1539, an attempt was made on his life. It occurred, ironically enough, while he was at mass. Eight Portuguese traders, led by a corrupt priest, burst into the church and took shots at him with their arquebuses but missed, and after that he became ever more reclusive, dreaming in private his grand dream of bringing the benefits of European civilization to the Kongo while in reality the realm fragmented and plunged ever deeper into the chaos and violence that Europe actually had brought.

Meanwhile, the Congo River remained unexplored. In the *regimento* of 1512, Manuel had specifically instructed his ambassador to Mbanza to investigate the possibility of sailing on the river above the cataracts to discover where it led. And we know that three of his ambassadors—Gregorio Quadra, Balthasar di Castro and Manuel

Pacheco—at different times attempted to carry out these instructions by building and launching brigantines on the Stanley Pool. Affonso, however, blocked all three attempts. He feared that any major expedition into the interior of his country could only lead to more chaos and trouble. However, it didn't much matter. Even had Affonso not prevented it, it is highly unlikely that any of these expeditions could have succeeded, given the reputation white men had made for themselves in the Congo forests. If the terrain and the fevers had not killed off the explorers, the tribesmen, in their fear and hatred of the Portuguese slavers, surely would have.

9

SLAVERS, CANNIBALS, AND A SAINT

While Affonso was still alive, the nobility of his character and his charismatic stature as monarch—if not his policies and politics—held the kingdom of Kongo together in the semblance of an independent, functioning political unity. But, once he died, sometime in 1542 or 1543, the forces of divisiveness that had developed in the half century since the Kongo's discovery burst loose and proceeded to tear the kingdom to pieces.

A battle for succession—between Nkanga Mbemba, baptized Pedro and believed to be Affonso's oldest son, and Nkumbi Mpudi a Nzinga, baptized Diogo and said to be either a second son or a nephew—erupted on Affonso's death and became the battleground for all the contending factions that intrigued around the ManiKongo's throne. It is impossible to reconstruct the politics in Mbanza at the time, who supported whom, how and why, but it appears that Pedro received the backing of the São Tomistas and he managed to take Affonso's crown. But his was a chaotic and short-lived reign. Diogo rallied his forces and, after two years of bloody conflict, he overthrew Pedro and began a 16-year reign of increasing dissolution and disintegration.

Diogo was no primitive savage, no jungle chieftain sprung from the bush. Quite the contrary; he was almost surely one of Affonso's relatives who had been educated at the College of Santo Eloi in Lisbon and was every bit as "civilized" as the old ManiKongo himself. But there the comparison with Affonso ends. For Diogo had no grand vision for the modernization and evangelization of his kingdom. Nor, on the other hand, had he any program for the expulsion of the Portuguese and the return of the Kongo to its original state. He had, in-

deed, no visions or programs of any kind. He was a monarch much like
any number of European kings of that time, beset by all sorts of problems, concerned with fighting off his enemies, maintaining his rule,
and deriving the greatest amount of profit from it.

He was not, for example, opposed to the slave trade that was ravag-
ing his kingdom. What he opposed was the fact that not enough of the
profits of that trade were reaching his royal treasury. And one of his
first actions on gaining the Kongo throne was to send a certain Diogo
Gomes, who seems to have been a mulatto born in Mbanza, to Europe
in an attempt to do something about it.

Gomes's mission was to get the Portuguese to agree to restrict their
trading activities in the Kongo to the port of Mpinda at the Congo's
mouth. The São Tomé slavers—and, to a lesser degree, the white
traders operating out of Mbanza—at this time roamed freely throughout the kingdom and traded directly with local chiefs and other vassals
of the ManiKongo as deep in the interior as the Stanley Pool and as
far south as the forests of today's northern Angola. The ManiKongo
wanted to reorganize the trade so as to confine the white slavers to a
single marketplace on the coast, in this case Mpinda, and force them to
do business strictly through his own Bakongo middlemen. This clearly
was not a scheme to reduce the slave traffic in the kingdom, but designed to give Diogo control over it.

Gomes, not surprisingly, failed in his mission. King John III was
no less eager now to get all the profit he could from slaving the Kongo
than he had been during Affonso's reign, and he turned Gomes down
on the spot. But, as some sort of gesture to the old alliance, he decided
to send four Jesuits to Mbanza, the first Portuguese priests to go out
there in a decade.

Throughout its long association with the Kongo, Portugal or,
more accurately, the Catholic Church never quite gave up its attempts
to Christianize the Bakongo. In the early years of Affonso's reign, the
attempt had a magnificently ambitious dimension to it—nothing less
than the establishment of the faith as the Kongo's church. As time
went on, however, the effort became ever more modest, diminishing to
the rather commonplace business of saving heathen souls from perdi-
tion. But, no matter how ambitious or modest the effort, it was always
a sporadic, intermittent affair, which was constantly being started all
over again from scratch. First the Franciscans came, then the Domini-
cans, then the Austin friars and the canons of Santo Eloi; later it

would be the Augustinians, the Carmelites, and Capuchins, but, no matter by which order, the effort always followed the same dismal cycle: huge enthusiasm and a burst of zealous activity at the outset, and then the good fathers would succumb to the corruption of slavery, and the effort would come to nothing until someone new came along to try it again. Now it was the Jesuits' turn.

We are told that when the Jesuits arrived at Mpinda the Kongo was in such a state of disorder that they had to be escorted by 10,000 armed warriors from the coast up to Mbanza. Nevertheless, they seem to have survived the trip with their enthusiasm intact and embarked on their missionary work with predictable zeal. In the first four months, 2100 baptisms were recorded; a school (those of Affonso's reign had fallen into ruins) was built for 600 students; and three new churches were erected, the principal one of which, dedicated to the Saviour, was called São Salvador, by which name the Jesuits rechristened Mbanza.

But, alas, even so disciplined and intellectual a group as the Jesuits could not resist the temptations of that wide-open, wicked town, and within the year we find them following their predecessors into the degrading business of buying and selling slaves and keeping concubines. And we find them also involving themselves in the political intrigues at the ManiKongo's court. To protect their slaving interests, the fathers allied themselves with the São Tomé faction and turned against Diogo. They attacked him for practicing polygamy, advised John III that he was an obstacle to their missionary work, and recommended that he be replaced. They denounced him from the pulpit as "a dog of little knowledge," and joined a São Tomista plot aimed at ousting him and returning Pedro to the throne. Diogo countered as best he could, first by limiting the Jesuits' activities, then by cutting off their allowances of food and quarantining their mission, finally by expelling them.

The expulsion of the Jesuits gave the Portuguese another self-righteous justification for further defying the ManiKongo. They boycotted Mpinda, then in the control of Diogo's middlemen, and built their own slaving port, Mboma (later more simply called Boma), on the Congo River's estuary. And, pushing further southward down the West African coast, they established yet another slave port in the Bay of Goats on the site of what is today Angola's capital of Loanda, and from there struck an alliance with the ManiKongo's most important

southern vassal—the Ngola or paramount chief of the Ndongo (from whose title the name Angola derives)—and induced him to revolt against the Kongo king. Diogo attempted to put down this revolt by main force. But, though some Portuguese from Mbanza fought on his side, the white forces against him proved far too strong and, in a battle on the Dande River, the Ngola routed the army of the ManiKongo in 1556. The defeat set an inescapable example, and by the time of Diogo's death, in 1561, vassal kings, province lords, tribal chiefs, and even village headmen were entering into separate slaving compacts with the Portuguese and rising in revolt against the Mani-Kongo.

Under the circumstances, the new succession struggle was a horrendous bloodbath. The Portuguese murdered Diogo's designated heir and put a nephew with the glorious name of Affonso II on the throne. This blatant power play seems to have led to a general insurrection, in the course of which Affonso II was assassinated by his brother Bernardo. Bernardo, however, didn't last much longer. He had the bad luck to seize the Kongo throne just at the moment the vassal state of the Bateke were in rebellion, and he was killed in battle against them at the Stanley Pool. His successor was named Henrique, and he went the way of Bernardo, killed in war against another rebelling vassal state. When *his* successor, Álvaro, took the crown in 1568 an even more terrible catastrophe befell the Kongo. Out of the dark forests to the south and east, the fearsome warrior hordes of the cannibalistic Yakas descended on the kingdom.

We don't really know who the Yakas (or Jagas) were. No such tribe or people exists today and there are no accounts of their origins. For all intents and purposes, they seem to have sprung mysteriously full blown on the West African scene in the mid-sixteenth century and, after a brief and terrible history of a hundred years or so, vanished from it just as mysteriously.

The best speculation is that they were a Bantu-speaking people who originated deep in the interior of Central Africa and who might just possibly have been related to the Masai or Galla of present-day Kenya and Tanzania. Why they moved from those highland savannas down through the forests of the Congo River basin toward the Atlantic Coast is unknown, but clearly theirs wasn't a mass migration of a people in search of land. The Yakas weren't farmers; nor were they pastoralists. Their main interest in things agricultural seems to

have been limited to the palm tree, which they cut down by the forestful and tapped to make intoxicating wine. As for being herders, it appears that they slaughtered and immediately ate whatever cattle they could lay their hands on.

No, what they seem to have been, and that apparently from the outset of their mysterious movement toward the West African coast, was a warrior army on the march. Much like the Nguni who came out of the Lake Malawi region to create the great Zulu empire of southern Africa, the Yakas organized themselves onto a permanent war footing early in their migration, lived in small mobile fortified camps, focused their entire social structure around their fighting men, and, attacking by surprise and exercising fierce discipline, conquered tribes more populous than their own. They killed their own babies, burying them alive at birth, so as not to be hindered on their relentless march, and, not unlike the Mamelukes of Egypt, adopted the children of the peoples they conquered and made them warriors in their army. They practiced cannibalism as much for the terror it inspired in their enemies as for the taste of it, and by the time they burst into recorded history they were a desperately feared and formidable military force.

Our best source on the Yakas is the remarkable chronicle of an English sailor who lived among them for nearly two years, called *The Strange Adventures of Andrew Battell.*

Battell was a pirate. In 1589, he shipped out as pilot aboard the privateer *Dolphin,* commanded by a certain Abraham Cocke, who made directly for the coast of Brazil to prey on vessels trading with the Portuguese settlements there. After several adventures in the region of the mouth of the Rio de la Plata, Battell and four mates went ashore to forage for food, were surprised by a gang of Indians in the Portuguese service and taken prisoners. Cocke, seeing what had happened, hastily put to sea, abandoning the men to their fate. Battell was kept prisoner for four months at the Portuguese settlement at Rio de Janeiro, then was shipped in chains to the new slaving port of Loanda on the Angola coast. There he was to spend nearly twenty years as a captive of the Portuguese, some of the time shackled in terrible dungeons, much of it serving as pilot or soldier on Portuguese trading expeditions along the West African coast and in the forests of the interior, attempting several times to escape and enduring extraordinary adventures. It was in the course of one such adventure that Battell fell in among the Yakas, whom he calls the Gagas.

The year was 1600 or 1601. Battell, with a group of Portuguese and mulatto slavers, had been on a trading mission to a tribe some two days' march into the interior from the Angola coast. When they had assembled their caravan and were ready to return to their ship on the coast, the chief of the tribe, a certain Mofarigosat

would not let us go out of his land till we had gone to the wars with him, for he thought himself a mighty man having us with him. For in this place they never saw a white man before, nor guns. So we were forced to go with him, and destroyed all his enemies, and returned to his town again. Then we desired him that he would let us depart; but he denied us, without we would promise him to come again, and leave a white man with him in pawn.

Battell tells us that at first

the Portugals and Mulatos being desirous to get away from this place, determined to draw lots who should stay; but many of them would not agree to it. At last they consented together that it were fitter to leave me, because I was an Englishman, then any of themselves. Here I was fain to stay perforce. So they left me a musket, powder and shot, promising this Lord Mofarigosat that within two months they would come again and bring a hundred men to help him in his wars, and to trade with him. . . . Here I remained with this lord till the two months were expired, and was hardly used, because the Portugals came not according to promise. The chief men of this town would have put me to death, and stripped me naked, and were ready to cut off mine head. But the Lord of the town commanded them to stay longer, thinking the Portugals would come. And after that I was let loose again, I went from one town to another, shifting for myself within the liberties of the Lord. And being in fear of my life among them I ran away.

Battell fled through the jungle only to be captured by a band of Yaka warriors and taken to their camp. "All the town, great and small," he tells us, "came to wonder at me, for in this place there was never any white man seen." The camp was overgrown with baobab trees, cedars, and palms so that its streets

are darkened with them. In the middle . . . there is an image, which is big as a man, and standeth twelve feet high; and at the foot of the image there is a circle of elephants teeth, pitched into the ground. Upon these teeth stand great store of dead men's skulls, which were killed in the wars.

Presently Battell was presented to the Yaka chief whom he calls the Great Gaga Calandola and who

hath his hair very long, embroidered with many knots of Banba shells, which are very rich among them, and about his neck a collar of *masoes,* which are also shells, that are found upon that coast, and are sold among them for the worth of twenty shillings a shell: and about his middle he weareth landes, which are beads made of the ostrich eggs. He weareth a palm cloth about his middle, as fine as silk. His body is carved and cut with sundry works, and every day anointed with the fat of men. He weareth a piece of copper across his nose, and in his ears also. His body is always painted red and white. He hath twenty or thirty wives, which follow him when he goeth abroad; and one of them carrieth his bows and arrows; and four of them carry his cups of drink after him. And when he drinketh they all kneel down, and clap their hands and sing.

Evidently the Great Gaga developed a liking for the Englishman, and especially for his musket. Battell was enlisted in the Yaka army and participated in their wars, burning towns down, drinking palm wine, dancing "and banquetting with man's flesh, which was a heavy spectacle to behold." In time, Battell tells us, "I was so highly esteemed with the Great Gaga, because I killed many negroes with my musket, that I had anything that I desired of him." Battell stayed with them for nearly two years in the hope that, in the course of their rampaging march, "they would travel so far to the westward that we should see the sea again; and so I might escape by some ship." And that did eventually occur, but until it did he was a rare eye-witness to the ways of these mysterious people.

He tells us, for example, that the Great Gaga Calandola

warreth all by enchantment, and taketh the Devil's counsel in all his exploits. . . . He believeth that he shall never die but in the wars. . . . He hath straight laws to his soldiers: for those that are faint-hearted, and turn their backs to the enemy, are presently condemned and killed for cowards, and their bodies eaten. He useth every night to make a warlike oration upon a high scaffold, which doth encourage his people. It is the order of these people, wheresoever they pitch their camp, although they stay but one night in a place, to build their fort, with such wood or trees as the place yieldeth. . . . They build their houses very close together, and have their bows, arrows, and darts standing without their doors; and when they give alarm, they are suddenly all out of the fort. . . .

When they settle themselves in any country, they cut down as many palms as will serve them wine for a month: and then as many more, so that in a little time they spoil the country. They stay no longer in a place than it will afford them maintenance. And then in harvest-time they arise

. . . and do reap their enemy's corn and take their cattle. For they will not sow, nor plant, nor bring up any cattle, more than they take by wars. When they come into any country that is strong, which they cannot in the first day conquer, then their general buildeth his fort, and remaineth sometimes a month or two quiet. For he saith, it is as great wars to the inhabitants to see him settled in their country, as though he fought with them every day. . . . And when the general mindeth to give the onset, he will, in the night, put out some one thousand men: which do ambush themselves about a mile from the fort. Then in the morning the Great Gaga goeth with all his strength out of the fort, as though he would take their town. The inhabitants coming near the fort to defend their country, the Gagas give the watchword with their drums, and then the ambushed men arise, so that very few escape. And that day their General overrunneth the country.

Before the Great Gaga undertook any great enterprise, Battell tells us he would make

a sacrifice to the Devil, in the morning, before the sun riseth. He sitteth upon a stool, having upon each side of him a man witch: then he hath forty or fifty women which stand round about him, holding in each hand a zebra tail wherewith they do flourish and sing. Behind them are great store of petes, ponges, and drums, which always play. In the midst of them is a great fire; upon the fire an earthen pot with white powders, wherewith the men-witches do paint him on the forehead, temples, 'thward the breast and belly, with long ceremonies and inchanting terms. . . . Then the witches bring his Casangula, which is a weapon like a hatchet, and put it into his hand, and bid him be strong with his enemies. And presently there is a man-child brought, which forthwith he killeth. Then are four men brought before him; two whereof, as it happeneth, he presently striketh and killeth; the other he commandeth to be killed without the fort. Here I was by the men-witches ordered to go away, as I was a Christian, for then the Devil doth appear to them, as they say.

The Kongo was helpless against these ferocious people. The Yakas erupted from the forests along the kingdom's southwest frontier, crossed the Kwango River, and began their pillaging advance northward to the royal capital. The ManiKongo Álvaro, his court, the entire Portuguese settlement, and much of the population fled São Salvador in abject terror. The Yakas took the city, set it afire, and slaughtered and ate whoever remained behind. Then they split their army into several regiments and proceeded to overrun the rest of the

realm, massacring the inhabitants, scourging the countryside and looting the villages. Álvaro and his black and white retainers scrambled down to the Congo River and took refuge on one of the islands in the stream.

The chroniclers of the period refer variously to this sanctuary as the Isle of Horses, Hippopotamus Island, and Elephant Island. We cannot tell for sure which of the many islands in the Congo's estuary it might have been, but we know that few of them are large enough to support the thousands of fugitives who must have sought refuge there. One can easily visualize the horrendous situation. The countryside was in turmoil. Hundreds of thousands were homeless, fleeing aimlessly through the forests, crowding down to the banks of the Congo in hopes of finding safety on the islands, while those already there, like survivors on a lifeboat, fought them off and cast them to the crocodiles in the river. Famine soon doubled the misery as the crops were left to rot in the fields or be ravaged by the Yakas. And then the bubonic plague broke out and the refugees, huddled like trapped animals on the islands, died of it by the thousands.

The only beneficiaries of this awful chaos were the slavers. Caravels from São Tomé anchored in the Congo's mouth, and the slavers rowed to the islands, their longboats loaded with food. And, Duarte Lopes tells us, "forced by necessity, the father sold his son, and the brother his brother, everyone resorting to the most horrible crimes in order to obtain food." Even the nobles of Álvaro's court were not above this practice. Lopes tells us, "Those who were sold to satisfy the hunger of the others were bought by the Portuguese merchants . . . the sellers saying that those they sold were slaves, and in order to escape further misery, the latter confirmed the story."

This situation lasted for nearly three years. But finally Álvaro managed to get a message through to the King of Portugal—Sebastião, the grandson of John III—and he responded by ordering the governor of São Tomé, Francisco de Gouvea, to go to the relief of the Kongo. In 1571, de Gouvea arrived at the river's mouth with an army of 600 soldiers, slavers, and assorted adventurers and renegades and, rallying the remnants of the ManiKongo's forces, embarked on a bloody campaign against the Yakas. It lasted for two years and in the end the Yakas were driven out of the kingdom and Álvaro was reinstated as king in São Salvador.

But he was now, in effect, a king without a kingdom. He may have

A. *Paleis des Konings*.

B. *Slaven en Slavinne die uit de Reviere water na de Stadt brengen*.

C. *Kerken*.

D. *Krygs-resting of Sterkte*.

E. *Spring-bron, met zeet zoet water*.

The River Lelunda

D

adt SALVADOR
n het Rijk
O.

the Chief

of

A. The Kings palace.
B. The Slaves men & women which
   carry Water from the River
   to y. City.
C. The Churches.
D. The Block house.
E. a Well Spring of very Sweet water.

RIEVIERE LELUNDA.

View of São Salvador

ruled in São Salvador but hardly anywhere else in the Kongo. The Yakas had been defeated but not destroyed, and they remained a force of chaos and turmoil in the Congo River basin for years. The country-side was stricken by plague and famine and torn apart by wars, every chief and province lord was in open revolt, and slavers, traders, sol-diers of fortune, and adventurers of every ilk infested the realm.

Moreover, the Portuguese, except for a handful of Dominican priests who came with de Gouvea's soldiers to try once again to resur-rect missionary work there, did not return to São Salvador after the fright of the Yaka terror. The slaving ports of Mpinda and Boma on the Congo's estuary thrived, but the main Portuguese base shifted now to Loanda, about 100 miles further south down the coast. In 1576, King Sebastião appointed Paolo Dias de Novais, grandson of the Bar-tholomeu Dias de Novais who had found the way round the southern tip of Africa, *donatário* of Loanda and dispatched him with seven ships and 700 soldiers to build a fort and establish a permanent Portuguese settlement there. This was to be Portugal's—and indeed Europe's—first colonization on the African mainland. For, unlike the settlement in Mbanza, the white presence here was not based on an alliance with a local monarch. Loanda was taken by force. Dias's soldiers embarked on a relentless war, which was to last for more than 30 years, against the tribes and states of the territory, conquering some, subjugating others, making vassals of still others, and, as always, harvesting slaves from among their people. In this war no boundaries were recognized, and the Portuguese soldiers, not infrequently with the cannibalistic Yakas as their allies, struck north into the Kongo and made war against provinces ostensibly under the sovereignty of the ManiKongo.

Álvaro did the best he could to resurrect his kingdom. He offered to become a vassal of the Portuguese crown. He tried to make an alliance with Dias's colony. He sent ambassadors to Lisbon. But all came to nothing; the kingdom continued its pitiable descent into anarchy. When Álvaro died in 1614, the struggle for succession was a bloody and tragic farce. In the next 27 years, eight kings occupied the ManiKongo's throne, one of them a boy barely thirteen years old, while the lords of the provinces made war against each other and conspired against each successive king.

It was during this period that Portugal lost its monopoly on the West African coast. To a large degree this was due to events in Eu-rope. Sebastião had turned out to be a foolhardy king. Trained by the

Jesuits, he visualized himself as a Christian knight and, harking back to the dreams of glory of a bygone era, he led a crusade against the Moorish infidels of Morocco, only to have his army destroyed and himself killed at the battle of Alcazarquivir. He was succeeded on the throne by his uncle, Cardinal Henrique, who, having no heir, was the last of the Aviz kings. On his death, in 1580, Philip II of Spain took the Portuguese crown, and the long so-called Spanish captivity began, involving the Portuguese in Spain's debilitating wars against the English and the Dutch. It is not surprising then that the Portuguese found it increasingly difficult and eventually impossible to protect their African, Brazilian, Indies, and other far-flung enterprises.

But the more important reason that the Portuguese lost their West African monopoly was the slave trade. With the market for slaves booming, and the fortunes to be made from them reaching astronomical proportions, it was impossible to keep other European maritime nations out of the lucrative traffic.

As early as the 1560s, French and English pirates were regularly raiding the African coast and seizing the cargoes of Portuguese merchantmen. We have the account of one such pirate, a certain John Hawkins, who "put off and departed from the coast of England in the month of October 1562 and . . . passed to the coast of Guinea . . . where he stayed some time and got into his possession, partly by the sword and partly by other meanes, to the number of three hundred Negroes at the least" from five different Portuguese vessels. Then he "sayled over the ocean sea to the iland of Hispaniola," where he went from port to port selling his cargo, for which he received "such quantities of merchandise, that he did not onely lade his owne three shippes with hides, ginger, sugars, and some quantities of pearles, but he fraighted also two other hulkes with hides and like commodities." We know that Hawkins sailed at least two more times, in 1564 and 1567, with like success, and when England went to war with Spain (and, perforce, Portugal) she gave her blessings to such pirates (Hawkins was knighted). In the 1580s and 1590s, Queen Elizabeth granted royal charters to companies to trade on the Barbary Shore, the Senegambia coast and Sierra Leone. In 1618, James I chartered 30 London merchants, who called themselves the Company of Adventurers of London Trading into Parts of Africa, to do business on the Guinea Coast; and in 1672 Charles II created the Royal African Company to trade from Morocco to the Cape.

The French followed suit, creating companies to exploit the mouths of the Sénégal and Gambia rivers, and hot on their heels came the Danes and Swedes and Prussians. In time all these countries would become major slavers along the entire West African coast. But for the moment they concentrated their activities on the coastline north of the equator. It was the Dutch who emerged in the first half of the seventeenth century to challenge the Portuguese south of the line.

In the 1570s, the Dutch were also at war with Portugal's Spanish king. Having just recently revolted against Philip II, they were fighting desperately to retain their independence, and were quite willing to carry the conflict to Africa. A highly efficient commercial and maritime people, they quickly realized that the best way to break into the rich trade was not by the interloping tactics of the English and the French but by following the Portuguese example and building settlements, forts, and factories on the coast itself. The first Dutch vessel to trade on the Guinea coast of which we have any record was in 1595, and by 1612 the Dutch had built their first African trading post. Five years later, making a deal with a local chieftain, they got permission to build two forts on an island called Goree smack in the middle of the Portuguese-held Cape Verde group, and then built a factory at Rufisque on the mainland opposite these islands. Emboldened by their success both in Africa and in Europe (the English had come to their side in their war against Spain), the Dutch attacked the Portuguese directly in 1637 and in the course of the next five years drove them from the Gold Coast entirely.

The Dutch now moved south of the equator. In August of 1641, an armada of twenty-one Dutch ships appeared off the Angolan coast at Loanda. The Portuguese, apparently, were not caught unawares, but the commander of the garrison made a serious blunder. Watching the Dutch vessels find their way into the harbor and beach at a point beyond the reach of his cannon, he concluded, rather improbably, that the Dutch had come merely to plunder the settlement, not capture it, so he ordered the evacuation of the port. The Portuguese withdrew into the interior to an upcountry post called Massangano to await the departure of the invaders. They, however, did not depart. A Portuguese counter-attack was organized, but the Dutch easily dispersed the force, and the records tell us that 200 Portuguese, including the garrison commander, were taken prisoner. Then a few months later another Dutch fleet sailed into the mouth of the Congo River, attacked

the port of Mpinda and, to confirm their conquest, tore down the stone pillar that Diogo Cão had erected there a century and a half before.

As a chronicler tells us, "the chiefs of the Kongo, Angola and Matamba, who had reason to complain of the Portuguese, rejoiced at their defeat and made common cause with the Dutch." The reigning ManiKongo of the moment, called Garcia II Affonso, entered into an alliance with the Dutch and sought their support in his efforts to stop the secession of the kingdom's vassals and restore control over the realm to the throne in São Salvador. What's more, he was cunning enough to exploit the fact that the Dutch were Protestants, alarming the Vatican about the fate of Catholicism in the kingdom. The Pope responded by sending the Kongo its first non-Portuguese priests, mainly Italian Capuchins. And for a moment it seemed as if the Kongo stood a chance of recovering some of its former glory.

But as abruptly as they had arrived the Dutch departed and the Portuguese returned. By 1648, Dutch interest had shifted to the Indies trade, Asian colonization, and the building of a port-of-call for their Indiamen at the Cape of Good Hope. Meanwhile, the Portuguese had thrown off the Spanish yoke—the House of Braganza, in the person of John IV, had ascended the Portuguese throne—and were eager to reclaim their Kongo holdings. And they reclaimed them with a vengeance in 1665, invading the kingdom outright.

We have the call-to-arms issued by the ManiKongo, Antonio, at the time of this invasion:

Listen to the mandate given by the King sitting on the throne at Supreme Council of war: and it is that any man of any rank, noble or base, poor or rich, provided he is capable of handling weapons, from all villages, towns and places belonging to my Kingdoms, Provinces and Domains, should go, during the first ten days following the issue of this Royal proclamation and public notice, to enlist with their Captains, Governors, Dukes, Counts, Marquises, etc., and with other justices and officials who preside over them . . . to defend our lands, wares, children, women and our own lives and freedoms which the Portuguese nation wants to conquer and dominate.

An army was raised and it marched into battle, carrying flags bearing the cross, and met the Portuguese at a place called Ambouila, near the headwaters of the Bengo River. The date was October 25, 1665.

View of Loanda

The Bakongo were massacred and the ManiKongo was killed and beheaded.

It would not be until the late nineteenth century that Portugal would formally annex the territory of the Kongo kingdom to its colony of Angola. And between the battle of Ambouila and then we could piece together a chronology of perhaps another score of ManiKongos. But, in fact, the battle of Ambouila marked the end of this once impressive African realm. After the death of Antonio, the kingdom shattered into a hundred pieces, and those who claimed the title of ManiKongo were little more than local chieftains who happened to rule in the vicinity of São Salvador. The once royal city itself fell rapidly into ruins. The Bishop of Loanda, who visited it in the 1670s, called it "a den of savage beasts," and by 1690 its churches had all

crumbled into dust and most of the population had fled. In 1701, a
Capuchin priest, Laurent de Lucques, wrote:

The news coming from the Kongo is always worse and the enmities between the royal houses are tearing the kingdom further and further apart.
At present there are four kings of the Kongo. There are also two great
dukes of Mamba; three great dukes in Ovando; two great dukes in Batta,
and four marquises of Enchus. The authority of each is declining and they
are destroying each other by making war among themselves. Each claims to
be chief. They make raids on one another in order to steal and to sell their
prisoners like animals.

Then in the midst of all this despair and desolation there arose improbably a Joan of Arc of the Kongo. Her name was Kimpa Vita,

baptized Beatriz, and the Capuchin Father de Lucques describes her
for us in this way:

This young woman was about twenty-two years old. She was rather slender
and fine-featured. Externally she appeared very devout. She spoke with
gravity, and seemed to weigh each word. She foretold the future and predicted, among other things, that the day of Judgement was near.

His confrère, a Father Bernardo de Gallo, from an interview he conducted with Beatriz, provides us with her own account of how she
discovered her mission:

The event occurred in this manner, she said. When she was sick and on
the point of death, at the last gasp, a brother dressed as a Capuchin appeared to her. He told her he was Saint Anthony, sent by God through
her person to preach to the people, hasten the restoration of the kingdom,
and threaten all those who tried to oppose it with severe punishments.
She died, because in place of her soul, Saint Anthony had entered her head;
without knowing how, she felt herself revive. . . . She arose then and
calling her parents, explained the divine commandment to go and preach,
teach the people, and hasten the departure toward São Salvador. So as to
do everything properly, she began by distributing the few things she
possessed, renouncing the things of this world, as the apostolic missionaries
do. Having done this she went up into the mountain and in complete
liberty fulfilled her duty, as God had commanded her to do, and with
great success.

Thus, in the early eighteenth century, the sect of the Antonians was
born. Within two years this extraordinary young woman developed a
dogma and doctrine, established a rudimentary church, and gathered
an immense following. She claimed Saint Anthony was the second
God, who held the keys to heaven and was eager to restore the Kongo
kingdom. She herself, as Father de Gallo tells us, "Was in the habit of
dying every Friday," in imitation of the passion of Christ, and going
up to heaven "to dine with God and plead the cause of the Negroes,
especially the restoration of the Kongo" and being "born again on
Saturday." She imitated the Virgin as well, and when she had a son she
told Father de Lucques, "I cannot deny that he is mine but how I had
him I do not know: I know however that he came to me from
heaven." She preached that there was a fundamental difference between whites and blacks, saying the former "were originally made
from a certain soft stone called fama" while the latter "came from a

tree called musenda," and her followers wore garments made from the bark of that tree (a species of fig) .

Moreover, she claimed the Kongo was the true Holy Land, that Christ was born in São Salvador and received baptism in Nsundi, that the Virgin "was born of a slave or servant woman of the marquis Nzimba Npanghi" and that Saint Francis belonged "to the clan of the marquis of Vunda." She exhorted her disciples "not to worship the cross because it was the instrument of the death of Christ"; she rejected baptism, confession, and prayer, and declared polygamy legal. She prophesied that the roots of fallen trees would turn into gold and silver, that the reconstructed ruins of São Salvador would reveal mines of precious stones and metals, and that the "rich objects of the Whites" would come to those who followed her faith.

In time, of course, she came to be regarded as a saint with miraculous powers. It was said of her that where she walked twisted or fallen trees straightened; her followers fought to possess anything she touched; the noblest ladies of the realm cleared the paths for her; and the "lords offered her the ends of their capes as mantillas or table-cloths."

Thus it came about [Father de Gallo tells us], that São Salvador was rapidly populated, for some went there to worship the pretended saint, others to see the rebuilt capital, some to see friends, others attracted by the desire to recover their health miraculously, others still out of political ambition and to be the first to occupy the place. In this manner the false saint became the restorer, ruler and lord of the Kongo.

The Capuchins, needless to say, were not happy with Beatriz and the Antonian sect. Nor, for that matter, was the reigning ManiKongo, a puppet in the hands of the Portuguese, named Pedro IV, and with a little prodding from the missionaries he had the young woman arrested. At first, fearing the outrage of popular sentiment, he thought to exile her to Loanda. But the Capuchins, motivated, they tell us, "solely by zeal for the glory of God," wouldn't hear of it, and so the ManiKongo pronounced "a sentence of death by fire on the false Saint Anthony and his guardian angel." The execution took place on July 2, 1706. Both priests were there to describe the scene.

Here is Father de Lucques:

Two men with bells in their hands . . . went and stood in the middle of the great multitude and gave a signal with their bells, and immediately

the people fell back and in the middle of the empty space the basciamu-cano, that is, the judge, appeared. He was clad from head to foot in a black mantle and on his head he wòre a hat which was also black, a black so ugly that I do not believe its like for ugliness has ever been seen. The culprit was led before him. The young woman, who carried her child in her arm, now appeared to be filled with fear and dread. The accused ones sat on the bare ground and awaited their death sentence. We understood then that they had decided to burn the child along with his mother. This seemed to us too great a cruelty. I hastened to speak to the king to see whether there was some way to save him. . . . The basciamucano made a long speech. Its principal theme was a eulogy to the king. He enumerated his titles and gave proofs of his zeal for justice. Finally he pronounced the sentence against Dona Beatriz, saying that under the false name of Saint Anthony she had deceived the people with her heresies and false-hoods. Consequently the king, her lord, and the royal council condemned her to die at the stake, together with the infant. . . . They were led to the stake. The woman did all she could to recant, but her efforts were in vain. There arose such a great tumult among the multitude that it was impossible for us to be of assistance to the two condemned persons. . . . For the rest all we can say is that there was gathered there a great pile of wood on which they were thrown. They were covered with other pieces of wood and burned alive. Not content with this, the following morning some men came again and burned the bones that remained and reduced everything to very fine ashes.

Father de Gallo tells us that Beatriz died "with the name of Jesus on her lips," and then adds: "The poor Saint Anthony, who was in the habit of dying and rising again, this time died but did not rise again." Nor did the Kongo.

Part Three

THE EXPLORATIONS

10

---◆•■•◆---

THE WAY TO TIMBUKTOO

It was now more than 200 years since the voyages of Diogo Cão and, while everything else in the Kongo had been catastrophically changed by them, one thing remained resolutely the same: the Congo River was still unexplored, its source and course and the lands it passed through as much a mystery as they had ever been.

Even the 100 miles of the river's estuary between the Cauldron of Hell and the sea, on which European vessels had trafficked since 1482, remained astonishingly inadequately mapped. We can see by the few mariners' charts of the river that were available in the eighteenth century that even such an obvious feature as the width of the river's mouth was still a matter of uncertainty, some making it as much as 30 miles across, others giving it as less than 10. An even greater degree of uncertainty existed about the falls and cataracts above the estuary. That they were there had been known, of course, ever since Diogo Cão first encountered them, but their full extent and true character had nowhere nearly been determined. As late as 1818, for example, the best that the renowned English geographer Jameson could offer about them, after noting plaintively that they "are nowhere particularly described," was that "They are said, however, to be of great magnitude, and their noise so tremendous, as to be heard at the distance of eight miles." He then went on to suggest, quite inaccurately, that they probably extended into the interior for no more than 70 miles.

As for what lay above the cataracts, that was open to the wildest speculation. Even though Portuguese soldiers, slavers, and missionaries had reached the Stanley Pool in the first decades after the Congo's discovery, this information had somehow been lost in the

intervening years. No map or description of the river in the eighteenth century makes mention of it. The most popular notion of the river's course and its source was that it rose out of a great lake deep in the heart of Central Africa—a lake fed by streams from the Mountains of the Moon and from which the River Nile was also believed to issue—and flowed from there almost due west in an unbroken line to the sea. It was a notion dating back to the fifteenth century (we first come across it on *L'Insularium illustratum Henriei Martelli Germani* of 1489) and, while it is true that the more learned geographers of the eighteenth century were tending to dismiss it at last as "fabulous" (they recognized the geological improbability of a lake outletting by two major rivers, one to the north and the other to the west), their own ideas on the subject were, if anything, even further off the mark. D'Anville, for example, in his celebrated map of Africa of 1731, imagined that the Congo was formed by the union of three rivers, the Kwango flowing from the south, the Vambre flowing from the east and the Bancaro flowing from the north, all joining in a great confluence at the head of the cataracts, with the one from the north probably the Congo's mainstream. But when it came to describing the origin and course of these rivers, he didn't have the smallest idea.

This sort of geographical ignorance was not limited to the Congo. The whole of the interior of Africa remained a blank for eighteenth-century Europe, a blank almost as complete as it had been for Prince Henry and for very much the same reason: no European had ever been there. The brutal terrain, alien climate, killing fevers, and hostile tribes continued to play their devastating part in blocking the white man's way inland, but by the eighteenth century so did something else: an almost total lack of interest in getting there. For a hundred years or more, Europeans had had no incentive for running the risks involved in attempting to penetrate the continent's forbidding interior. For they had organized themselves quite efficiently to get from the relative safety and comfort of their coastal posts the only thing they wanted of Africa: her slaves.

The eighteenth century has been described as the cruelest hundred years of the slave trade. With the European colonies of the New World firmly established and flourishing, the demand for forced labor for the plantations of the West Indies and the Americas had become insatiable. The most conservative estimates have it that no fewer than 7 million and quite possibly as many as 10 million African slaves were

landed in the New World during this bloody century. The Portuguese were still the major slavers of the Congo River basin; they took some 2 million slaves from there between the time of Diogo Cão's discovery and the end of the seventeenth century and shipped at least that many again during the 1700s, mainly to Brazil. But theirs was only a fraction of the total African trade. The Danes, settled in the sugar-rich Virgin Islands, and the French with their colonies in Mauritius, Haiti, and Guadeloupe, accounted for hundreds of thousands more. The Dutch, supplying not only their own colonies in Ceylon, Surinam, and the East Indies but those of other nations in the New World, shipped at least as many as the Portuguese. But it was imperial Britain, newly emerged as the undisputed maritime and mercantile power of Europe, that overwhelmingly dominated the trade, and more than half the slaves taken from Africa during those hundred years were carried in her ships, both to her own and to other's colonies.

Those ships sailed by the hundreds each year on what was called the Great Circuit, carrying cheap manufactured goods from the ports of Liverpool, London, and Bristol to the trading posts strung down the West African coast, there to be traded at handsome profits for slaves. They in turn were carried across the Atlantic, the infamous Middle Passage, to the West Indies and the Americas, where they were exchanged, at still greater profit, for the products of the mines and plantations the slaves worked. And these were then brought back to England to be sold for the most enormous profits of all. "How vast is the importance of our trade with Africa," an anonymous English pamphleteer wrote in 1772; "[it] is the first principle and foundation of all the rest; the main spring of the machine, which sets every wheel in motion."

But there is, of course, something else that needs to be said about the eighteenth century. If it marked the zenith of the slave trade, it also saw the flowering of the Enlightenment. This was, after all, the century of Rousseau and Voltaire, Montesquieu and the *Encyclopédie* of Diderot, of Hume and Swift and the economics of Adam Smith, of Kant and Lessing and Tom Paine. It was the century of such ideas as the Noble Savage and the Rights of Man, such movements as humanitarianism and Protestant nonconformism, such events as the American and French revolutions. Newspapers, periodicals, books, encyclopedias circulated widely and literacy spread as never before. The developments of the previous century—the discoveries of Newton, the ra-

tionalism of Descartes, the empiricism of Bacon—became part of the
mainstream of thought, and the ideas of the age fostered belief in
natural law, universal order, and human reason. It was a century of
immense intellectual creativity and intense scientific curiosity, a century for which both the bloody traffic in slaves and the abysmal ignorance of the African interior were at first paradoxes, then insults, and
finally unacceptable.

Perhaps just because she was the preeminent slaving nation, England gave rise to the antislavery movement. For a century and more,
isolated protests had been heard in the land. For example, in the mid-
seventeenth century, Robert Baxter, a nonconformist preacher, attacked the slave trade in his *Christian Directory,* and George Fox, the
founder of the Society of Friends, made antislavery a tenet of his
Quaker sect. Aphra Behn's novel *Oroonoko,* published in 1678 and
turned into a play by Thomas Southerne in 1696, which described the
miseries of slaves in the West Indies, stirred up the kind of public
outrage that *Uncle Tom's Cabin* would a century and a half later, and
such writers and philosophers of the Enlightenment as Locke, Pope,
Defoe, and Adam Smith, some by satire, others by logical argument,
still others by appeals to humanitarian and religious sentiment, carried the attack well into the eighteenth century. But one can fairly say
that antislavery as a political movement didn't get underway until
1772, and the man who got it moving was a young, well-born civil
servant by the name of Granville Sharp.

At that time there were more than 10,000 African slaves in England. They had been taken there by planters from the West Indies
and the Americas who, regularly traveling back and forth across the
Atlantic, expected to enjoy the services of their blacks in England just
as they did at home in the colonies. The story is told that Sharp, in
1765, came across such a slave who had been savagely beaten by his
master and thrown out into the street. Sharp had the black attended to
and then found him a job. But the slave's master reclaimed him and
then turned around and sold him to a friend. Sharp, very much a child
of the Enlightenment, was outraged. He could not believe that there
was any legal basis for such an action or indeed that English law
sanctioned the owning of slaves in England at all, and it was on this
basis that he set about bringing a challenge to slavery in the courts.

The test case he chose involved a runaway slave named Somersett
who had been recaptured by his master. It was a long and arduous

battle, draining on emotions and finances, and Sharp fought it with tenacity. He was vindicated for his efforts and secured the decision he had so desperately sought. In 1772, the Lord Chief Justice Mansfield handed down the judgment that "the state of slavery is so odious that nothing can be suffered to support it but positive law." And as no such positive law existed at the time, slavery forthwith became unlawful in England and any slave who set foot there automatically became a free man.

It was truly a momentous ruling, and the antislavers were quick to realize—and seize on—the opening it provided. For, after all, if slavery under English law was regarded as too odious to be legally practiced in England, it surely followed that it must be too odious to be legally practiced anywhere or by anyone subject to English law. And around this line of argument a formal antislavery movement crystallized. The Quakers led the way, forming a committee for "the relief and liberation of the Negroe slaves in the West Indies and for the discouragement of the Slave Trade on the coast of Africa." Sharp joined the committee, and soon the men who were to become the heroes of English antislavery—notably Thomas Clarkson and William Wilberforce—were part of it too.

In 1787, with Sharp as chairman, the committee made the politically astute judgment that it was unrealistic to attack the entire institution of slavery, and set itself the more limited goal of outlawing the slave traffic. Wilberforce, a Member of Parliament known because of his brilliance in debate as the nightingale of the House, carried the battle to the heart of the British government. Clarkson, recently down from Cambridge, where he had won a prize for a Latin essay on the subject "Is it right to make men slaves against their will?," visited the slave ports of Liverpool and Bristol and gathered the statistics and horror stories about the trade which served as the documentation for Wilberforce's arguments in Parliament. Others held meetings, issued pamphlets and stirred up public debate. Within a year, Clarkson wrote later, "the nature of the Slave Trade had, in consequence of the labours of the Committee and of their several correspondents, become generally known throughout the kingdom. It had excited a general attention, and there was among people a general feeling on behalf of the wrongs in Africa." In 1791 the government chartered the Sierra Leone Company to resettle in Africa those slaves in England who had been freed by Lord Mansfield's ruling, and popular support for the

abolitionists reached such a peak in the following year that 300,000 people signed petitions resolving to boycott slave-produced West Indian sugar.

It is not to minimize the heroic work of the abolitionists to say that, by the beginning of the nineteenth century, political and economic changes in England and Europe substantially helped their cause. But certainly with American independence Britain's direct vested interest in the slave trade diminished, and the bloody slave revolt in Haiti in the wake of the French Revolution made slave owning a less appealing prospect. Moreover, as industrialization boomed, Europe's economy came to depend less and less on the import of plantation products and more and more on the export of manufactured goods. Thus, within a few years the slave lobby in Europe found itself isolated and with little influence. And, in 1807, Britain ruled the slave trade illegal for her subjects. (Denmark had anticipated her by three years.) The next year the United States followed suit. The Dutch outlawed the traffic in 1814, the Swedes in 1815; in 1818 a Napoleonic decree did the same for the French; and Spain joined the trend in 1820. Portugal, it is true, dragged her feet. In 1815 she agreed to restrict the traffic to her own possessions, but in 1836 she too finally felt obliged to prohibit the trade altogether.

Legislation, of course, did not halt the brutal business or, for that matter, much reduce it. In fact, the numbers of slaves shipped annually actually increased for several years in the mid-nineteenth century. Britain sent armed naval squadrons to police the West African coast but there were plenty of pirates willing to try to run her blockades so long as slavery itself, and thus profitable markets for slaves, still existed. Nonetheless, the die was cast. It took another half-century, but it was perfectly plain that the end of the profits to be made from the sale of slaves was now inevitable. And, with that, so was the end of the sole commercial value Africa held for Europe.

Indeed, ever since Lord Mansfield's ruling there had been a growing recognition that this was so and, concomitantly, a growing interest in whether or not Africa could be made to yield any other commercial possibilities. Might it not, for instance, prove to abound in "immense treasures," as Malachi Postlethwayt, the leading English economic journalist of the period, suggested, in minerals and raw materials with which to feed Europe's industrial machine? Might it not, furthermore, be developed into a huge new market for the products of that ma-

chine? "The Continent of Africa is of great extent, the Country extremely populous," Postlethwayt wrote, and then went on to ask rhetorically, "If we could so exert our commercial policy among these people [the Africans], as to bring a few hundred thousand of them to cloath with our commodities, and to erect buildings to deck with our furniture, and to live something on the European way, would not such traffic prove far more lucrative than the slave-trade alone?" All logic seemed to argue that it would. But no one could know for sure until someone at last went beyond the limits of the coastal stations and found out what was actually there.

Unquestionably then, the hope for trade to replace the dying slave traffic provided a powerful new incentive for Europe to attempt the penetration of the African interior, but it would be misleading to leave the impression that it was the only one. The antislavery campaign had stirred an intense interest in Africa and in Africans. People were suddenly avidly curious about these blacks, about who they were and where they came from. Moreover, the initial humanitarian concern for the African's political and material rights awakened a religious concern for his spiritual salvation. Churches, especially the nonconformist and evangelical sects, which had been involved in the Abolition Movement from the outset, began forming those great missionary societies which would send preachers into the heart of Africa and play a vital role in opening the continent's interior for Europe.

But perhaps the single most powerful incentive was the desire for knowledge and the confidence that not only could everything be known but that it should be, that abiding belief in science which so characterized the Enlightenment. It was considered then not only a sufficient reason but a supremely sensible one to go somewhere merely because no one had ever been there before and discover something that no one had ever known. Britain's Royal Society, its very founding an illustration of the spirit of the Enlightenment, sent astronomers to Sumatra to observe the transit of Venus. The Society of Dilettanti, a dining club of rich young English nobles, organized archeological expeditions to Ionia. Louis XVI of France dispatched Comte de La Pérouse round Cape Horn to map the coasts of Japan and Australia. Captain James Cook, in ten years of ceaseless voyaging, sailed to Tahiti and Australia, the Easter Islands and Hawaii, and meticulously recorded all the exotica he saw. In such a time, then, it is anything

but surprising that the vast blank which was the map of the interior of Africa should represent an irresistible challenge.

All these forces were very much in play when, on June 9, 1788, a group of Englishmen sat down to dine at St. Albans Tavern off Pall Mall in London. They were members of the Saturday's Club, one of those small (this one had a total membership of twelve, of whom nine were present that day), elitist eating clubs to be found in London in those years, where friends of equal social standing and common interests would gather informally to enjoy an excellent roast and fine old port and discuss the ideas of the day. The members were all extremely wealthy and from the highest ranks of the establishment, but they were also wonderfully representative of the enlightened spirit of their times.

For example, Sir Joseph Banks, who was to emerge as their leader, was then president of the Royal Society as well as secretary of the Society of Dilettanti and was an accomplished botanist who had sailed on Cook's first expedition. Henry Beaufoy, a Quaker, was an active abolitionist, as was the Earl of Galloway. The Bishop of Llandaff was both an abolitionist and a scientist, holding the chair of chemistry at Cambridge. Sir John Sinclair is credited with pioneering the science of statistics and later would become governor-general of India.

Given the informal nature of the club there are, of course, no records of their discussions before the June 9th gathering, but it isn't difficult to imagine that men of this sort must have often turned their conversations to Africa, speculating on its commercial and scientific value and deploring the lack of information about it. What we do know is that on June 9 they made a decision to do something about it. Beaufoy wrote later:

While we continue ignorant of so large a portion of the globe, that ignorance must be considered as a degree of reproach on the present age. Sensible of this stigma, and desirous of rescuing the age from a charge of ignorance, which, in other respects, belongs so little to its character, a few Individuals, strongly impressed with a conviction of the practicability and utility of thus enlarging the fund of human knowledge, have formed the Plan of an Association for promoting the Discovery of the Interior parts of Africa.

And with this they founded what was to become known as the African Association and set in motion the greatest age of African exploration since the days of Prince Henry.

Before they broke up that evening the members formed a committee of five with Beaufoy as secretary and Banks as treasurer (a chairman among peers apparently wasn't deemed necessary). They were aware that the British government was unlikely to sponsor their enterprise but, with their impeccable credentials and influential connections, they knew they could count on a measure of official cooperation and would have no problem finding financing privately. Each member agreed to pay a subscription of five guineas a year for three years and "to recommend . . . such of his Friends as he shall think proper to be admitted to the new Association." (In time, more than 200 such friends, well represented by dukes and earls and generals, would become patrons.) There was nothing, in fact, to prevent the discovery of the interior parts of Africa from getting started right away. All that had to be done was to pick which interior part was to be discovered first.

They did not pick the Congo. Although the explorations initiated by the African Association ultimately would focus on the river, at the time there was nothing about it to attract the attention of Banks and Beaufoy as they scanned the map of Africa, hunting for a likely goal for their first expedition. We have to remind ourselves that Banks and Beaufoy knew little if anything about the Kingdom of Kongo, of its rich history and tragic fate, nor that it had existed at all for that matter. Nor were they more than dimly aware of the size and power of the river. Information of that kind belonged then almost exclusively to the Portuguese. For Banks and Beaufoy, in fact, the most striking thing about the Congo was that the Portuguese had already been there and that was reason enough for them to be uninterested in it at the start. For what they were looking for was a place where no European had ever been before; what they wanted was a grand challenge, an intriguing mystery, a geographical puzzle so fascinating as to have defied repeated attempts at its solution, a discovery so worthwhile as to increase immediately the fund of human knowledge and promise practical benefits to mankind. The Congo seemed to offer none of these, but there was a place that did: Timbuktoo and the River Niger, on whose banks the fabled golden city was said to stand.

Unlike the Congo and its kingdom, Timbuktoo and the Niger were part of the classic literature familiar to the scholarly gentlemen of the Enlightenment. Herodotus had written about the Silent Trade conducted by the kings of Timbuktoo, Claudius Ptolemy had specu-

lated on the Niger's course, and such Arab geographers as Al-Idrisi and Ibn-Batuta had described this interior part of Africa as the source of the gold the Saharan caravans brought. One need read only this passage from Leo Africanus, the sixteenth-century Granada Moor, to get an inkling of the magical excitement this part of Africa generated for these Englishmen:

Tombuto [Timbuktoo] is situate within twelve miles of a certaine branch of Niger . . . there is a most stately temple to be seene, the wals thereof are made of stone and lime, and a princely palace also built by a most excellent workman. . . . Here are many shops of artificers and merchants and especially of such as weave linen and cotton cloth. . . . The inhabitants, and especially strangers there residing are exceeding rich. . . . The rich king of Tombuto hath many plates and scepters of gold, some whereof weigh 1,300 pounds; and he keeps a magnificent and well-furnished court. . . . He hath alwaies 3,000 horsemen, and a great number of footmen that shoot poysoned arrowes, attending upon him. They have often skirmishes with those that refuse to pay tribute, and so many as they take they sell unto the merchants of Tombuto. . . . Here are great stores of doctors, judges, priests and other learned men, that are bountifully maintained at the kings cost and charges. And hither are brought diverse manuscripts or written bookes out of Barbarie, which are sold for more money than any other merchandize.

Surely alluring enough, but the best part of it all was that no European had ever been there. Moreover, the Niger posed so dark a geographical mystery that not only were the locations of its source and mouth unknown but no one knew even in which direction the river flowed. And, as Beaufoy wrote, its exploration was "made doubly interesting by the consideration of its having engaged the attention and baffled the researches, of the most inquisitive and most powerful nations of antiquity." So it was chosen as a most suitable object for the association's first expeditions.

Amazingly little time was wasted. Within four days of the inaugural supper, an explorer, John Ledyard, was recruited, and within a month he was on his way. Ledyard, an American soldier-adventurer who had sailed on Cook's last voyage and who just that year had returned from a failed attempt to cross Europe and Asia to North America, set out to traverse the African continent east to west, from Cairo to Timbuktoo and the Niger. While he was en route, the association sent a second explorer, Simon Lucas, a one-time wine mer-

chant, who had been enslaved by Moorish pirates for three years and, after his release, had served for sixteen years as British vice consul to the Moroccan court. He was to try to make the crossing from Tripoli to the river, north to south.

The expeditions were ill equipped and ill prepared. The men went off alone into the unknown without maps, with hardly any supplies and very little money. Lucas and Ledyard each started out with only £100 and the right to draw that much again once in Africa because, curiously, Banks and Beaufoy were "persuaded that in such an undertaking poverty is a better protection than wealth." Under the circumstances, their courage was incredible and the forces driving them—a sense of adventure, a degree of curiosity—of such power as to seem unimaginable in this day.

Ledyard got only as far as Cairo, and there died of an unknown disease. Lucas, disguised in Turkish dress, managed to join a Moorish caravan in Tripoli but was turned back by warring tribes in the Fezzan. The failure of the first two missions did nothing to discourage the association but it did force a reconsideration of the plan of attack. Recognizing the difficulty of passing through the Moslem-controlled desert, Banks and Beaufoy decided to dispatch the next expedition from the West African coast. Daniel Houghton, a retired army major who had served at the British fort at Goree off the coast of Sénégal, was sent to the mouth of the Gambia, with instructions to go up that river as far as possible, learn whatever he could about "the rise, the course, and the termination of the Niger, as well as of the various nations that inhabit its borders." Houghton followed these instructions to the best of his ability, but from the outset he was in constant danger from native traders trying to rob and kill him. They finally succeeded. But before they did Houghton had penetrated further into the African interior than had any other previous European. Years later it was discovered that he had died at a village named Simbing (in present-day Mali), about 160 miles north of the Niger and perhaps 500 miles short of Timbuktoo. In the dispatches he sent to London during his journey, we see that he had correctly surmised that the Niger rose in the mountains south of the Gambia and that its course was probably west to east.

The explorer the African Association next sent out was Mungo Park, the man who would turn British interest toward the Congo. Park was a young Scottish physician with an itch for travel, who had

sailed in 1791 as ship's surgeon on an East India Company vessel
bound for Sumatra. When he returned two years later, he offered his
services to the African Association, and the association accepted, finding him "a young man of no mean talents . . . sufficiently instructed
in the use of Hadley's quadrant to make the necessary observations;
geographer enough to trace his path through the wilderness, and not
unacquainted with natural history." In May 1795, Park sailed aboard
the brig *Endeavour,* bound for the Gambia for a cargo of ivory, and
reached Jilifree, on the river's northern bank, thirty days later. From
there he struck inland, following Houghton's route.

Park was gone more than two and a half years, and his adventures
and accomplishments rank among the greatest in the annals of African
exploration. Like Houghton, he was constantly harassed by tribesmen
demanding bribes for the right to pass through the regions they controlled. And, as he pressed further inland and reached territories
under Moslem influence, his life as well as his supplies were threatened. In the Moorish kingdom of Ludamar, where, he learned,
Houghton had been robbed of all his belongings and left to die, the
tribesmen, he later wrote, "hissed, shouted, and abused me; they even
spit in my face, with a view to irritating me, and afford them a pretext
for seizing my baggage. But finding such insults had not the desired
effect, they had recourse to the final and decisive argument, that I was
a Christian, and that my property was lawful plunder." Not long
afterward he was taken prisoner by a band of Moorish horsemen and
brought to the camp of a local chieftain, who ordered his right hand
cut off, his eyes plucked out, and his life ended. Park escaped only
because, at just the opportune moment, an enemy tribe attacked the
camp. He pressed on, ridden with fever, bereft of supplies, tormented
by thirst and sandstorms. But at last he was out of Moorish territory
and entered the country of the Bambara. The Bambara proved
friendly and he followed a group from a place called Kaarta heading
east toward the town of Ségou. "As we approached the town," Park
wrote in his *Travels in the Interior of Africa,*

I was fortunate to overtake the Kaartans . . . and we rode together
through some marshy ground, where, as I was looking round anxiously
for the river, one of them called out, *"Geo affili"* (see the water) ; and looking forward, I saw with infinite pleasure the great object of my mission, the
long-sought and majestic Niger, glittering to the morning sun, as broad
as the Thames at Westminister, and flowing slowly *to the eastward.* I

hastened to the brink, and, having drank of the water, lifted up my fervent thanks in prayer to the Great Ruler of all things for having thus crowned my endeavours with success.

The date was June 20, 1796, and Park had become the first European on record to have laid eyes on the Niger. His task now was to follow it to Timbuktoo and then on to its mouth, wherever that might be. He did not succeed. His circumstances deteriorated rapidly as he once again moved into Moorish country. The heat was unbearable, his horse collapsed, the tropical rains began, and on August 25 he was jumped by a gang of thieves and stripped naked. "I was now convinced," he wrote, "that the obstacles to my further progress were insurmountable." He had reached Silla on the Niger, still some 400 miles from Timbuktoo, when he decided to turn back. His struggle to the coast took him nearly a year. In June 1797, he reached the mouth of the Gambia and there boarded an American slaving vessel, which got him to Antigua, where he was able to catch a packet making for Falmouth. He arrived back in England just a few days before Christmas of 1797.

The African Association and, indeed, all of England were thrilled by Park's accomplishment. He was, after all, the first man to have penetrated the forbidding interior of Africa for the sole purpose of finding out what was there and to have come back alive. And, in a sense, by doing that he had invented a new and glorious calling, created a new and adventurous species of hero, the lone, brave African explorer, who was to capture the imagination, feed the fantasies, and fill the literature of Europe for a century to come. He was lionized by the best of English society, and the book he wrote about his adventures became an instant best-seller. And Banks, with Park's success to point to, launched an ultimately successful campaign to involve the British government in African exploration.

Speaking strictly geographically, Park had barely scratched the surface of the interior of Africa. Timbuktoo still had not been reached, and the puzzle of the Niger's course and the location of its mouth remained unsolved. No one was more acutely aware of this than Park himself, and no sooner had he returned than he began making plans for a second expedition. But, as it turned out, that would have to wait for nearly six years. For Park married and began having children. Considering the meager wages the African Association paid its ex-

plorers (Park was offered ten shillings a day for his next journey), this meant settling down and earning a living.

While practicing medicine in Scotland, Park had plenty of time to sort out what he had learned from first-hand experience and develop his own theory about the geography of the Niger, especially the location of its mouth. There were at this time three contradictory theories about the river's ultimate destination. The oldest and perhaps the most venerated "supposed," as a geographer of the period wrote,

that the Niger has an inland termination somewhere in the eastern part of Africa . . . and that it is partly discharged into inland lakes, which have no communication with the sea, and partly spread over a wide extent of level country, and lost in sands or evaporated by the heat of the sun.

Against this theory, it was argued:

To account for such a phenomenon, a great inland sea, bearing some resemblance to the Caspian or the Aral, appears to be necessary. But besides that the existence of so vast a body of water without any outlet into the ocean, is in itself an improbable circumstance . . . such a sea, if it really existed, could hardly have remained a secret to the ancients, and entirely unknown at the present day.

Another idea was that the Niger flowed into the Nile. But the geographers of the period tended to dismiss this theory as

rather a loose popular conjecture, than an opinion deduced from probable reasoning; since nothing appears to be alleged in its support, except the mere circumstance of the course of the river being in the direction of the Nile.

The third hypothesis held

that the Niger, after reaching Wangara [present-day Mali], takes a direction towards the south, and being joined by other rivers from that part of Africa, makes a great turn from thence towards the southwest, and pursues its course till it approaches . . . the gulf of Guinea, when it divides and discharges itself by different channels into the Atlantic; after having formed a great Delta.

This was to turn out to be an amazingly accurate description of the river's course and termination, but at the time the reasoning in support of it was regarded as "hazardous and uncertain," and a host of geographical objections were raised, resulting in the widely held con-

clusion, as one geographer of the period put it, that "the data on which it is grounded are all of them wholly gratuitous." So it was a fourth theory entirely that Park, while not its originator, came to adopt and champion. That theory held that the Niger, taking the turn to the south after Wangara or Timbuktoo, as proposed above, but persisting in that direction rather than turning southwest, terminated through the estuary of the Congo. The two rivers, it said, were one and the same.

This idea appears to have been first put forward by a certain George Maxwell, a Scotsman who had traded on the Congo and who, more than any other person, managed to attract Britain's attention to it. For years he had proselytized among his influential friends in London about the river's importance, pointing out the then little known facts about the river's powerful current and flow, ranking it accurately as second only to the Amazon in this regard, deducing its immense size from that, and arguing that it offered a natural way for the exploration of and trade with the African interior. But it wasn't until the question of the Niger's geography became a lively subject of inquiry after Park's first expedition that he succeeded in getting the right London circles to pay him and the Congo any serious heed.

Maxwell himself had never traveled above the estuary but, as he wrote, he had long concluded, "before even the Niger came to be the topic of conversation . . . that the Congo drew its source far to the northward," and in a letter to a mutual friend of his and Park's, which he asked to be passed on to Park, he set forth his conviction that "if the Niger *has* a sensible outlet, I have no doubt of its proving the Congo, knowing all the rivers between Cape Palmas and Cape Lopes to be inadequate for the purpose." He was so convinced of this that in another letter, this one written directly to Park, he described a plan he had formulated for exploring the river which involved bringing out from England "six supernumerary boats, well adapted for rowing and sailing; each being of such a size as to be easily carried by thirty people, and transported across several cataracts, with which the course of the river is known to be impeded.

Park, as his first biographer was to write, "adopted Mr. Maxwell's sentiments relative to the termination of the Niger in their utmost extent, and persevered in that opinion to the end of his life." He was well aware of the geographical objections that could be raised against this theory, but was quick to find solutions by which to overcome each.

For example, if the Niger and Congo were one, it would have a length of well over 4000 miles (thus making it the longest river in the world) . To this, Park's answer was essentially, well, why not? After all, the Amazon was then accepted to be more than 3500 miles long. As to the objection that the river would have to flow through a great mountain chain, which was then supposed to run through the middle of the continent, this was dismissed on the grounds that there was no real evidence that these mountains existed. And to get around the difficulty that the great rises and falls in the level of the Niger did not correspond to the relatively even flow of the Congo, Park supposed that the river passed through a series of 17 or 18 lakes. Moreover, as he wrote to Earl Camden, then the British colonial secretary, "the quantity of water discharged into the Atlantic by the Congo cannot be accounted for on any other known principle but that it is the termination of the Niger."

By 1804 Park was tired of his sedentary family life as a country doctor and came down to London to present a plan to Banks and Earl Camden for a second Niger expedition. This one was not to be a lone adventure. He wanted an escort of thirty English soldiers, a half-dozen carpenters to build the boats he would need to travel on the river, and authority to hire up to twenty Africans to serve as porters. Though he was convinced of Maxwell's ideas, Park chose not to follow the trader's plan of exploration up the Congo estuary. More familiar with the route he had taken on his first expedition, he planned to start again from the Gambia, strike overland to the Niger, and then sail down the river to its end. If, indeed, the river did terminate in a great lake in Wangara, he would then return across the desert to the coast at the Bight of Benin. But he was sure that he would wind up in the Congo's estuary and planned to sail from there to the West Indies and then back to Europe. If he proved correct, he told Earl Camden,

the expedition though attended with extreme danger, promises to be productive of the utmost advantages to Great Britain. Considered in a commercial point of view, it is second only to the discovery of the Cape of Good Hope, and in a geographical point of view is certainly the greatest discovery that remains to be made in the world.

A number of distinguished geographers regarded Park's ideas as wrong and tried to discourage him from embarking on such a dangerous enterprise. But Banks backed him fervently:

I am aware that Mr. Park's expedition is one of the most hazardous a man can undertake but I cannot agree with those who think it is too hazardous to be attempted; it is by similar hazards of human life alone that we can hope to penetrate the obscurity of the internal face of Africa; we are wholly ignorant of the country between the Niger and the Congo and can explore it only by incurring the most frightful hazards.

Park set off at the end of January 1805 aboard the troopship *Crescent* and arrived at Goree at the mouth of the Gambia two months later. He had brought with him five navy carpenters, who had been convicts in Portsmouth and had received pardons in exchange for volunteering for the expedition. In Goree, he recruited 32 soldiers and 2 sailors from the Royal Africa Corps garrison there, men who were also convicts—service in Africa was their punishment—and who joined the party on the promise of double pay and a discharge from the corps at the completion of the expedition. In addition, Park, who had been commissioned a brevet captain, had with him an army lieutenant, his brother-in-law, and a friend from Scotland. He, however, discovered that, as he wrote, "No inducement could prevail on a single Negro to accompany me." Nevertheless, Park and his party sailed up the Gambia aboard the *Crescent* to the town of Kayee, where an English-speaking Mandingo guide named Isaaco was hired, and from there, in April, struck out overland toward the Niger.

Park had reckoned on reaching the Niger by the end of June. In fact, he didn't get there until August 19, and by that time three-quarters of his party were dead. The rains had come and, more than the Moorish tribesmen who attacked the caravan all along the way, fever and dysentery proved the great killers. So terrible was the journey that the dead were not buried and the ailing were left behind to be stripped and killed by bandits. But on seeing the Niger again, "rolling its immense stream along the plain," although he had only ten men left and his own health was badly undermined, Park was too excited to acknowledge the seriousness of his situation and, against all common sense, decided to press forward with the journey.

Canoes were hired to take Park and the remnants of his caravan downriver as far as Ségou, where they arrived in September. There they had to wait several weeks while suspicious tribesmen argued about providing new canoes. During that time, the party suffered further losses, including the death of Park's brother-in-law. By the time the natives agreed to let Park have two canoes, his escort was

down to the army lieutenant, three soldiers, and the guide Isaaco. Nevertheless, Park was determined to go on. He sent the guide Isaaco back to the coast with letters to his wife and to Banks. He wrote to Banks that it was his intention "to keep to the middle of the river and make the best use I can of winds and currents till I reach the termination of this mysterious stream." To his wife: "I think it is not unlikely that I shall be in England before you receive this . . . the sails are now hoisting for our departure to the coast." That was November 20, 1805, and it was the last anyone ever heard from Park.

We don't know exactly what happened to him, what fate he met, or how far he got before he met it, but a few years later, in 1810, the Mandingo guide Isaaco volunteered to return to Ségou in an attempt to find out, and the story he heard gives us some clues. Apparently Park, realizing that he was now moving into country controlled by Moorish tribes and remembering their hostility from his previous expedition, had been expecting trouble. He had taken fifteen muskets and plenty of ammunition aboard the two canoes, as well as enough provisions so that his party would not have to land until they were safely out of Moorish country.

From the outset, Park and his men came under attack from the shore and were required to shoot their way down the river. According to Isaaco's account, they managed to get to Timbuktoo, but there was absolutely no question of going ashore and visiting the city because of the hostility of its inhabitants. Park pushed on and, it seems, managed to sail down some 1500 miles of the Niger's total course of 2600 miles and reach a point barely 600 miles from its outlet to the sea. But it was at this point, a place called Bussa rapids, where the Kainji dam in present-day Nigeria stands, that the party was ambushed and all were killed.

Park's death, however it actually occurred (questions persisted about Isaaco's version, and it wasn't until 1819 that the London *Times* finally wrote, "The death of this intrepid traveller is now placed beyond any doubt"), did not kill off the belief that the Niger and Congo were one and the same river. To be sure, Park himself, if he did in fact get as far as Isaaco tells us, would have been forced to abandon the idea, seeing that the river, having turned to the south after Timbuktoo, turned again soon thereafter, at Gao, to the southwest and flowed in a direction that couldn't possibly have brought it to the Congo's estuary. But no one else knew this at the time; the last

reports from Park were sent from Ségou, and he was then even more convinced about the rightness of the theory. For he had learned there that the until then eastward-flowing river would soon turn to the south (not yet knowing that it would later turn again to the southwest). In a letter to Banks, which Isaaco had brought back, we find Park writing, "I have hired a guide . . . he is one of the greatest travellers in this part of Africa: he says that the Niger, after it passes Kashna [presumably near Timbuktoo], runs directly to the right hand, or to the south," and in his last letters to his wife and Lord Camden he repeated his conviction that he would return to England via the West Indies from the Congo's mouth.

Ten years were to pass before Britain again would try to prove the connection between the Niger and the Congo, mainly because the Napoleonic Wars came along to divert her attention from Africa. But interest in the question had been so heightened by the drama and mystery of Park's disappearance that in 1815 an ambitious, two-pronged attack on the problem was launched. One expedition, under the sponsorship of the Colonial Office, was sent out to follow Park's course down the Niger. The second, organized by the Admiralty, was to start at the Congo's mouth and follow that river upstream. The hope, of course, was that the two would meet somewhere in the middle.

11

---◆◈◆---

THE TUCKEY EXPEDITION

The Admiralty's expedition was the first real attempt to explore the Congo River ever undertaken by Europeans. And, it must be said, having waited more than three hundred years to get around to it, they undertook it in a wholly admirable manner. The expedition, like no other effort of African exploration until that time, was meticulously planned, conscientiously organized, and generously financed.

To be sure, its main purpose was to establish the identity of the Niger's mouth. Sir John Barrow, who was then the secretary of the Admiralty and the driving force behind the expedition, underscored this goal repeatedly in a memorandum he prepared for the expedition's commander. For example, at one point he noted:

The usual flooded state of the Zaire [the names Congo and Zaire were used interchangeably by this time] . . . would seem to warrant the supposition, that one great branch, perhaps the main trunk, descends from the tropical regions to the northward of the Line; and if in your progress it should be found, that the general trending of its course is from the north-east, it will strengthen the conjecture of that branch and the Niger being one and the same river. It will be adviseable, therefore, as long as the mainstream of the Zaire shall be found to flow from the northeast . . . to give the preference to that stream; and, to endeavour to follow it to its source.

Nevertheless, Barrow and the Admiralty also recognized that the Congo was in and of itself a worthy object of exploration. Barrow wrote:

It is not to be understood, that the attempt to ascertain this point [the

identity of the Congo and the Niger] is by any means the exclusive object of this expedition. That a river of such magnitude as the Zaire, and offering so many peculiarities, should not be known with any degree of certainty, beyond, if so far as, 200 miles from its mouth, is incompatible with the present advanced state of geographical science, and little creditable to those Europeans, who, for three centuries nearly, have occupied various parts of the coast near to which it empties itself into the sea, and have held communication with the interior of the country through which it descends, by means of missionaries, and slave agents; so confined indeed is our knowledge of the course of this remarkable river, that the only chart of it which can have any pretension to accuracy [it was one drawn by George Maxwell], does not extend above 130 miles, and the correctness of this survey, as it is called, is more than questionable. There can be little doubt, however, that a river, which runs more rapidly and discharges more water, than either the Ganges or the Nile, and which has this peculiar quality of being, almost all seasons of the year, in a *flooded* state, must not only traverse a vast extent of country, but must also be supplied by large branches flowing from different, and probably opposite directions; so that some one or more of them must, at all times of year, pass through a tract of country where the rains prevail. To ascertain the sources of these great branches, then, will be one of the principal objects of the present expedition.

James Kingston Tuckey, a captain in the Royal Navy, was named the expedition's commander. He was then not quite forty years old, a tall, gangling man, prematurely gray and nearly entirely bald. "His countenance" as a contemporary described him, "was pleasing, but wore rather a pensive cast; but he was at all times gentle and kind in his manners, cheerful in conversation, and indulgent to every one placed under his command." His early navy service was in Britain's empire-building skirmishes against the Dutch and the French in India and Ceylon and then later against the French in the Red Sea and off the East African coast. In 1802, sent out to New South Wales to participate in the establishment of a British colony there, he gathered his first experience as an explorer, making a survey of the harbors, coasts, and adjacent unmapped country.

His career, however, appeared to come to an abrupt halt with the outbreak of the Napoleonic Wars. His ship, the *Calcutta,* escorting a British convoy from St. Helena in 1805, was captured by the French, and Tuckey spent the next nine years in imprisonment. But, in fact,

he made remarkably good use of those years. "To pass away the tedious hours of a hopeless captivity," as he later wrote, he compiled a massive, four-volume *Maritime Geography and Statistics,* a work which presented

a comprehensive view of the various phenomena of the ocean, the description of coasts and islands, and of the seas that wash them; the remarkable headlands, harbours and port towns; the several rivers that reach the sea, and the nature and extent of their inland navigations that communicate with the coasts.

It was not long after his release, at the end of the war with France, that the Admiralty began planning its Congo expedition. Tuckey requested its command. He was not the only one. In a time of peace, the Admiralty's expedition provided a naval officer with the best, if not only, opportunity to distinguish himself, and several applied for the coveted position. Tuckey was selected because of his impressive *Maritime Geography and Statistics,* which gave proof that "he had stored his mind with so much various knowledge and . . . had given so much attention to the subject of nautical discovery and river navigation" as to be considered "most eligible for the undertaking." Still, in retrospect, one can't help wondering about the choice. Though still relatively young, Tuckey was not a strong man. His health had been undermined by fevers he had contracted during his service in the tropics and was seriously if not permanently damaged by his long imprisonment in France. What's more, he seems to have been a typically conservative, careful, strait-laced military man. He does not seem to have had the flair, the imagination, the innovative daring one expects of an explorer. For example, a contemporary Admiralty historian has noted:

As so very little was known of the course of the Zaire, and nothing at all beyond the first cataracts, it was at first intended to leave Captain Tuckey entirely to his own discretion, to act as circumstances might appear to require . . . but Captain Tuckey pressed with such urgency for specific instructions, that, as he observed, he might be satisfied in his own mind when he had done all that was expected of him, that his wishes in this respect were complied with.

Tuckey chose for his second-in-command John Hawkey, a navy lieutenant of about his own age who had also spent the entire Napoleonic war in captivity and whom Tuckey had befriended when they

Captain Tuckey's voyage in Africa. The market village near Embomma

shared the same prison compound in France. A party of scientists was assembled. It included a botanist by the name of Smith; a "Collector of Objects of Natural History" called Cranch; a surgeon and comparative anatomist named Tudor; the gardener from His Majesty's Gardens at Kew by the name of Lockhart; and a man named Galwey who is listed in the log simply as a "Volunteer and Observant Gentleman" and appears to have been a boyhood chum of Tuckey's. In addition, the expedition consisted of five other navy officers, eight petty officers, four carpenters, two blacksmiths, fourteen able seamen, an escort of fourteen Royal Marines, and two freed slaves who were natives of the Congo, named Benjamin Benjamin and Somme Simmons, to act as guides and interpreters.

The plan for the expedition took much of its inspiration from George Maxwell. Two ships, loaded with provisions, arms, and equipment, as well as presents for the natives such as iron tools, knives, glassware, beads, and umbrellas, would sail to the Congo's mouth. One of these, a 350-ton transport store ship christened the *Dorothy,* was meant to help carry supplies to the river, and once these were transhipped at the river's mouth to the other vessel, appropriately christened the *Congo,* she was to return to England. The *Congo* then would sail up the river until she met the impediment of the rapids

and cataracts. At this point, smaller, lighter vessels, capable of being transported overland, were to be brought into play. Two double-boats, drawing very little water, were designed and built; each was 35 feet long, fitted with a canopy to keep off sun and rain and, when assembled, capable of carrying 20 to 30 men and three months' provisions. With them, the party was supposed to get around the cataracts, find where the river became navigable again, and sail on it to its source, expected to be the Niger.

The expedition departed from Deptford on February 16, 1816. The ships had some trouble getting out of the English Channel but by March they were at last on the high seas, making for Madeira, then the Canaries, and then the Cape Verde Islands. There they laid over for caulking and sail repairs and reached the mouth of the Congo on July 5, early in the dry season.

Tuckey now issued a memorandum of regulations "for our conduct in the country," which gives us another insight into his careful character. He warned:

It is highly necessary to be guarded in our intercourse with [the natives]; that, by showing we are prepared to resist aggression, we may leave no hope of success, or no inducement to commit it. . . . In the event of the absolute necessity of repelling hostility for self-preservation, it will certainly be more consonant to humanity, and perhaps more effectual in striking terror, that the first guns fired be only loaded with small shot.

Tuckey also worried about theft, which, he had learned from his studies of the experiences of other African explorers,

has been one of the most frequent causes of unhappy catastrophes that have befallen navigators; it is therefore urgently advised, not to expose anything unnecessarily to the view of the natives, or to leave any object in their way that may tempt their avidity.

He then pointed out that another

great cause of the disputes of navigators with uncivilized people is in unauthorized freedoms with their females; and hence every species of curiosity or familiarity with them, which may create jealousy in the man, is to be strictly avoided.

Tuckey was aboard the *Dorothy* and, while the more maneuverable *Congo* under Hawkey's command had little difficulty anchoring at Tall Trees (the name that British traders on the river had given the

old slaving port of Mpinda), the captain spent three days getting his "brute of a transport" around the headlands of the river's mouth and into the estuary. At last he reached Shark's Point a short way upstream from the point where Diogo Cão had erected his pillar, and there he remained. For all his efforts, Tuckey could not get the *Dorothy* any further upriver than that.

Tuckey and his party, as it turned out, weren't the only Europeans on the river. "At four o'clock," he noted in his log for July 8,

a schooner appeared off the point, hoisted Spanish Colours, and fired a gun. . . . A boat was immediately sent from her to ask what we were, and on being informed, they made some excuse for firing the shot, intended as they said, to assure the colours; their vessel, by their account, was from the Havana for slaves.

Tuckey had been forewarned by the Admiralty to expect to run into slavers on the river and specifically ordered not to get involved with them. At this time, as we've seen, most European nations had outlawed the traffic. The notable exceptions were Spain and Portugal, and the most popular ruse of pirate slavers, when they encountered vessels of the British naval squadrons policing the trade on the West African coast, was to hoist the colors of one or the other of these nations. Tuckey was convinced that this was the case with this ship. As he noted in his log, "It was perfectly evident, from their answers to my questions, that she was illicity employed in this trade, and prepared to carry it on by force, being armed with 12 guns, and full of men." However, under his orders from the Admiralty, he was obliged to assure the slavers that he had no intention of interfering in their business. Even so, the sight of a vessel flying the Union Jack commanded by a British naval officer and carrying Royal Marines made the pirates uneasy. And that they didn't entirely believe Tuckey was "put out of doubt," he noted in his log, by the slaver "getting underway and running out of the river." Seven other slavers, three schooners and four pinnaces, all flying the Portuguese flag, were anchored at the slave port of Embomma (Boma) further upriver. And, when they learned of the presence of the two British vessels, they too "precipitately . . . quitted the river, passing us no doubt in the night."

While stuck aboard the *Dorothy* at Shark's Point, Tuckey made his first contacts with the Bakongo of the lost kingdom's Soyo province,

and his unflattering observations provide a striking reminder of how the centuries of the slave trade had corrupted and destroyed these once noble people.

The Mafook [trading agent of the local chief] of Shark Point came on board with a half dozen of his myrmidons [Tuckey wrote], and though the most ragged, dirty looking wretch that can be well conceived, he expected as much respect as a prince. . . . Seating himself at the tafferel, he certainly made a very grotesque appearance, having a most tattered pelisse of red velvet, edged with gold lace, on his naked carcass, a green silk umbrella spread over his head, though the sun was completely obscured, and his stick of office headed with silver in the other hand. It being our breakfast hour, he notified his desire to be asked into our cabin, to partake of our meal; but he smelt so offensively, and was moreover so covered with a cutaneous disorder, that my politeness gave way to my stomach, and he was obliged, though with great sulkiness, to content himself on deck. To bring him into good humor, I however saluted him with one swivel [the firing of a musket], and gave him a plentiful allowance of brandy. He seemed indeed to have no other object in coming on board than to get a few glasses of this liquor, which he relished so well that he staid on board all night and the five following days.

Others quickly followed. Tuckey noted with contempt:

Several of the Soyo men were Christians after the Portuguese fashion, having been converted by missionaries of that nation; and one of them was even qualified to lead his fellow negroes into the path of salvation, as appeared from a diploma with which he was furnished. This man and another of the Christians had been taught to write their own names and that of Saint Antonio, and could also read the Romish litany in Latin. . . . The Christian priest was however somewhat loose in his practical morality, having, as he assured us, one wife and five concubines; and added, that St. Peter, in confining him to *one* wife, did not prohibit his solacing himself with as many handmaidens as he could manage. . . . Our Soyo visitors were almost without exception sulky looking vagabonds, dirty, swarming with lice, and scaled over with the itch, all strong symptoms of their having been *civilized* by the Portuguese.

After more than a week at Shark's Point, Tuckey chased all the brandy-imbibing Mafooks off the *Dorothy,* gave up trying to get the transport any further upriver, and set about transhipping her stores to the *Congo.* The operation took until July 18, and now the expedition's real business of exploration could begin.

Tuckey's first object was to get the *Congo* to Embomma. But again the river current and the precarious sea breeze worked against him, and so he left the job to Hawkey and set out with the scientists in one of the double-boats. It appears to have been a pleasant trip. At one point, Tuckey noted in his journal:

This evening's sail along the banks was particularly agreeable, the lofty mangroves overhanging the boat, and a variety of palm trees vibrating in the breeze; immense flocks of parrots alone broke the silence of the woods with their chattering towards sun-set.

At another he records:

Two women, an old and a young one, came on board . . . by their dress and ornaments they appeared to be of a superior class; I therefore gave them some beads and a glass of rum, which they swallowed as greedily as the men; and, in return, the old lady offered, through our interpreter, to leave the young one on board, pour m'amuser; a civility which, under existing circumstances, I thought proper to decline; though the young lady seemed much chagrined at such an insult to her charm.

On July 25, the party reached the marketplace of Embomma, where a remarkable incident occurred concerning Somme Simmons, one of the freed slaves with the expedition, who had worked as a cook's mate on the voyage out and had served as the chief interpreter since its arrival on the river.

It was, of course, known that Simmons was from the Congo, but "the story of this man," Tuckey confessed, "I never thought of inquiring into." As it turned out, this man, who had "performed, without any signs of impatience or disgust, his menial offices" with the expedition, was from Embomma and the son of "a prince of the blood, and counsellor to the King of Embomma." His father, Tuckey learned,

intrusted him, when eight or ten years old, to a Liverpool captain . . . to be educated (or according to his expression to learn to make book) in England; but his conscientious guardian found it less troublesome to have him taught to make sugar in St. Kitts, where he accordingly sold him.

For eleven years, his father had awaited his son's return, making inquiries of every European ship that came to trade at Embomma. But it was only in the previous year that Simmons had contrived to escape his enslavement in the West Indies and get aboard an English ship and

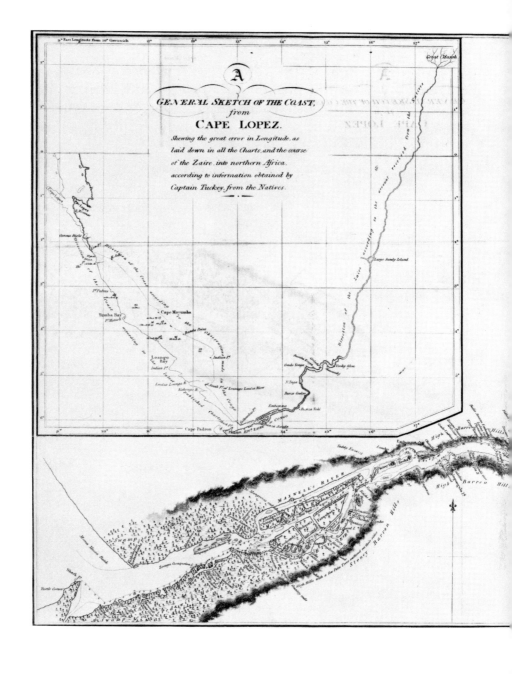

A

GENERAL SKETCH OF THE COAST,
from
CAPE LOPEZ.

Shewing the great error in Longitude, as
laid down in all the Charts, and the course
of the Zaire into northern Africa,
according to information obtained by
Captain Tuckey, from the Natives.

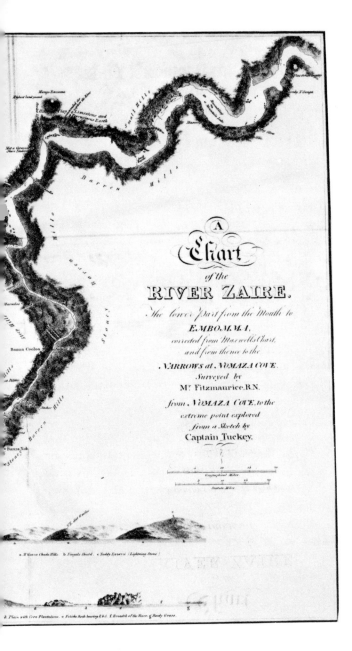

A
Chart
of the
RIVER ZAIRE.

The lower Part from the Mouth to

E.MBO.M.M.A,

corrected from Maxwells Chart,
and from thence to the

NARROWS at NOMAZA COVE.

Surveyed by
Mr. Fitzmaurice, R.N.

from NOMAZA COVE, to the
extreme point explored
from a Sketch by
Captain Tuckey.

by that win his freedom. And the commander of that ship, hearing of the Admiralty's expedition to the Congo, had arranged to have Simmons signed over to Tuckey.

Now once again, with news of the presence of English ships on the river, Simmons's father made his hopeful inquiries about his long-lost son, and this time, we read in the journal of the botanist Smith,

unexpectedly got intelligence of his being with us, and came on board the first evening of our arrival [at Embomma]. His excessive joy, the ardour with which he hugged his son in his arms, proved that even among this people nature is awake to tender emotions.

Tuckey tells us that

The transport of joy, at the meeting was much more strongly expressed by the father than by the son, whose European ideas, though acquired in the school of slavery, did not seem to assimilate with those of Negro society, and he persisted in wearing his European jacket and trowsers; he however went ashore with his friends, and throughout the night the town resounded with the sound of the drum and the songs of rejoicing.

The next day, Tuckey informs us,

Mr. Simmons . . . paid us a visit, in so complete a metamorphosis that we could with difficulty recognize our late cook's mate; his father having dressed him out in a silk coat embroidered with silver . . . on his head a black glazed hat with an enormous grenadier feather, and a silk sash . . . suspending a ship's cutlass, finished his costume. He was brought to the boat by two slaves in a hammock, an umbrella held over his head, preceded by his father and other members of his family, and followed by a rabble escort of 20 muskets. His father's presents to me consisted of a male goat, a bunch of plantains, and a duck.

Tuckey was escorted to the compound of the Chenoo or king of Embomma and led to a seat

prepared of three or four old chests, covered with a red velvet pall, an old English carpet with another velvet pall spread on the ground. Having seated myself . . . the Chenoo made his appearance from behind a mat screen, his costume conveying the idea of Punch in a puppet-show, being composed of a crimson plush jacket with enormous gilt buttons, a lower garment in the native style of red velvet, his legs muffled in pink sarcenet in guise of stockings, and a pair of red Morocco half-boots; on his head an immense high-crowned hat embroidered with gold; and surmounted

by a kind of coronet of European artificial flowers; round his neck hung a long string of ivory beads, and a very large piece of unmanufactured coral.

With Simmons as his interpreter, Tuckey explained his mission. The Chenoo and his counselors were, however, suspicious. "For two hours they rung the changes on the questions, are you come to trade and are you come to make war." Dissatisfied with Tuckey's responses, they went off to palaver among themselves. They returned and

after again tiring me with questions as to my motives, the old man, starting up, plucked a leaf from a tree, and holding it to me said, if you come to trade, swear by your God, and break the leaf; on my refusing to do so, he then said, swear by your God you don't come to make war, and break the leaf; on my doing which, the whole company performed a grand *sakilla.*

After this all seemed well. There was a grand banquet, an exchange of gifts, the offer of women, even the offer of land on which to build an English settlement. In this congenial atmosphere, Tuckey decided to set up camp and, while waiting for Hawkey, who was making slow but steady progress bringing the *Congo* upstream, spend the time surveying the river and learning whatever he could of the country.

It is striking to see how utterly lost, even among the Bakongo themselves, was the history of the ancient Kingdom of Kongo by this time.

The country named Congo, of which we find so much written in collections of Voyages and Travels, appears to be an undefined tract of territory, hemmed in between Loango on the north, and Angola on the south; but to what extent it stretches inland, it would be difficult to determine. . . . All that seems to be known at present is, that the country is partitioned out into a multitude of petty states or Chenooships, held as a kind of fiefs under some real or imaginary personage living in the interior, nobody knows exactly where.

This personage or paramount sovereign, Tuckey was told, "is named Lindy, or Blindy N'Congo, and resides at Banza Congo, six days journey from Tall Trees." There, Tuckey learned, the Portuguese once had a "fixed settlement, the natives speaking of their having soldiers and white women there."

Despite the vagueness of the information available to him, Tuckey proved a careful observer and provides a vivid picture of what the life and customs of the people along the river had come to since their contact with Europe:

The natives are, with very few exceptions, drest in European clothing, their only manufacture being a kind of cape of grass, and shawls of the same material; both are made by men, as are their houses and canoes, the latter of a high tree. . . . Their drinking vessels are pumions or gourds, and their cooking utensils, earthen pots of their own making. . . . Both men and women shave the head in ornamental figures. . . . The women seem to consider pendent breasts as ornamental, the young girls, as soon as they begin to form, pressing them close to the body and downwards with bandages. They also sometimes file the two front teeth away, and raise cicatrices on the skin as well as the men. . . . The two prominent features, in their moral character and social state, seem to be the indolence of the men and the degradation of the women! the latter being considered as perfect slaves, whose bodies are at the entire disposal of their fathers, or husbands, and may be transferred by either of them, how and when they may please.

At one point, Tuckey came upon a funeral. The corpse of a woman was lying in a hut

drest as when alive; inside the hut, four women were howling, and outside, two men standing close to the hut, with their faces leaning against it, kept them company in a kind of cadence, producing a concert not unlike the Irish funeral yell. These marks of sorrow, we understood, were repeated for an hour for four successive days after the death of the person.

Apparently though, the corpse would not be buried for several years, not until it had

arrived at a size to make a genteel funeral. The manner for preserving corpses, for so long a time, is by enveloping them in cloth . . . the smell of putrefaction being only kept in by the quantity of wrappers, which are successively multiplied as they can be procured by the relations of the deceased, or according to the rank of the person; in the case of a rich and very great man, the bulk acquired being only limited by the power of conveyance to the grace; so that the first hut in which the body is deposited, becoming too small, a second, a third, and even to a sixth, increasing in dimensions, is placed over it.

On August 1, the *Congo* at last reached Embomma and the next

morning Tuckey "shook hands with the Chenoo, giving him, as a parting token of friendship, one fathom of scarlet cloth, an amber necklace, two jars of spirits, and some plates and dishes." In return, the Chenoo sent three of his sons and a half-dozen of his men to accompany the expedition as guides and pilots. Four days later the *Congo* got up to a point just below the Cauldron of Hell and "finding that we should be much retarded by persevering in the attempt to get much higher, I ordered her to be moored and directed . . . the purser to remain in charge of her; together with the surgeon, a master's mate and 15 men." In the middle of the next day, the rest of the party, in the double-boats, a long boat from the *Dorothy,* two gigs and a punt, set off to take on the rapids.

The going was tricky but not impossible. Tuckey's journal notes strong eddies and rocky outcroppings, but he also found channels, stretches of calm water, and sheltered reaches, and his party made decent headway. On August 8, they reached a village called Noki, where they "received their first coherent information respecting . . . a great cataract named Yellala" that was said to pose a formidable obstruction to further navigation. Tuckey sent his interpreter Simmons to the Chenoo of Noki

to request he would send me a person acquainted with the river higher up; but on his return in the evening, I found that nothing could be done without my own presence, and the usual *dash* of a present of brandy.

The next morning, after "a two hour's fatiguing march" into the interior from the river's left bank,

I was ushered into the presence of the Chenoo, whom we found seated . . . in much more savage magnificence, but less of European manner, than the king of Embomma, the seats and grounds being here covered with lions' and leopard skins, the treading on which, by a subject of the highest rank, is a crime punished with slavery.

Once again Simmons was called upon to explain the expedition's motives and much to Tuckey's gratification,

the Chenoo, with less deliberation or questioning than I had been plagued with at Bomma, granted two guides to go as far as the cataract, beyond which the country was to them terra incognita, not a single person of the banza having ever been beyond it. The palaver being over, the keg of brandy I had brought was opened, and a greater scramble than even at Bomma took place for a sup of the precious liquor.

Tuckey and his men returned to their boats on the river to await the Chenoo's guides, but it wasn't until the following evening that they at last arrived. The next day Tuckey set off, trying still to keep to the river.

With the aid of the oars, and a track rope at times, we got the boats up along the south shore, until we came to a large sand bank extending two-thirds across the river; here we crossed over to the other side, and ran along it as far as a little island. . . . Here we found the current so rapid, that with a strong breeze and the oars we could not pass over it. . . . In crossing the river we passed several whirlpools, which swept the boat round and round in spite of her oars and sails. . . . These vortices are formed in an instant, last but a few minutes with considerable noise, and subside as quickly. The punt got into one of them and entirely disappeared in the hollows.

Tuckey went ashore and climbed the highest hill to see what lay ahead. He reported:

From hence our upward view of the river was confined to a single short reach, the appearance of which, however, was sufficient to convince us, that there was little prospect of being able to get the double boats up much farther, and none at all of being able to transport them overland. Both sides of the river appeared to be lined by rocks above water, and the middle obstructed by whirlpools, whose noise we heard in a constant roar.

Tuckey made one more reconnaissance in the gig, which convinced him of the utter futility of trying to proceed further on the river. So on the morning of August 14 he had the boats anchored in a safe cove and, with a party of twenty and provisions to last four days, struck out overland. At noon they reached a village called Cooloo,

from whence we understood we should see Yellala. Anxious to get a sight of it, I declined the Chenoo's invitation to visit him, until my return. On the farthest end of the banza we unexpectedly saw the fall almost under our feet, and were not less surprised than disappointed at finding, instead of a second Niagara, which the description of the natives, and their horror of it had given us reason to expect, a comparative brook bubbling over a stony bed.

Tuckey climbed down to the river and on a closer inspection of the cataract realized that it was nevertheless impassable.

The party was utterly exhausted by its first march overland across

the Crystal Mountains. It was not so much a matter of climate. At this time of year, in the dry season, although the sky was almost constantly overcast and the air hung with heavy, oppressive humidity, temperatures during the day didn't get much above 80 degrees Fahrenheit and at night dropped to a pleasant 65 degrees. What proved so punishing was the terrain, the "scrambling up the sides of almost perpendicular hills, and over great masses of quartz and schistus" and the slipping and stumbling down into precipices and ravines. So Tuckey had the party pitch their tents for the night in Cooloo and he went to make the obligatory call on the local Chenoo, where he

found less pomp and noise, but much more civility and hospitality, than from the richer kings I had visited. This old man seemed perfectly satisfied with our account of the motives of our visit, not asking a single question, treating us with a little palm wine, and sending me a present of six fowls without asking for anything on return.

At Cooloo, Tuckey had reached deeper into the interior along the river itself than any other white man. Smith notes in his journal that "we are constantly followed by a number of people, chiefly boys. They said they had never seen white men before," and Tuckey writes,

The higher we proceed the fewer European articles the natives possess; the country grass-cloth generally forms the sole clothing of the mass of people. . . . The women approach nearer to a state of nudity; their sole clothing being a narrow apron . . . before and behind, so that the hips on each side are uncovered . . . they flocked out to look at the white men, and without any marks of timidity came and shook hands with us. . . . We in no instance . . . found the men *allant en avant* in their offer of their women.

The next morning Tuckey engaged a guide from Cooloo and set off with the party overland to get around the cataract.

After four hours most fatiguing march we again got sight of the river; but to my great vexation, instead of being 12 or 13 miles as I expected, I found we were not above four miles from Yellala. . . . Here we found the river still obstructed with rocks and islets sometimes quite across, but at one place leaving a clear place, which seems to be used as a ferry, as we found here a canoe with four men; no inducement we could offer them had however any effect in prevailing on them to attempt going up the stream.

The party pushed a bit further, crossing through deep ravines, and at sunset camped on the side of a steep hill.

The next morning, Tudor, the comparative anatomist, and several other members of the party awoke with fever, unable to go on. Tuckey had them sent back to Cooloo and with the rest tried to proceed further.

We went across a valley and the hills on the other side, which were last night illuminated by fires [Smith tells us]. Towards the north, the country is more level and more woody. Elephants are reported to be plentiful here. A wild boar rushed forth in a valley, and though it broke through the whole line, the sailors, from their hurry and want of skill, all fired amiss. . . . We continued our route over the steep hills.

By noon though, "the people being extremely fatigued," Tuckey agreed to halt. He climbed a hill from which he had a view of a five-mile stretch of the river. It

presented the same appearance as yesterday, being filled with rocks in the middle, over which the current foamed violently; the shore on each side was also scattered with rocky barren islets. . . . Upwards my view was stopped by the sudden turn of the river from north to S.E. . . . Just where the river shuts in . . . on a high plateau of the north shore, is the banza Inga, which we understood was two days march from Cooloo (though its direct distance is not above 20 miles) and that it is out of the dominions of the Congo.

Tuckey decided to return to Cooloo, resupply his party and attempt to reach Inga along the opposite bank. The march back took eight hours; they reached the village at dark. At Cooloo, Tuckey found Tudor "in a most violent fever," unable to move on his own, and more than half the rest of the party complaining of fatigue and blistered feet. The invalids were carried down to the river where the expedition's boats had been left anchored and Tuckey had them sent back downriver to the *Congo,* anchored just below the Cauldron of Hell, and had additional supplies brought back. With a half-dozen guides and porters recruited from Cooloo and a party of about a dozen relatively fit whites, Tuckey was ready to set off for Inga on the morning of August 22.

He had awakened feeling "extremely unwell . . . directly swallowed five grains of calomel, and moved myself until I produced a strong perspiration." He hoped to be off by daybreak but it wasn't

until ten o'clock that the guides and porters showed up. And then he learned that Simmons, his valued interpreter, now called Prince Schi, had deserted. The reason, as the Chenoo came to tell Tuckey, was that Simmons, "having bargained with two of the head gentlemen for their wives (one the first time I was at Cooloo, and the other the night preceding), for two fathoms a night, which having no means of paying, he had concealed himself, or ran off to Embomma." To replace him, Tuckey hired "a man whom we had picked up at Embomma and employed as one of the boat's crew," and to whom Tuckey promised to pay "the value of a slave and other etceteras on my return, if he would accompany me; to which he at last acceded, all his countrymen attempting to deter him, by the idea of being killed and eaten by the bushmen" who lived outside the Congo realm at Inga.

The party, after a march that was now becoming depressingly familiar in its punishing difficulty, reached Inga at noon the following day. The Chenoo there turned out to be blind, and the affairs of the village were in the hands of a committee of headmen. Here Tuckey ran into a degree of hostility that he had not met before and it is difficult to tell, from either his or Smith's journals, why. It may have been because these people were not Bakongo; indeed, there is some suggestion, from the repeated reference to them as cannibalistic bushmen, that they may have been descendants of the Yakas, who had once overrun the ancient kingdom. But it is more likely that the trouble was with Tuckey rather than with the tribesmen. He was ill; as we've noted, his health had not been good at the outset anyway. Added to that were the punishing difficulty of the terrain and the depressingly slow progress that he was making, all of which would have been enough to make him short-tempered. But, whatever the cause, it was from this point that we see the expedition starting to go dangerously awry.

What Tuckey wanted from the headmen at Inga was a guide who knew the river still further upcountry, but to get one here, he reports,

I found it would be necessary to deviate from my former assertions of having nothing to do with trade, if I meant to go forward; and accordingly I gave these gentlemen to understand, that I was only the forerunner of other white men, who would bring them everything they required, provided I should make a favorable report of their conduct on my return to my own country. At length I was promised a guide to conduct me to a place where the river again became navigable for canoes, but on the express

condition that I should pay a jar of brandy and dress four gentlemen with two fathoms of bast each. These terms I complied with, stipulating on my part that the guide should be furnished immediately . . . but was now informed that I could not have the guide till the morning. Exasperated by this intolerable tergiversation, being unable to buy a single fowl, and having but three days' provisions, I remonstrated in the strongest manner, and deviated a little from my hitherto patient and concilliating manners . . . ordering the ten men with me to fall in under arms; at the sight of which the palaver broke up. . . . The women and children, who had flocked to see the white men for the first time, disappeared, and the banza became a desert; on inquiring for the men who had come with me from Cooloo, I also found that they had vanished . . . in short, I was left sole occupier of the banza. Finding that this would not at all facilitate my progress, I sent my interpreter with a conciliating message . . . which shortly produced the re-appearance of some men, but skulking behind the huts with their muskets. After an hour's delay, the regency again appeared, attended by fifty men, of whom fourteen had muskets. The Mamoom, or war minister, first got up, and made a long speech, appealing now and then to the other people . . . and who all answered by a kind of howl. During this speech he held in his hand the war kissey, composed of buffaloes' hair, and dirty rags; and which (as we afterwards understood) he invoked to break the locks and wet the powder of our muskets. As I had no intention of carrying the affair to any extremity, I went from the place where I was seated . . . and familiarly seating myself alongside the headman, shook him by the hand, and explained, that though he might see that I had the power to do him a great deal of harm, I had little to fear from his rusty muskets; and that though I had great reason to be displeased with their conduct . . . I would pass it over, provided I was assured of having a guide.

This dispute went on for several days, with Tuckey sometimes threatening, sometimes conciliatory. The Europeans had set up camp on the outskirts of the village, and from time to time small parties were sent out to see whether they could manage without a guide, but all they succeeded in doing was exhausting themselves in the unknown, brutal terrain. Fever and illness spread, morale collapsed, and nerves frayed, and what was worse, as Smith noted on August 26, "Last night . . . we had the first shower of rain since our arrival in Africa."

At last, having paid an exorbitant price to the headmen, Tuckey secured the services of a guide and set off upriver with a few of the healthier men in his party on August 28.

We ascended the hills that line the river, and which are more fatiguing than any we had yet met with, being very steep, and totally composed of broken pieces of quartz. . . . At four o'clock we came in sight of the river . . . it is crossed by a great ledge of slate rocks . . . the stream runs at least eight miles an hour, forming whirlpools in the middle, whose vortices occupy at least half the breadth of the channel, and must be fatal to any canoe that should get into them.

With night falling, the guide suggested "a banza not much higher up, where we might get some victuals" and they proceeded toward it, "scrambling over the rocks with infinite fatigue . . . nearly choked with thirst . . . until it became quite dark" only to discover that either the guide had lost his way or the banza was no longer situated where it once had been. However, they came upon a group of bushmen camped on the hillside: "The little water brought us by the wives of these bushmen . . . was our supper, and the broken granite stones our bed." The following morning, "after a small portion of roasted manioc and a draught of water for breakfast," the party returned to Inga.

For the next few days, Tuckey continued making forays of this sort from Inga in hopes of finding the point where the cataracts ended or at least where the brutal terrain of its banks eased and overland travel became feasible. On September 2, a major attempt in this respect was organized. The seriously sick were sent back to Cooloo and all the remaining fit members of the party—now numbering only twelve— along with a handful of porters from Inga, set out. It was Tuckey's last desperate try. It lasted five days and they managed to reach perhaps another 40 miles upriver, but chances for success were doomed at the outset. All the white men, Tuckey, Hawkey, and Smith included, were sick to a greater or lesser extent. Morale was abysmally low. The countryside remained unrelenting in its cruelty and the river unyielding in its impassability.

By the second day out, Tuckey tells us,

the Inga men desired to go back, on pretence of being afraid to proceed. . . . They had not walked above a mile before they laid down their loads, and refused to go on; and in this manner they plagued me . . . putting down their loads every ten minutes, walking back fifty or sixty yards as if to return, taking them up again, and so on, with a palaver of half an hour between each stoppage.

The next day, the Inga men quit entirely and Tuckey had to hire porters from a village along the way. They did not prove more cooperative. In Tuckey's entry for September 6 we read:

After a constant battle with the natives from daylight, and after using every possible means, by threats, persuasions, and promises, I at last, about two o'clock, got them underway.

The next day the party got down to the river at a stretch where it was navigable and Tuckey managed to hire some canoes from local fishermen.

About three miles from the place of departure we passed two small rapids, but the other side of the river was clear. We came to a bay in which were ten hippopotami; as the canoes could not venture to come on until these huge creatures were dispersed, we were obliged to fire volleys at them from the shore. . . . At four, reached one of the rocky promontories, round which the current set so strong, that the canoe men refused to attempt passing it. . . . I was therefore under the necessity of attempting to haul the canoes up the stream by the rocks with our own people . . . but by the neglect of one of the men, the stern of the second canoe stuck fast in the rocks, and the current taking her on the broadside, broke her right in two, and several of the articles that were in her sunk, and others were swept away. . . . All was now confusion among the canoe men, who first ran off, and then, after a long delay, came back again, but nothing could induce them to go forward.

September 9:

In the morning some rain. . . . At two P.M. we reached the head of a deep reach . . . here we stopped to dine. After dinner I wished to proceed, but our bearers refused. . . . Finding all persuasions useless, I was obliged to pitch tent at this place, and with Dr. Smith and Lieutenant Hawkey walked to the summit of a hill, where we perceived the river winding again to the S.E. but our view did not extend above three miles of the reach: the water clear of rocks, and, according to the information of all the people, there is no impediment whatever, as far as they know, above this place.

And here we were under the necessity of turning our back on the river, which we did with great regret, but with the consciousness of having done all that we possibly could.

One has to read the entry a second time. Just at the moment Tuckey at last finds the river clear of rocks and all reports assure him

that there are no further impediments upstream he decides to turn his back on the river. Just when he seems at last within sight of his goal, he decides to admit the river has defeated him. Why? It was a question that never was to be answered adequately. To be sure, illness had taken a very heavy toll of the party. Moreover, it was by then short of supplies, and there was all that trouble with the native bearers. But none of these seems an adequate explanation. After all, they were not very far into the interior. It would have taken only a week or two, three at the most, to get further provisions brought up from the *Congo* and the ailing back down to her for medical attention. The struggle to get this far had been great but not really greater than expected. An expedition of this sort was expected, on the past experiences of such explorers as Mungo Park, to be gone for years, and they had been under way only just over two months. Indeed, one might feel they were just getting started. Yet the next day, September 10, the heart for some mysterious reason gone out of him, Tuckey started back.

The return to Inga took four days. There Tuckey learned that the Inga men who had deserted "had reported that one half of us had been drowned in canoes, and the rest killed by black bushmen." The next day they got back to Cooloo.

Though ill myself, I intended to proceed; but Dr. Smith and two of our people are too ill to be moved; remained therefore this day. . . . I passed a miserable and sleepless night . . . being very weak myself and wishing to get on before the sun became too hot, I set off with Dr. Smith, leaving Mr. Hawkey behind to bring on the people. . . . Terrible march; worse to us than the retreat from Moscow."

Sept. 16. Unable at daylight to procure any canoe men, I set off with our own people, and at three P.M. reached the *Congo*.

Terrible report of the state on board: coffins.

Sept. 17. At daylight sent off all the sick in double boats . . . to the transport; hired fifteen black men to assist in taking the Congo down the river. . . .

Sept. 18. Reached the transport. . . .

Flocks of flamingos going to the south denote the approach of the rains.

This was Tuckey's last journal entry. He was taken aboard the *Dorothy,* which was anchored at Tall Trees, "in a state of extreme exhaustion." He never recovered and died on October 4. By that time

Smith, Cranch, Tudor, and Galwey were also dead, and Hawkey died two days later. Before the expedition reached England again twenty-one of the original fifty-four white men in the company (Simmons and Benjamin had remained in their homeland) were dead. In his report, the surviving assistant ship's surgeon stated "that though the greater number were carried off by a most violent fever . . . some of them appeared to have no other ailment than that which had been caused by extreme fatigue, and actually to have died from exhaustion."

The catastrophe of Tuckey's expedition came as an incredible shock to England. "It may not, perhaps, be too much to say," an Admiralty historian wrote two years later (in 1818), "that there never was in this or any other country, an expedition of discovery sent out with better prospects or more flattering hopes of success. . . . Yet, by a fatality that is almost inexplicable, never were the results more melancholy and disastrous." Its high rate of mortality and the almost embarrassing shortness of its duration were bad enough. But its lack of accomplishment was overwhelming. Not only had Tuckey come no-where near solving "the grand problem respecting the identity of the Niger and the Zaire," his magnificently equipped expedition had failed to explore and map the latter river much more than 150 miles further than had lone, haphazard European traders before him.

Under the impact of this disaster England and Europe seem to have recoiled from the Congo. They continued their exploration of the Niger. The other prong of the expedition sent out by the Colonial Office at the same time as Tuckey's, under the command of Major John Peddie, which was to follow Park's route down the Niger and which was as expensively mounted and manned, in fact failed as miserably as Tuckey's. Yet, curiously, the reaction to that failure was not the same. In the course of the next fifteen years, expedition after expedition was sent out, until the Lander brothers finally reached the Niger's mouth in 1830 and proved once and for all that it had nothing to do with the Congo. And then, when adventurous men began look-ing around for another geographical puzzle to solve, they did not turn to the still mysterious Congo. Tuckey's failure was too overwhelming.

12

DR. LIVINGSTONE AND THE NILE

No sooner had the riddle of the Niger been solved than nineteenth-century men, as if they could be happiest only when faced with the challenge of *the* superlative geographical mystery, transferred all their age's impassioned curiosity to the Nile. Barely fifty years after Mungo Park had pronounced the discovery of the Niger's mouth "certainly the greatest discovery that remains to be made in the world," Englishmen were declaring, without the least sense that they were contradicting themselves, that the location of the sources of the Nile was in Sir Harry Johnston's phrase, "the greatest geographical secret after the discovery of America."

That Europe's next great adventure in African exploration should have been the Nile, rather than the Congo, is as easily explicable as that the Niger should have been its first. For like the Niger, and so very unlike the Congo, which after Tuckey's disaster had been condemned to the darkest regions of vile savagery, the Nile had long fascinated Europe. Its delta and lower valley were, after all, the cradle of Western civilization, its flow and flood the life blood of that civilization, and the location of the source of those life-giving waters a mystery that had tantalized and defeated mankind for more than 2000 years.

As long ago as 460 B.C., Herodotus had attempted to ascend the Nile to find where it began, only to be turned back by the cataracts at Aswan. The Roman Emperor Nero, in the first century of the Christian era, sent two centurions beyond the confluence of the Blue and White Niles on the same errand, but they too were stopped, this time by the impenetrable papyrus swamps of the Sudd. A few years later,

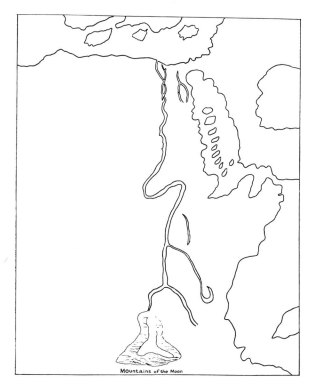

Mountains of the Moon

The course of the Nile according to the oldest extant version of Ptolemy's map

the Syrian geographer Marinus of Tyre tells us, a Greek merchant by the name of Diogenes, returning from a trading voyage to India, landed on the East African coast and then journeyed inland for 25 days in search of "two great lakes, and the snowy range of mountains whence the Nile draws its twin sources," an idea that was enshrined in Claudius Ptolemy's celebrated *mappimundi* which showed the Nile flowing from two such lakes, hidden away in the heart of Africa and fed by streams from the legendary snow-capped Mountains of the Moon.

But it wasn't until the second decade of the seventeenth century that any real headway was made in cracking the secret of the Nile sources, when two Portuguese Jesuits, on that quest for the realm of Prester John, reached Lake Tana in the Ethiopian highlands, the source of the Blue Nile. Some 150 years later, just about the time the Saturday's Club in London was forming the African Association, James Bruce, a rich and eccentric Scotsman, traveling alone from Cairo, duplicated the Jesuits' feat. In subsequent decades, Europe's abiding interest in the Nile sharpened and took on an increasingly political and economic cast with Napoleon's campaign in Egypt, Me-

hemet Ali's conquest of the Sudan, the Anglo-French competition for control of the Red Sea, and the first glimmerings of a grand plan to build a canal through the Suez isthmus. Then, with the Niger's mouth at last found and Europe yearning for a new geographical conundrum to solve, along came the sensational reports of three German missionaries in East Africa to rivet attention on the still undiscovered source of the river's parent stream, the White Nile.

Johann Ludwig Krapf, born in Württemberg but sent out to Africa by the London Church Mission, initially had set up a mission station in Ethiopia, but, because of the hostility of the native Coptic priests, he had been obliged to withdraw and establish himself near Mombasa, on the coast of present-day Kenya. There he was joined by two of his countrymen, Johannes Rebmann and Jakob Erhardt, and they proved a remarkable trio. Not only were they the first Protestant missionaries in this part of Africa, but they brought to their work an intelligent curiosity about the continent, inquiring ceaselessly about the geography of the interior, listening carefully to every report, rumor, myth, and tale. One story they heard repeatedly was of a mountain whose peak was said to be covered in silver but a silver so strange that when men brought it down from the mountain top it turned into water. Rebmann, a farmer's son and the strongest of the trio, was chosen to go inland, like the legendary Diogenes, and try to find that obviously snow-capped mountain. On May 11, 1848, he did. It was Mount Kilimanjaro, the tallest in Africa. The following year, Krapf, pushing beyond Kilimanjaro, discovered still another snow-covered peak, the Kenya massif, and Erhardt, following up on Krapf's work, learned that further westward was the land of Uniamwezi—the Country of the Moon—in which, it was said, lay a vast inland sea from which a river flowed northward toward the "land of the Turks."

The missionaries' findings, published in the periodicals of the London Church Mission between 1848 and 1855, created a sensation in England. After all, the map they drew of their discoveries bore a stunning resemblance to Ptolemy's, and their commentaries on it, replete with references to snow-capped mountains, great lakes, and the Country of the Moon, seemed a confirmation of the ancients' view of the White Nile's source. What's more, after centuries of futile attempts to reach that source by ascending the river from its delta, they suggested a promising new way of getting there. In 1856, Britain's Royal Geographical Society, which had absorbed the African Associa-

tion, took up that suggestion and launched a campaign to find the White Nile's source by striking not southward through the desert but westward from the East African coast, a campaign which, like the African Association's missions to the Niger a half century before, though for rather different reasons, would once again awaken Europe's interest in the Congo.

The first expedition sent out by the Royal Geographical Society was that of Richard Francis Burton, although only 36 already a famous explorer for his journeys to the forbidden cities of Mecca and Harar, and John Hanning Speke, a 30-year-old officer in the Indian Army, who had accompanied Burton on the Harar expedition. Sailing on the monsoon from Bombay aboard a British sloop, the pair arrived in Zanzibar in December 1856, spent several months making a geographical reconnaissance—they took a side trip to visit Rebmann at the mission near Mombasa—outfitted and assembled a caravan, and in June 1857 crossed over from Zanzibar to the East African mainland at the village of Bagamoyo in present-day Tanzania, just up the coast from Dar es Salaam.

These were the last great years of Arab domination in East Africa, and the island of Zanzibar was the major entrepôt of their thriving ivory and slave trade with the African interior. The Zanzibari sultans, in a vague and general way, laid claim to what today is Tanzania, Kenya, Uganda, the South Sudan, Malawi, Zambia, Mozambique and even Zaire, and each year, with the onset of the dry season, Arab caravans would set out from Bagamoyo into those (at least from Europe's standpoint) unmapped parts, following well-traveled trading routes, visiting their upcountry trading stations and returning perhaps a year or two later with their harvest of slaves and ivory. It was along one of these trading routes that Burton and Speke now set off with their own caravan of locally hired porters and guides and a herd of pack animals, and by August they had ascended the escarpment from the coastal plain and struck westward across the savanna plateau toward the vast lake or lakes of Uniamwezi, from which the White Nile arrived in June.

The going wasn't particularly rough. For the most part, the track they followed led from one village to another, from one watering place to another. Still, their progress was slow. At every village the local chief would delay them with a demand for the payment of a tax for the privilege of passing through his territory. What's more, as they

got further from the coast, porters deserted, and much time was wasted in hiring replacements. And then there were the fevers and disease of the African interior. One by one the pack animals died, and both Burton and Speke were soon constantly sick. So it wasn't until November that they reached Tabora, in the middle of present-day Tanzania, and, as we know now, just about equidistant from Lake Victoria toward the north and Lake Tanganyika toward the west.

Tabora was then the most important Arab town in the African interior, the crossroads of caravan routes radiating throughout Central Africa, and Burton and Speke decided to take advantage of its comparative luxury to rest up and recover their health, and to gather information from its Arab residents about the geography of the country. It was during the month they spent in Tabora that they heard the encouraging news that great lakes did indeed lie ahead, both to the west and to the north of them.

As the leader of the expedition, it was for Burton to choose in which of these directions to head. And, as it turned out, he chose wrongly. When they left Tabora in December, Burton and Speke headed west toward Lake Tanganyika, reaching the Arab trading village of Ujiji on its eastern shore in February 1858. To be sure, this was a major discovery. Burton and Speke were the first Europeans to have penetrated this far into the interior of Africa, the first to lay eyes on the great lake, the first to prove that, just as the ancients and later the German missionaries had believed, great lakes did exist in these parts, one of which might very well be the source of the White Nile. But Lake Tanganyika wasn't it.

By the time they reached Ujiji, both men were seriously sick again. Besides malaria, Speke was suffering from ophthalmia so that he could barely see and Burton from an ulcerated jaw so that he could barely eat. When they recovered enough, they hired some native canoes and sailed to the north end of the lake in hopes of finding a river issuing from it which could be the Nile. They didn't. They heard of a river further on, the Ruzizi, but the local tribesmen told them that it flowed not out of but into the lake, so they didn't bother to investigate it. The two explorers returned to Ujiji "sick at heart" as Burton wrote later, and from there made their way back to Tabora, where they arrived in June.

Here Burton made yet another wrong choice. He decided to spend some time in Tabora resupplying the expedition's caravan and com-

piling his notes on the discovery of Lake Tanganyika. Speke, on the other hand, was anxious to investigate the lake that they had heard lay to the north of Tabora, a lake which the Arabs claimed to be far larger than Lake Tanganyika, and Burton let him go off on his own. Speke's journey took three weeks. He arrived on the shore of Lake Victoria, near present-day Mwanza, in early August, and at the first sight of it was seized by an amazing conviction. "I no longer felt any doubt," he wrote, "that the lake at my feet gave birth to that interesting river, the source of which has been the subject of so much speculation, and the object of so many explorers." He was correct, of course, but in fact he had no right to be. He spent only three days on the lake and viewed only a tiny portion of it. He did not find any river outletting from it to the north, nor could he even be sure that the vast sheet of water he saw was a single lake and not several. Even so, he returned to Tabora in an ecstasy of enthusiasm, declaring to Burton that he felt "quite certain in my mind I had discovered the source of the Nile."

Now the green serpent of jealousy reared its ugly head. Burton wasn't about to concede to his younger, less experienced companion this most cherished prize of African discovery. He immediately pointed out Speke's failure to explore the lake properly and rejected his reasons for claiming the discovery as "weak and flimsy." Moreover, Burton had been having second thoughts about Lake Tanganyika, of which he could claim himself the discoverer, and he was now no longer willing to rule it out altogether as a possible source of the White Nile. Speke's lake, christened by him in honor of the reigning British monarch, might provide a feeder stream to the Upper Nile, Burton was willing to allow, but if so only after the Upper Nile had emerged from *his* lake, Tanganyika, perhaps as that unexplored river, the Ruzizi.

The traveling companions fell out bitterly over the issue, and with neither speaking to the other and both again stricken with fever, their return to the coast was a nightmare. They arrived back in Zanzibar in March 1859, proceeded to Aden and there parted forever. Burton chose to continue his convalescence in Aden. Speke returned to England and, going directly to Sir Roderick Murchison, president of the Royal Geographical Society, was able to make his argument for Victoria as the White Nile's source without Burton's interference. Murchison and the society were excited by the report and agreed to sponsor an expedition to follow up Speke's discovery. Speke was to head it,

and James Augustus Grant, another Indian Army officer, the same age as Speke and a former hunting companion of his, was to be his traveling companion this time.

The Royal Geographical Society's second attempt to find the White Nile's source from the East African coast left the following year and Speke, now with Grant, arrived again in Zanzibar in October 1860. His plan was to follow the same caravan route to Tabora, turn north from there to Victoria, then work his way along the lake's western shore until he reached the north end, where he fully expected to find a river outletting into the Nile, which he would then follow north into the Sudan. It was a sensible plan and, except for some unexpected delays, he and Grant carried it through to a remarkable extent.

Because of tribal wars in the interior, it took the pair over a year after leaving Zanzibar to get as far as Speke and Burton had gotten in five months, and it wasn't until November 1861 that they were at last on their way northward from Tabora. Then came further and, in many ways, wonderful delays in the kingdoms of Uganda, especially at the fabulous court of Mtesa, the Kabaka (king) of Buganda, on the western shores of Lake Victoria. It wasn't until July 1862 that they were actually on the march to the northern end of the great inland sea. And here Speke again contrived to separate from his expedition partner. Unlike Burton, however, Grant never raised any complaint. He was at that time suffering from an agonizingly painful infection in one of his legs and, recognizing that he was slowing Speke down, agreed to let his companion go on ahead without him. Speke then led a column on a forced march, traveling at the rate of 20 miles a day, and on July 21, 1862, at a place called Urondogani about 40 miles from Victoria, he found a river flowing from the lake toward the north and "at last," he concluded, "I stood on the brink of the Nile."

A month later, Speke rejoined forces with Grant and then, since they had been in Africa for nearly two years, his main concern was to get back to England and report his momentous discovery to the world. For the next six months he and Grant marched to the north, sometimes in sight of the river found outletting from Victoria but, because of the rugged terrain, usually not. At one point they heard reports of still another great lake to the west of them, called Luta Nzige, which they realized might prove to be another source of the Nile, but with their supplies running low and their health failing they couldn't

afford the detour to find out. In February 1863, they reached Gondo-koro, in the southern Sudan, where a relief column sent by the Royal Geographical Society was waiting for them. From there they sailed down the Nile to Khartoum, on to Cairo, and finally back to England, where they arrived in June 1863.

Speke had in fact discovered the source of the White Nile, but that was not to be conclusively proved or finally conceded for nearly fifteen years. He had left too many unanswered questions and there were still too many rival explorers coveting the honor for themselves. Burton, for example, once again charged Speke with "an extreme looseness of geography." He argued that what Speke had done was catch a glimpse of a large sheet of water at Mwanza in 1858, then catch a glimpse of another large sheet of water at the court of the Kabaka of Buganda in 1862 and conclude that the area between the two points, covering nearly 30,000 square miles, comprised a single lake. But he had no right to jump to such a fantastic conclusion because he still had not circumnavigated the lake, still had not demonstrated that what he had discovered was not two different lakes or more. In addition, Burton went on, while it was true that Speke had found a northward-flowing outlet from the lake (or lakes), he had no basis for declaring it to be the Nile because he had not followed it downstream into the Sudan; he had marched overland to Gondokoro and though, from time to time, he caught sight of a river along the march, he had no way of knowing that what he saw was always the same river. But finally, Burton contended, even granting it was the same river, even granting that Victoria was a single vast lake and not several, there was still no proof that it was the source of the Nile. For, after all, Speke could not say what river might flow *into* the lake, a river rising to the south of the lake, rising perhaps in another lake like his Tanganyika, a river whose source, by virtue of lying further south, would more properly be the Nile's source than Victoria's outlet.

Arguments like these split England into two passionately contending camps. And then Samuel Baker came along to confuse matters even further.

Baker, a rich man's son who had spent his youth in idle travel and big-game hunting, decided in his late thirties to get in on the excitement of African exploration. In June 1861, outfitted with delicacies from Fortnum & Mason's and equipment from the best London shops and traveling with his beautiful Hungarian wife, he arrived in Cairo

to spend a year journeying up the Nile, shooting big game and observing the exotic ways of the natives, reaching Khartoum in June 1862. And there his aimless wandering came to an end. The Royal Geographical Society had charged the British vice consul in Khartoum, a certain John Petherick, with the job of organizing a relief column to meet Speke and Grant in Gondokoro. A few months before Baker and his wife arrived at Khartoum, Petherick and *his* wife had set off for Gondokoro. Nothing had been heard from them since, and rumors had filtered back that they were dead. What's more, nothing had been heard from Speke and Grant for more than a year, and there was a growing belief that they too had perished. So the Royal Geographical Society asked Baker to take over the job of leading the relief column to Gondokoro and, if he learned there that Speke and Grant were dead, to take up their task of finding the Nile's source.

Baker delightedly accepted the dual assignment. It took him six months to assemble and outfit the relief column, and he and his wife led it out of Khartoum in December. After a journey of over 1000 miles southward on the Nile—first through the waterless waste of the desert, then through primeval swamp of the Sudd—a journey that took forty days, they reached Gondokoro in February 1863.

As it turned out, no one had died. Two weeks after the Bakers' arrival in Gondokoro, Speke and Grant turned up, and a few days later so did the Pethericks. As a result, Baker considered "my expedition as terminated," he later wrote, "but . . . Speke and Grant with characteristic candour and generosity gave me a map of their route, showing that they had been unable to complete the actual exploration of the Nile, and that a most important portion still remained to be determined." That portion was the large lake, Luta Nzige, of which Speke and Grant had heard, lying to the west of them, during their march to Gondokoro. So, as soon as Speke and Grant left for Khartoum, Baker and his wife set out to find it. Just over a year later, in May 1864, they did. "The waves were rolling upon a white pebbly beach," Baker wrote. "I rushed into the lake, and thirsty with heat and fatigue, with a heart full of gratitude, I drank deeply from the Sources of the Nile." And so Lake Albert, as Baker named Luta Nzige in honor of Queen Victoria's recently deceased consort, was added to the dispute over the origins of the river.

In September 1864, at a meeting of the British Association for the Advancement of Science at Bath, an attempt was to be made to settle

the dispute by debate. The principal contestants in what the popular press called the Nile Duel were to be the two greatest rivals on the issue, Burton and Speke. Before an audience of several hundred of the nation's most eminent geographers and scientists, they were to face each other for the first time since they had parted in Aden more than five years before. They never did. On the day before the Nile Duel, Speke killed himself. It was, as it turned out, a tragic accident. Speke had gone out that afternoon with some friends to shoot partridges on his uncle's estate and, while climbing over a wall, had fallen and his rifle discharged into his chest. But so hot were the emotions on the question of the Nile that the immediate reaction was that Speke, fearing to face Burton's arguments, had committed suicide, a view that persisted for years.

Obviously, the Nile Duel was off. (In its place, Burton read a paper on the *Ethnology of Dahomey.*) But, equally obviously, even had it taken place it would have accomplished little more than inflame the controversy even further. For the question of the Nile's source could not be resolved in a lecture hall in England by debaters. The only place it would be settled finally was in the field in Central Africa by an explorer. No one understood this better than Murchison, the president of the Royal Geographical Society, and for that job he now turned to another participant at the Bath meeting: the missionary doctor David Livingstone.

At the time of the Bath meeting, where he delivered a paper on the evils of the slave trade, Livingstone was almost 52 years old and had spent nearly half those years in Africa. He had been born in Blantyre, Scotland, the son of a respectable but desperately poor traveling tea salesman, and had worked in the textile mills of that city, from six in the morning to eight at night, six days a week, from the age of 10 until he was 23. He escaped from that Dickensian life by gaining admission to Anderson's College in Glasgow, and there he trained for a career as a medical missionary.

That was the time, at the height of the abolitionist movement, of the first real surge of Protestant mission activity in Africa. For the Scottish and English nonconformists the main field of that activity was in and around the Cape Colony, which the British government had seized from the Dutch at the outbreak of the Napoleonic Wars in order to protect its shipping lanes to India. As early as 1805, the London Missionary Society had established a mission station north

of the Orange River, and by 1841, when Livingstone completed his medical studies in Glasgow and was ordained a Congregationalist minister at Albion Chapel, Finsbury, the society had a station at Kuruman, nearly 600 miles further into the African interior. And that was where Livingstone asked to be sent.

From the outset, Livingstone was an unusual sort of missionary. The London Society's prevailing practice then was to have its missionaries settle down at their first station and proceed to spend if not exactly their entire lives then at least twenty or thirty years there, devoted to the task of converting the tribesmen in the immediate region. But Livingstone had been in Kuruman barely a month when he was already restlessly looking further afield. He quarreled with his superior, found that he couldn't get along with his fellow missionaries, developed an insatiable curiosity to discover what lay beyond the confines of the station's territory, and was immediately ambitious to run a mission of his own. Indeed, it was this early in his African career that he first used the phrase that was to be the guiding light of the rest of his life. In a letter home to Scotland, he wrote, "I would never build on another man's foundation. I shall preach the gospel *beyond every other man's line of things.*"

And Livingstone got his chance far sooner than he had any right to expect. Convincing the society's directors that the tribes to the north of Kuruman offered a promising field for missionary work, he received permission to undertake a series of expeditions in search of a suitable site for a new station. And from the end of 1841 to the middle of 1843 he traveled north and northeast, often as much as 500 miles further into the interior from Kuruman, entering country where no white man had been before. Though the mission station that he finally did establish, at Mabotsa, ultimately turned out to be a failure, these travels proved decisive to his career: during them Livingstone began the steady, inevitable transformation from a missionary with an interest in geography to an explorer with an interest in religion.

Livingstone spent a little less than two years running the mission station at Mabotsa, during which time he married a missionary's daughter from Kuruman, but, having no success in converting the local tribesmen there, he abandoned it and moved further northeast and established another one at Chonunane. As this turned out just as dismally as the last, he moved on once again and set himself up in Kolobeng where he remained for two more years.

David Livingstone (From a photograph taken by Thomas Annan, of Hamilton and Glasgow)

It was at Kolobeng that he first heard of a large lake lying north-westward from the station, a lake which, he wrote to a friend, "everyone would like to be the first to see." And in 1849, determined to be that first one, he set off on the first of three expeditions which were to establish his reputation as an African explorer. Between June and October of 1849, he journeyed more than 300 miles from Kolobeng, crossing the Kalahari Desert, and reached Lake Ngami in the north-western corner of what is today Botswana. His account of this journey, which was published in the March 1850 issue of *Missionary Magazine*, brought Livingstone to the attention of the Royal Geographical Society, and Murchison, just then elected its president, arranged to have a small sum raised for a second expedition. So, between April and August of 1850, Livingstone repeated the journey, this time taking his family along (there were three children by now and his wife was five months pregnant with the fourth) and this time heard of a great river lying several hundred miles further to the northeast. Because his wife and children had fallen ill, Livingstone had to turn back without attempting to find that river. But the next year, again with his wife and children in tow, he set off on the third and what was to prove the crucial journey, for in August 1851, at the town of Sesheke where the Caprivi Strip of South-West Africa divides modern Botswana from Zambia, he came upon the Zambezi River.

The discovery of the Zambezi is one of the great achievements of African exploration, and Livingstone devoted the next twelve years of his life to the river's exploration. After taking his family back to Cape Town, he returned to the Zambezi in May 1853, and, in the course of the next year, followed the river upstream into Angola and then proceeded all the way to Loanda on the West African coast, where he arrived in May 1854 half-dead with fever. Then, after five months in the Portuguese settlement recovering his health, he turned around, retraced his steps across Angola and returned to his starting point in September 1855. But he was not done yet. In November of that year he set out to follow the river downstream, to its mouth, discovering Victoria Falls along the way, and arrived in Quelimane in present-day Mozambique in May 1856. By this stupendous journey he became the first European ever to have crossed the African continent from coast to coast and the most famous African explorer of his day. When he returned to England, he was treated as a national hero. The Royal Geographical Society awarded him its gold medal; Oxford University

gave him an honorary doctorate; Queen Victoria granted him a private audience; and wherever he appeared in public, he was mobbed by crowds fighting to shake his hand.

But Livingstone was not yet through with the Zambezi. He believed that in the river he had found a great highway into the interior of Africa, along which "Christianity and Commerce" could be brought to the continent. And he used his popularity, fame, and prestige to promote a government-sponsored expedition to the river which was meant to open the way for missionaries and mission stations, traders and trading posts, and for the eventual British colonization of the regions adjacent to its shores. That expedition left England in March 1858, it lasted until July 1864, and it was a terrible failure. In the first place, Livingstone discovered that the Zambezi, far from being a highway into the interior, was navigable for only 400 miles from its mouth. During his journey *down* the river in 1856, he had heard about the Kebrabassa Rapids but, seeking then to avoid some rough terrain, he had left the river and bypassed them without actually seeing them. When he returned and laid eyes on the rapids for the first time, he realized that what he had heard—that they were merely "a number of rocks which jut out across the stream"—was utterly false. In fact, they turned out to be 30 miles of thundering cataracts, through which no vessel of any sort could pass. Moreover, even the short navigable stretch of the river posed problems for his expedition's boats. The Zambezi's mouth is a delta, clogged with sandbars and mudflats through which Livingstone's vessels had a devilish time entering, and not far upstream the river becomes shallow, with its channels shifting from month to month, so that the boats were constantly going aground.

After a year of struggling hopelessly with this troublesome river, Livingstone admitted defeat and turned his attention to the Shire, a major tributary which flows into the Zambezi about 100 miles above its mouth. At first this seemed a promising prospect, and, indeed, it was in the process of exploring the Shire that Livingstone scored his next noteworthy discovery, that of Lake Nyasa (now called Lake Malawi), out of which the Shire flows. But it was to be the expedition's only positive achievement. All too soon a host of problems beset the explorer. The Shire turned out to be only slightly more navigable than the Zambezi, being clogged with vegetation and blocked by rapids of its own. Moreover, the shores of the river and lake were a

major hunting ground of the Arab slavers, and as a consequence the tribes in the region were extremely hostile to strangers and defeated all attempts to establish missions or trading posts among them. Then too, because of the flooding of the river and the lake, the shorelines were swampy and proved to be breeding grounds for disease, and members of the party rapidly came down with fever and dysentery. Men became delirious; Livingstone's wife died; morale plummeted. The ugliest sort of petty quarrels broke out. Defeat and failure were inevitable.

When Livingstone returned to England this time, in July 1864, he met with an entirely different reception. It would be too much to say that he was in disgrace. Among geographers at least there was a fair appreciation for his accomplishments. He had discovered an important new lake; he had mapped the Zambezi to the Kebrabassa Rapids and all of the Shire; he had provided useful new information about the tribes, the Arab slave trade, and the geographical problems of south-central and southeast Africa. Nevertheless, there were no banquets, no visits with the Queen, no medals, no mobs hailing him in the streets. For the public, at least, his expedition seemed worthy of little attention, especially since something far more exciting in the way of African exploration had come along in the meantime.

During the six years Livingstone had been struggling on the Zambezi and Shire, the search for the Nile's source had developed into the passionate issue of the day. Burton and Speke had gone out to Africa and returned during those years, and so had Speke and Grant and Baker. In fact, it was barely six weeks after Livingstone's return that the great Nile Duel was scheduled to take place at Bath.

Nevertheless, Livingstone was still accorded enough respect as an explorer for Murchison to select him to go out to Africa and settle the dispute about the Nile's source, and it was a choice that was universally applauded. For there was Livingstone's vast experience in Africa to commend him for the job. But, more important, on the touchy issue of the Nile, he was a neutral. To have sent out Burton or Grant (in lieu of the dead Speke) or Baker would have made nonsense of the project. Each too passionately had his own axe to grind, his own theory to prove. Livingstone, presumably, had none. In all his years in Africa, he had never come near the region of the supposed source of the White Nile, had never laid eyes on any of the contending lakes, and so could bring a fresh, objective view to the problem.

What Murchison wanted Livingstone to do was to proceed to Burton's Lake Tanganyika and determine whether the Ruzizi flowed from it, and, if it did, find out whether it flowed north into Baker's Lake Albert and issued from there as the Upper Nile. Furthermore, he wanted him to explore Speke's Lake Victoria and establish once and for all its relationship to the Nile watershed.

But Livingstone was the man who had written more than twenty years before that he "would never build on another man's foundation," that he would always work "beyond every other man's line of things." For him to have proceeded as Murchison suggested would have meant that he would be building on Burton's and Speke's and Baker's foundations, would be remaining within their line of things. And this simply wasn't in Livingstone's character. If he was going to settle the issue of the Nile, he would not do it by confirming one or another man's work; if he was going to find the river's origin, he would find it where other men had never looked for it before. Livingstone, as a matter of fact, wasn't quite the neutral on the question that everyone believed. Almost as soon as Murchison involved him in the great debate, he began to develop his own ideas about where the Nile's source was to be found: south of Lakes Victoria and Albert, south even of Tanganyika, further south than Burton or Speke or Baker or any other man had dreamed. Livingstone would look for the Nile's source in those savanna highlands where not the Nile but the Congo rises.

13

THE SACRED ORACLES

Livingstone did not immediately accept Murchison's proposal to undertake an expedition to settle the Nile dispute. It was not from any lack of desire on his part to return to Africa. Of that there was never any question. He had spent more than twenty years, virtually his entire adult life, on the continent, and Africa was far more a home to him than England or Scotland. At 52 he was still youthful enough and intellectually vigorous, and his health, though it had been undermined on his last expedition, seemed fully recovered after his rest in Britain. And besides, with his wife dead and his children grown, he had no family duties to hold him back. No, it was something else that caused Livingstone to hesitate: the purely geographical purpose of the enterprise.

Livingstone had long before this severed his ties with the London Missionary Society and had so thoroughly evolved away from his original calling as a medical missionary that it was hard to think of him as anything but an explorer by this time. Yet, oddly enough, this was not how Livingstone thought of himself. If he was no longer a missionary in the classic sense, he also was not, at least in his own mind, someone for whom geographical discovery for its own sake was sufficient reason to lead an expedition into the heart of Africa. He had to have a larger, more noble reason, and on all his previous journeys he had managed to come up with one. In his earliest years, for example, he had justified his restless wanderings as the search for new and more promising fields for missionary work. And later on, when he was no longer even nominally in the pay of the London Society, he insisted that his expeditions were less matters of discovering and mapping the Zambezi

or the Shire than grand pioneering ventures to open up those rivers as highways which missionaries and traders could follow to bring the civilizing influence of Christianity and commerce to the African tribes of those parts.

But no such reasons, Livingstone realized, could be used to justify an expedition searching for the Nile's source. Such an expedition would be constantly on the move, and where it went would be dictated by such strictly geographical considerations as the locations of lakes, the flow of rivers, the pattern of watersheds. As this might lead it into the remotest, most unlikely regions, it would be ridiculous to claim that its purpose was the reconnaissance of promising fields for missionary stations or commercial settlements. So other justifications entirely had to be found and, though it took him a year, Livingstone eventually found them.

The first was the Arab slave trade. On his previous expedition, while traveling up the Shire to Lake Nyasa, he had come into contact with it and witnessed the terrible havoc it wrought, and he was aware that, wherever a search for the Nile's source might otherwise lead, it surely would pass through the bloody hunting grounds of the Arab slavers. At this time, Europe cared very little about the Arab slave trade, primarily because little was known about it, so Livingstone could allow himself to believe that he was undertaking Murchison's assignment, at least in part, to make Europeans aware of this bloody traffic and arouse them to take the same sort of measures to abolish it that they had taken to end the slave trade from the West African coast.

But Livingstone found yet another reason for agreeing to take up the search for the Nile's source, a reason that infused the enterprise with a far grander significance than even the abolition of the Arab slave trade did. For he had come to believe that the agelessly elusive source of what he called, quoting Homer, "Egypt's heaven-descended spring" was somehow holy and its discovery an almost divine undertaking.

It is impossible to know when the seeds of this fantastic belief first took root in Livingstone's mind because he revealed it only after it was in its fullest flower, when he had been on his divine quest for several years. What we do know is that he was familiar with and fascinated by the ancient geographers' accounts of the mystery of the Nile's sources. For example, at one point in his journals he tran-

scribed an account of the Nile's origin, given to Herodotus by an Egyptian scribe, in which it is described as rising from "fountains fathomless in depth" between two mountains, half of whose water "flowed to Egypt, towards the North Wind, the other half to Ethiopia and the South Wind." And we know too that, with his missionary training, Livingstone was an avid Bible student and was particularly intrigued by a story in Exodus which tells of Moses, accompanied by Merr, the Pharaoh's daughter, going up the Nile to Inner Ethiopia to found the mysterious city of Meroe, going up so far that he might possibly have reached the great river's source. And this allowed Livingstone to dream, as he wrote, of discovering "evidence of the great Moses in those parts." Apparently these Biblical and classical allusions melded in Livingstone's mind into a mystical sense of mission "to confirm the Sacred Oracles," a mission so compelling that it was to blind him to his expedition's true accomplishment: the discovery of the source and headwaters of the Congo.

Livingstone departed from England on August 13, 1865, and, traveling by way of India, arrived in Zanzibar on January 28, 1866. This

A View of Zanzibar

was still the capital of the Arab slave trade, where anywhere from 80,000 to 100,000 captives were brought from the African interior each year and, given Livingstone's stated intention of campaigning against this trade, it is rather a paradox that not only did his expedition start out from this teeming slave port but from the very outset its success depended on the help of Arab slavers.

On Livingstone's side, the paradox is not difficult to explain. There can be no question of his hatred for the island and everything he saw there. In one of his first journal entries he called the place "Stinkibar" and described the humiliations that the Africans were subjected to in its slave market: "The teeth are examined, the cloth lifted up to examine the lower limbs, and a stick is thrown for the slave to bring, and thus exhibit his paces. Some are dragged through the crowd by the hand, and the price is called out incessantly." But Livingstone really had no choice. This was the only place he could properly outfit his expedition, and since all the island's firms, directly or indirectly, dealt in slaves he had no way of avoiding doing business with slavers. Moreover, all the caravan routes he would be following into the interior were controlled by the Arab slavers, as were all the trading posts upcountry where he would be calling for resupply, so he was obliged to stay on reasonably good terms with them.

What is far more difficult to understand is why the Arabs cooperated with Livingstone. They were aware of his view of the slave trade and knew well enough that one of his main objects in coming to Africa was to incite a campaign to destroy it. And yet they helped him. They outfitted his expedition with first-class goods at decent prices. The Sultan of Zanzibar loaned him a handsome house for his stay on the island and provided him with a *firman* to the sheikhs in the interior, instructing them to render Livingstone any assistance he might require. And time and again, once he was in the interior, slavers went out of their way to render him just such assistance and, in fact, on more than one occasion saved his life. Partly, one can suppose, this amiable attitude toward a man who ostensibly was their enemy was rooted in the Arabs' desire to stay on good terms with the British. But, to a greater extent, it had something to do with the kind of man Livingstone was, his courage, his indomitable will, his patience and gentleness, that quality in him which the Arabs called *baraka* and which attracted them to him and made them genuinely want to help him.

Livingstone spent seven weeks on Zanzibar organizing his caravan. He had brought out 22 members of the party from India, 13 sepoys from the Bombay Marine Battalion and 9 young freed African slaves from the British government school at Nassick. Now he recruited 13 more, including ten Johanna men sent over from the Comoro Islands and he would later bring the complement up to 60 by hiring local tribesmen once he landed on the African mainland. Among his initial party were a number of men who had served with him before. Chuma, for example, one of the Nassick schoolboys, was a slave Livingstone had freed during his explorations of Lake Nyasa, and Susi, a young Zanzibari, had worked on the boat used in the expedition up the Shire River. In addition, Livingstone assembled a train of baggage animals. He was the only white man in the party.

It was an astonishingly small party. To appreciate just how small it is only necessary to point out that Burton and Speke, who traveled nowhere nearly the great distances Livingstone now intended, never had fewer than 130 men in their caravan. The small size of the party reflected Livingstone's ideas on the best way to travel in Africa. He believed that to march in "grand array" was only to stir up the greed and hostility of the tribesmen, provoke demands for larger *hongo* or bribes, and offer greater temptations for thieving. Even so, the reality of African travel in Livingstone's time was that the larger the caravan the farther it could go, for it had to carry not only all the equipment the expedition itself needed but enough trading goods— bales of cloth, bags of beads, and items of manufacture—to buy fresh food and the right of passage along the way. Thus, to make up for the fact that he didn't have a sufficiently large party to carry as much goods as he needed, Livingstone arranged to have an advance post set up in the interior, where additional supplies were to be sent for him. And the post he chose was Ujiji, the Arab trading town on the eastern shore of Lake Tanganyika, which he hoped to reach within a year.

In March 1866 his little party landed on the East African coast at the port town of Mikindani, just north of the mouth of the Rovuma River in what is today Tanzania, and set off for the interior. "Now that I am on the point of starting another trip into Africa I feel quite exhilarated," he recorded in his journal on March 26.

The mere animal pleasure of travelling in a wild unexplored country is very great. When on lands of a couple of thousand feet, brisk exercise im-

parts elasticity to the muscles, fresh and healthy blood circulates through the brain, the mind works well, the eye is clear, the step is firm, and a day's exertion always makes the evening's repose thoroughly enjoyable. We have usually the stimulus of remote chances of danger either from beasts or men. Our sympathies are drawn out towards our humble hardy companions by a community of interests and, it may be, of perils, which makes us all friends.

Livingstone, as we've seen, was convinced that the Nile's source lay much further south than any of his predecessors had thought to look. And so his plan was to march almost due westward from Mikindani, following the Rovuma River much of the way, until he reached Lake Nyasa, cross it, and then begin working his way northward toward the southern tip of Lake Tanganyika, in the full expectation that before he got there he would come across a system of rivers and lakes which would be the watershed of the Nile and from which he would find a river flowing northward, very possibly into Lake Tanganyika, and from there on into Lake Albert or, alternatively, along the western shores of those lakes. Having established that, he would then thoroughly explore the watershed until he isolated the particular stream which fed it and then find that particular stream's source, and thus discover the precise fountain of the Nile.

But things turned sour almost immediately, and the exhilarating tone of the early entry vanished tragically quickly from Livingstone's diary. The area he was passing through proved to be far more brutally ransacked by the Arab slavers than even Livingstone had expected. He records at one point:

We passed a woman tied by the neck to a tree and dead, the people of the country explained that she had been unable to keep up with other slaves in the gang, and her master had determined that she should not become the property of anyone else if she recovered after resting for a time. I may mention here that we saw others tied up in a similar manner, and one lying in the path shot or stabbed, for she was in a pool of blood. The explanation we got invariably was that the Arab who owned these victims was enraged at losing his money by the slaves becoming unable to walk, and vented his spleen by murdering them.

But Livingstone's real troubles developed within his own caravan. Barely ten days after leaving the coast, he became aware that the sepoys were mistreating the baggage animals, flogging, goading, and

Slavers revenging their losses

stabbing at them with such ferociousness that he suspected that they
were deliberately bent on killing the beasts and sabotaging the expedition. What was worse, they dawdled incorrigibly, constantly making
excuses for stopping or falling back.

At one point, his patience tried to the breaking point, Livingstone
gave two of the sepoys "some smart cuts with a cane." But this was
very much not in the gentle Livingstone's style, and he wrote after the
incident, "I felt I was degrading myself, and resolved not to do the
punishment myself again." Discipline meted out so half-heartedly
served more to encourage than discourage defiance and the rot spread,
slowing the march, destroying the baggage animals, which died off one
by one, and finally infecting the Nassick boys and Johanna men. "It is
difficult to feel charitable to fellows," Livingstone wrote of the sepoys,
"whose scheme seems to have been to detach the Nassick boys from me
first, then, when the animals were all killed, the Johanna men, afterwards they could rule me as they liked, or go back and leave me to
perish; but I shall try to feel as charitably as I can in spite of it all."

In June, some 200 miles inland from the coast, the caravan entered
a region suffering from famine and ravaged by tribal wars as well as by
Arab slavers. Under these conditions, the porters whom Livingstone
had hired at Mikindani refused to go further, saying they feared capture by the slavers or death in the tribal wars, and Livingstone was
obliged to pay them off and let them return to the coast. It was a

serious loss. The party had been small enough to begin with and now it was more than halved in size. Then a few weeks later there was another devastating blow. Believing they had gained the upper hand because of the loss of the porters from the coast, the sepoys became increasingly mutinous, until Livingstone had no choice but to get rid of them as well. Thus, with the Johanna men, Nassick boys, some locally hired porters, and his young servants from previous expeditions, such as Chuma and Susi, Livingstone's party was down to twenty-three and growing alarmingly short of food as it marched through the famine-stricken country toward the shores of Lake Nyasa.

We came to the Lake . . . and felt grateful to That Hand which had protected us thus far on our journey [reads the entry for August 8 in Livingstone's journal]. It was as if I had come back to an old home I never expected to see again; and pleasant to bathe in the delicious waters again, hear the roar of the sea, and dash in the rollers. Temp. 71 degrees at 8 A.M., while the air was 65 degrees. I feel quite exhilarated.

But, alas, this exhilaration also was to pass quickly. Livingstone had planned to get passage for his party across the lake in one of the Arab dhows that regularly crossed it as part of the slaving route from the interior down to the coast. But here was a case—the only serious one—where the Arab slavers refused to aid Livingstone. Showing them the *firman* of the Sultan of Zanzibar was no help. "Very few of the coast Arabs can read," Livingstone discovered. "All Arabs flee from me, the English name being in their minds inseparably connected with recapturing of slaves." So, after two weeks of useless negotiations for a dhow, Livingstone was obliged to make a long detour around the southern end of the lake. He crossed the Shire, where it outlets from Nyasa, on September 13 and started up the lake's western shore toward Lake Tanganyika.

And now there were still more setbacks. On September 25, the Johanna men quit. They claimed that they had heard from a passing Arab, we read in Livingstone's journal, "that all the country in front was full of Mazitu [a tribe of nomadic warriors] . . . and all the Johanna men now declared that they would go no further. Musa [their leader] said, 'No good country that; I want to go back to Johanna to see my father and mother and son.' " Livingstone tried to convince them that the Arab's story was false and took them to a local chieftain, who told them, " 'There are no Mazitu near where you are going'; but Musa's eyes *stood out* with terror, and he said, 'I no can

believe that man.' . . . When we started, all the Johanna men walked off, leaving the goods on the ground." The party was now down to a dangerously small complement of eleven as the caravan moved from the open savanna into ever more thickly forested regions.

And then the rains began. Within a matter of a few weeks Livingstone was writing, "It rains every day . . . the cracks in the soil then fill up and everything rushes up with astonishing rapidity . . . we spent a miserable night . . . wetted by a heavy thunder-shower . . . Morning muggy, clouded all over, and rolling thunder in the distance." And with the onset of the rains came diseases and fevers, taking their toll of the members of the dwindling party, including Livingstone himself. His entry for December 6: "Too ill to march." In the subsequent weeks: "We could get no food at any price . . . the men grumbled at their feet being pierced by thorns . . . we have no grain, and live on meat alone . . . we had so little to eat that I dreamed the night long of dinners I had eaten, and might have been eating." On New Year's Eve he wrote: "We now end 1866. It has not been so fruitful or useful as I intended. Will try to do better in 1867, and be better—more gentle and loving; and may the Almighty, to whom I commit my way, bring my desires to pass, and prosper me! Let all the sins of '66 be blotted out for Jesus' sake."

Barely a week into the new year there was yet another serious mishap. A porter, clambering down into a ravine along a steep path slippery from the incessant rain, fell and damaged Livingstone's chronometers, making it impossible for him to know for sure that his longitude readings were accurate, and thus where he was. Two weeks after that, a still more dangerous blow fell. Two porters deserted with their loads—and the load one carried was the expedition's medicine chest. With little exaggeration Livingstone wrote, "I felt as if I had now received the sentence of death."

He had now been more than nine months under way and had traveled more than 800 miles. He was suffering from dysentery and malaria, both of which were sure to get worse with the rains and the lack of decent food and, unchecked by drugs, they could prove fatal. To go on without the medicine chest was almost suicidal. And yet Livingstone decided to go on. He believed that he was very near his goal, that within a reasonable amount of time he would come upon that watershed of lakes and rivers where he would find the source of the Nile. He was wrong only in the name of the river. On January 24,

he reached the Chambezi, the source of the Congo.

It is difficult to understand how Livingstone could have made the gross geographical error he now made. The Chambezi flows southwest into Lake Bangweolo, from which, as the Luapula, it turns to the north to flow into Lake Mweru, the outlet of which is the Luvua, which flows into the Lualaba, which is the Upper Congo. Yet Livingstone believed—perhaps wanted to believe—that the Chambezi flowed north, that it was the river he was seeking that flowed into Lake Tanganyika and thus was the beginning of the Nile. He would not realize his mistake for months, and by that time he had marched northward all the way to the southern shore of Lake Tanganyika.

It was a beastly trek. He was hungry all the time, his health deteriorated alarmingly, and added to his woes was an attack of rheumatic fever. "Every step I take jars the chest," he wrote, "and I am very weak; I can scarcely keep up the march, though formerly I was always first, and had to hold in my pace not to leave the people altogether." The only moment of consolation came when the party encountered a caravan of Arab slavers headed for the coast and its leader offered to take a packet of letters with him to Zanzibar. This was Livingstone's first opportunity to make contact with the outside world in nearly a year and he used it to describe the dismissal of the sepoys and the defection of the Johanna men, then went on to describe his own situation:

We have lately had a great deal of hunger, not want of fine dishes, but want of all dishes except mushrooms. . . . The severest loss I ever sustained was that of my medicines; every grain of them, except a little extract of hyoscyamus. We had plenty of provisions after we left Lake Nyassa, but latterly got into severe hunger. Don't think please, that I make a moan over nothing but a little sharpness of appetite. I am a mere ruckle of bones.

On April 1, Livingstone reached the southern shore of Lake Tanganyika. There was no exhilaration this time. He writes, "I feel deeply thankful at having got so far. I am excessively weak—cannot walk without tottering, and have a constant singing in the head." The next day he fell dangerously ill. "I had a fit of insensibility, which shows the power of fever without medicine. I found myself floundering outside my hut and unable to get in; I tried to lift myself from my back by laying hold of two posts at the entrance, but when I got nearly

upright I let them go, and fell back heavily on my head." Chuma and
Susi, who were daily becoming Livingstone's most devoted followers,
got their leader into the hut "and hung a blanket at the entrance . . .
that no stranger might see my helplessness; some hours elapsed before I could recognize where I was." A month elapsed before he could
get up and move around again.

He had by this time realized, of course, that the Chambezi did not
flow into Lake Tanganyika. What's more, he had also learned of Lake
Bangweolo, into which it did flow, and of Lake Mweru, into which
Bangweolo drained via the Luapula. The existence of this system of
lakes and rivers suggested the very watershed Livingstone had expected to come across in his march north from Lake Nyasa, and he
recognized that what he ought to do was return there and explore it.
But he could not bring himself to turn away from Tanganyika—and
his advance post at Ujiji 300 miles to the north, where he could hope
to get medicines and other supplies. But, when he was well enough to
undertake the trek to Ujiji, he discovered that the way was blocked by
wars that had broken out between local tribes and Arab slavers.

For a month, Livingstone tried to decide what to do, and we find
him confessing in his diary, quite uncharacteristically, "I am perplexed how to proceed." Then in May he fell in with a party of Arabs
who proved extremely hospitable. Their leader, Livingstone wrote,
"has been particularly kind to me in presenting food, beads, cloth
. . . [and] is certainly very anxious to secure my safety." So, in his
perplexed state and undermined physical condition, Livingstone decided to attach his party to the Arab caravan and let it dictate the
direction of his march for the time being.

The leader of the caravan was Hamidi bin Muhammad, a Zanzibari Arab better known by his nickname Tippoo Tib, who was to
become the greatest slaver and trader in Central Africa within the
next few years and play, as we shall see, a crucial role in the exploration of the Congo. Now, though, he was merely an agent of his father's
firm in Zanzibar, and he was headed westward to Lake Mweru. So it
was to Mweru, rather than back to the Chambezi and Bangweolo, that
Livingstone went. It was a journey of little more than 100 miles, but
with constant stops to conduct business along the way the caravan
didn't reach the lake's northern shore until November. Livingstone's
interest in Mweru centered on its relationship to Bangweolo and the
pattern of the rivers and streams in the watershed around it. And,

piecing together information he gathered from the local tribesmen, he learned that "round the western end flows the water that makes the river Lualaba, which, before it enters Mweru, is the Luapula, and that again (if the most intelligent reports speak true) is the Chambezi before it enters Lake Bemba, or Bangweolo."

Moreover, Livingstone heard that the Lualaba was a major river, and a northward-flowing one at that, and he concluded that it could be the river he had been searching for. Now two obvious tasks faced him. One was to go south and confirm with his own eyes the geography he had learned second-hand of the Lualaba's origin in the Chambezi. The other was to go north and follow the Lualaba from Mweru as far as necessary to see if in fact it was the mainstream of the Nile. But which of the two he would undertake depended on which direction the Arab caravan chose to go. His party was now down to nine members, he was drastically short of supplies, food, and trading goods, and his health, in the absence of any proper medicines, continued to decline dangerously. Under such conditions, it was utterly impracticable for him to set off on either exploration on his own. So, when Tippoo Tib chose to move southward down the eastern shore of Lake Mweru, Livingstone went along, and on November 20 he reached the lake's southern end, not far from the banks of the Luapula, and the royal kraal of the King of Casembe.

The plain extending . . . to the town of Casembe is level [Livingstone recorded], and studded pretty thickly with red anthills, from 15 to 20 feet high. Casembe has made a broad path from his town . . . about a mile-and-a-half long, and as broad as a carriage path. The chief's residence is enclosed in a wall of reeds, 8 or 9 feet high, and 300 square yards, the gateway is ornamented with about sixty human skulls; a shed stands in the middle of the road before we come to the gate, with a cannon dressed in gaudy cloths. A number of noisy fellows stopped our party and demanded tribute. . . . Many of Casembe's people appear with the ears cropped and hands lopped off: the present chief has been often guilty of this barbarity. One man has just come to us without ears or hands: he tries to excite our pity making a chirruping noise, by striking his cheeks with the stumps of his hands."

November 24:

We were called to be presented to Casembe in a grand reception. The present Casembe has a heavy uninteresting countenance, without beard or whiskers, and somewhat of the Chinese type, and his eyes have an outward

squint. He smiled but once during the day, and that was pleasant enough, though the cropped ears and lopped hands, with human skulls at the gate, made me indisposed to look on anything with favour. His principal wife came with her attendants . . . to look at the Englishman. She was a fine, tall, good-featured lady, with two spears in her hands; the principal men who had come around made way for her, and called on me to salute: I did so; but she, being forty yards off, I involuntarily beckoned her to come nearer: this upset the gravity of all her attendants; all burst into a laugh, and ran off. Casembe's smile was elicited by a dwarf making some uncouth antics before him. His executioner also came forward to look: he had a broad Lunda sword on his arm, and a curious scizzor-like instrument at his neck for cropping ears. On saying to him that his was nasty work, he smiled, and so did many who were not sure of their ears at the moment; many men of respectability show that at some former time they have been thus punished.

The town of Casembe was a major trading post for Arab caravans and, as Tippoo Tib had a great deal of business to conduct there, Livingstone was obliged to idle away his time for more than a month. To occupy himself, he wrote letters which he hoped to get to the outside world by a chance Arab caravan headed for the coast. In one of these, he provided an accurate description of the Mweru-Bangweolo watershed, and, though he was not yet quite ready to make the claim publicly that this was the Nile's source—he wouldn't do that formally for another year—the implication was there and the task that he saw before him clear. "Since coming to Casembe's," he wrote, "the testimony of natives and Arabs has been so united and consistent that I am but ten days from Lake Bemba, or Bangweolo, that I cannot doubt its accuracy." But we also find him writing, "I am so tired of exploration without a word from home or anywhere else for two years, that I must go to Ujiji on Tanganyika for letters before doing anything else. The banks and country adjacent to Lake Bangweolo are reported to be now very muddy and very unhealthy. I have no medicine." So when, at the end of December, he heard of an Arab caravan heading north again for Ujiji—Tippoo Tib planned to go westward into Katanga— Livingstone turned his back on Bangweolo and joined it.

He didn't get very far. For nearly three months the caravan trudged north along the eastern shore of Lake Mweru but managed to cover barely 50 miles. Once again the rains had set in, and they turned the land into a terrible swamp. On the last day of 1867, he wrote: "I

was taken ill. Heavy rains kept the convoy back. . . . It is well that I
did not go to Bangweolo Lake, for it is now very unhealthy to the
natives, and I fear that without medicine continual wettings . . .
might have knocked me up altogether." The next morning, New
Year's Day 1868, he wrote: "Almighty Father, forgive the sins of the
past year for Thy Son's sake. Help me to be more profitable during
this year. If I am to die this year prepare me for it." A month later: "I
am ill with fever. . . . We must remain; it is a dry spot. . . . *Hoop-
ing-cough* here." At the end of February: "Some believe that Kilimanjaro Mountain has mummies, as in Egypt, and that Moses visited it of
old." On March 17, the caravan at last reached the northern end of
Lake Mweru, and that was as far as it would go. The land to the north
toward Tanganyika and Ujiji was by now an impassable swamp and
the Arabs decided to wait for the end of the rains before proceeding
any further.

For a few weeks Livingstone seemed to have accepted the Arabs'
decision and resigned himself to another long period of inactivity and
delay. But then on April 2 we find this entry in his journal:

If I am not deceived by the information I have received from various
reliable sources, the springs of the Nile rise between 9 degrees or 10
degrees south latitude [the region of Bangweolo], or at least 400 or 500
miles south of the south end of Speke's Lake, which he considered to be
the sources of the Nile.

With that he seems suddenly to have realized that for nearly a year
now he had been wandering pointlessly in the tow of Arab caravans.
By some inexplicable bolt of energy, he resolved to put an end to that
state and turn back to find Bangweolo after all. The leader of the
caravan was appalled by the decision and attempted to dissuade Livingstone by promising that the departure for Ujiji would not be
much longer delayed. But Livingstone responded that even if that
were the case "I would on no account go to Ujiji, till I had done all
in my power to reach the Lake I sought." On April 13, he announced
his plans to his nine followers. Five of them pointblank refused to go.
So the next day he set off with only Chuma, Susi, and two others.

It was a heroic undertaking, a journey of 200 miles under the
worst possible conditions, and miraculously it succeeded. Retracing
his steps, wading waist deep through rivers and swamps for hours at a
time, slogging through "black tenacious mud," floundering through

Chuma and Susi

water-filled ruts, he reached Casembe at the end of May. There, by a splendid stroke of luck, he came upon an Arab caravan making for Bangweolo, and on June 11 he headed southeast with it. It took another month, a month of suffering, constant peril, and thoughts of death. At one point, the party was surrounded by tribesmen "poising their spears at us, taking aim with their bows and arrows, and making as if about to strike with their axes." At another point,

We came to a grave in the forest; it was a little rounded mound as if the occupant sat in it in the usual native way; it was strewed over with flour, and a number of large blue beads put on it; a little path showed that it had visitors. This is the sort of grave I should prefer, to lie in the still, still forest, and no hand ever to disturb my bones.

Livingstone reached Bangweolo on July 18 and, although an attempt to circumnavigate it failed, he confirmed all the information he had heard about its geography and felt free to announce publicly that he had reached his goal. In a dispatch to the foreign office, which he hoped to send out by Arab caravan, he wrote:

I may safely assert that the chief sources of the Nile, arise between 10 and 12 degrees south latitude, or nearly in the position assigned to them by Ptolemy . . . the springs of the Nile have hitherto been searched for very much too far to the north. They rise some 400 miles south of the most southerly portion of Victoria Nyanza, and, indeed, south of all the lakes except Bangweolo.

In another letter to a friend around the same time he acknowledged:

I still have to follow down the Lualaba, and see whether, as the natives assert, it passes Tanganyika to the west, or enters it and finds exit into Baker's lake.

Livingstone was now ready to go to Ujiji to get his much-needed medicines and supplies and from there take up the exploration of the Lualaba. The rainy season had ended, and by October Livingstone was back at the northern end of Lake Mweru. The Arab caravan he had left in April was still there and so were his five deserters, and they all once again joined forces and in November set off for Ujiji.

That miraculous burst of energy, which had gotten Livingstone to Bangweolo and back proved to be just that—a burst. He had not recovered his health, and on the long, hard journey to Ujiji it steadily

deteriorated. The diary entry for New Year's Day 1869 omits the usual prayers and expressions of hope for the coming year: "I have been wet times without number, but the wetting of yesterday was once too often: I felt very ill." Two days later: "I marched one hour, but found I was too ill to go further . . . I had a pain in the chest . . . my lungs, my strongest part, were thus affected. . . . I lost count of the days of the week and month after this. Very ill all over." The next entry: "About 7th January.—Cannot walk: Pneumonia of right lung, and I cough all day and night: sputa rust of iron and bloody: distressing weakness." The Arabs rigged up a litter and had him carried. "I am so weak I can scarcely speak. . . . This is the first time in my life I have been carried in illness, but I cannot raise myself to a sitting posture. . . . The sun is vertical, blistering any part of the skin exposed, and I try to shelter my face and head as well as I can with a bunch of leaves, but it is dreadfully fatiguing in my weakness."

That was the last inscription Livingstone made until February 14, when the caravan at last reached the western shore of Lake Tanganyika and set about trying to get canoes for the passage across to Ujiji on the opposite shore. "Patience was never more needed than now," Livingstone scribbled. But at last the necessary canoes were acquired, and after nearly three weeks of paddling they brought him to Ujiji on March 14, emaciated, toothless, desperately sick, practically three years to the day since he had landed on the East African coast and after traveling more than 2000 miles totally out of contact with the outside world.

And now drama turns to melodrama. There were only three things Livingstone wanted and needed at Ujiji: medicines to cure his illness, letters to soothe his loneliness, and supplies to carry on his explorations. And none of these were there.

As we have seen, Livingstone, before leaving Zanzibar, had made arrangements for goods to be sent up to Ujiji, and these arrangements had been faithfully carried out. But the goods had arrived two years before and what happened to them in the meantime is easily enough imagined. As the weeks turned into months and the months into years and Livingstone didn't arrive and the conviction grew that he was dead somewhere in the interior and would never arrive, the goods were pilfered, plundered, and finally stolen outright by the Ujiji inhabitants. "The disappointment," Horace Waller, who edited Living-

stone's *Last Journal,* annotated on the page with the entry for March 14, "must have been severe indeed." But, curiously, there's no indication of the disappointment in Livingstone's own writing. It is possible that he had all along realized that setting up a depot at Ujiji was risky business and had steeled himself against the possibility that he wouldn't find his stores once he got there. Besides, when he did get there he was in terrible physical condition, and by the time he was up and around again, in the early summer, the disappointment was well behind him and he had turned his attention to other things.

It is now that we realize what a fantastic hold the quest for the Nile's source had on him. For surely the wisest thing that he could have done would have been to join one of the Arab caravans going down to the coast and return to Zanzibar for proper medical care and supplies. But he doesn't seem to have given this possibility a serious second thought. Instead, he merely sent a message to Zanzibar asking for new supplies to be dispatched to Ujiji and set off to explore the Lualaba.

Livingstone's tiny expedition party was in as bad shape as it had been for the last two years, which meant that in order to embark on any further journey of exploration he again had to rely on the help of the Arabs. On July 12, a caravan did turn up in Ujiji headed across Lake Tanganyika for a slave and ivory hunt along the banks of the Lualaba, and Livingstone attached his small party to it. He expected to be gone four or five months, long enough to determine the course of the Lualaba and be back just about the time his new shipment of supplies from Zanzibar reached Ujiji. In fact, he was gone for more than two years and in all that time never did learn where the Lualaba flowed.

He had no idea into what kind of country he was going. No European had ever been there and it was utterly unlike any Livingstone himself had ever been in before. For where he went was the rain forest of Maniema (Manyuema, in Livingstone's spelling), the forbidding home of cannibal tribes. What's more, it was a region which the Arab slavers and ivory hunters had only just barely begun to penetrate, and their shocking impact was still new enough to be met with resistance by the forest tribesmen, turning the jungle into a doubly hostile and dangerous place.

Almost as soon as he set foot on Lake Tanganyika's western shore,

we find those, by now, all-too-familiar pitiful entries in his journal about the difficulties: "Marched $3\frac{1}{4}$ hours . . . very fatiguing in my weakness. . . . Any ascent, though gentle, makes me blow since the attack of pneumonia." But this was still not yet the Maniema, and the caravan made decent progress. On September 21, it reached the town of Bambarre (Kabambare in today's Zaire), about 100 miles west of Tanganyika and 100 miles east of the Lualaba, where Livingstone rested for over a month while his Arab hosts went about their business of collecting slaves and ivory. On November 1, Livingstone, resuming the westward march, entered the outskirts of the Maniema forests: the vegetation thickened and the cannibal tribesmen, never having seen a European before, became increasingly wary; then the rains came and with them the fevers. Three weeks after leaving Bambarre, the party reached the Luama, a tributary of the Lualaba, but couldn't cross it. The region ahead had been plundered by slavers, and the tribesmen were openly hostile to strangers and wouldn't let them have canoes. They were obliged to return to Bambarre. It was December 19, 1869.

The plan now was to circumvent the troubled regions by striking northwest and reaching the Lualaba further downstream. On December 25, Livingstone wrote, "We start immediately after Christmas: I must try with all my might to finish my exploration before next Christmas." And his prayer for New Year's Day, 1870: "May the Almight help me to finish the work in hand, and retire . . . before the year is out." But six months later he was back in Bambarre, again having failed to reach the Lualaba, defeated by the Maniema forests.

Trees fallen across the path formed a breast-high wall which had to be climbed over; flooded rivers, breast and neck deep, had to be crossed, the mud was awful. . . . The country is indescribable . . . an elephant alone can pass through it . . . reeds clog the feet, and the leaves rub sorely on the face and eyes. . . . Full grown leeches come on the surface.

Then two blows fell that made pushing on impossible. Six of Livingstone's nine followers deserted him (one, he later learned, was killed and eaten by the cannibals), leaving him with only the faithful Chuma and Susi and a Nassick boy named Gardner. And his feet

for the first time in my life failed me. . . . Instead of healing quietly as heretofore, when torn by hard travel, irritable-eating ulcers fastened on both feet. . . . If the foot were put to the ground, a discharge of bloody

ichor flowed, and the same discharge happened every night with considerable pain, that prevented sleep.

Livingstone stayed in Bambarre for eight months, three of which he was confined to a hut unable to move. It was a terrible time. In a letter he confessed that "I am made very old and shaky—my cheeks fallen in—space around the eyes—the mouth almost toothless." And, unquestionably, his mind was also damaged by all his suffering. For it was here, in his awful isolation and loneliness, able to do little else than read and reread his Bible, that his strange, mystical conception of the sources of the Nile, and his quest for it, came into full flower.

He wrote on August 25:

One of my waking dreams is that of the legendary tales about Moses coming up into Inner Ethiopia with Merr, his foster mother, and founding a city which he called in her honour 'Meroe,' may have a substratum of fact. . . . I dream of discovering some monumental relics of Meroe, and if anything confirmatory of sacred history does remain, I pray to be guided thereunto. If the sacred chronology would thereby be confirmed, I would not grudge the toil and hardships, hunger and pain, I have endured—the irritable ulcers would only be discipline.

Several weeks later, after what we can imagine to be wandering speculation in his fevered solitude, we find him writing:

My course has been an even one, turning neither to the right hand nor to the left, though my route has been torturous enough. All the hardship, hunger, toil were met with the full conviction that I was right in persevering to make a complete work of the exploration of the sources of the Nile. . . . I had a strong presentiment during the first three years that I should never live through the enterprise, but it weakened as I came near to the end of the journey, and an eager desire to discover any evidence of the great Moses having visited those parts bound me, spellbound me, I may say, for if I could bring to light anything to confirm the Sacred Oracles, I should not grudge one whit all the labour expended.

Around this time, two Arab traders who had come to Bambarre from a journey to Katanga, visited Livingstone and told him that they had seen the "fountains" of four great rivers in that region. One flowed northward through a chain of lakes; the second, seven days away, also flowed northward but to the west of the first; the other two, about ten miles away, flowed to the south and "a mound rises between them, the most remarkable in Africa." As a matter of fact, this was

reasonably accurate geography. Four rivers do rise within a few hundred miles of each other in the Katanga region: the Lomami and the Lualaba both flowing northward, the first eventually becoming a tributary of the Congo, and the Zambezi and the Kafue flowing southward. But Livingstone's mind, in its agitated state, leaped to a fabulous conclusion: "Were this spot in Armenia it would serve exactly the description of the garden of Eden in Genesis, with its four rivers, the Ghison, Pison, Hiddekel, and Euphrates." But, as it was not, Livingstone decided rather that "It possibly gave occasion to the story told to Herodotus by the Secretary of Minerva in the City of Sais, about two hills with conical tops, Crophi and Mophi. 'Midway between them,' said he, 'are the fountains which it is impossible to fathom: half the water runs northward into Egypt; half to the south towards Ethiopia.' "

And so the idea was fixed. Though he still planned to go northward and trace the course of the Lualaba to confirm that it was the Nile, he would be drawn always more obsessively by those four fountains of Herodotus, by his search for evidence of the great Moses, by his desire to confirm the Sacred Oracles, and in the end they would kill him.

His chance to try for the Lualaba again came early in the new year. On New Year's Day, 1871, he had written, "O Father! help me to finish this work in Thy honour. Still detained at Bambarre, but a caravan of 500 muskets is reported from the coast: it may bring me other men and goods." It did. The message he had sent to Zanzibar nearly two years before had gotten through, and, at the beginning of February, having been directed there from Ujiji, ten porters with supplies arrived in Bambarre for Livingstone. He was fairly well recovered and the medicines that now arrived made him feel fit enough to again undertake his explorations.

The going was as rough as ever, but now with a party of thirteen, decent supplies, and the continuing assistance of the Arabs, Livingstone made good time, and on March 30 he reached the Lualaba at Nyangwe, an Arab trading town on its banks. The next day, "I went down to take a good look at the Lualaba here. It is . . . a mighty river, at least 3000 yards broad, and always deep: it can never be waded at any point, or at any time of the year; the people unhesitatingly declare that if any one tried to ford it, he would assuredly be lost." The next step was clear: to get canoes and follow it to the north.

But he didn't. And here we see how seriously undermined, in physical and mental powers, Livingstone was after all his years of torturous wandering. The problem was acquiring canoes; the tribesmen wouldn't give, rent, or sell him any. "They all think," Livingstone wrote, "that my buying a canoe means carrying war to the left bank." It was not an unreasonable fear. Nyangwe was the furthest into the Maniema forests that the Arab traders had penetrated, and on the basis of their performance so far, it is hardly surprising that the tribesmen didn't want to see them penetrate any further. They did not distinguish Livingstone from the Arabs. They had never seen a European, so he was for them just another stranger who would unleash all the horrors of the slave and ivory hunts.

Still, given all the obstacles he had overcome to get this far, it is hard to accept the idea that getting canoes should have been such an impossible task. And yet, curiously, it seemed so to Livingstone. He settled down in Nyangwe, built himself a house, and waited passively for the canoes somehow to materialize. And he was still waiting two and a half months later when an event occurred that finally broke his spirit and caused him to turn his back on the Lualaba forever.

During his weeks of helpless waiting, Livingstone's only real pleasure had been to visit Nyangwe's marketplace. It was a lively and colorful place, jammed with hundreds, sometimes thousands of people, mainly women, for whom

it seems to be a pleasure of life to haggle and joke, and laugh and cheat: many come eagerly . . . many are beautiful . . . all carry very heavy loads of dried cassava and earthen pots which they dispose of very cheaply for palm-oil, fish, salt, pepper, and relishes for their food. The men appear in gaudy lambas, and carry little save their iron wares, fowls, grass cloth, and pigs.

After making a few visits, he felt himself very welcome there

for all are pleased to tell me the names of the fishes and other things. Lepidosirens are caught by the neck and lifted out of the pot to show their fatness. Camwood ground and made into flat cakes for sale . . . are offered and there is quite a roar of voices in the multitude, haggling. It was pleasant to be among them . . . vendors of fish run about with potsherds full of snails or small fishes . . . each is intensely eager to barter food for relishes, and makes strong assertions as to the goodness or bad-

ness of everything: the sweat stands in beads on their faces—cocks crow
briskly, even when slung over the shoulder with their heads down, and
pigs squeal. . . . They deal fairly, and when differences arise they are
easily settled by the men interfering or pointing at me.

On July 15, Livingstone made his usual visit to the market. "It was
a hot, sultry day," he tells us but there was a good attendance, perhaps
as many as 1500 people, mostly women. He noticed three Arabs and

was surprised to see these three with their guns, and felt inclined to re-
prove them . . . for bringing weapons into the market, but I attributed it
to their ignorance, and, it being very hot, I was walking away to go out
of the market, when I saw one of the fellows haggling about a fowl, and
seizing hold of it. Before I got thirty yards out of the market, the discharge
of two guns in the middle of the crowd told me that slaughter had begun:
crowds dashed off from the place, and threw down their wares in confusion, and ran. At the same time . . . volleys were discharged from a
party down near the creek on the panic-stricken women, who dashed at the
canoes. These . . . were jammed in the creek, and the men forgot their
paddles in the terror that seized all . . . men and women, wounded by
the balls . . . leaped and scrambled into the water, shrieking. . . . Shot
after shot continued to be fired on the helpless and perishing.

The massacre went on for two days, spreading through the town,
to surrounding villages, and across the river. A gang of slaves broke
loose and went on a rampage of looting. Huts were set afire, entire
villages went up in flames. At least 400 people and probably far more
were killed.

The open murder perpetrated on hundreds of unsuspecting women fills me
with unspeakable horror: I cannot think of going anywhere. . . . I cannot stay here in agony. . . . I see nothing for it but to go back to Ujiji.

The return trip took three months and Livingstone arrived there
on October 23, "reduced to a skeleton." And once again there was
nothing waiting for him. As before, whatever goods might have been
sent up to Ujiji from Zanzibar had been stolen.

This was distressing [Livingstone wrote]. I had made up my mind . . . to
wait till men should come up from the coast, but to wait in beggary was
what I never contemplated, and I now felt miserable. . . . But when my
spirits were at their lowest ebb, the good Samaritan was close at hand, for
one morning Susi came running at the top of his speed and gasped out,

The massacre of the Manyuema women at Nyangwe

"An Englishman! I see him!" and off he darted to meet him. The American flag at the head of the caravan told of the nationality of the stranger. Bales of goods, baths of tin, huge kettles, cooking pots, tents, etc., made me think, "This must be a luxurious traveller, and not one at his wits' end like me."

The interpreter for the luxurious traveler at that moment called out, "I see the Doctor, sir. Oh, what an old man! He has got a white beard." And the luxurious traveler, as he later would write, thought,

And I—what would I not have given for a bit of friendly wilderness, where, unseen, I might vent my joy in some mad freak, such as idiotically biting my hand, turning somersault, or slashing at the trees, in order to allay those exciting feelings that were well-nigh uncontrollable. My heart beats fast, but I must not let my face betray my emotions, lest it shall detract from the dignity of a white man appearing under such extraordinary circumstances.

So I did that which I thought was most dignified. I pushed back the crowds, and, passing from the rear, walked down a living avenue of people, until I came in front of the semi-circle of Arabs, in front of which stood the white man with the grey beard. As I advanced slowly towards him I noticed he was pale, looked wearied, had a grey beard, wore a bluish cap with a faded gold band around it, had on a red-sleeved waistcoat, and a pair of grey tweed trousers. I would have run to him, only I was a coward in the presence of such a mob—would have embraced him,

only, he being an Englishman, I did not know how he would receive me; so I did what cowardice and false pride suggested was the best thing— walked deliberately to him, took off my hat, and said: "Dr. Livingstone, I presume?"

"Yes," he said, with a kind smile, lifting his cap slightly.

I replace my hat on my head, and he puts on his cap, and we both grasp hands, and I then say aloud:

"I thank God, Doctor, I have been permitted to see you."

He answered, "I feel thankful that I am here to welcome you."

14

STANLEY AND LIVINGSTONE

Henry Morton Stanley was the first European to see Livingstone in nearly six years—and he would be the last—but he was not the only one to have tried to find Livingstone in all those years.

It will be remembered that in September of the expedition's first year, 1866, when Livingstone was making his way up the western shore of Lake Nyasa, the Johanna men in his party had downed their loads and refused to proceed further in fear of the hardships that lay ahead. Unlike the sepoys, whom Livingstone had fired and paid off, the Johanna men were deserters. So, when they got back to Zanzibar in December, they were obliged to come up with a story to explain their desertion. And they came up with a cunning one. Calculating that the sepoys had already given their version of what had happened, the Johanna men told the truth about events up to the time the sepoys were dismissed. But then the self-serving lies began. They claimed that after the party had crossed Lake Nyasa it was attacked by a band of marauding tribesmen. Livingstone was at the head of the caravan, as usual, while they were at the rear and, they admitted by way of adding a convincing touch, had just grounded their loads and stopped to rest when the attack began. What happened next they saw from the hiding places they rushed into in the long grass. The tribesmen charged, shouting war cries and rattling their spears against their shields. Livingstone managed to shoot two, but, as he was reloading his rifle, a third felled him with an axe blow to the back of his neck, and the rest of the party was massacred. That evening, at sunset, the Johanna men said they had crept to the site of the battle, found Livingstone's body and buried it. There was no trace of any survivor

and all the expedition's baggage had been stolen, leaving nothing for them to bring back to Zanzibar as proof of the occurrence.

The initial reaction to the story was disbelief, but the Johanna men had apparently rehearsed it so well and in such convincing detail during their march back to the coast and stuck to it so unshakably under the closest questioning that it gradually won acceptance. In March 1867, while Livingstone was struggling to Lake Tanganyika, the *Times* of London printed a letter from Murchison saying, "If this cruel intelligence should be substantiated, the civilised world will mourn the loss of as noble and lion-hearted an explorer as ever lived." Less than two weeks later, in another letter to the *Times,* Murchison had to concede, "I can now scarcely cling to the hope my dear friend should still be alive." At a meeting of the Royal Geographical Society on March 25, which had been called to discuss the matter, Murchison suggested that a search expedition be sent to Africa to determine Livingstone's fate, one way or another, as "doubt was not to be endured."

E. D. Young, a naval lieutenant who had served with Livingstone on the second Zambezi expedition, headed the search party. It departed from England in June, reached the mouth of the Zambezi in July, pushed upstream to the confluence with the Shire, reached Lake Nyasa in mid-August, and by the beginning of September was in the region where Livingstone reportedly had been killed. Once on the scene, Young was able to give the lie to the tale told by the Johanna men. He found evidence of Livingstone's passage—a spoon, a knife, a razor, a mirror, a cartridge case, and other such items which had been traded at one village or another for food—well beyond where the Johanna men claimed they had buried him. Then he met and interviewed chiefs and tribesmen who had seen Livingstone alive months after the Johanna men had deserted him. With that he concluded that his mission had been satisfactorily completed. It is true he had no proof that Livingstone was *still* alive but, in all fairness, that proof would have been virtually impossible to come by. Young hadn't the least idea where Livingstone might be at that time—he was, in fact, wandering aimlessly with the Arabs 500 miles to the north—and Young's party wasn't equipped to set off on a blind search into the interior of Africa. So they made their way down to the coast, where, in December, a ship picked them up for the voyage back to England.

No sooner had Young returned than the letter which Livingstone had dispatched a year before, while he was still making his way for the

first time toward Lake Tanganyika, arrived, setting forth the details of
the desertion of the Johanna men and providing information on his
plans and whereabouts. And in May 1868, Murchison convened a
meeting of the Royal Geographical Society for the purpose of com-
municating the "glorious tidings" that the lion-hearted explorer was
alive, then went on to caution the members that it might be years
before Livingstone emerged from the African interior.

There was no further word of Livingstone for more than a year.
From time to time, in the course of 1869, while Livingstone was struggling to Ujiji from Lake Bangweolo near to death, the Royal Geographical Society and letters in the *Times* speculated on his whereabouts or reported rumors of his fate. One suggested that he was on his
way down the Nile and would soon emerge at Aden. Another cau-
tioned that it was likely that he was being held prisoner by the King of
Casembe. Yet another believed he had been diverted to the west and
could be expected to reappear on the continent's Atlantic coast. But
by and large it seems to have been a case of "out of sight, out of mind"
and public interest in the lone wanderer waned. Even Murchison took
a surprisingly apathetic view. In September 1869, he wrote to the
Times, "I hold stoutly to the opinion that he will overcome every
obstacle" and advised that the only reasonable course was to wait patiently until he was heard from again. The fact is that no one knew
whether Livingstone was alive or dead, lost or safe, and no one seemed
to care enough to send someone to find out. Except one man.

The genius of James Gordon Bennett, Jr., heir of the proprietor of
the New York *Herald* and himself the newspaper's general manager,
was his uncanny instinct for what made a story. Under his editorial
direction the *Herald* had gained a world-wide notoriety—and a booming circulation—with its flashy, sensationalist coverage of events and its
endlessly astonishing scoops and features. It was this remarkable jour-
nalistic instinct that told Bennett that Livingstone was a story, despite
the general public's apparent indifference to the explorer's fate. He
was convinced that if someone actually found out what had happened
to Livingstone and put an end to the vague, uninteresting speculation
on the matter, the news would jolt the public out of its apathy and the
newspaper that carried the news would have the scoop of the century.
And so on October 16, 1869, while visiting in France, Bennett fired off
a telegram to his star reporter, ordering him to Paris "on important
business."

The star reporter was, of course, Henry Morton Stanley. He was in Madrid at the time, covering the Carlist uprising against the Spanish throne and had just returned "fresh from the carnage at Valencia" when Bennett's telegram arrived. "Down come my pictures from the walls of my apartments," he later wrote, "into my trunks go my books and souvenirs, my clothes are hastily collected, some half washed, some from the clothes-line half dry and after a couple of hours of hasty hard work my portmanteaus are strapped up, and labelled for Paris."

He arrived in the French capital the following afternoon and was ushered into Bennett's suite at the Grand Hotel. Bennett was in bed. "Who are you?" he asked, Stanley tells us.

"My name is Stanley," I answered.

"Ah, yes. Sit down; I have important business on hand for you."

After throwing over his shoulders his robe-de-chambre, Mr. Bennett asked, "Where do you think Livingstone is?"

"I really do not know, sir."

"Do you think he is alive?"

"He may be, and he may not be," I answered.

"Well, I think he is alive, and that he can be found, and I am going to send you to find him."

Stanley was flabbergasted. "Wondering at the cool order of sending one to Central Africa to search for a man whom I, in common with almost all other men, believed to be dead," he asked Bennett,

Have you considered seriously the great expense you are likely to incur on account of this little journey?"

"What will it cost?" he asked, abruptly.

"Burton and Speke's journey to Central Africa cost between 3,000 and 5,000 pounds, and I fear it cannot be done for under 2,500 pounds."

"Well, I will tell you what you will do. Draw a thousand pounds now; and when you have gone through that, draw another thousand, and when that is spent, draw another thousand, and when you have finished that, draw another thousand, and so on; but FIND LIVINGSTONE."

Stanley was 28 years old when Bennett handed him the assignment. Although only 5 feet 5 inches tall, he was powerfully built and in prime physical condition; he had a handsome head of chestnut hair, a flamboyant Victorian mustache, intense gray eyes and a swaggering style. He was something of a romantic and very much the rough-and-ready adventurer, a combination that nicely suited his identity as the

Henry Morton Stanley

daring newspaperman, dashing off from one war zone to another, from one perilous situation to another.

But Stanley was also an extremely ambitious young man. He had acquired his reputation as Bennett's star reporter only recently—indeed, had won a staff position on the *Herald* less than two years before—and he realized, in accepting Bennett's improbable assignment, that if he succeeded at it, if he did find Livingstone, his career would be made, fame and fortune would be his, and, most of all, what he had struggled for all of his life—respectability, social standing, prestige—might at last be achieved. For Stanley was a bastard and that condition haunted him, drove him, and more than anything explains his incredible accomplishments.

He was born in Denbigh, Wales, in 1841 to a rather feckless 19-year-old daughter of a butcher; Elizabeth Parry (she was to go on and have three more illegitimate children before she was done), christened him John Rowlands, after a young farmer who was willing to admit paternity but not responsibility, and then abandoned him. Her father and brothers looked after the child, but when the father died the brothers refused to continue with the arrangement and the boy was sent to the St. Asaph Union Workhouse.

St. Asaph's, "into which I had been so treacherously taken," Stanley wrote in his *Autobiography*, "is an institution to which the aged poor and superfluous children of that parish are taken, to relieve the respectabilities of the obnoxious sight of extreme poverty, and because civilization knows no better method of disposing of the infirm and helpless than by imprisoning them." Stanley received in this institution all the formal education he was ever to get. He was six when he entered and fifteen when he left. And he left by escaping over its walls. The headmaster of the workhouse, a certain James Francis, who years later was to die in a lunatic asylum, was a brutal and violent man, and one day, Stanley tells us, "fell into a furious rage, and uttered terrific threats with the air of one resolved on massacre," then set about birching the entire senior class. When Stanley's turn came, "I felt myself hardening in resistance. He stood before me vindictively glaring, his spectacles intensifying the gleam of his eyes." Stanley refused to submit to the birching and, as a result,

I found myself swung upward into the air by the collar of my jacket, and flung into a nerveless heap on the bench. Then the passionate brute pum-

meled me in the stomach until I fell backward. . . . Recovering my
breath, finally . . . I aimed a vigorous kick at the cruel Master . . . and,
by chance, the booted foot smashed his glasses, and almost blinded him
with their splinters. Starting backward with the excruciating pain, he
contrived to stumble over a bench, and the back of his head struck the
stone floor.

Stanley believed that he had killed the master. And so he scampered
over the garden wall and fled "as though pursued by bloodhounds."

Stanley's hope was to find some kind relatives to take him in, but
the fatherless boy was no more wanted now than he had ever been. So,
after two years of shuttling from one family to another, he wandered
off to Liverpool and signed on as a cabin boy aboard a packet bound
for America. But at the packet's first port-of-call, New Orleans, he
jumped ship because the captain's cruelty to his crew was no less than
the headmaster's at St. Asaph's.

A long-standing legend, based on Stanley's *Autobiography* but recently called into doubt, tells us what happened next. He was then
still John Rowlands, a fatherless, friendless, penniless youth of eighteen in a strange city in a foreign country, walking the streets looking
for work. One day he saw a gentleman sitting in front of a general
goods store, reading the morning newspaper.

"From his sober dark alpaca suit and tall hat," Stanley tells us, "I
took him to be the proprietor of the building. . . . I ventured to
ask,—'Do you want a boy, sir?'

" 'Eh?' he demanded with a start; 'what did you say?'

" 'I asked if you wanted a boy.' "

As it turned out, the gentleman wasn't the proprietor of the store
but, the legend has it, he was a childless man who had long regretted
never having a son and, startled from his newspaper reading, he
thought the youth was offering to make up for this lack. In the next
few words it became clear that what the youth was doing was asking
for work and not offering himself for adoption, but the gentleman was
so taken by his initial misunderstanding that he expressed an immediate and deeply paternal interest in the youth. This gentleman's name
was Henry Morton Stanley.

The elder Stanley was a prosperous cotton broker and, although he
never formally adopted the youth, he outfitted him with a new wardrobe, set about improving his education, took him into his business,
and told him: "As you are wholly unclaimed, without a parent, rela-

tion, or sponsor, I promise to take you for my son . . . and, in future, you are to bear my name." The workhouse boy was overjoyed.

Before I could quite grasp all that this declaration meant for me, he had risen, taken me by the hand, and folded me in a gentle embrace. My sense seemed to whirl about for a few half-minutes: and, finally, I broke down, sobbing from extreme emotion. It was the only tender action I had ever known, and, what no amount of cruelty could have forced from me, tears poured in a torrent under the influence of the simple embrace. The golden period of my life began from that supreme moment!

It was, however, a pathetically brief period. For two years, Stanley traveled with his "father" learning the cotton brokerage business, studying the books the elder Stanley gave him, developing into a "complete gentleman." But in the autumn of 1860 the elder Stanley visited a brother in Cuba and died in Havana the next year. Stanley was fatherless and adrift again.

The Civil War broke out. After some hesitation, Stanley enlisted in a volunteer brigade called the Dixie Greys and saw his first combat at the battle of Shiloh.

I cannot forget that half-mile square of woodland, lighted brightly by the sun, and littered by the forms of about a thousand dead and wounded men, and by horses, and military equipments [Stanley wrote years later]. For it was the first Field of Glory I had seen . . . and the first time that Glory sickened me with its repulsive aspect, and made me suspect it was all a glittering lie.

Stanley was wounded and captured on the second day of battle and shipped, along with several hundred other Confederate soldiers, to Camp Douglas, a prisoner-of-war center near Chicago. He was held there nearly a year and then took his only chance for escape. He deserted the Confederate cause, took an oath of allegiance to the Union, and was sworn into a regiment of the Illinois Light Artillery. He, however, never got to fight with the unit. Within days of donning his Federal army blues, he collapsed with dysentery and was discharged. And he began a period of wandering that was to last most of his life.

He returned to Wales, where he found himself as unwelcome as ever, sailed from Liverpool again to New York, there signed on as a

deckhand aboard a merchant vessel trading between Boston and the Mediterranean, worked as a scribe for a time in Brooklyn, and then, in 1864, enlisted in the Federal Navy with the petty officer rating of ship's writer. He was aboard the frigate *Minnesota* at the time of the last major battle of the Civil War, the Union's combined land-and-sea attack on Fort Fisher in North Carolina, and turning his official duty of recording the engagement for the ship's log to his own account, he sent an eye-witness report of the battle to a group of provincial newspapers and launched his career as a journalist.

Though he had still two and a half years to serve, Stanley deserted the U.S. Navy at the end of the Civil War and, heeding Horace Greeley's grand cry of the times, headed west. In St. Louis he persuaded the Missouri *Democrat* and then later a string of other newspapers, including eventually the New York *Herald,* to sign him on as a free lance. For the next three years he roamed the American wilderness, covering the Rocky Mountain mining boom, the Indian wars, the coming of the railroad, the settlement of the plains, America's expansion from coast to coast. He was adventurous, recklessly brave, with a vivid writing style, a keen nose for news, and a sharp eye for the telling detail; his reputation rapidly grew and with it so did his ambition. His first big chance came when he heard that Britain was preparing to invade Ethiopia.

Theodore, the tyrannical and half-mad emperor of Ethiopia, believing himself to have been insulted by Queen Victoria, had imprisoned the British consul along with a number of other Europeans residing in his realm, and for several years all efforts to negotiate their release had failed. So in 1867 Britain declared war on the ancient kingdom of Prester John and organized, under the command of Sir Robert Napier, the largest European army to invade Africa since the days of Imperial Rome. It had all the makings of an exciting story, and Stanley hurried to New York and persuaded James Gordon Bennett to send him to cover it for the *Herald.*

On the way to Ethiopia, in January 1868, Stanley stopped in Suez and made arrangements that would assure his success. Suez had the only telegraph office anywhere near Ethiopia, and Stanley bribed the head telegraphist to send his dispatches ahead of everyone else's. Then, at the end of the campaign, with the death of Theodore and the fall of his mountain fastness at Magdala in April, Stanley sped back to

Suez ahead of Napier's army (with which the other journalists were traveling) and, even though the city was in quarantine because of a cholera epidemic, managed to smuggle his dispatches to the bribed telegraphists for transmission to the *Herald*'s bureau in London.

It was an astonishing scoop. For a time, Stanley's was the only account of Napier's campaign, and the *Herald* was accused of fabricating the news. But at last the official messages from Napier arrived confirming everything the *Herald* had published, and the delighted Bennett signed Stanley on as a staff correspondent. "I am now a permanent employee of the Herald," Stanley rejoiced in his diary on June 28, 1868, "and must keep a sharp look-out that my second coup shall be as much of a success as the first." It was, and then some.

Stanley did not set off to find Livingstone straight away. First Bennett wanted him to cover the inaugural ceremonies of the opening of the Suez Canal. Then, as Samuel Baker was planning to take an expedition up the Nile from Cairo, Stanley was to file a dispatch on that, and, while he was at it, he should also write up a practical guide on Lower Egypt for tourists. "Then you might as well go to Jerusalem," Stanley tells us Bennett ordered.

Then visit Constantinople, and find out about that trouble between the Khedive and the Sultan. Then—let me see—you might as well visit the Crimea and those old battle-grounds. Then go across the Caucasus to the Caspian Sea, I hear there is a Russian expedition bound for Khiva. From thence you may get through Persia to India; you could write an interesting letter from Persepolis. Bagdad will be close on your way to India; suppose you go there and write up something interesting about the Euphrates Valley Railway. Then, when you have come to India, you can go after Livingstone.

The reason Bennett came up with this roundabout itinerary, which would take Stanley fourteen months to complete, was simple. Just three days before Bennett had summoned Stanley to Paris, Livingstone had been heard of again. Some Arab traders had arrived in Zanzibar with news that they had seen the explorer in Ujiji a few months before. Not long after that, a letter from Livingstone from Ujiji, dated May 13 of that year (1869), was received, and yet another report from traders placed Livingstone, correctly, in Ujiji as late as July (shortly after which, as we've seen, he set out for the Lualaba).

None of this particularly bothered Bennett. He was perfectly convinced that, if he let enough time pass, Livingstone would surely get
"lost" again. And he was right. By the time Stanley completed his
roving assignment from the Suez to Bombay and arrived in Zanzibar
on January 6, 1871, Livingstone, then making his second vain attempt
to reach the Lualaba from Bambarre, hadn't been heard from for over
a year. The last report anyone had was in a letter to the *Times,* in
which a gentleman in Donegal said that his son-in-law, the captain of
the H.M.S. *Petrel,* then on naval patrol off the West African coast, had
been told by a Portuguese trader that Livingstone had been eaten by
cannibals. It was up to Stanley to prove otherwise.

Stanley had a few problems. He had been to Africa only once
before in his life, and then in the company of Napier's well-provisioned army. He had no experience as an explorer. He had never led
an expedition of any sort; in fact, he had never led men under any
circumstances before, and he was going into country that not only he
hadn't seen but only three Europeans (Burton, Speke and Grant)
before him had. What's more, as a journalist in search of a scoop, he
felt constrained to keep secret what he was up to. Even worse, his
casual inquiries in Zanzibar led him to believe that Livingstone didn't
want to be found and that, if he heard, as the acting British consul on
the island told Stanley, "fellows were going after him . . . Livingstone would put a hundred miles of swamp in a very short time between himself and them." So Stanley thought it best to go about
assembling his expedition on the pretext that he was planning only a
modest news-gathering excursion along the East African coast.

Against these handicaps, however, Stanley had an advantage that
no other traveler into the African interior had ever had: that flamboyant offer by Bennett of virtually unlimited funds. And Stanley
made liberal use of it. In the six weeks he was on Zanzibar readying his
expedition, he spent £4,000. He bought almost 6 tons of supplies and
equipment, including nearly 350 pounds of brass wire, 20 miles of
cloth, and a million beads to use as trading currency, 2 collapsible
boats, 71 cases of ammunition, 40 rifles, tents, cooking utensils, silver
goblets, champagne, Persian carpets, and a bathtub. He hired 192
porters to carry this massive load, getting many who had served with
Burton and Speke, as well as two British seamen he had met on his
recent travels and a young Christianized Arab, Selim Heshmy, whom
he had picked up in Jerusalem to act as his interpreter. In the first

week of February, he landed his party on the coast at Bagamoyo, saying, "We are all in for it now, sink or swim, live or die—none can desert his duty," and to the sound of rifles fired in celebration struck into the interior at the head of the caravan carrying the American flag.

Stanley, who was to become the greatest of all the African explorers of the nineteenth century, was described by a contemporary as "a man remarkable for strength of character, resolution, promptness of thought and iron will. . . . Difficulties did not deter him, disasters did not dismay him. With an extraordinary readiness of mind he improvises means, and draws himself out of difficulty." For all his lack of experience, these qualities—plus his physical strength, his rough-and-ready courage, his innate if untested leadership abilities, his ambition—emerged full-grown on his first African adventure. He set as his goal Ujiji, for that was where Livingstone had been last heard from, and though all the usual trials and tribulations of African travel beset him—malaria, tribal wars, mutiny in his own ranks, the death of his white companions, hunger, and dysentery (he lost 40 pounds during the trek) —he made excellent time. On November 10, the 236th day from Bagamoyo, he saw Lake Tanganyika.

It is a happy, glorious morning, [he wrote]. The air is fresh and cool. The sky lovingly smiles on the earth and her children. . . . A little further on—just yonder, oh! there it is—a silvery gleam. I merely catch sight of it between the trees, and—but here it is at last. . . . An immense broad sheet, a burnished bed of silver—lucid canopy of blue above—lofty mountains are its valances, palm forests form its fringes! The Tanganyika! —Hurrah!

Stanley had Selim lay out a new flannel suit, oil his boots, chalk his pith helmet, and fold a new puggaree around it and, shedding the tattered clothing he had worn throughout the march, changed into this fresh outfit "to make as presentable an appearance as possible." Then he ordered the American flag unfurled and volleys fired by his rifle men to announce the coming of the caravan. "We are now about three hundred yards from the village of Ujiji, and the crowds are dense about me. Suddenly I hear a voice on my right say, 'Good morning, sir!' " Startled to hear the English greeting, Stanley turned sharply to see "a man dressed in a long white shirt, with a turban of American sheeting around his woolly head."

"Who the mischief are you?" he asks.

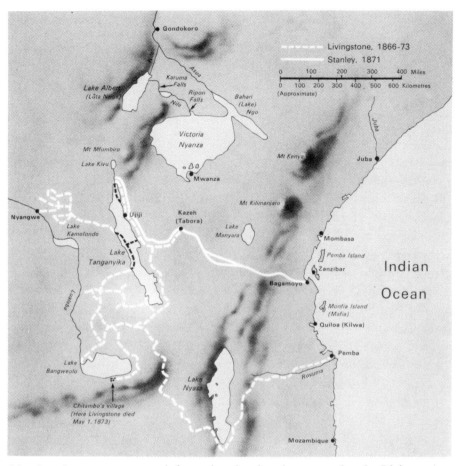

Map based on contemporary information showing the route taken by Livingstone, 1866–1873, and the route taken by Stanley, 1871

"I am Susi, the servant of Dr. Livingstone," said he, smiling and showing a gleaming row of teeth.

"What! Is Dr. Livingstone here?"

"Yes, sir."

"In this village?"

"Yes, sir."

"Are you sure?"

"Sure, sure, sir. Why, I leave him just now."

Stanley's incredulity that he should find Livingstone the very first place he looked for him was thoroughly justified. It was an amazing coincidence. One only has to remember that Stanley had been under way in an outlandishly rambling fashion for more than two years and that Livingstone had arrived in Ujiji not much more than a week and

probably only a few days before Stanley got there. (The reason for doubt on the matter is that both men had lost track of time during their African travels. Livingstone's journals give October 24 as the day he got back to Ujiji and October 28 as the day Stanley arrived, but later realized his calendar could have been off by as much as three weeks. Stanley's diary gives November 10 as the day he reached Ujiji but he later discovered that he had lost a week during his travels and might have arrived there as early as November 3.)

Had Stanley arrived in Ujiji only a week or two earlier "Livingstone would not have been found there," as he himself acknowledged, "and I should have had to follow him on his devious tracks through the primeval forests of Manyuema, and up along the crooked course of the Lualaba for hundreds of miles . . . [and] I might have lost him." And had he arrived only a few weeks later, an equally likely supposition, Livingstone almost surely wouldn't have been there either. He very well might have set off on his restless wanderings again or, in his dire physical and mental condition, he might very well have been dead. As he himself told Stanley on the first day of their meeting, "You have brought me new life. You have brought me new life."

Stanley remained with Livingstone for over four months, and that

"Dr. Livingstone, I presume."

time had a profound impact on him. When he first arrived he was an ambitious journalist in search of a scoop, and his plan was to stay a week or two, provide Livingstone with supplies in return for an exclusive interview, then race back to the coast, catch a boat for Aden, from where he would telegraph his sensational story. At dinner on the first day of their meeting, even before Stanley had revealed to Livingstone who he was and why he had come, he was tempted, as he tells us, "to take my note-book out, and begin to stenograph his story." And during that night, as he records, he carried on this delighted conversation with himself:

> "What was I sent for?"
> "To find Livingstone?"
> "Have you found him?"
> "Yes, of course; am I not in his house? Whose compass is hanging on the peg there? Whose clothes, whose boots are those? . . ."
> "Well, what are you going to do now?"
> "I shall tell him in the morning who sent me, and what brought me here. I will then ask him to write a letter to Mr. Bennett, and to give what news he can. . . . It is a complete success so far."

And the next morning at breakfast he was happy to see that Livingstone

was not an apparition . . . and yesterday's scenes were not the result of a dream! and I gazed on him intently, for thus I was assured he had not run away, which was the great fear that constantly haunted me as I was journeying to Ujiji. "Now, Doctor," said I, "you are, probably, wondering why I came here?"

Livingstone had, indeed, been wondering but, he said, "I did not like to ask you yesterday, because it was none of my business." And so Stanley said: "Now don't be frightened when I tell you that I have come after—you!" And not long after that he did at last take out his notebook and begin scribbling down the story Livingstone had to tell.

But it wasn't long before Stanley came to believe that what he was acquiring in Livingstone's company was not merely a story, albeit the scoop of the century, but something far more precious and personal. "I knew him not as a friend before my arrival," wrote the erstwhile workhouse orphan who had been moved to tears by a paternal embrace in New Orleans less than a decade before.

He was only an object to me—a great item for a daily newspaper . . . but never had I been called to record anything that moved me so much as this man's woes and sufferings, his privations and disappointments.

And in the days and weeks that followed we find Stanley writing,

Livingstone's was a character that I venerated, that called forth all my enthusiasm, that evoked nothing but the sincerest admiration. . . . I grant he is not an angel, but he approaches to that being as near as the nature of living man will allow. . . . He is sensitive. . . . His gentleness never forsakes him; his hopefulness never deserts him . . . he has such faith in the goodness of Providence. . . . His is the Spartan heroism, the inflexibility of the Roman, the enduring resolution of the Anglo-Saxon.

Now these certainly were the qualities that the young reporter could wish for in an idealized father. And the difference in their ages—Livingstone was approaching 60, Stanley nearing 31—conspired to foster just such a relationship between them. At one point Stanley was delighted to tell Livingstone that "my men call you the 'Great Master,' and me the 'Little Master,' " and years later confessed, "I loved him as a son, and would have done for him anything worthy of the most filial."

For his part, Livingstone responded to Stanley with almost as much warmth and affection. He too acknowledged their paternal relationship and wrote of the young reporter, "He behaved as a son to a father—truly overflowing with kindness." He unhesitatingly agreed not only to the interview but to Stanley's request that he write a couple of letters himself for publication in the *Herald*. And he took it upon himself to instruct Stanley in the customs of Africans and how best to get along with them. When Stanley fell ill with malaria he nursed him with such care that Stanley would write, "But though this fever . . . was more severe than usual I did not much regret its occurrence, since I became the recipient of the very tender and fatherly kindness of the good man whose companion I now found myself." But perhaps the best measure of the closeness that Livingstone felt for Stanley is the fact that he confided to him the secret of the Nile.

Stanley recorded in his notebook:

That this river [the Lualaba] flowing from one lake into another in a northerly direction, with all its great crooked bends and sinuosities, is the Nile—the true Nile—the Doctor has not the least doubt. For a long

time he entertained great scepticism, because of its deep bends and curves west, and south-west even; but having traced it from its head waters, the Chambezi . . . he has been compelled to come to the conclusion that it can be no other other river than the Nile. He had thought it was the Congo . . . but the Lualaba, the Doctor thinks, cannot be the Congo, from its great size and body, and from its steady and continued flow north-ward. . . . Livingstone admits the Nile sources have not been found, though he has traced the Lualaba through seven degrees of latitude flow-ing north; and, though he has not a particle of doubt of its being the Nile not yet can the Nile question be said to be resolved and ended. For two reasons: 1. He has heard of the existence of four fountains. . . . Several times he has been within 100 and 200 miles of them, but some-thing always interposed to prevent his going to see them. . . . These fountains must be discovered, and their positions taken . . . he says. These four full-grown gushing fountains, rising so near each other, and giving origin to four large rivers, answer in a certain degree to the description given of the unfathomable fountains of the Nile . . . to the father of all travelers—Herodotus . . . 2. The Lualaba must be traced to its connection with some portion of the old Nile. When these two things have been accomplished, then, and not till then, can the mystery of the Nile be explained.

Stanley and Livingstone undertook a bit of joint exploration and, although it lasted only four weeks and covered only 300 miles, it had its significance. It concerned the question, dating back to Burton's day, whether the Ruzizi River at the northern end of Lake Tangan-yika flowed into or out of the lake. Burton had heard that it flowed into the lake, but never having actually seen it he later theorized that it flowed out and thus could be the Nile, with Tanganyika the river's source. Livingstone, who was perfectly satisfied that the Nile rose far south of Lake Tanganyika, was interested in the Ruzizi's direction to determine whether it connected Tanganyika with Baker's Lake Al-bert, the outlet of which Livingstone believed joined the Lualaba, and so made Tanganyika part of the Nile watershed. Stanley and Living-stone discovered that the Ruzizi flowed into Tanganyika and not out of it into Lake Albert. Thus they removed Tanganyika from Living-stone's geography of the Nile and confirmed his belief in the four fountains of Herodotus as the river's true source.

Stanley enjoyed this, his first experience with geographical explo-ration, but he was still very much the journalist and he was anxious to get to civilization, file his scoop, and enjoy the fruits of his success. But

he was also worried about leaving his new-found father in the wilds. During the excursion on Tanganyika, he had seen how seriously Livingstone's health was undermined and, using "some very strong arguments," as Livingstone noted, urged the doctor to return to England with him. This was very much to Stanley's credit because surely the return of Livingstone himself would take the drama out of his scoop and shift the limelight from Stanley to the long-lost explorer. But Livingstone refused to go home. He was by now completely possessed by his quest for the fountains of the Nile, and the most he would agree to was to accompany Stanley to Tabora, where he could rest and recuperate in greater comfort than in Ujiji while Stanley arranged for a well-provisioned caravan to be sent up to him for his future explorations. The two men arrived in Tabora in mid-February 1872, and on March 14 Stanley departed for the coast.

It was an emotional parting. Stanley seems to have sensed that he would be the last European to see Livingstone alive. On the night before the final day, he wrote, "I feel as though I would rebel against the fate which drives me away from him . . . the farewell may be forever!" The next morning, "We had a sad breakfast together. I could not eat, my heart was too full; neither did my companion seem to have an appetite." Livingstone chose to accompany Stanley's caravan a little way down the road from Tabora. "We walked side by side. . . . I took long looks at Livingstone, to impress his features thoroughly on my memory." Then they stopped and made their last farewells. "We wrung each other's hands, and I had to tear myself away before I unmanned myself; but Susi, and Chuma . . . the doctor's faithful fellows—they must all shake and kiss my hands before I could quite turn away. I betrayed myself!" Bursting into tears, Stanley shouted to his men: "March! Why do you stop? Go on! Are you not going home? And my people were driven before me. No more weakness. I shall show them such marching as will make them remember me."

Stanley reached Bagamoyo on May 6 and the following day took a dhow across to Zanzibar. There he spent two weeks assembling the caravan he had promised Livingstone, taking every pain to make sure it was well outfitted and that it would reach Tabora quickly. Then he filed his story to the *Herald* and caught a mail steamer for England, where he arrived on August 1, 1872.

Stanley's reception was a mixed one. Bennett, of course, was de-

lighted. Even before Stanley reached England he had received a cable from the boss saying, "You are now as famous as Livingstone, having discovered the discoverer. Accept my thanks and the whole world's." By the time he got to London, the news of his exploit had swept all others from the front pages. "He sets off and does it," wrote the *Times,* "while others are idly talking or slowly planning. Africa is a very wide target, but Mr. Stanley hit the bull's-eye at once." Other British papers echoed the sentiment: "We could, of course, have wished," wrote one, "that the honour of that discovery had fallen to countrymen of our own. But it is only in the generous sense of the word that we can be said to envy the honour which the American press has fairly won and well deserved." He was presented to Queen Victoria, he was modeled in wax for Madame Tussaud's, he was invited to address the Royal Geographical Society and awarded its gold medal. He went on a lecture tour, there were cheering crowds at railway stations, toasts and tributes at civic banquets, and his book, *How I Found Livingstone,* became an overnight best seller. It would seem that the illegitimate workhouse boy had achieved all he had hoped for when he had taken the assignment.

But the acclaim, in fact, was far from universal. Most of the British press was a great deal less sporting than the *Times.* They could barely contain their jealousy at having been scooped by the *Herald* and its American journalist. An editorial in the *Standard* stated, "We cannot resist some suspicions and misgivings in connection with his story. There is something inexplicable and mysterious about its incidents and conclusions." Other papers picked up on the line, going so far as to suggest that Stanley had never found Livingstone at all, that the whole thing was a hoax, and the letters Livingstone had written for the *Herald* were Stanley's forgeries.

The acclaim of the scientific community, though more gentlemanly than Fleet Street's, was also riddled with doubts. Henry Rawlinson, who had succeeded as president of the Royal Geographical Society on Murchison's death the year before, commented in a letter to the *Times,* "If there has been any discovery it is Dr. Livingstone who has discovered Mr. Stanley," and other members of the society held to this view, maintaining, in order to excuse their own inaction, that Livingstone couldn't have been found by Stanley because he had never been lost. But the most devastating criticism focused on Stanley's assertion that Livingstone believed the Lualaba to be the main-

stream of the Nile. James Grant (of the Speke-Grant expedition) led the way in questioning this geography, theorizing, quite correctly as it would turn out, that the Lualaba was more likely the Congo than any other river.

Stanley was deeply wounded by all this and reacted rather vehemently.

Gentlemen, editors [he wrote], you have no right to feel jealous of me. . . . The whole world is as open to you as to the New York Herald. . . . The traveller whom I sought for was . . . alive. . . . I found him ailing, and destitute; by my mere presence I cheered him—with my goods I relieved him. Is the fact that I cheered and relieved him a source of annoyance to you? . . . Some of you first doubted the truth of my narrative; then suspected that the letters I produced as coming from him were forgeries; then accused me of sensationalism; then quibbled at the facts I published, and snarled at me as if I had committed a crime. With a simple tale—unvarnished, plain, clear, literal truth—you could find fault! What weakness! What puerility!

But what hurt most were the attacks on his reports on Livingstone's view of the Nile sources, for these were not only insults to him but to his new-found father. To answer them was difficult but he did his best to defend Livingstone. "What have you to say for yourselves, gentlemen geographers?" he wrote in his sharpest style.

A paper written by Colonel Grant . . . was to the effect that Livingstone had conceived a most extravagant idea when he believed that he had found the Sources of the Nile. . . . Colonel Grant was the companion of Speke . . . and he believes implicitly that Speke discovered the Nile source in the river issuing from Victoria. . . . As a friend of Speke's, and as his companion during the expedition, the gallant gentleman dislikes to hear any other person claiming to have discovered another Nile source.

The rancorous controversy raged for a few months but as with all such matters the public soon tired of it, and before the end of the year interest in Stanley and his scoop had waned, and he returned to New York to resume his career as a foreign correspondent for the *Herald*. He was confident that Livingstone would have the last word on the Nile.

15

THE LAST JOURNEY

Livingstone, alone and isolated again in Africa, had of course no inkling of the doubts his theories about the Nile's geography had raised in England. And, while waiting for the caravan that Stanley had arranged to send up to him at Tabora, he made a stunning—and thoroughly unwarranted—leap of faith in his fantastic belief.

As we have seen, when Livingstone turned back from Nyangwe and returned to Ujiji the year before, he had been on his way to prove that the Lualaba became the Nile somewhere downstream of Lake Albert, and it would be reasonable to expect that his plan, after he had been properly re-equipped and resupplied by Stanley, would be to resume that task and trace the Lualaba as far northward as necessary to find, as he told Stanley, "its connection with some portion of the old Nile." But, amazingly enough, even before Stanley left him, he had abandoned this plan. He seems to have entirely forgotten about it or simply to have taken it to be a foregone conclusion that the Lualaba flowed into the Nile. Or, what is more likely, his mind had been finally overcome by his mystical desire to reach the four fountains of Herodotus.

A month before Stanley left for the coast, we find this entry in Livingstone's journal:

It is all but certain that four full-grown gushing fountains rise on the watershed eight days south of Katanga, each of which at no great distance off becomes a large river; and two rivers thus formed flow north to Egypt, the other south to Inner Ethiopia. . . . It may be that these are not the fountains of the Nile mentioned to Herodotus . . . but they are worthy of discovery. . . . I propose to go . . . round the south end of

Tanganyika . . . then across the Chambezi, and round south of Lake Bangweolo, and due west to the ancient fountains. . . . This route will serve to certify that no other sources of the Nile can come from the south without being seen by me.

Livingstone had to wait five months for Stanley's caravan to reach him, and it was a difficult time. March 19, four days after Stanley left, was his fifty-ninth birthday, and he wrote: "My Jesus, my king, my life, my all; I again dedicate my whole self to Thee. Accept me, and grant, O Gracious Father, that ere this year is gone I may finish my task." But he was acutely aware that if he were to finish his task within the year he couldn't afford to be sitting idly in Tabora month after month. First of all, he realized that his health, though improved by the food and medicines Stanley had brought, was in fact incurably undermined, and it could not stand the rigors of African exploration too much longer. Secondly, there was the matter of weather. It soon would be the dry season in the part of Africa where he intended to travel (at the end of April) and he wanted to take advantage of that. The longer he delayed, the more of his traveling would take place after the rains started (in the beginning of December), and that would mean facing impassable terrain and killing fevers again.

But, perhaps most worrisome, the longer he delayed the more he was assailed by doubts.

Ptolemy [he wrote] seems to have gathered up the threads of ancient explorations, and made many springs (six) flow into two Lakes situated East and West. . . . If the Victoria Lake were large, then it and the Albert would probably be the Lakes Ptolemy meant, and it would be pleasant to call them Ptolemy's sources, rediscovered by the toil and enterprise of our countrymen Speke, Grant, and Baker.

A few weeks later he wrote,

I pray the good Lord of all to favour me so as to allow me to discover the ancient fountains of Herodotus, and if there is anything . . . to confirm the precious old documents, the Scriptures of truth, may He permit me to bring it to light, and give me wisdom to make proper use of it.

But then:

I wish I had some of the assurance possessed by others, but I am oppressed with the apprehension that after all it may turn out that I have been following the Congo; and who would risk being put into a cannibal pot and converted into black man for it?

And then ten days later:

In reference to the Nile source I have been kept in perpetual doubt and perplexity.

A month later:

The medical education has led me to a continual tendency to suspend judgement. What a state of blessedness it would have been had I possessed the dead certainty of the homeopathic persuasion, and as soon as I found the Lakes Bangweolo, Moero . . . pouring out their waters down the great central valley, bellowed out, "Hurrah! Eureka!" and gone home in firm and honest belief that I had settled it, and no mistake. Instead of that I am even now not at all "cock-sure" that I have not been following down what may after all be the Congo.

In a letter to London, in which he described the route he intended to take to the fountains of Herodotus, he wrote: "But what if these fountains exist only in my imagination!"

But all he could do now was wait, read books Stanley had brought him, write in his journal, organize and reorganize his notes, conduct Bible classes for native children under the mangoes, count the days.

Dr. Livingstone at work on his journal

If Stanley arrived the 1st of May at Zanzibar—allow 20 days to get men and settle with them = May 20th, men leave Zanzibar 22nd of May. . . . On the road may be 10 days, still to come 30 days . . . ought to arrive 10th or 15th July . . . then engage pagazi half a month = August, 5 months of this year will remain for journey, the whole of 1873 will be swallowed up in work, but in February or March 1874, please the Almighty Disposer of events, I shall complete my task and retire.

Then: "Stanley . . . 100 days gone: he must be in London now." In July: "Wearisome waiting, this; and yet the men can not be here before the middle or the end of the month." A few days later: "Weary! weary! . . . Waiting wearily here, and hoping that the good and loving Father of all may favour me, and help me to finish my work quickly and well."

But then at last the wearisome waiting was over. On August 9 an advance party arrived, and on August 14 the full caravan Stanley sent marched into Tabora. It was, in Stanley's best style, a splendidly outfitted party: 57 carefully chosen porters (one of whom, Jacob Wainwright, deserves to be mentioned by name because of the role he was later to play in Livingstone's service), plus muskets, ammunition, flour, sugar, tea, canned foods, riding donkeys, thousands of yards of trading cloth, and hundreds of pounds of beads and wire. Added to the 5 men, including of course Susi and Chuma, who had remained loyal to Livingstone from the beginning, he now commanded a caravan that would last at least two years, the most luxurious he had ever had in his whole life.

Because wars between Arab slavers and tribesmen blocked the route west back to Ujiji, Livingstone struck off to the southwest and, in early October, reached Lake Tanganyika a little more than halfway between Ujiji and the lake's southern end and there turned southward. All the familiar hardships and mishaps beset the caravan during this leg of the journey: a couple of porters decamped carrying off precious loads of trading cloth; the tsetse fly got to the baggage animals and killed them off one by one; food became increasingly hard to come by; the climate and the terrain along the mountainous eastern shore of Tanganyika proved brutally punishing. And it became quickly apparent just how superficial Livingstone's recovery had been, how unequal his health was to the rigors of African travel. Within a month of setting off he was suffering from malaria, and by the beginning of November from dysentery and anal bleeding. Nevertheless, it

was at least still the dry season and, plodding steadily on, the caravan rounded the southern end of Lake Tanganyika in the second week of November, turned west and then south toward Lake Bangweolo.

But then the rains came. For some weeks Livingstone had been listening to the thunder in the east with growing anxiety. On October 30, he had recorded, "Thunder all the morning, and a few drops of rain fell." Then, on November 19: "There are heavy rains now and then every day." By the end of that month: "Very heavy rain and high gusts of wind, which wet us all." And, from the beginning of December onward, the rains became the lamenting refrain of his days, falling in a steady drizzle, bursting from the heavens in sudden, violent downpours, lashing across the land in blinding, impenetrable sheets. "Rain, rain, rain as if it never tired on this watershed." Rivulets and rivers flooded their banks; the terrain was transformed into vast and terrible swamps (which he called sponges) ; snakes and leeches came out; and there was never ever getting dry and warm again.

A leech crawling towards me in the village this morning elicited the Bemba idea that they fall from the sky. . . . 29th or 1st January, 1873.—I am wrong two days. . . . The sponges here are now full and overflowing, from the continuous and heavy rains. . . . Detained by heavy continuous rains. . . . Got off in the afternoon in a drizzle; crossed a rill six feet wide, but now very deep, and with large running sponges on each side . . . then one hour beyond came to a sponge, and a sluggish rivulet 100 yards broad with broad sponges on either bank waist deep, and many leeches. . . . Never was in such a spell of cold rainy weather. . . . The country is covered with brackens, and rivulets occur at least one every hour of the march. These are now deep, and have a broad selvage of sponge. . . . I don't know where we are. . . .

    . . . Carrying me across one of the broad deep sedgy rivers is really a very difficult task. One we crossed was at least 2000 feet broad. . . . The first part, the main stream, came up to Susi's mouth, and wetted my seat and legs. One held up my pistol behind, then one after another took a turn, and when he sank into an elephant's foot-print, he required two to lift him, so as to gain a footing on the level, which was over waist deep. Others went on, and bent down the grass, to insure some footing on the side of the elephant's path. Every ten or twelve paces brought us to a clear stream, flowing fast in its own channel, while over all a strong current came bodily through all the rushes and aquatic plants.

"The main stream came up to Susi's mouth."

Under these conditions, Livingstone's health, not surprisingly, steadily disintegrated. From time to time, he would note in his journal:

I lose much blood. . . . I remain because of an excessive haemorrhagic discharge. If the good Lord gives me favour, and permits me to finish my work, I shall thank and bless Him, though it has cost me untold toil, pain, and travel; this trip has made my hair all grey.

And equally unsurprisingly, in his weakness and pain, his mind began to play tricks on him. He started composing imaginary dispatches:

I have the pleasure of reporting to your Lordship that on the —— I succeeded at last in reaching your remarkable fountains, each of which, at no great distance off, becomes a large river. They rise at the base of a swell of land or earthen mound, which can scarcely be called a hill, for it seems only about —— feet above ground level. . . . Possibly these four gushing fountains may be the very same that were mentioned by Herodotus. . . . The geographical position of the mound or low earthen hill, may be for the present taken as latitude —— and longitude ——. The altitude above the sea, ——.

In mid-February, Livingstone reached Lake Bangweolo, but he now had only the vaguest notion where he was. Because of the cease-

less rains, the lake had monumentally overflowed its banks, giving it a
configuration far different from what it had had when Livingstone
had seen it five years before. Because of the relentlessly overcast sky, he
couldn't fix his position by shooting the sun or stars. And the bleak,
featureless marshland all around him provided no landmarks to help
him out. All he knew was that he was somewhere on the lake's northeastern shore. His plan was to go round to the southern end, from
where he would strike out to the southwest toward Katanga and his
fabulous fountains, but he could not see the way to get around. In
fact, he could not properly see the lake's shoreline at all because the
waters of the lake merged imperceptibly with the waters of the flooded
marshland, in places seven feet deep and broken only occasionally by
islets, the crowns of anthills, clumps of reeds, and lotus plants. The
only course that seemed open was to go into the lake, that is, to cross it
from the northeastern to the southeastern shore. But for that canoes
were required.

Canoes could be gotten, apparently, only from a certain Matipa,
the leading chief of the neighborhood, and that involved endlessly
tedious negotiations. In the meantime Livingstone was forced to camp
in the dreadfully unhealthy mosquito-ridden swamps, suffering the
relentless rains and cold, the attacks of driver ants, the painful anal

Discovery of Lake Bangweolo

bleeding. At one point Matipa agreed to hire out some canoes in return for five bundles of brass wire, but reneged on the arrangement. At another, after Livingstone had given him a sharp talking-to, he again agreed but again no canoes were produced. "Matipa says 'Wait' . . . Time is of no value to him. His wife is making him pombe, and will drown all his cares, but mine increase and plague me. . . . I spoke sharply to Matipa for his duplicity. He promises everything and does nothing. . . . Ill all day with my old complaint. . . . The delay is most trying." Livingstone's sixtieth birthday came, March 19: "Thanks to the Almighty Preserver of men for sparing me thus far on the journey of life. Can I hope for ultimate success? So many obstacles have arisen. Let not Satan prevail over me, Oh! my good Lord Jesus."

That morning, nerves stretched to the breaking point, Livingstone, in an uncharacteristic act of violent desperation, marched into Matipa's village, took possession of the chief's hut, and fired a pistol through the roof. That did the trick, for in a few days Livingstone had six canoes and on March 24 had them loaded with his men and goods and set off into the lake.

We punted six hours to a little islet without a tree, and no sooner did we land than a pitiless pelting rain came on. We turned up a canoe to get shelter. . . . The wind tore the tent out of our hands, and damaged it too; the loads are all soaked, and with the cold it's bitterly uncomfortable. . . . Nothing earthly will make me give up my work in despair. I encourage myself in the Lord my God, and go forward.

For some two weeks, he went forward, southeasterly, the canoes trying to follow as closely as possible the reed marshes that vaguely marked the lake shore, each night stopping at another sodden islet in the endless expanse of water.

The flood extends . . . for twenty or thirty miles, and far too broad to be seen across . . . got into a large stream. . . . One canoe sank in it, and we lost a slave girl. . . . Fished up three boxes, and two guns, but the boxes being full of cartridges were much injured. . . . A lion roars mightily. The fishhawk utters his weird voice in the morning, as if he lifted up to a friend at a great distance . . . it is quite impossible at present to tell where land ends, and Lake begins; it is all water, water everywhere. . . . I am pale, bloodless, and weak from bleeding profusely ever since the 31st of March last: an artery gives off a copious stream, and takes away my strength.

That last was the entry under April 10. The party had reached the southeastern shore of the lake, had abandoned the canoes, and was preparing to set off southwestward through the endless marshlands. But Livingstone was now slowly bleeding to death, and it was virtually impossible for him to walk.

Tottered along nearly two hours, and then lay down quite done. Cooked coffee—our last—and went on, but in an hour I was compelled to lie down. Very unwilling to be carried, but on being pressed I allowed the men to help me along by relays.

Two days later he wrote:

After the turtle doves and cocks give out their warning calls to the watchful, the fish-eagle lifts up his remarkable voice. It is pitched in a high falsetto key, very loud, and seems as if he were calling to someone in the other world. Once heard, his weird unearthly voice can never be forgotten—it sticks to one through life.

He had to submit to being carried, and Chuma and Susi constructed a litter for him. His diary entries become shorter, punctuated with pathetic confessions of weakness, the copious loss of blood, the relentlessness of the driving rains, the murderous difficulty of making way through the flooded lands. On April 19, he wrote, "It is not all pleasure this exploration. . . . No observations now, owing to great weakness; I can scarcely hold the pencil." But he still had not given up his quest. On April 25, upon reaching a village where the party intended to spend the night, Livingstone called some of the tribesmen around him and asked them if they knew of a hill around which four rivers took their rise. The chief replied that they had no knowledge of such but went on to explain that they themselves were not travelers and all those who once went on the trading expeditions from their tribe were now dead. Livingstone thanked them and asked them to leave him. On April 27 he scrawled his final diary entry: "Knocked up quite and remain—recover—sent to buy milch goats. We are on the banks of the Molilamo."

Livingstone lived four days longer, and our knowledge of what happened in those days comes from an account provided by his most faithful followers, Chuma and Susi. On April 29, after a day of rest, Livingstone ordered the party to march on southwestward, obviously still in quest of his mystical fountains. He himself was, however, com-

The last mile of Livingstone's travels

pletely unable to walk, and since the door of the hut in which he rested was too small for his litter to be brought through, the walls of the hut had to be broken down before he could be carried from his cot. That day's traveling was brutal. A small river had to be crossed, but Livingstone was unable to sit up in the canoe, and he had to be lifted off his litter, put down gently in its bottom and then lifted again onto the litter after the crossing. Chuma and Susi tell us that his pain was so great from the movements of the march that he repeatedly begged them to set him down and allow him to rest. But, just when it seemed that he wouldn't be able to stand the anguish of being carried a step further, the outlying huts of a village came into sight, Ilala, the village of a chief called Chitambo.

Livingstone was set down under the eaves of a hut to shelter him from the rain while a lodging of reeds and grass was built for him. It took until nightfall, and inquisitive villagers gathered around to peer at the prostrate white man. At last he was moved into the hut. The cot was placed on sticks to keep it out of the muddy water; a crate beside it held the medicine chest and a young boy was put on guard outside the hut to listen in case the master called out for something during the night. But Livingstone slept.

The next morning the chief, Chitambo, came to pay a courtesy call on the white man, but Livingstone was too weak to speak to him and

was obliged to ask him to return the next day, when he hoped to be better. In the afternoon he sent for Susi and had him bring his watch so that he could wind it. Then he dozed off again and, as night fell once more, a fire was lighted outside the hut, and the boy took up his vigil there. Around 11 P.M. Livingstone sent for Susi and inquired about some sounds he heard off in the distance. "Are our men making the noise?" he asked faintly. "No," Susi replied, "I can hear from the cries that the people are scaring away a buffalo from their fields." After a few moments, Livingstone asked, "Is this the Luapula?" Susi told him they were at Chitambo's village. *"Sikun' gapi kuenda Lua-pula?* (How many days is it to the Luapula?)" Livingstone asked, reverting to Swahili. *"Na zani zikutatu, Bwana* (I think it is three days, master)," Susi replied. After a few seconds, Livingstone said, "Oh dear, dear," and dozed off again. An hour later Susi was called again and Livingstone asked him to boil some water, and then, with great difficulty, Livingstone took a dosage of calomel from his medicine chest and had Susi mix it with the hot water in a cup so he could take it. "All right," he said, "you can go now." Those were his last words.

Around 4 A.M. the following morning, May 1, with the first pastel shades of the sun streaking the horizon, the boy who had been placed on guard outside Livingstone's hut called for Susi and Chuma. He said that before he had fallen asleep by the fire he had seen Livingstone pull himself off the cot and kneel by it in prayer. Now, when he awakened a few hours later, he saw that the master was still in the same position. Susi, Chuma, and a few others hurried to the hut. A candle stuck by its own wax to the crate by the cot shed sufficient light for them to see. Livingstone was kneeling by the side of the cot, his body stretched forward, his head buried in his hands on the pillow. They watched him for a moment, not sure whether to disturb him at his prayers. But they saw that he didn't move; there was no sign of breathing. At last one went into the hut and placed his hand gently against Livingstone's cheek. It was nearly cold. Livingstone had been dead for some time.

What happened now remains one of the most remarkable stories in the annals of African exploration. By all rights, Livingstone's death should have shattered his party. The sixty or so Africans of the caravan were hundreds and in some cases thousands of miles from their homes. For more than eight months they had followed Livingstone from

Tabora, going where he chose to go, wandering through the endless swamps with him, suffering the cold and the rain and the fevers with him, facing all the terrors he led them into, leaving all the decisions to him, relying completely on him to get them to their goal and back again. And now suddenly he was dead and they found themselves stranded in the middle of the wilderness, in a strange land with no real idea where they were. There would be every reason to expect them to panic, to abandon Livingstone's body and his journals, to plunder the stores of the caravan for its most precious goods, and set off in a disorderly and desperate flight in whatever direction they thought might lead them homeward. But they did none of these things. Rather they acted with a calm and courage and discipline and intelligence that must still elicit admiration a century later.

The news of Livingstone's death was quietly spread to each member of the caravan, and in the first light of morning they all gathered in front of the master's hut to discuss what they should do. Two decisions were made without any hesitation. The first was that Susi and Chuma, who had been with Livingstone for more than seven years and who, in the words of the others, were "old men in travelling and in hardships," were to take over as the leaders of the caravan. The second was that they would not abandon Livingstone: they would take him home. The second of these decisions was remarkable enough in revealing just how profound was the affection Livingstone had elicited from his followers. But it is all the more remarkable in that these followers were well aware of the problems they would create for themselves by trying to carry a corpse halfway across Africa. The tribesmen through whose regions they intended to pass believed that the spirits of the dead caused terrible trouble and destruction among the living. Thus, to carry a stranger's corpse through a tribe's territory was extremely dangerous. At the very best, the punishment for such a horrendous deed would be the payment of a stiff fine. At the worst, the bearers of the corpse could expect, if discovered, to be attacked and killed as evil witches. Nevertheless, Livingstone's followers resolved to run the risks. What they had to do, however, if they hoped to have any chance of succeeding, was keep what they were doing a secret.

The first person they had to keep it a secret from was Chitambo, the chief of the village they were in. So Chuma went to the chief later that morning and, telling him that Livingstone was still too ill to be seen, asked Chitambo for permission to move the white man out of the

village to a quieter, more secluded place. Chitambo consented, and so that afternoon a new hut was built and Livingstone's corpse, covered with cloth and a blanket, was carried to it on a litter. However, not long after, Chitambo learned the truth and hurried to the new hut to confront Susi and Chuma. The two men stood their ground tensely, ready for the first of the series of troubles they could expect from their extraordinary decision. But it seems that Chitambo himself had somehow been affected by the force of Livingstone's personality. And we find him saying, "Why did you not tell me the truth? I know that your master died last night. You were afraid to let me know, but do not fear any longer. . . . I know that you have no bad motives in coming to our land, and death often happens to travellers in their journeys." Encouraged by his attitude, Chuma and Susi then told him of their plan to carry Livingstone home. Chitambo tried to dissuade them, urging them to bury the body then and there. But, when he saw the two men's determination, he agreed not to interfere with whatever they wanted to do and brought a party of mourners, including his wives, drummers, and warriors with bows and arrows, to Livingstone's hut and led them in wailing lamentations for the dead white man.

Within, Susi, Chuma, and another member of the caravan held a thick blanket as a screen in front of the emaciated body lying on the cot. Jacob Wainwright, who had joined the party in Tabora and could read and write English, stood to one side with his prayer book. And a porter by the name of Farijala, who had worked as a servant for a doctor on Zanzibar, stepped forward to begin the operation. He made a careful incision upward from the abdomen. Then he removed Livingstone's heart and viscera and poured a quantity of salt into the body. (During this process all noticed a clot of coagulated blood as large as a man's fist blocking the lower intestines, which, if it was not the reason for Livingstone's death, must have caused him horrifying pain in his final days.) The heart and internal organs were then placed in a tin box, and, while Jacob Wainwright read the service from his prayer book, the box was buried in the earthen floor of the hut. Some brandy was then poured into the corpse's mouth as an additional preservative and, as at long last the dry season was returning again, the roof of the hut was removed so that the body could be exposed to the drying power of the sun. This took fourteen days, and once each day Susi or Chuma would go into the hut and change the position of the corpse. When the body was judged tolerably dry, it was

wrapped in calico and then placed in a cylinder of bark. Over this, sailcloth was sewn and heavily tarred to make it waterproof, and this strange bier was then lashed to poles so it could be carried by two men. Wainwright now carved an inscription on a tree near where the body had lain—Livingstone, May 4, 1873. Two strong posts with a crosspiece were erected in the form of a doorway, and Chitambo promised to guard both the tree and this doorway from destruction. And so, sometime in the middle of May, Susi and Chuma led the caravan out of Chitambo's village on the more than 1000-mile journey back from whence it had come. It is a measure of Susi's and Chuma's magnificent leadership abilities that, despite the ruggedness of the terrain, the ravages of disease, and the hostilities of tribesmen to the strange burden they carried, the caravan reached Tabora, with the loss of only ten men, in five months' time.

Meanwhile, back in England, ever since Stanley's successful expedition, the Royal Geographical Society had been suffering from a guilty conscience for having taken a far too sanguine view of Livingstone's fate and for having left it to an American newspaperman to find and help him. Determined never to let that happen again, the Royal Geographical Society decided to send out *two* relief expeditions just to make doubly sure that Livingstone was all right. Both departed from England the same day, November 30, 1872, when Livingstone was, in fact, still all right, making his way around Lake Tanganyika toward Lake Bangweolo before the rains had fully set in.

One of these, headed by a young naval lieutenant by the name of William J. Grandy, is of interest only because it reveals that at last there was a growing recognition of the true significance of Livingstone's discoveries. More and more geographers were coming around to the opinion that the system of rivers and lakes that Livingstone had found formed the watershed not of the Nile but the Congo. Convinced that Livingstone himself would come to realize this as well, they believed that he would ultimately trace the Lualaba along its great westward arc, and therefore the most likely way to meet up with him would be in his inevitable journey down to the Atlantic. Thus it was Grandy's task to push up toward Livingstone along the Congo River and provide him with whatever assistance he might need. But, even if he failed to meet Livingstone by this route, the expedition would not be a waste because Grandy was further instructed to explore and map the Congo's course upstream into the interior as far as

he possibly could. This was the first expedition to the Congo since Tuckey's and, if it wasn't as terrible a catastrophe as Tuckey's, it was even less successful.

Grandy's party arrived at Loanda, in Angola, on January 22, 1873, and from there struck overland northeastward toward the Congo. Because by then the rainy season had started in this part of Africa, because too of the difficulties of getting porters, and perhaps mainly because of Grandy's inexperience, it wasn't until October that the party reached the old royal capital of the vanished Kingdom of Kongo, São Salvador. By this time Livingstone, of course, was dead and his body was on its way home with his faithful followers. But Grandy could not know this, and he pushed his caravan down to the banks of the Congo. There he was stopped for the next six months, engaged in interminable negotiations for guides and porters and canoes for the journey upriver. By the time he was ready to move on upriver into the interior, however, the news of Livingstone's death had at last reached him, and he abandoned the project.

The second expedition was under the command of Verney Lovett Cameron. He also was a young naval lieutenant (28 years old) but he had had some experience in Africa before this assignment. He had served with Napier in the British punitive campaign against Theodore in Ethiopia, after which he had been posted to Zanzibar, where he participated in the British fleet's efforts to blockade the Arab slave traffic. Often taking his shore leaves to visit the East African mainland, he developed an appetite and ambition for African exploration. This was his first chance and, unlike Grandy, he wasn't going to let anything—even Livingstone's death—deter him from making a success of it. As a consequence, he in fact was to add more to Europe's understanding of the Congo's geography than Grandy or Tuckey ever did, even though he was never expected to come anywhere near the river. For he was sent out to meet Livingstone by the conventional route from the East African coast westward into the interior.

Cameron's party, which included three other white men—a naval surgeon by the name of Dillon, an army lieutenant by the name of Murphy, and Robert Moffat, a nephew of Livingstone's by marriage—arrived in Zanzibar just about the same time that Grandy arrived in Angola. Following what was then an increasingly routine procedure, Cameron assembled his supplies and porters, including some who had served with Stanley, then took a dhow across to Bagamoyo, where he

arrived in the beginning of February, and, after all the usual delays, struck off inland along the familiar Arab caravan route at the end of March 1873. During the trek, Cameron and his white companions were struck down with severe cases of malaria. By May, Moffat was dead of it, and by August, when the caravan reached Tabora, the others were half crazed and half blind from the fever, so they halted the march until they were sufficiently recovered to go on. It was a painfully slow recovery and, indeed, never completed—within a few months Dillon was to blow his brains out and Murphy was to desert the expedition—and on October 20 they were still there, bedridden and virtually helpless.

Then, Cameron tells us,

as I lay on my bed, prostrate, listless, and enfeebled from repeated attacks of fever; my mind dazed and confused with whirling thoughts and fantasies of home and those dear ones far away . . . my servant . . . came running into my tent with a letter in his hand. I snatched it from him, asking at the same moment where it came from. His only reply was, "Some man bring him."

Tearing it open, this is what Cameron found:

Sir, We have heard in the month of August that you have started from Zanzibar for Unyenyembe, and again and again lately we have heard your arrival—your father died by disease beyond the country of Bisa, but we have carried the corpse with us. 10 of our soldiers are lost and some have died. Our hunger presses us to ask you some clothes to buy provisions for our soldiers, and we should have an answer that when we shall enter there shall be firing guns or not, and if you permit us to fire guns then send some powder. We have wrote these few words in the place of the Sultan or King Mbowra. The writer Jacob Wainwright. Dr. Livingstone Exped.

Cameron tells us that

Being half-blind, it was with some difficulty that I deciphered the writing, and then, failing to attach any definite meaning to it, I went to Dillon. His brain was in much the same state of confusion from fever as mine, and we read it again together, each having the same vague idea—Could it be our own father who was dead?

At last, Cameron thought to have the bearer of the letter brought to him. It was Chuma, and then Cameron understood. Susi, Chuma, and the others, on their long hard journey bearing Livingstone home, had

come across an Arab caravan from Bagamoyo which told them that an English expedition had arrived on the east coast, headed for Tabora, commanded by one of Livingstone's sons. It is not clear how this misunderstanding arose. It is possible that the Arabs misunderstood Moffat's relationship to Livingstone and converted the nephew by marriage into a son. But in any case, on hearing the news, Chuma had run on ahead with Jacob Wainwright's letter, and a few days later the rest of the troop arrived, carrying Livingstone's body into Tabora.

The reaction to the arrival of Livingstone's body was curious. Murphy immediately seized on the occasion to quit the expedition and return to the coast, on the grounds, as Cameron tells us, "that nothing further remained for us to do." Dillon was clearly too sick to consider doing anything, and it was agreed that he should be carried back to the coast in a litter (he would kill himself before he got there). But Cameron was all for going on. He intended to make a name for himself as an explorer and he wasn't about to let Livingstone's death forestall him. He rummaged through Livingstone's effects and took a number of instruments that he felt would be useful for his explorations, and though Chuma and Susi were appalled at this there was nothing they could do to prevent him. But, when Cameron went on to suggest that they bury Livingstone's corpse in Tabora and not bother to carry it down to the coast, they firmly declined. They were taking Livingstone home and they would not stop until they had completed the sacred task they had set for themselves. On November 9 they once more took up their burden and, with Murphy and Dillon now a part of their caravan, set off on the final leg of their journey to the coast while, Cameron tells us, "my cry was 'Westward ho!' "

Cameron reached Ujiji just about the same time that Livingstone's cortege reached Bagamoyo, February 15, 1874. Chuma had gone ahead to Zanzibar, and the next day, February 16, a British cruiser, the H.M.S. *Vulture* arrived at Bagamoyo and took Livingstone's body aboard and transported it to the island. There it was taken from its coffin of sailcloth, bark, and calico, and a medical examination revealed a skull of European shape with white straight hair and, though the features were no longer recognizable, there could be no doubt that this was Livingstone's body. It was then laid in a simple coffin of zinc and wood and put aboard the next mailboat bound for England, where it arrived on April 15.

Only one of the Africans—Jacob Wainwright—accompanied Liv-

ingstone on this journey. Chuma and Susi and the others, who had shown themselves so brave and devoted and who would never understand the callous lack of response to their courage and devotion, were paid off and sent on their way. To be sure, a few months later Susi and Chuma were taken to England to help edit Livingstone's last journals and fill in the narrative of the days after his death, but by that time they were too late to attend his funeral. A year later the Royal Geographical Society thought to strike commemorative medals for the sixty men who had carried Livingstone out of the heart of the interior, but by that time those men were scattered all over East Africa, and most never received the medals. When Livingstone's journals were published, an attempt was made to acknowledge the remarkable and noble deed of these men.

Nothing but such leadership and staunchness as that which organized the march home . . . and distinguished it throughout, could have brought Livingstone's bones to our land or his last notes and maps to the outer world. To none does the feat seem so marvellous as to those who know Africa and the difficulties which must have beset both the first and the last in the enterprise. Thus in his death, not less than in his life, David Livingstone bore testimony to that goodwill and kindliness which exists in the heart of the African.

16

THE EXTRAORDINARY ENTERPRISE

Stanley learned of Livingstone's death on February 25, 1874, ten days after the explorer's body had been brought to Zanzibar and the news had been telegraphed around the world. As it happened, Stanley was himself just returning from Africa. He had spent the preceding four months in the Gold Coast, covering a British punitive campaign against the Ashantee for the *Herald,* and it was on his way home, when the British warship H.M.S. *Dauntless* on which he was traveling called at St. Vincent in the Cape Verde Islands that he received the cable telling him that he had once again lost a father.

Stanley reached England a month before Livingstone's body, and, taking rooms at the Langham Hotel in London, he used that time to go through all the file stories at the *Herald*'s office on Livingstone's death to convince himself that it was really true and not just another of those many false reports that had dogged the explorer in his last years of wandering. And, once he was, he wrote, "Dear Livingstone! another sacrifice to Africa! His mission, however, must not be allowed to cease; others must go forward and fill the gap." And then: "May I be selected to succeed him in opening up Africa to the shining light of Christianity!"

On April 15, Stanley went down to Southampton to meet the funeral cortege. It was a wet and windy day, but massive crowds, the mayor and aldermen of the town, a military band, a company of the Royal Horse Artillery and a procession of black-draped carriages had been waiting on the quay since dawn. At nine o'clock the mail steamer from Zanzibar entered the harbor with Livingstone's coffin, draped in the Union Jack, on the open deck. Then, as it was brought down the

gangway, the Royal Horse fired the first of a series of twenty-one-gun salutes and the band began the mournful refrain of the "Death March" from *Saul*. The waiting carriages escorted the coffin to the railway station, where a special train carried it to London. There it lay in state in the map room of the Royal Geographical Society for two days. On the morning of April 18, declared a day of national mourning, it was transported through the crowded silent streets to Westminster Abbey, where, down the nave beyond the tomb of the Unknown Soldier, it was interred. Stanley was one of the pallbearers. Another was Jacob Wainwright.

Stanley confided to his diary that day that the effect the news of Livingstone's death had on him "after the first shock had passed away, was to fire me with a resolution to complete his work, to be, if God willed it, the next martyr to geographical science, or, if my life was to be spared, to clear up not only the secrets of the Great River throughout its course, but also all that remained still problematic and incomplete."

Stanley's desire to finish Livingstone's work was for him unquestionably genuine. He loved and admired the man; he could deeply sympathize with Livingstone's tragic disappointment at having failed to settle the mystery of the Nile; and as the last European to have spoken to the explorer, he felt personally called upon to vindicate Livingstone's geographical theories.

But there was something else at work in Stanley's psyche at this time. He was still suffering bitterly from the mixed and often insulting reception he had received when he had returned from Africa after finding Livingstone. He could not forget that his accomplishment at first had been dismissed as a hoax and then belittled as a publicity stunt, and he was painfully aware that he remained in the eyes of the geographers and social establishment and the educated public merely a journalist, a daring and adventurous journalist to be sure, but merely a journalist nevertheless. He had gained a certain kind of fame and something of a fortune but he had not acquired the respect and reputation accorded to the true heroes of African exploration. And more than anything else that was what he craved. "What I have already endured in that accursed Africa," he wrote, "amounts to nothing in men's estimation. Surely if I can resolve any of the problems which such travelers as Dr. Livingstone, Captains Burton, Speke, and Grant, and Sir Samuel Baker left unsettled, people must needs believe

that I discovered Livingstone." And it was this, perhaps more than his love for Livingstone, that inspired him to plan the most amazingly audacious journey of African exploration that had ever been conceived let alone undertaken, one that would make him inarguably the greatest African explorer of them all.

It consisted of three parts. First, he would resolve the problems left unsettled by Speke. As we've seen, Speke believed Victoria to be a huge single sheet of water whose outlet was the source of the White Nile. Since Speke's death, this view, although correct, had fallen into disrepute. The most definitive map of Africa published around this time—that of Georg Schweinfurth's in *The Heart of Africa*—showed Victoria as five separate lakes, and even Grant, Speke's faithful companion on his second expedition, had tired of arguing otherwise. So Stanley proposed to settle this matter one way or the other by doing what no one else had yet done: circumnavigate the lake.

Second, there were the disputes about Burton's Lake Tanganyika and Baker's Lake Albert. Each of these men also believed *his* lake was a single body of water and the Nile's source. Baker was willing to concede that Albert might share the distinction with Victoria, that its outlet might join Victoria's to form the great river. But Burton held that Tanganyika was the Nile's only source, arguing that its effluent river, which neither he nor anyone else had yet found, flowed into Albert. So Stanley decided to undertake answering these questions as well.

And, finally, there was Livingstone's Lualaba. From the explorer's last journals, which had been brought home with his body, Stanley could see that Livingstone had done a fairly complete job of mapping the watershed of this river. What he hadn't done, however, allowing his obsessive quest for the four fountains of Herodotus to divert him, was to trace the Lualaba far enough northward to prove whether it was the Nile, as he had contended, or the Congo, as a growing number of geographers now believed. So Stanley planned, after settling all the outstanding questions about Victoria, Albert, and Tanganyika, to follow the Lualaba wherever it took him, down the Nile to the Mediterranean or down the Congo to the Atlantic Ocean.

This was the scheme for a journey of more than 5000 miles, most of it through country where no European had ever gone before and further in distance than Livingstone had traveled in all the seven years of his final wanderings. Stanley realized that it would require massive

financial backing. He estimated it at over £12,000 sterling or $60,000 and he knew that the New York *Herald* could not be expected to put up that much. (For all Bennett's largess when he sent Stanley off to find Livingstone he had been appalled at the amount of money the scoop had cost him.) So Stanley first turned to the London *Daily Telegraph.* The *Telegraph,* which around this time had emerged as the leading British newspaper, had a popular, racy style much like that of the *Herald,* and what's more its deputy editor, Edwin Arnold, was a fellow of the Royal Geographical Society and one of the few backers Stanley had in that group. Thus, Stanley could count on an intelligent hearing for his plans from Arnold, and he could expect Bennett's competitive spirit to be aroused by the idea that an opposition newspaper might beat him to a scoop.

As Stanley tells the story, he was out strolling the streets of London not long after Livingstone's funeral and decided to look in on Arnold at the *Telegraph*'s offices. Their conversation drifted to Livingstone and from there to the work he had left incomplete. "What is there to do?" Arnold asked. Stanley outlined his threefold scheme. "Do you think you can settle all this, if we commission you?" Arnold asked. Stanley tells us he replied: "While I live, there will be something done. If I survive the time required to perform all the work, all shall be done." A telegram was sent off to Bennett in New York asking him if he would be willing to split the cost with the *Telegraph* of "sending Stanley out to Africa to complete the discoveries of Speke, Burton, and Livingstone." There was only a twenty-four-hour wait. Stanley had judged his boss's temper correctly. Bennett's cable in reply contained only one work: "Yes."

Stanley was anxious to get started as quickly as possible so as to be under way in Africa by the beginning of the dry season. He made a brief trip back to New York in June to put his personal affairs in order and then spent the next two months in London preparing the extraordinary enterprise. He bought every available book on Africa and African exploration, more than 130 he tells us, and cluttered up his rooms at the Langham Hotel with maps and newspapers and manuscripts. "Until late hours I sat up, inventing and planning, sketching out routes, laying out lengthy lines of possible exploration." During the day, he went out shopping in the London stores for the hundreds of items on the endless lists of supplies he drew up. As he intended to spend so much of his time exploring lakes and rivers, he decided to

bring along his own boats and put in orders for a yawl, a gig, and a barge, the last of which he designed himself so that it could be disassembled into sections for easier portage.

Stanley also used this time to recruit some white assistants. There was no dearth of volunteers. At the time the papers announced the joint Anglo-American enterprise, "applications by the score poured into the offices of the *Daily Telegraph* and the *New York Herald* for employment," Stanley tells us.

Over 1200 letters were received from generals, colonels, captains, lieutenants, midshipmen, engineers, commissioners of hotels, mechanics, waiters, cooks, servants, somebodies and nobodies, spiritual mediums and magnetizers, etc., etc. They all knew Africa, were perfectly acclimatized, were quite sure they would please me, would do important services, save me from any number of troubles by their ingenuity and resources, take me up in balloons or by flying carriages, make us all invisible by their magic arts, or by the science of magnetism would cause all savages to fall asleep while we might pass anywhere without trouble.

At the end, though, Stanley chose three rather conventional young British lads. The brothers Edward and Francis (Frank) Pocock were Kentish fishermen and accomplished boatsmen, "who bore the reputation of being honest and trustworthy," while Frederick Barker was a desk clerk at the Langham Hotel, "who, smitten with a desire to go to Africa, was not to be dissuaded by reports of its unhealthy climate, its dangerous fevers, or the uncompromising views of exploring life given to him." Additionally, and for some inexplicable reason, Stanley bought five dogs to take with him, and then after a few farewell dinners departed from England on August 15, 1874. Six weeks later he was once again in Zanzibar, 28 months after he had left it with the scoop of the century, but this time he was there as an explorer and not a journalist.

The island was in the midst of great changes. Since the opening of the Suez Canal, it was no longer quite the remote, exotic, clove-scented outpost. The island's European colony now numbered over 70, and America as well as practically every major European power maintained a consulate there. A mail steamer called every month, and the harbor was jammed with the vessels of a dozen nations plying the Indies trade. But the biggest change that had occurred since Stanley left it was the end of the island's booming market in slaves. Largely

owing to Livingstone's propaganda, and most especially his vivid, heart-breaking account of the massacre at Nyangwe, the British government had been incited to threaten the sultan of Zanzibar with a naval blockade if he didn't shut down the island's slave market. And, though slaving continued in the African mainland, with the bloody traffic passing through other markets, Zanzibar's marketplace had been bought up by the Anglicans, and a huge red-brick church was under construction on the site when Stanley arrived.

In characteristic fashion, he immediately set about assembling his caravan, recruiting first a reliable cadre from among the men who had served with him or Livingstone before and with whose help he meant to select and hire the rest of his force. But, before this could begin, Stanley tells us, "a preliminary deliberative palaver" or *shauri* was necessary. "The chiefs arranged themselves in a semicircle . . . and I sat *a la Turque* fronting them." After a few minutes of formalities, a spokesman for the group said, "A traveller journeys not without knowing whither he wanders. We have come to ascertain what lands you are bound for." Stanley, using a

low tone of voice, as though the information about to be imparted to the intensely interested and eagerly listening group were too important to speak it loud . . . described in brief outline the prospective journey, in broken Kiswahili. As country after country was mentioned of which they had hitherto but vague ideas, and river after river, lake after lake named, all of which I hoped with their trusty aid to explore carefully, various ejaculations expressive of wonder and joy, mixed with a little alarm, broke from their lips, but when I concluded, each of the group drew a long breath, and almost simultaneously they uttered admiringly, "Ah, fellows, this is a journey worthy to be called a journey!"

"But, master," said they, after recovering themselves, "this long journey will take years to travel—six, nine or ten years." "Nonsense," I replied. "Six, nine, or ten years! What can you be thinking of? It takes the Arabs nearly three years to reach Ujiji, it is true, but, if you remember, I was but sixteen months from Zanzibar to Ujiji and back . . . If I were quick on my first journey, am I likely to be slow now? Am I much older than I was then? Am I less strong? Do I not know what travel is now? Was I not like a boy then, and am I not now a man? You remember while going to Ujiji I permitted the guide to show the way, but when we were returning who was it that led the way? Was it not I . . . ? Very well then, let us finish the shauri, and go."

By mid-November they were ready to go. Some 356 pagazis (porters) and askaris (armed soldiers for an escort) had been hired and, though he planned to travel nearly three times as far and had almost twice as many men as on his previous expedition, Stanley assembled only 8 tons of supplies versus the 6 tons the last time. He had learned from experience what was really needed and, what's more, this time he wanted to travel light for speed. The goods were broken down into 60-pound loads for each porter to carry, and they included (among the usual wire, beads, cloth, bedding, ropes, tents, medicines, ammunition, guns, scientific instruments, and so on) photographic equipment (the first ever to be taken into Africa), five cut-throat razors in a case, shaving mirrors, ivory-backed hairbrushes, eau de cologne, and a few meerschaum pipes, one with Stanley's monogram on the bowl. But clearly the centerpiece of the caravan was the portable barge that Stanley had designed. It was 40 feet long, 6 feet wide and 30 inches deep, made of Spanish cedar, equipped with oars and a sail and capable of being disassembled into five sections, each light enough to be carried by two men. It was to prove to be the single most valuable piece of equipment on the expedition, and Stanley christened it the *Lady Alice.*

Who the lady named Alice was has long been a titillating mystery of the Stanley expedition, and only recently, in Richard Hall's biography of the explorer, was it at last cleared up. It seems that Stanley, just a few weeks after Livingstone's funeral, had fallen in love. The girl who had won his heart was Alice Pike, the 17-year-old daughter of an American whiskey millionaire, who was visiting London with her family at the time. They met at a dinner party at the Langham Hotel arranged by a mutual friend, and they seem to have seen each other practically every day after that. Although Alice had other suitors, Stanley was able to write only a few days after meeting her, "I fear that if Miss Alice gives me as much encouragement long as she has been giving me lately, I shall fall in love with her." Stanley, whom Alice preferred to call by his middle name Morton because it had a more melodious ring, was then already in the midst of his preparations for his African journey, but when the Pikes returned to New York, Stanley, on the pretext of needing to see Bennett, followed shortly thereafter. In mid-July he proposed to Alice and they signed a marriage pact: "We solemnly pledge ourselves to be faithful to each other

and to be married to one another on the return of Henry Morton Stanley from Africa. We call God to witness this our pledge in writing." On their last evening together, they took a walk in Central Park and "She raised her lips in tempting proximity and I kissed her on her lips, on her eyes, on her cheeks and her neck, and she kissed me in return." She gave him two photographs of herself to carry with him on his travels, and he promised that he would return in two years.

And so, on November 17, when he set off from Bagamoyo, he was intent on keeping this rendezvous with love.

The bugle mustered the people to rank themselves. . . . Four chiefs a few hundred yards in front; next the twelve guides clad in red robes of Jobo, bearing the wire coils; then a long file 270 strong, bearing cloth, wire, beads, and sections of the Lady Alice; after them thirty six women and ten boys, children of some of the chiefs and boat-bearers, following their mothers and assisting them with trifling loads of utensils, followed by the riding asses, Europeans and gun-bearers; the long line closed by sixteen chiefs who act as rearguard . . . in all, 356 souls. . . . The lengthy line occupies nearly half a mile of the path which at the present day is the commercial and exploring highway into the Lake regions.

Stanley knew that he was not the only European traveling in those regions at this time. As we have seen, Verney Lovett Cameron, who had been sent out to assist Livingstone and who, after learning of Livingstone's death, had decided to continue on his own expedition of exploration, had reached Ujiji in February, nine months before Stanley left Bagamoyo. Moreover, as Stanley knew at this time, Cameron had sailed from Ujiji down the eastern shore of Lake Tanganyika, around its southern end, and part way up the western shore, and had then returned to Ujiji in May. From there, Cameron could be expected to have set off from Ujiji again, this time in an effort to reach the Lualaba and do what Livingstone had failed to do, sail northward on it to see if it was really the Nile or rather the Congo. All reports indicated that Cameron was having a very difficult time of it, and his progress was desperately slow, but he had eighteen months' headstart on Stanley, and by the time Stanley completed his explorations of Victoria and Albert, which he intended to do before ever heading for the Lualaba, that lead would have lengthened to over three years. So, as Stanley now led his caravan into the African interior, he was a man not only hurrying to a rendezvous with love, but in a terribly handi-

capped race with a rival for the most cherished prize of African exploration.

And the way he proceeded showed it. Nothing could have been more different from Livingstone's march into the interior. He himself had acknowledged it would be. "My methods will not be Livingstone's. Each man has his own way," he had written before setting out, and his way was a series of forced marches, an overpowering of obstacles, harsh, relentless discipline, a heavy loss of life, but finally a speedy attainment of the objective. He reached the town of Mpwapwa, about halfway between the coast and Tabora, in less than a month, whereas it had taken Cameron four. Here Stanley turned off the well-beaten track of the Arab caravan route and blazed a new trail north for Lake Victoria.

The rains began and with that all the Europeans, including Stanley, came down with fevers, and, to make matters worse, the country they were passing through was beset by famine. The further northward they went the more difficult it became to acquire food. The local tribesmen either just didn't have any or what little they had was too precious to barter away for Stanley's beads, wire, and cloth at anything less than exorbitant prices. On Christmas, he wrote to Alice Pike:

How your kind woman's heart would pity me and mine. . . . I am in a centre-pole tent, seven by eight. As it rained all day yesterday, the tent was set over wet ground. . . . The tent walls are disfigured by large splashes of mud, and the tent corners hang down limp and languid, and there is such an air of forlornness and misery about its very set that it increases my own misery. . . . I sit on a bed raised about a foot above the sludge, mournfully reflecting on my condition. Outside, the people have evidently a fellow feeling with me, for they appear to me like beings with strong suicidal intentions or perhaps they mean to lie still, inert until death relieves them. It has been raining heavily the last two or three days, and an impetuous downpour of sheet rain has just ceased. On the march, rain is very disagreeable; it makes the clayey path slippery, and the loads heavier by being saturated, while it half ruins the cloths. It makes us dis-spirited, wet, and cold, added to which we are hungry. . . . I myself have not had a piece of meat for ten days. My food is boiled rice, tea and coffee, and soon I shall be reduced to eating native porridge, like my own people. I weighed 180 lbs. when I left Zanzibar, but under this diet I have been reduced to 134 lbs. within thirty-eight days. The young Englishmen are in the same impoverished condition of body, and unless we reach some more flourishing country . . . we must soon become mere skeletons.

But it would be some time before more flourishing country would be reached, and in the meantime matters steadily deteriorated. Porters deserted, others were killed off by disease or hunger, the riding donkeys and the dogs Stanley had brought with him dropped off one by one, and on January 17 the first of the Europeans, Edward Pocock, died of typhus. Then, when it appeared that the situation couldn't possibly get any worse, the local tribesmen turned openly hostile. Bands of warriors armed with spears and knobsticks began harassing the caravan, attacking and killing stragglers and stealing their loads, and in one pitched battle, which lasted three days, 22 of Stanley's men were killed. Yet through it all Stanley never once faltered in his harsh, disciplined, single-minded methods, and with bulldog persistence he reached his objective. The cost was high: of the 356 men who had started out with him from Bagamoyo only 166 were left. But on February 27, 1875, having covered the 720 miles in the record-breaking time of 103 days, Stanley reached Lake Victoria at the town of Kagheyi, near present-day Mwanza in Tanzania. He was only the fourth European to lay eyes on it since Speke discovered it nearly seventeen years before, and he would be the first to prove that it was a single lake and not several, map its shoreline, and establish its incredible extent. (At 26,000 square miles in area, Victoria is the largest lake in Africa and the second largest, after Lake Superior, in the world.)

Food was plentiful here and the people of Kagheyi friendly, so Stanley selected the spot to set up a base camp for the second stage of his expedition: the circumnavigation of Lake Victoria. He gave himself a week to recuperate from the grueling march from the coast, during which time he hired on additional pagazis and askaris to bring the party's strength up to about 280, resupplied the caravan, and had the *Lady Alice* assembled and launched on the lake. His plan was to leave the bulk of his caravan at Kagheyi under the command of the two remaining Englishmen, Fred Barker and Frank Pocock, while he sailed once around the lake with a small party and, on his return, collect all the men for the next stage of the expedition: the exploration of Lake Albert.

The day he was ready to depart, he called for volunteers. There were none. Victoria had a fearful reputation among the tribesmen.

There were, they said, a people dwelling on its shores who were gifted with tails; another who trained enormous and fierce dogs for war; an-

other tribe of cannibals, who preferred human flesh to all other kinds of meat. The lake was so large it would take years to trace its shores, and who then at the end of that time would remain alive?

Again he asked for volunteers and again the response was dead silence. "Will you let me go alone?" he then asked. "No," was the reply. "What am I to do?" Stanley asked. Manwa Sera, the chief captain of the caravan, said: "Master, have done with these questions. Command your party. All your people are your children, and they will not disobey you. While you ask them as a friend, no one will offer his services. Command them, and they will go."

So Stanley selected eleven men, had the *Lady Alice* provisioned with flour and dried fish, bales of cloth and beads and other odds and ends, gave final instructions to Barker and Pocock, wrote a love letter to "my darling Alice," signing it Morton, and set sail on March 8, traveling in a counter-clockwise direction up the lake's eastern shore. The first half of the circumnavigation was essentially uneventful. On a few occasions, lakeshore peoples launched war canoes from their villages and made as if to attack the *Lady Alice,* but in every case the encounters ended amicably, without any shots being fired and with an exchange of gifts. But what it lacked in adventure this leg of the journey made up for in its contribution to geography. By the time Stanley reached the Kingdom of Buganda at the northern end of the lake in the beginning of April, he could report that it was indeed a vast single expanse as Speke had guessed, and he wrote:

Speke has now the full glory of having discovered the largest inland sea on the continent of Africa, also its principal affluent as well as outlet. I must also give him credit for having understood the geography of the countries we travelled through better than any of those who so persistently opposed his hypothesis.

Stanley spent a little less than two weeks in Buganda. The same Kabaka or king, Mtesa, was on the throne as when Speke and Grant had visited the kingdom in 1862 but he was apparently a much changed man. Mtesa then was a slim, well-built youth in his early twenties, who affected a weird stiff-legged walk, which he imagined resembled that of a lion, and who was given to having people killed in the most atrocious ways for the perverse fun of it. He ruled by pure terror and Speke regarded him as a savage, blood-thirsty monster. But the intervening thirteen years had done much to mature the king, for

we find Stanley writing in his diary on the evening of his first visit with him:

Speke described a youthful prince, vain and heartless, a wholesale murderer and tyrant, one who delighted in fat women. Doubtless he described what he saw, but it is far from being the state of things now. Mtesa has impressed me as being an intelligent and distinguished prince . . . a prince well worthy the most hearty sympathies Europe can give him.

Mtesa treated Stanley grandly. He sent out a fleet of six beautiful war canoes to escort the *Lady Alice* to his royal capital, on the Victoria lakeshore (near present-day Kampala in Uganda), where 1000 warriors greeted the arrival of the white man with volley after volley from their muskets while drums sounded, banners waved, and another thousand people roared cheers of welcome. A compound of handsome grass huts was put at Stanley's disposal, and he was loaded down with gifts. A naval display was arranged in which 40 war canoes containing a total of 1200 men "went through the performance of attack and defence on water." The Kabaka took him on a crocodile hunt accom-

Mtesa, the Emperor of Uganda

Stanley is received by King Mtesa's bodyguard

panied by 200 riflemen and invited him each day to his sumptuous palace for hours of discussion on every conceivable topic. Stanley's admiration grew.

He has very intelligent and agreeable features [he wrote after a few days], reminding me of the great stone images at Thebes, and of the statues in the museum of Cairo. He has the same fulness of lips, but their grossness is relieved by the general expression of amiability blended with dignity that pervades his face, and the large, lustrous, lambent eyes that lend it a strange beauty.

Stanley was so overwhelmed that he himself felt constrained to suggest that

either Mtesa is a very admirable man, or that I am a very impressionable traveller, or that Mtesa is so perfect in the art of duplicity and acted so clever the part, that I became his dupe.

Stanley, of course, didn't believe for a moment that he was being played for a dupe. Everything he saw in Buganda—the magnificence of the court, the richness of the dress, the abundance of goods including manufactured items of all kinds, the immensity of the army (the Kabaka was said to be able to raise a force of at least 150,000), the

beauty and intelligence of the people, the sense of law and order in the realm—all this convinced him that Mtesa was

the Foremost Man of Equatorial Africa . . . I think I see in him the light that shall lighten the darkness of this benighted region. . . . In this man I see the possible fruition of Livingstone's hopes, for with his aid the civilization of Equatorial Africa becomes feasible.

There was one problem. Mtesa was a Muslim, converted to the faith by the Arab traders who did business at his court, and much of the grandeur and prosperity of the court and much of the change in the Kabaka's character since Speke's day were, as Stanley himself had to admit, a result of the influence of Islam. But Stanley had no trouble rationalizing this away. In his view, since Christianity was infinitely superior to Mohammedanism, even greater improvements could be wrought if Mtesa would embrace Christ. And so Stanley set out to convert the Kabaka of Buganda.

Since 5th April [he tells us], I had enjoyed ten interviews with Mtesa, and during all I had taken occasion to introduce topics which would lead to the subject of Christianity. Nothing occurred in my presence but I contrived to turn it towards effecting that which had become an object to me, viz. his conversion. There was no attempt made to confuse him with the details of any particular doctrine. I simply drew for him the image of the Son of God humbling himself for the good of all mankind, white and black. . . . I showed the difference in character between Him whom white men love and adore, and Mohammed, whom the Arabs revere; how Jesus endeavoured to teach mankind that we should love all men, excepting none, while Mohammed taught his followers that the slaying of the pagan and the unbeliever was an act that merited Paradise. I left it to Mtesa and his chiefs to decide which was the worthier character.

Mtesa proved an interested pupil. Not unlike the ManiKongos hundreds of years before, the Kabaka was perfectly aware of the practical values of European civilization and perfectly willing to consider adopting Christianity if by that he could bring those values to his kingdom. In years to come, Mtesa would reveal that his conversion was little more than a useful bit of politics, but at the time Stanley was elated by the progress he was making in his daily Bible classes with the king. "I have, indeed, undermined Islamism so much here," he wrote, "that Mtesa has determined henceforth, until he is better informed, to observe the Christian Sabbath as well as the Muslim Sabbath, and the

great captains have unanimously consented to this."

But, just a few days after having written this, Stanley abruptly abandoned his missionary role. In one of those incredible coincidences that no novelist could write into his story without blushing, another white man turned up at Mtesa's court. This was Linant de Bellefonds, a young French colonel in the service of Charles Gordon, who was then the governor of Equatoria, with his headquarters at Gondokoro (and who would later, as governor-general of the Sudan, die in the siege of Khartoum by the fanatical Mahdists). Gordon's main mission was to extend Egyptian control as far up the Nile as possible, including the annexation of Buganda, and he had sent Linant de Bellefonds to make a reconnaissance of the situation. The young French officer's arrival jolted Stanley out of his missionary fantasies. For the very first words Linant de Bellefonds addressed to him on meeting him at Mtesa's court were: "Have I the honor of speaking to Mr. Cameron?" And that served as reminder enough of the vast amount of work that still lay in front of him, work of exploration, which he feared Cameron might beat him to.

On April 15 he departed from the Kabaka's court to complete his circumnavigation of Lake Victoria. This leg of the journey, however, wasn't quite as uneventful as the first. Sailing down Victoria's western shore, the *Lady Alice* put into an island called Bumbireh (offshore of the present-day town of Bukoba) on April 28 to barter for food. But the tribesmen weren't particularly friendly. About 200 gathered around the cove which the *Lady Alice* entered, with spears and shields, bows and arrows. Stanley was certain he could master them. He was wrong. When the *Lady Alice* came within the tribesmen's reach, Stanley tells us,

with a rush they ran the boat ashore . . . seizing hawser and gunwale, dragged her about 20 yards over the rocky beach high and dry. . . . Then ensued a scene which beggars description. . . . A forest of spears was levelled; thirty or forty bows were drawn taut; as many barbed arrows seemed already on the wing; thick, knotty clubs waved above our heads; two hundred screaming black demons jostled with each other and struggled for room to vent their fury, or for an opportunity to deliver one crushing blow or thrust at us.

Stanley sprang to his feet, brandishing a cocked revolver in each hand, "to kill and be killed," but he quickly realized the hopelessness

of the gesture and instead ordered his Zanzibari interpreters to try to negotiate with the tribesmen, invoking the name of Mtesa, while he scooped up beads and cloth and wire to offer to them. This had the effect of calming the warriors momentarily. A *shauri* was called. Half the tribesmen remained surrounding the boat while the other half retreated to talk things over. But, just as Stanley was beginning to relax, six men suddenly seized the boat's oars and rushed off with them. The situation was now dangerous. The *shauri* went on. A messenger arrived and demanded the payment of cloth and beads as tribute, but no sooner was this paid than drums began to beat and hundreds of other warriors gathered on a hill overlooking the beach in full war costume, their faces smeared with black and white paint.

Stanley decided to take a reckless gamble. He gave one of his men two expensive pieces of red cloth and told him to walk slowly toward the enemy as if to barter but to turn and run back to the boat as soon as he was called. To the others of his crew he said, "And you, my boys, this is for life and death, mind; range yourselves on each side of the boat, lay your hands on it carelessly, but with a firm grip, and when I give the word, push it with the force of a hundred men down the hill

The reception at Bumbireh Island

into the water." He waited for his man with the cloth to get fifty yards up the beach, then gave the signal, and, when the boat began to move, leaped into it, snatched up his double-barreled elephant gun, and shouted for his decoy to return. But "the natives were quick-eyed. They saw the boat moving, and with one accord swept down the hill uttering the most fearful cries." The boat reached the water's edge and shot out into the lake with the men swimming after it. The decoy raced back with the warriors in hot pursuit. "Spring into the water, man, head first," Stanley shouted, and then fired into the ranks of the tribesmen, killing two with a single shot. "The bowmen halted and drew their bows. I sent two charges of duck-shot into their midst with terrible effect." The crew now scrambled into the boat and were about to take up their rifles, "but I told them to leave them alone, and tear the bottom-boards out of the boat and use them as paddles; for there were two hippopotami advancing upon us open-mouthed." Stanley whirled and killed one with a shot between the eyes and wounded the other severely enough to drive it off. Then he turned back to the Bumbireh warriors, who had launched four canoes in pursuit of the *Lady Alice*. "My elephant rifle was loaded with explosive balls for this occasion. Four shots killed five men and sank two of the canoes. The two others retired to assist their friends out of the water. They attempted nothing further." Stanley, however, would not forget this incident and, vowing revenge the first chance he got, completed his voyage around the lake, and on May 6 was back at Kagheyi.

Fred Barker was dead. He had died of fever only twelve days before Stanley returned and so had a number of the Zanzibaris. Then Stanley himself came down with a severe attack of malaria, which reduced his weight to under 110 pounds and put him out of action for nearly a week. Then came still further delays. Stanley's plan now was to take his entire caravan back to Buganda, from where he would strike out for Lake Albert. But, rather than make the return trek overland, he intended to take them by water back up the western shore of Lake Victoria. For all the people of his party, though, he needed more boats than he had with him and he had arranged with Mtesa to have Buganda canoes sent down to him at Kagheyi. But weeks turned into months before they arrived, and it wasn't until the end of July that Stanley at last was on his way back to Buganda with his entire caravan.

Stanley had not forgotten Bumbireh, and when he passed it on his

way up the lake's western shore he stopped there to settle the score. In his writings he gives an elaborate justification for what he subsequently did, claiming in effect that it was necessary to assure the safe passage of his expedition up the lake. But what it really seemed to come down to was that Stanley, still in a pique over his treatment at the hands of the island's warriors, sent an ultimatum to their chief to make amends, and when this was ignored he attacked. On August 4, he took a force of 250 of his men in six canoes, led by the *Lady Alice,* around to the western side of the island so that his foes would have the setting sun in their eyes, and arrayed his fleet in a line of battle across the entry of a large cove about 100 yards from the land. Anywhere from 2000 to 3000 warriors were massed on the beach and on the surrounding hills. Stanley tells us he made one last effort to parley, but the Bumbireh responded, "We will do nothing but fight." So he gave his men the order to fire. The result was a massacre.

The savages, perceiving the disastrous effect of our fire on a compact body, scattered, and came bounding down to the water's edge, some of the boldest advancing until they were hip-deep in water; others, more cautious, sought the shelter of the cane-grass, whence they discharged many sheaves of arrows, all of which fell short of us. We then moved to within 50 yards of the shore, to fire at close quarters, and each man was permitted to exercise himself as best he could. The savages gallantly held the water-line for an hour, and slung their stones with better effect than they shot their arrows . . . the spear, with which they generally fight, was quite useless.

Some 30 or 40 tribesmen were killed and at least 100 wounded before the Bumbireh gave up the fight and Stanley could feel that "Our work of chastisement was complete." Not one of Stanley's men had suffered so much as a scratch.

It would take over a year for the news of this battle to reach the outside world—via Stanley's own dispatches to the New York *Herald* and the London *Daily Telegraph*—but when it did it raised a furor. The Royal Geographical Society called protest meetings; liberal groups like the Anti-Slavery Society and intellectual journals like the *Saturday Review* vehemently expressed their disapproval of "this outrage on a peaceful and comparatively unarmed people." "Even Stanley's best friends," James Grant wrote to the Royal Geographical Society, "cannot but regret his pugnacity and want of discretion."

Stanley, of course, remained ignorant of the outcry and at the time

had no expectation that it would provoke such a hostile reaction. If anything, he seems to have thought that he would be admired for the incident, and he described it in his newspaper accounts with much buccaneering gusto, justifying it on the grounds that "the savage only respects force, power, boldness, and decision." And, as he proceeded on his way up the western shore of the lake, he felt quite vindicated in this view. For the news of the Bumbireh massacre spread rapidly before him, and the lakeshore peoples, fearful of being the next victims of Stanley's riflemen, did all they could to keep from offending him, pressing gifts of food on him, lining the shores unarmed to cheer the passage of his canoes. And so, on August 14, Stanley reached the Kingdom of Buganda, ready to strike off from there northwestward to Lake Albert.

But Mtesa was at war with a vassal chief. "When I heard this news," Stanley writes, "I felt more than half inclined to turn back, for I knew by experience that African wars are tedious things, and I was not in the humour to be delayed." But on reflection Stanley realized that he couldn't do this, for he was counting on Mtesa's assistance in his exploration of Lake Albert. The region he intended to traverse, between the northwestern shore of Victoria and the southeastern shore of Albert, was populated by warrior tribes, and Stanley knew he couldn't get his caravan through without a substantial military escort of the Kabaka's soldiers. So Stanley decided to join in Mtesa's war, rationalizing that with his assistance the war, and the delay it would cause him, would be significantly shortened.

Nevertheless, for all his tactical advice and the devastating effect of his guns, the war dragged on for two months, and it wasn't until mid-October that the enemy chief sent two of his daughters to Mtesa's harem by way of tribute and the peace was concluded. Stanley was anxious to get off, but it took yet another month of negotiations with Mtesa before he succeeded in arranging for his military escort—more than 2000 Buganda warriors under the command of a young general of the Kabaka's army by the name of Sambuzi—and so he didn't set out until late in November.

This was to be the only part of his grand plan of exploration at which Stanley failed: he never reached Lake Albert, let alone explored it. One obstacle certainly was the swampy, malarial, heavily forested terrain he had to cross toward the foothills of the towering Ruwenzoris, the Mountains of the Moon. His men, after spending

nearly nine months in relative immobility camped on the shores of Lake Victoria, weren't in shape for the hard march. But the main problem was the fierce hostility of the Wanyoro tribesmen along the way and the utter inadequacy of Sambuzi and his army to deal with them.

On Christmas Day, the first spear came hurtling out of a forest ambush, wounding a Buganda warrior, and by the first days of the New Year, 1876, the caravan was under constant attack. Stanley's account of this leg of his journey is anything but explicit, and it is quite impossible to trace exactly the route he took. One senses on reading his diaries that he didn't really know himself; he was probably quite lost. And Sambuzi was of no help. The Wanyoro of these forests were mortal enemies of the Bugandans, and the further from Lake Victoria they got the more fearful Sambuzi became. On January 11, however, Stanley believed that he was in sight of his goal. Gazing down from the edge of a plateau, he saw the blue waters of a lake lying 1500 feet below, which he wanted to believe was the southeastern corner of Albert. It wasn't. From the latitude and longitude he scribbled in his diary, what he was looking at was probably what years later would be named Lake George, a then unknown small body of water nearly a hundred miles to the south of Lake Albert. But it didn't really matter. Whatever lake it was, Stanley never got to it.

By this time, Sambuzi was in a complete panic. He was convinced that to descend to the lake would be to walk into an ambush of hostile tribesmen. Stanley tells us:

Large numbers of natives, posted on every hill around us, added to the fear which took possession of the minds of the Waganda [Bugandans], and rumours were spread about by malicious men of an enormous force advancing from the south. . . . The members of the Expedition even caught the panic, and prepared in silence to follow the Waganda, as common-sense informed them that, if a force of over 2000 fighting men did not consider itself strong enough to maintain its position, our Expedition of 180 men could by no means do so.

Stanley did everything he could to stem the rising panic. He called a council-of-war and tried to shame Sambuzi into pressing forward, but to no avail. Sambuzi and his lieutenants "were of the opinion that it would be best to fly at once, without waiting for night or for morning." Sambuzi said,

Stamlee, you are my friend, the Emperor's friend, and a son of Uganda, and I want to do my duty towards you as well as I am able to; but you must hear the truth. We cannot do what you want us to do. We cannot wait here two days, nor one day. We shall fight tomorrow, that is certain; and if you think I speak from fear, you shall see me handle the spear. . . . We shall fight tomorrow at sunrise, and we must cut our way through the Wanyoro to Uganda . . . once the war is begun, it is war which will last as long as we are alive—for these people take no slaves as the Waganda do. Then the only chance for our lives that I see is to pack up tonight, and tomorrow morning at sunrise to march and fight our way through them.

Stanley toyed with the idea of going down to the lake with his own men, but he discovered that, except for his last white assistant, Frank Pocock, and a handful of his most loyal Zanzibaris, they wouldn't follow him either. And so he was forced to turn away from the lake.

At dawn we mustered our force. . . . A thousand spearmen with shields formed the advanced-guard, and a thousand spearmen . . . composed the rear-guard. The goods and Expedition occupied the centre. The drums and fife and musical bands announced the signal to march. The natives, whom we expected would have attacked us, contented themselves with following us at a respectful distance . . . they permitted us to depart in peace.

By the beginning of February, they were back within the frontiers of the Kabaka's kingdom and Stanley sent off a letter to Mtesa, sharply condemning Sambuzi's cowardice, which got the young general into an awful lot of trouble with his king. But apart from this Stanley showed remarkably little disappointment over his failure to reach and explore Lake Albert. Increasingly, that part of his grand plan had become unimportant to him. His months on and around Lake Victoria had steadily moved him toward the conclusion that Victoria was, if not certainly the source of the White Nile, the river's most important watershed, and whatever Lake Albert's role might be it was surely secondary and not worth the expenditure of any more time and effort. For there were far more important questions he was determined to answer, and he was in a race with Cameron to be the first to answer them. So, without visiting Mtesa, he undertook a four months' march south to Lake Tanganyika.

At noon of the 27th May the bright waters of the Tanganyika broke upon the view, and compelled me to linger admiringly for a while, as I did on the day I first beheld them. By 3 P.M. we were in Ujiji. . . . Nothing was changed much, except the ever-changing mud tembes [houses] of the Arabs. The square or plaza where I met David Livingstone in November 1871 is now occupied by large tembes. The house where he and I lived has long ago been burnt down, and in its place there remains only a few embers and a hideous void. The lake expands with the same grand beauty before the eyes as we stand in the marketplace. . . . The surf is still as restless, and the sun as bright; the sky retains its glorious azure, and the palms all their beauty; but the grand old hero, whose presence once filled Ujiji with such absorbing interest for me was gone!

Stanley had been traveling in Africa for 17 months, covering almost 3500 miles on land and water, and he was very much looking forward to finding letters from home awaiting him at Ujiji. There were none and he was deeply disappointed.

As I thought of Ujiji I flattered myself daily that I should receive letters and newspapers. I daily fed and lived on that hope [he wrote to Alice Pike]. You may imagine how I felt . . . what would you have done, oh my Alice? Tear your hair, clothes, and shriek distractedly, run about and curse the Fates? I did not do anything so undignified, but I soberly grieved and felt discouraged. . . . My cheeks are sunk, my eyes large and sickly, my bones feel sore even lying on two blankets. . . . Yet the same heart still throbs with deepest love, as it did long ago.

Stanley still held out some hope of hearing from her before he vanished again into the unreachable depths of Africa. His plan now was to circumnavigate Lake Tanganyika, which he calculated would take him about two months, so there was a chance that there would be mail waiting for him when he returned again to Ujiji. He hurriedly had the *Lady Alice* reassembled and launched on Tanganyika and, leaving Frank Pocock in charge of the bulk of the expedition at Ujiji, set sail in mid-June, with a crew of thirteen, southward down the lake's eastern shore. In 51 relatively pacific and uneventful days he mapped 810 miles of the lake's 930 miles of coastline and was back in Ujiji with virtually positive proof that Tanganyika had no outlet river which possibly could connect it with Lake Albert and make it part of the headwaters system of the Nile. And with that he destroyed Burton's theory and was obliged to take yet another step toward accepting Speke's contention that Victoria was the White Nile's true source. The

only other possibility left was Livingstone's Lualaba, but it is clear that by this time Stanley was entertaining serious doubts about his grand old hero's theory. Nevertheless, he did not waver for a moment in his determination to explore it, to complete Livingstone's work no matter what the cost or where it took him.

And he was now desperately eager to get on with it. No letters had arrived while he'd been away and there was no chance of any arriving. A smallpox epidemic had broken out in Ujiji, making the town extremely unsafe to stay in. And besides there was a growing problem with desertions; a score of his men had quit the caravan while he was away circumnavigating Tanganyika, and the longer he stayed in Ujiji the more men he lost (his party would be reduced to under 140 before he finally got away).

But most important was his sense that time was running out on him. There was his race with Cameron. Stanley learned in Ujiji that Cameron had reached Nyangwe, Livingstone's furthest point down the Lualaba, a full two years before, making his chances of catching up desperately slim. And there was his rendezvous with Alice Pike. As he wrote her in mid-August, "It is now within a few days of twenty-five months since I parted from you, and nearly twenty months since leaving Zanzibar," and then he went on to confess that he now had to figure that it would take him a total of three years to complete his expedition.

just a year longer than I estimated. But the estimates are invariably wrong, and it is not fair to tie a man down to mere estimates. We have all done our best. . . . Then, my own Darling, if by that name I may call you, let us hope cheerfully that a happy termination to this long period of trial of your constancy and my health and courage await us both. . . . Grant then that my love towards you is unchanged, that you are my dream, my stay and my hope, and my beacon, and believe that I shall cherish you in this light until I meet you, or death meets me. This is the last you will get, I fear, for a long time. Then, my darling, accept this letter with one last and loving farewell.

He signed it "Morton."

A few days later, he led his party across Lake Tanganyika and struck westward on the grueling march into the Maniema forests.

Suddenly from the crest of a low ridge we saw the confluence of the Luama with the majestic Lualaba. The former appeared to have a

breadth of 400 yards at the mouth; the latter was about 1400 yards wide, a broad river of a pale grey colour, winding slowly from south and by east. We hailed its appearance with shouts of joy, and rested on the spot to enjoy the view. . . . A secret rapture filled my soul as I gazed upon the majestic stream. The great mystery that for all these centuries Nature had kept hidden away from the world of science was waiting to be solved. . . . My task was to follow it to the Ocean.

The date was October 17, 1876.

17

DOWN THE LUALABA TO THE SEA

Verney Lovett Cameron had reached the Lualaba in August 1874, more than two years before Stanley, and had every intention of following the river to its end. What's more, and very much to his credit, he had a far clearer notion where that end might be than Stanley. While still in Ujiji, Cameron tells us, "I had many long yarns with the Arabs who knew these parts . . . and learned that in their opinion the Lualaba is the Kongo." Indeed, one of these Arabs boasted to Cameron that he had once traveled "fifty-five marches" along the river "and came to where the water was salt and ships came from the sea, and white men lived there who traded much in palm-oil and had large houses." Cameron calculated 55 marches at about 500 miles, added another 300 miles for the distance from Ujiji to Nyangwe and, supposing the river turned west after Nyangwe, came up with a journey of some 800 miles, which, he believed, "gives about the distance to the Yellala Cataracts. This looks something like the Kongo and West-coast merchants." Then, once he had himself reached Nyangwe, he measured the volume of river water flowing past the town and found it to be "123,000 cubic feet per second in the dry season, or more than five times greater than that of the Nile at Gondokoro, which is 21,500 feet per second." From this fact he made the wonderfully accurate assessment:

This great stream must be one of the head-waters of the Kongo, for where else could that giant among rivers, second only to the Amazon in its volume, obtain the two million cubic feet of water which it unceasingly pours each second into the Atlantic? The large affluents from the north would explain the comparatively small rise of the Kongo at the coast; for

since its enormous basin extends to both sides of the equator, some portion of it is always under the zone of rains, and therefore the supply to the main stream is nearly the same at all times, instead of varying, as is the case with tropical rivers whose basins lie completely on one side of the equator.

Cameron's only real error was his supposition that the Lualaba turned west a short distance downstream of Nyangwe, whereas it continues northward for hundreds of miles before making its westward and southwestward arc to the sea. But his assumptions were based purely on hearsay, and as such, Cameron knew, would never meet the exacting standards of the Royal Geographical Society or the acceptance of rival explorers. They would demand a map of the river's course drawn from first-hand observation, and to do that he would have to penetrate along the Lualaba into the regions north of Nyangwe. And that, like Livingstone before him, he could not do.

In the first place, he too could not get canoes. From time to time, chiefs and tribesmen, Cameron tells us, "made some show of affording aid, but they always said, 'Slowly, slowly; don't be in a hurry; tomorrow will do as well as today'; and so the matter dragged along." The paramount chief of the town, named Dugambi, promised Cameron each market day that he would go to the Nyangwe marketplace and use his influence to induce local tribesmen to sell him canoes. "And he would leave me apparently on this errand. But I afterward found that he used to slip into one of the houses of his harem by a back way, and remain there until the market-people had gone." On a few occasions, boatmen agreed to make a sale but only if payment was made in slaves, knowing full well that the white man had none, and, because of his beliefs, would not acquire any. Once a man agreed to take payment in cowries, but "when I counted out before him the correct number of cowries," Cameron tells us, "he quietly looked them over and then returned them, remarking that if he took home such a quantity of cowries they would only be appropriated by his wives as ornaments. and he would be poorer by a canoe." "One hoary-headed old fellow" told Cameron quite bluntly why he'd never acquire any canoes.

No good had ever resulted from the advent of strangers, and he should advise each and all his countrymen to refuse to sell or hire a single canoe to the white man; for if he acted like the strangers who had gone before him, he would only prove a fresh oppressor . . . or open a new road for robbers and slave-dealers.

But, even had he been able to get the canoes, it is doubtful that Cameron would have gone down the Lualaba. For, with each passing day in Nyangwe, he and, more to the point, the members of his caravan heard fresh horror stories of what lay ahead on the river. "They described the natives as being very fierce and warlike, and using poisoned arrows, a mere scratch from which proved fatal in four or five minutes, unless an antidote, known only to the natives, was immediately applied." And they were cannibals, "more cruel and treacherous than any with whom we had yet met. Consequently stragglers would most certainly be cut off, killed and probably eaten." As for the terrain, it was, they said, "a country of large mountains wooded to the summits, and valleys filled with such dense forests that they travelled four and five days in succession without seeing the sun." So forbidding was the prospect that even the Arab caravans, despite their greed for slaves and ivory and despite their armies of riflemen, did not dare venture into those regions.

Cameron's party consisted of about 100 men, including 45 askaris armed with Snider rifles, the best weapon of the day, but Cameron considered it as "being far too small . . . to make the journey by itself." And, he discovered quickly enough, he would never be able to hire an escort.

The settlers at Nyangwe declared themselves to be too short of powder and guns to spare a sufficient force to accompany me and return safely by themselves, so no volunteers were forthcoming. In addition to this, they were very much afraid to travel by roads north of the Lualaba; for several strong and well-armed parties had been severely handled by the natives in that direction, and had returned to Nyangwe with the loss of more than half their numbers. One party . . . had especially suffered, having lost over two hundred of their total strength of three hundred.

So, within a few weeks, Cameron's resolve to go down the Lualaba eroded, and when the first opportunity came along to turn away from the terrible challenge of the river, he seized it.

That opportunity came along in the person of Tippoo Tib, the very same Tippoo Tib who had met Livingstone at the southern end of Lake Tanganyika seven years before and had assisted him during his journey to the headwaters of the Lualaba. The Arab trader had prospered mightily during the years since, having amassed a huge fortune in ivory and slaves, a fearsome following of armed riflemen, and a

terrible reputation for efficient cruelty. Cameron describes him as "a good-looking man, and the greatest dandy I had seen among the traders," and in his own memoirs, Tippoo Tib confessed that he always enjoyed playing the role of grand seigneur and had always felt an intense attraction toward Europeans. When he marched into Nyangwe at the head of his impressive caravan, he immediately called on Cameron and, with a show of great chivalry and courteousness, declared himself at the white man's service.

Cameron made one last, although not too convincing request for help in securing canoes for a water journey or for an armed escort for an overland trek down the Lualaba, but Tippoo Tib, for all his eagerness to ingratiate himself with this lone European, turned him down. Despite his rapacious reputation and military might he too considered it suicidal to venture into those fearsome regions to the north but, by way of compensation, he offered to escort Cameron's party *westward* from the Lualaba at least as far as the trading camp he maintained on the banks of the Lomami River, some "ten marches" from Nyangwe. From there, Tippoo Tib claimed, Cameron would have no difficulty continuing to the west all the way to the Atlantic, since native caravans constantly made that journey to trade with the Portuguese on the Angola coast.

Cameron accepted the offer. It was either that, he realized, or return via Ujiji to Zanzibar, having accomplished nothing more than Livingstone before him. So, at the end of August, 1874, Cameron set out with Tippoo Tib's caravan, and fifteen months later, in November 1875, arrived at the Portuguese settlement of Benguela on the Atlantic Ocean. It was, unquestionably, a brilliant feat of African travel. Cameron became the second European, after Livingstone, to traverse the continent from coast to coast. In the course of this monumental journey, he crossed through a substantial portion of the Congo River basin and filled in a large portion of the map of Africa. But he had left the mystery of the Lualaba unsolved, and so the way was open for Stanley.

Stanley, of course, knew nothing of this. As he made his way along the banks of the Lualaba from its confluence with the Luama toward Nyangwe in October 1876, although Cameron had in fact been back in England for nearly six months, he still very much felt himself in a race with the British naval lieutenant. And it wasn't until Stanley himself met with Tippoo Tib on the outskirts of Nyangwe, nearly two

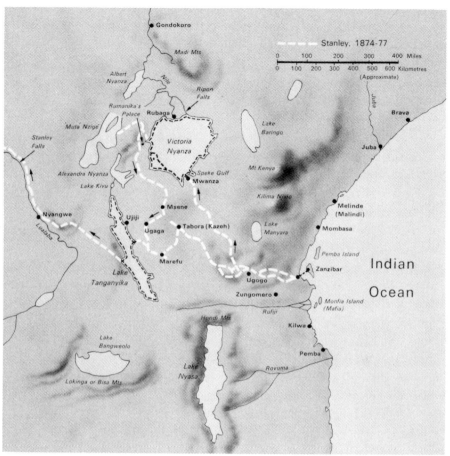

Map based on contemporary information showing the route taken by Stanley,
1874–1877

years after Cameron had parted from the Arab trader, that he at last
learned it and could heave a huge sigh of relief.

He was a tall, black-bearded man, of negroid complexion, in the prime
of life, straight, and quick in his movements, a picture of energy and
strength [Stanley wrote of Tippoo Tib at their first meeting]. He had a fine
intelligent face, with a nervous twitching of the eyes, and gleaming white
and perfectly formed teeth. . . . With the air of a well-bred Arab, and
almost courtier-like in his manner, he welcomed me . . . and his slaves
being ready at hand with mat and bolster, he reclined vis-a-vis, while
a buzz of admiration of his style was perceptible from the on-lookers.
After regarding him for a few minutes, I came to the conclusion that this
Arab was a remarkable man—the most remarkable man I had met among
Arabs, Wa-Swahili, and half-castes in Africa. He was neat in his person, his

clothes were of a spotless white, his fez-cap brand-new, his waist was encircled by a rich dowle, his dagger was splendid with silver filigree, and his *tout ensemble* was that of an Arab gentleman in very comfortable circumstances.

Stanley wasted no time in putting the question that was uppermost in his mind, inquiring of Tippoo Tib

as to the direction that my predecessor at Nyangwe had taken. The information he gave me was sufficiently clear . . . the greatest problem of African geography was left untouched at the exact spot where Dr. Livingstone had felt himself unable to prosecute his travels. . . . This was momentous and all-important news to the Expedition. We had arrived at the critical point in our travels: our destinies now awaited my final decision.

But, before he made that decision he wanted to know why Cameron had turned away from the Lualaba. And he was told in no uncertain terms: want of canoes, reluctance of the Arabs to help, cowardice of Cameron's followers, but most importantly the difficulty of the terrain and the hostility of the tribesmen ahead. To illustrate these last points, Tippoo Tib had a young Arab brought before Stanley to tell of his adventures with one of the few caravans that had ever attempted to penetrate those regions. It was, the youth related, "a forest land, where there is nothing but woods, and woods, and woods, for days, and weeks, and months. There was no end to the woods." He went on to tell of cannibal warriors, of monstrous boa constrictors, gorillas that "run up to you and seize your hands, and bite the fingers off one by one." "It is nothing but constant fighting," the youth warned.

Only two years ago a party armed with three hundred guns started north . . . they only brought sixty guns back, and no ivory. If one tries to go by river, there are falls after falls, which carry the people over and drown them. A party of thirty men, in three canoes, went down the river half a day's journey from Nyangwe. . . . They were all drowned. . . . Ah, no. Master, the country is bad, and the Arabs have given it up. . . . They will not try the journey into that country again, after trying it three times and losing nearly five hundred men altogether."

Stanley listened attentively. "These were difficulties," he realized, "for me also to surmount in some manner not yet intelligible. How was I to instil courage in my followers, or sustain it, to obtain the assistance of the Arabs to enable me to make a fair beginning, and

afterwards to purchase or make canoes?" But that he would find the
means to surmount the difficulties, that he would in fact go on, he was
never in doubt. And he tells an anecdote that makes the point dramatically.

That night he called Frank Pocock into his hut and said to him,
"Now Frank, my son, sit down. I am about to have a long and serious
chat with you. Life and death—yours as well as mine, and those of all
the Expedition—hang on the decision I make tonight." He then went
on to review the dangers in attempting to go down the Lualaba, pointing out that "Livingstone, after fifteen thousand miles of travel, and a
lifetime of experience among Africans, would not have yielded the
brave struggle without strong reasons; Cameron, with his forty-five
Snider rifles, would never have turned away from such a brilliant field
if he had not sincerely thought that they were insufficient to resist the
persistent attacks of countless thousands of wild men." Then he asked,
"Now, what I wish you to tell me, Frank, is your opinion as to what
we ought to do. . . . Think well, my dear fellow; don't be hasty, life
and death hang on our decision." And before Frank could properly
answer, Stanley sketched out an alternative route the expedition could
take, south to Katanga and down the Zambezi, which in itself would
represent a major feat of exploration. The young Kentish fisherman,
struggling to follow Stanley's conversation, agreed that to go to Katanga and the Zambezi "would be a fine job, Sir, if we could do it."
"Yet, if you think of it, Frank," Stanley said, "this great river which
Livingstone first saw, and which broke his heart almost to turn away
and leave a mystery, is a noble field too. Fancy, by-and-by, after buying
or building canoes our floating down the river day by day, either to
the Nile . . . or to the Congo and the Atlantic Ocean!" Finally,
Frank came up with an idea: "I say, sir, let us toss up: best two out of
three to decide it. . . . Heads for the north and the Lualaba; tails for
the south and Katanga."

Stanley gave Frank a rupee coin. The youth flipped it; he flipped
it in fact six times and six times it came up tails for the south and
Katanga. Fate may have been trying to tell Stanley something, but he
refused to listen. He decided that instead of flipping the coin they
should draw straws to decide, long for the north and the Lualaba,
short for the south and Katanga. Stanley held the straws and Frank
drew them from his hand, and each time he drew a short straw, for the
south and Katanga. But then, abruptly, Stanley flung the straws and

coin away. "It is of no use, Frank," he said. "We'll face our destiny, despite the rupee and the straws. With your help, my dear fellow, I will follow the river."

Stanley had a plan. He would not bother to try to obtain canoes in Nyangwe. "Livingstone could not. Cameron failed. No doubt I shall fail," he decided realistically. Instead, he would push northward along the Lualaba overland until he came to a place where he could get canoes. But, for this to work, he would have to persuade his expedition to strike into those terrible regions from Nyangwe in the first place. He was perfectly aware that, after only a day of listening to the horror stories told about those regions, his men were fast losing courage, and he was in danger of mass desertions when he informed them of his plan. To prevent this, he would have to provide them with a large and comforting military escort. And that, he decided, he would have to get from Tippoo Tib. It would be sufficient, he felt, to have the Arab's riflemen accompany his party only a relatively short distance down the river, just far enough into the wild country so that, once they were alone again, his men would find it as dangerous to desert and try to make their way back again as they would to go on.

Tippoo Tib must have seen something special in Stanley, something he hadn't seen in Livingstone or Cameron or any other white man. It is true that when Stanley first made the proposition to him he raised all the predictable objections and concluded, "If you Wasungu [white men] are desirous of throwing away your lives it is no reason we Arabs should. We travel little by little to get ivory—it is now nine years since I left Zanzibar—but you white men only look for rivers and lakes and mountains, and you spend your lives for no reason, and to no purpose."

Stanley answered: "I know I have no right to expect you to risk your life for me. I only wish you to accompany me sixty days' journey, then leave me to myself . . . all I am anxious for is my people. You know the Wangwana [Zanzibaris] are easily swayed by fear, but if they hear Tippoo Tib has joined me, and is about to accompany me, every man will have a lion's courage."

Tippoo Tib agreed to think about it, and that night he held a *shauri* with his relatives and principal chiefs. In his memoirs, the Arab tells us that all his associates and family strongly advised him against assisting Stanley. But, at the end of the *shauri*, Tippoo Tib tells us, he declared, "Perhaps I am mad and it is you who are sane. Mind your

own concerns." And the next day he told Stanley that, for a payment of $5000, he would accompany him with 200 armed soldiers plus that many more porters for a distance of 60 camps or marches, each camp to be four hours' march from the preceding camp, with the understanding that the total journey would not take longer than three months.

Stanley readily agreed, a contract was signed, and the next few weeks were spent in preparation for the extraordinary journey. Stanley's party consisted of about 150; 60 of these were askaris armed with Snider or Winchester rifles, percussion-lock muskets, double-barreled elephant guns or revolvers; the rest were pagazis (or porters) plus a handful of wives and children of the chiefs and headmen. Tippoo Tib's force numbered at first 700; 300 of these, however, were to strike off to the east after a few days on a separate ivory and slave-hunting expedition. Of the remaining 400, more than half were soldiers, armed with flintlocks, bows and arrows, spears and shields; the rest were porters, gunbearers, scouts, house servants, cooks, carpenters, and slaves. In addition, Tippoo Tib, "bland and courteous, enthusiastic, and sanguine," brought along twenty women from his harem. On November 5, 1876, the immense caravan set off from Nyangwe. Stanley writes:

We saw before us a black curving wall of forest, which, beginning from the river bank, extended south-east, until hills and distance made it indistinct. . . . What a forbidding aspect had the Dark Unknown which confronted us!

The terrain was killing.

The trees kept shedding their dew upon us like rain in great round drops. Every leaf seemed weeping. Down the boles and branches, creepers and vegetable cords, the moisture trickled and fell on us. Overhead the wide-spreading branches, in many interlaced strata, absolutely shut out the daylight. We knew not whether it was a sunshiny day or a dull, foggy, gloomy day; for we marched in a feeble solemn twilight. . . . To our right and left, to the height of about twenty feet, towered the undergrowth, the lower world of vegetation. . . . The tempest might roar without the leafy world, but in its deep bosom there is absolute stillness. . . . Every few minutes we found ourselves descending into ditches, with streams. . . . The dew dropped and pattered on us incessantly. . . . Our clothes were heavily saturated with it. My white sun-helmet and puggaree

appeared to be weighted with lead. . . . Added to this vexation was the perspiration which exuded from every pore, for the atmosphere was stifling. The steam from the hot earth could be seen ascending upward and settling in a grey cloud above our heads.

Day after day the caravan fought its way through the primeval forest.

We had a fearful time of it today. . . . Such crawling, scrambling, tearing through the damp, dank jungles, and such height and depth of woods. . . . Our Expedition is no longer the compact column which was my pride. It is utterly demoralized. . . . It was so dark sometimes in the woods that I could not see the words which I pencilled in my notebook.

The men were soon grumbling and

all their courage was oozing out, as day by day we plodded through the doleful, dreary forest. . . . The constant slush and reek which the heavy dew caused in the forest . . . had worn my shoes out, and half the march I travelled with naked feet. I had then to draw out of my stores my last pair of shoes. Frank was already using his last pair of shoes. Yet we were still in the centre of the continent. What should we do when all were gone?

On November 16, barely 10 marches and 50 miles from Nyangwe, Tippoo Tib came to Stanley and said,

It is of no use. . . . Look at it how you may, those sixty camps will occupy us at the rate we are travelling over a year, and it will take as much time to return. I never was in this forest before, and I had no idea there was such a place in the world; but the air is killing my people, it is insufferable. You will kill your own people if you go on. . . . This country was not made for travel; it was made for vile pagans, monkeys, and wild beasts. I cannot go farther.

Stanley argued with him for two hours and at last persuaded him to continue for just 20 marches further. Three days later they camped on the bank of the Lualaba, which Stanley had decided to rechristen the Livingstone, at a point where the river was 1200 yards wide.

Downward it flows into the unknown [he wrote in his diary], to the night-black clouds of mystery and fable. . . . Something strange must surely lie in the vast space occupied by total blankness on our maps . . . we have laboured through the terrible forest, and manfully struggled through the gloom. My people's hearts have become faint. I seek a road.

Why, here lies a broad watery avenue cleaving the Unknown to some
sea, like a path of light!

It still proved impossible to acquire or even build canoes but Stanley
decided that he could at least launch the *Lady Alice* on the river.
Some thirty of the party joined him in the boat while the rest under
Tippoo Tib's command, continued overland along the river's left
bank.

Although the traveling was slightly eased by this, the expedition
now began to encounter the other great terror of the forest—its inhabitants. At first the villages they passed were deserted, the tribesmen
fleeing into the dark forests at the news of the advance of the strange
caravan, but there wasn't any question about what kind of people
lived in them. Row upon row of human skulls lined the palisades
around the villages, and bones from every part of the human anatomy
could be seen scattered around the cooking sites. From time to time, a
solitary, grotesquely painted savage would be caught sight of peering
out from the thick undergrowth, and throughout the day and night
they heard the drums beating, telling of their progress, the shrill, eerie
cry—Ooh-hu-hu! Ooh-hu-hu!—calling warriors to assemble in the
gloom of the woods and the blare of ivory war horns sounding from
another world.

On November 23, the *Lady Alice* reached the confluence of the
Ruiki with the Lualaba, and Stanley, realizing that the land party
would have to be ferried across it, decided to camp there until Tippoo
Tib's people caught up. Throughout the evening, warriors gathered
in the forests around the camp but the night passed without incident.
The next morning, as Tippoo Tib's party still had not arrived, Stanley went off to explore the Ruiki, but he had barely left when he
heard the forest silence shattered by the crack of rifle fire. Rushing
back to the camp, he found his men under attack by 100 screaming
tribesmen. The Snider and Winchester rifles drove them off, but from
then on hardly a day or night went by without trouble of this sort.

Morale disintegrated and problems multiplied. "The march
through the jungles and forests, the scant fare, fatigue, and consequent
suffering," Stanley tells us, "resulted in sickness." A small pox epidemic broke out; dysentery killed others. "Thorns had also penetrated
the feet and wounded the legs of many of the people, until dreadful
ulcers had been formed, disabling them from travel." Then there were

typhoid fever, pneumonia, pleurisy. "Over fifty were infected with the itch. . . . Every day we tossed two or three bodies into the deep waters of the Livingstone." Six leaky canoes were found abandoned along the river bank and Stanley had these lashed together to form a floating hospital. Other abandoned canoes were picked up along the way or captured from the local tribesmen in the sporadic battles, but then the river turned nasty. Periodically, stretches of fast-moving rapids or whirlpools would suddenly break up "the broad watery avenue" and canoes would be overturned and precious cargo lost. And in December the rains began.

Tippoo Tib and the Arab advanced to me for a shauri [Stanley writes]. They wished to know whether I would not now abandon the project of continuing down the river—now that things appeared so gloomy, with rapids before us, natives hostile, cannibalism rampant, small-pox raging, people dispirited. . . . "What prospects," they asked, "lie before us but terrors, and fatal collapse and ruin? Better turn back in time."

But Stanley, of course, had no intention of turning back.

The river widened; sizable islands stood in its stream; the jungle all around was "a prey to gloom and shade, where the hawk and the eagle, the ibis, the grey parrot, and the monkey, may fly and scream and howl, undisturbed"; and the attacks of the natives intensified, became unrelenting.

We heard the warhorns sounding . . . we saw eight large canoes coming up river along the islands in mid-stream, and six along the left bank. . . . When they came within thirty yards, half of the men in each canoe began to shoot their poisoned arrows, while the other half continued to paddle in-shore. . . . On the 14th, gliding down the river . . . the natives made a brilliant and well-planned attack on us, by suddenly dashing upon us from a creek; and had not the ferocious nature of the people whom we daily encountered taught us to be prepared at all times against assault, we might have suffered considerable injury. . . .

On the 18th, after floating down a few miles . . . the aborigines at once gathered opposite, blew war-horns, and mustered a large party, preparing to attack us with canoes. . . . While rowing down, close to the left bank, we were suddenly surprised by hearing a cry from one of the guards of the hospital canoes, and, turning round, saw an arrow fixed in his chest. The next instant, looking towards the bank, we saw the forms of many men in the jungle, and several arrows flew past my head in ex-

tremely unpleasant proximity. We sheered off instantly, and, pulling hard down stream, came near the landing place of an untenanted market-green. Here we drew in-shore, and, sending out ten scouts to lie in wait in the jungle, I mustered all the healthy men, about thirty in number, and proceeded to construct a fence of brushwood, inspired to unwonted activity by a knowledge of our lonely, defenceless state. . . . The scouts retreated on the run, shouting as they approached, "Prepare! prepare! they are coming!" About fifty yards of ground outside our camp had been cleared, which . . . was soon filled by hundreds of savages, who pressed upon us from all sides . . . we were at bay, and desperate in our resolve not to die without fighting. Accordingly, at such close quarters the contest soon became terrific. Again and again the savages hurled themselves upon our stockade, launching spear after spear with deadly force. . . . Sometimes the muzzles of our guns almost touched their breasts. The shrieks, cries, shouts of encouragement, the rattling volleys of the musketry, the booming war-horns, the yells and defiance of the combatants, the groans and screams of the women and children in the hospital camp, made together such a medley of hideous noises as can never be effaced from my memory. For two hours this desperate conflict lasted. . . . At dusk the enemy retreated . . . but the hideous alarums produced from their ivory horns, and increased by the echoes of the close forest, still continued; and now and again a vengeful poison-laden arrow flew by with an ominous whizz to quiver in the earth at our feet. . . . Sleep, under the circumstances, was out of the question. . . . Morning dawned. . . . We were not long left unmolested. . . . The combat lasted until noon, when, mustering twenty-five men, we made a sally, and succeeded in clearing the skirts of the village for the day. . . . The next morning an assault was attempted. . . . About noon a large flotilla of canoes was observed ascending the river close to the left bank, manned by such a dense mass of men that any number between five hundred and eight hundred would be within the mark . . . blowing their war-horns and drumming vigorously. At the same moment, as though this were a signal in concert with those on land, war-horns responded from the forest, and I had scarcely time to order every man to look out when the battle-tempest of arrows broke upon us from the woods. This was a period when every man felt that he must either fight or resign himself to the only other alternative, that of being heaved a headless corpse into the river.

Just a few days before Christmas, some 200 miles downriver from Nyangwe and still eight marches short of the twenty they had agreed to, Tippoo Tib and the Arabs

declared their intention of returning to Nyangwe by another route, and with such firmness of tone [Stanley tells us], that I renounced the idea of attempting to persuade them to change their decision. Indeed, the awful condition of the sick, the high daily mortality, the constant attacks on us during each journey . . . had produced such dismal impressions on the minds of the escort that no amount of money would have bribed the un-disciplined people of Tippoo Tib to have entertained for a moment the idea of continuing the journey.

Not so Stanley; all the awful conditions hadn't for a moment dis-suaded him. What's more, he had led his men so deep into the wild country that the prospect of returning seemed to them every bit as dreadful as proceeding further. But what most gave Stanley and his men the heart to go on without the Arab escort was the fact that they had by now found or captured more than twenty canoes. Repaired and christened with such names as *Livingstone, Stanley, Telegraph, Herald, London Town,* and *America,* they formed a fleet large enough to transport the entire party on the river.

Before parting, Stanley and Tippoo Tib took a few days off to celebrate Christmas. Canoe races were organized; there were foot races, including one between Frank Pocock and Tippoo Tib which the Arab won by fifteen yards; there was a banquet of rice and roasted sheep, with dances by the tribesmen around a bonfire. On the night of December 27, 1876, Stanley had one of his earnest chats with his youthful lieutenant, and in it he revealed his steadily changing view of Lualaba's geography.

Here we are at an altitude of sixteen hundred and fifty feet above the sea [he told Frank]. What conclusions can we arrive at? Either that this river penetrates a great distance north of the Equator, and, taking a mighty sweep round, descends into the Congo . . . or that we shall shortly see it in the neighborhood of the Equator take a direct cut towards the Congo . . . or that it is the . . . Nile. I believe that it will prove to be the Congo; if the Congo then, there must be many cataracts. Let us only hope that the cataracts are all in a lump, close together.

At dawn, a heavy gray mist hung over the river and Stanley waited for it to lift before embarking the expedition. It numbered 149 men, women and children, 2 donkeys, 2 goats and a sheep, loaded into 22 canoes; the canoes were lashed together in pairs and the *Lady Alice* took her position at the head of the flotilla. Stanley concedes that the morale of his men was anything but high. "Sons of Zanzibar," Stanley

shouted to them. "the Arabs . . . are looking at you. They are now telling one another what brave fellows you are. Lift up your heads and be men." But "with what wan smiles they responded to my words! How feebly they paddled." An attempt was made to raise a song but the voices died out into "piteous hoarseness" and the eerie silence of the jungle again descended. And again all the troubles started.

The drums beat along the river banks; the war-horns sounded their dreadful cry in the jungles; the cannibals gathered along the banks, rattling their spears against their shields, brandishing their bows and arrows, shrieking, "Bo-bo-bo-bo-o-o! Meat! Meat! We shall have plenty of meat!" Every day the flotilla had to run a gauntlet of arrows and spears, every night the party had to build fortifications around its camp and fight off attacks, and the further north Stanley went, the bolder the cannibals became. Painted half red and half white, with broad black stripes streaked across them, they came out into the river in their giant war canoes—one, which Stanley captured, was 85 feet long with a bas relief of a crocodile adorning its side. Stanley soon arranged to have all the shields taken from the enemy affixed to the sides of the boats of his flotilla so that his boats came to resemble miniature Viking ships. New Year's Day, 1877, passed as all the rest: fighting off cannibals, drenched in the rains, suffering fevers and disease. And then in the midst of all these horrors yet another horror loomed. On January 4, Stanley heard the distant roar of rapids on the river, and the next day he reached the first of the seven cataracts of the Stanley Falls.

It took him just over three weeks to descend the falls, and it was an amazing feat. Wherever there was a stretch of relatively calm water, Stanley would make use of it and relaunch the *Lady Alice* and his fleet of canoes, but no sooner were they floating downstream than they would again hear the roar of the next cataract in the series, and all hands would begin paddling for dear life to make the bank and avoid being swept to destruction. Then the horrendous labor of portage would begin again. A path fifteen feet wide had to be hacked through the jungle, sometimes two and three and four miles long, to circumvent a cataract. Half the expedition worked at this exhausting task, all day and, by the light of torches, all night as well, while the other half of the expedition dragged the boats after them. And throughout it all they had to fight off the continual, relentless, terrifying attacks of hordes of cannibals.

"Lady Alice" over the falls

On January 23, the party circumvented the sixth cataract and once again relaunched the boats on the river. They had, Stanley discovered from his solar observations, crossed to north of the equator, and a stretch of calm water lay in front of them. They halted the next day on an island to make some repairs on the *Lady Alice* and resumed their journey on the 25th. Around midday, the roar of the seventh cataract

burst upon our ears with a tremendous crash. . . . As the calm river, which is 1300 yards wide one mile above the falls, becomes narrowed, the current quickens, and rushes with resistless speed for a few hundred yards, and then falls about 10 feet into a boiling and tumultuous gulf, wherein are lines of brown waves 6 feet high leaping with terrific bounds, and hurling themselves against each other in dreadful fury. . . . I have seen many waterfalls during my travels in various parts of the world, but here was a stupendous river flung in full volume over a waterfall only 500 yards across. The river . . . does not merely *fall:* it is precipitated downwards.

So again the boats raced for the banks. Again the killing work of cutting a path for the overland portage was undertaken. Again a desperate battle with the cannibals was joined. And then on January 28,

we hastened away down river in a hurry to escape the noise of the cataracts which, for many days and nights, had almost stunned us with their deafening sound. . . . We are once again afloat upon a magnificent stream, whose broad and grey-brown waters woo us with its mystery.

Stanley realized that he had cleared the last of the cataracts.

And he realized something else as well: the Lualaba could not possibly be the Nile. He was now 40 miles north of the equator and, by measuring the temperature at which water boiled, he determined that the river's elevation had dropped to 1511 feet above sea level, some 20 feet *below* that of the Nile at Gondokoro. Thus, for the Lualaba to be the Nile, as Livingstone had so fervently believed, it would have to flow uphill from here on. But, even if by some miracle it could perform such a feat, Stanley saw that "The Livingstone now deflected to the west-northwest."

For the next 1000 miles, the river, making its great sweeping arc from northwest to west and then to southwest back across the equator again, widening out from about a mile across to six and even nine miles in places, would be wholly navigable and provide Stanley's flotilla with that ideal "broad watery avenue cleaving the Unknown" of which he had dreamed months before. But even so it would take him nearly seven weeks to make the journey, for if the river itself no longer impeded his travels, the peoples of the river still did. Stanley calculated that, between the first cannibal attack at the confluence with the Ruiki River back in November and the bottom of the Stanley Falls at the end of January, he had fought twenty-four pitched battles with river tribes. He would now have to fight eight more.

We were getting weary of fighting every day [he wrote]. The strain to which we were exposed had been too long, the incessant, long-lasting enmity shown us was beginning to make us feel baited, harassed, and bitter . . . [these] combats which we had with the insensate furies of savage-land began to inspire us with a suspicion of everything bearing the least resemblance of man, and to infuse into our hearts something of that feeling which possibly the hard-pressed stag feels, after distancing the hounds many times, and having resorted to many stratagems to avoid them, wearied and bathed with perspiration, he hears with terror and trembling the hideous and startling yells of the ever-pursuing pack. We also had laboured strenuously through ranks upon ranks of savages, scattered over a score of flotillas, had endured persistent attacks night and day while struggling through them, had resorted to all modes of defence, and yet at

every curve of this fearful river the yells of savages broke loud on our ears, the snake-like canoes darted forward impetuously to the attack, while the drums and horns and shouts raised a fierce and deafening uproar. We were becoming exhausted. Yet we were still only on the middle line of the continent! We were also being weeded out by units and twos and threes. There were not thirty men in the entire Expedition that had not received a wound. To continue this fearful life was not possible. Some day we should lie down, and offer our throats like lambs to the cannibal butchers. . . . Livingstone called floating down the Lualaba a foolhardy feat. So it has proved, indeed, and I pen these lines with half a feeling that they will be never read by any man.

At the confluence with the Aruwimi River, after two days of cease-less fighting, Stanley's party was attacked by a fleet of 54 monster canoes carrying a total of at least 2000 cannibals. The lead canoe had

two rows of upstanding paddles, forty men on a side, their bodies bending and swaying in unison as with the swelling barbarous chorus they drive her down towards us. In the bow, standing on what appears to be a platform, are ten prime young warriors, their heads gay with feathers of the parrot, crimson and grey: at the stern, eight men with long paddles, whose tops are decorated with ivory balls, guide the monster vessel; and dancing up and down from stem to stern are ten men, who appear to be chiefs. . . . The crashing sound of large drums, a hundred blasts from ivory horns, and a chilling chant from two thousand throats, do not tend to soothe our nerves or to increase our confidence.

When the first spears began to fly, Stanley gave the order to fire. Despite their more than ten-to-one superiority, the tribesmen were no match for the rifles, and after five minutes of awful slaughter they broke off the attack and retreated. But, Stanley tells us,

Our blood is up now. It is a murderous world, and we feel for the first time we hate the filthy, vulturous ghouls who inhabit it. We therefore lift our anchors, and pursue them up-stream along the right bank, until rounding a point we see their villages. We make straight for the banks, and continue the fight in the village streets with those who have landed, hunt them out into the woods.

And then, in a maddened frenzy brought on by nerves shredded to the breaking point, Stanley gave permission to his men to loot and plunder the villages.

The fight below the confluence of the Aruwimi and the Livingstone Rivers

The attack of the tribesmen in their sixty-three canoes

A week later, Stanley found momentary respite at the village of Rubunga, whose chief proved friendly and willing to barter food for beads and cloth. And here the expedition found its first evidence of European civilization since Nyangwe: four ancient Portuguese muskets. At the sight of these, the men "raised a glad shout. These appeared to them to be certain signs that we had not lost the road, that the great river did really reach the sea, and that their master was not deluding them when he told them that some day they would see the sea." But this, Stanley realized, was a double-edged omen. To be sure, the presence of the muskets, which had been traded up the river along the old slave trails over the centuries, meant that the European settlements that had existed for centuries at the Congo's mouth could not be too far away. But it also meant that the one overwhelming advantage he had had in the ceaseless battles with the river tribes—his firearms—was about to come to an end. From now on, his attackers would come at him with muskets as well as spears. And only a few days later that was what happened.

"Suddenly I heard a shot, and a whistling of slugs in the neighborhood of the boat. I turned my head, and observed the smoke of gunpowder drifting away from a native canoe." Sniping of this sort steadily intensified and at one point escalated into a pitched battle, in which 63 canoes, armed by Stanley's estimate with at least 315 muskets, swarmed around his boats. All that saved the expedition from total annihilation was the fact that the tribesmen didn't have proper ammunition for their weapons, loading them with scraps of copper and iron, which couldn't do much damage except at close range.

The unrelenting hostility of the river tribes also threatened the expedition with starvation. By now, of course, Stanley's own provisions were virtually exhausted, and he had to count on trading with local people to get food. But each time he went ashore to barter there was new trouble and we find him writing:

We have been unable to purchase food, or indeed approach a settlement for any amicable purpose. The aborigines have been so hostile that even fishing canoes have fired at us as though we were harmless game. God alone knows how we shall prosper . . . we regarded each other as fated victims of protracted famine, or the rage of savages.

But fearing famine more, on March 9 Stanley took an armed party ashore to forage for food. Almost immediately,

several loud musket-shots startled us all, and six of our men fell
wounded. Though we were taken considerably at a disadvantage, long
habit had taught us how to defend ourselves in a bush, and a desperate
fight began, and lasted an hour, ending in the retreat of the savages, but
leaving us with fourteen of our men wounded.

It was, by Stanley's reckoning, the 32nd fight he had had, and it was
the last. Three days later,

the river gradually expanded . . . which admitted us in view of a mighty
breadth of river. . . . Sandy islands rose in front of us like a sea-beach,
and on the right towered a long row of cliffs, white and glistening. . . .
The grassy table-land above the cliffs appeared as green as a lawn. . . .

While taking an observation at noon of the position, Frank, with my
glass in his hand, ascended the highest part of the large sandy dune that
had been deposited by the mighty river, and took a survey of its strange
and sudden expansion, and after he came back and said, "Why, I declare,
sir, this place is just like a pool; as broad as it is long. There are mountains all round it, and it appears to me almost circular."

"Well, if it is a pool, we must distinguish it by some name. Give me
a suitable name for it, Frank."

"Why not call it Stanley Pool?"

Stanley had reached the end of the longest single navigable stretch
of the Congo River and had entered a region of peaceable tribes at
last. Around him was the Bateke Plateau, on the frontier of the
ancient Kingdom of Kongo with its centuries-old familiarity with
Europeans. The sea was less than 400 miles away; the long-established
European settlement at Boma less than 200. In effect, Stanley had
accomplished all he had set out to accomplish. He had mapped the
great lakes of Central Africa, settled the mystery of the Nile's sources,
and proved that the Lualaba was the Congo. All he had to do now was
get home. And that, he realized, would prove the most difficult task of
all. For he now stood at the barrier which, albeit from its other side,
had blocked all explorers from Diogo Cão to Tuckey from exploring
the Congo until now.

Taking his boiling-point measurements, Stanley determined that
the river's elevation at Stanley Pool was nearly 1150 feet above the sea.
How it would make the descent Stanley had no real idea. He knew
that the distance to the Atlantic was now too short for the river to
make the descent in easy, gradual stages. There would have to be falls,

and, indeed, after half a day of floating down the length of the Pool "we heard for the first time the low and sullen thunder of the first cataract." In the best of all possible worlds, the plunge would occur in a single, albeit dreadfully precipitous fall, for then, with the expenditure of an enormous final burst of energy, the boats could be portaged around it and refloated on the river's estuary for the happy last leg of the journey by waterway to Boma. But Stanley was perfectly aware that he lived in anything but the best of all possible worlds. He had studied the maps drawn by the Tuckey expedition and realized that "Tuckey's Farthest," the Yellala Falls where the ill-fated British naval captain had abandoned his attempt to ascend the river in 1816, had to be a considerable distance from the cataract he now found plunging over the southern edge of the Stanley Pool. Thus he could be sure that there were at least two falls between him and the sea, and all he could hope and pray was that there weren't too many more than that. In this he was encouraged by a local chieftain, Itsi of Ntamo; he said there were only three, the Child, the Mother, and the Father. As we now know, there are thirty-two.

On March 16, Stanley began the descent on "a furious river rushing down a steep bed obstructed by reefs of lava, projected barriers of rock, lines of immense boulders, winding a crooked course through deep chasms, and dropping down over terraces in a long series of falls, cataracts, and rapids." It was a descent into what Stanley called "a watery hell" and he would later confess that

there is no fear that any other explorer will attempt what we have done in the cataract region. It will be insanity in a successor. Nor would we have ventured on this terrible task, had we the slightest idea that such fearful impediments were before us.

The three cataracts which Itsi of Ntamo had forecast turned out to be only the first bunch.

The Child was a two hundred yards' stretch of broken water; and the Mother consisted of a half a mile of dangerous rapids. . . . But the Father is the wildest stretch of river I have ever seen. Take a strip of sea blown over by a hurricane, four miles in length and a half a mile in breadth, and a pretty accurate conception of its leaping waves may be obtained. Some of the troughs were a hundred yards in length, and from one to the other the mad river plunged. There was first a rush down into the bottom of an immense trough, and then, by its sheer force, the enormous

volume would lift itself upward steeply until, gathering itself into a
ridge, it suddenly hurled itself 20 or 30 feet straight upward, before rolling down into another trough. If I looked up or down along this angry
scene, every interval of 50 or 100 yards of it was marked by wave-towers—
their collapse into foam and spray, the mad clash of watery hills, bounding
mounds and heaving billows, while the base of either bank, consisting of
a long line of piled boulders of massive size, was buried in the tempestuous surf. The roar was tremendous and deafening. I can only compare
it to the thunder of an express train through a rock tunnel. . . . The
most powerful ocean streamer, going at full speed on this portion of the
river, would be as helpless as a cockle-boat. I attempted three times, by
watching some tree floated down from above, to ascertain the rate of the
wild current by observing the time it occupied in passing between two
given points, from which I estimated it to be about thirty miles an hour!

Stanley devised a scheme of leashing the boats with rattan hawsers
to hold them back from the rapids while teams of men on land
dragged them along the bank. Where that didn't work, he had the
boats manhandled over the jagged and slippery rocks and boulders
along the shore. By these methods, he managed to get downstream of
these cataracts by March 24, only to discover an even more terrible
cataract awaiting him, which he named the Cauldron. Hawsers parted,
canoes were torn loose from the hands of fifty men and were swept
away to destruction. "Accidents were numerous. . . . One man dislo-
cated his shoulder, another was bruised on the hips, and another had a
severe contusion of the head." Stanley himself fell feet first "into a
chasm 30 feet deep between two enormous boulders, but fortunately
escaped with only a few ribs bruised." On March 28 came the first
fatalities in the roaring river. The Cauldron had been bypassed and
the next rapid was about to be attempted and

I was beginning to congratulate myself . . . when to my horror I saw the
Crocodile [the huge canoe captured above the Stanley Falls, now with
six men in it] in mid-river . . . gliding with the speed of an arrow towards
the falls. Human strength availed nothing now, and we watched it in
agony. . . . We saw it whirled round three or four times, then plunged
down into the depths, out of which the stern presently emerged pointed
upwards, and we knew then that the canoe-mates were no more.

That afternoon three more men were lost in the raging torrents. "On
the 3rd April . . . I myself tumbled headlong into a small basin, and

saved myself with difficulty from being swept away by the receding tide."

Often the boats had to be portaged.

If the rapids or falls were deemed impassable by water, I planned the shortest and safest route across the projecting points, and then, mustering the people, strewed a broad track with bushes, over which . . . we set to work to haul our vessels. . . . The rocks rose singly in precipitous masses 50 feet above the river, and this extreme height increased the difficulty and rendered footing precarious.

On April 12, the *Lady Alice,* with Stanley in her, was almost lost.

Strong cane cables were lashed to the bow and stern, and three men were detailed to each, while five men assisted me in the boat. . . . We had scarcely ventured near the top of the rapids when . . . the current swept the boat from the hands [of the men holding the canecables on the bank]. Away into the centre of the angry, foaming, billowy stream the boat darted, dragging one man into the maddened flood . . . we rode downwards furiously on the crests of the proud waves, the human voice was weak against the over-whelming thunder of the angry river. . . . Never did rocks assume such hardness, such solemn grimness and bigness, never were they invested with such terrors and such grandeur, as while we were the cruel sport and prey of the brown-black waves, which whirled us round like a spinning top, swung us aside, almost engulfed us in the rapidly subsiding troughs, and then hurled us upon the white rageful crests of others. . . . The flood was resolved that we should taste the bitterness of death . . . we saw the river heaved bodily upward, as though a volcano was about to belch around us. . . . I shouted out, "Pull, men, for your lives."

And as by a miracle the *Lady Alice* was tossed up on the sandy bank of a small inlet.

On April 21, 37 days after the party had begun the descent, it had advanced a mere 34 miles from the Stanley Pool. And the cataract that now faced it, the Inkisi Falls, was utterly impassable. The boats would have to be portaged around it. But the banks were utterly impassable as well, "heaps of ruin, thick slabs, and blocks of trap rock." The only way to bypass Inkisi was to back away from the river and go up and over a 1200-foot mountain. To appreciate the magnitude of the task, one need only realize that, of the some dozen or so canoes that remained, several were well over 70 feet long and, made of teak,

weighed upward of three tons. Stanley hoped to recruit 600 local tribesmen to assist in the work, but they considered the project complete madness. So Stanley set out with just his own men, half of them cutting a path up the mountain while the other half dragged the canoes after them; 500 to 800 yards of advance in a day was considered good going. Ultimately, "the native chiefs were in a state of agreeable wonder and complimentary admiration of our industry" and they delegated tribesmen from their villages to help the undefeatable white man. Nevertheless, it took the caravan nearly a month to get over the mountain and back down to the river on the other side.

The further downriver the expedition moved, the greater was the evidence of the long European presence at the river's mouth. So far the tribesmen had never actually seen Europeans themselves, but the marketplaces of their villages contained Delft ware and British crockery, Birmingham cutlery, gunpowder and guns, cloth and glassware and other such items of European manufacture. To a degree, of course, this was a heartening sight, since it proved that the party was advancing, no matter how painfully slowly, ever closer to its destination. But, as was the case with the appearance of those four Portuguese muskets at Rubunga, it created new problems. For, with European merchandise fairly abundant, Stanley found that his own trading goods were not in much demand. In effect, his currency was devalued; the prices for everything, and most especially food, skyrocketed.

In the absence of positive knowledge as to how long we might be toiling in the cataracts, we were all compelled to be extremely economical. Goat and pig meat were such luxuries that we declined to think of them as being possible with our means . . . chickens had reached such prices that they were rare in our camp. . . . Therefore—by the will of the gods—contentment had to be found in boiled duff, or cold cassava bread, ground-nuts, or pea-nuts, yams, and green bananas.

On this sort of diet, the caravan became increasingly prey to ravages of dysentery and disease.

Another devastating affliction was foot ulcers, and Frank Pocock was among the first to fall victim to them. He had finally worn out his last pair of shoes and after them a series of improvised sandals. Though Stanley—who himself was down to his last pair of boots, held together by bits of brass wire and worn through at the soles—continually urged him to make new sandals, Frank had taken to going bare-

foot most of the time. As a result, ants, mosquitos, vermin, and insects
of all kinds swarmed into every cut or bruise his feet sustained scrambling over the rocks and crags of the river bank. Infections developed;
they soon turned into festering ulcers, steadily eating down to the
bone, and by the end of May he was too crippled to walk, and whenever the party could not travel by boat he had to be carried in a
litter.

On June 3, the party reached a long stretch of rapids and cataracts
called Zinga Falls and Stanley went ahead to make a reconnaissance.
The plan was for the canoes to shoot the rapids one by one in those
portions where it was feasible, to portage them around where it
wasn't. But Frank, because of his crippled condition, was to come the
entire way overland carried in his litter. The youth, however, seems
to have taken this as an affront to his manhood, and no sooner was
Stanley gone than he countermanded the order and had the men lift
him into one of the canoes. The first stretch of rapids was run successfully, but then they came to a booming cataract and the boatmen
pulled for the bank. Ordinarily what they would have done now was
portage the canoe overland, but with the crippled youth they couldn't
do that. What they decided, therefore, was to leave Frank where he
was while they portaged the canoe downriver, then return with the
litter to carry him the rest of the way. But the youth wouldn't hear of
it. "What, carry me about the country like a worthless Goee-Goee for
all the natives to stare at me? No, indeed!" Then he went on to argue,
"I don't believe this fall is as bad as you say it is." For some minutes he
and the boatmen debated the advisability of shooting the cataract in
the canoe. The boatmen insisted the river was impassable; Frank,
fearful of being made a laughingstock by allowing himself to be carried, insisted that it wasn't and finally called them cowards for not
daring to attempt it. Goaded beyond endurance, one of the boatmen
at last turned to the others and said, "Boys, our little master is saying
we are afraid of death. I know there is death in the cataract, but come,
let us show him that black men fear death as little as white men."

So the canoe was relaunched.

There was a greasy slipperiness about the water that was delusive, and it
was irresistibly bearing them broadside over the falls. . . . Roused from
his seat by the increasing thunder of the fearful waters, Frank rose to his
feet, and looked over the heads of those in front, and now the full danger

of the situation burst on him. But too late! They had reached the fall, and plunged headlong amid the waves and spray. The angry waters rose and leaped into their vessel, spun them round as though on a pivot, and so down over the curling, dancing, leaping crests, they were borne, to the whirlpools which yawned below. Ah! then came the moment of anguish, regret, and terror.

Eight days later Frank's body was found washed up on the bank, "the upper part nude, he having torn his shirt away to swim."

The death of the youth was an appalling blow to the morale of the caravan. Every man sensed in it his own approaching death on this hopeless enterprise. Stanley grieved as blackly as the rest. In the almost three years that he had been traveling with Frank, he had developed a deep affection for him, had come to count heavily on his assistance, and now felt himself terribly alone. "We are all so unnerved with the terrible accident . . . that we are utterly unable to decide what is best to do. We have a horror of the river now." It took him nearly three weeks to rouse himself and the rest of his party out of a paralyzed state of despair and get them struggling onward again. Hunger and fever plagued them; more men drowned in the raging torrents or dropped from disease; mutinies were repeatedly threatened, and thirty men deserted. By July, the situation had become so desperate that the men took to thieving. The only items the local tribesmen were interested in trading for were rum and guns, and as Stanley had no rum and would not sell his guns, his party was edged ever closer to the brink of outright starvation, and the men took to stealing from the villages they passed. When they were caught, Stanley had to pay heavy ransoms of cloth, beads, and wire to free them and when, as finally happened, he had exhausted his supplies, he was forced to abandon them to slavery.

At last, at the end of July, Stanley decided he had to abandon the river. He had been making latitude measurements for the last several days, and when he reached a cataract called Isangila on July 30 he concluded this was Tuckey's Farthest. "As the object of the journey had now been attained, and the great river of Livingstone had been connected with the Congo of Tuckey, I saw no reason to follow it farther, or to expend the little remaining vitality we possessed in toiling through the last four cataracts." More important, he had learned from the local people that by striking away from the river he could reach Boma in five days, and given the condition of his party every day

was a matter of life and death. So, on July 31, the canoes were beached for the last time and, as a final tribute to "the brave boat, after her adventurous journey across Africa," the *Lady Alice* was carried to the summit of some rocks and "consigned to her resting place above the Isangila Cataract, to bleach and to rot to dust!" The next morning "a wayworn, feeble, and suffering column" set off for Boma.

They couldn't make it. For three days they struggled forward through the cruel, punishing Crystal Mountains, which had defeated Tuckey.

Up and down the desolate and sad land wound the poor, hungry caravan. Bleached whiteness of ripest grass, grey rock-piles here and there, looming up solemn and sad in their greyness, a thin grove of trees now and then visible on the heights and in the hollows—such were the scenes which every uplift of a ridge or rising crest of a hill met our hungry eyes.

On the fourth day, they reached a village named Nsanda, and here Stanley called a halt. The party was finished; the people were dying.

"To any Gentleman who speaks English at Embomma," he wrote:

Dear Sir, I have arrived at this place from Zanzibar with 115 souls, men, women, and children. We are now in a state of imminent starvation. We can buy nothing from the natives, for they laugh at our kinds of cloth, beads, and wire. . . . I do not know you; but I am told there is an Englishman at Embomma, and as you are a Christian and a gentleman, I beg you not to disregard my request. . . . We are in a state of the greatest distress; but if your supplies arrive in time, I may be able to reach Embomma within four days. . . . The supplies must arrive within two days, or I may have a fearful time of it among the dying. . . . What is wanted is immediate relief; and I pray you to use your utmost energies to forward it at once. . . . Until that time, I beg you to believe me.

He signed the letter "Yours sincerely, H. M. Stanley" and then added rather pathetically, "P.S. You may not know me by name; I therefore add, I am the person that discovered Livingstone in 1871."

He prepared two other versions of the letter, in French and in Spanish (as a substitute for Portuguese), and then called for volunteers from among his men to carry them to Boma. Four stepped forward. "If there are white men in Embomma," they said, "we will find them out. We will walk, and walk, and when we cannot walk we will crawl." Two guides were recruited from the village to accompany them.

The reply was not long in coming. Boma turned out to be just a day's journey away, and on August 6 the men returned at the head of a luxuriously provisioned caravan.

Pale ale! Sherry! Port wine! Champagne! Several loaves of bread, wheaten bread, sufficient for a week. Two pots of butter. A packet of tea! Coffee! White loaf-sugar! Sardines and salmon! Plum-pudding! Currant, gooseberry, and raspberry jam! The gracious God be praised for ever! The long war we had maintained against famine and the siege of woe were over, and my people and I rejoiced in plenty!

After feasting for a day, Stanley and his expedition set off once again and "On the 9th August, 1877, the 999th day from the date of our departure from Zanzibar, we prepared to greet the van of civilization." Four white men, three Portuguese and a Hollander, came out to meet the caravan.

They brought a hammock with them, and eight sturdy, well-fed bearers. They insisted on my permitting them to lift me into the hammock. I declined. They said it was a Portuguese custom. To custom, therefore, I yielded.

He had come 7000 miles through the dark continent to be carried the final steps into Boma.

He spent two days there, and then he and his party were transferred to the larger Portuguese trading settlement at Cabinda.

Turning to take a farewell glance at the mighty river on whose brown bosom we had endured so greatly, I saw it approach, awed and humbled, the threshold of the watery immensity, to whose immeasurable volume and illimitable expanse, awful as had been its power, and terrible as had been its fury, its flood was but a drop.

Stanley and the Congo had reached the sea.

Toward the end of August, a Portuguese gunboat took the expedition to the still greater comforts of Loanda in Angola, where it spent a month for much-deserved rest and recuperation, and from there, this time aboard a British naval vessel, they went on to Cape Colony. It was everyone's expectation that Stanley at last would part from his men here. For surely his most sensible course now would be to take a British ship from Cape Colony to England. But he had made a promise to his men when they first set out and, as he told them now,

nothing shall cause me to break my promise to you that I would take you home. You have been true to me, and I shall be true to you. If we can get no ship to take us, I will walk the entire distance with you until I can show you to your friends at Zanzibar.

On November 6, 1877, the H.M.S. *Industry* sailed from Cape Colony, and two weeks later

the boat-keel kissed the beach, and the impatient fellows leaped out and upwards, and danced in ecstasy on the sands of their island; then they kneeled down, bowed their faces to the dear soil, and cried out, with emotion, their thanks to Allah! To the full they now taste the sweetness of the return home. The glad tidings ring out along the beach, "It is Bwana Stanley's expedition that has returned."

Stanley had another reason for returning to Zanzibar. He knew there must be a packet of letters waiting for him there and he was eager to read those that had accumulated during his three years in the wilderness from his beloved Alice Pike. And this is what he read: "I have done what millions of women have done before me, not been true to my promise."

Part Four

———◆—◆——

THE EXPLOITATION

18

EUROPE AND THE CONGO

When Stanley returned to England from his conquest of the Congo, there was—so unlike the mixed reception he had met after he had found Livingstone five years before—absolutely no quibbling with the magnificence of his accomplishment. The dispatches he had sent from Boma and Cabinda, Loanda, Cape Town, and Zanzibar had preceded him by several months, and by the time he set foot in Europe in January 1878 the world was in a state of almost hysterical excitement and hero worship. Geographical societies heaped their highest honors upon him; kings and queens, presidents and prime ministers vied to grant him audiences; the U.S. Congress convened especially to accord him a unanimous vote of thanks; newspapers queued up to get interviews; and publishers competed to sign up his memoirs. Even his arch-rivals in the field—Burton, Grant, Baker, Cameron—were unstinting in their praise. He had done more than all of them put together; he had filled in the great blank spaces of the map of Africa and had solved the outstanding geographical mysteries of the dark continent. He was, inarguably, the greatest African explorer of them all.

It was everything that Stanley had ever hoped for, but he was unable to enjoy it. He was, as he wrote, "so sick and weary . . . I cannot think of anything more than a long rest and sleep." The grueling three-year, 7000-mile journey had exhausted him and wrecked his health. His hair had turned totally white, he was emaciated in the extreme, and although he was only 37 he looked 15 years older. Worst of all, his heart had been broken by the betrayal of his betrothed. She had been "my stay and my hope, my beacon" throughout the years of his terrible travels, but now he knew himself to have been a fool;

Alice Pike had been married in January 1876, when Stanley had been under way barely a year. He excised every reference to the faithless woman from his journals, and a friend found him "very lonely and depressed" when they met at a banquet in his honor: "He was evidently suffering acutely from a bitter disappointment . . . 'What is the good of all this pomp and show,' were his words. 'It only makes me the more miserable and unhappy.' " In his own journal Stanley described his mood in this way:

When a man returns home and finds for the moment nothing to struggle against, the vast resolve, which has sustained him through a long and difficult enterprise, dies away, burning as it sinks in the heart; and thus the greatest successes are often accompanied by a peculiar melancholy.

In his melancholy mood, Stanley secluded himself for a few months to write a massive, 1000-page account of his epic journey, and then set out to try to amuse himself with the pleasures of civilization.

I had indulged in luxurious reveries while imprisoned in the rocky cañon of the Congo, and banqueted blissfully on thoughts of how I should enjoy myself. . . . I thought the art lay in dressing *à la mode,* sipping coffee with indolent attitudes on the flagstones of Parisian boulevards, or testing the merits of Pilsen and Strasburg beer; but my declining health and increasing moody spirits informed me that these were vanities, productive of nothing but loss of time, health, and usefulness.

He went on to Trouville, Deauville, and Dieppe "but my wretchedness increased. I explored those famed seaside resorts, and discovered that I was getting more and more unfit for what my neighbors called civilised society." Then he spent three weeks in Switzerland, where he did finally recover his health but where he also concluded that his "liberty" was "joyless and insipid," that the luxury of lounging about had become "unbearable." He had to get back to work, and he had a piece of work that he wanted to get back to.

Unlike explorers in Africa before him, Stanley was determined to see his explorations profitably exploited. In the spirit of Livingstone, he believed his mission now was to "pour the civilization of Europe into the barbarism of Africa." In the tradition of the Victorian age, he was convinced that the way to do that was through commerce. In the light of his discovery, he regarded the Congo River as the perfect artery by which that commerce could be carried into the long-inaccessible heart of the continent. And, in character with his tough-minded,

wholly practical nature, he counted on the "legitimate desire for gain" to serve as the motivating force for Europeans to underwrite the enterprise.

Even while he was still in Africa he had written, in a dispatch to the London *Daily Telegraph:*

I feel convinced that the question of this almighty water-way will become a political one in time. As yet, however, no European Power seems to have put forth the right of control. Portugal claims it because she discovered the mouth; but the great Powers—England, America, and France —refuse to recognize her right. If it were not that I fear to damp any interest you may have in Africa, or in this magnificent stream, by the length of my letters, I could show you very strong reasons why it would be a politic deed to settle this momentous question immediately. I could prove to you that the Power possessing the Congo, despite the cataracts, would absorb to itself the trade of the whole of the enormous basin behind. This river is and will be the grand highway of commerce to West Central Africa.

Of all the great powers, it was Britain that Stanley most wanted to take possession of the Congo. Since his expedition, financed by a pair of newspapers, had had no official standing, he had not attempted to lay claim to the lands he discovered for the British, but he now set out to convince them that they should lay claim to it themselves. He was well aware of the problems posed to the commercial exploitation of the Congo by those 200 miles of murderous cataracts between the Stanley Pool and the river's estuary but he had a straightforward plan for doing something about them. Quite simply, a road, and in time a railroad, had to be built around them to connect the 1000 miles of navigable inland waterway above the Pool with the estuary and the sea. Then, a fleet of boats would be transported up that road and set sailing between the Stanley Pool and the Stanley Falls, and a string of trading stations would be established along the riverbanks, from which commerce and civilization would radiate out into the vast hinterland of the river basin and through which huge profits would be harvested home.

Stanley took every opportunity to proselytize for this plan—in newspaper articles, on the lecture circuit, in private conversations with powerful political and financial figures. He met a number of times with the Prince of Wales and Baron Rothschild; he addressed

the Chambers of Commerce of Manchester and Liverpool and other industrial cities.

There are 40,000,000 of naked people beyond that gateway [he argued], and the cotton-spinners of Manchester are waiting to clothe them. . . . Birmingham's foundries are glowing with the red metal that shall presently be made into ironwork in every fashion and shape for them . . . and the ministers of Christ are zealous to bring them, the poor benighted heathen, into the Christian fold.

The reaction to all this at first dumbfounded Stanley and then ultimately infuriated and embittered him. To be sure, the French statesmen Léon Gambetta told him, "Not only, sir, have you opened up a new Continent to our view, but you have given an impulse to scientific and philanthropic enterprise which will have a material effect on the progress of the world." And a number of missionary societies, especially the English and American Baptists, were inspired to send brethren to the lands of the old Kongo kingdom. But as for "the redemption of the splendid central basin of the continent by sound and legitimate commerce," no one responded. Again and again, the merchants and politicians with whom he discussed his plans dismissed them as impractical and dismissed him as a dreamer.

A wise Englishman [Stanley wrote] has said that pure impulses and noble purposes have been oftener thwarted by the devil under the name Quixotism than by any other insinuating phrase of obstruction . . . that word was flung in my teeth. . . . The charge of Quixotism, being directed against my mission, deterred many noble men . . . from studying the question of new markets, and deepened unjustly their prejudices against Africa and African projects.

In part, this was due to Stanley's personality and personal history. For all the honor and acclaim the British establishment was willing to shower on him, it still couldn't take this one-time bastard poorhouse boy and erstwhile scoop-seeking journalist quite seriously. In the back of all those well-bred minds, Stanley's reputation as something of a "mere penny-a-liner," something of a buccaneer, still lingered, and enough had happened on his last African journey to keep that reputation alive. The relish with which he had described his massacre of the natives of Bumbireh island in Lake Victoria hadn't helped nor did the vivid and flamboyant accounts which he later wrote of his 32 running battles with the cannibals down the Lualaba. In fact, there were those

who suggested that because of Stanley's pugnacious methods the tribesmen in the Congo interior were now wildly up in arms against all white men, making any enterprise like the one Stanley proposed doubly dangerous. What's more, gossip had it, utterly falsely, that the Africans whom Stanley had captured in those ceaseless wars he had often sold into slavery and just as often he had taken their women for his personal concubines. Now and again some bejeweled lady in an establishment drawing room, raising an eyebrow innocently, could be heard to inquire how it was that of all the white men Stanley had taken with him on his African journeys (two in his search for Livingstone and three on his exploration of the Congo) not one had got out alive.

But none of this really accounts for the lack of interest in Stanley's plan. Even had his reputation been as pure as the driven snow and his social credentials as impeccable as a lord's, his ideas would have been dismissed. The best proof is the fact that Cameron, a highly respectable officer of the Royal Navy with a highly respectable family background, had met with much the same indifference when he had returned to England two years before. Like Stanley, Cameron had been enthusiastic about the commercial possibilities of the Congo River basin and had described in ecstatic and exaggerated detail the beautiful scenery, the healthy climate, and the "incalculable wealth in tropical Africa." What's more, unlike Stanley's, his expedition had had an official status, and in his enthusiasm he had formally annexed the lands he had passed through in the name of the queen. But when he got back, he was told, in effect, thanks a lot but no thanks; Britain wasn't interested in the Congo. Nor, for that matter, was any other great power. It wasn't a question of his or Stanley's reputation. It was rather that the times were all wrong for their schemes. For Europe's view of Africa just then was in transition, passing from the old but not yet having reached the new, at one of those turning points in history where for a brief moment nothing can be done.

In a very real sense, Stanley's epic journey marked the end of the old. It had solved the most intriguing geographical secrets of the continent, and with that, perforce, the great age of African exploration, impelled by adventurous intellectual curiosity, was over. What's more, the suppression of the slave trade and the abolition of slavery were by now virtually completed, and so the humanitarian enthusiasm for Africa, which had played such a vital role in awakening Europe's

interest in the continent, had also much waned. But the next era—the European colonization of Africa—had not yet quite begun.

At the time, in the late 1870s, with the notable exception of South Africa (which would remain the notable exception in everything about Africa to this day), Europe still had almost no colonies worthy of the name south of the Sahara, and those few that it did have were either unimportant or unsuccessful. For example, British abolitionists had established Sierra Leone as a settlement for freed slaves and when it failed the British government felt obliged to take it over, but its only real use was as a base for its antislavery naval patrols. British colonial administrations had also been set up on the Gold Coast, at the Niger delta, and at the mouth of the Gambia River, but their prime function was to provide military protection for private traders rather than to govern natives. Similarly, France's only colonial activity on the continent at the time was in Senegal, for the protection of French traders on that river, and at Libreville in Gabon, where it too had been obliged to take over when an abolitionist attempt to set up a freed-slave settlement failed. Portugal continued to hold on to its centuries-old settlements, but these too were less colonies in the modern sense than sprawling trading stations under a governmental umbrella, with little real jurisdiction or control over the natives of the region.

And that was just about how most Europeans were content to allow it to remain. Certainly the white traders in Africa were. A rough-and-ready, individualistic band, including such legendary characters as Trader Horn, Mary Kingsley, John Holt, Du Chaillu and Douville, they were ardent advocates of laissez faire and, while they acknowledged the need for their governments' protection from time to time, they were nevertheless anxious to limit their governments' involvement in their freebooting affairs.

For their part, European governments were not anxious to get any more deeply involved in black Africa than they already were. The lucrative legitimate trade with the continent, which was expected to have boomed after the end of the slave traffic, hadn't materialized. Britain's exports to black Africa at the time, for example, amounted to less than one-hundredth of its exports to the rest of the world; apart from palm oil, groundnuts and the old standby ivory, no especially valuable imports had been developed; and because of the brutal climate, nothing in the way of meaningful white settlement had even been tried. Moreover, there wasn't any political or military advantage

King Leopold II

to be gained. Black Africa had not yet become a stage on which Europe's traditional rivalries were played out (the situation, of course, was much different in North Africa, Egypt, and along the Red Sea, since the opening of the Suez Canal). No major power exercised any greater political influence or derived any greater economic benefits than any other, nor did anyone's territorial claims, which in any case were modest, come into geographical conflict with anyone else's.

For the moment at least, what today would be called a balance of power existed in sub-Sahara Africa, and it would not be until that balance was upset, until it began to appear that one power was gaining an upper hand, that European governments would abandon their indifference toward Africa and the wild, almost hysterical scramble for colonies would suddenly get under way. But that wasn't to happen for another ten years, and when it did the force that caused it was so unexpected, so unlikely, indeed so bizarre that no one can be too seriously criticized for not anticipating it. For that force was Leopold II, king of the Belgians.

At the time of Stanley's return from the Congo, Leopold was 42 and had been 12 years on his throne, a tall, imposing man with a huge spade beard and an enormous nose, enjoying a reputation for hedonistic sensuality, cunning intelligence (his father once described him as subtle and sly as a fox), overweening ambition, and personal ruthlessness. He was, nevertheless, an extremely minor monarch in the *realpolitik* of the times, ruling a totally insignificant nation, a nation in fact that had come into existence barely four decades before and lived under the constant threat of losing its precarious independence to the great European powers around it. He was a figure who, one might have had every reason to expect, would devote himself to maintaining his country's strict neutrality, avoiding giving offense to any of his powerful neighbors, and indulging his keenly developed tastes for the pleasures of the flesh, rather than one who would have a profound impact on history. Yet, in the most astonishing and improbable way imaginable, he managed virtually single-handedly to upset the balance of power in Africa and usher in the terrible age of European colonialism on the black continent.

He began fashioning this infamous destiny in his earliest youth. While crown prince, he traveled widely, from Egypt and North Africa to India and the lands of the Far East, including China itself, and what appeared at first a harmless fascination with geography proved to

be the germ of a policy for acquiring power which was to be the central obsession of his life and reign. He believed that the only road to greatness open to little Belgium and, more especially, to her insignificant king was the acquisition of colonies. Long before he became king, he wrote:

Surrounded by the sea, Holland, Prussia and France, our frontiers can never be extended in Europe. The sea bathes our coast, the universe lies in front of us, steam and electricity have made distances disappear, all the unappropriated lands on the surface of the globe may become the field of our operations and of our successes. . . . Since history teaches that colonies are useful, that they play a great part in that which makes up the power and prosperity of states, let us strive to get one in our turn.

Leopold was related to Queen Victoria through the House of Coburg (she was a cousin) and he was influenced by this connection to believe that Belgium could achieve a measure of Britain's wealth and power by emulating her imperial policies. After all, he argued, both Britain and Belgium were small countries, both were highly industrialized, and the only real difference between them was that Britain, in her overseas possessions, had ready markets for her products and inexpensive raw materials for her industries. Belgium had lost hers when she split from the Netherlands in the 1830s, and since the Dutch had contrived to retain the entire overseas empire of the United Provinces, including the rich East Indies, Belgium had to make up for this lack. What she needed, in Leopold's words, was "some new Java." In the late 1850s and early 1860s, he set himself the task of finding one.

At one point, he expressed interest in "the Argentine Province of Entre Rios and the little island of Martin-Garcia at the confluence of the Uruguay and the Parana. Who owns this island?" he asked. "Could one buy it, and set up there a free port under the moral protection of the King of the Belgians?" Later his attentions focused on the Far East. He came up with a plan to buy Borneo from the Dutch; he offered to rent the Philippines from Spain; he suggested schemes for Belgian colonies in China, Indo-China, Japan, Fiji, the New Hebrides, and a host of other places. "I believe that the time has come to spread ourselves outwards," he wrote with growing eagerness and impatience while still prince; "we cannot afford to lose any more time, under penalty of seeing the best positions, which are already

becoming rare, successively occupied by nations more enterprising than our own."

Leopold ascended the throne, in December 1865, just at the moment when the excitement generated by the exploration in search of the Nile sources was at its height. Burton, Speke, Grant, and Baker were not long back from their travels, the Nile debate raged throughout Europe, and Livingstone was about to set off on his last journey. And quite naturally, the new Belgian king's attention shifted from the far East to the dark continent. Here were "unappropriated lands" which could become the field for his operations. And here too, he saw, the best positions were not becoming rare; indeed, the great powers were making no move to occupy the territories newly opened up by their explorers and seemed to have no intention of doing so. Leopold became an Africa enthusiast. He read all the explorers' books, he joined geographical societies, he donated money for future expeditions, and he began hatching colonial schemes for Belgium in Africa. He studied the possibilities along the West Coast, between Senegal and Cape Masuradi; he proposed the foundation of an East Africa Company to operate in Mozambique and later in other Portuguese territories; he took an interest in the Lualaba question and met with Cameron; he came up with plan after plan. Yet, ten years later, in 1875, Belgium was still without a colony.

Leopold's problem was that, as much as he wanted a colony for Belgium, Belgium didn't want one for herself. Like all European governments at the time and, given her small size, with better reason, the government in Brussels was strongly opposed to incurring the costs and risks involved in establishing colonies in Africa. Since the king of the Belgians was a constitutional monarch, he was powerless to force his will on the nation. And that, by all rights, should have been the end of that. But it wasn't, and the fact that it wasn't was where the situation took its bizarre turn. For this minor and essentially powerless monarch was so determined that he decided if he couldn't acquire a colony for his country then he was going to acquire one for himself.

This was then as incredible an idea as it would be today. No individual, be he even a king, could have, would be allowed to have, his own personal colony. Leopold was perfectly aware of this. But it didn't deter him. Calling on all his cunning, all his ambition, all his ruthlessness, he devised the means by which he could have it anyway.

In September 1876, Leopold, as a well-known African enthusiast

and member of a number of geographical societies, sponsored an international geographical conference in Brussels. Delegations from the scientific societies of Britain, France, Germany, Austria, Italy, and Russia attended. The purpose, Leopold stated in his speech opening the conference,

is one of those which must be a supreme preoccupation to all friends of humanity. To open to civilization the only area of our globe to which it has not yet penetrated, to pierce the gloom which hangs over entire races, constitutes, if I may dare put it in this way, a Crusade worthy of this century of progress. . . . Gentlemen, many of those who have made the closest study of Africa have come to the conclusion that their common purpose would be well served by a meeting and a conference designed to get their work in step, to concert efforts, to share all resources, and to avoid covering the same ground twice. It seemed to me that Belgium, a neutral and centrally placed country, would be a suitable place for such a meeting. . . . Need I say that in bringing you to Brussels I was guided by no motives of egoism? No, gentlemen, Belgium may be a small country, but she is happy and contented with her lot; I have no other ambition than to serve her well.

The agenda for the conference was every bit as deceptively high-minded. Only the most disinterested scientific and philanthropic topics were to be discussed: for example, the prospects for setting up supply bases and medical posts in the African interior to assist future expeditions, the methods necessary for the correlation and dissemination of maps and data gathered by past explorations, measures to be taken to accomplish the final eradication of the Arab slave trade, and so on. As the last item, Leopold called for the establishment of a permanent international committee to coordinate and oversee all these useful projects. The delegates couldn't but be favorably impressed. They threw themselves with enthusiasm into the work of the conference and, at the end, voted the formation of the Association Internationale Africaine, with headquarters in Brussels, a banner of blue with a gold star on it, and none other than Leopold II as its chairman.

The association, as it was to turn out, was a complete fiction. It, in fact, met only one more time, in 1877, and then was never heard from again. Which was precisely the way Leopold wanted it. What he had set out to create was a front organization through which he could pursue his improbable personal ambitions in Africa. And, with the

subtle and sly skill of a fox, that was exactly what he had done. As the head of an ostensibly international, scientific, and philanthropic institution dedicated to good works on the continent, and not as the king of the Belgians, he was free to undertake all manner of activities in Africa without the interference of the Belgian government and without arousing the suspicions of the European powers.

Leopold's ambition had fixed on the Congo River basin. His interview with Cameron had convinced him of the potential wealth of the region, and the dispatches from Stanley, which filtered out of Africa during 1876 and 1877 and which the Belgian king read avidly, served to sharpen his appetite. So when Stanley, en route back to England in January 1878, stopped at Marseilles, Leopold sent two emissaries to meet him and, as Stanley later reported, "before I was two hours older I was made aware that King Leopold intended to undertake to do something substantial for Africa, and that I was expected to assist him." What precisely that might be Leopold was still keeping secret, but in a remarkably candid letter written at this time to a close intimate he put it this way:

I think that if I entrusted Stanley publicly with the job of taking over part of Africa in my own name, the English would stop me. If I consult them, they will again try to stop me. So I think that at first I shall give Stanley an exploring job which will not offend anybody, and will provide us with some posts down in that region and with a high command for them which we can develop when Europe and Africa have got used to our "pretensions" on the Congo.

Stanley wasn't interested. He was exhausted, sick and heartbroken, as we've seen, and, what's more, still believed that he was going to be able to interest England in backing his scheme for the exploitation of the Congo. So he politely brushed off the two Belgian emissaries, refused to pay even a courtesy call on Leopold, and went on his way to London. Leopold wasn't discouraged. He correctly judged what the British government's and, for that matter, the other great powers' reaction to Stanley's ideas would be. There was the precedent of Cameron's failure, and Leopold guessed that Stanley's somewhat soiled reputation would make him an even less convincing advocate. So, after biding his time for a bit, Leopold in June 1878 again invited Stanley to Brussels. Stanley, although by no means yet ready to give up altogether on the British but getting increasingly discouraged by their attitude, accepted. The two men discussed Stan-

ley's ideas and especially his view that nothing substantial could be done until a road and, better yet, a railroad were built around the Livingstone Falls. Leopold agreed and revealed that he was prepared to arrange the financing of such an enterprise under the auspices of his International Association. But even so nothing definite came of the meeting, and Stanley returned to London to pursue his cause for another few, frustrating months.

In the meantime, Leopold made another cunning move. Using the umbrella of the International Association, but without consulting any of its members, he formed something called the Comité d'Études du Haut-Congo with himself as chairman. Ostensibly, this study committee was meant to sponsor a new expedition "with an essentially philanthropic and scientific point of view and with the intention of extending civilization and finding new outlets for commerce and industry by the study and explorations of certain parts of the Congo." In fact, it was simply a highfalutin name for a commercial syndicate which Leopold had formed to finance that road or railway around the Livingstone Falls and go on from there to build trading stations on the Congo. The principal stockholder in this syndicate was Leopold. Within a year, after he had changed the syndicate's name to the Association Internationale du Congo so as to deliberately confuse it with the Association Internationale Africaine, Leopold in fact became its sole stockholder. But when Stanley, early in November, once again responded to an invitation to meet with the king at the royal palace in Brussels, he tells us,

I there discovered various persons of more or less note in the commercial and monetary world, from England, Germany, France, Belgium, and Holland. . . . This body of gentlemen desired to know how much of the Congo River was actually navigable by light-draught vessels? What protection could friendly native chiefs give to commercial enterprises? Were the tribes along the Congo sufficiently intelligent to understand that it would be better for their interest to maintain friendly intercourse with the whites than to restrict it? What tributes, taxes, or imports, if any, would be levied by the native chiefs for right of way through their country? What was the character of the produce which the natives would be able to exchange for European fabrics?

But central to all their questions were those about building a way around the cataracts. Stanley suggested that, before they attempted to lay 200 miles of railway track through the rugged Crystal Mountains,

a survey should be made, a wagon road built, and a string of supply stations erected for the use of the crews that would come afterward. Moreover, he pointed out, arrangements would have to be made with local chiefs, by treaty, purchase, or lease, for the acquisition of lands for the supply stations and right-of-way in order to avoid unnecessary hostilities. Once this was done, he went on, a fleet of vessels could then be transported up the wagon road and launched on the Stanley Pool, and trading, supply, and scientific stations could be erected along the Congo all the way to the Stanley Falls.

The commercial and monetary gentlemen agreed that this seemed an eminently practical approach to begin with. They were prepared to finance an expedition to implement it and Stanley was invited to head it under a five-year contract at a salary of £1000 a year. By now his hopes of interesting the British in this plan had been completely dashed and he accepted. Throughout the winter of 1878 he again engaged in the complicated business of mounting an expedition to the Congo.

There was someone else in Europe that winter who was also busily engaged in mounting an expedition to the Congo. He was Count Pierre Savorgnan de Brazza, a tall, slim, almost embarrassingly handsome 26-year-old French naval officer, who, like Cameron, was to engage Stanley in a race for the Congo but who, unlike Cameron, would win it.

Brazza by birth was an Italian from one of the most distinguished families of Rome (his correct name was Pietro Paulo Francesco Camillo Savorgnan di Brazza), and claimed descent from the Emperor Severus and from the Doges. But as a youth he had developed a passion for and joined the French Navy, and after seeing service in the Franco-Prussian War had applied for and received French citizenship. He first set foot in Africa in 1871, when the ship he was aboard carried reinforcements to French troops fighting rebel tribesmen in Algeria, and then for the next three years he served on a vessel that made frequent calls at Libreville and Port Gentil in France's Gabon colony. Though his duties as an auxiliary ensign usually confined him to his ship during these visits, he did manage on three occasions to make short excursions up the Ogowe and Gabon rivers, and in June 1874, when he was only 22 and Stanley was planning the epic journey that would discover the Congo, Brazza came forward with his own plan of exploration. "I have acquired the conviction that the Ogowe, even above

Count Pierre Savorgnan de Brazza

the first rapids, is still a very considerable river that stretches into the interior," he wrote to the French Minister of Marine, and then went on to propose an expedition, led by himself and accompanied by a couple of other navy officers and a party of Senegalese sailors, to explore the river and discover its commercial possibilities for the Gabon colony.

Three things conspired in Brazza's favor. One was that the Minister of Marine was a close personal friend of his family and had, in fact, been instrumental in getting the Italian-born youth into the French Navy in the first place. Another was that the strikingly good-looking, exquisitely mannered youth, with his impeccable noble lineage, was charmingly persuasive and made an irresistible impression wherever he went. But third and most important was the fact that there was a growing uneasiness in some influential quarters in Paris that France was allowing herself to be outdistanced, in the matter of African exploration, by her archrival Great Britain. For nearly two decades now, British expeditions, sponsored by the Admiralty, Foreign Office, or Royal Geographical Society, had been winning honors and glory for Queen Victoria with their magnificent and highly publicized quests for the Nile sources, while France had been standing aside doing absolutely nothing. Surely the time had come for the French to get into the field and take some of the prizes for their own monarch. To be sure, not everyone agreed, and it took well over a year for the Minister of Marine to win approval for Brazza's plan. But in the end the combination of these three factors won out, and by August 1875 the young count was on his way.

Stanley, who by this time had circumnavigated Lake Victoria and was headed toward Lake Albert, was completely unaware of Brazza's expedition; the only rival he knew he had in the field then was Cameron. Brazza, for his part, was aware of both Stanley and Cameron, but he did not regard himself as their rival. In his heart of hearts, he hoped that the Ogowe would stretch eastward from the coast so far into the African interior that it would bring him to the region of the great lakes and allow him to make some grand discovery in connection with the Nile sources. But he was realistic enough not to count on it. His was a modest and modestly financed expedition, and he seems to have been content just to be under way, enjoying the heady excitement of traveling in the wilds, seeking to solve the minor mystery of the Ogowe's source.

The going was rough; the terrain was thickly jungled; the tribes became increasingly hostile the deeper he penetrated from the coast; disease claimed its usual ghastly toll; and the cruelty of the slave traffic in the interior was shockingly depressing for the young, refined nobleman. It took him nearly two years to reach the point where the river, having turned from the east to the south, became unnavigable and dwindled to a stream near its source. "The Ogowe had no more secrets from us," he wrote. "It was now clear that its course was only of secondary importance, with no direct access to the center of the African continent." Although this was not unexpected, Brazza did not now turn back, for during the last several weeks of his travels he had been hearing reports of a "big water" lying further eastward in the interior, and he had begun to hope that it might turn out to be one of the great lakes. So, leaving the Ogowe, he pressed on eastward.

Early in 1878, by which time Stanley had returned to England, Brazza reached the land of the Bateke tribesmen, who showed him a river, called the Alima, which they said flowed into the big water. In fact, they claimed, the big water was only five days' journey away, but they also warned Brazza that the tribes he would now encounter were the most ferocious of all, and cannibals into the bargain. Though he was running short of supplies and, most especially, ammunition, Brazza was willing to chance it and, hiring canoes from the Bateke, set off with his party down the Alima. The first day on the river they heard the eerie and unnerving sound of the cannibal war drums beating along the jungled banks, but the first village let them pass without trouble. In the evening, however, they were fired on from shore. Fearful of traveling in the dark on the unknown river, they camped that night, and at dawn they awoke to find thirty war canoes bearing down on them in a fearsome attack. Brazza's rifles managed to drive the tribesmen off, but he decided his expedition was in no condition to survive even five days of such conditions. Leaving most of the baggage and all of the canoes, Brazza fled with his men overland through the swampy forests back from whence he had come.

Had Brazza been able to keep going, had he been, one is tempted to say, Stanley with all the latter's bulldog persistence and unflinching courage, he would have made a magnificent discovery. For the Alima is a tributary of the Congo. Five days' journey down it would have brought Brazza to the "big water" he had heard about, some 200 miles upstream of the Stanley Pool.

Brazza arrived back in France in the last days of 1878, nearly a year after Stanley's return. His reception was warm and congratulatory, and the French made something of a national hero of him as their first African explorer. But obviously his achievement was minor and the honors and acclaim bestowed on him pale in comparison to Stanley's. It wounded the young nobleman's pride. When he read Stanley's account of his journey and realized just how close he had come to reaching the Congo himself, he turned somewhat nasty. He claimed then—and, later in life, he would elaborate and embroider on his claim—that his failure was Stanley's fault. Seizing on Stanley's own accounts of the 32 battles he had fought in his progress down the river, Brazza tried to make the case that the hostility he had encountered from the tribesmen during his journey, which finally forced him to turn back from the Congo, was a result of the hostility Stanley had aroused among the tribesmen against all whites. Out of his bitter envy, Brazza became, unbeknown to Stanley, Stanley's most ferocious rival.

Brazza had a plan. He had found, although quite inadvertently, he realized, a completely new and, until now, unthought-of route to the Congo. By following the Ogowe from the Gabon coast, and then the Alima or any of a number of other tributaries that flow into the Congo from the north, he could reach Stanley's "grand highway of commerce to West Central Africa" without having to surmount the terrible cataracts of the Livingstone Falls. What Brazza wanted to do was mount a well-equipped and well-financed expedition to open that newly discovered route. He was as convinced as Cameron and Stanley had been of the commercial potential of the Congo, and he wanted to exploit that potential for France.

Unfortunately, for all his charming persuasiveness, Brazza found it as difficult to get a serious hearing for his ideas as Cameron and Stanley had for theirs. The French government was as reluctant to get involved in a colonial enterprise in Africa as the British and, for that matter, the Belgian governments had been. For months after his return Brazza raced around Paris trying to arouse support for his scheme, calling on influential friends of his family, writing articles, addressing chambers of commerce, lobbying statesmen, using every argument he could think of. He held out the prospect of a great French African empire stretching from Algeria to the Congo, promised mammoth profits from trade in the river basin, argued France's responsibility to undertake a civilizing mission among the savages

there, called for the assertion of French power and glory. And all in vain.

But then Brazza got a break. The news leaked out that Stanley, having been rejected by the British, had hired on with Leopold and was to lead an expedition for the Belgian king's Association Internationale Africaine. To be sure, according to Leopold's cover story, this was meant to be a purely scientific and philanthropic undertaking, but Brazza was able to arouse suspicion in the right circles. His good friends at the Ministry of Marine were willing to sponsor a second expedition on a modest scale much like the first, lightly equipped and minimally financed, in order to give Brazza a chance to demonstrate the feasibility of reaching the Congo from the Gabon coast. And so a second race to the Congo began.

19

BULA MATARI

Stanley's expedition was cloaked in immense secrecy. So great were the stealth and deception with which Leopold surrounded it that, by the time Brazza got any inkling of it and hurriedly began preparing his own expedition in August 1879, Stanley had been under way for more than half a year.

Toward the end of January, Leopold had dispatched a chartered steamer, the *Albion,* to Suez. But Stanley wasn't on it. He left a few days later alone, traveling incognito as Monsieur Henri, on what appeared to be a private citizen's holiday ramble through France and Italy. It was only when he was sure that he had shaken off any interest in his movements and his whereabouts in Europe was generally unknown that he made a dash for Suez to rendezvous with the *Albion.* From there he sailed aboard her through the canal and down the Red Sea to Zanzibar. Meanwhile, the bulk of his expedition—a massive assemblage of over 80 tons of stores and equipment, including prefabricated houses, a fleet of 8 boats, and a party of a dozen European assistants—was dispersed in various European ports. It wouldn't set off for the Congo until May—and then by an entirely different route.

Stanley's unexpected arrival in Zanzibar in April startled the European community on the island and set it buzzing with speculations. It was obvious, of course, that he must be considering another one of his stupendous African journeys, but where or why no one could fathom. And Stanley himself deliberately deepened the mystery. Without saying a word to anyone, he hired 68 Zanzibaris—three-quarters of whom had served with him before—and then made a series of utterly pointless and completely misleading excursions with them to the East African mainland. The puzzled American consul on the

island cabled Washington: "Mr. H. M. Stanley has been hovering between this place and the coast for over a month, and will leave soon for Mombassa. We don't know for what reason he is here, but presume it has some concern with some grand commercial scheme."

Then, to further compound the confusion, yet another unannounced expedition turned up on the island. It was headed by a Belgian army captain and was said to be under the auspices of King Leopold's scientific, philanthropic, and thoroughly defunct Association Internationale Africaine, sent out to establish a chain of supply stations in the African interior for the use of future explorers. Stanley busied himself helping outfit this party, as if this might have been the reason for his visit to Zanzibar, but when it departed for the mainland at the end of May (where it attached itself to a White Fathers' mission and conveniently dropped out of public view) he, of course, did not go along. Instead, he boarded his Zanzibaris on the *Albion* and steamed, not round the Cape of Good Hope toward the Congo's mouth, but once again misleadingly back up the East African coast and into the Red Sea.

For all this hugger-mugger, the biggest secret about Leopold's audacious scheme was one that Stanley himself didn't know anything about. And it was only when he was so deeply committed and so far under way that he was unlikely to pull out of the venture that Leopold felt free to let him in on it.

During his passage back through the Red Sea, Stanley received two telegrams from Brussels. The first, at Aden, informed him that Leopold had taken over all the shares of the Comité d'Études du Haut-Congo and was now the sole proprietor of the international syndicate. The second, at Suez, requested him to proceed to Gibraltar. There he was met by a certain Colonel Maximilian Strauch, a stiff-necked, pince-nezed staff officer from the Belgian War Ministry and a devoutly loyal servant of Leopold's, whom the Belgian king had designated as the secretary-general of his Comité d'Études du Haut-Congo and through whom he would henceforth communicate with Stanley about his devious Congo schemes. Strauch took Stanley to his rooms at a Gibraltar hotel and there passed on to him Leopold's latest and most startling set of instructions. Stanley was to go ahead and build that wagon road around Livingstone Falls and erect a string of trading stations up the river, as he had been instructed to do by the Comité. But now that Leopold was the sole owner of the Comité he was to do something

else: create a Confederation of Free Negro Republics in the Congo River basin.

This was to be an independent black African state, taking for its precedent and bearing a superficial resemblance to the then recent American experiment in Liberia. It was to be formed through the signing of treaties with local chiefs; under the treaties they were to agree to combine in this confederation and surrender their individual sovereignties to it. And it was to have as its ruler Leopold II. "It is not a question of Belgian colonies," Stanley was told.

It is a question of creating a new State, as big as possible, and of running it. It is clearly understood that in this project there is no question of granting the slightest political power to the negroes. That would be absurd. The white men, heads of the stations, retain all power. They are the absolute commanders. . . . Every station would regard itself as a little republic. Its leader, the white man in charge, would himself be responsible to the Director-General of Stations, who in turn would be responsible to the President of the Confederation. . . . The President will hold his powers from the King.

Here then, bluntly put, was the outline of Leopold's plan to acquire his own African colony. If Stanley was in any doubt, a subsequent letter to him from Leopold reemphasized the central point:

The King, as a private person, wishes only to possess properties in Africa. Belgium wants neither a colony nor territories. Mr. Stanley must therefore buy lands or get them conceded to him, attract natives on to them, and proclaim the independence of his communities, subject to the agreement of the *Comité*.

There is no indication that Stanley found anything incredible about this idea. It is true that, knowing what he knew about African tribes, he did not think it would be an easy matter to get them to agree to any sort of political union among themselves, and in a letter to Brussels from Gibraltar he told Leopold as much. But, as his subsequent actions were to prove, he was certainly willing to give it his best try. In the context of the ideas of the times, which is to say Europe's ignorant concept that the African was too primitive to govern himself, Stanley could allow himself to believe that a confederation of this sort, ruled by a presumably enlightened European monarch, might serve to "pour the civilization of Europe into the barbarism of Africa." And so, sailing from Gilbraltar down the West African coast to the Congo's mouth, he could view his expedition as having

the novel mission of sowing along [the Congo's] banks civilized settlements, to peacefully conquer and subdue it, to remould it in harmony with modern ideas of National States, within whose limits the European merchant shall go hand in hand with the dark African trader, and justice and law shall prevail, and murder and lawlessness and the cruel barter of slaves shall for ever cease.

Stanley, with his company of 68 Zanzibaris, reached the Congo on August 14, 1879. The rest of his expedition which included a polyglot crew of Belgians, Danes, Englishmen, Americans, and Frenchmen, were already there, and some 100 additional local tribesmen were hired. The flotilla of boats—three steamers, *La Belgique, Espérance,* and *Royal;* a paddle boat, *En Avant;* two steel lighters; a screw launch; and a wooden whale boat—were launched on the estuary. The massive amount of supplies and equipment, contained in over 2000 packing cases, were loaded on the boats. And on August 21 the expedition started upriver, "an event," as Stanley would later write, "that may well be called the inauguration of a new era for the Congo basin."

Stanley's first job in opening this era was the establishment of a main base camp, the first in the string of stations he was to build up the Congo. For it, he selected a village called Vivi, located on a hill on the estuary's right bank, just across the river from the present-day seaport of Matadi and just below the Cauldron of Hell. And here he took the first step to implement Leopold's ambition to bring the Congo basin under his personal sovereignty. Gathering the chiefs of Vivi together for a palaver, Stanley announced,

I want ground to build my houses, for I am about to build many. . . . I want to go inland, and must have the right to make roads wherever it is necessary, and all men that pass by those roads must be allowed to pass without interruption. No chief must lay his hand on them. . . . You have no roads in your country. It is a wilderness of grass, rocks, bush. . . . If you and I can agree, I shall change all that.

This was the first of literally hundreds of such palavers Stanley was to have in the next five years, and out of that experience he was moved to write:

In the management of a bargain I should back the Congoese native against Jew or Christian, Parsee or Banyan, in all the round world. Unthinking men may perhaps say cleverness at barter, and shrewdness in trade, consort not with their unsophisticated condition and degraded customs.

Unsophisticated is the very last term I should ever apply to an African child or man in connection with the knowledge of how to trade. . . . I have seen a child of eight do more tricks of trade in an hour than the cleverest European trader on the Congo could do in a month. . . . Therefore when I write of the Congo native, whether he is of the Bakongo, Byyanzi, or Bateke tribes, remember to associate him with an almost inconceivable amount of natural shrewdness, and power of indomitable and untiring chaffer.

The palaver went on for two days before a bargain was finally struck. Under it, Stanley agreed to make a payment of £32 sterling worth of cloth down and £2 sterling worth of cloth per month. In return, the Vivi chiefs agreed to sell him a 20-square-mile tract for his base station, granted him the right-of-way through their domains for whatever roads he wanted to build, and ceded their sovereignty over those lands to Leopold's Comité. This bargain set the pattern for the hundreds of others to come and, considering the ghastly price that they would cost the peoples of the Congo, one has to wonder about the cleverness in barter and the shrewdness in trade with which Stanley credited them. It would seem that even the American Indians made a better deal with their sale of Manhattan Island. Nevertheless, Stanley tells us, "We had the usual scenes of loud applause" at the conclusion of the negotiations.

The real work began on October 1. The local chiefs and populace gathered along the river banks "in gay robes and bright colours." Stanley had tools unloaded from his boats and then he himself picked up a sledgehammer and, in a way of instructing his men, struck the first blow. A great cry of admiration arose from the crowds and, we are told, it was for this act that the Vivi chiefs "bestowed on me the title Bula Matari—Breaker of Rocks—with which, from the sea to Stanley Falls, all natives of the Congo are now so familiar." It was a title which in time would fall into disrepute because it was to become synonymous with the governors and governments of the terrible colony which Stanley was now setting out to found for Leopold. But when it was originally bestowed on Stanley it was meant to be one of great honor, and it was then one that was richly deserved. For in the course of the next fourteen months—from October 1879 to February 1881—Bula Matari and his rock-breaking crews built a road up from the river to the Vivi hill, erected a major settlement at the Vivi station, then cut a 52-mile road around the first set of rapids and cataracts to

Isangila (where the *Lady Alice* had been abandoned), and transported by man-hauled wagons a number of the boats and more than
50 tons of equipment and supplies up it.

It was a grueling period. Stanley reckoned, what with all the
marching and countermarching, that he walked 2352 miles to cover
the distance from Vivi to Isangila. Ravines had to be bridged, mangrove swamps crossed, mountains surmounted, forests felled. Fevers
and accidents killed 6 of the Europeans and 22 Africans, and scores of
the party had to be invalided out and scores more hired to replace
them. The work went on ten hours a day, six days a week, on a diet
consisting of beans and goat meat and bananas. Quarrels broke out
among the Europeans. Unused to commanding so many white men,
Stanley found himself repeatedly embroiled in petty disputes with
them over the terms of their contracts, the prerogatives of their ranks,
and the perquisites of their service.

Almost all of them [Stanley later wrote in disgust], clamoured for expenses
of all kinds, which included, so I was made to understand, wine, tobacco,
cigars, clothes, shoes, board and lodging, and certain nameless extrava-
gances. One said that he would not stay on the Congo unless these were
granted to him freely; another asserted that if he was expected to drive
a steam-launch unassisted, he must have higher pay. . . . Another—an
engineer—asserted that he was engaged as sub-commander of the expedition; that he . . . would never have ventured into Africa upon such a
miserable stipend; he had come for honour, reputation, fame; he would
write to the newspapers, etc. Another engineer complained that he was
not accorded his proper rank . . . he certainly was equal to the general
accountant of the expedition. The gentleman in charge of the smallest
steam-launch thought himself superior to the sailor in charge of a rowing
boat, and considered himself disparaged by being requested to mess at
the same table as the latter.

But most irritating of all for Stanley was the constant stream of harassing communications from Brussels.

Leopold was growing increasingly uneasy about Stanley's slow
progress up the river, for at the end of December 1879, when Stanley
had not yet completed the construction of Vivi station, Brazza had
reached Gabon and, traveling light, was advancing swiftly up the
Ogowe toward the Congo. Leopold was desperately afraid that Brazza
would reach the Stanley Pool and claim it for France before Stanley
got there. "Serious rivalry is threatening on the Upper Congo," he

wrote, "Brazza will try to follow the Alima down to its junction with the Congo and hopes to get there before you. There is not a moment to lose." And Strauch followed up with a barrage of goading, complaining letters. Stanley responded with undisguised annoyance; he explained in detail the nature of his problems, the reasons for delays, the obstinacy of some local chiefs, the ruggedness of the terrain, the bad weather.

These and similar facts have been repeated to you since February of this year. The truths they describe should by this time be clearly obvious, so that I am ashamed to iterate and repeat them. . . . My dear Colonel, when will you believe that this is the hardest-worked expedition that ever came to Africa?

And then addressing Leopold's anxieties, he wrote haughtily,

Relative to your information about the French Expedition going over from the Ogowe River to the Stanley Pool . . . I beg leave to say that I am not a party in a race for the Stanley Pool, as I have already been in that locality just two and a half years ago, and I do not intend to visit it again until I can arrive with my fifty tons of goods, boats, and other property. . . . If my mission simply consisted on marching for Stanley Pool, I might reach it in fifteen days, but what would be the benefit of it for the expedition or the mission that I have undertaken?

On November 7, 1880, a Sunday, while the road to Isangila was still under construction, Stanley returned to his tent camp to take the day off. Around ten o'clock in the morning, he tells us, after having bathed, shaved, "dressed as becomes the Sabbath," breakfasted, and sat down to do some Bible reading, one of the local tribesmen rushed into the camp

and coming to me hastily, he hands a paper to me, on which I find traced with a lead pencil the words "Le Comte Savorgnan de Brazza, *Enseigne de Vaisseau.* . . . An hour later the French gentleman appears, dressed in helmet, naval blue coat, and feet encased in a brown leather bandage, and a following of fifteen men, principally Gabonese sailors, all armed with Winchester repeating rifles. The gentleman is tall in appearance, of very dark complexion, and looks thoroughly fatigued. He is welcome, and I invite him into the tent, and a dejeuner is prepared for him, to which he is invited. I speak French abominably, and his English is not of the best, but between us we contrive to understand one another.

And what Stanley contrived to understand was that Brazza had beaten him to the Stanley Pool. The French party had not followed the Alima to the Congo, which, as we've seen, would have brought it to the river some 200 miles above the Pool. This time, with geographical information he hadn't possessed on his previous journey, Brazza was able to strike directly for the Pool from the Ogowe and reached its right bank at a village called Mbe—site of the present-day city of Brazzaville, capital of the Congo Republic—in September 1880, less than a year after setting off from the Gabon coast.

Preceded by a bugler and by the French flag [Brazza wrote in his diary], I went into the village. . . . In front of the door of the chief's compound, we stopped, to wait for the chief to receive me. . . . At last, preceded by his wives, Makoko appeared. . . . The chief wore a big cloth robe, big bracelets on his feet and arms, a woollen hat with tapestry which is fixed to his head with an iron pin in which two long feathers are stuck. . . . Chief Makoko sat on a big carpet four metres wide, in blue and red squares, in serge, on which there was a rug with a lion. He was leaning on a big cushion of red serge. Then the men who brought me in went to kneel before him, placing their hands on the ground by his carpet, very respectfully. . . . That finished, I told Makoko that . . . hearing he was chief of all the land between Ngampe and N'coma [the right bank of the Pool], I had come to see him to talk of the views of the French about the country, where they wished to establish themselves.

Brazza was improvising. At this point the French government had no intention of establishing itself on the Pool or, for that matter, anywhere else on the river, and regarded Brazza's expedition as purely exploratory. But he spent about a month with Makoko and persuaded the chief to give him permission to build a French "fort" at his village and to put his mark on a document, which Brazza had drawn up, placing Makoko's lands and peoples under the protection of the French flag. Although nowhere nearly as impressively substantial as Stanley's stations, roads, and treaties, this piece of paper and the mud-and-grass "fort" Brazza built were to be the basis for France's claim—when a few years later she felt compelled to make it—to the north shore of the Stanley Pool and laid the foundation for her future sub-Saharan African colony, French Equatorial Africa, including what is today Congo-Brazzaville, Gabon, the Central African Republic, Cameroon, and Chad.

Having established France's presence on the Congo, Brazza was anxious to get back to Paris and pressure the French government into ratifying his improvised treaty with Makoko. He had, by then, a fairly good idea what Stanley was up to and was worried that Stanley, with his far superior force, would undo his work for France on the river. But as he had traveled with a lightly equipped expedition, which after the year's journey was much thinned out and short of supplies, the best he could do to protect his claim was to leave behind the French flag, two Gabonese sailors under the command of a Senegalese sergeant by the name of Malamine, and a copy of the document signed by Makoko, which Malamine was instructed to show to any white man who came along. "I can't give you any money or supplies," Brazza told the Senegalese. "You have your men, your hands, and your firearms . . . don't abandon your post." Then Brazza departed. He didn't return to the coast via the Ogowe, however, but chose instead to follow the Congo down to the sea. It was then, on that Sunday morning in November, that he met Stanley.

Brazza spent two days at Stanley's road camp. Stanley behaved, if not exactly warmly, then altogether correctly toward his rival. He replenished Brazza's supplies, loaned him some porters and a guide to Vivi, and provided him passage aboard one of the Belgian steamers from Vivi to Banana Point, where Brazza could catch a mailboat back to Gabon. In return, Brazza was rather less correct in his behavior toward Stanley: he never once mentioned the treaty he had struck with Makoko or the "fort" he had built at Makoko's village or the claim to the Congo he was planning to press in the name of France. Stanley was to learn all this only when he reached the Stanley Pool, and that wouldn't be for another nine months.

First the road to Isangila had to be completed and then a second station built there. Then came an 88-mile stretch of fairly navigable waterway along which the boats and goods were sailed upriver to a village called Manyanga, where a third station was to be built. But just as Stanley was about to enter his first palaver with the Manyanga chiefs he came down with a severe attack of malaria. It put him out of action for over a month and at times was so bad that he was certain he would die. But huge doses of quinine in hydrobromic acid, mixed in Madeira wine, ultimately had their effect, and in mid-June 1881 he was up and about again. He concluded his negotiations for the Manyanga station, set his crews to building it, went off on a reconnaissance

trip upriver with a party of Zanzibaris, and on July 26, "we came to a square-browed hill, from whose high open summit we saw Stanley Pool far away in the hazy distance, like a blurred mirror obscured by gauze set in a gauze-covered frame of dark wood."

No sooner had he arrived, he tells us, than "we saw borne high up, a French tri-coloured flag approaching, preceded by a dashing Europeanised negro (as I supposed him to be, though he had a superior type of face), in sailor costume, with stripes of a non-commissioned officer on his arm." This was Malamine, the Senegalese sergeant whom Brazza had left behind. And with him were the two Gabonese sailors. Stanley tells us:

Malameen [sic], spoke French well, and his greeting was frank and manly. After a few words had been said on either side, he showed to me a paper, which duly translated, turned out to be a treaty, whereby a certain chief called Makoko ceded to France a territory extending . . . on the north bank of Stanley Pool, and which M. de Brazza notified, to all whom it might concern, that he took possession of the said territory in the name of France. Malameen knew a great deal about the transaction. Makoko had been generous, and for very trifling gifts had parted with a territory which, as far as I could learn, extended along the river about nine miles; the extent of it inland, was not indicated.

Later, when he heard of how Stanley had handled this situation, Leopold was furious. One of his key associates in his schemes, Baron Solvyns, the Belgian ambassador in London, declared:

Stanley is held to have been stupid to the highest degree. He ought to have begun by securing the most important part of the Congo, namely Stanley Pool, and one wonders why, as a Californian [this is in reference to Stanley's adventures as a young reporter in the wild and woolly American West], he did not think fit to lay his rival low with a rifle shot. He proved as gentle and tractable as those wretched savages that have to be civilized.

But naïve Stanley behaved gently in this instance and didn't think to shoot down Malamine and the two Gabonese sailors because he quite sincerely believed that his was a peaceful philanthropic and civilizing mission and it would be dreadfully out of character to take possession of lands by force. Besides, he didn't think that the treaty with Makoko was any good. Perfectly aware of the importance of securing the right as well as the left bank of the Pool, he crossed over two days after meeting Malamine and visited with some local chiefs

there to see whether they recognized Makoko's action. One of these, a certain Gamankono, told him of Brazza's visit: "He had a few men from Makoko with him; he sent word to all of us . . . to come and see him. We went and talked with him, but I heard nothing of selling or giving away a country." Stanley asked: "But is not Makoko the great king of all this country?" Gamankono responded: "There is no great king anywhere. We are all kings—each a king over his own village and land. Makoko is chief of Mbe; I am chief of Malima . . . no one has authority over another chief. Each of us owns his own lands. Makoko is an old chief; he is richer than any of us; he has more men and guns, but his country is Mbe." On the strength of this, Stanley entered into negotiations with Gamankono for the establishment of a station at Malima. At first it seemed to be going well, but when Brazza's man Malamine got wind of what Stanley was up to he started a propaganda campaign to undermine the effort.

What fables Malameen uttered about our fondness for the meat of tender children will never be published perhaps [Stanley tells us]; but the effect of what he told them was known when the crier beat his tom-tom in the night, and shouted out along the river bank and amid the huts of the scattered village that Gamankono . . . resolved that none of the people should speak with us, or sell us anything more. By morning this notice was magnified into a mediated rupture. A woman was caught selling fish to one of my people, and beaten by some of the villagers, while some bold fellows crowded around the tent with broad knives like butchers' cleavers in their hands. The good feelings of yesterday had become replaced by suspicion, if not hatred.

Stanley made three attempts to reopen negotiations with Gamankono, then finally abandoned the effort. He realized that serious trouble could be brewing and, though his force was certainly large enough to handle it, he was not prepared to press matters to a bloody conflict. His reputation for "scrapping instincts" was, as he well knew from his previous expeditions, bad enough without adding to it now, and so, for the moment at least, he decided to withdraw and concentrate his efforts on the Pool's left bank.

The chief he had to deal with there was called Ngalyema now but he was, in fact, the Itsi of Ntamo whom Stanley had met during his first passage down the Pool in 1877.

During the four years that had elapsed, he had become a great man . . . grown richer by ivory trade . . . and become powerful by investing his

large profits in slaves, guns, and gunpowder. . . . Success in life had considerably developed other ambitions. Itsi aspired to become known as the greatest chief of the country. . . . He was now about thirty-four years old, of well-built form, proud in his bearing, covetous and grasping in disposition, and, like all other lawless barbarians, prone to be cruel and sanguinary whenever he might safely vent his evil humour.

The initial meeting between Stanley and Ngalyema had all the flavor of a grand reunion. Blood brotherhood was proclaimed, toasts in palm wine were drunk, rich gifts were exchanged. Stanley gave the chief two donkeys, a large mirror, a gold-embroidered coat, brass chains, pieces of fine cloth, and a japanned tin box. Ngalyema in return presented Stanley with goats, pigs, loaves of bread, gourds of palm wine, and his own scepter, "a long staff, branded profusely with brass, and decorated with coils of brass wire, which was to be carried by me, and shown to all men as a sign that I was the brother of Ngalyema of Ntamo!" But the fraternal relationship began to fray badly as the palaver over a treaty for a station on the Stanley Pool dragged on for days and then weeks. Ngalyema very much resisted the idea of a permanent settlement of whites in his lands. At the same time, though, he coveted the white man's goods and throughout the palavering constantly demanded more. He wanted another japanned tin box, more and finer pieces of cloth, a Newfoundland dog Stanley had with him, iron boxes, cases of gin, guns, gunpowder, then Stanley's own best black suit, which the white man wore for ceremonial meetings with great chiefs. Stanley, realizing he was getting nowhere acceding to these ever-escalating demands, put an end to it by refusing to give Ngalyema the suit. The chief was infuriated; he broke off the palaver and stomped angrily out of Stanley's camp.

A few days later, word reached Stanley that Ngalyema had assembled a band of some 200 warriors armed with muskets and was returning to the camp in a foul mood. Anxious as ever to retain the peaceful, diplomatic character of his expedition, Stanley decided to deal with this threat by a clever ruse. He figured that Ngalyema would come into the camp, pretending to want to resume negotiations, then, with Stanley off his guard, attempt a surprise attack. Stanley's stratagem was to appear to be taken in by the chief, then spring an even greater surprise. He had all but twenty of his Zanzibaris hide in the trees and bushes outside the camp; the remaining twenty were told to lounge around in the camp, appearing very much off their guard and indeed

half asleep. Then he had a Chinese gong, which was used to awaken the party in the mornings and call them to breakfast, placed in front of his tent and instructed all his men, those hiding and those in the camp, not to make a move until they heard the gong sounded. Finally, he seated himself next to the gong and, pretending to read a book, awaited Ngalyema's arrival.

"Ngalyema was moody-browed, stiff, most unbrotherly in his responses to my welcome," Stanley tells us, "while I looked like one almost ready to leap into his arms with an irrepressible affection." Ngalyema, as Stanley had anticipated, pretended to resume the palaver. But after only a few moments he declared abruptly, "We have no objections to trade with white men if they come for trade, but you do not come for trade; therefore you cannot come to Ntamo. My brother must go back the way he came." Stanley persisted: "I only want to get near the river and build a village of my own, whither many white men will come to trade. White men will do you no harm." But Ngalyema cut him off. "Enough, enough," he shouted. "I say for the last time you shall not come to Ntamo; we do not want any white men among us." Ngalyema turned to leave. This was the crucial moment. The chief had been carefully appraising the seeming lack of preparedness in Stanley's camp, and Stanley braced himself for a sudden attack by Ngalyema's 200 warriors. But just then, exactly as Stanley had hoped, Ngalyema's attention was drawn to the Chinese gong.

"What is this?" he asked. "It is fetish," Stanley answered. "Bula Matari, strike this; let me hear it." "Oh, Ngalyema, I dare not," Stanley said; "it is the war fetish." "Beat it, Bula Matari, that I may hear the sound," the chief insisted. "I dare not, Ngalyema. It is the signal for war; it is the fetish that calls up armed men; it would be too bad." But Ngalyema continued insisting: "Strike—strike it, I tell you." So, with feigned reluctance, Stanley relented.

With all my force I struck the gong, the loud bell-like tone sounding in the silence caused by the hushed concentrated attention of all upon the scene, was startling in the extreme. . . . They had not recovered from the first shock of astonishment when the forms of men were seen bounding . . . and war-whooping in their ears . . . a stream of frantic infuriates emerged as though from the earth . . . a yelling crowd of demoniac madmen sprang out one after another, everyone apparently madder than his neighbor. The listless, sleep-eyed stragglers burst out into a perfect frenzy of action . . . there streamed into view such a frantic mob of

armed men, that to the panic-struck natives the sky and earth seemed to be contributing to the continually increasing number of death-dealing warriors.

Ngalyema's men dropped their weapons and fled the terrifying scene. Ngalyema himself dodged behind Stanley and, clutching him around the waist, cried, "Save me, Bula Matari; do not let them hurt me!" "Hold hard, Ngalyema," Stanley called out, "keep fast hold of me; I will defend you, never fear." Stanley shouted an order and his shrieking, jumping Zanzibaris suddenly formed into orderly ranks. With calm restored, Stanley let Ngalyema in on the joke. The chief, for all the humiliation he had suffered, took it in good spirits. His warriors returned to the camp somewhat sheepishly but

half-an-hour later they were all . . . retailing to one another, amid boisterous merriment, their individual experiences, while Ngalyema's loud laugh was heard above all others. . . . Over palm-wine we mutually swore faithful brotherhood and everlasting peace; and the doughty warriors of Ngalyema embraced in a fraternal manner the jolly good fellows of Bula Matari.

Stanley loved to tell this story and doubtless it played some role in softening up Ngalyema. But it took several more palavers and a number of touchy incidents with the chief before a treaty was signed that permitted Stanley to build a station on the Stanley Pool.

By the end of 1881, the road around the Livingstone Falls from the Manyanga station was completed and the paddle boat *En Avant* and a few of the smaller vessels, along with some 50 tons of supplies and equipment, were hauled up and launched on the Stanley Pool. Then, in the next four months, the fourth station was built between Ngalyema's village of Ntamo and another one called Kinshasa, on the left bank of the Pool. It was the largest and most elaborate so far, a neat settlement centered around a one-story wooden blockhouse, with broad streets, a promenade along the river front, gardens of banana trees and vegetables, prefabricated storehouses. And it was the most important. From here, with the river providing a navigable highway for more than 1000 miles, the entire Congo basin was accessible. Stanley named the station Leopoldville.

Until now, he had been totally occupied with the enormous task of building the wagon road around Livingstone Falls and erecting the four stations along it, but with the completion of Leopoldville he had

his first opportunity to do some exploration. So, taking a small party aboard the *En Avant,* he sailed up the river to the confluence with the Kwa, about 100 miles above the Pool, and exploring this tributary he discovered a lake which he also named for his employer. But his heart doesn't seem to have been in the work. He had, by this time, been in Africa close to three years. He was exhausted and edgy, his quarrels with his European assistants continued unrelentingly, and then he came down with a second severe bout with malaria, complicated by gastritis, which laid him low for more than a month. "I could not disguise from myself," he wrote in his journal, "that I was not now the hardy, energetic pioneer I once was." And so, when he had sufficiently recovered from his illness, he decided to go home.

Leopold was enraged. Under his contract, Stanley had two more years to serve in the Congo, and that was where the Belgian king wanted him. By this time Brazza had been back in France for four months and had been hard at work persuading the Paris government to ratify the treaty with Makoko and stake a colonial claim to the Congo. Leopold had done his best to forestall this. At one point he even tried to hire Brazza away from France, but Brazza, fiercely patriotic, turned him down, and all he accomplished by making the approach was to give Brazza more of an insight into Leopold's Congo scheme and more fuel for his own arguments in Paris. In a sharply sarcastic document to the French government, reporting on his meeting with Leopold, Brazza wrote:

Doubtless the King of the Belgians . . . gave his millions with the sole aim of civilizing the savage tribes. I thought, however, that there was a political idea at the back of the humanitarian sentiments of the King of the Belgians. I was far from blaming him for this, but that did not prevent me from having a political idea of my own, and mine was very simple. Here it is: if it was a good thing to get hold of the Congo, I would prefer that it was the French flag, rather than the Belgian "international" flag. that floated over this splendid African territory.

Although the French government continued to be extremely suspicious of any colonial venture in Africa, imperialist notions were certainly stirred up by Brazza's campaign. And in November 1882, shortly after Stanley's return to Europe, Paris finally agreed to ratify Brazza's treaty with Makoko and back him on a third expedition to the Congo.

Leopold saw all his plans for the Congo dangerously threatened by

this, and when he met with Stanley on the latter's return he is reported as saying, "Surely, Mr. Stanley, you cannot think of leaving me now, just when I most need you?" Stanley tried every argument.

I pointed out that by strenuous effort we had achieved more than we intended . . . five stations had been constructed, a steamer and sailing boat launched on the Upper Congo, while another small steamer and lighter maintained communications between the second and third station. A wagon-road had also been made at great expense and time between Vivi and Isangila, and Manyanga and Stanley Pool.

He also complained of the quality of his European assistants and the impossibility of continuing the work without better men. And he brought up the matter of his health, saying that a physician he had consulted had told him that he would be running a great risk returning to the Congo. But to no avail. Leopold promised to get Stanley an outstanding deputy to assist him in the work—Leopold, in fact, was then in communication with Charles "Chinese" Gordon, who had resigned his post in the Sudan and had expressed interest in going to work for the Belgian king—but he insisted that Stanley return to the Congo immediately.

It is indispensable that you should purchase for the *Comité d'Etudes* as much land as you can obtain, and that you should successfully place under the sovereignty of the *Comité*, as soon as possible and without losing a minute, all the chiefs from the mouth of the Congo to Stanley Falls.

So, in December 1882, Stanley was back on the Congo. To his despair, he saw that, in the short time he had been away, much of his work had fallen into disrepair because of the incompetence of his European assistants. Leopoldville was in the worst shape of all, with the streets and gardens overgrown and buildings falling into ruin. So he was forced to spend the next few months restoring order, traveling back and forth between the stations, getting crews working again, putting out fires. As he points out,

the day's notes of the 24th of March . . . will serve to show the desperate nature of my duties about this time. . . . Dispatched Lieutenant Orban with thirty-one men to Vivi, to hurry up by forced marches a caravan with brass rods. . . . Lieutenant Grang departs with sixty-four men . . . to haul the boilers of the Royal to Leopoldville. Received news today that a Mons. Callewart had been killed and decapitated at Kimpoko. . . . Second chief at Vivi declaims against asking him to manage the duties of

chief, second chief, and storekeeper, and declares he will not—suffer who may. His letter is remarkable for impoliteness, and is replete with gross accusations against a number of people. The officer in charge of the transport of a whaleboat from Vivi to Isangila, having fifty-eight men with him, writes that he cannot and will not carry the boat with such a limited number. The Chief of Manyanga writes that the chief in charge of Vivi is acting an "infamous comedy." . . . He also writes that Mons. Luksic, an Austrian marine officer, has committed suicide by shooting himself through the head.

Finally, in May 1883 Stanley was able to get on with the work of building new stations and signing more treaties, and with a party of 80 men and 6 tons of material aboard the *En Avant* and *Royal* (which, along with 6 other vessels had by now also been launched on the Pool), sailed upriver from Leopoldville. A station was built on the Equator, and in November, six years since he had last been there, he neared the site of the farthest outpost he proposed to build on the river, the Stanley Falls.

The area was strangely silent and deserted.

On my old map [Stanley noted], it is marked Mawembe, and was strongly palisaded; but now, though I looked closely through my glass, I could detect no sign of palisade or hut. . . . As we advanced we could see the poor remnants of banana groves; we could also trace the whitened paths from the river's edge leading up the steep bank, but not a house or living thing could be seen anywhere . . . all had vanished. When we came abreast of the locality, we perceived that there had been a late fire. The heat had scorched the foliage of the tallest trees, and their silver stems had been browned by it. The banana plants looked meagre; their ragged fronds waved mournfully their tatters, as if imploring pity. . . . Six years before we had rushed by this very place without stopping, endeavoring by our haste to thwart the intentions of our foes. . . . Surely there had been a great change! As we moved up the stream slowly, another singular sight attracted our gaze. This was two or three long canoes standing on their ends, like split hollow columns, upright on the verge of the bank. What freak was this, and what did the sight signify? A few miles higher up on the same bank we came abreast of another scene of desolation, where a whole town had been burnt, the palms cut down, bananas scorched, many acres laid level with the ground, and the freak of standing canoes on end repeated. In front of the black ruin there were a couple of hundred people crouched down on the verge of the bank, looking woefully forlorn and

cheerless, some with their hands supporting their chins, regarding us with stupid indifference, as though they were beyond further harm.

And then Stanley learned what had happened. The Arab slavers had come. Six years before, Tippoo Tib had watched Stanley vanish into the jungles down the Lualaba convinced that he would never be heard from again. But, when Tippoo Tib learned that he was, the thrall of horror that had kept Arab and European out of the region was broken and Tippoo Tib had sent his slaving gangs to follow in Stanley's footsteps and wreak their bloody havoc along the river he had opened up to them.

As Stanley continued the journey up to the falls, "every three or four miles we came in sight of the black traces of the destroyers. The charred stakes, upright canoes, poles of once populous settlements, scorched banana groves, and prostrate palms, all betokened ruthless ruin." At one point, "we detected some object, of a slaty colour, floating down stream." When a sailor on the *En Avant* turned it over with a boat-hook, "we were shocked to discover the bodies of two women bound together with a cord!" A few days later, they reached the camp of the Arab slavers.

There are rows upon rows of dark nakedness, relieved here and there by the white dresses of the captors. . . . On paying more attention to detail, I observe that mostly all are fettered; youths with iron rings around their necks, through which a chain . . . is rove, securing the captives by twenties. The children over ten are secured by three copper rings, each ringed leg broke together by the central ring. . . . The mothers are secured by shorter chains. . . . Every second during which I regard them the clink of fetters and chains strike my ears. My eyes catch sight of the continual lifting of the hand to ease the neck in the collar, or as it displays a manacle exposed through a muscle being irritated by its weight, or want of fitness. My nerves are offended with the rancid effluvium of the unwashed herds within this human kennel. The smell of other abominations annoy me in the vitiated atmosphere. For how could poor people, bound and riveted together by twenties, do otherwise than wallow in filth!

Stanley discovered that there were 2300 captives in this camp taken in raids on 118 villages, during which at least another 4000 Africans had been killed. "How many are wounded and die in the forest, or drop to death through an overwhelming sense of their calamities, we do not know," but Stanley reckoned that perhaps 33,000 die for every 5000 captured and enslaved.

And such slaves! they are females, or young children who cannot run away.
. . . Yet each of the very smallest infants has cost the life of a father and
perhaps his three stout brothers and three grownup daughters. An entire
family of six souls have been done to death to obtain that small, feeble,
useless child.

Stanley at first was seized by the impulse to revenge "these wholesale outrages" but then decided against it. "Who am I that I should
take the law into my hands and mete out retribution," he rationalized.
"I represented no constituted government, nor had I the shadow of
authority to assume the role of censor, judge and executioner." Moreover, he felt it was necessary to stay on good terms with the slavers,
who were clearly the true chiefs in the area. So he entered into
friendly negotiations with the Arabs and, without raising a word of
protest about their ghastly activities, went ahead and built his station
just below the last cataract of the Stanley Falls—which was to be
known as Stanleyville—and then returned downriver, making treaties
and building further stations along the way.

When he got back to Leopoldville, in January 1884, his five-year
contract with Leopold was just about up. He had hoped that by this
time Gordon would have come out to the Congo, but the British
general had decided to accept the post of governor-general of the
Sudan (where a year later he would die in the fall of Khartoum to the
Mahdists) and Leopold sent out a Belgian army officer, Lieutenant
Colonel Francis de Winton of the Royal Artillery, to relieve Stanley.
By the time he departed for Europe in June, Stanley had connected
the Congo with the sea and opened it to European exploitation. He
had signed some 400 treaties with local chiefs and brought them under
the *Comité's* sovereignty. And, while he had been unable to dislodge
the French from the north shore of Stanley Pool, he had secured the
whole of the river's left bank and most of its right bank from its
mouth well over 1000 miles into the interior to the Stanley Falls, and
had firmly built the foundation for Leopold's private Kingdom of the
Congo, a kingdom that was to be formally recognized as such by all the
great powers hardly more than half a year after Stanley returned to
Europe.

20

THE PERSONAL KINGDOM OF LEOPOLD II

Pretty much against their will, Leopold had forced the European powers to pay attention to Africa again. Stanley's stupendous pioneering work in the Congo on the Belgian king's behalf had not only awakened commercial interest in the potential of the great river basin but it also had stirred up political rivalries that had long lain dormant. The precarious balance of power in the continent was in danger of being upset, and what was to be known as the Scramble—that feverish seizure of colonies which was to bring all of Africa under European rule within the next three decades—was about to be set off.

France, albeit still reluctantly, was already moving in that direction. Even before Stanley returned to Europe, Brazza was back in Africa at the head of a third expedition to follow up on the treaty he had made with Makoko. Britain didn't like this a bit. The traditional Anglo-French rivalry had been sharpened perceptibly by Britain's recent occupation of Egypt (1882), and Britain viewed France's moves on the Congo as her way of striking back. To forestall the French, the British considered reactivating the formal claim that Cameron had made to the Congo basin. But the cabinet, under Lord Salisbury, was as opposed as ever to further colonial commitments in sub-Saharan Africa, and when another ploy came to hand for frustrating the French the cabinet grabbed for it.

Portugal provided the ploy. Awakened by Stanley's successes, the Portuguese now suddenly remembered their own centuries-old right to the Congo, based on the fact that they had discovered the river in the first place and that, in Angola and Cabinda, they currently had settlements near its estuary. At first it seemed that Portugal would do a deal with France, recognizing her claims to the Stanley Pool in

exchange for recognition of Portugal's claims to the estuary. But the British moved in and offered to conclude an Anglo-Portuguese treaty, under which Britain would recognize Portugal's sovereignty over the whole river, cutting out the French, in return for Portuguese guarantees of free trade for the British.

Before this treaty could be signed, the Germans entered the picture. United under Bismarck for a little more than a decade and recently triumphant in the Franco-Prussian War, Germany was developing imperial ambitions of its own and, in an eighteen-month period between the end of 1883 and 1885, established missions and trading posts in the Tanganyika region of East Africa, in South-West Africa, and in Togoland and the Cameroons on the West African coast. Bismarck didn't want to see either France or Britain, through its deal with Portugal, control the Congo. Until now, the river's mouth had been open to the trade of every nation without the customs or duties of any, and, if Germany wasn't to control it, then that was how Bismarck wanted to keep it.

All of this represented a threat to Leopold's personal ambitions in the Congo but, as the Belgian king was cunning enough to realize, it also presented an opportunity—an opportunity to play off the contending powers against each other to his own ultimate advantage. And that is what he did, setting out in every direction at once.

He went to the French and, harping on their fears of the British, offered them a secret deal under which, in exchange for their recognition of his association's sovereignty over the Congo, he promised not only to concede their claims on the river's right bank but also to turn over to them the rest of the Congo in the event (which most thought likely) that his own personal resources proved insufficient for him to hold on to it. At the same time, he launched a provocative campaign against Portugal, reminding the world, and especially the still-influential humanitarian interests in Britain, of the Portuguese's notorious record as slavers. And to further undermine Britain's support of Portugal, Leopold let it be known in British commercial circles that if his association controlled the Congo he was prepared to grant them the same most-favored-nation trading rights on the river that Portugal had promised. Then he went to Bismarck and, conveniently forgetting about his promises to Britain, blandly assured him that under his association's control the Congo would remain a free port open to trade of every nation, including especially Germany.

But perhaps Leopold's most ingenious tack was the one he used on the United States. Though America was relatively disinterested in the brewing African Scramble, the canny Belgian king knew that her backing would influence the European powers. Sending Chester Arthur, the U.S. president, laundered versions of the treaties Stanley had signed with the Congo chiefs (and making much of the fact that Stanley was an American), Leopold emphasized the apparent similarity between his Confederation of Free Negro Republics and the American-supported state of Liberia. He argued that his association, a nongovernmental, privately financed philanthropic organization, was intended to provide the administrative, political, and technical know-how for the fledgling independent black African state, just as a private American society was doing for Liberia. Once that state was able to handle these matters for itself Leopold and his association would fade out of the picture. So convincingly did Leopold argue this case that on February 25, 1884, the beguiled U.S. Congress passed a resolution recommending that the blue flag with gold star of Leopold's association be recognized as that of a friendly government, the Congo Free State.

By now it was clear that a serious crisis over the Congo was shaping up. But it was a crisis that, for the time being at least, the major powers were anxious to avoid. For, while each was intensely suspicious of the other's expansionist plans, none was really ready yet to run the political and military risks or make the huge capital investments in expanding itself. The situation had to be defused, and on November 15, 1884, with Bismarck taking the lead, an international conference was convened in Berlin to find a way of doing that. Fourteen nations attended—Austro-Hungary, Belgium, Denmark, Britain, Holland, Italy, Norway, Portugal, Russia, Spain, Sweden, Turkey, the United States, and the host, Germany—with Bismarck himself in the chair. Leopold's association had no official representation, but Stanley, with his special knowledge, attended in the role of a technical consultant.

The meeting dragged on for over three months, but its outcome was never really in much doubt. Leopold had done his work well. He had convinced each of the major contending powers that it could expect to gain if the issue was settled in his favor. As for the others, with the United States in the lead and again thanks to Leopold's clever propaganda, they had come to believe that the safest way to cool the crisis would be by taking the Congo out of the arena of big-power

confrontation and putting it under the trusteeship of a neutral, in-
offensive, and philanthropic agency such as Leopold's association professed itself to be. And so, on February 26, 1885, the Berlin Act on the
Congo was signed. Under it, France was given 257,000 square miles of
the river basin, including a substantial stretch along the right bank,
Portugal was granted sovereignty over 351,000 square miles, including
a stretch along the estuary's left bank; all the rest, comprising nearly
1 million square miles and encompassing perhaps 15 million people,
was officially recognized as the Congo Free State and handed over to
Leopold personally. To be sure, under the agreement, Leopold was
obliged to keep this vast area open to the trade of all nations, to
welcome there missionaries of all churches, and to confine the activities of his association to the administration of the new independent
black African state. But there was no doubt whatsoever that he personally, as a private individual, was to be its sovereign.

One feels obliged to reemphasize just what an incredible arrangement this was. The Congo had not been taken as a colony by Belgium,
nor was Leopold to rule it as the king of the Belgians. A brand-new
state had been created essentially by fiat out of a vast African territory,
unbeknown to the overwhelming majority of the people who lived
there. And a private individual, whom an even greater number of
those people had never heard of, had been given that state to own
personally and had been made its king. "The sovereignty of the Congo
is invested in the person of the Sovereign," a Belgian lawyer of the
time wrote. "His will can be resisted by no juridical obstacle whatsoever. Leopold II could say with more justification than Louis XIV
did: *L'état, c'est moi.*" Leopold himself, somewhat later, put it even
more bluntly: "My rights over the Congo are to be shared with none;
they are the fruit of my own struggle and expenditure . . .   the King
was the founder of the state; he was its organizer, its owner, its absolute sovereign." Perhaps an American newspaperman at that time
summed up this peculiar situation most succinctly: "He [Leopold]
possesses the Congo just as Rockefeller possesses Standard Oil."

With the establishment of the Congo Free State, Leopold dis-
carded the façade of the Association Internationale du Congo or the
Comité d'Études du Haut-Congo or whatever else people had been
misled into calling it. In its place, he erected his own personal government. The president of the new state and its "cabinet"—consisting of a
secretary of state, three secretaries-general and a treasurer-general—

were, like the king who appointed them, resident in Brussels (in all his life, Leopold was never to set foot in the Congo). Boma was selected as the capital (it would be later transferred to Leopoldville when the railroad was built to Stanley Pool), and there Leopold sent a governor-general, a vice governor-general, and a commander-in-chief of a Congo gendarmerie, known as the Force Publique. The state itself was divided into fourteen districts, each with a Leopold-appointed district commissioner in command. In turn, each district was divided into zones, each zone into sectors, and each sector into posts, with each again in the charge of a Leopold appointee, and each, it goes without saying, a white man.

Leopold's first task was to establish the authority of the new Free State as widely and as unmistakably as possible throughout the Congo River basin. The delegates at the Berlin conference might have blithely drawn a red circle around a vast territory in the heart of Africa and handed it over to Leopold, but at the time of its creation the Congo Free State in reality consisted of only the eight stations Stanley had built along the river itself from Vivi to Stanley Falls. All the rest of the basin remained pretty much terra incognita, unsurveyed rain forests for the most part, where few if any Europeans had ever gone (Cameron and some Portuguese traders being the only exceptions) and where few if any black men had ever heard of Leopold as the Belgian king, let alone as the new Congo king. Thus, expeditions had to be sent out, the numerous tributaries of the Congo explored and mapped, the commercial potential of the forests surveyed, administrative stations and military garrisons built, hundreds more treaties with local chiefs signed, the state's borders defined and secured, its gold-starred blue flag planted everywhere.

One place that Leopold would have dearly loved to plant that flag was on the Nile. His ambition was to extend his state's northeastern frontier across the Lualaba into the great lakes region and take possession of the southern Sudan itself. And barely a year after the Berlin conference he thought he saw a chance to realize that ambition.

The opportunity arose as a result of the fall of Khartoum, the death of General Gordon, and the occupation of the Sudan by the fanatical Mahdists in 1885. The catastrophe had caused a furious outcry in England, the public and the newspapers blaming the British government for failing to get a rescue expedition to Khartoum in time to save the heroic Gordon from his grisly martyrdom (he was decapi-

tated and his head paraded around on a pole in the Mahdi's camp).
Queen Victoria herself had joined in the protest: "That the promises
of support [to Gordon] were not fulfilled—which I so frequently and
constantly pressed on those who asked him to go—is to me *grief inex-
pressible!* indeed, it has made me ill." But then, just as it seemed that
the government must fall over the issue, it got a chance to redeem
itself. In the summer of 1886, a startling letter arrived in London by
way of Zanzibar. It was from a certain Eduard Schnitzer, a remarkable
German physician, who had disguised himself as a Turk, converted to
Islam, taken the name Emin Pasha, and been appointed by Gordon to
the post of governor of Equatoria, the most southerly province of the
Sudan. And what his letter revealed was that, although all the other
provinces had fallen in the wake of Gordon's death, he and his garrison were still holding out against the Mahdi's hordes at Lado, near
present-day Juba, on the Upper Nile.

Instantly, Emin Pasha became the hero of the hour; he became the
surrogate for the martyred Gordon, and the cry went up that he must
be saved. An Emin Pasha Relief Committee was formed. Tens of
thousands of pounds sterling were subscribed for an expedition. An
army of hundreds of riflemen was to be recruited, a dozen British
army officers and gentlemen volunteered for the mission, and, what
seemed a most obvious and natural choice, Stanley was invited to
head it.

Stanley, however, was still in the employ of the Belgian king. Although he had been relieved of his duties in the Congo and had spent
the last couple of years lecturing, Stanley continued to receive an
annual salary of £1000 sterling from Leopold as a retainer on his
services. So, before he could accept the command of the Emin Pasha
Relief Expedition, he was obliged to get Leopold's permission. Leopold was only too happy to grant it. He had been looking for an
excuse to get to the Nile, and, in fact, if the British hadn't beaten him
to it he would have put Stanley in charge of a rescue mission to Emin
Pasha on his own. The British-sponsored expedition, with his own
employee at its head, would serve his purposes just as well, and at a
secret meeting in Brussels he instructed Stanley what he was to do. In
the first place, he was to lead the expedition to Equatoria not from the
East African coast, which would have been the obvious and easier
route, but from the West African coast up the Congo River to the
Stanley Falls, then across the Lualaba northeast through the Ituri rain

forests to Lake Albert and from there along the Nile to Lado. Leopold was prepared to provide the expedition with all the resources of the Congo Free State—transport by its boats on the river and use of its stations along the banks—because he wanted to demonstrate the geographical integrity and easy accessibility between the Congo and the southern Sudan and by that make a case for his claim to it. What's more, once he reached Emin Pasha, Stanley was instructed to offer him, in Leopold's name, the governorship of an equatorial province of the Congo Free State.

In January 1887, Stanley set off on what was to be his last (he would be nearly 50 when he returned) and most difficult African adventure. It took very nearly three years; and it covered well over 5000 miles. It cost the lives of some 400 members of the party, who suffered all the horrors of disease and starvation and calamitous accident and all the terrors of attacks by hostile tribesmen. The expedition experienced mass desertions and violent mutinies and indulged in the worst sort of brutalities, including fatal floggings and summary executions, to contain them; it became lost time and again in the lethal jungles; it saw men go mad, murder one another, and turn into cannibals. And, in the end, it accomplished nothing.

Emin Pasha refused all offers Stanley made him on Leopold's behalf. What made the enterprise even more ludicrously pointless, Emin Pasha didn't want to be rescued. His letters to London had been meant to get him supplies and reinforcements so that he could remain in Equatoria, not be carried out of it. But by the time Stanley's ravaged column reached him it was in such desperate straits that it had only a slim chance of surviving itself, let alone providing support against the Mahdists. So Stanley was forced to rescue Emin Pasha against his will, taking him virtually as a captive down to the coast. But it was to the East African coast that he took him. On top of everything else, the expedition wound up demonstrating exactly the opposite of what Leopold had intended. The Sudan was in fact so utterly inaccessible by way of the Congo that Stanley didn't dare return from Lado the way he had come. Then, as the final irony of the entire debacle, on arriving at Bagamoyo, Emin Pasha fell and fractured his skull and had to be hospitalized on the spot. So Stanley, after all his frightful experiences, didn't even have the satisfaction of returning to Europe with the hero he had saved.

Leopold was greatly disappointed, but he did not have the luxury

to dwell on his disappointment. For, although he would never entirely give up his ambition of extending the Congo Free State's northeastern border to the Nile, by the time Stanley returned from the abortive Emin Pasha expedition Leopold was engaged in a desperate struggle to hang on to the state's southwestern border in Katanga.

The year was 1890, the Scramble by now was on in earnest, and the British, in the person of one of the most ruthlessly successful empire builders of all, Cecil Rhodes, had shed their reluctance about getting involved in Africa and had taken the lead in the acquisition of colonies. Rhodes, who was at this time prime minister of Cape Colony and head of the crown-chartered British South Africa Company, sent his agents always deeper into the interior, building trading posts and mission stations, signing treaties with local chiefs, and laying claim to territories that would become Southern Rhodesia and Northern Rhodesia (today's Zambia), and then, ignoring the Berlin Act in the piratical spirit of the Scramble, on into the headwaters region of the Lualaba and Katanga. Leopold's protests to London were of no avail, and he realized that the only way to forestall Rhodes was to occupy Katanga and establish an unchallengeable Congo Free State military and political presence there, on the reasonable assumption that the British wouldn't allow Rhodes, whatever else they permitted him, to drag them into a war in the depths of Africa.

This, however, proved to be a far more difficult thing to do there than anywhere else in the Congo River basin. For at the time Katanga was under the rule of a wily, sophisticated, and powerful paramount chief by the name of Msiri. Msiri had amassed a huge fortune trading in ivory, copper, and slaves with the Portuguese on both the east and west coasts, had bought guns, assembled a great army, and had united the petty chiefdoms of the savanna plateau under his control in a series of tribal wars. His capital was at the village of Bunkeya (near today's city of Likasi), virtually at the center of the Lualaba watershed, and though his rule was despotic and unpopular it was unchallenged. He was universally acknowledged as the king of Katanga, and it was clear that any white man who hoped to possess the region would have to treat with him.

British missionaries had been the first to reach Bunkeya, and while they found Misri "a thorough gentleman" they failed to convert him to Christianity. Rhodes's agents had little better luck. At first it seemed that he might be willing to place his territories under British

protection, but when he read the fine print of the treaty he balked. He couldn't see any reason why he should sign away his sovereignty for a few bits of colored cloth and some cases of gin. Leopold, however, had no intention of engaging in this sort of sham diplomacy. He was determined to secure Katanga either by cajolery or force, and he sent three well-equipped military expeditions to Bunkeya to impress this fact on Misiri. The first built a garrison near the king's capital, the second, arriving a few months later, reinforced it, and the third, coming in from the east coast, marched straight into Bunkeya itself and, without consultation, hoisted the gold-starred blue flag of the Congo Free State over Msiri's palace.

The Katanga king could see he was in trouble and retreated with his court to a neighboring village. Leopold's soldiers pursued him, brought him back to Bunkeye, and presented him with the treaty he was to sign ceding the sovereignty of his kingdom to the Congo Free State. A brief period of negotiations ensued. Misiri made one last desperate attempt to hold out, trying to amend the treaty's terms in his favor. But Leopold was impatient. The order from Brussels came down. Under mysterious circumstances, a Free State officer provoked a quarrel with the king of Katanga, and, using it as a pretext, shot Misiri dead in his palace and installed in his place a pliant puppet chief, who hastily put his mark on every document presented to him. With these, which he showed in the capitals of Europe, Leopold secured his hold on Katanga.

He was now free to turn his attentions once again to his northern and eastern frontiers. He was still dreaming of gaining a foothold on the Nile, and in the course of the next decade he would send expedition after expedition there to stake his claim. Lobbying relentlessly in Europe, he would make one arrangement after another with the British, French, and Germans in an effort to cut himself in on the regions of the Nile watershed in the Sudan, Uganda, and Tanganyika which they were partitioning out among themselves in the ferociously escalating Scramble. But his most pressing problem in the early 1890s was the challenge to the sovereignty of the Congo Free State then posed by the Arabs. For Tippoo Tib's ivory and slave hunters, following Stanley down the Lualaba from Nyangwe, had established themselves in the forests of the northern and eastern frontiers and formed a separate state within Leopold's state, interposed between the Upper Congo and the Upper Nile.

In the first years of the Congo Free State, Leopold tried a policy of coexistence and alliance with the Arabs. At one point he went so far as to appoint Tippoo Tib governor of the Stanley Falls district and enlist his aid in extending the state's borders to the Nile, encouraging the Arab to establish trading stations northeastward from Stanley Falls to the southern Sudan. But this coexistence couldn't last. The Arabs were in direct commercial competition with Leopold for the riches of the Congo River basin. And, with their highly sophisticated methods of organizing, administering, and operating their trading enterprises, they were also in direct conflict with Leopold's attempts to establish the state's political authority over its population. Tippoo Tib's satraps would not take orders from Leopold's officers nor were they willing to accept the Free State's control over their operations. What's more, the alliance was a constant source of embarrassment for Leopold in Europe. In teaming up with the last of the world's active slavers, Leopold made a public farce of the ostensible high-minded character of the state. So, professing moral indignation over their slaving but aiming at ending their political and commercial rivalry, Leopold decided to drive the Arabs out of his realm.

The Arab war was just another grisly episode in the unredeemingly grisly history of Leopold's Free State. The armies on both sides were made up largely of African tribesmen, and for the most part these Africans came from the cannibal tribes of the Lualaba forests. Stories are told of the orgies of man-eating that occurred after each battle, of how the fallen were scavenged and consumed on the battlefields, of how the captives while still living were prepared for the pot (arms and legs were broken and the prisoners were submerged in streams chin-deep, since suffering was believed to tenderize the meat for the cooking), of how some European officers developed a taste for human flesh. Both sides were undoubtedly equal in the performance of these atrocities, but in everything else Tippoo Tib's army was no match for Leopold's. The Free State's Force Publique was armed with the latest machine guns and artillery, and in battle after battle against the Arab muskets, it drove Tippoo Tib's forces back up the Lualaba. In March 1893 Nyangwe was taken, a few months later the great Arab center at Ujiji fell, and by early 1894 the war was over.

All this cost a great deal of money and, although Leopold was one of the richest men in Europe—he had made a fortune speculating in Suez Canal shares, among other things—even he didn't have enough,

personally, to finance expeditions of exploration, build stations and pay their staffs, raise armies and fight wars. And he certainly didn't have the huge sums of investment capital needed for the development program—the construction of that railway around the Livingstone Falls, for example—to exploit the commercial potential of the Congo River basin. Such sums could only be had on the traditional European money markets and, at the outset, obtaining them proved to be a difficult task. It would take a few years before any of the several Congo bond issues Leopold floated would be subscribed, before any of the railway and mining syndicates he tried to form actually came into existence, before the commercial trading companies and merchant bankers that he approached were willing to take the risk and invest in his Congo enterprise. In the meantime, his personal fortune was suffering a heavy drain. Indeed, it got so bad that he is said to have melodramatized his problems by ostentatiously selling off the livery of his servants, cutting out courses at his banquets, and dunning fellow royalty for money at state funerals. His wife is said to have wailed, *"Mais, Léopold, tu vas nous ruiner avec ton Congo."* Clearly something had to be done, some other source of revenue had to be found to tide him over the first hard years, and, to his everlasting infamy, Leopold decided to find it in the Congo itself.

He had toyed with this approach before. While Stanley was still rock-breaking his way up to Stanley Pool, Leopold had suggested that European traders and missionaries be required to pay tolls for the use of the roads and stations he was building. But Stanley dissuaded him. "The mere rumour of such a course in Europe," he warned, "would bring general condemnation on our heads." Obviously, the association's philanthropic image would be damaged and just when Leopold was presenting that image as his best argument why the European powers should let him have the Congo. But now that he had it—and in view of what it was costing him to hold on to it—he was less concerned about preserving that image. So, in a clear violation of the Berlin Act, which had mandated him only to administer and police the new state, he put his Congo governmental apparatus into the business of doing business. All Free State officials—from the governor-general down to the lowliest post commander—became his personal trading agents.

He started modestly enough—and, characteristically, in secret—with the concept of *terres vacantes.* What constituted vacant or un-claimed land was left deliberately vague; presumably it represented

areas where Africans didn't actually live, but it could include regions where they might hunt or farm. In any case that land was designated Free State property and Free State officials were authorized, and indeed encouraged, to engage in trade there in competition with private operators. This worked out quite nicely. One official, for example, discovered that ivory could be bought from Africans for 82 centimes a pound and sold in Liverpool for 12 francs 50 centimes, a profit, before deducting transport costs, of over 1500 percent. These transactions were meant to be secret, but the private traders of course were aware of them and they protested to their governments, arguing that besides being in violation of the Berlin Act, Leopold's officers enjoyed a grossly unfair advantage in being able to bring the full force of the state apparatus and the Force Publique into the trade. But the European powers took no notice. So, undeterred in this first experiment, Leopold got greedier. In 1891 and 1892, he issued a series of decrees—also in secret—which laid the foundation for a hugely lucrative scheme by which he could realize the maximum profits from his Congo enterprise.

The Free State was divided into two separate economic zones. The first of these was a free trading zone, which was open to the exploitation of private entrepreneurs of all nations. To attract them and their much-needed development capital, Leopold instituted a system of monopoly concessions in this zone. Under varying term leases (ten to fifteen years seems to have been average), investors were guaranteed exclusive commercial rights over a specific service or industry, product or region. And the investors responded. With the Scramble heating up, Europe's financiers and merchants, eager to get in on the profits that Africa promised, now began flocking to the Congo. An international syndicate was formed to build the railway around Livingstone Falls (it was completed and the first locomotive reached Leopoldville in 1898). The Anglo-Belgian India-Rubber Company was granted monopoly rights over vast tracts of rubber-rich forest regions; other concessionaires took over the trade in ivory, in hides, in palm oil, in forestry products. Union Minière du Haut-Katanga was created to develop the mineral wealth of Katanga, a consortium was organized to exploit the diamond fields of the Kasai, and in all of these trusts and corporations Leopold contrived to retain control of 50 percent of the voting stock.

But this Free Trading Zone, unbeknown to most, comprised less

than half, probably not more than a third, of the land area of the Free State. All the rest, as a natural extension of the *terres vacantes* concept, was designated Domaine Privé, the private property of the state. And, in this zone, the state and only the state had the right to do business.

Government officials ran the state's trading monopolies, and in one of his secret decrees Leopold made it clear that their paramount duty—that is, above their administrative, military, or judicial duties— was the collection of revenue and the production of profits. As an incentive, the officials' wages consisted of direct annual salaries (pegged very low) and commissions based on how much profit their post or sector or district made for the state. To ease the job of making money, yet another secret decree stipulated not only that the native populations could not sell their products to any trader except the state's agents but that they *had* to sell to them. A quota system was installed: every village or tribal group was required to sell so much ivory or rubber to the state and, as the state held the monopoly, sell it at the state's fixed price. Failure to meet the quota was a crime punishable under the state's laws and enforced by the Force Publique. What's more, under the euphemism of taxation, Leopold also introduced a system of forced labor. Every tribal grouping of forty people was obliged to donate four people a year on a full-time basis to serve the government—one of whom was taken into the military—and ten other people part time for public-works projects. In addition, each such community was also required to provide food for the state's local post.

The money generated by this system—and it soon became substantial—went into the treasury of the Congo Free State and was used to pay its administrative and operating expenses. As this halted the drain on his personal fortune, Leopold was satisfied with it for a while. But then he became greedier still. In 1893 he created a third economic zone. It was cut out of the Free Trade Zone, centered around Lake Leopold II and Lake Tumba in the heart of the river basin, and was five times the size of Belgium. This he designated the Domaine de la Couronne. Here all the same rules and regulations as in the Domaine Privé applied and all the same operational methods were used, but the profits generated in the Crown Domain went not into the Free State treasury but into Leopold's pocket.

It is impossible to know how much money Leopold made out of the Congo. All sorts of ways have been tried to come up with a realis-

tic number. For example, one source has pointed out that the state's exports of rubber soared from 241 tons, worth 1 million francs, in 1893, to 6000 tons, worth 47 million francs, in 1906, and Leopold owned more than half of that rubber. Another source has estimated that in a ten-year period the Crown Domain alone yielded a clear profit of over 90 million francs, and all of that went into Leopold's pocket. Still another way to look at it is that the value of each share of the Anglo-Belgian India-Rubber Company, of which Leopold owned 50 percent, rocketed in the first six years from about £5 sterling to £35. Putting it in dollars, one source has calculated that Leopold cleared at least $20 million in pure profit in the twenty years he owned the Congo. What we know for sure is that during this period he bought $13 million worth of real estate in such choice resort areas as the Riviera, Belgian beaches, German spas, and the French Midi; that he built palaces, chased young girls, kept mistresses, and won the sobriquet the King of Maxim's; and that when he died, in 1909, his will was probated at $80 million. The point is of course that he made an incalculable fortune out of his personal kingdom before it was finally taken away from him. And it was finally taken away because of that fortune—and the way he had made it.

In order to get the Congo in the first place, Leopold had kept secret his true intentions, and now he tried to keep secret what he was doing there in order to hold on to it. Independent explorers and geographers were discouraged. Casual travelers were barred. He carefully selected his officials and agents from the ranks of his most abject supporters and from the most disreputable elements in Europe—mercenaries, soldiers of fortune, adventurers, and profiteers, whom nothing was likely to shock. He even tried to control the missionaries who were allowed to enter his kingdom, giving preference to Belgian Catholics on whose loyalty he believed he could count, while hanging the threat of expulsion over the others if they did anything to cross him. But the secret he was trying to keep couldn't be kept; the things that were happening in the Congo under his personal rule were far too atrocious even for his most loyal priests, his most abject supporters, his most immoral agents, to keep from the eyes of the world.

The atrocities centered primarily on rubber, which, with the newly rising demand for bicycle and then automobile tires, was then the single most valuable product of the Congo. At the time, rubber was not cultivated on plantations; it still grew in the wild, and to

harvest it natives went into the forests, located the rubber trees amid the profusion of other species, tapped their trunks, waited for the slowly running sap to collect, then brought it back to the state's agents. The work was hard and unrewarding, given the low prices the state monopoly paid for the latex, and there was very little enthusiasm for it. Thus, as often as not, the state-imposed quotas—which constantly escalated as the profits to be made in rubber escalated—were not met. So the state resorted to coercive methods.

As early as 1890, reports about these methods began to reach the outside world. They came at first from English Baptist missionaries, who were initially rather tentative in fear of Leopold's wrath, but as time went on they grew bolder and were joined by other missionaries, including the Belgian priests, and then even by officials of the state apparatus. And what they told of were the most unspeakable, inhuman cruelties. The soldiers of the Force Publique—recruited for the most part from the cannibal tribes of the Lualaba—were used to enforce the rubber quotas. Like their commanders, they were paid low salaries but handsome commissions based on how well they did their jobs—that is to say, how much rubber they coerced out of the local population—and they were taught by their white officers that terrorism was the most efficient way of getting it done. "I have the honour to inform you," a district commissioner in the late 1890s wrote to his sector and post commanders, "that you must succeed in furnishing 4000 kilos of rubber every month. To this effect I give you *carte blanche.* . . . Employ gentleness first, and if they [the natives] persist in not accepting the imposition of the State employ force."

One common use of force was the taking of hostages, usually women and children, who could be bought back by their husbands and fathers only with stipulated amounts of rubber. To make sure that they would be bought back, the conditions under which these hostages were held were awful. "In stations in charge of white men," an American missionary wrote, "one sees strings of poor, emaciated women, some of them mere skeletons . . . tramping about in gangs with a rope around their necks and connected by a rope one and a half yards apart." Brutal floggings, often fatal, with a bullwhip called the *chicotte* were freely meted out to encourage the rubber collections. If a village failed or was slow in meeting its quota, a punitive raid was staged, accompanied by rape, plundering, and wanton killing, and any protest or rebellion was dealt with by mass executions. A white officer

described such a raid: "We fell upon them all and killed them without mercy . . . he [a Monsieur X who was in command] ordered us to cut off the heads of the men and hang them on the village palisades, also their sexual members, and to hang the women and children on the palisade in the form of a cross." As the American missionary wrote in 1896, "War has been waged all through the district of the Equator, and thousands of people have been killed and twenty-one heads were brought back to Stanley Falls, and have been used by Captain Rom [the station commander] as a decoration around a flower-bed in front of his house."

One particularly widespread punishment was the cutting off of hands.

If the rubber does not reach the full amount required the sentries attack the natives. They kill some and bring the hands to the Commissioner [a Danish missionary wrote]. That was about the time I saw the native killed before my own eyes. The soldier said, "Don't take this to heart so much. They kill us if we don't bring the rubber. The Commissioner has promised us if we have plenty of hands he will shorten our service." These were often smoked to preserve them until they could be shown to the European officer.

For the most part, the hands (and, for that matter, the cut-off heads) served as proof that the Force Publique soldiers were doing their job, that they were actually killing people who failed to meet the rubber quotas and not just going off into the forests and shooting off their bullets in pretense. But horribly often the hands were taken from the living.

The scenes I have witnessed [another American wrote], have been almost enough to make me wish I were dead. The soldiers are themselves savages, some even cannibals, trained to use rifles. . . . Imagine them returning from fighting rebels; see on the bow of the canoe is a pole, and a bundle of something on it. These are the hands (right hands) of sixteen warriors they have slain. "Warriors?" Don't you see among them the hands of little children and girls? I have seen them. I have seen where the trophy has been cut off, while the poor heart beat strongly enough to shoot the blood from the cut arteries at a distance of fully four feet.

The baskets of severed smoked hands, set down at the feet of the European post commanders, became the symbol of Leopold's Congo Free State. In the degenerate, brutalized atmosphere of the Congo

forests—the atmosphere out of which Joseph Conrad created that chill-ing masterpiece *Heart of Darkness* and the malevolently evil figure of Kurtz, a station agent in the vicinity of Stanley Falls—the collection of hands became an end in itself. Force Publique soldiers brought them to the stations in place of rubber; they even went out to harvest them instead of rubber. Hands took on a value in their own right. They became a sort of currency. They came to be used to make up for short falls in rubber quotas, to replace the food that hadn't been delivered to the stations or the people who were demanded for the forced-labor gangs; and the Force Publique soldiers were paid their bonuses on the basis of how many hands they collected. A native might save his life by surrendering his right hand, but more often than not the harvesting of hands meant wholesale murder, and there are estimates that in the twenty years of Leopold's personal rule at least 5 million people were killed in the Congo.

Leopold mounted a massive propaganda campaign to counter these devastating reports. He created a phony Commission for the Protection of the Natives, which ostensibly was to track down what he maintained might be a few isolated cases of atrocities and have them corrected. He set up a secret press bureau, whose job was to influence and buy off prominent newspapers and newspapermen. He imputed ulterior motives to his accusers, claiming, for example, that the English were attacking his rule in the Free State because they wanted to take it over for themselves or that the Protestant mission-aries were sending out those reports in order to undermine the Catho-lics. And in the Congo itself he used all his powers to terrorize to prevent the reports from getting out. An Italian officer in the Force Publique, for example, who finally had become disgusted with what he had been forced to participate in, discovered that a white man wasn't free to quit Leopold's service.

If he insists [he reported], and leaves his station, he can be prosecuted for desertion, and in any case, will probably never get out of the country alive, for the routes of communication, victualling stations, etc., are in the hands of the Administration, and escape in a native canoe is out of the question—every native canoe, if its destination be not known and its move-ments chronicled in advance from post to post, is at once liable to be stopped, for the natives are not allowed to move freely about the con-trolled water-ways.

As these horror stories circulated ever more widely and the evi-

dence supporting them mounted always more irrefutably, Europe, and especially Britain, at last became exercised. And by the turn of the century, something amounting to a concerted political and propaganda campaign against Leopold's Congo misrule was underway, spearheaded by such men as H. R. Fox Bourne, Herbert Samuel, John Holt and Edmund D. Morel.

Morel had started his career as a clerk at the Liverpool shipping line of Elder Dempster, which imported rubber from the Congo Free State, and it was while in this relatively lowly job that he first became suspicious of what was going on in the Belgian king's personal realm. Specifically, what Morel noted was that, although the Free State had ostensibly been created and given to Leopold for the humanitarian purpose of bringing the benefits of European civilization to the peoples of the river basin, in fact very little if any European goods were exported to the Congo in exchange for the increasingly huge quantities of rubber that were being taken out. This statistic alone—the Free State's disastrous export-import imbalance—forced Morel to draw the only possible conclusion: that Leopold was stealing the Congo blind. Turning into a muckraking, investigative journalist, Morel set about substantiating this contention. He scoured the ledgers of other shipping firms and those of the Congo monopoly trusts for further damaging statistics; he collected fresh eye-witness accounts of Leopold's atrocious *modus operandi* from missionaries and disaffected Free State agents. And he published what he found in inflammatory newspaper articles and in such devastating polemical books as *Red Rubber, The Congo Scandal* and *King Leopold's Rule in Africa.*

John Holt, a Liverpool merchant who headed one of the largest West African trading companies of the time, took a keen interest in Morel's work. His interest, it is only fair to point out, wasn't entirely philanthropic. Like all British merchants, Holt was extremely annoyed at being shut out of the Congo's rich trade by Leopold's monopolistic practices and was eager to find a way of breaking the Belgian king's hold on the river basin. So, not surprisingly, he encouraged and supported Morel in every way he could, publishing Morel's articles in his company's newspaper, *West Africa,* and helping Morel start his own newspaper, *West African Mail.* At the same time, he lobbied energetically among his fellow merchants and succeeded in getting the British Chambers of Commerce to pass a reso-

lution calling on the British government to launch an inquiry into the abuses in the Congo Free State.

Herbert Samuel, a Liberal party member of Parliament, following up on this line of attack, carried the anti-Leopold campaign into the House of Commons. Again and again he introduced the subject for formal debate and, using Morel's writings in support of his arguments, stressed Leopold's violation of the Berlin Act in not allowing free trade in the Congo and pointed out the huge, often 500 percent profits being made by Leopold's monopoly concessions and the atrocious methods by which they were making them. H. R. Fox Bourne entered the fight as the leader of the Aborigines Protection Association—the direct descendant of England's venerable anti-slavery and abolitionist movement—and he brought all the righteous fervor and propaganda techniques of that movement to the Congo cause, writing such blistering tracts as "Civilization in Congoland: A history of wrongdoing" and staging, along with Morel and Holt, fiery public rallies.

All this together ultimately aroused public opinion to a furious pitch. But unquestionably the fatal blow to Leopold's personal kingdom was delivered by Roger David Casement.

"A tall, handsome man of fine bearing," Herbert Ward, the sculptor, who knew him in his Congo days, wrote of Casement; "mere muscle and bone, a sun-tanned face, blue eyes and black curly beard. A pure Irishman he is, with a captivating voice and a singular charm of manner. A man of distinction and great refinement, high-minded and courteous, impulsive and poetical."

Casement's greatest popular fame, of course, came years later as one of the authentic martyr-heroes of the Irish rebellion. Then, just before the Easter Uprising of 1916, having gone to Berlin on the quixotic errand of trying to secure armed assistance from the Germans for the Irish independence movement, he was arrested by the British, tried for treason and hanged. But before he met this tragic and romantically futile destiny, he performed a service to the peoples of the Congo far more important than any he ever performed for the Irish.

Born in 1864 in Sandycove near Dublin, Casement developed his interest in the Congo in much the same way as Morel. Orphaned as a child and raised by guardians in Ulster, he was sent as a teenager to live with an uncle in Liverpool who was an agent for a West

African trading firm and who got the youth a job as a clerk at the
Elder Dempster shipping line where Morel was to work ten years
later. During his employment there, Casement shipped out as a
purser on one of the line's packets for a rubber-hauling voyage to
Boma and though the journey started out as a lark it gave him a
taste for African adventure which he was to pursue for the next
quarter century.

He began in the Congo itself. In 1884, at the age of twenty, he
left Elder Dempster and joined that band of Europeans who were
then working for Stanley on the river. This was nearly a year before
the Berlin Act created the Free State, while Leopold was still cun-
ningly manipulating the European Powers into granting him sovereignty over the river basin and while Stanley's forces were still
building a roadway and stations around Livingstone Falls to the
Stanley Pool. Very much a believer then in the humanitarian and
philanthropic purpose of Leopold's enterprise, Casement first was
employed at the road-building expedition's supply base at Matadi,
then was transferred to the trading station that had been built at the
equator on the river's left bank (today's Mbandaka). In 1886, after
the Free State had been established and Stanley had departed, Casement returned to Matadi to take charge of the survey for the railway
that was to be built from there to Leopoldville.

On completion of this work, in 1887, Casement found himself
without a job. Leopold by then was growing wary of having idealists
like Casement around and was weeding out all but the most hardened
adventurers from the Free State's employ. Casement, however, wasn't
yet ready to return to Europe so he took a post as lay helper at a
British mission on the Stanley Pool, looking after the station's river
transport and managing its accounts and correspondence. But then,
in 1890, when it seemed he would at last have to leave Africa, construction on the Matadi-to-Leopoldville railway began and, despite
the Belgian king's unease with Casement's type of idealistic enthusiasm, he was signed to a one-year contract on the project because of
his experience in preparing the original survey. And it was while on
this job that Casement met the young Polish-born sea captain, Teodor
Jozef Konrad Korzeniowski, who was to gain literary fame under the
pen name of Joseph Conrad.

Since boyhood, Conrad had been drawn to the Congo—in *Heart of
Darkness,* his protagonist, Marlow, reminiscing on "when I was a

little chap," remembers thinking then that the river resembled "an immense snake uncoiled, with its head in the sea, its body at rest curving afar over a vast country, and its tail lost in the depths of the land. And as I looked at the map of it in a shop-window, it fascinated me as a snake would a bird"—and in the fall of 1890 he signed on as captain on one of the Free State's steamers plying the Congo from Leopoldville to Stanley Falls. All things considered, this was a very brief interlude in Conrad's relentlessly adventurous life, lasting in fact barely four months. But the impact of the experience was enormous. Out of it came his masterpiece, *Heart of Darkness*, which, when published in 1902, gave literary expression to an entire age's perception of the Congo as a place of horror and dread and which forever characterized in men's minds Leopold's agents as sadistic lunatics. And out of it also came his life-long friendship with Casement which was to stand the anti-Leopold cause in good stead in the years to come.

I can assure you [Conrad wrote of Casement], that he is a limpid personality. There is a touch of the conquistador in him too; for I've seen him start off into an unspeakable wilderness swinging a crook-handled stick for all weapons, with two bulldogs, Paddy (white) and Biddy (brindle), at his heels, and a Loanda boy carrying a bundle for all company. A few months afterwards it so happened that I saw him come out again, a little leaner, a little browner, with his stick, dogs, and Loanda boy, and quietly serene as though he had been for a stroll in a park.

Returning from his last such stroll on the Matadi-to-Leopoldville railway project, Casement, now twenty-seven, joined the British foreign service and, though he remained in Africa, it was eight years before he again returned to the Congo. His first posting, in 1892, was to Britain's Niger Coast Protectorate where he was put in charge of a survey of regions until then unexplored and, in some cases, never visited by Europeans. Then, in 1895, he was named Her Majesty's Consul in Lourenço Marques, capital of Portuguese East Africa (today's Mozambique), where he got involved in the Boer War, then raging just across the frontier in South Africa, by planning a raid on the Pretoria railroad. And three years later, in 1898, he was assigned as Consul to Loanda in the Portuguese colony of Angola.

By this time, concern about what was going on in the neighboring Congo Free State was rapidly on the rise so, while still in Loanda, Casement unofficially began checking out the situation there and

became increasingly horrified by what he found. For example, about this time on a visit to his old base of Matadi, he made the same discovery that Morel was to make a few years later: namely, that no European goods beneficial to the peoples of the Congo were being imported to the Free State. Instead, he learned, the loads of rubber on the Matadi wharfs, destined for Antwerp, were being exchanged for guns and ammunition with which to arm the forest sentries of the Force Publique who in turn used them to terrorize the populace into harvesting ever more rubber. Casement's disturbing dispatch to this effect convinced London to transfer the consulate from Angola to the Free State and so, in 1900, Casement once again returned to the Congo, now as British Consul in Boma.

Once officially on the job, Casement followed up on his initial discoveries and began looking into all the alleged abuses of Leopold's rule and firing off sharply worded dispatches to London. "There is no free trade in the Congo today," he wrote at one point. "There is, it might be said, no trade, as such, at all in the Congo. There is ruthless exploitation at the hands of a savage and barbarous soldiery of one of the most prolific regions of Africa, in the interest of and for the profit of the Sovereign of that country and his favoured Concessionaires." At another point he complained angrily that the entire Congo "has become by the stroke of the pen the sole property of the governing body of that State, or, it should be said, in truth, the private property of one individual, the King of the Belgians." And throughout these dispatches, he repeatedly urged the British government to intervene, to take action so that the Free State's "rotten system of administration either be mended, or ended."

Casement's scorching dispatches from Boma came pouring into Whitehall just as the anti-Leopold campaign of Morel, Holt, Fox Bourne and the others—Conrad's *Heart of Darkness* appeared at this time—was reaching a fever pitch. And the combination proved irresistible. In 1903, under the management of Herbert Samuel, the British Parliament voted a motion stating that

the Government of the Congo Free State, having at its inception guaranteed to the Powers that its native subjects should be governed with humanity, and that no trading monopoly or privilege should be permitted within its domains, and both these guarantees having been constantly violated, this House requests His Majesty's Government to confer with the

other Powers signatories of the Berlin General Act by virtue of which the Congo Free State exists, in order that measures may be adopted to abate the evils prevalent in the State.

The British government then sent a note to the thirteen other powers of the 1885 Berlin Convention, requesting a meeting to discuss their possible intervention. And it also instructed Casement to undertake an extensive tour of inspection of the Free State and make a detailed official report of what exactly was going on there.

Traveling light—just with his crook-handled stick, two bulldogs and Loanda boy—Casement set off in June 1903. He was gone just a little over three months but what he saw and heard in this brief period confirmed at first-hand all the atrocity stories that had been circulating for years. He saw women chained in sheds with their babies, being held hostage for the delivery of their village's rubber quota. He saw men beaten mercilessly with the *chicotte* for having brought insufficient latex to the collecting point. He heard of whole tribes migrating across the Congo River to escape the Force Publique's brutalities, of mass executions by the state's agents, of punitive raids in which obscene mutilations were committed.

He interviewed a handless boy of eleven or twelve who had been wounded in such a raid on his village and who, while playing dead, had been "perfectly sensible of the severing of his wrist, but lay still fearing that if he moved he would be killed." Another youth, taken prisoner in a raid, told Casement that he had had his hands tied so tightly with thongs that they "had swollen terribly in the morning, and the thongs had cut into the bone. . . . The soldiers beat his hands with their rifle butts against the tree. His hands subsequently fell off." And a woman told of fleeing with her son from soldiers "when he fell shot dead, and she herself fell down beside him—she supposed she fainted. She then felt her hand being cut off, but she made no sign."

All this, and more, Casement described in chilling detail in his official report, "confident that once any decent man or woman . . . learns and appreciates the ghastly truth of the wrong done to the Congo man and woman—aye, and the poor hunted child!—they will not desert them." And when the report was published, in February 1904, the effect was electrifying. A contemporary English statesman declared that "no external question for at least thirty years has

moved the country so strongly and vehemently as this in regard to the Congo." Of the report itself, Moral wrote,

The scenes so vividly described seemed to fashion themselves out of the shadows before my eyes. The daily agony of an entire people unrolled itself in all the repulsive and terrifying details. I verily believe I *saw* those hunted women clutching their children and flying panic-stricken through the bush; the blood flowing from those quivering black bodes as the hippopotamus-hide whip struck again and again; the savage soldiery rushing hither and thither amid burning villages; the ghastly tally of severed hands.

And Conrad wrote,

It is an extraordinary thing that the conscience of Europe, which seventy years ago has put down the slave trade on humanitarian grounds, tolerates the Congo State today. It is as if the moral clock has been put back many hours. . . . In the old days, England had in her keeping the conscience of Europe. The initiative came from her. But I suppose we are busy with other things—too much involved in great affairs to take up the cudgels of humanity, decency and justice.

An immediate consequence of the Casement Report was the founding of the Congo Reform Association. Led by Morel (Casement, as a civil servant, could not participate but he gave it considerable behind-the-scenes support) and using the organizational set up of Fox Bourne's Aborigines Protection Association, it soon had active chapters not only in Britain but throughout Europe and the United States as well, lobbying their governments and marshalling their citizenry's outrage against Leopold. And nowhere was that outrage greater than in Belgium.

The Belgians had never been happy with their king's African adventure and now they found themselves embroiled in a nightmare of ugly worldwide publicity because of it. Something had to be done. Under pressure from his own Parliament, Leopold was forced to agree to the creation of a Commission of Enquiry—consisting of distinguished lawyers from Belgium, Italy and Switzerland—to investigate the conditions revealed in the Casement Report. The king hoped, of course, that the Commission would refute or, at least, ameliorate the charges against him. But that wasn't the case. When the international panel returned from an on-the-scene tour of inspection in 1905, it confirmed every one of Casement's findings.

Leopold made one last-ditch attempt to hang on to the Congo by promising to undertake a program of wide-ranging reforms. But it was rejected. In the first place, it was clear that the promised reforms would not go to the source of the problem: the state's participation in and monopoly control of the Congo's trade. In fact, with incredible imperial arrogance, at the very moment that the furor was at its height, Leopold had the audacity to extend his Crown Domain and reorganize his monopoly trusts so as to increase his personal profits from the river basin. But, additionally, the European powers had at last recognized the outlandishness of a situation in which an individual owned a country and ruled it as the most absolute of absolute monarchs without even the pretense of democratic controls. And they decided that the Congo must be taken away from him. The only question was to whom should it be given. In those days of the Scramble and ruthless colonialism, it never occurred to anyone that it might simply be given back to the Congo people. No, the belief then was that Africans couldn't rule themselves, that it was the God-given right and duty of European governments to do the job for them. And in this case the European government that seemed the natural choice for the task was that of Belgium.

Belgium, however, was no more eager now for an African colony than it ever had been and so for the next two years the matter was a subject of intense national debate. Elections were fought over it, governments fell because of it and the Parliament was occupied with no other question. But the outcome was inevitable. In August 1908, the Belgian Parliament, albeit reluctantly, voted an annexation treaty and on November 15, 1908, twenty-three years after its formation, the Congo Free State became the Belgian Congo.

EPILOGUE

In retrospect, we know that there never was any such thing as a good colony, and the Belgian Congo proved to be among the worst, but it was a considerable improvement over the Congo Free State. It couldn't help but be.

The Belgian government dismantled Leopold's apparatus of personal rule and put the administration of the Congo in the charge of a colonial ministry, answerable to the democratically elected Parliament, and set about correcting the most flagrant abuses. For a while many of Leopold's agents remained at their posts, especially at the more remote jungle stations, but in time the worst of them, the foreign mercenaries, soldiers of fortune, and sadistic adventurers, were weeded out and a conventional colonial service of Belgian civil servants and military personnel was created. The government was removed from the business of doing business. The rights of the Congolese to own and work their lands and to trade in their products were restored. The system of forced labor was abolished. The state's monopoly in trade was ended. The Domaine Privé and Crown Domains were thrown open to all comers. And they came.

Missionaries and entrepreneurs, settlers and traders flocked into the Congo. The European population rose from about 3000 in 1908, when Belgium took over from Leopold, to more than 100,000 on the eve of independence in 1960. Thousands of businesses were established. Huge plantations were put into cultivation for rubber, cotton, coffee, and palm oil. Banking consortiums were formed. The diamond fields of south Kasai, the tin and gold deposits of Kivu, the rich copper and uranium ores of Katanga were developed. Mines, factories, roads

and railways, and astonishingly modern industrial cities were built. Passenger and cargo steamers were launched on the rivers, hydroelectric power dams were constructed at the cataracts, dock facilities and port towns burgeoned along the navigable stretches. In the great rush of development, the Congo became something very close to "the grand highway of commerce to West Central Africa" that Stanley had visualized, and its vast basin seemed at last to have received the wonders of European civilization of which the ManiKongo Affonso had so long ago dreamed.

There was a time, especially during the fifteen years after the Second World War, when the Belgian Congo was considered the very model of an African colony. Its economy boomed. Its colonial service seemed to administer its affairs with even-handed justice. The missionaries and mission stations offered primary and secondary education. The business concerns and industrial conglomerates provided an admirable array of enlightened social services—employment, housing, medical care, decent wages and working conditions—and the Congolese were said to be the happiest and most prosperous of all of Africa's colonized peoples.

But it was a tragic illusion; the "civilization" that Belgium appeared to have cast over the Congo proved the most fragile of façades, behind which seethed the savage anger of a people too long abused, of tribal nations too much invaded, and when the opportunity came this savagery and anger erupted in what was the bloodiest epoch of the Congo's relentlessly bloody history.

"The winds of change" was how Harold Macmillan termed the demand for independence from European rule that arose among the colonized of Africa in the wake of World War II. But those winds, with amazing swiftness, gathered the strength of a howling hurricane and, from the guerrilla wars in Algeria to the Mau Mau terror in Kenya, ripped across the continent with such irresistible force that it swept away all but a remnant of Europe's colonial power within little more than a decade. Nowhere in Africa, however, was the transition from colonialism to independence quite so agonizing as in the Congo.

Blame for the horrors of that era falls heavily on Belgium's shoulders. Having corrected the most outrageous abuses of Leopold's reign, it settled self-righteously into fifty years of what it regarded as enlightened colonial administration, never once giving a thought to the possibility, let alone the necessity, of eventual decolonization. And, when

that eventuality was suddenly at hand, it did next to nothing to prepare the Congolese for it. As late as 1958, the Belgian government
officially—and proudly—was describing its colonial policy as "paternal-
istic." No civil rights were thought necessary for the Congolese. They
were citizens neither of Belgium nor of the Congo. They participated
not one jot in the governing of the colony. The highest ranks they
were allowed to attain in the colonial administration were as minor
clerks in the civil service and as noncommissioned officers in the Force
Publique. Elections were unheard of. Political parties and publications were banned. Racial segregation was the order of the day. Until
1955, Congolese were forbidden to go to college, and even after that
they were not permitted to study at universities abroad; a special
native school, Lovanium University, under close colonial supervision,
was created in Leopoldville to insulate the "children" from dangerous
foreign influences.

Nevertheless, the Congo was no more impervious to the winds of
change than any other African colony. Political unrest stirred first
among the so-called *évolués*—Congolese with secondary-school educa-
tions. Barred from organizing politically, they formed social, religious,
and cultural clubs, usually along tribal or regional lines, and at clan-
destine meetings, discussed, planned, and plotted how to get better
pay, improve working conditions, end racial discrimination, gain civil
rights, and ultimately, win independence. These clubs became the
Congo's political parties of the 1960s. In the 1950s they served as the
training ground for the country's future political leaders. For example, out of the government workers' club in Stanleyville emerged a
charismatic postal clerk by the name of Patrice Lumumba. In the
Bakongo tribal club in Leopoldville, a pudgy civil servant named
Joseph Kasavubu won popularity by stirring up memories of the lost
greatness of the Kingdom of Kongo. In Katanga, at the Union Minière
mining complex, a white-collar worker named Moise Tshombe organized a club among the Luba-Lunda tribesmen. And the leader of a
soldiers' club in the Force Publique garrison at Thysville was a young
NCO by the name of Joseph Mobutu.

Belgium's view of the *évolué* clubs and their leaders was remarkably sanguine, and its response to the political discontent that they
signified was confined to token gestures. For example, a system of
immatriculation was introduced by which a Congolese "who demonstrated a state of civilization implying the aptitude for enjoying laws

and fulfilling duties" could gradually gain Belgian citizenship. The idea, essentially, was to defuse any political threat posed by the *évolués* by making a privileged class of them and thus separating them from the masses they might lead. "The time will come which will assure to each, white or black, his proper share in the country's government, according to his own qualities and capacity," the Belgian King Baudouin, on a trip to Leopoldville in 1955, declared. "But before we realize this high ideal, gentlemen, much remains to be done." Just how much, in the Belgian view, was revealed by a University of Antwerp professor. In a scholarly article in 1956, he outlined a scenario for the Congo's gaining independence—in thirty years.

But the winds of change were blowing too hard for such a leisurely timetable. In 1957, Britain granted Ghana its independence. In August 1958, Charles de Gaulle chose Brazzaville, just across the Stanley Pool, to announce that France was granting independence to all her colonies. In December 1958, newly-independent Ghana held an All-African People's Conference in Accra, at which the call went out to all the continent's blacks to rise up and throw off their colonial chains. Patrice Lumumba managed to attend that conference, and when he got back to the Congo the drive for independence surfaced in earnest. The *évolué* clubs revealed their true political character. They sent petitions to Brussels, organized rallies, staged demonstrations and strikes, circulated inflammatory pamphlets, clashed with the police.

Under the impact of this unexpected political activity, the Belgian government in January 1959 vaguely promised that "Belgium intends to organize in the Congo a democracy capable of exercising its prerogatives of sovereignty and deciding on its independence." To the nationalists, this sounded like a meaningless placebo, and the wave of rallies and strikes went on. In October, Belgium took another step to mollify the nationalists: it set a timetable under which independence would be granted in 1964. But the nationalists rejected this as not soon enough. So in January 1960, Belgium convened a conference in Brussels with black delegates from 62 *évolué* clubs and 19 tribal associations and, in a stunning capitulation, agreed to grant the Congo its independence virtually immediately.

Why Belgium reversed herself so abruptly is a question that will probably never be answered to everyone's satisfaction. There are those who say that Brussels feared that revolutionary violence would rapidly escalate and draw Belgium into a long, debilitating guerrilla war that

she could ill afford, and so, never particularly happy about having an African colony anyway, decided to abdicate all further responsibility and be rid of the problem once and for all. On the other hand, there are those who believe that Belgium was perfectly aware that the Congo was in no way yet ready for independence, that chaos would surely follow its granting on such short notice, and that, as a result, she could expect to be called back to restore order and, in effect, to resume her rule. Whichever the true reason, Brussels set independence for June 30, 1960. This allowed barely six months for the Congolese to formally organize political parties, choose slates of candidates, conduct elections for a bicameral national assembly and a host of provincial and local governments, and take over the civil service bureaucracy and colonial administration from the Belgians. Considering that at the time there were hardly a score of Congolese college graduates in the country—and among them not a single military officer, engineer, lawyer, architect, doctor, economist, or anyone with any practical experience or training in government—it was a patently impossible job.

The troubles began during the election campaign. Candidates made wild promises of miracles to come. In one case, a candidate advised his constituents to bury stones because they would be turned into gold once the Congo was independent. Another promised that, if elected, he would resurrect all his voters' dead relatives. More dangerously, candidates used the campaign to vent long-repressed hostilities against whites, and they sought to gain political advantage by stirring up old tribal feuds. By Independence Day, the country was in a state of high nervous excitement. Crowds roamed the streets of the major cities, impatient for the miracles of freedom to begin, nursing tribal grudges, eager to become lords over the whites and take vengeance for past injustices.

King Baudouin, either out of gross ignorance or even grosser insensitivity, intensified the country's edgy mood when at the Independence ceremonies in Leopoldville he devoted much of his formal address to paying homage to King Leopold. Patrice Lumumba, the newly elected prime minister, was enraged, and when his turn came to speak on behalf of the new Congo government, he launched into a vitriolic diatribe on the cruel and inhuman rule of the Belgians. Joseph Kasavubu, the republic's new president, rebuked Lumumba and later Lumumba tried to calm the situation in a second speech, but his original words had touched a raw nerve in the Congolese people.

As Independence Day wore on, the crowds turned into mobs, there were repeated clashes with the Force Publique, attacks on whites, outbreaks of tribal feuding. The mood rapidly worsened during the first week. With the wholesale departure of Belgian civil servants—and the lack of trained blacks to replace them—the public services broke down. And, when government employees didn't get their paychecks, wildcat strikes erupted which turned into riots when the Force Publique attempted to quell them. But the most devastating blow fell when the Force Publique itself mutinied.

At the time, Lumumba, who was eager to replace Belgians with Congolese in every other sector of the new administration, was unwilling to risk running the Force Publique with inexperienced blacks. He believed that, for the obviously difficult times ahead, he had to have a well-disciplined gendarmerie and so intended to keep the 1000 Belgian officers in command of the 24,000-man force until Congolese could be trained to replace them. To the NCOs and soldiers, though, this was discrimination, and on July 1 the Force Publique garrison at Leopoldville staged a protest demonstration against the policy. When they refused to obey orders to return to barracks, the Belgian commanding general ordered out the Thysville garrison. But that garrison mutinied as well and, as if a string of dynamite had been set alight, one by one so did virtually every other garrison in the country.

The soldiers went on a rampage, attacking their officers, raping officers' wives, looting stores. On July 6, Lumumba capitulated and agreed to replace all Belgian officers with Congolese NCOs and promote everyone else at least one rank, thus creating an army without a single private. But he was too late. The mutinies had started a tidal wave of violence. Blacks attacked whites and each other as anti-European hatreds and intertribal rivalries exploded with savage fury. The sudden chaos was exacerbated by the panicked flight of whites. In the first week some 40,000 Belgians fled. All services shut down, food shortages developed, epidemics broke out. Then another disastrous blow fell.

Moise Tshombe, who had been elected premier of Katanga Province, called on Lumumba and Kasavubu to ask Brussels for troops to restore order. Fearing that this would bring back Belgian rule, they refused, and so, on July 11, Tshombe declared the secession of Katanga. He called for and got Belgian paratroopers to round up and disarm the Force Publique mutineers in his province. And he also

asked for and got Belgian civil servants to take over the shattered administration in Katanga.

Lumumba was desperate. The Congo's richest province had seceded, and violence was sweeping the rest of the country. He had only one place to turn. On July 15, he appealed to the United Nations for help.

While overall the UN's performance in the Congo must be judged positively, at the outset its presence only further complicated the rapidly deteriorating situation. Lumumba wanted the UN troops to attack Katanga and end Tshombe's secession, but the UN wanted to avoid a military confrontation with a member nation, Belgium. First the Belgian paras had to be gotten out of Katanga. In the meantime, the polyglot army of soldiers from Ghana, Tunisia, Guinea, Mali, and Ethiopia concentrated on bringing the Force Publique mutineers under control and on putting down the tribal warfare. While it did, the whirlwind of chaos raged throughout the summer.

In September, the situation took another bizarre turn. Declaring him unable to handle the affairs of state, Kasavubu fired Lumumba. Hearing this, Lumumba commandeered the Leopoldville radio station and broadcast to the nation that he had fired Kasavubu. The bewildered Congolese assembly didn't know which of the leaders to support so it wound up supporting neither. All pretense of a functioning government came to an end. And, as might be expected in such a situation, a military man stepped in. Joseph Mobutu, the young former NCO of the Force Publique who had been promoted to the command of the army when Lumumba ousted the Belgians in July, seized power.

His first move was to arrest Lumumba. On hearing this, Antoine Gizenga, a close associate of Lumumba's, declared the secession of Oriental Province, of which Lumumba's hometown and power base, Stanleyville, was the capital. The soldiers of the province's garrisons opened an attack on Mobutu's forces, and by Christmas they had overrun Kivu Province and northern Katanga. A renewed wave of savagery ravaged the country; whites were murdered and the most horrendous kind of tribal warfare, marked by wholesale massacres and cannibalism, raged in the rain forests. Blaming Lumumba, Mobutu decided to get rid of him. In January 1961, he had Lumumba flown to Katanga. What he had in mind in turning Lumumba over to Tshombe has never been made clear. Perhaps he only meant to exile

him to a distant corner. But in February the news came that Lumumba was dead, killed by Katangese soldiers. The world-wide outcry—which made Lumumba a martyr-hero of Africa—was so furious that Mobutu resigned and Kasavubu resumed command.

In the midst of the turmoil, the United Nations at last began to make some progress. Belgium had been persuaded to withdraw its troops from Katanga and, though Tshombe recruited white mercenary soldiers to replace them, the UN troops were finally authorized to attack Katanga and bring its secession to an end. That war lasted eighteen months. On several occasions, Tshombe was ready to concede defeat and offered a ceasefire with the United Nations (it was while flying out to meet Tshombe to negotiate one such ceasefire that the UN Secretary-General Dag Hammarskjöld was killed in a plane crash) only to reneg and keep the bloody fighting going. But finally in January 1963, with his mercenary troops in full retreat, Tshombe threw in the towel and fled into exile in Spain. The Katanga secession was over and, after two years of political controversy about their presence there, the UN forces withdrew.

But the Congo's agony was not over. The economy had collapsed; strikes and riots were endemic in the cities and towns; tribal warfare raged in the jungles. And, above all, Oriental Province was still in secession and had fallen into the grip of an increasingly savage rebel regime. In an attempt to bring the province back into the fold, Kasavubu had arrested Gizenga, but his place in Stanleyville had been taken by a wild-eyed revolutionary named Christophe Gbenye, who received military aid from Russia and China and who claimed to be in possession of "the magic Golden Book containing all the powerful secrets of the Congo, given by Lumumba to Gizenga and by Gizenga to me." He enlisted witch doctors in his cause, called his rebel soldiers Simbas (Swahili for "lions") and convinced them that a special *dawa* (magic) he dispensed made them impervious to bullets. Dressed in monkey furs, armed with poisoned arrows and spears as well as Russian rifles, largely recruited from the once-cannibal tribes of the Lualaba, and often doped up on *mira* (a local marijuana-like drug), the Simbas struck terror before them as they marched through the jungles to the beat of the ju-ju drums. The Congo army fled before their horrifying advance, and in the course of some eighteen months they overran more than half of the Congo.

Kasavubu declared a state of emergency, and, in June 1964, in yet

another bizarre twist in the Congo melodrama, he called Tshombe out of exile to head a government of national unity to meet the frightening threat of Gbenye's Simbas. Tshombe's idea of how to meet that threat was brutally simple: he would put into the field an army even more terrible than that of the Simbas. As it was clear that the Congo's own soldiers weren't up to the job, he turned to those who had helped him in the Katanga secession: wiite mercenaries. The call went out; the pay was $300 a month, all you could loot, and the most savage kind of excitement. And the mercenaries answered the call. Former French Foreign Legionnaires, ex-Nazis, white racists from Southern Rhodesia and South Africa, soldiers of fortune, demented sadists, adventurers and fugitives of every description—the descendants, in spirit and temperament, of the brutal agents of Leopold's Free State—enlisted in Tshombe's army. Once unleashed into the rain forests, they proved more than a match for the Simbas in savagery. Looting, massacring, raping, committing atrocities, they rolled back the Simba tide.

By September, Gbenye's forces had been driven into the northeastern corner of the Congo basin. All they held of any consequence was Stanleyville itself. In this desperate situation, Gbenye played one last horrifying card. He held 1300 white hostages from 25 countries in Stanleyville and, in a message to the United Nations, he warned that unless the mercenaries' drive on the city was halted, all the hostages would be executed and "we will wear their hearts around our necks like fetishes and dress ourselves in their flayed skins."

The fate of the hostages riveted the world's attention. An attempt was made to negotiate for their lives. But Gbenye remained adamant: Tshombe's advance on Stanleyville had to be turned back first. The negotiations dragged on, frustratingly, frighteningly, for weeks. And each day the hostages' situation grew more menacing. They were herded into barracks. They were manhandled, brutalized, tortured. Groups of them were periodically taken out to face firing squads, surrounded by howling mobs. Though no whites were executed yet, the Simbas began machine-gunning blacks whom they considered "enemies of the revolution." As the mercenaries tightened the siege around Stanleyville, water and food ran low and the Simbas turned ever more savage.

On November 24, 1964, a lightning military blow was struck at Stanleyville in a desperate gamble to save the hostages' lives. Using planes supplied by the U.S. Air Force, 600 Belgian paratroopers

jumped on the city center as the mercenaries smashed into its outskirts in a coordinated attack. As soon as they realized what was happening, the Simbas drove the hostages into the streets and, as loudspeakers blared hysterically, "Kill them, kill them all—men, women, and children," the Simbas opened fire with rifles and Sten guns. A wild melee broke out; the paras and mercenaries moved in fast, the hostages scrambled for cover. It was a brief battle. The Simbas were no match for the modern military force thrown against them, and they soon broke and ran for the darkness of the rain forests. Gbenye himself fled, never to be heard of again. Twenty-nine hostages were found dead. Later, 51 more bodies of whites were found, hacked to pieces and cannibalized. The secession of Oriental Province was over.

The Congo smelled of the graveyard. It has been estimated that at least 200,000 Congolese had been killed in the less than five years since independence. The roads, bridges, railways, and communications network were a shambles. The rubber and palm-oil plantations had been abandoned, the mining industries crippled. There were shortages of everything, refugees everywhere, and every sort of tribal, racial, and regional strife had been stirred up to a killing pitch. Despite the submission of Oriental Province, the conditions in the Congo in 1965 were such that the chaos and bloodshed of the past five years seemed likely to go on for five years more. And they very well might have. For, in a chilling reprise of his action with Lumumba, Kasavubu suddenly fired Tshombe; and this immediately threatened to lead to still another round of tribal and civil wars. But then, just as he had done in the first year of independence, Joseph Mobutu stepped in. This time, though, the army chief made sure his seizure of power would last.

Mobutu's second regime can be taken to mark the Congo's final passage—for better or worse—from the mysterious mythological darkness of its savage past into the rather banal light of the modern age and, as such, provides an entirely appropriate point at which to end this book. For, from 1965 onward, the story of the river belongs less to the history of its discovery, exploration, and exploitation by Europe than to the politics of modern independent Africa. This politics is characterized by the struggle going on all over the continent—with some admirable successes and many dismal failures but always with much agony and hope—to recover the virtues and values that prevailed in Africa before the white man came, to combine them with the inarguable advantages of the civilization the white man brought,

and out of that combination to forge a new but genuine African identity and society. It is a struggle that has seen, on the one hand, the undertaking of such monumental industrialization projects as a multibillion-dollar hydroelectric complex to harness the enormous power of the Livingstone Falls and, on the other hand, the introduction of Mobutu's *authenticité* campaign to change not only all the European place names but all the river people's Christian names as well. (Mobutu changed his from Joseph to Sese Seko.) It is, in short, the struggle by which the Congo is, in fact as well as name, being transformed into Zaire.

SELECTED BIBLIOGRAPHY

Anstey, Roger. *Britain and the Congo in the Nineteenth Century.* Oxford, 1962.

Anstruther, Ian. *I Presume: Stanley's Triumph and Disaster.* London, 1956.

Archer, Jules. *Congo: The Birth of a New Nation.* New York, 1970.

Armattoe, R. E. G. *The Golden Age of West African Civilization.* Londonderry, 1946.

Ascherson, Neal. *The King Incorporated.* London, 1963.

Axelson, Eric. *Congo to Cape.* New York, 1973.

Axelson, Eric. *Portuguese in Southeast Africa.* Johannesburg, 1960.

Axelson, Eric. *Southeast Africa.* London, 1940.

Balandier, Georges. *Daily Life in the Kingdom of the Kongo from the Sixteenth to the Eighteenth Century.* London, 1968.

Beazley, C. Raymond. *Prince Henry the Navigator.* New York, 1894.

Bell, Christopher. *Portugal and the Quest for the Indies.* London, 1974.

Bentley, William Holman. *Pioneering on the Congo.* London, 1900.

Blake, John W. *European Beginnings in West Africa, 1454–1578.* London, 1937.

Bovill, E. W. *The Golden Trade of the Moors.* London, 1958.

Boxer, C. R. *Four Centuries of Portuguese Expansion, 1415–1825.* Johannesburg, 1961.

Brode, Heinrich. *Tippoo-Tib: The Story of His Career in Central Africa.* London, 1907.

Burton, Richard Francis. *The Lands of Cazembe: Lacerda's Journey in 1798.* London, 1873.

Burton, Richard Francis. *Two Trips to Gorilla Land and the Cataracts of the Congo.* London, 1876.

Cameron, Verney Lovett. *Across Africa.* New York, 1877.

Campbell, Reginald John. *Livingstone.* London, 1929.

Clarkson, Thomas. *History of the Rise, Progress and Accomplishment of the Abolition of the African Slave Trade* (2 vols.) . London, 1808.

Conrad, Joseph. *Heart of Darkness.* New York, 1923.

Coupland, Reginald. *The British Anti-Slavery Movement.* London, 1933.

Coupland, Reginald. *East Africa and Its Invaders.* Oxford, 1938.

Coupland, Reginald. *The Exploitation of East Africa, 1856–1890.* Evanston, Ill., 1967.

Coupland, Reginald. *Livingstone's Last Journey*. London, 1945.

Crone, G. R. *The Voyages of Cadamosto*. London, 1937.

Cuvelier, Jean. *L'Ancien Royaume de Congo*. Brussels, 1946.

Davidson, Basil. *The African Awakening*. London, 1955.

Davidson, Basil. *Black Mother: The African Slave Trade, 1450–1850*. London, 1961.

Debenham, Frank. *The Way to Ilala: David Livingstone's Pilgrimage*. London, 1955.

Donnan, Elizabeth. *Documents Illustrative of the History of the Slave Trade to America*, Vols. I and II. Washington, D.C., 1930.

Dos Passos, John. *The Portugal Story*. Garden City, N.Y., 1969.

Duffy, James. *Portuguese Africa*. Cambridge, Mass., 1968.

Eannes de Azurara, Gomes. *Conquests and Discoveries of Henry the Navigator*. London, 1936.

Farwell, Byron. *The Man Who Presumed*. London, 1958.

Fisher, H. A. L. *A History of Europe* (2 vols.) . London, 1938.

Foran, W. Robert. *African Odyssey: Life of Verney Lovett Cameron*. London, 1937.

Gramont, Sanche de. *The Strong Brown God: The Story of the Niger River*. Boston, 1976.

Hall, Richard Seymour. *Stanley: An Adventurer Explored*. Boston, 1975.

Hallett, Robin. *Africa to 1875*. Ann Arbor, Mich., 1974.

Hallett, Robin. *The Penetration of Africa*. London, 1965.

Hallett, Robin. *Records of the African Association, 1788–1833*. London, 1964.

Hird, Frank. *The Authorized Life of Henry Morton Stanley*. London, 1935.

Ihle, Alexander. *Das Alte Koenigreich Kongo*. Leipzig, 1929.

Jameson, Robert. *Narrative of Discovery and Adventure in Africa*. New York, 1831.

Jeal, Tim. *Livingstone*. London, 1973.

Johnston, Harry H. *A History of the Colonization of Africa by Alien Races*. Cambridge, 1905.

Johnston, Harry H. *Livingstone and the Exploration of Central Africa*. London, 1891.

Johnston, Harry H. *The River Congo*. London, 1884.

July, Robert W. *A History of the African People*. New York, 1970.

Laman, Karl. *The Kongo*. Uppsala, 1953.

Legum, Colin. *Congo Disaster*. Baltimore, 1961.

Leo Africanus. *History and Description of Africa*. London, 1896.

Livingstone, David (Horace Waller, ed.) . *The Last Journals of David Livingstone in Central Africa*. London, 1864.

Livingstone, David. *Missionary Travels and Researches in South Africa*. London, 1857.

Livingstone, David. *Narrative of an Expedition to the Zambesi and Its Tributaries*. New York, 1866.

Major, Richard Henry. *The Discoveries of Prince Henry the Navigator*. London, 1877.

Martekki, George. *Leopold to Lumumba: A History of the Belgian Congo*. London, 1962.

Moorehead, Alan. *The Blue Nile*. London, 1962.

Moorhead, Alan. *The White Nile*. London, 1960.

Morel, Edmund D. *King Leopold's Rule in Africa*. London, 1904.

Morel, Edmund D. *Red Rubber*. London, 1907.

Morison, Samuel Eliot. *Admiral of the Ocean Sea: A Life of Christopher Columbus*. Boston, 1942.

Murray, Hugh. *Historical Account of Discoveries and Travels in Africa*. Edinburg, 1818.

Oliveira Martins, J. P. *The Golden Age of Prince Henry the Navigator*. London, 1914.

Oliver, Roland A. *The Dawn of African History*. London, 1961.

Oliver, Roland A., and J. D. Fage. *A Short History of Africa*. New York, 1963.

Pacheco Pereira, Duarte (G. H. T. Kimble, trans.). *Esmeraldo de Situ Orbis*. London, 1937.

Park, Mungo. *A Journal of a Mission to the Interior of Africa*. London, 1815.

Park, Mungo. *The Life and Travels of Mungo Park*. New York, 1840.

Perham, Margery, and Jack Simons (eds.). *African Discovery: Anthology of Exploration*. London, 1942.

Pigafetta, Filippo, from Duarte Lopes. *A Report of the Kingdom of Congo*. London, 1597.

Prestage, Edgar. *The Portuguese Pioneers*. London, 1933.

Ravenstein, E. D. (ed.). *The Strange Adventures of Andrew Battell of Leigh, in Angola and the Adjoining Regions*. London, 1901.

Robinson, Ronald, John Gallagher and Alice Denny. *Africa and the Victorians*. London, 1961.

Sanceau, Elaine. *The Land of Prester John*. New York, 1944.

Schiffers, Heinrich. *The Quest for Africa*. New York, 1957.

Silverberg, Robert. *The Realm of Prester John*. Garden City, N.Y., 1972.

Slade, Ruth. *King Leopold's Congo*. London, 1962.

Stanley, Henry Morton (Dorothy Stanley, ed.). *The Autobiography of Henry Morton Stanley*. Boston, 1909.

Stanley, Henry Morton. *The Congo and the Founding of Its Free State* (2 vols.). New York, 1885.

Stanley, Henry Morton. *How I Found Livingstone*. New York, 1872.

Stanley, Henry Morton. *In Darkest Africa* (2 vols.). New York, 1890.

Stanley, Henry Morton. *Through the Dark Continent* (2 vols.). New York, 1878.

Stanley, Henry Morton. (Albert Maurice, ed.). *Unpublished Letters*. London, 1957.

Stanley, Richard, and Alan Neame (eds.). *The Exploration Diaries of H. M. Stanley*. London, 1961.

Sterling, Thomas L. *Stanley's Way*. New York, 1960.

Stevenson, E. L. (trans. and ed.). *The Geography of Claudius Ptolemy*. New York, 1932.

Tuckey, J. K. *Narrative of an Expedition to Explore the River Zaire*. New York, 1818.

Vansina, Jan. *Kingdoms of the Savanna*. Madison, Wisc., 1966.

West, Richard. *Brazza of the Congo*. London, 1972.

INDEX

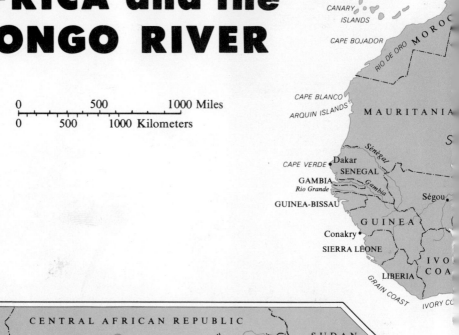

AFRICA and the CONGO RIVER

0		500		1000 Miles
0	500		1000 Kilometers	

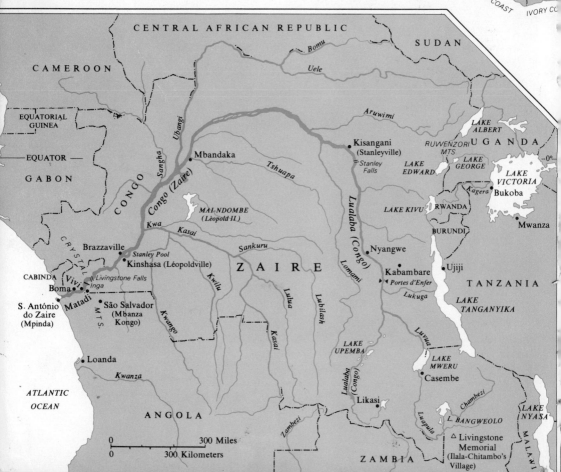

PORTU
Sa
CAPE ST. VIN

CANARY
ISLANDS

CAPE BOJADOR

RIO DE ORO

MOROC

CAPE BLANCO
ARQUIN ISLANDS

MAURITANIA

S

Sénégal

CAPE VERDE • Dakar
SENEGAL

GAMBIA
Rio Grande

Gambia

Ségou

GUINEA-BISSAU

GUINEA

Conakry •

SIERRA LEONE

IVO
COA

LIBERIA

GRAIN COAST

IVORY CO

CENTRAL AFRICAN REPUBLIC

SUDAN

Bomu

CAMEROON

Uele

Aruwimi

LAKE
ALBERT

EQUATORIAL
GUINEA

Ubangi

Kisangani
(Stanleyville)

RUWENZORI
MTS.

UGANDA

EQUATOR

Sangha

Mbandaka

Tshuapa

Stanley
Falls

LAKE
EDWARD

LAKE
GEORGE

0°

GABON

CONGO

Congo (Zaire)

MAI-NDOMBE
(Léopold II)

Lualaba (Congo)

LAKE
VICTORIA

Kagera • Bukoba

Kwa

Kasai

LAKE KIVU

RWANDA

Mwanza

CRYSTAL

Brazzaville

Sankuru

BURUNDI

Stanley Pool

Nyangwe

Lomami

Kinshasa (Léopoldville)

ZAIRE

Kabambare • Ujiji

CABINDA

Vivi

Kwilu

Kwango

Lukuga

TANZANIA

Boma

Livingstone Falls
Inga

Portes d'Enfer

Matadi

MTS.

São Salvador
(Mbanza
Kongo)

Lulua

Lubilash

LAKE
TANGANYIKA

S. António
do Zaire
(Mpinda)

Kasai

Luvua

• Loanda

Kwanza

LAKE
UPEMBA

LAKE
MWERU

• Casembe

ATLANTIC
OCEAN

Lualaba
(Congo)

Chambezi

LAKE
NYASA

ANGOLA

Zambezi

Likasi

Luapula

L. BANGWEOLO

△ Livingstone
Memorial
(Ilala-Chitambo's
Village)

MALAWI

0		300 Miles
0	300 Kilometers	

ZAMBIA

MICHAEL CRICHTON was born in Chicago in 1942. His novels include *The Andromeda Strain, Jurassic Park, Timeline,* and *Prey.* He is also the creator of the television series *ER*.